RICHARD ROHMER

O M N I B U S

ULTIMATUM

EXXONERATION

PERISCOPE RED

THE DUNDURN GROUP
TORONTO

Printer: Webcom

National Library of Canada Cataloguing in Publication Data

Rohmer, Richard, 1924-
  A Richard Rohmer omnibus.

Ultimatum was published originally: Toronto: Clarke Irwin, 1973;
Exxoneration: Toronto : McClelland & Stewart, 1974;
Periscope red: Don Mills, Ont. : General, 1980.
Contents: Ultimatum — Exxoneration — Periscope red.

ISBN 1-55002-460-4

I. Title. II. Title: Ultimatum. III. Title: Exxoneration. IV. Title: Periscope red.

PS8585.O3954A6 2003   C813'.54   C2003-905011-4

1   2   3   4   5   07   06   05   04   03

Canada

THE CANADA COUNCIL | LE CONSEIL DES ARTS
FOR THE ARTS | DU CANADA
SINCE 1957 | DEPUIS 1957

ONTARIO ARTS COUNCIL
CONSEIL DES ARTS DE L'ONTARIO

We acknowledge the support of the **Canada Council for the Arts** and the **Ontario Arts Council** for our publishing program. We also acknowledge the financial support of the **Government of Canada** through the **Book Publishing Industry Development Program** and **The Association for the Export of Canadian Books**, and the **Government of Ontario** through the **Ontario Book Publishers Tax Credit** program, and the **Ontario Media Development Corporation's Ontario Book Initiative.**

Care has been taken to trace the ownership of copyright material used in this book. The author and the publisher welcome any information enabling them to rectify any references or credit in subsequent editions.

J. Kirk Howard, President

Printed and bound in Canada.⊛
Printed on recycled paper.
www.dundurn.com

Dundurn Press
8 Market Street
Suite 200
Toronto, Ontario, Canada
M5E 1M6

Dundurn Press
2250 Military Road
Tonawanda NY
U.S.A. 14150

CONTENTS

ULTIMATUM   7

EXXONERATION   243

PERISCOPE RED   455

ULTIMATUM

To my beautiful daughters,
Cathy and Ann

PORTER, Rt. Hon. Robert Maitland, P.C., Q.C., M.P., Prime Minister of Canada since August, 1980; b. Winnipeg, 7 May, 1935; s. Wilfred Martin and Nora (Carter) P.; B.A. University of Manitoba, 1956; LL.B. University of Alberta, 1960; LL.M., 1967; called to Bar of Alberta, 1960; m. Min Carpenter, 1967 (deceased); no children; practised law with Simpson & Crane, Calgary, 1960-66; mem. law firm Porter & Smith, Inuvik, 1966-74; elected to House of Commons, 1974; Minister of Energy, Mines and Resources, 1977-80. Member Arctic Institute of North America, the Law Society of Alberta and the Northwest Territories. Publications: A Proud People, 1969; Reconquering Our Land, 1971. Recreations: riding, fishing, snowshoeing. Address: Prime Minister's Residence, 24 Sussex Drive, Ottawa, Canada.

———————————————, President U.S.; b. Houston, Tex., Sept. 17, 1921; s. James Howard and Margaret (Stafford) B.; LL.B. University of Texas; m. Jennifer Harley, May 3, 1949; children — James Everett, Marian Stafford (Mrs. Walter Morton). Mem. law firm Whitfield, Harley, Wilkinson & Steele, Houston, 1949-53; atty for Masefield, Warfield, Hamilton & Smith, ind. oil operators, Ft. Worth, 1953-60; mem. 87th, 88th, 89th U.S. Congresses; senator, 1967-71; elected President of United States, Nov., 1976, took office, Jan. 21, 1977. Served to lt. col., U.S.A.F., 1941-45, ETO. Decorated DFC, Air medal with three oak leaf clusters. Democrat. Home: The White House, 1600 Pennsylvania Ave. N.W., Washington.

Day One

9:00 a.m., EDT = 8:00 a.m., CDT = 7:00 a.m., MDT

The Prime Minister's intercom buzzed. His secretary sounded excited. "Prime Minister, the President of the United States is calling. The President himself is on the line."

Robert Porter hesitated a moment, then he picked up the telephone.

"Good morning, Mr. President. To what do I owe the honour of being called by the President of the United States at nine o'clock on a Monday morning?"

"Good morning, Mr. Prime Minister. I'll come to the reason for my call in a moment. But first let me say that, while you and I haven't met, I've read a great deal about you. For a man who has just taken on the job — seven weeks I think it is now, isn't it?"

"That's right, Mr. President."

"Well, you seem to be getting things done, putting your team together, reorganizing policies and departments. We Texans like people who can move fast, and make decisions."

Suddenly the President's voice hardened. "Now, Mr. Prime Minister, let me tell you why I'm calling. As you're aware, I'm facing re-election next month. As a politician, you'll appreciate that I want to clean up as many loose ends as I can before the beginning of November so I can show the voters...."

"I understand, Mr. President."

15

"I thought you would. Well, what I want to talk to you about is natural gas. I should tell you at this point that I've discussed what I'm going to say with the leaders of the Senate and the House of Representatives, and with my Cabinet and my experts in the State Department. I have the full concurrence of all of them.

"Let me give you the background, Mr. Prime Minister. The United States is heading for another winter of disastrous shortages of natural gas. As you know, the energy crisis has been building up over the last decade. We've been able to offset it to a certain extent by increasing our imports of crude oil, but natural gas represents a far greater problem. Over 32% of the energy in this country is supplied by natural gas. We must have it if we are to survive. This year we expect a shortage of 2.7-trillion cubic feet. My advisers and the Federal Power Commission expect that in the area from Chicago and Detroit through to New York and Boston alone 20% of our industrial capacity will have to be shut down for the extremely cold parts of the winter. Apartment buildings and houses will be without heat; schools, hospitals and homes for the aged will have to be closed. In other words, Mr. Prime Minister, we are facing a national disaster.

"I recognize that there is absolutely nothing I can do in the short term to overcome this problem completely, but what I want to put to you is a long-term program that we can get working on right away."

Robert Porter leaned forward in his chair. "Mr. President, we're tremendously concerned about the problem up here. If there is any way Canada can help . . ."

The President cut him short. "That's just the trouble. For years now we've been trying to get you people to help, and all we get is a lot of talk. Now let me finish. I realize that you have most of the facts, but I want to get across

16

to you the position exactly as I see it.

"Our shortage of natural gas is caused largely by lack of transportation. While gas is produced in Algeria, the Middle East and Venezuela, there is no existing tanker fleet large enough to carry it to the United States. We've been trying desperately to build ships of our own. In late '72 we gave two contracts worth $569-million to General Dynamics and Newport News. We now have ten tankers in operation and ten more near completion, but that's only a drop in the bucket.

"Therefore, it's absolutely essential for us to obtain natural gas on the North American continent or in the Arctic Islands. And the gas is up there, all right. I'm told we can get 1½-trillion cubic feet a year out of Prudhoe Bay and the Mackenzie Delta by the Mackenzie Valley pipeline. The fact is, you have natural gas, and we're suffering because you've consistently refused to give us access and you've failed to plan intelligently. Look at the Mackenzie Valley pipeline. Almost all the financing has come from the United States, and we've worked with you people all the way to see that the economic impact of the construction would be good for Canada, and that the environmental boys would be kept happy. That pipeline is still being tested. It should be finished by now. I was counting on it being ready to start delivering gas next month. Now God knows when it will be completed. It must be at least six months behind schedule. And what's worse, because you didn't take our advice in dealing with the claims of the native peoples in the Northwest Territories, they started blowing up the pipeline ten days ago."

"Mr. President, you know the RCMP are investigating the bombings."

"Hell, you don't have a hope of finding anything. Those people can move in and blow up the pipe any place they like and any time they like, and there's no way you can do a thing about it.

"For years we tried to convince Canada to follow our example and recognize aboriginal rights to a share of the natural wealth. When we settled with the people of Alaska in the early 70's we gave them $500-million, 40-million acres of land, and another $½-billion from a royalty of 2% on the oil and gas production from Prudhoe Bay.

"What did you people do? You got on your high horse and denied that the Indians and Eskimos had any claim to compensation, even though your government had signed treaties with some of the native groups in the Mackenzie Valley Corridor. I tell you, you have a moral obligation to them just as you have a moral obligation to see that the rest of us have natural gas so we can live and so our industries can keep going. But not one cubic foot of gas will flow in that pipeline until an agreement has been reached with the natives.

"Now, let's look at the Arctic Islands. Firms such as Imperial Oil, Tenneco, Columbia Natural Gas, and a host of others have poured more than $300-million into Panarctic's exploration program. The proved up gas reserves now total at least 60-trillion cubic feet. Melville Island is sitting on a bed of natural gas, and enormous finds have been made on King Christian, Ellef Ringnes, Thor, Axel Heiberg, Ellesmere, and other islands in the Sverdrup Basin. There's absolutely no doubt that by the time a transportation system is set up from the Islands to the mainland, the reserves will far exceed the 60-trillion mark. And virtually all the money for this exploration and development has come from the United States.

"The fact is, Prime Minister, Canada has the natural gas. The United States has paid for its discovery, and by rights we own the stuff. We must have it, and must have it fast."

Porter interrupted. "Now just a minute. I realize you people have put money into the Arctic. So have we. We're prepared to make a deal to supply gas from the Islands on fair terms, but we have to protect...."

"Now, Prime Minister, you know that's not true. God knows we've been trying for years to get your government to come to grips with the situation. We've cajoled, wheedled, got on bended knee, and got absolutely nowhere. All we hear is the maddening response that Canada won't let us have any gas until its own needs for the future are determined and you see if there is any surplus you can afford to sell."

The President paused and cleared his throat. "Now let's get down to brass tacks. The United States can't put up with this situation any longer, and we're not going to. We must have three unconditional commitments from the Parliament of Canada, and we must have them by six o'clock tomorrow night.

"The first is that the aboriginal rights of the native people of the Yukon and the Northwest Territories will be recognized and that a settlement will be worked out with them at once along the lines of the Alaskan model.

"The second is that Canada will grant the United States full access to all the natural gas in the Arctic Islands without reference to Canada's future needs.

"And finally, I want a commitment that the United States will be allowed to create the transportation system necessary to move the gas as quickly as possible from the Arctic Islands to the United States. This commitment will have to include free access to the Islands across any Canadian territory which may provide a practical route.

19

"Now let me make this clear. I want these commitments by six o'clock tomorrow night, and they must be given by the Parliament of Canada, not simply the government. I know your Parliament isn't in session, but that's your problem, not mine."

The Prime Minister's eyes were wide with disbelief, and his voice betrayed his anger.

"Now hold on. If you think you can try to blackmail us into giving you people the right to take control of our resources, you'd better do some more thinking."

"Well, Mr. Prime Minister, it's up to you. I've given Canada an ultimatum. As you know, we have plenty of muscle to back it up — economic levers too numerous to list. I expect to hear from you by six o'clock tomorrow night. Good-bye."

The Prime Minister put the receiver down. His face was white with anger and astonishment. He reached for the intercom and punched the button for his chief executive assistant.

Tom Scott responded immediately. "Yes, sir."

"Tom, get in here fast, and alert your entire staff to stand by. We've got real trouble on our hands."

Scott burst into the office. The Prime Minister motioned for him to sit down.

"Tom, I've just had a telephone call from the President of the United States, and this is what he said. . . ."

When he had finished, all Scott could say was, "Good God! He must be crazy."

"No. He means business. He meant exactly what he said.

"Tom, get Mike and Tony in here. I want them to sit in a corner, take notes, and keep quiet. Also, I want your two best secretaries. Before you bring them in they must swear not to say a word to anybody about what is going on. They're going to have to know exactly what is in my mind up to a point, and I don't want any leaks. Nothing is to be said unless I authorize it.

"Also, have someone phone the cabinet ministers most closely concerned — that would be Energy, Northern Development, External Affairs, Defence, Environment, Transport and Finance. Ask them if they could be here with their deputies in twenty minutes. And advise the

Leader of the Opposition and the leaders of the other two parties that I would be obliged if they would meet with me on a matter of urgent national importance one hour from now, at 10:15. Tell each of them, Tom, that I have invited the others to attend, so they'll know they're not alone. I'll see the leaders here and the ministers in the Cabinet Room."

As Tom turned to go, he muttered, "Christ, he can't do this to us!"

The Prime Minister heard him. "Sure he can and he is. Furthermore, I can see why. I have enormous sympathy for him in the position he's in and for the thousands of Americans who are going to suffer this winter. But that doesn't make it any easier for us."

The Prime Minister turned to look out the window of his East Block office across Parliament Hill.

Robert Porter was new to the office of Prime Minister, but he had already established himself as a strong, forceful leader who had brought to his election campaign imaginative national goals with which almost all Canadians could personally identify. One of his main objectives was that the people of Canada should own all the crude oil and gas and all the exploration leasing rights for the natural resources in the Canadian Arctic. In Porter's view, the existing system under which foreign exploration firms were able to pick up drilling rights for between five and twenty cents an acre and pay royalties of only five to ten per cent on the well-head price when the oil and gas was finally found, left Canada with a "pittance" and put the ownership of control in foreign hands. Under Porter's program, control of the development in the Arctic would remain in Canadian hands, and the yearly revenue from

22

the sale of gas and oil from the Arctic Islands and the Mackenzie Delta, which could eventually range as high as $40-billion, would produce profits which could be used to reduce personal taxation and increase the standard of medical and other social services. Now it was clear that he was faced with a crisis which could threaten his whole program and require all his skills as a leader.

"Sir, we're ready."

It was Tom Scott, with his two young staff men and the secretaries.

The Prime Minister turned away from the window and repeated to the group what he had already told Scott, outlining the President's position.

"The reason I have brought you all in is this: I want to set out the course of action we must take within the next few hours so that a decision can be made on the ultimatum. Since you, Mike and Tony, will be working directly under Tom, I thought it was best that you should hear my instructions. Marie, I want you and Louise to take down what I say so that we'll have a record. I asked for both of you because, as you know, I sometimes speak rather quickly and I don't want to be interrupted. What I say will also be tape-recorded, so that you can double-check.

"Now Tom, there's no question in my mind that the House will have to be reconvened at once. The response to the ultimatum will have to come by a decision of Parliament on a free vote.

"One of the major problems is to make sure that every member of the House and the Senate is fully briefed on the state of Canada's relations with the United States and on the status of the oil and gas finds, as well as on the pipeline situation in the Mackenzie Valley Corridor. They must also be filled in on the specifics of the current energy shortage in the U.S., and what has been happening since the early 70's.

"I want the premiers of each of the provinces informed as soon as possible, and I want them brought here to Ottawa immediately for consultation. When I decide on a course of action, I will have to clear with the Governor-General and also the Leader of the Opposition and the leaders of the other parties. I want their full concurrence and understanding so that we can work this thing out together."

Tom Scott nodded. "The party leaders will be here at 10:15, sir. The Governor-General is on his way back from Victoria. I'll leave word at Government House that you're to be informed immediately on his arrival."

"Good. I also want to meet with the leaders of the television and radio industry and the press, to see if I can get them to cool it. This situation will have to be handled carefully. I don't want anyone to panic.

"Tomorrow's agenda is even more important. It's the key to the whole thing. I have to get the decision to the President before six o'clock. The House and the Senate must meet and there has to be a reasonable time for debate. But the most important thing I have to do is to make sure that everyone understands the background of this whole situation.

"So here's what we're going to do. I want a briefing organized for eight o'clock tomorrow morning in the Commons Chamber. You can set that up with the Speaker, Tom.

"The briefing will be for all members of the House, the Senate, the premiers who can get here, and anyone else we think appropriate. It will be given by the ministers and deputy ministers of the departments which have an interest in the North and in oil and gas — Energy, Mines and Resources; Indian Affairs and Northern Development; Environment; Transport; External Affairs; Defence — also Finance. I want the lead-off to be External Affairs. The briefing must be over by eleven o'clock, because I want the House and the Senate to meet at twelve noon. As it is, that only gives us five hours for debate — less, actually, because the motion will have to be put before the House and I'll need half an hour at the end to close off. But we must be finished by five so that a vote can be taken in both houses before 5:30 and I can get back to the President with a decision by six.

"I'll ask the Leader of the Opposition and the other party leaders to help me draft the motion. I think that it should be put forward by all of us jointly."

Scott interjected, "Prime Minister, how in the hell are you going to sort out who's to speak during the debate, how long people are going to take and that sort of thing, so you can get through in time?"

"I don't see that as a real problem. The leaders are reasonable people, and I think the seriousness of the situation is such that we can set up a system that will be acceptable to all of them. Mind you, each of them is going to have to work out with his own people who is going to speak and for how long. That's one of the understandings I'll have to get from them when we meet, but I'm sure they'll cooperate.

"For now the major effort is to get Parliament reconvened and every member back here as fast as possible, wherever he is."

Porter turned to Mike Cranston. "Mike, I think you'd better get going. Phone the Chief of the Defence Staff immediately. Tell him to be prepared within an hour to divert all his Hercules transport aircraft to pick up members of the House and the Senate who are at places off the main airline routes. We'll advise him as soon as possible where they'll have to go.

"Would you also tell the president, or the top man you can find at Air Canada, Canadian Pacific, and the regional carriers, that seats should be cleared for all members of Parliament, senators, and people whom we provide with special priority ratings. Also tell them that we may require special flights to be made off schedule.

"Then get on to the executive assistants of the leaders of the other parties so that they can communicate with their members to get back here. Tell them to let you know where their people are so that they can be picked up if they're off-route. And of course have someone get in touch with our own people."

As Mike Cranston headed for the door, the Prime Minister flicked the intercom switch for his secretary.

"Joan, would you please call and speak to the presidents of the National Press Gallery, the CBC, CTV, and Global Television. Ask them if they or their senior representatives can be at this office within an hour. Tell them I have an emergency on my hands that I must speak to them about and get their advice. Say they may have to wait, and I hope they won't mind. And find out exactly who will be coming."

"Yes, sir."

The Prime Minister turned back to Scott. "Tom, you'd better get on to the premiers now. I want them all here as quickly as possible. I guess the premiers from Ontario and Quebec won't need any help from us, but those from the West and the Maritimes may have to be given a hand getting here. That includes the Commissioners from the Northwest Territories and the Yukon, of course. I'd like you to make every effort to get them here by six tonight, because I want them involved in this decision."

Scott interjected, "What about the Cabinet, sir?"

"You're quite right, I've got to get the whole Cabinet together as soon as possible after I've met with the key ministers. I should be clear of the press by 12:15, so I'll call a Cabinet meeting for that time. Look after it, please.

"Now, one final thing. You've got a hell of a lot of work to do. We're going to have to schedule everything down to the minute. As we work toward the briefing at eight o'clock tomorrow morning, I don't want anyone to be talking to the press without my direct authority, and I want you to stay within shouting distance. Get in more staff if you need it."

Scott was already on his way to the door. He paused long enough to say, "I'll be here, sir. By the way, the press will be after you for a statement. What shall I tell them?"

"I don't see a press conference as being possible. Really, there isn't time. Anyway, I want to discuss that whole question with the news people when they're here."

When Scott and his assistants had left, Porter picked up the telephone and dialled a familiar number. In a moment he was through to John Thomas, a close and trusted friend whom he had appointed to the Senate.

"John, I've got real trouble. I've just had a call from the President of the United States. They're forecasting an even worse energy shortage this winter than our experts had predicted. On top of that he's really worried about the bombings along the Mackenzie pipeline. He's dropped a real crusher on us. By six o'clock tomorrow night we have to agree to settle with the native people and get the bombings stopped. We must also give him free access to the natural gas in the Arctic Islands and the right to set up a transportation system to get it out.

"You said once that if ever I needed your personal counsel I was to let you know. Well, I need it now. I'd like you to drop everything and give me a hand until this whole thing is over with.

"I want you to sit in on all the meetings, listen and take notes. If something crosses your mind, scribble a message and pass it to me. I'm just going into the Cabinet Room now to meet my key ministers. If you could join me there as soon as possible I'd appreciate it."

"I'll be there in five minutes, Bob."

Sam Allen's eyes opened slowly as he wakened. Their dark brown pupils moved slightly from side to side as he focused on the white material of the tent just a few inches from his face. Then he remembered where he was.

His eyes closed again. They never opened very wide, for Sam Allen, like his Eskimo forefathers, had been raised on the land and the ice and the snow. The slitted eyes were those of the hunter who lived off the harvest of the sea and the animals which moved across the barren tundra.

But for young Sam, lying half asleep in his small white tent, pitched on the snow under a stand of jackpine next to the swath the gas pipeliners had made as they passed on their construction journey to the south two years before, life was not that of a hunter. In 1962 Sam's father, old Joe Allen, had moved, along with twelve other Eskimo trappers, from Tuktoyaktuk northeast across the ice to Sach's Harbour on Banks Island. There, it was said, white fox existed in abundance.

It was a good move. The white fox did indeed abound on Banks Island, and the white man paid good prices for the magnificent furs. The families at Sach's Harbour flourished and were prosperous. Sam's father had built a primitive but comfortable house for his wife and nine children. Sam, the oldest, went for his schooling to Inuvik with hundreds of other Eskimo and Indian children from the Mackenzie Delta region, brought there each fall to be educated according to the white man's plan. There they lived for nine months of the year, from the time each was the age of six until they finished high school, or decided, at the age of fifteen or sixteen, to drop out and stay with their families in the settlements or maybe get a job at Inuvik or with the pipeliners — or maybe not work at all.

Sam Allen had lived through that cruel process of education which the white man had decided was best for the Indian and Eskimo. He had survived the wrench of being taken from his family at such a young age to live under the benign regimentation of the Anglican priests who ran the hostel to which he was assigned. As Sam grew older, his education increased far beyond that of his father, Joe Allen, and it became much more difficult for Sam and his classmates to return home at the close of the school year to their families living in tents or shacks in the settlements all along the Arctic coast.

Sam Allen had indeed survived the educational system. He was a determined, headstrong, intelligent, inventive young man. Unusually proficient in mathematics, he had been encouraged to go south to the University of Alberta at Edmonton to take a degree in civil engineering. His tuition and expenses were paid for by the government of the Northwest Territories. Sam worked hard, and graduated near the top of his class. Long before he finished at the university, he had been approached by several of the major oil companies who all wanted the first Eskimo ever to graduate as an engineer. He would be very valuable to the company which got him as a symbol that they were co-operating with the Eskimo people. Sam listened carefully to each of the proposals, thanked each of the company representatives, and said he would be in touch before the end of his final year. Then he kept on with his studies.

It had been 1970 when Sam, still a teenager, had become

deeply involved in the work of COPE, the Committee for Original People's Entitlement. The government, without any consultation with the Eskimo trappers who occupied Banks Island, had granted rights to a French company to drill exploration wells and do seismic tests. When the oil exploration people arrived with their first equipment, all hell broke loose. COPE became immediately involved in an attempt to protect the Sach's Harbour Eskimos. They retained a Yellowknife lawyer and eventually, after the threat of an injunction, an agreement was worked out between the government and the local people. Even then it was apparent to Sam that the main intention of the government departments was not to protect the native people but to push for exploration and development. This meant that the native people had to organize to protect themselves. So Sam had become involved in the work of COPE while he was still at school in Inuvik, and was soon recognized as a born leader. At Inuvik, too, he had met the new lawyer who had come to practise there, Robert Porter. Porter had taken an interest in Sam, and it was he who had encouraged him to go on to university.

Now Robert Porter was Prime Minister, and Sam Allen a graduate civil engineer working with Imperial Oil in the Mackenzie Delta, leader of COPE, and a militant spokesman for the native people. Although Robert Porter had made a full commitment to recognize the aboriginal rights of the Eskimos and Indians of the Northwest Territories and the Yukon and to provide a settlement similar to that made by the United States with the Alaskan native people, negotiations had not yet got under way. The native people, even Sam Allen, felt that Porter ought to move more quickly, because the pipeline was now almost finished. After three years, the southern section from the United States border near Killdeer, Saskatchewan, north to

31

Yellowknife was complete. The last sections near Camsell Bend, northwest of Yellowknife, were under construction linking Yellowknife to Prudhoe Bay and the Mackenzie Delta. But no settlement had been made with the native people. When the construction jobs were gone, nothing would be left. The Indians and Eskimos would be as poor as before, while the white man drained away their natural wealth. Something had to be done. Sam Allen was doing it.

Sam turned over on his right side to look into the sleeping face of his woman. Bessie Tobac was a Loucheux Indian girl whom he had known from the time they were both at school in Inuvik. She was three years younger than Sam, and he had not paid much attention to her then. But when he arrived back from university and had started to work for COPE, he found that Bessie was already a vice-president of the organization. She had been working at the craft shop at Inuvik for about five years, and had become the first native person to be promoted to be assistant manager of that store. Like Sam, she was bright, and totally dedicated to the cause of her people.

As Sam looked at her still sleeping, he could see wisps of her raven black hair sticking out from under the parka hood which framed her somewhat angular face, thin nose and full red lips. He gently put his arm around her and moved his bare left leg to wedge it between Bessie's, and forced them gently apart. At his touch, Bessie's eyes opened to look into Sam's. She smiled at him and put her arm around him, and her legs opened in response to his pressure. It was time to make love. It was time to begin the day.

In the hours ahead they would finish laying the last of the ten packages of high explosive they had brought with them out of Inuvik the day before.

The Prime Minister entered the Cabinet Room. After greetings were exchanged and everyone was seated, he said, "Gentlemen, I have brought you here to advise me. We are facing an emergency of the first magnitude. Since you represent the ministries most closely involved in the crisis, I felt that I should consult with you first."

He then went on to report the telephone call from the President and the nature of the ultimatum from the United States. When he was finished, his audience was shocked and incredulous.

Without pausing for comment, the Prime Minister continued quickly, "We will, of course, discuss the situation in detail at the full Cabinet meeting later today. Now I want you to prepare for a briefing to be held tomorrow morning at eight o'clock.

"The briefing will be for all members of Parliament, including the Senate, and the provincial premiers who can get here. It should be a crash course for everyone on the status of the Arctic Islands gas and oil discoveries and development. For example, it should cover the number of rigs in operation there, the number of people involved, the ownership and control of the gas and oil fields, the interests of Panarctic, and the position of Tenneco, Columbia Gas, and other major American firms that have been advancing money to Panarctic for exploration work. It should deal with the estimated reserves of natural gas and oil and the commitments made by Panarctic and the other owners in the islands to United States firms. And it should also give the National Energy Board's figures on what they calculate will be surplus to Canada's requirements.

"Then I want the same information for the Mackenzie Delta region, and I want growth and demand figures for the United States itself, an analysis of their energy crisis and of the long-term efforts they've taken to cope with it.

"The next thing we'll need is a status report on the Mackenzie Valley pipeline, the problems that have occurred, both in building it and financing it. We should also be brought up to date on the state of the government's discussions with the native people concerning aboriginal rights, and on the sabotage which has been taking place.

"Then I would like to have an informed guess on the type and scope of the economic sanctions that the United States might impose if we refuse to give in to their ultimatum, and a review of the sanctions and other measures they've used in the past two decades to protect their economy and world trading position.

"A similar survey showing what forms of military pressure have been invoked by the United States in various parts of the world since 1945 would be useful. External and National Defence could work that out for us.

"Finally we should have a review of the United States' position concerning our sovereignty in the Arctic, dating back to the *Manhattan* voyages in 1969 and '70, and the enactment of the Arctic Waters Pollution Prevention Act at that time.

"The objective I have in mind, gentlemen, is to give every member of the House a factual briefing on the background behind each element of the ultimatum. I think you'll be surprised at how little most members know about what is going on in the Canadian Arctic about oil and gas, and about our ongoing relationship with the United States and with our native people.

"The briefing will be in the Commons Chamber. As I said, it will start at 8 a.m. Each of you will have twenty-five minutes to make your presentation and answer questions. That's really very little time, but it's the best we can do under the circumstances. I want the briefings to be precise and to the point. They must be finished by eleven o'clock because the House will sit at twelve noon to debate the ultimatum. I have no objection if a deputy minister rather than the minister makes the presentation, and of course you can be assisted by any other advisers you wish."

At this point, Tom Scott entered the room and spoke quietly to the Prime Minister. After receiving instructions, he nodded and departed. The Prime Minister turned back to his colleagues.

"Mr. Scott has just informed me that the office of the President has been on the line. He requests permission to make a flight over Canadian territory to inspect the Polar Gas Study experimental station on Melville Island and to inform himself of conditions in the North generally. I can see nothing to be gained by refusing this permission. Indeed, we may gain by granting it. The President may have more understanding when he sees the difficulties under which we've been operating. I've therefore told Tom to give the President clearance. I trust this meets with your approval."

There was a general murmur of consent, and the Prime Minister continued. "Now to get back to the briefing session: Bob, I want you to start off."

The Prime Minister was speaking to Robert Gendron, Minister for External Affairs. Gendron was the Prime

35

Minister's right-hand man in the Cabinet, the leader of the Quebec sector of the party, and by far the most experienced of all the ministers.

"I think it's important for you to give a broad overview of our relationship with the United States. I don't care who follows after that. It might be a good idea if you carried on with this meeting now to sort out the details. There is to be a full Cabinet meeting at 12:15, so as soon as you can get your staffs going on the briefing material the better.

"I have asked for a meeting with the Leader of the Opposition and the other parties. They should be waiting for me now. I hope you will excuse me."

Sam Allen bent over to strap on his second snowshoe. As he did so he said to Bessie, "We've got a tough day ahead of us. I've planned to set these last five charges along a fifteen-mile stretch. We're going to have to hurry to finish and meet Freddie at Rat Lake at six." He straightened up and looked southwest down the 120-foot swath cut by the pipeliners to where the pipe emerged at the river's edge. Although the pipe had not been buried completely in the permafrost and tundra, it had been sunk halfway down, and the part above the surface covered over with a mound of earth or "berm" of gravel and soil so that the natural vegetation could grow and cover over the pipe. In this way it was hoped the wildlife would not be impeded and that the whole corridor could return to an apparent state of nature. Because of the covering, Sam had had to set the charges at water-crossings. He knew there was no natural gas in the pipe yet but that it was under pressure for testing, and that the moment the first explosion went off, the company would get reconnaissance helicopters out to locate the break and find any other explosives which they had set. This was what had happened when the first set of five bombs had blown the pipe successfully two weeks before.

Sam and Bessie slipped their heads through the holes in the white sheets which they had brought to provide some camouflage against a possible survey helicopter patrolling

37

the line. Bessie said, "I'm ready to go. Shall we leave the tent and packs here, Allen, while we set this charge?"

"I think so." Sam reached into the small tent and dragged out an old and much-used knapsack. From inside he carefully drew out a small blue plastic bag. The package was about the size and weight of a 32-ounce bottle of booze. But, as Sam had said to Bessie, it packed one hell of a lot more wallop. The plastic explosives were powerful enough to rip out a five-foot section of 48-inch steel pipe cleanly. Attached to the explosive was an arming device and a timer mechanism, both of which had to be delicately engaged once the bomb was in place.

With the timer, Sam had planned to set the bombs to go off at random intervals down the line over a twelve-day period. Although this bomb was the sixth to be placed, it actually would explode two days later.

The arming mechanism had a fail-safe device designed to prevent anyone from disarming the bomb once the charge was in place and the timer set. Projecting through the casing of the unit was the rim of a small wheel. To disarm the bomb, the wheel had to be turned fully clockwise and the connecting wires removed between the explosive and the timer. If the wheel were turned counter-clockwise it would detonate the explosive charge and, with it, the person turning the wheel.

When they reached the pipe, Sam handed the explosives to Bessie and, taking the shovel, chopped away at the snow around the base of the pipe where it re-entered the berm. Then he laid the plastic bag out on the snow between his snowshoes, squatted down on his haunches, and set out the arming device, timer and plastics in front of him. He connected the two wires running from the plastic charge through the detonator to the timing unit and pulled back his sleeve to check the time. It was 7:50. He reached inside his pocket to fish out the piece of paper on which he had marked the locations of the ten bombs, together with the date and times selected for their explosion. The list confirmed a time of eleven o'clock two days from now.

He set the timer for 51 hours, and then wrote down on the list the number and date of the bomb, the time at which it was planted, and the time delay. He set the marker on the disarm wheel and pushed in the red arming button. He could feel it engage. The bomb was armed, the timer was set.

He turned to Bessie and nodded. At the signal she stooped over and gingerly lifted the explosive package while Sam picked up the arming device and timer. They lowered the bomb back into the plastic bag. Then Sam eased it into the opening he had made in the snow and covered it over, smoothing out the surface.

"That's it," he said. "Let's pick up the stuff and move on."

As they turned to go back to the tent, they suddenly stopped. In the distance there was a faint chopping sound. Bessie shouted, "Helicopter!"

In their clumsy snowshoes they raced for the edge of the clearing and the protection of the trees. They knew from the sound that the helicopter was very close and flying low. They threw themselves in the snow between the trees and pulled the white sheets up over their heads, covering themselves completely, except for their snowshoes. As they lay in the snow barely daring to breathe, Sam could hear the blades of the helicopter whacking through the air just above the treeline as it passed straight over top of them. He knew that the pilot and the observer in the helicopter had probably been airborne for at least two hours out of the Canadian Arctic gas base near Arctic Red River. By this time, their eyes would be tired from the bright sunlight and they probably wouldn't be able to see very much, even the snowshoe tracks. Sam was right. The helicopter went straight on, without pausing.

When they were certain that the helicopter was gone, Sam and Bessie got up, went quickly back to the tent, packed up, and then set off at a fast pace down the pipeline corridor.

When the Prime Minister returned to his office following his meeting with the key cabinet ministers, he found the leaders of the opposition parties waiting for him.

The Leader of the Opposition, George Foot, a man whom Porter respected, greeted the Prime Minister warmly as they shook hands. So did Donald Walker, the Leader of the New Democratic Party, and Pierre Johnson, of the Social Credit. All three men had been in the House of Commons for many years — a good deal longer than the Prime Minister — and they let him know it from time to time during the heat of debate. But though he was much younger than any one of them, they clearly recognized his ability.

As the Prime Minister was about to explain the urgent reason for the meeting, John Thomas entered the office. Porter introduced him. "Gentlemen, this is Senator Thomas. I don't think any of you have met him personally, but I'm sure you all know who he is. He is not only my close friend, but my personal counsel as well. I've asked him to sit in on all my meetings during the next few hours. I hope you don't mind if he joins us. When I get through explaining what is going on, I think you will understand why I need his presence."

Without waiting for reply, the Prime Minister went straight on. "At nine o'clock this morning I received a telephone call from the President of the United States. As you are all aware, the United States faces an unparalleled energy shortage this coming winter, most particularly a shortage of natural gas. The President, facing re-election next month, has given me an ultimatum which has to be answered unconditionally by Parliament by tomorrow night at six o'clock."

The Prime Minister quickly outlined the three conditions of the ultimatum. When he had finished, George Foot exclaimed, "Why, that's straight blackmail!"

All three opposition leaders were clearly appalled by what they had heard. Johnson stuttered, "Did he say what the United States would do if Canada refused to give in?"

"No," the Prime Minister replied. "I asked him, but all he would say was that he had economic levers too numerous to list. I can think of two or three right off the top. I will be instructing the President of the Treasury Board and the Governor of the Bank of Canada to get their staffs going on estimating the kind of sanctions they think the President can impose, and the probable effect, but just for openers the Americans could levy a prohibitive tax on all manufactured goods coming from Canada. They could prohibit American investors from buying Canadian securities, or in any other way investing money in Canada. By itself, that sanction would practically destroy the Canadian economy, because we need the inflow of U.S. and other foreign capital in order to stay alive."

The Leader of the Opposition agreed. "No question about it. And I suppose they could even stop taking our natural resources, except of course the commodities which they desperately need in their energy crisis, the gas and oil."

It was Pierre Johnson's turn. "They could even go so far as to cut off our shipping or prevent goods from crossing the border. But they would never do that, do you think? We've been on the best of terms with the Americans always. I can't conceive of their doing such things."

"I can," said the Prime Minister. "And I can also see why they're taking this course of action. What we must discuss now are the steps we can take to handle this situation.

"First, I hope we can agree to put aside party considerations. I do not expect you to give up your right to quarrel with anything I do or say, but at this moment bear in mind that what I need is your advice and counsel, not criticism."

George Foot immediately responded, "Prime Minister, there are many differences between us and there always will be, but in this situation my party will do its utmost to co-operate with the government." Johnson and Walker made similar announcements, much to the relief of the Prime Minister.

"Thank you, gentlemen, I hoped you would agree. Now, to get down to business. I think it is obvious that Parliament must be recalled. I have already issued instructions that this step be taken and that emergency transportation be arranged under the direction of the Chief of the Defence Staff. I want every member of the House and Senate here in time for a briefing in the Commons at eight o'clock tomorrow morning. Following the briefing, which will provide information for the members on all matters relevant to Arctic development and the current energy crisis in the United States, the House should convene in emergency session at twelve noon. The Senate can sit at the same time, and I will ask the Government Leader of the Senate to make sure that the motion which is debated is exactly the same as the one the House considers and that no vote is taken by the Senate until the House has voted.

"We must conclude debate by five o'clock, so the vote can be completed by 5:15 to allow the Senate to vote by

5:30. I propose that the vote in the House be a free vote so that no one is tied to party lines."

All three party leaders nodded their agreement.

"Good. The ideal thing would be for the four of us to prepare a motion and present it jointly to the House. The way we put it forward should be no indication whatsoever of the way in which any one of us is going to vote on the question. In introducing the motion I'll make that perfectly clear."

The Prime Minister was interrupted as Tom Scott quietly entered the room and handed him a note. Porter read it, whispered briefly to Scott, then carried on.

"If we open the House at twelve noon and commence the vote at five o'clock, that leaves just five hours for debate; actually, somewhat less than that, because I would like to have thirty minutes at the end to sum up and ten minutes at the beginning to get the ball rolling. Obviously we are going to have to control the number of speakers and the time for debate very rigidly. I would suggest that each of you take fifteen minutes and that all other speakers be limited to ten."

Pierre Johnson broke in. "Good heavens, Prime Minister, in fifteen minutes I can't even get started!"

His colleagues all laughed. Johnson was a notoriously long-winded though colourful speaker.

"Sorry, Pierre, this is one time when your eloquence will have to be contained."

None of the other leaders had any objection to the proposal. The Prime Minister continued.

"I also suggest that the number of speakers from each party be in proportion to the seats in the House. If we four take a total of fifty-five minutes for our remarks, that brings us to 12:55. Between 12:55 and 4:30 there are 215 minutes. At ten minutes per speaker, that works out to twenty-one speakers, more or less. Based on the present proportion in the House, that should give us ten speakers from the government, six from the Opposition, three from the NDP and two from Social Credit.

"For myself, I would open the debate by putting forward the motion in our joint names, and take that opportunity to provide the House with the background of the President's telephone call. Although this will have been extensively covered at the eight o'clock briefing, I think it should be repeated for Hansard."

"That's fine as far as my party is concerned, Prime Minister," said George Foot. "But we would very much appreciate knowing something about the line which you are going to take at the opening. If you could let us have a brief sketch of your remarks, it would be helpful. We will then be in a position to prepare our speeches so they will not cut across your approach or be contradictory. If I *have* to take a position on any point which is contrary to what you say in your remarks, that would also give me the opportunity of letting you know before the debate starts.

"Let me put it to you another way. I'm personally most anxious that all of us in the House present a solid front to the Americans and to our own public, as far as possible, but at this moment I don't know what the motion is going to be and I don't know all the facts. So I can't tell you now, Bob, what the final position of my party is going to be, or, for that matter, since it is a free vote, what my own position is going to be. However, as a matter of principle, I do feel very strongly that if Parliament can come out of this with a unanimous decision, or one which is close to it, it will strengthen Canada's position in negotiating with the representatives of the United States in the future. To have Parliament split in a crisis of this magnitude would be a disaster."

"I certainly agree, George. What do you think, Donald?" Donald Walker had been the Leader of the NDP for many years. He had led his party in opposition to the building of the Mackenzie Valley gas pipeline and the sale of Arctic natural gas and oil to the United States. Furthermore, he had encouraged his party to take a position of strong economic nationalism, and he frequently made heavy attacks on corporations under foreign control. For Donald Walker, this moment of confrontation with the United States was an event which he had long and eagerly anticipated. His grey, sallow face, topped by a thatch of white hair, reflected little emotion, however, when he said, "Prime Minister, you and all of Canada know fully the position which my party has historically taken against the export of natural gas to the United States and against the building of the Mackenzie Valley pipeline. We have long expected that the American corporations, and the U.S. government, having failed completely to plan for their country's future energy requirements, and having taken no steps toward controlling their escalating population, would inevitably take such a step. The New Democratic Party has few members in the House, but our voice is strong. I can tell you one thing, and that is that I will do my best to persuade my party to stand against this intolerable American threat regardless of the consequences.

"So far as I am concerned, the proposals for the briefing tomorrow morning and the handling and timing of the debate are satisfactory. Subject only to seeing the form of the motion you propose, I will be pleased to move it jointly with the three of you."

The Prime Minister smiled and nodded. "Thank you, Donald. Your position is one which has not come as a complete surprise to me. Your willingness to co-operate is much appreciated.

"Now, Pierre, how about you?"

Pierre Johnson cleared his throat. "Prime Minister, so far as the arrangements are concerned, they sound fine to me. I am not going to say what my position will be until the debate. I want my own members to make up their own minds, since it is to be a free vote. I do feel that this is no time for Canadians to cling to regional or cultural differences, and I offer you my co-operation and my support."

"Thank you, Pierre.

"Well, gentlemen, I won't keep you any longer. I will try to keep you informed as matters develop, and to consult with you as the circumstances require. I have also asked the provincial premiers to be in Ottawa by six o'clock tonight. I feel that their views should be solicited and that they should take part in the decision-making process over the next few hours. I hope this meets with your approval."

The other party leaders nodded their heads in assent.

"One final thing," said the Prime Minister. "I've asked the President of the National Press Gallery, and the networks, or their senior representatives, to meet with me. Tom Scott has just informed me they are here. I'm going to ask them to play down as much as possible the ultimatum given to us by the President. The last thing I want is for the country to panic, so we'll need maximum restraint from the media."

As the opposition leaders rose to go, George Foot said, "Well, I wish you luck, Prime Minister. You'll do well to keep the press under control with a news story as big as this one. But you can rest assured that I and my party will do nothing to make this situation more difficult. If we stand together we will show the President that we have some muscle too."

The President loped across the green lawn of the White
House toward the huge Navy helicopter waiting for him,
its blades already starting to turn.

A tall, angular, athletic man, he moved quickly and
decisively. His white hair blew wildly in the down-draught
from the idling blades as he entered the door, followed by
a retinue of six aides and secret service agents, all lugging their briefcases and green army-issue parkas, a
strange sight on a warm autumn morning in Washington.

The President acknowledged the salute of the chief
crewman as he entered the aircraft. He shoved his mane
of hair back in place. As he walked toward the cockpit of
the monster helicopter, he stripped off his coat and threw
it on one of the passenger seats. Without breaking stride,
he ducked his head as he entered the cockpit.

"Are we all set to go, Mac?"

The pilot replied, "Yes, we are, Mr. President. I've got
all the taps on, and we've got traffic clearance across to
Dulles at 3,000 feet."

"O.K., let's go. I'll ride as a passenger on this one."

Flying the helicopter, flying Air Force One, flying anything he could get his hands on was an enormous release
for the President. He had been a pilot, and a first-class
one, from the time he was twenty, when he joined the
USAF. He had become one of their top fighter pilots in the
European theatre, flying P51's in the Eighth Air Force as

escort for the B17 Flying Fortresses. During his tour of operations he had shot down eight enemy aircraft and eventually had commanded his own squadron. There were times when, after long escort flights of six or seven hours, the ground crew would have to lift him out of the airplane. He would be so stiff from being cramped into the small cockpit that he couldn't move.

After the war, when he had graduated from law school and started to practise law in Houston, he kept up his flying. He had also begun to take part in his family's oil business, and the firm's fleet of aircraft provided him with an opportunity to maintain his standards. Even now, at the age of fifty-nine, the President of the United States flew as often as he could.

After the short hop from the White House lawn to Dulles, the helicopter set down with a bit of a bump about fifty yards away from the enormous silver Boeing 747, Air Force One, which was sitting waiting for him on the ramp. He and his six companions immediately transferred to the giant aircraft to join the large staff already on board. The President went directly to the cockpit.

The captain of the 747, Colonel Mike Wypich, with whom the President had flown so many times, had Air Force One set up for him in the usual way and was just completing the pre-flight checks. Finally Wypich said, "It's all yours, sir."

The President responded, "Good." Then he changed his mind. "No, you taxi out, Mike. I need practice in taking down the clearance."

He called Dulles Ground Control for taxi clearance, then switched to Departure Control for flight clearance. Both came through immediately. The President's pen moved rapidly as he copied down the details on his route pad. When the controller had finished reading the message to him, the President read it back to confirm that he had it correct. "ATC clears Air Force One to the Resolute Bay airport via direct Westminster, Jet 75 Plattsburgh, high level 567 Montreal, high level 570 Chibougamau, high level 572 Poste de la Baleine, INS direct Resolute, to maintain flight level 410. Depart Runway One right. After take-off maintain runway heading for radar vectors." The voice of the Air Controller came back. "Your clearance checks. Go to Dulles tower frequency now." Then, in a rare lapse of procedure, the controller said to one of his buddies, "Hey that sounds like the man himself!" The President chuckled as he dialled up Dulles tower on the radio and took control from Mike Wypich.

At 10:32 Eastern Daylight Saving Time, the President got the huge 747 smoothly off the ground, rotating to pick it up cleanly at 160 knots. He climbed away on runway heading in accordance with his clearance.

The captain raised the landing gear on signal and changed over to departure frequency, contacted Departure Control, and received instructions to turn left to a heading of 350 degrees for vectors to the Westminster VOR. The President started a gentle left turn, and after rolling the 747 out on the assigned heading, asked for the after-take-off checks.

The route Air Force One was to follow today would take it over Albany and Plattsburgh, and then on northward over Canadian air space to Montreal's St. Eustache VOR, Chibougamau, Poste de la Baleine on the south-east coast of Hudson Bay, and then across Hudson Bay and the Boothia Peninsula on a course directly to Resolute Bay, on the 747's Inertial Navigation System.

When the aircraft reached its assigned flight altitude, the captain and engineer settled it to cruise at 480 knots. At that point the President said, "Give me your ETA for

Montreal, Mike, so that I can report as we pass over Albany VOR. When I've done that she's all yours. I've got to get back and get to work again."

The Albany VOR station was Air Force One's first check-point where, by international flight rules, they were obliged to report to the air traffic control people their position, altitude, and their estimated time of arrival (ETA) at the next check-point.

The captain responded immediately, "ETA over Montreal is 11:35, sir."

"Check."

As the big aircraft sliced through the clear air on course and at designated altitude, the President checked his flight director instruments and his radio magnetic indicator needles. Their VOR receivers were tuned in to a frequency of 117.8 MHz, and as the aircraft passed over Albany the RMI needles moved from pointing towards the nose of the aircraft through 180 degrees until they pointed to the tail. Observing this station passage, the President pressed his transmitter switch and spoke into the microphone. "Boston Centre, this is Air Force One. Over."

The reply was instantaneous. "Air Force One, this is Boston Centre. Go."

"Air Force One is by Albany at 11:08, flight level 410 IFR, estimating Montreal at 11:35 en route to Resolute Bay."

"Roger. Air Force One, we read two fast-moving aircraft your altitude at this time, moving your direction on intercept course about 50 miles from you at one o'clock position."

"Roger," the President replied. He turned to the captain. "You get that, Mike?"

"Yes, sir, I sure did. We'll keep an eye open."

"O.K.," the President said. "You have control. I'm going

51

to go back to my paperwork. I have to address the nation from this old bird at 12:30, and I've got to find out what my staff want me to say. You know how much us Texans like to be told what to say." The President's long angular face broke into a grin.

The captain laughed. "I sure do, Mr. President."

With that the President took off his head-set, unstrapped it, and left the cockpit.

As the three party leaders left his office, the Prime Minister motioned to Senator Thomas to stay. He went back to his desk, pushed the intercom button for his secretary, and asked, "Have you any messages I should know about?"

"No, Prime Minister, but I can tell you that Mr. Scott has been on the phone constantly, with people calling and trying to find out what's been going on."

"I'll bet he has. Tell me the names of the people who've turned up from the press."

"Peter Forbes, President of the National Press Gallery is here. You know him, Prime Minister. And the Executive Vice-President of the CBC, James Laing, came. He's agreed also to represent CTV and Global, so there are just these two gentlemen."

"Would you ask them to come in, please."

The Prime Minister turned to Senator Thomas. "We can have a few words when these people leave, John."

From the chair in the corner of the room which was to be his listening post, Thomas replied, with a wry smile, "Bob, I wouldn't miss this for the world."

The Prime Minister moved toward the main entrance door to greet Forbes and Laing as they entered the office.

"Peter, good to see you, and you, Jim. Have you people met Senator John Thomas? I've asked Senator Thomas to sit in on all the meetings I will be having in the next few hours so he can assist me in keeping some balance and perspective as well as give me advice."

When they were seated, the Prime Minister gave them a rapid-fire rundown on the President's ultimatum, the action he had already taken, and the plans to recall Parliament, bring in the premiers, carry out the major briefing the next morning, and convene the House and Senate during the afternoon.

Peter Forbes was almost beside himself with excitement. When the Prime Minister completed his explanation of the situation, Forbes practically shouted, "This is a fantastic story. Good God, I've got to get to my paper fast!" He looked around the room as if he were trying to figure out the quickest exit.

"Now wait a minute, Peter," Porter said calmly. "That's the real reason I want to talk with you and Jim. This might be the story of your lifetime, but it's also the worst and most disastrous crisis this country has had to face outside wartime. You people are in highly responsible positions, and you'll be among the first to recognize that if this story goes rocketing off, there could well be panic across Canada. I don't want that to happen, and I'm sure you don't either. So what I want to talk to you about is how the press can help control the situation."

James Laing put in cautiously, "What do you have in mind, sir?"

"I guess what I have in mind is something that really can't be done." The Prime Minister turned away from the two men facing him and looked out the window as he thought the question over. "What I really would like to see is a conscious effort by the press, TV and radio people to play this situation down. I don't want the newspapers to have four-inch headlines saying, 'Crisis Canada' or 'U.S. Ultimatum.' I don't want the television and radio pro-

54

grams to be interrupted with emergency bulletins. I would like to see a sort of normal, everyday reporting of the U.S. proposals and how we are dealing with them, just as if we had a routine situation on our hands. I'm not suggesting for one moment that the facts be suppressed or that the news be controlled. My concern is that the people of Canada should not be panicked."

Forbes, a peppery, excitable little fellow, the senior Ottawa Hill reporter with one of the Montreal papers, took the stance Porter had expected. In a rather hostile voice he said, "Are you suggesting, sir, that the press in this country are irresponsible or that we would deliberately go out of our way to over-emphasize the importance of this story just to sell newspapers? The press has always treated you fairly, Prime Minister, and I don't see why you think...."

The Prime Minister broke in. "I'm not making any such suggestion, Peter, but what I do recognize is that there are human beings running the newspapers and the newsrooms and television stations across this country. How they react to this whole situation will largely dictate how they will print the story.

"Let me lay the thing right on the table for you. I am very much afraid that there will be a strong and possibly violent anti-American reaction among the people of Canada, especially among those who live close to the American border. The last thing I want is to see the people of this country worked up to such a state that some foolish acts of reprisal will be taken against American citizens in Canada by wild-eyed nationalistic Canadians whose emotional juices are turned on, not only by the ultimatum itself, but by inflammatory reporting."

Laing raised a calming hand toward Peter Forbes and said to the Prime Minister, "I see your point, sir. What you say about reaction by the Canadian people is probably quite true. The last thing in the world I would want to see would be some act of violence against American nationals. That would set up a valid reason in the President's mind for some sort of reprisal, perhaps even military action, against Canada. Maybe that's just what he'd like to see at this time, and it's exactly the sort of thing that might happen, not only between now and tomorrow night but for some time after that." Laing hesitated. "But the problem is, sir, that I don't know what can be done about it."

"I agree, Prime Minister," said Forbes. "But how can I, or anyone in the Press Gallery, for that matter, convince his editor to play it cool? Frankly, sir, I don't think there's a hope in hell that you can keep the lid on this."

Senator John Thomas' voice rumbled from the corner, startling all three of them. "Prime Minister, I wonder if you might permit me to put in a word."

"Sure, John, please do."

"Well, it seems to me that there's only one person in Canada who can explain the situation to the people and make them see matters in the proper light, and that's you.

"I suggest that rather than place the burden upon Mr. Laing and Mr. Forbes or their colleagues, you take the matter before the whole country. I think you should appear on national television some time later today and make a statement to the nation. You should outline the seriousness of the situation and directly suggest to the press, radio and TV people that every effort should be made to keep all the facts in perspective, that the American position in the energy crisis should be understood, and that typical Canadian calmness and coolness should prevail."

Laing nodded his head in agreement. "I think that's an excellent idea, Prime Minister. The CBC will clear its national TV network for you at any time, and I know CTV and Global will do the same. In fact, I would be pleased to speak to them for you if you wish."

The Prime Minister turned to Forbes. "What do you think, Peter?"

"Sounds good to me, sir, but I suggest that you get something out to the public as quickly as possible."

"All right, then. I'll need some time to prepare a statement. What about nine o'clock this evening? Could you clear half an hour at that time for me, Jim?"

Laing replied, "No problem, sir, but is there any possibility of your doing it earlier?"

"I don't think so. There's just too much to be done. However, I think I can put together a press release, although there isn't time for a press conference now. You can alert your people that a release will be made in half an hour. In the meantime, I'd like both of you to keep this discussion in confidence, and, Jim, if you will check with CTV and Global and clear the network time with them as well, I'd appreciate it. Would you get in touch with Tom Scott, my chief executive assistant, when the matter has been arranged? Also would you let him know if there are any snags? I think it would be appropriate to carry the program on your radio network as well."

As the Prime Minister stood up to terminate the meeting, there was a quick knock on the door, and Tom Scott entered.

"Sir, we've just had word that the President is going on television at 12:30. It looks as though he's going to make a public announcement about the ultimatum."

Porter was silent for a moment or two. Then he turned to Laing and Forbes and said, "Well, gentlemen, it looks as though the time-table is now somewhat out of our hands. Jim, I would appreciate it if you could clear your television network for me to speak immediately after the President's address. I'll try to deal with the points he raises at that time and make it as short as I can. In any event, I will still want to do the lengthy and considered statement at nine o'clock. Can you arrange it?"

Laing looked at his watch and exclaimed, "My God, it's now two minutes to twelve. We've just a little over half an hour. If you can let me use the phone I think we can arrange for you to follow the President, but we'll have to hustle. As far as nine o'clock tonight is concerned, that's no problem. I'll get onto our technical people immediately to get a TV camera and crew up here. I understand you have a cable and hookup for transmission in the Conference Room down the hall."

Tom Scott said, "That's right."

"Good. We'll use that room for your broadcast. Now, Mr. Scott, if you can get me to a telephone I'll get everything set up."

After getting Laing started on his calls, Scott returned to the Prime Minister's office and reported, "Sir, all the members of the Cabinet are now in the Cabinet Room. I've also arranged for the six deputy ministers of the key departments and the Governor of the Bank of Canada to be present."

Porter nodded. "Good. You'd better get the Deputy Minister of National Defence, too, if he's available. How are the arrangements for transportation coming?"

"Very well, sir. Things seem to be going smoothly. Also the premiers are on their way now."

"That's fine. Now if you'll look after Mr. Forbes, I want to have a brief word with Senator Thomas before I meet the Cabinet. "Thanks again, Peter. I appreciate your advice and co-operation."

As the door shut behind them, Porter said, "Well, John, what do you think of the situation?" He walked over to a massive easy chair in front of the great stone fireplace, lowered himself into it, and put his feet up on the coffee table.

Thomas sat down opposite him, put his notebook and pen on the table, and said, "I think you've got all the bases covered, Bob. While you're dealing with the Cabinet, do you want me to put together the draft press release? You remember you told Forbes you'd have one in half an hour."

"I forgot about that when I heard the President was going to speak. No, it won't be necessary now that I'm going on TV. My shot at that time will be more than sufficient, so don't waste your time putting anything together."

Thomas nodded. "Right. Now the only other question I have is this. Do you think there's any possibility of getting the President to extend his time limit? It seems to me that after all these years of negotiating and haggling another day or two shouldn't matter much to him. But it would give you and the whole country a far better opportunity to assess the ultimatum before a final answer is given. If there's any chance at all of getting him to change the time, it must be done before he gets on television. He won't do it after that."

"You're right. I think you'd better try to get the President on the phone for me while I go to meet with the Cabinet. If you'll let me know when the call comes through, I'll go to the office across the hall and take it there."

The Prime Minister gathered up the papers on his desk and headed for the Cabinet Room. As he entered the dignified, elegant panelled room lined with portraits of past prime ministers, the buzz of conversation ceased abruptly and everyone in the room stood up. Porter went directly to the high-backed chair at the end of the long highly polished table, said, "Thank you, gentlemen," and sat down.

With great shuffling and scuffling of chairs, the ministers seated themselves at the table in order of seniority, with the deputy ministers and other staff ranged round the outside of the room.

The Prime Minister opened the meeting without preliminaries. "Gentlemen, I am sure that by this time all of you have been informed that the President of the United States, on behalf of the government of that country, presented to me in a telephone conversation this morning a three-part ultimatum, the answer to which must be given by Parliament no later than six o'clock tomorrow evening.

"At this moment my staff are trying to get through to the President so that I may speak with him and ask that the time be extended. The President is scheduled to address the United States on television at 12:30. Once he informs the American people of the action he has taken, it will be impossible to get him to extend the time, so if we can't get it done now we won't get it at all.

"As soon as I receive word that the President will speak with me, I'll leave the Cabinet Room to talk to him, but I'll come back here as soon as we're finished. I suggest we watch the President's address here so that I can get your immediate reaction. The CBC are setting up a television camera in the Conference Room next to my office, and I will go on live immediately following the President. Unfortunately I will not have time to consult with you about my response, but I hope you have enough confidence in me to back me up in what I say."

Robert Gendron, the Minister for External Affairs, broke in, "Prime Minister, despite the relatively short time you have held office, I know I can assure you that every one of your colleagues here has the utmost faith in you and will stand behind whatever response you see fit to make." There were immediate cries of "Hear, hear!"

60

As Gendron was speaking, John Thomas had entered the room. He whispered to the Prime Minister, "The President has agreed to speak with you, but it must be very brief because he is attempting to put the finishing touches to what he is going to say on television. If you come with me now, everything is set up."

Air Force One / 11:50 a.m., EDT

The President made his way from the cockpit of the 747
to the circular stairs which took him down to the office in
the forward cabin of the aircraft.

When it was built, Air Force One had been designed to
make it possible for the President to carry on the nation's
business almost as easily from the aircraft as from the
White House. At the front, normally the first-class area,
the President had his private office. In the midsection was
a complex of offices housing the secretarial staff and communications centres for telex and telephone links to the
ground, as well as a sophisticated system of computers,
radar, ground and satellite communication which linked
Air Force One with the military surveillance and communication network. Here, too, was the small, sound-
insulated TV studio from which the President would
broadcast to the nation. At the rear of the aircraft were
the President's sleeping quarters and accommodation for
the staff.

As he came down the stairs, the President could see
Irving Wolf and Al Johnston sitting opposite each other
at a desk on the port side of the aircraft. These were his
two top advisers. Through them the President maintained
his contact with the world. From them came the ideas,
analyses, considerations and judgments upon which the
man in the world's top position of power had to rely.

Wolf got up and moved towards him, breaking off an

animated discussion with Johnston. He was clutching a sheaf of papers. "We've been having an argument on one or two points, Mr. President."

The President smiled. "I can certainly see that, Irving."

Wolf looked slightly embarrassed. "I guess you can, but this is an important statement we're putting together, and we just aren't seeing eye to eye on it."

The President reached for the papers in Wolf's hand and said, "If you two didn't have different opinions, neither one of you would be worth a damn to me. Let's see what it's all about."

Suddenly there was a startled shout from Al Johnston. "For God's sake, look at that! What the hell do they think they're doing?" He was looking out the window on the port side, just a little ahead of where the President and Wolf were standing by the staircase. The President went immediately to the window.

A fighter aircraft was there, its wing-tip fitted closely under the wing of the 747. He recognized the plane immediately. It was a Canadian CF5 fighter, one of the American-designed, Canadian-built aircraft that had come down the production line in the early 70's. The fighter pilot, whoever he was, certainly knew how to fly. The CF5 was tucked in solid as a rock, just as if it was tied to the 747. The plane gleamed silver in the sunlight, its maple leaf markings boldly defined, and a blazing white vapour trail stretched out behind it. To the President it was a spectacular sight.

Suddenly a thought struck him. He went quickly over to the starboard side of the aircraft and looked out toward the wing-tip. Johnston followed. Sure enough, there was another CF5 in exactly the same position. The President was almost beside himself with admiration and envy. Without taking his eyes off the CF5 he said, "Al, that's one

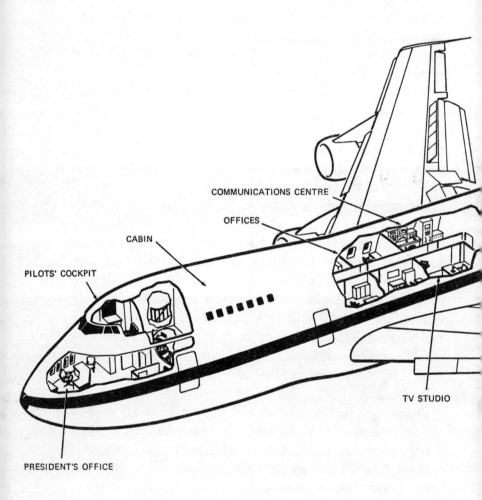

COMMUNICATIONS CENTRE

OFFICES

CABIN

PILOTS' COCKPIT

TV STUDIO

PRESIDENT'S OFFICE

64

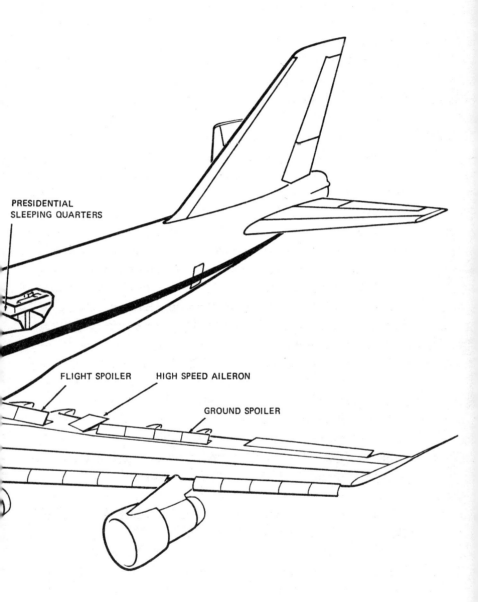

PRESIDENTIAL
SLEEPING QUARTERS

FLIGHT SPOILER   HIGH SPEED AILERON

GROUND SPOILER

of the most beautiful sights in the world. Look at the way that boy's flying that airplane!"

Johnston, who was not an airman, could only say, "How the hell can we get those bastards away from us? They're going to kill us for sure."

The President patted his right shoulder reassuringly. "Don't you fuss, Al. The boy in that plane knows exactly what he's doing. I'm going to try to talk to him." He walked forward to a telephone sitting on the desk and punched the button marked "Captain." When Wypich responded he said, "Mike, I want to talk to those two boys sitting on your wing-tips."

"What two boys?"

"Haven't you seen them? We've got two of the neatest, shiniest CF5's you've ever seen, one on each wing-tip. I guess they're a bit far back for you to spot."

There was a pause. "Well, I'll be damned. I guess those are the two aircraft that Boston Control reported to us about three minutes ago, just as you were leaving the flight deck, Mr. President."

"Must be, Mike. It looks as if the Canadians are telling us we're over their real estate. Try to make contact, will you?"

"Yes, sir. Stand by one."

The President could hear the captain talking to his co-pilot. "What's the serial number of the aircraft on the starboard side?"

"It's 411."

Then the captain transmitted, "Canforce 411, this is Air Force One on 117.8. Do you read me?"

Immediately a voice came back. "Air Force One, this is Canforce 411. Good morning. We're instructed to welcome you and your distinguished passenger to Canada. My wing man and I will fly with you for the next half hour, then

66

you'll be picked up by two other aircraft from my base. We will have someone with you all the way to Resolute, purely as a matter of courtesy, you understand, Colonel Wypich."

The President, listening to the conversation, grinned broadly when the fighter pilot casually let it be known that he knew the name of the captain of the 747. He spoke into his telephone, "Mike, can I transmit using this telephone?"

"Yes, Mr. President. Just push the button on the top right-hand corner."

The President pushed the button, and looking out the window at the sleek fighter said, "Canforce 411, good morning. This is the President speaking. Give me your ident, please."

"Good morning, sir. I'm Colonel Jack Prince. I command the Canadian forces base at Bagotville, Quebec. I was instructed by Ottawa to take charge of this escort operation. On the port wing-tip is Lieutenant Colonel Jean Belisle. He commands 433 squadron at Bagotville."

Belisle broke in. "Good morning, sir."

"Good morning, son. We're sure glad to have you boys along. We're going from here across to Churchill. First I want to take a look at the big new deep-water port you people are building up there. Then I'm going straight north to Resolute."

Colonel Prince's voice came back. "Sorry we won't be going all the way, sir. We'll be with you for the next half hour, then you'll be picked up by another team."

"Fine, Colonel, fine," responded the President. "But now I'd be obliged if you'd do me a favour. My staff on this big bird aren't really used to seeing airplanes fly so close and they're getting a little uptight about it. It doesn't bother me one bit, but I'd appreciate it if you'd park your aircraft about two hundred yards out in battle formation. It would make everybody here just a little more comfortable."

"Wilco, sir," said the Colonel, and passed the word to his wing man. "Battle formation, Jean. Go!"

With that, both fighters turned outward. The Colonel took up his position about two hundred yards abreast of Air Force One on the starboard side, while Belisle's aircraft did the same on the port.

As the President put down the telephone Wypich entered the cabin from the cockpit. "Sir, you mentioned Churchill to the Canadian pilots but I don't have that in your instructions."

"That's right, Mike. It struck me as I talked to those young fellows that we would be passing pretty close to Churchill, so I thought it would be a good idea just to go by and take a look at the new port from low level. When we get there let's go down to about two thousand feet and then head for Resolute."

The captain said, "Yes, sir," and went back up the circular stairs.

The President walked over and sat down beside his aides. "O.K., Irving," he said. "The pilots have given us lots of room. Now you two can relax."

Wolf nodded. "Here's your speech, Mr. President. Your rough draft was excellent in parts but, if you'll pardon the expression, pretty damn awful in others. When you read this draft you'll probably say I've screwed up the excellent parts and left in the bad ones. Anyway, here it is."

The President smiled. He found Irving's dry wit refreshing.

Wolf had first impressed him more than a decade earlier when he had testified before the Senate Foreign Relations Committee regarding the pressure being brought to bear on the United States by the OPEC countries. On that occasion, Wolf had presented a superb exposé of the increasingly-difficult and complex problem confronted by the U.S. in its relationship with the Organization of Petroleum Exporting Countries. Many of these nations were Arab and, as Wolf had skilfully explained, had combined to exert leverage on the United States to cease supporting Israel by supplying it with money and military equipment.

After the testimony, the Senator had sought out Wolf, befriended him and asked for the opportunity, readily granted by Wolf, to consult with him from time to time on questions of international trade and world diplomacy. So it was only natural that when he began his drive for the presidency he invite Irving Wolf to become part of the team. After the election, the President selected Wolf, not as a member of the Cabinet but as his special assistant and adviser on a broad range of matters assigned to him. With that recognition, real power came into the hands of Irving Wolf, power which he did not hesitate to use.

When the native people of the Northwest Territories and Yukon had begun, only a few days before, to blow up sections of the Mackenzie pipeline, it was Wolf who had recognized that the President would have to take action immediately to protect American interests in the area. It was Wolf who proposed the ultimatum and who drafted its terms. Despite the President's reluctance, Wolf had convinced him and the Cabinet at the meeting which had taken place the evening before, and it was Wolf who had secured agreement on the strategy of sanctions which the President could impose to enforce the ultimatum.

Now he sat watching the President, his scythe-like nose pinched between his index fingers, a gesture of contemplation for which he was now famous. He was not worried that the President would reject or alter the draft speech; that seldom happened. Rather he was considering the implications of the economic sanctions he had proposed against Canada, the first of which was to take effect at twelve noon.

As he expected, the President, when he had finished reading, took off his glasses, sat back and put his hands behind his head. After a few moments' silence he drawled, "That's fine, Irving. Looks good to me. But I tell you I'm still not happy about threatening to put a bullet between the eyes of the Canadians. It makes me very uneasy. I'm concerned about the ultimatum, and I'm concerned about the sanctions."

He stood up. "However, we've done it, and we'll stick by it. How much time have we got until I do the broadcast?"

Wolf looked at his watch and said, "Seventeen minutes, Mr. President. The networks have cleared you for 12:30. The TV studio back there is all set."

"You mean aft, Irving, not back," the President chuckled. "Don't forget, you're on a ship."

Wolf smiled and shrugged. "The studio aft is all set. They've got the Presidental Seal in place and the flag behind the table so that everybody who is watching you will think you're right in the White House. They'll get a hell of a shock when they find out you've been broadcasting from Air Force One over Canadian territory via the Canadian satellite Anik 3."

"Why are we using that satellite and not one of our own?"

"Oh, I gather the orbit is a little better for our position and the transmission will be clearer. Some time ago we rented two of the surplus TV channels on Anik 3. We'll use one of them this morning."

As the President turned toward the tail of the aircraft, Al Johnston came up behind him and said, "Mr. President, Prime Minister Porter wants to speak with you. His office says it's very urgent."

70

The President checked his watch. "There isn't much time. It'll have to be short." He followed Johnston back to the telephone. Johnston picked it up.

"Senator Thomas, the President will speak with the Prime Minister but it's got to be short because, as you know, he's going to address the nation in a very few moments."

Senator Thomas' voice came back. "We understand. I'll get the PM. Hang on, please."

In a few seconds the Prime Minister came on the line. When he was on, the President took the telephone from his aide and the two exchanged terse greetings.

The President said, "What can I do for you?"

Porter replied, "You gave me an arbitrary deadline of six o'clock tomorrow night. I've talked to my people here and I don't know if we can get Parliament reconvened and all the steps properly taken in such a short time so that I can give you an answer which reflects the view of the people of Canada. The Arctic question is not a new one. We've been haggling over it for years, and in the interests of fairness I think you should give us more time, even an additional twenty-four hours."

The President replied quickly, "I expected you'd be back to me on this point, and I've already discussed it thoroughly with my advisers. The answer has got to be No, there can be no extension. I've given you an ultimatum, and I've given you what I consider to be a reasonable length of time for your decision-making process to function. There's no way that, having stipulated at nine o'clock in the morning what the United States wants, I'm going to start backing off three hours later. No, Mr. Prime Minister, the terms of the ultimatum stand and the timing with it. Furthermore, just to show you that we mean business, at twelve noon the Secretary of the Treasury was instructed to place

71

an immediate embargo on the movement of any and all U.S. investment or other funds into Canada. At the present rate, that will mean a cut-off of $30-million of capital investment money a day. That's just for openers."

The Prime Minister started to protest but the President cut him short, "I'm sorry, Mr. Prime Minister, I'm due on television in just a few minutes, as you know. My staff tell me that you are going to respond as soon as I have finished. All I can say is, Be careful!"

He hung up.

As the President and Wolf entered the communications cabin the five men manning it glanced up, then carried on with their work. Pete Young, the President's Television Director, was giving final instructions at the main control console, so the President and Wolf waited, looking around at the familiar but still amazing setup.

Against the port wall were banks of telex equipment carrying reports from the State Department, the Pentagon, and the news wires. Two of the crew monitored these messages at all times, and delivered batches of the most significant items to the President's secretarial staff at half-hour intervals. Ranged against the forward wall were the high-frequency radio transmitters and receivers. To the President's left, under the arched roof of the cabin, were the computer terminal and control units which were hooked into the master defence computer system at the Pentagon. Through this terminal the President alone could issue the final command codes for missile interception or even nuclear retaliation. To the rear of the cabin, behind a glass panel, the President could see the TV studio, with its three cameras set up facing the desk, complete with Presidential Seal and Flag.

When Peter Young had completed his work at the control console he looked up and nodded.

"All ready to go, Pete?" the President asked.

"All set, Mr. President. We're locked on to the satellite, we've run a transmission check, everything looks good. The networks are standing by. There'll also be a feed-in to all the Canadian networks."

"That's good, Pete. How much time have we got?"

"Two minutes and thirty seconds, Mr. President."

"I guess I'd better get in there." The President headed for the studio door. In a few moments he was installed behind the desk with his papers in front of him.

Young flicked a switch on the console. "Are you all set, Mr. President?"

"Yes, Pete."

"Would you give me your voice level please, sir?"

"O.K. I'll do it by asking you to give me the countdown as we come up to 12:30. I understand that, as usual, you'll show the Presidential Seal for five seconds and do the intro over the Seal."

"Right. We're coming up to fifteen seconds. All network clearances established. Coming up to ten seconds . . . five, four, three, two, one." He flicked the switch for transmission of the Presidential Seal and spoke into the microphone in front of him. "Ladies and gentlemen, the President of the United States." Then he switched to the President and pointed to him.

"My fellow Americans, I want to inform all of you about certain actions I have decided to take to meet the serious energy crisis which confronts this nation. . . ."

Following his phone call to the President, Robert Porter stood for a moment deep in thought, his head down, shoulders slumped. Then he turned and walked slowly back into the Cabinet Room. The din of many voices ceased abruptly as he entered. The tension and anger shown on his face told his colleagues what had happened even before he began to speak.

"The President has given a flat No to my request for an extension of time. Furthermore, the United States has gone further than I thought they would at this stage to show us that they mean business. He has, as of twelve noon today, instructed the Secretary of the Treasury to place an immediate embargo on the movement of all U.S. investment capital into Canada."

The voice of young Michael Clarkson, the Minister of Finance, broke through the shouts of outrage which greeted this announcement. "The country can't survive without that capital!"

The Prime Minister hesitated a moment, then replied, "Now listen to me. We can survive, and we must, Michael. We've got to show at once that we will not be intimidated. Since the President has chosen to invoke sanctions against us even before the expiry of his deadline, he'd better learn that sanctions can go both ways. You should instruct your deputy, Angus Stone, and the Governor of the Bank of Canada — are they both here? — ah, yes, gentlemen —

74

you should instruct them right now to take all necessary steps to prevent the transfer of any Canadian funds into the United States, directly or indirectly. I have in mind dividends, return of capital, investment money, and the like. And all the stock exchanges should be directed to cease trading immediately and to remain closed until further notice."

The two financial officials huddled briefly with the Minister, then quickly left the room.

Glancing at his watch, the Prime Minister pressed a button under the table in front of him to activate the large television set mounted high on the wall at the far end of the room. As the panelling slid quietly open, the screen was already showing the words, "Special Bulletin, Stand By." Porter said, "Now gentlemen, our time is short. During the President's address, if a point occurs to you which you think I should cover in my response, make a note and pass it up to me. I want to have the benefit of your ideas and I'll try to incorporate any point you wish me to make.

"As soon as I have finished my televised statement, I'll come back here so that we can discuss the entire situation and make some decisions as to how the matter should be handled. As you know, I have taken steps to recall Parliament, bring in the provincial premiers, and hold a briefing session at eight o'clock tomorrow morning, to be followed by an emergency sitting of the House at twelve noon."

At this point the Presidential Seal flashed on the screen. Porter pressed the button to bring up the volume.

"Ladies and gentlemen, the President of the United States."

The President's familiar craggy countenance appeared on the screen. He displayed no sign of nervousness; he was, as always, calm and confident, a man who wore power with

75

dignity, directness, and assurance. Years before, when he had been first a senator and then a member of the Cabinet, he had had no hesitation in voicing tough and sharply critical views of Canada. He clearly considered Canada a bothersome colonial attachment to the United States' empire, worth putting up with only because of its rich treasury of mineral and fossil fuel resources. Everyone in the room knew he was watching a man who would pay no attention to Canada or the Canadian point of view, when they came into conflict with U.S. interests.

The President began, "My fellow Americans: I want to inform all of you about certain actions I have decided to take to meet the serious energy crisis which confronts this nation.

"This morning at nine o'clock Washington time, I telephoned the Prime Minister of Canada to discuss with him the urgency of the situation. I pointed out that this winter approximately 20% of all the industries in the United States which rely upon natural gas would have to be shut down. I made it plain to him that hospitals would have to be closed, that homes and apartments would be without heat, and that the American people would suffer, and indeed many would die this winter, because of a shortage of natural gas in the United States.

"My fellow Americans, the responsibility for this shortage rests primarily on the shoulders of the Canadians.

"The Canadians have vast reserves of natural gas in their Arctic regions, especially in the Mackenzie Delta and on the Arctic Islands. Because Canada could not put up the necessary capital, United States' money has paid for the construction of a pipeline to bring gas from Mackenzie and Prudhoe Bay in Alaska down to the Chicago and Detroit areas, one of the most critically affected regions of this country.

"Since 1970, American firms have poured millions upon millions of dollars into exploration and development. To date, more than 60-trillion cubic feet in proven reserves of natural gas has been discovered in the Arctic Islands alone.

"Because the Mackenzie pipeline will not meet all our requirements, Tenneco and the other major United States gas distribution firms, which have financed the discoveries in the Islands, are prepared to buy gas at the well-head and to create their own transportation system to deliver it to United States markets.

"For the past three years, American scientists have been carrying out an extremely costly and dangerous experiment to test a prototype pipeline system to transport gas between the Arctic Islands under water. As an alternative solution, we have spent approximately one billion dollars to develop a prototype Resources Carrier aircraft which has just been test-flown at the Boeing factory in Seattle. When fully operational, this aircraft, three times the size of a Boeing 747, will be capable of carrying 2¼-million pounds of liquid natural gas. Although the Canadians at one time had contracts which would have allowed them to control the building, financing and operation of these aircraft, they were once again unable to muster the initiative and financial resources to carry through with the project, and we have therefore taken it over. To sum up, American know-how, and American dollars, have discovered nearly all the reserves of natural gas. We need that gas desperately, right now. American engineering has developed the facilities to bring it to market. This is a great achievement, and we have every right to be proud of what we have accomplished.

"Why, then, do we find ourselves facing the present energy crisis? Quite simply, the Canadian government refuses to let us have any of the natural gas on the Arctic Islands. Negotiating teams from the United States government have been attempting for years to work out an agreement with the Canadians to purchase one-third of the crude reserves on the Islands, that is to say, 20-trillion cubic feet. At the same time, we have been trying to establish a comprehensive continental energy policy under which both countries would have mutual access to all of the electricity, crude oil, natural gas, nuclear power, and any other sources of energy which might be available.

"Unfortunately, we have been totally unsuccessful in our dealings with the Canadians, not because they have at any time said No to our legitimate requests, but because the Canadian bureaucracy is in such a state of division that they find it impossible to agree on a course of action which they are prepared to present to their political masters.

"The result is that no Canadian government since 1970, when the first evidence of the growing energy crisis began to emerge, has been able to come to grips with the reasonable demands of the United States for a commitment on the gas of the Arctic Islands or a continental energy agreement. Despite our eagerness to work out a plan which would be to the benefit of all Canadians, Americans and American industry are now facing an intolerable situation because of the inability of departments of the Canadian government to work with each other.

"Canada is a country which has long been regarded as a friendly trading and cultural partner of the United States. Most of its major manufacturing industries are subsidiaries of multi-national U.S.-controlled firms, and most of its resource industries, including minerals such as nickel and iron, which are essential to the United States, are controlled by American interests. Furthermore, much of the high standard of living enjoyed by the Canadian people must be directly credited to their favoured position as the first and largest trading partner of the United States.

"Under all these circumstances, it is not unreasonable for you and me as American citizens to expect, when we are suffering from a shortage of a commodity which the Canadians have in abundance, that they should adopt an open-handed policy.

"I have referred earlier to the Mackenzie Valley pipeline. I must now tell you that approximately ten days ago I was informed that acts of sabotage were occurring along the pipeline route. Let me give you the background.

"When large-scale oil development began in Alaska, almost a decade ago, the United States government recognized the legitimate demands of the native people to a share in the natural wealth of their land. We made a settlement with the native people of $500-million in cash, and 40-million acres of land. And we provided an additional $500-million to come from a 2% royalty on all the gas and oil production from Prudhoe Bay. This was a fair and a just settlement.

"Unfortunately, despite our strong recommendations, the Canadian government has refused to settle justly and fairly with their native peoples. Even now, as the Mackenzie Valley line nears completion, no settlement of any kind has taken place. As a result, the radicals within the native peoples' organizations have begun to blow up the pipeline.

"There is little the Canadian government can do to prevent these acts of sabotage, and it is clear that in American interests as well as Canadian a settlement must be reached at once.

"And so, my fellow Americans, time has run out in our

negotiations with Canada. The United States can no longer tolerate either a failure or a refusal by Canada to come to terms concerning natural gas and to settle their problems with their own people so that gas can be delivered to meet American needs. I am sure none of you would wish me to be harsh or vindictive with the Canadian government. On the other hand, it is my responsibility as your President to press the United States' case in the most direct and forthright manner.

"In the face of this emergency, I have been forced to take strong action. After receiving advice from the leaders of the Senate and the House of Representatives, and after conferring with the Chief Justice of the United States, I took the following steps at nine o'clock this morning. . . ."

As the President described the ultimatum he had given to the Prime Minister, Porter was rapidly making notes. His colleagues sat watching the President transfixed. Some scribbled short notes which were passed up to the Prime Minister. No one spoke.

Now there was no way back. The President had informed his people and the world that the U.S. demands would have to be met.

The President was moving to the conclusion of his address. "I have stipulated that unconditional, affirmative answers must be given to each of these three requirements no later than six o'clock tomorrow evening. We have prepared a series of economic sanctions which can be invoked against Canada should our reasonable ultimatum be refused. My fellow Americans, it is in your interests and in the interests of stopping this needless suffering by our people that I am fully prepared to impose such sanctions should it be necessary.

"In order to demonstrate our firm resolve in this matter, I have instructed the appropriate government officials that as of twelve noon today an embargo should be placed on the transfer of any funds by United States persons or corporations into Canada. This includes the lending of money, the purchase of shares or securities, or any other method of investment. Canada needs these monies from the United States in order to survive economically. By the same token, the United States needs access to the Arctic Islands natural gas in order to survive economically and physically. The principle is the same in both cases — survival.

"In conclusion I wish to say to the Canadian people that the United States wishes none of you individually any harm whatsoever. If there is any difference between us, it is not between our peoples but rather between our respective governments. Americans deeply regret that you must now be called upon to suffer for the ineptitude and stubbornness of an inflexible and unimaginative bureaucracy which has your new federal government paralyzed by its incompetence.

"And to the world I say that the United States and Canada must resolve this crisis between us. Interference or involvement by other nations is unnecessary and unacceptable.

"My fellow Americans, this great nation, the finest country in the world and the largest and most powerful, was founded and lives upon the fundamental principles of liberty and justice for all. I am sure that you will want me to maintain those principles in our dealings with Canada over the next few hours, but I want each of you to understand that I have first in mind the health and wellbeing of every American citizen. The interests of the United States and its citizens must be upheld.

"Thank you, and good afternoon."

Someone on the Prime Minister's right muttered, "Bullshit!"

For a few moments after the first outburst, there was silence in the Cabinet chamber. Then bedlam broke loose. Everyone was talking at once.

The Prime Minister sat, oblivious to the noise around him, rapidly making notes. Abruptly he got up and left the room, followed by Senator Thomas. Cries of "Give him hell, Bob" and "Don't submit to blackmail" followed him as he went out the door.

As he reached the Conference room, he was met by Tom Scott, who reported that everything was set. The conference table had been moved toward one end of the room opposite the TV camera and a chair placed behind it so the Prime Minister would be facing the camera with a panelled wall as background.

The producer, Al Price, who had covered many of the Prime Minister's speeches, was well known to Porter. They exchanged greetings.

Price said, "Would you sit over here, sir? We've got the camera set up to cover you face on. You can put your notes on the table in front of you." He led the Prime Minister around behind the long conference table and slipped a neck microphone over his head. Porter sat down and glanced at his notes.

"How much time do we have?"

"You're on in thirty seconds, sir."

The cameraman and the other two crewmen, who had

been muttering among themselves, quieted down. The Prime Minister took off his glasses, and with an automatic motion put them in his left shirt pocket. He sat up a little straighter and looked the camera in the eye. He was ready.

Al Price held up his outspread hand. "Five seconds." At the final cue, he pointed to the Prime Minister.

"The President of the United States has just informed the American people — and those in Canada who were able to see or hear him — of the ultimatum which he presented to me and the government of Canada this morning.

"Originally I had planned to speak with you this evening at nine o'clock. I still intend to do so, because by that time the situation will be much clearer and the steps taken by your government to meet this crisis will be firmly established. However, when I learned that the President was going to address the American nation at this time, I felt it appropriate to follow his statement with one of my own.

"As the President pointed out, the people of the United States are indeed caught in a severe energy crisis. Some years ago it became apparent that because of bad planning, or failure to provide for future energy needs, heavy shortages of oil, natural gas and electricity were about to occur. The first serious shortage was felt in the winter of 1972, when some factories, schools, and other institutions in various parts of the United States were shut down because of lack of fuel. You are all aware, I am sure, of the continuing problems which have increased since that time, of electrical "brown-outs," of gasoline rationing and of shortages of heating fuels, which have occurred regularly, winter and summer, since that time. During this period two things have happened: First, the population of the United States has grown rapidly over the last decade from 209-million to about 229-million this year, an increase almost equivalent to Canada's entire present population. In other words, the energy needs of the United States at this time is at least equal to its 1970 needs plus the entire energy requirements of Canada.

"During this time, the United States has continued to expand its industrial and manufacturing capacity without restraint, thereby further increasing its insatiable demand for energy.

"The United States moved as quickly as it could to overcome the energy crisis. It was successful in increasing its supply of crude oil but not in obtaining additional natural gas. That is the reason why the United States is much more concerned about getting its hands on Canada's natural gas resources than on the crude oil reserves that have also been found in the Mackenzie Delta and in our Arctic Islands.

"The Americans have been able to keep up with their oil demands as they have risen because they have been able to purchase crude oil from various places in the world such as Venezuela, Algeria and the Middle East, and to transport it in the fleet of oil tankers which they began to build in the 60's.

"The situation regarding natural gas is more complicated. The background is simply this: Natural gas represents a little over 30 per cent of the energy consumed by the United States on an annual basis. At the beginning of this decade, there was a shortage of natural gas amounting to 900-billion cubic feet per year. Today the figure is more than two and a half times that amount.

"The world appears to have adequate reserves of natural gas available, and the problem facing the Americans is not that there is a short supply but that there is no adequate transportation system in existence which can carry the natural gas to the United States from overseas.

"Tankers of the kind necessary to transport natural gas are still in very short supply. The gas must be cooled to the point at which it becomes liquid (–260°F), and it must be kept at that intense cold in special uncontaminated containers during transportation. The tankers required to carry liquid natural gas did not even exist a decade ago, and though the Americans and Japanese are building them as quickly as they can, there are still very few in operation. The Americans have twenty, but they could use a hundred.

"In the light of this situation, the United States has no choice but to make every effort to gain immediate access to the reserves in the Mackenzie Delta and the Arctic Islands, where it is possible to transport the gas by pipeline or the special airlift tankers to which the President referred.

"Let me say to all Canadians and to every American that I have great sympathy for the dilemma in which the President finds himself and for the American people.

"When I came to the office of Prime Minister only seven weeks ago, I took on the legacy of action or inaction of all my predecessors of whatever party. I fault none of them. On the other hand, there is little doubt that the President is quite correct when he complains of the inaction of the Canadian bureaucracy. That bureaucracy is the product of a system which has given the country great stability and has permitted the various government departments to function effectively despite frequent political shifts. But inevitably over the years the system has become excessively rigid. It has failed to keep pace with the changing times. I've proposed to make a number of reforms in this area, but that is a matter for discussion on another occasion.

"The point is this. Canada must accept some of the blame for the failure of which we stand accused by the President. We *have* been negligent in dealing with our native people. It is perfectly clear that they have a moral right to share in the returns from the resources of their lands, and we should have dealt with them long ago. And we did, in fact, fail to make an arrangement with the Americans to give them access to the Canadian Arctic Islands gas. In part, this was due to a natural concern that our own requirements should be taken into consideration, but in part it was also a failure to come to grips with what was obviously an emergency situation. The President is right. Canada is largely to blame.

"But having conceded this, the question remains: Is the President justified in suddenly giving Canada an ultimatum and enforcing that ultimatum by economic reprisals even before the deadline? This question is of major concern to me. I do not propose to attempt to answer it at this time, but I will do so when the House of Commons meets in emergency session tomorrow."

The Prime Minister then outlined the steps which had already been taken to recall Parliament, to consult with the provincial premiers, and to brief the members of the Senate and the House of Commons prior to the emergency sitting of the House the following afternoon. Then he continued.

"There is no doubt that this is the most difficult and important crisis Canada has ever faced. What the outcome will be I cannot predict, but I am most anxious that the Canadian people remain calm, that there should be no panic, and that there should be no reaction of an anti-American nature. Any acts of physical retaliation against any United States citizen in Canada would cause irreparable damage to our already-delicate position in relation to the United States.

"I ask every journalist, editor and copy writer to maintain a high calibre of responsible, factual reporting of the news and to refrain from any kind of comment which might inflame emotions.

"This is a time when the nation and its leaders should abandon partisan positions or regional attitudes, so that we can all reply to the United States with one voice.

"This crisis demands of all of us courage, strength, and patriotism. I am sure the Canadian people will respond."

The Prime Minister then spoke in French, covering the same ground. Finally he said, "I have asked the radio and television networks to permit me to speak with you again tonight at nine o'clock. At that time I will review the situation as it then exists.

"Thank you."

The two ravens flew soundlessly overhead in the brilliant sunlight of the early afternoon as Sam and Bessie trekked along the pipeline cutting. The two enormous black birds had joined them early on the first day, and Sam had recognized their presence as a good omen. They were his favourite birds, and among the most intelligent. They live and fly usually in pairs, talking to each other much like crows but in a more guttural fashion. They make a good team. In the settlements of the treed parts of the Arctic they are the scavengers which scour the communities and keep them much cleaner than they would otherwise be.

They particularly delight in driving the husky dogs mad. A pair of ravens can strip a dog of his food in the twinkling of an eye, one landing in front of the dog just beyond the length of his chain, flapping his wings and muttering obscenities at the animal. With great howling, barking, and mighty pulls against the restraining chain, the dog uses all his efforts to get at the bird to destroy it, forgetting all about his food. The more frantic he becomes, the louder the raven shouts at him, and goads him on.

Meanwhile, just behind the frustrated dog, the second raven is quietly but quickly gulping down his dinner, pausing once in a while only long enough to smile quickly up at the wild, well-plotted scene. When it is finished, the two birds fly swiftly off, leaving the dog hungry, frustrated and angry.

"Yes," Sam thought, "two ravens make a pretty good team, and if Bessie and I can get these last two bombs set up, we'll have done a good job too. At least we'll wake up those northerners in Ottawa who keep forgetting there are people up here."

As the Prime Minister and Senator Thomas returned to the Cabinet Room, there was a wave of applause and congratulation as everyone stood while the Prime Minister moved to his chair at the head of the table. When the commotion had died down, he motioned them to be seated and sat down himself.

"Thank you, gentlemen, I appreciate your support."

"Prime Minister," said the Minister for External Affairs, "you can see that we're pleased with what you said. We support totally the position you took. We're proud that you're the leader of our party at this critical time."

"Thanks, Robert. Thank you all. Now let's get down to business. There's a lot to be done.

"I've told you that there will be a major briefing starting at eight o'clock tomorrow morning. I have asked each of the ministers responsible for the departments most directly concerned to prepare a status paper for presentation at that time. The Ministers for External Affairs, Energy Mines and Resources, Northern Development, Transport, Environment, Finance, and National Defence will all make presentations.

"A question period will follow each briefing. Since we have only three hours, I've suggested that the combined statement and question period should not exceed twenty-five minutes per ministry. I have asked the Minister for External Affairs and his deputy to lead off.

"I met with all the ministers concerned and their deputies this morning. I assume that preparations are now well under way. Is this so, gentlemen?"

The seven ministers and their deputies all nodded.

"Good. The House will sit at twelve noon. I will introduce a motion made jointly by myself, the Leader of the Opposition, and the NDP and Social Credit leaders. I'd like the Minister of Justice to draft the motion.

"Could you do that for us, Ken, in the next few hours?"

Kenneth Locke, down the table on the Prime Minister's right-hand side, said, "Certainly, sir."

The Prime Minister continued. "I suggest, Ken, that the motion restate the ultimatum and move that it be rejected. This of course is a matter of form. The fact that I present it does not necessarily mean I support it. I want to listen to the debate in the House, to hear the briefing, and to talk with quite a number of people before I decide whether to vote for or against the motion. The stakes are far too high for me to make up my mind conclusively one way or the other until I have had a full opportunity to assess every aspect of the situation.

"As soon as you have the motion drafted, Ken, I would be obliged if you would bring it to me. We can work it over together and then perhaps you could take it to the leaders of the other parties for approval or amendment."

Otto Gunther, Minister of Energy, Mines and Resources, spoke up. "Prime Minister, I think it would be appropriate to suggest that the Cabinet have a look at the wording of the motion before it is taken to the leaders of the other parties. While I am quite sure that what you and the Minister of Justice put together will be satisfactory, I think it would give the motion added weight if it carried the approval of the entire Cabinet."

The Prime Minister thought for a moment and then

said, "All right, Otto. Once Ken and I have settled the draft and before it goes to the other parties, copies will be delivered to each of you with instructions that your comments will have to be back in Ken's hands within an hour.

"The final thing that we have to discuss at this point is the list of speakers from our party during the debate on the motion. The number of speakers in each party will be in proportion to the number of seats held in the House. There will be eleven from our party. According to the plan agreed on with the other parties each speaker, apart from the party leaders, will have ten minutes.

"I suggest that James Campbell, as House Leader, be responsible for organizing the speakers for our party.

"Jim, you might want to consider asking all the members who wish to speak to let you know by a certain time. After that, the choice can be made by lot. This may be an unusual approach, but it will be a fair one under the circumstances.

"Now, gentlemen, I've been doing a lot of talking and you've been doing a lot of listening. Do you have any comments on the course of action I've outlined?"

As he was asking this question, Tom Scott entered the room and handed the Prime Minister a note. Porter scanned it briefly and nodded to Scott, who left the room.

Silence had greeted the Prime Minister's invitation to comment.

Gendron of External Affairs broke in. "Obviously, Prime Minister, the fact that there are no questions indicates general agreement with the steps you have proposed. Might I suggest that if any of us do have comments or questions we get in touch with Tom Scott. He can pass anything straight on to you if required."

"Thank you, Bob. That's a good suggestion."

"Well, there's one thing that bothers me, Prime Minister." It was Otto Gunther from Newfoundland again, Robert Porter's main competitor at the leadership convention eight weeks before. Gunther's defeat by Porter still rankled. After all, he was an older, more experienced and senior member of the party, and as far as he was concerned Porter was only a johnny-come-lately. "What I don't understand is that you haven't given us any indication of what you think about this ultimatum. It's all very well to say that you want to wait until you've heard the briefing and the debate, but I don't think that's good enough. We're in a difficult situation and you ought to exercise some leadership and give the country some direction."

Porter smiled a tight, hard smile. "I suppose what you're saying, Otto, is that if you were the Prime Minister you'd be telling us where to go."

"You're damn right I would. The leader of this country has to be prepared to show where he stands, not wait for somebody else to make up his mind in a debate." Otto Gunther returned the smile, but he meant what he said.

Porter nodded. "I understand your point of view, but I must say I don't agree with it. I feel very strongly that I should stand by my intention of hearing and considering every opinion and every factor before I state my position.

"Now, gentlemen, if there are no other comments, I have one final thing. In my television talk I spoke about the importance of keeping calm and unemotional. May I suggest that when you are talking with the press you make no derogatory remarks about the United States, the President, or the action they are taking. Anything you or I say at this time which is inflammatory can only serve to harm the interests of Canada, and severely damage our ability to negotiate.

"I have just received word that the Governor-General has arrived from Victoria. I want to see him as soon as possible, so I will leave the meeting in the hands of the Minister for External Affairs. Thank you."

Neither Robert Porter nor John Thomas spoke as they walked quickly back to the Prime Minister's office. There Porter called his secretary and instructed her to have his car ready and standing by in front of the East Block. Then he asked Tom Scott to phone Government House and find out whether His Excellency could receive him in about twenty minutes.

Scott replied, "I'll do that right away, sir, but first I should tell you that the Chief of the Defence Staff called about two minutes ago and said that he had information he wanted to pass on to you personally."

"O.K., have somebody get him on the line for me as soon as possible."

As he turned away from the intercom, Thomas said, "I don't know about you, Bob, but I'm hungry as hell. Do you think we could have something sent in? We haven't had a thing to eat, not even coffee."

Porter laughed. "Too bad, John, you probably could stand to lose a few pounds anyhow. I don't think I'm going to have anything, but I'll get my secretary to find some sandwiches and coffee for you.

"While I'm seeing the Governor-General, do you think you could rough out a sketch of what I might say in my television address tonight? I want to tell the people exactly what's going on and how we propose to deal with the situation, and I want to stress again the need for a calm approach. You might get Bob Gendron of External Affairs to give you a hand. He's a pretty wise old bird, and he's had lots of experience. Also, he understands the Americans very well."

"Sure, at least I'll make a stab at it. I can't guarantee anything, but having listened to you for a good part of the day and watched what's going on, I'm sure I can get something down on paper. It won't be the first speech I've drafted for you."

"Thanks, I'd appreciate it."

Porter turned to gaze out the office window. "I've got something else on my mind. I wonder how we could get a good reading of what the people of Canada think we should do about this ultimatum. Surely with the fantastic communications systems today there must be some way to do a representative sampling of opinion fast. Maybe Davies of Bell Telephone would have an idea. He's a good friend of mine. You know him, don't you?"

"Yes, I do. I met him in Montreal with you just before the leadership campaign started. We had lunch at the Beaver Club in the Queen Elizabeth."

The intercom buzzed. It was Tom Scott. "Sir, the Chief of the Defence Staff, General Adamson, is on the line."

"Thanks, Tom."

The Prime Minister picked up the telephone. "General, you were calling me."

The General answered. "Yes, sir. Two things: First of all, I want to report that the airlift for the members of Parliament and the Senate is going very well. We should have everyone in for the eight o'clock briefing tomorrow morning except for those who are too ill to travel — there are a couple — and three from the Senate who are out of the country and can't make it back in time."

"That's a very good turnout."

"The second thing is that I think you should know that in the past twenty-four hours we have noticed a substantial increase in the number of practice flights carried out by USAF bombers over Canadian territory. The same thing applies to fighter interception practice. As you know, Prime Minister, under the NORAD arrangements, the Americans have to get final clearance from us to over-fly Canadian territory. They've been doing this, so there's no secret about the flights, but I thought I ought to draw the matter to your attention.

"We have no intelligence that there is any ground activity, troop movements, or anything of that kind anywhere in the United States, but there certainly is a lot of activity in the air."

"Thank you for telling me, General. The President knew very well that you would report to me the increase in the overflights. Obviously it's another piece of pressure.

"Since I have you on the line, General, there's a matter I should take up with you. I have been quite concerned that the military be ready to come to the aid of the civil power should any anti-American reaction develop in the next few hours — protest parades, or acts of violence against American citizens or property in Canada. I understand that the emergency structure that was set up in the early 70's after the FLQ trouble in Quebec is designed to cope with this kind of situation, and I just want to make sure that the military are on the alert."

The CDS responded, "We certainly are, sir. I've already issued instructions and the machinery is in operation. I've kept the Minister of Defence and his deputy fully informed, including the information I have just passed on to you, sir. They have approved of what we're doing."

"Thank you, General. Keep a close eye on the situation. For what it is worth, I think the Canadian mouse should put all its military forces on the alert in case the American elephant decides to get nasty, although I can't conceive of such a possibility."

The General chuckled. "I will, sir."

The Prime Minister hung up and said to Thomas, "I guess you could gather what that was all about. The Americans are rattling their planes at us. And the members and senators are on their way back.

"Now I should be off."

He touched the intercom. "Tom, is my car ready?"

"Yes, sir, and there are four RCMP officers here waiting to escort you through the gang of reporters and photographers lying in wait out in the hall."

"O.K., I'm leaving right now."

As he headed for the door, Porter said to Thomas, "I suggest you stay and work here, John, rather than go back to your own office. You can use any of my staff. But suit yourself."

The Prime Minister went through the reception area, where he collected the four RCMP officers, resplendent in their traditional red-coated uniforms. Two of the men preceded him and the other two walked one on each side.

As they opened the door to the corridor, the Prime Minister was confronted by a mass of pushing reporters, most of them holding out microphones. All were shouting questions, none of which he could make out. The Prime Minister and his bodyguard wedged their way through the milling throng to the top of the staircase, but there they were blocked. Finally Porter held his hands in the air and waved vigorously. Gradually the commotion died down and the shoving subsided. The RCMP officers cleared a space of a few feet between the Prime Minister and the reporters, but he still had to shout to be heard.

"If you will all be quiet for a minute, I'll tell you what I am doing and where I am going. There's no time for interviews at this point."

A score of hungry microphones were thrust toward the Prime Minister, and television cameras ground away.

"The Governor-General has just arrived back from Victoria and I am on my way to advise him of the ultimatum and to let him know what steps the government is taking. Also, of course, I will seek his advice. I've known His Excellency for many years and there is no man in the country whose counsel I would value more at a time such as this.

"I have nothing more to add to what I said on television a short while ago except that all the machinery is in operation to ensure that a decision will be made by Parliament within the time frame set down by the United States."

Someone shouted, "How are you going to vote on the ultimatum question, Prime Minister?"

Porter did not respond immediately. When he did, he spoke slowly. "I am not in a position to say how I will vote, and will not be until the House has completed its debate tomorrow afternoon. By that time I will have heard what the members of the House have to say, I will have had opinions from all across the country, and I will have had counsel from the premiers of the provinces. When I finish off the debate in the House tomorrow, you will know my decision on the ultimatum."

Another question. "Prime Minister, do you think the Americans are justified in putting a gun to our heads?"

This was a question that the Prime Minister clearly did not want to answer. He held up his hands and said, "Sorry, I can't take any further questions. There's no time." With that he turned and moved quickly down the stairs and out the heavy doors into the waiting limousine. An RCMP car with the four officers in it followed the Prime Minister's as it moved away from the East Block.

Air Force One (Churchill)
1:07 p.m., CDT

Air Force One, with the President at the controls, had slowed down to 250 knots. To the citizens of Churchill, Manitoba, 2,000 feet below, the Boeing 747 appeared to be hovering there like some great goose followed at a respectful distance by a brace of ducks. The new pair of Canadian Armed Forces CF5 fighters trailed the 747 in formation, about four hundred yards behind and a thousand feet above.

The President banked the big bird in a shallow turn to the left. On the approach to Churchill coming in from the south he had passed over the entrance to the harbour, north of the grain elevators, over the Old Fort on the west side of the Churchill River, and then circled so that he could have a good view of the inner harbour. There were no buildings on the west side of the narrow river mouth, but on the east there were the rail marshalling yards and dock facilities with huge cranes. There was still one ship in the port taking on a load of grain, probably the last of the year. The navigation season at Churchill, which had begun at the end of July when the ice broke up, was just about over.

To the south of the dock facilities lay the town of Churchill, and beyond it the single CNR line that led south to Thompson and Winnipeg. To the east of the town was Fort Churchill, a military base and airport during World War II. The airport, which had survived the post-war years, was paved with an east-west runway sufficiently large to take even the 747.

The airport was bustling with activity as the President swung the big plane in a wide arc overhead. Several vehicles were working on the loading of five Hercules aircraft and several other smaller planes. The President said to the captain, "Ever been here before, Mike?"

"No, sir, I haven't."

"Well, let me tell you a little about this place. You can see that the river flows north into Hudson Bay. It's very narrow. The port is right at the river mouth. During spring break-up, the ice which flows down the river piles up against the ice which is blown in from the north, and so Churchill, which was supposed to be a major ocean port for the Provinces of Western Canada, has been restricted to a shipping period of from 50 to 80 days a year, depending on the weather. What's more, the water is so shallow in the port that only ships under 30,000 tons can get in. As a result, Churchill has never really been able to attract much business except the shipping of grain from the Prairies. There are a few ships that move to and from Europe and bring in booze and things like that, but Churchill has been severely hampered by the short shipping season, the shallowness of the harbour, and by the high insurance rates on ships entering Hudson Bay.

"But things are beginning to happen pretty fast here. The Hercs on the ramp there are running drilling rigs straight north into Baker Lake and beyond, and also into the Chesterfield Inlet region, about 350 miles north. There have been three major copper finds and one nickel discovery in the area, and more exploration work is being done. You may have noticed that about 15 miles south there's a bridge under construction. It's a combined railway and motor vehicle bridge, which will make it possible for the

CNR to continue north right up to Chesterfield and Baker Lake. That railway is under construction now and should be ready in the next year. Alongside it there will be a highway.

"The whole thing is built on eskers. They're long beds of gravel that were left behind after the last ice age. They stretch all the way from Churchill straight north."

"Sir, how on earth do you know all that?"

The President chuckled. "Mike, right now it's my business to know. I was here a few years back and had a good look around then, and I made sure I was well briefed before this trip. Before we left, I thought I might take a look at Churchill, and in the next three or four minutes you'll see why. We'll do one more circuit around the town and the airport and then head out due east."

He went on. "The railway and road I told you about are really the beginnings of a transportation and development corridor that'll stretch all the way from here straight north to Resolute and the centre core of the High Arctic Islands. That corridor already exists as far as air transportation is concerned. An enormous amount of machinery and equipment is now moving from Chicago, Detroit, Toronto and Winnipeg straight into Resolute, and a lot of that supply comes into Churchill for transfer into the Baker-Chesterfield Inlet area.

"Just about the time I was here last, the Canadian government had a special committee called the Great Plains Group. They came up with a proposal to build a new deepwater port on the west coast of Hudson Bay to take ice-strengthened ships up to 500,000 tons which could move ore or liquid natural gas and minerals from the High Arctic. Some bright boy on the committee remembered the eskers, and suggested why not take this fantastic supply of gravel and build a causeway from Churchill straight

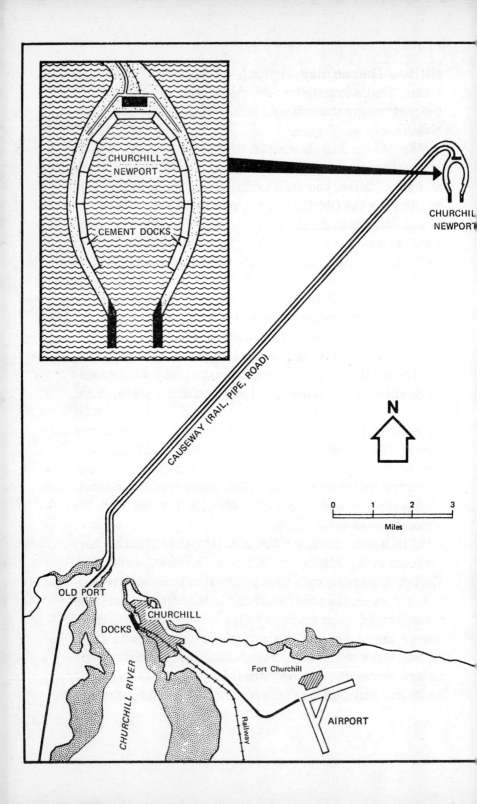

CHURCHILL
NEWPORT

CEMENT DOCKS

CHURCHILL
NEWPORT

CAUSEWAY (RAIL, PIPE, ROAD)

N

0 1 2 3
Miles

OLD PORT

CHURCHILL

DOCKS

CHURCHILL RIVER

Fort Churchill

Railway

AIRPORT

out into Hudson Bay to the point where there is deep water. That's exactly what they've done, Mike. It's about the only imaginative thing the Canadians have done in the North in the last decade."

The 747 was to the east of the airport now, heading north. The President pointed west toward the old harbour and said, "Mike, you see the west side of the old harbour mouth near the Old Fort location? That's where the automated railway and road lead out to the causeway. It goes north about a mile into the bay, turns east-northeast and runs in a straight line for twelve miles. We'll follow it out."

With that the President put the wheel of the 747 gently over to the right, turning the aircraft until it was running parallel to the causeway. The dull gray strip of gravel matched the overcast sky which hung low above the plane.

"There, Mike, you can see the setup now — a three-track railway, a six-lane roadway, and a double pipeline.

"The railway was used to build the causeway. It has an automated loading and off-dumping system that was hooked into the eskers to the west. They moved millions of tons over the period of two years that it took to get the causeway and the basic framework of the port built. We should be able to see the port any minute now."

The captain said, "Mr. President, why are you so interested in looking at this port? Is it of some particular importance to the U.S.?"

"That's a good question, Mike, and the answer is, It sure is. See those pipes on the causeway? One is for crude oil and the other is for natural gas. The southern end of each of those pipes plugs straight into the Chicago-Detroit area. The northern end, just up ahead of us, will plug into crude oil and liquid natural gas tankers coming in from Venezuela, the Middle East and Algeria, as well as from the

High Arctic Islands if the Canadians will get off their butts and give us access."

The captain nodded and pointed straight ahead. "There's the port, sir, at twelve o'clock."

Churchill Newport began to appear out of the haze. From the end of the causeway the port faced south like a huge wishbone. Each arm, like the causeway itself, was a great long pyramid of gravel stretching from its broad base on the floor of the Bay to the surface of the water and then above it to a height of thirty feet above high tide. The top of this great structure, 400 feet wide, carried the road, rail and pipes that had been built for loading and off-loading, and around the entire inner edge were huge docks made of cement which had been floated in and sunk.

The President pointed and said, "Do you see those big cement caissons, Mike? They're built like that because of the ice. If an ice-breaker has to be used to open the port, it could ram its way past those things, and because their walls are sloped rather than vertical, the ice would ride up instead of jamming.

"It's ingenious, isn't it? You have to hand it to them. They've thought it all out. They've even got a system inside that pre-fab port to keep the water from freezing. They drive compressed air through a series of pipes laid under water, and if that's not enough, they pump heated effluent from the town of Churchill to keep the water above freezing point. Between that and the fact that the new port faces south away from the prevailing winds, they should be able to prolong the shipping season well beyond the normal period.

"When you consider all this, you can see why I think this is so important for the United States and why I want to take a good look at it. I can sit on my can in the White House and have people tell me all about it, but I'm the one that has to deal with the energy crisis and I've got to know what I'm talking about."

Col. Wypich nodded in agreement. "I get the picture now, Mr. President, and you're dead right."

"I only wish I'd been able to come up before," the President added. "I would have if I'd been able to shake myself clear. When the native people began blowing up the Mackenzie Valley pipe ten days ago I knew that the time had come to get hold of the situation before it was too late."

He brought the aircraft out of the turn and said to Wypich, "O.K., Mike, if you'll plug in the latitude and longitude of Resolute Bay on the INS and get clearance from Churchill tower I'll set her up for the climb to 40,000 feet, and tell the fighter boys we'll meet them on top."

Leaving a trail of black smoke and diminishing noise, Air Force One climbed sharply and disappeared into low gray cloud just north of Churchill Newport. The faithful Canforce CF5's fell in behind and entered the cloud cover at the same time.

Ottawa / 2:13 p.m., EDT

As his driver slowed to pass through the narrow entrance gate of Rideau Hall, the Prime Minister reflected on the close relationship which had existed for many years between the Governor-General and himself. As a law student, Robert Porter had articled in the large Calgary law firm of Simpson and Crane. Alexander Simpson, the senior partner, had taken an immediate liking to the bright, aggressive young man, and the fact that Porter was deeply involved in the work of the same political party that Simpson supported only served to increase his interest. When he was called to the bar after heading his law school class, Bob Porter accepted a generous offer to join the law firm and work with Simpson as his junior. In large measure, he became the son that Alexander Simpson had never had, and during the years in which they worked closely together, the two formed a strong bond of mutual respect which had continued.

On his appointment to the Senate six years after Porter joined the firm, Simpson decided to retire from the practice of law to devote his time to work of the Senate and to the interests of the University of Alberta, of which he had become Chancellor. As well as being a distinguished lawyer, he was known for his deep concern for the cultural, social and physical development of Canada and its people. He had established a Chair of Nationology at the University and gave an annual lecture there on the state of

Canada. This yearly event had become an occasion of major importance in the life of the University.

Soon after entering the Senate Simpson was chosen as its Speaker. His fluency in the French language and his knowledge of French-Canadian culture, combined with a remarkable sense of fair play, and an equitable perception in dealing with the sittings of the Senate, made him universally regarded as one of Canada's most distinguished and respected citizens. He had never fought to uphold the hard party line. In point of fact, he was looked upon by many of his peers as being above politics, but at the same time his allegiance to his party was never in question.

Consequently, when the previous Governor-General, an able French-Canadian, retired from office, Robert Porter's predecessor had reached across party lines and recommended to the Queen the appointment of Senator Simpson. As is the custom, she accepted the Prime Minister's advice and made the appointment, one which was well received throughout Canada, and particularly in the West.

When Alexander Simpson had left the firm to take up his duties in the Senate, Porter decided to make his move into the Northwest Territories. Simpson's work had been in the field of corporation law, chiefly on behalf of the oil and gas firms engaged in exploration and development in Alberta and the Arctic. With the considerable experience he had gained in dealing with these companies and the service firms which supported them, it was not long before Robert Porter's decision to practise in Inuvik, the centre of the oil and gas finds in the Mackenzie Delta, proved to be a rewarding one.

When Bob Porter became Prime Minister, both he and Simpson were delighted to be able to work together again. Porter found the Governor-General unfailingly kind, wise and helpful during the days when he was getting his bearings in office, but never had he needed the counsel and understanding of his old friend more than he did today.

The car swung around the circle in front of Rideau Hall and stopped under the porte-cochere. The Prime Minister got out of the car and acknowledged the salute of the RCMP officer on duty. He mounted the few steps to the front door, which was opened by a young Canadian Forces officer, one of the aides-de-camp to the Governor-General. He said, "I'm Capt. Robillard, sir. His Excellency is expecting you. He's in the drawing room at the end of the hall, if you'd be good enough to follow me."

With the aide leading the way, the two of them left the entrance foyer of Rideau Hall and walked through the reception room and down the long hallway past the formal dining room, reception and writing rooms, to the drawing room which His Excellency used as an office. It was a large, comfortable room lined with bookshelves. At one end there was an ornate, carved stone fireplace, before which a settee and chairs had been placed in a semi-circular arrangement around the coffee table. At the other end, between two windows, there was a beautifully-carved desk at which the Governor-General was sitting.

As the Prime Minister was announced, the Governor-General got up immediately and moved around the desk toward Robert Porter, his hand outstretched in welcome, clear delight and pleasure beaming from his face. He was a man who showed few signs of his age. His piercing eyes and firm chin conveyed strength and authority, and brought warmth and confidence to the Prime Minister. As they shook hands, he said, "I can't tell you how glad I am you're here, sir. If ever I have needed your help and advice it's now."

"Well, Bob, as you know, one of the great delights of my life is to be of service to you. Whether or not I can be in this instance remains to be seen. I'll do what I can, but remember my gratuitous advice is probably worth what you pay for it."

Both men laughed lightly and easily.

The Governor-General took Porter by the arm and said, "Come and sit down over here by the fireplace. I've ordered some tea—or would you prefer a glass of sherry?"

"As a matter of fact, Your Excellency, I would prefer the sherry."

The instructions were given to the aide and the two men sat down, facing each other across the coffee table. The Governor-General leaned back and took out a small cigar. "Well, Bob, I understand we have a crisis on our hands."

"A crisis of the first order, sir. If I may, let me fill you in on everything that has happened and tell you about the plan of action for the rest of today and tomorrow."

The Governor-General nodded his approval and puffed at his cigar.

The Prime Minister began with the telephone call from the President and traced the events and plans through to the point of his proposed discussion with the President the next evening, at which time he would inform him of the decision made by the Canadian Parliament.

The sherry was silently served. The Prime Minister took a sip from time to time as he proceeded. His host sat back and puffed occasionally on the cigar as he listened intently to everything that was being said.

When it was over, the Governor-General slowly shook his head. "Incredible, simply incredible."

Nothing was said for a few moments. Finally His Excellency broke the silence. "You know, Bob, in one way you are in a fortunate position whether you realize it or not. You said you're going to meet with the provincial premiers at six o'clock. Has it struck you that the two main points of the ultimatum come strictly within federal jurisdiction rather than provincial? The first has to do with native rights, an area of responsibility which no province has ever claimed. The second—the demand for Arctic Islands gas—has to do with the Northwest Territories and the Yukon, which are still under direct federal jurisdiction since they have not yet received full provincial status.

"So I think that in regard to the first two points, the Parliament of Canada and you as Prime Minister can speak exclusively and without interference from the provinces.

"On the third matter—the one having to do with granting the Americans free access to any part of Canada to enable them to transport gas from the Arctic Islands—things might be more difficult. If they're talking about a pipeline—and I presume they are—then that pipeline will have to come from the Islands either down the west coast of Hudson Bay and through Manitoba and Ontario into New York State or Michigan. Or it will have to come down across Baffin Island, then across Hudson Strait into the Ungava area of Northern Quebec and on from there. If it is to be a pipeline, can you and Parliament commit the provinces, or do you think you have to get their consent?"

The Prime Minister took his last drop of sherry, put down the glass, and replied, "I hadn't thought of the problem in exactly those terms, but it was in my mind that I would have to have the advice and, if necessary, the consent of the premiers. That's why I asked them to come to Ottawa. The question of jurisdiction will very likely be raised by Quebec and possibly Ontario, but perhaps I should raise the matter with them first."

The Governor-General nodded. "Yes, I think you should."

The Prime Minister went on. "One thing is certain. If

110

I do have to obtain consent of any one of the provinces, it will have to be from the premier alone. He can check with his cabinet, but there's no way the legislatures could be convened in time to endorse or reject that consent. The whole responsibility for the decision will have to be taken by the individual premier.

"And if any one of them balks, I suppose we—that is, Parliament—will have to override the objection. On the other hand, if Parliament rejects the ultimatum, then the question of provincial consent becomes academic.

"In any event, I don't think the Americans will bring the gas out of the islands by pipe, because I don't think it's technically possible. A consortium called the Polar Gas Study Group has been trying for years to lay pipe between Melville and Byam Martin Islands. They have had one failure after another. I understand they are running a final test now on a new plastic pipe, but I doubt whether it will be successful. It's my guess that they'll choose to take the gas out by air, using the fleet of huge aircraft which Boeing and the American gas companies have been developing."

The Governor-General said, "Oh, yes, the Resources Carrier. That's the plane we initiated some years back and then lost out on."

"That's right, sir. The Americans carried through with the project and the prototype had its maiden flight in Seattle about six weeks ago.

"Panarctic and Tenneco plan to use the aircraft to fly the gas off the Islands if the pipe doesn't work. They would carry it out on relatively short hauls to Ungava in Quebec or Cochrane in Ontario, say, and then feed it into pipelines there for transmission to New York State. Or, on the other hand, they could decide to extend its range and airlift directly to the United States.

"In any event, they're going to use the RCA to haul the oil from the new Melville wells to market."

The Governor-General thought for a moment. "Bob, there's another question that's been going through my mind. What about the formality of my presence at the opening of the emergency session of Parliament tomorrow?"

"I haven't checked with the Speaker yet, but I think your presence will be required. If a Speech from the Throne is necessary, I'll prepare a one-liner for you. I'll confirm it, but I think you should plan to be present."

The Prime Minister went on. "I think I should tell you, in your capacity as Commander-in-Chief of the Armed Forces, that I have asked the Chief of the Defence Staff to alert the entire military establishment with a view to containing any possible outbreaks or demonstrations of anti-Americanism that might occur as a result of the President's ultimatum.

"The CDS tells me there has been a marked escalation in U.S. military flights over Canada since this morning. I'm not really worried about that; it's obviously part of their game plan. What really worries me is what the President can do to us by economic sanctions. The one he has already imposed is serious enough by itself, but when you get down to it, he could practically destroy our economy overnight if he chose to do so. Whether this will be sufficient to persuade Parliament that it should give in is the real question.

"The other side of that question is whether or not Canadians, and in particular the members of the Commons and the Senate, are sufficiently nationalistic to refuse the ultimatum and face the consequences."

"Well, you'll know soon enough," said the Governor-General. "I can certainly understand the Americans' predicament, but I wish they hadn't chosen this big-stick blackmail-type approach. It just isn't in keeping with their traditional way of doing things."

"Perhaps it is consistent if you look at their track record since World War II," said the Prime Minister as he stood up. "Now, sir, if you'll excuse me, I must go to my meeting with the premiers."

The Governor-General also rose, walked around the coffee table, and taking the Prime Minister by the arm, led him toward the door. He said, "Well, Bob, I don't know that I've given you much help during this visit or any advice, for that matter, but maybe I've given you a chance to review the whole situation and perhaps see the implications of the President's actions and your own in a better perspective."

"Yes, I think you're right. It's a great help to me to know that you're here and ready to back me up."

By this time they had reached the entrance foyer of Rideau Hall. The young aide was holding open the door.

The Governor-General turned and faced the Prime Minister, looking him squarely in the eye. "Now remember, Bob, I'm available to you at any time of the day or night. I will do anything I can to help, anything at all."

The Prime Minister turned and went out the door, quickly passing the saluting RCMP officer, and turned to wave to the Governor-General as he got into his car and was gone.

When the Prime Minister arrived back at his office, he found that Senator Thomas had left.

"He didn't feel comfortable in your office, sir, so he went back to his own," Scott explained on the intercom. "He said to call him when you want him."

"O.K. Where are the premiers, Tom? Have they arrived in town yet?"

"They're all here but Post of Nova Scotia. He's somewhere in Europe and they can't find him, so Margaret Cameron, the acting premier, has come in his place. I've booked them all in at the Chateau Laurier. They'll be here at six. I've set up the Cabinet Room for you.

"And whether you like it or not, sir, I have arranged for steak to be brought in at seven. I know that you will want to get right on to the final preparation of the nine o'clock statement. Do you think you'll be through with your meeting with the premiers by that time?"

"Yes, I must be clear by then. If the meeting hasn't broken up, come in and get me. Say another emergency has arisen so that I can wrap it up. Arrange for some food for yourself; then the three of us can have a bite to eat together and you can bring us up to date on what has been going on.

"After that, we can go over Senator Thomas' draft. Have my secretary stand by to retype as we put on the finishing touches. Would you remind her to use the extra-large type so that I can read the speech without my glasses?"

Tom Scott laughed. "I'll tell her, sir. I don't think she would ever forget, though."

"Have there been any urgent calls?"

"No, none that are really urgent. I've had several calls from your ministers and a lot of other people, but there have been no direct calls for you. I think people realize the importance of the situation and don't want to bother you."

"Good. I'm going to take the next few hours to make some notes about what I want to say in the House tomorrow.

"By the way, have you heard anything from the Minister of Justice about the draft resolution? We should have that by now."

"It's just arrived on my desk this moment. Shall I bring it in?"

"Yes, please do."

By six o'clock the Prime Minister had gone back and forth over the draft motion and made a few minor changes. He called in Tom Scott. "Here's the motion, Tom. I'm satisfied that it's in acceptable form now. Would you please have it retyped and deliver it back to the Minister of Justice as quickly as possible. He's going to circulate it to the other Cabinet ministers. If they will let him have their comments by nine o'clock tonight, he should be able to give me a final draft by 9:30. It might be a good idea if he sent a copy to the party leaders at the same time so that we can arrange a meeting if they have any objections."

"Will do, sir."

The Prime Minister stood up. He looked pale and tired. Scott said, "You've been under a terrible strain today, sir. Are you going to be able to get some sleep tonight?"

"I'll try, but it will have to be here in this office. I want to be near the hot line and close at hand in case I'm needed."

The Prime Minister glanced at his watch. "Good Lord, I'm five minutes late for the meeting with the premiers. They're a sensitive bunch at the best of times, so I'd better get going. Remember to come and get me, Tom, if the meeting hasn't broken up by seven."

After leaving Churchill, Air Force One climbed back up to 40,000 feet. The President levelled it off and turned the controls over to the pilot, then went down to the office to be briefed on events as they were happening in Ottawa. He scanned the summary of the Prime Minister's remarks made in response to his own, snorted a couple of times, and said to Wolf and Johnston, "Well, you've got to give that young fellow credit. He's certainly trying hard."

They had reached the south end of the Boothia Peninsula and were starting down. The cloud cover below had disappeared and they were able to see the vast reaches of the Canadian Arctic eastward to Baffin Island and westward towards Victoria and Banks Island. Stretching out in front of them was the great channel which separated the mainland from the Arctic Islands — the historic Northwest Passage.

The President pointed out the channel and said, "I came up here to see the *Manhattan* sail past Resolute Bay in September '69 with a group of people from Montreal who were making the trip at the invitation of Nordair.

"We found her to the west of Resolute Bay, steaming through a great pan of ice. She was a pretty sight, looked right at home in that setting, but the Canadians weren't very happy that she was here. She represented a threat to their claim that the waters of the Northwest Passage belonged to them. They've passed all sorts of legislation since, claiming sovereignty, which they can't possibly enforce, but the voyage gave notice that we intend to back up our position that the Passage is high seas."

Soon Air Force One came in for a landing on the new 10,000-foot runway at Resolute Bay. In the years since his last trip, only the centre core of Resolute had changed appreciably. The single-storey, red-coloured prefabricated buildings that had been brought in by ship to serve as offices, hotel, and administrative buildings were still there, but there was now also a high-rise building like the one in Frobisher. And there were several new hangars lying to the west of the runway, and a great many more fuel-storage tanks.

Resolute Bay had become, in fact, an Arctic boom town. Though it was a poor airport because of uncertain weather conditions, it made an excellent naval base, and had developed into the major regional centre serving the growing gas and oil developments in the Sverdrup Islands. The recent discovery of a massive pool of oil on Melville Island had added to the already enormous discoveries of gas on the Sabine Peninsula and on King Christian, Ellef Ringnes, Thor, Axel Heiberg, and Ellesmere Islands. The number of rigs drilling in the area had increased from thirteen to fifty within a ten-year period. Resolute was for the President just a transfer point, however, the last possible landing space for the giant 747 in that part of the world. With no more than a quick look around to survey the changes which had come about since he was there before, the President went aboard the Hercules transport that was ready and waiting for him. Wolf and Johnston and the rest of the staff would remain on Air Force One to provide the link between the President and the outside world.

The Canadian fighter planes, the fifth pair to join them,

scrambled to refuel and took off shortly after the President. It was by then four o'clock in the afternoon local time, but the sun was still high in the sky. The weather was "ceiling and visibility unlimited." The Herc flew low at 2,000 feet so that the President could clearly see the geological formations, especially the huge salt domes which dotted the islands from Melville to Ellesmere. It was at the edge of these domes that the oil and gas finds were occurring with such remarkable frequency.

They had taken off in a northerly direction, but at Bathurst Island they turned left to swing over the Magnetic North Pole and then due west toward Melville Island. The President wanted to take a look at the main base of Panarctic at Rea Point and at the work going on at Drake Point and Hecla, where development wells were now being drilled.

When they reached Drake Point the President said, "Circle around, Captain. I want to have another look. It was right about here that the first big gas discovery was made in January '70. It came up under such enormous pressure that it blew. It took several months before they could bring it under control. The same sort of thing happened elsewhere in the Arctic, too. No one had the knowhow or the technology then to cope with high-pressure finds like that.

"Well, I guess I've seen all I need. We can head south now."

As the captain lined up for the final approach to the Polar Gas base, the President said, "Are you going to land on the ice?"

The captain nodded, "Yes, sir. I checked it out when we were on our way across from Fairbanks earlier today. The strip is serviceable, the ice moves and opens up a bit here and there in August and September, but with freeze-up on it's real solid and no problem."

When they had landed and had taxied up to the cluster of four shacks which served the airstrip, the captain said, "You could probably communicate directly with Air Force One using the base camp radio, sir, but we should really be the master ground net because of the extra communications we have on board. They give us more flexibility."

"Fine," said the President. "Bear in mind that I may want to get the hell out of here fast if something big comes up." He unstrapped his seat-belt and with the help of the navigator, put on his army parka. He hoisted himself down a ladder to the cargo deck and moved quickly toward the passenger door on the port side of the aircraft. The crew chief had put down the steps by the time he reached the door.

As the President stepped out of the aircraft he was hit by a blast of freezing air whipped up by the propellers, which were still turning. He ran quickly to get out of the propwash toward a tall figure, dressed in muskrat parka and mitts, caribou mukluks and heavy dark trousers, waiting to meet him.

"Welcome to Polar Gas, Mr. President," the man said. "I'm Harold Magnusson. I'm with Tenneco out of Houston, assigned to Polar Gas Study as Chief Engineer, trying to pick up the pieces here."

"Mighty proud to meet you, son. Glad to find a fellow Texan, even in these parts."

They walked toward the Polar Gas helicopter, which started up as they approached. When they had climbed in, Magnusson said, "What I'd like to do, sir, is take you to the base camp, show you a model of the under-water pipeline we've been working on, explain the system, and brief you on the test we're running tomorrow morning."

The President said, "That sounds fine, Harold. I'd like

to hear and see as much as I can while I'm here." He turned to look at Magnusson and smiled. "I bet you could even find a big Texas steak in the freezer if you looked."

"I wouldn't be at all surprised, Mr. President. We're real proud to have you here as our guest. This is a big event for us at Polar Gas. We have a visit from the President, and we've finally got the line installed under the ice in a new system that I've put together in the last year and a half. We were going to run the first test this morning, but when we got word that you were coming, we put it off until early tomorrow morning so you could see it."

The President turned to Magnusson and said, "Son, let me tell you something. For the last four years I've been watching the work at this station with an eagle eye. I've heard about every failure and every disaster. I've also heard a lot about you since you got here, and they tell me if anybody can make this thing work you can. I knew you were going to be running the experiment, and that's what helped me make the decision to come up here. The success or failure of this test is of tremendous importance to us. If it fails, I don't think we've a hope in hell of licking this energy crisis. If it succeeds, we've got a real fighting chance. So I'm mighty pleased, Harold, that you waited until I got here."

The Prime Minister glanced at his watch. He would have to wind up his meeting with the premiers soon, and they certainly weren't making much progress.

From the moment Porter had finished his report on the emergency, the discussion had been hot and heavy, and the premiers were still arguing, pounding the table and shouting at each other when their local interests clashed.

As never before, the Prime Minister could see the weakness of Canada's constitution, created in 1867. Regional differences had been strong then, too, and the provinces which had joined together to form Canada had seen to it that under the terms of Confederation they would retain much of the legislative authority, particularly over the natural resources within their own boundaries.

Under the American federal system, the powers of the states had been made secondary to the power of the Congress in all areas of national interest. Thus the President could deal from strength in this war of intimidation, while the Prime Minister had the difficult job of bringing the premiers to a consensus in support of his position.

Robert Porter was tired. Time was running out. He had to rally his strength and bring the meeting to a conclusion. In a firm voice he broke into the heated discussion. "Miss Cameron, gentlemen! I wonder if I might attempt to sum up where we stand. It's nearly seven o'clock. Most of you have travelled a long way today under trying circumstances. I'm sure you'd like to have dinner, talk with your people back home, and get ready for the briefing tomorrow morning.

"I've given you the wording of the resolution to be presented in the House formally tomorrow. Listening to your remarks, it seems, at the moment at least, that five of you will likely favour accepting the ultimatum and five will be for rejecting it.

"May I suggest that each of you let me have your decision before I rise to conclude the debate in the House tomorrow afternoon so that I will have your viewpoint before me. Arrangements will be made to have your opinions delivered to me. A special section in the Spectators' Gallery opposite my seat will be reserved for you and a page will be assigned to carry your messages."

The Premier of Manitoba, Boris Wegeruk, broke in. "If I give you my opinion on what should be done with the ultimatum, Prime Minister, I'm not sure I want it made public or referred to in the House."

That drew a retort from Stewart Andrews, Premier of Alberta. "Look, if you're going to take a position, take it so that the members of the House and the people of your province know what you're thinking. This is the time to stand up and be counted, Boris!"

The Prime Minister said, "Why don't we leave it this way — if you don't want me to refer to your position in the House, let me know."

Margaret Cameron put it right on the line. She looked at the Prime Minister with animosity, her dark eyes flashing. She was a vital and dynamic woman, intellectually far superior to most in the room. Robert Porter found her stimulating as an adversary as well as tremendously attractive physically.

She said heatedly, "So far as I am concerned, Prime

Minister, and so far as Nova Scotia is concerned, we'll take a stand on this issue and you can let anybody in the world know what our position is. These people"— she waved her hands in a sweeping gesture at Boris Wegeruk —"from the West who are too frightened to tell it like it is are not living up to their responsibilities as Canadians and as leaders in their own provinces.

"For that matter, Prime Minister, you've been hedging on this issue too. Where do you stand?"

The Prime Minister laughed. "You may not agree with me, Margaret, but I've decided to keep an open mind for the moment. I want to hear what you people have to say and what the Cabinet wants to do, and what the people of the country think, before I give my opinion publicly. Obviously I have very strong feelings myself, and I've been under a great deal of pressure from the Cabinet to make my position known even before the debate. But I'm sorry, I simply will not take that approach."

He waited for a biting response, but Margaret Cameron simply shrugged her shoulders, sat back in her chair, and said nothing.

"Now let me see if I can sum up where I think you all stand. Miss Cameron of Nova Scotia, Mr. Renault of New Brunswick, Mr. MacGregor of Prince Edward Island, and Mr. Tallman of Newfoundland are of the view that the American ultimatum should be accepted. They feel that the long history of Maritime connection with the United States has forged a bond that is too strong to be broken. More importantly, the substantially lower level of the economy of their provinces, combined with a widespread feeling that they continue to get the short end of the stick from Ottawa, makes them unwilling to risk the effects of American economic sanctions.

"On the other side of the country, Mr. Ramsay of British

123

Columbia feels that his province, with its emphasis on resource industries, has had traditionally close ties with Washington and California, its major trading partners to the south, and that it too has been remote from Central Canada and Ottawa. He feels that to attract economic sanctions by telling the Americans they can't have the natural gas to which they feel entitled would be sheer folly.

"Premiers Charbonneau of Quebec and Michael Harvey of Ontario, and the premiers of the other western provinces, Mr. Wegeruk of Manitoba, Mr. Lipson of Saskatchewan, and Mr. Andrews of Alberta, all favour flat rejection of the ultimatum. Indeed, Mr. Andrews of Alberta has put forward the strong recommendation that we should tell the United States that unless the ultimatum is withdrawn we will begin a program of counter-sanctions immediately. Specifically, he proposes that we threaten to cut off our current supply of gas and oil to the United States. In my view, this is an unselfish and statesmanlike proposal. Alberta has by far the biggest stake in this situation. Together with Saskatchewan, they already provide vast quantities of gas and oil to the American market. And yet they are prepared to accept the economic consequences of the counter-sanction."

Andrews, on the Prime Minister's left, broke in. "Prime Minister, what you say is right. We in Alberta have by far the biggest stake in the counter-sanction. If it goes into effect, our market for oil and gas goes right down the drain, and so does our entire provincial economy. But let me tell you that we are Canadians first, and Albertans second. So far as my government and the people of Alberta are concerned, this is a sacrifice we're ready to make."

The Prime Minister paused briefly and then continued. "Well, gentlemen, Miss Cameron, while we seem to be evenly split on the matter of the ultimatum, I take it you are all agreed that we should start to fight back by counter-sanction."

There was a general murmur of assent.

"Very well, then, I'll advise the President immediately."

As they entered the main building of the Polar Gas Study base camp, Magnusson said, "I know there's a lot riding on the test tomorrow. I hope we don't let you down, Mr. President."

Ten members of the staff had gathered in the reception room. After appropriate introductions and a few minutes' conversation, Magnusson said, "Mr. President, I wonder if I might drag you away from these people and show you the model of our system? I've ordered a real Texas steak for you — rare. It should be ready in about fifteen minutes."

"That sounds fine." The President nodded, thanked the group, and accompanied Magnusson down a long hall into a briefing room complete with a blackboard, motion picture and slide projectors. At the front of the room were scale models of the experimental under-water under-ice pipeline crossing. Magnusson said, "Sir, if you'd like to sit on that stool, I'll explain the set-up to you."

The President dutifully perched on the stool next to the models and said, "Harold, what I really need before you start is a large bourbon and soda. It's long past that time of day. I've got to have something to keep the old pump going."

Magnusson ordered two bourbon-and-sodas from the canteen bar and then began.

"Please ask me any questions that come to your mind, Mr. President."

"Sure will."

"The first model is really a vertical view to scale of the crossing that we have to make.

"The line goes from a pumping station here at Consett Head, east across the Byam channel twelve miles to a landfall at May Cove on the west coast of Byam Martin Island. In fact, we've laid two sets of pipe in the water. I'll explain why in a minute. If we're successful, we will put together a system that can pick up all the gas on Melville Island and take it straight across to Resolute on Cornwallis. Then the plan is to hook up with a route to the south. We can go from Resolute across to Devon Island to the east, then across the Northwest Passage to Baffin Island, and then down into Northern Quebec and into New York State. The alternative is from Resolute south across the Northwest Passage to Somerset Island, down the Boothia Peninsula and the west coast of Hudson Bay through Ontario to New York State.

"The reason we started off with our experiment between Melville and Byam Martin is that Melville has a bigger volume of gas than any other island in the Canadian Arctic."

The President said, "Yes, I understand that. I also understand that from 1975 until you came on the scene, several attempts were made to put a metal pipe under the ice, and those experiments were total disasters."

"Yes, sir, that's true. What we have had to do is find a system to put a pipe or a series of pipes under the water deep enough down to be out of reach of the moving ice. There's evidence of ice scouring on the bottom down to depths of 250 feet, and there are pressure ridges which

127

cause formations to a depth of anywhere from thirty to a hundred feet. When we lay pipe under the water we have to do it under the worst conditions in the world. You can get temperatures ranging down to 50° below zero here, and with any kind of a wind the chill factor can go down to 100 or 120 below. Those are temperatures which can kill a man and destroy equipment. Metal becomes brittle, and machinery and pipe can crack and become useless. For a rigid metal pipe, the ice has to be opened in long sections and the pipe has to be contoured exactly to the bottom. It has to be ballasted, not only to get it down as far as we might have to go, which could be up to 2,000 feet in some channel crossings, but because when you get it down there the gas itself has so much lifting power.

"In addition you have to make a trough in the bottom to take the pipe so that if the ice does scrape along the bottom in the shallower areas it won't rip it up.

"There's another problem with metal pipe, too. Once you get it down a thousand or two thousand feet, how do you maintain it? Or if you make a mistake, how do you get it back up again for repair? On top of all that, there are other natural hazards. In some of the channels between the islands there are currents which have to be dealt with above the 600-foot level, and of course you have to do much of your work in total darkness during the dead of winter. There's no sunlight at all here except a bit of twilight around noon. The summer months, July, August and September, are just as bad, because then the ice tends to open, leaving stretches of water. It shifts, but it never goes away.

"So you can see that putting a pipeline beneath the ice is a hundred times more difficult than laying pipe across tundra and permafrost. It's little wonder that from the beginning of this research work we've had many failures and no successes."

The President nodded his agreement and took a long sip of his bourbon and soda. Magnusson went on.

"One thing I want to stress, Mr. President, is that no matter what we come up with in an operational under-ice pipe, there's no way that pipe can be used to carry oil. The ecology here is very delicate. Bacteriological activity is virtually non-existent and the amount of wildlife that lives on the ice and in the water is enormous. If we had an oil-spill under the ice, there'd be no way of getting it out. It would be permanent and a total disaster for the eco-system.

"So we're not talking about oil, Mr. President, although there has now been a major oil pool discovered here on Melville. Moving the oil is a job for the big airplane."

The President said, "I agree. We're damn lucky that the Resources Carrier is in prototype and it looks as if it will be ready to go soon. We're going to be able to use it to carry crude oil from Melville to New York State direct. That's the only thing we've been able to get out of the Canadian government in the last four years — consent to take the crude oil from Melville — but it's the gas that's the key."

The President stopped, took a long sip, and said, "But don't let me interrupt, Harold. You have the floor."

"Well, sir, let's look at the next model. It's a working model, because I can move some of the parts as we go along, particularly at the location of the pipe in the water. This is a side view of the channel between Melville and Byam Martin, the 12-mile stretch. It's as much as 750 feet deep in places. At the top of the water is a layer of ice ranging from four to nine feet thick, although there are some pressure ridges as thick as one hundred feet. That's the ice we had to get through in order to get the pipe down.

"Now what I've gone for is the use of a flexible plastic pipe rather than metal. My predecessors — and there were three of them — were locked to the use of metal pipe, rang-

129

ing from a big one 148 inches in diameter to a series of smaller ones in spaghetti form. Apparently they hadn't even thought of the potential of plastic. Certainly they never tried it. In their work the metal became so brittle before it was put into the water that it cracked under the ice. Or, if they could get it down without cracking, the joints broke. They ran into problem after problem. In fact, it got so bad that after the third man quit, the Polar Gas group almost gave up. But by that time they'd sunk about $70-million into the project and didn't want to quit without one more try.

"Now here's a sample of my pipe. The plastic is plain, old-fashioned neoprene. It's enormously flexible and impervious to the cold. It's thick enough to stand a lot of internal pressure, but not strong enough on its own to take the fourteen hundred pounds per square inch that these pipes have to carry in order to get the natural gas through them in volume. So what I've done is to strengthen the outside walls by encasing the tube in a sheath of stainless steel mesh.

"When the pipe is lowered to the operational level of 600 feet below the surface, the plastic will collapse like a tube in a tire, but of course the stainless steel mesh will not. And the steel, being in mesh form, allows the pipe to remain totally flexible, which makes it easier for the divers to handle.

"We have it shipped in here in 50-foot lengths, and we set it in the water in spaghetti fashion, as you can see from the model. We need the capacity of a 48-inch diameter pipe. That's the size they've used for the land pipelines. My plastic pipe is twelve-inch, so we tie sixteen of them together once they're in the water.

"Now we've got a pipe that's flexible enough and can still stand the pressure we have to put through it. But there's

130

one major problem with any pipe under water, and that is the enormous lifting force of the gas inside. What we have to do is to create a ballast system all along the line and tie the pipe to it. Then it gets to be quite a tricky job, because the ballast system has to be capable of letting the pipe up for servicing work and at the same time keeping it under control despite the buoyancy. This is the thing we can't really predict with certainty without a live test, so I've run two lines, using different ballast and control systems, as you can see.

"The first system is really quite simple in principle, and it's the one I hope will work because it's by far the easiest to lay. What it boils down to is a series of enormous cement blocks resting on the bottom and attached to the pipeline by a cable system, running through pulleys at the pipeline and at the block. The end of the cable is held up by a buoy floating just under the ice. We can get at it very easily. The pulleys on the cement blocks have locks on them. To lower the pipe, I can pull up on the cable at the surface, and then when I release the pull the locks operate and the pipe is held in its new position. To raise the pipe, I release the locks with a separate control cable.

"Frankly, I'm concerned about that system. With the currents and other forces operating on the pipe, I'm not sure that it's going to work, so we've designed an alternative system which is more complicated but gives us greater control.

"You can see from the model that the second pipeline is attached to a series of towers every few hundred feet. The towers are approximately 120 feet high, although we've adjusted that in places where the floor of the channel is very uneven. The towers are a little like water-towers. At the top there's a tank which is the key to the whole system. Each tower carries many tons of ballast, and when I lower

UNDER WATER TOWER SYSTEMS

1. **FLOTATION TANK SYSTEM**
   ⍺) MAIN TANK
   b) FLOTATION PRESSURE CONTROL LINE

2. **GAS PIPE LINE SUPPORTS AND DEVICES**
   ⍺) HOUSING SYSTEM
   b) ELECTRONIC SENSING DEVICE
   c) COLUMN
   d) GAS PIPE LINES

3. **LANDERS**
   ⍺) COLUMNS
   b) PADS
   c) CONCRETE BALLAST

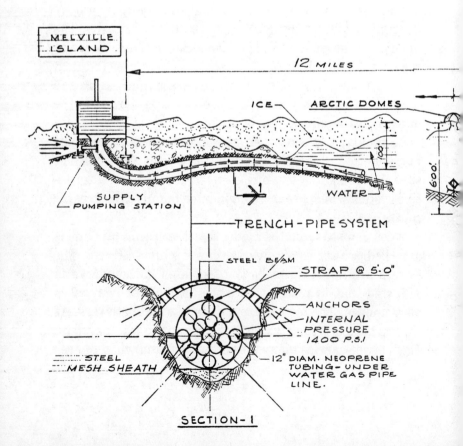

MELVILLE ISLAND

12 MILES

ICE   ARCTIC DOMES

WATER

600'

SUPPLY PUMPING STATION

TRENCH-PIPE SYSTEM

STEEL BEAM

STRAP @ 5'-0"

ANCHORS
INTERNAL PRESSURE 1400 P.S.I

STEEL MESH SHEATH

12" DIAM. NEOPRENE TUBING - UNDER WATER GAS PIPE LINE.

SECTION-1

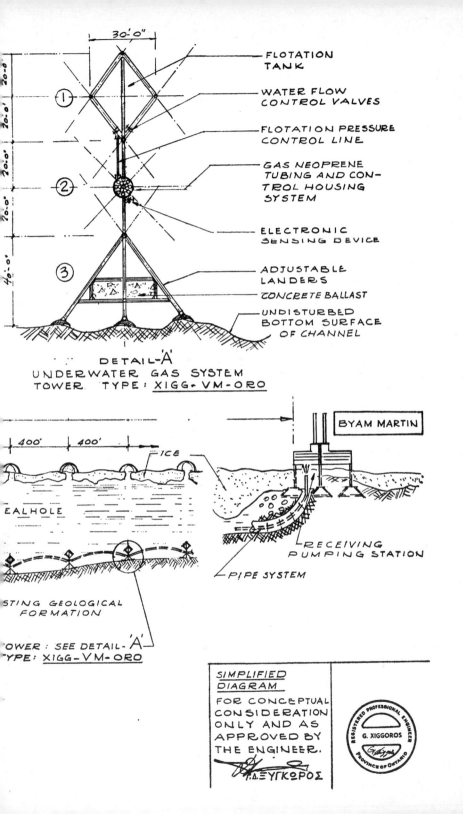

30'-0"

① FLOTATION TANK

WATER FLOW CONTROL VALVES

FLOTATION PRESSURE CONTROL LINE

GAS NEOPRENE TUBING AND CONTROL HOUSING SYSTEM

② ELECTRONIC SENSING DEVICE

③ ADJUSTABLE LANDERS

CONCRETE BALLAST

UNDISTURBED BOTTOM SURFACE OF CHANNEL

DETAIL-'A'
UNDERWATER GAS SYSTEM
TOWER TYPE: XIGG-VM-ORO

400'   400'

ICE

BYAM MARTIN

EALHOLE

RECEIVING PUMPING STATION

PIPE SYSTEM

STING GEOLOGICAL FORMATION

OWER : SEE DETAIL-'A'
YPE: XIGG-VM-ORO

SIMPLIFIED
DIAGRAM
FOR CONCEPTUAL
CONSIDERATION
ONLY AND AS
APPROVED BY
THE ENGINEER.

Γ.Δ.ΞΥΓΚΩΡΟΣ

REGISTERED PROFESSIONAL ENGINEER
G. XIGGOROS
PROVINCE OF ONTARIO

the towers into the water, the tanks are filled with air to provide buoyancy. When the pipeline has been attached to the tower just under the surface and all the towers are hooked on, we lower the whole thing at once. As I indicted, in the Byam Martin Channel the deepest point is about 750 feet. Once the system is resting on the bottom, we flood the tanks on the towers and let the ballast take effect. It's really just like a submarine. When I want to raise the pipeline, I can open valves from the line into the tanks on each tower, blow the water out, and make the system sufficiently buoyant to come to the surface.

"Both the tower system and the cement block system have control valves along the pipeline, of course, so that in case of a break we can shut the flow of gas off instantly and bring the pipeline to the surface for repairs.

"Near the shoreline we have to be very careful because of ice scouring. We lay the pipe in a trench which we dig, using an automated dredge called The Crab, which can crawl along the bottom."

The President shook his head in disbelief. "Son, I've got to hand it to you." He finished off his bourbon and soda and asked, "How do you get the pipes put together and into the water?"

Magnusson replied, "We do it this way. Here at Melville we've carried the trench out to a point where the bottom is 200 feet down. Then we've made a series of holes in the ice all the way across to the other side. These sealholes, as we call them, are about 10 feet in diameter. We've set up domes over each one of them which can be heated and keep the surface of the water free of ice for as long as we want. Then we work our way across, feeding sections of the pipe through the sealholes to the divers working underneath. When we get a line completely across, we can then attach the next 12-inch section, and so on, until we build up the sixteen pipes we need in each line.

"Both pipeline systems are complete now and in position. The pipes are presently filled with seawater. When we're ready to go with the experiment, we'll put a plug of oil through to clean out the water. It will be blown from the Melville side straight across to the Byam Martin end, and out behind the water it's shoving through. Behind the plug will come the gas which we'll take up to operating pressure of 1400 pounds per square inch."

The President broke in. "By the way, Harold, I've got to be out of here as quickly as possible when the experiment is finished. It want to be back in Resolute airborne by 8:15."

"No problem there, Mr. President. We'll get up shortly after five and be out to the main dome at the centre of the channel by six. We're due to start to bring the line under pressure at 6:10, and we should know by 6:30 how things are going to go."

"That's fine, Harold, just great," said the President. "You know, this is a fantastic effort. You've come up with a really ingenious arrangement. I'm looking forward to seeing how it goes tomorrow."

"Well, Mr. President, we'll be able to see, all right. I've got a television rig set up at the main sealhole and lighting down to pipe level, 600 feet, so that we can watch as the pressure is applied. And of course we've got all sorts of sensors set along the pipe to check on the effects as the pressure builds up."

The President slid off his perch, straightened up, and said, "Son, I think you'd better let me at that steak. I'm starved."

As the two men moved toward the door the telephone

rang. Magnusson answered and then turned the phone over to the President. "It's for you. Mr. Wolf calling from the 747."

The President took the phone and said, "Yes, Irving."

Wolf's voice came back. "Prime Minister Porter has been trying to reach you, Mr. President."

"Well, I can't talk to him right now, Irving. We're just going to eat. Let his people know that I'll be available at 7:45, that's 8:45 their time. I'll be in touch with you then. O.K.?"

"I'll pass the word, Mr. President."

"By the way, Irving, the experiment that I want to see will take place here tomorrow morning shortly after six, so I'll get back to Resolute by 7:45 and we can be out of there immediately."

"I'll tell Wypich, Mr. President. We'll be set to go as soon as you get here."

Robert Porter was back in his office, eating the steak Scott had produced and working on the draft of the TV address for nine o'clock. He had discussed the counter-sanction with both John Thomas and Scott, with Michael Clarkson, the Minister of Finance, and finally had reviewed it carefully with the Governor-General. They had all agreed that cutting off the oil and gas supply to the United States was a powerful weapon which stood a good chance of forcing the President's hand and making him lift the ultimatum.

At 7:45 a call was placed to the President. The two exchanged terse greetings, and the President said, "Well, what can I do for you?"

"Mr. President, you've hit Canada hard today, first with your ultimatum and then with the decision to cut off the flow of investment capital even before we had a chance to respond."

"Yes, it was a little rough, but I want to let you people know I mean business."

"We already knew that. It takes a lot to get Canadians excited, but I think you've certainly been able to do it today. Now Mr. President, let me put it to you straight. We are by no means as helpless in this country to resist blackmail as you think. As the United States' largest trading partner, we have very powerful economic weapons of our own, and since you have chosen to invoke sanctions against us without any prior discussion or warning, I am now going to give you a counter-sanction. But I intend to be fair about it; I won't impose the sanction if you agree to the condition I suggest."

"Well, let's hear it."

"Your country is currently receiving about 1½-million barrels of oil and three-billion cubic feet of gas per day from Western Canada. While Montreal and the Maritime Provinces used to be dependent upon oil supply from the United States, they too have a direct pipeline connection now with the West. Therefore, I'm going to order the flow of Canadian oil and gas into the United States cut off immediately unless you agree to lift the ultimatum."

There was silence for a few moments. Then Porter could hear the President chuckling. "You know, down in Texas we like cool poker players, and you do pretty well, young fellow. That's a pretty good card you've played, but not quite good enough. I'll tell you what I'll do. If you agree not to impose the counter-sanction, I'll agree to lift the embargo I put on at noon and not to put on the further sanction I was going to impose at midnight. In fact, I agree not to order any other sanctions between now and six o'clock tomorrow evening. The midnight sanction, by the way, was to close the border to the movement of all goods."

It was Porter's turn to pause as he thought over the President's move. Reluctantly he said, "I'm afraid you won that hand, Mr. President, but if nothing else, I think you've got the message that we have some weapons of our own."

"Yes," the President replied, "but I think you'll find you're outgunned. Is there anything else, Mr. Prime Minister?"

"No, that's all for the moment. You'll hear from me."

"I'm sure I will." The President hung up, while Porter muttered to himself, "Half a loaf is better than none, I guess."

John Thomas said, "You've got a real tough cookie at the other end of that telephone. He's going to play this one right down to the wire."

Porter nodded. "Yes, you're certainly right. But now I've got to get that speech finished. Let's go over it once again."

Freddie Armstrong picked up the mike in the single engine Otter and said, "Inuvik Tower, this is Romeo November Echo, 10 miles northwest at 3,000 feet VFR from Aklavik, landing at the town strip. Over."

"RNE. This is Inuvik Tower. You are cleared to the town strip. The wind is 330 at five. The altimeter setting is 3019. I have no other local traffic in the area."

"Roger, Tower. Will you please close my flight plan?"

"Roger, wilco."

Freddie put the VHF mike back on its holder. It was dark now, and he peered ahead into the twinkling lights of Inuvik for his marker, the wafting white plume of the steam from the power plant. He would turn left over the power plant on his final leg inbound to the airstrip northwest of the town along the west arm of the Mackenzie.

Freddie Armstrong was a living legend in the Arctic. An Indian who had competed successfully in a white man's field, he had graduated from high school, saved his money, and gone outside to Edmonton to take flying lessons. Back in Inuvik he had worked hard to save enough money to buy his own airplane, a Cessna, had obtained a Class 4 charter licence and started to work to build up his firm, Caribou Air Services Limited, at a time when no other operators were in the area and nobody gave a damn about the prospects of Inuvik or oil or gas in the Mackenzie Delta. The discoveries in the North brought so much business that he had been able to enlarge his fleet to ten aircraft, but they had also brought increased competition, and the Air Transport Committee in Ottawa had granted charter licences freely to the well-financed carriers from the south who soon moved in with their Twin Engine Otters and other sophisticated machines.

On top of that, his crews had cracked up two of his larger aircraft just as things were reaching their peak, and this financial setback had almost put him out of business.

But Freddie Armstrong was a determined man. He stuck to his guns and now had a reputation, all through the Arctic, as someone who really knew his job.

He glanced over at Sam Allen in the right-hand cockpit seat and thought, not for the first time, that Sam was a heck of a nice guy. He was glad he'd been able to do him a favour. Funny, though, that Sam and Bessie didn't have any pelts with them. When he dropped them off about twenty miles west of Aklavik the morning before, Sam had told him that they were going out to look after some muskrat traps set by Sam's brother Pete, who was sick in Aklavik. So he'd expected them to have at least two dozen skins when he picked them up. He asked Sam if they'd got any rats. And Sam replied, "Sure did, Freddie, got plenty, but I bagged them and hung them off the ground in a tree just north of Rat River, so Pete can pick them up there as soon as he's better."

Freddie saw that Sam's harness was done up, and turned back to check on Bessie. She was sitting in the passenger compartment on the right of the aircraft, and at his glance nodded and pointed to the harness. Freddie lined up on the runway lights and decided he'd do a full-flap landing because there was no wind. He pumped the flaps down and the nose of the aircraft came down in response. He checked his air speed, cutting back to 58 knots. He cranked on a bit more power to get ready for the roundout which was fast approaching, and as he passed the end of the airstrip, pulled back on the throttle and the wheel. The aircraft rotated beautifully and sank gently onto the snow. The skis squeaked and squealed as the plane slowed abruptly. A short landing was a trademark of the old Otter, and Freddie Armstrong was still one of the best pilots in the business.

Freddie cranked up the flaps and made a wide, sweeping turn into the dispersal area on the east side of the town strip. "Well, Sam, another successful non-crash."

Sam smiled, "Beautiful landing, Freddie, just great."

As they unstrapped and began to get ready to move out of the aircraft, there was a sudden pounding at the rear right-hand door. It was jerked open from the outside. Sam looked back into the ruddy, black-moustached face of Staff Sergeant Ray of the Inuvik detachment of the RCMP. Fear gripped him. He glanced quickly over at Bessie. Her eyes were wide with fright. Ray clambered up into the cabin next to Bessie and stopped, his hand on the green knapsack which contained a spare explosive charge, a timer and arming mechanism Sam had brought back with him. He said, "Sam, we've been looking all over for you. The Prime Minister has been trying to get hold of you all day. They tell me it's really urgent."

Sam moved quickly to get out of the Otter. As he passed by Bessie, who was still strapped in her seat, he said, "I'll take the knapsack with me, Bessie, if you and Freddie can bring the rest of the stuff." He followed Staff Sergeant Ray out the door, jumped down onto the snow, pulled up his parka around his head, and strode rapidly toward the shack Caribou Air Services called its office. Parts and pieces of aircraft were strewn about the area. Freddie's mechanics had to do a lot of their work outside now, since their original hangar had been sold to keep the business going. When they entered the office the Sergeant went immediately to the desk and handed a strip of paper to Sam.

"Here's the number. The Prime Minister's secretary said that he would probably be at a meeting when you called, but he gave her instructions to get him out. It sounds to me as though it's pretty important."

Sam asked, "Did she say why he was calling?"

"No. I asked if there was a message, but all she would tell me was that it was urgent to find you as soon as possible. Apparently they called your house, the Eskimo Inn, your office, and, from what I can gather, two or three other places in town. I guess your office told them you were out in the bush trapping."

Sam picked up the phone and was soon through to the Prime Minister's secretary. She said, "Oh, Mr. Allen, the Prime Minister will be very pleased we've finally got you. He's just finishing the meeting. If you'll hang on for a minute, I'll let him know you're on the line."

As he waited for the Prime Minister, Sam looked out into the darkness toward the aircraft where he could see Bessie and Freddie unloading the tent, the portable stove and sleeping bags. As they reached the office, Porter came on the line. "Sam, how are you? I haven't talked to you for a long time."

Sam shifted from one foot to the other and said, "Hi, Bob — I mean, Prime Minister. I'm fine. How does it feel to be the Chief?"

"Well, being the Chief is sometimes good and sometimes bad. Today's a bad day, Sam. I need your help, and I need it fast. I haven't time to give you all the details, but the President of the United States has dumped a real problem in my lap. He's given Canada an ultimatum. We have to agree to let the U.S. have all the gas it wants from the Arctic, and we have to give the Americans free access to the area so that they can get it out. On top of that, we have to guarantee to settle with the native people in the Northwest Territories and the Yukon immediately to get the bombings stopped. As you know probably better than anyone, I want to see us make a proper arrangement on native rights, and I've been trying to make plans for serious discussions, but with the pressure of everything else in Ottawa since I became Prime Minister I couldn't move as quickly as I wanted."

Sam broke in, "Yes, I know, Bob. The Indian Brotherhood and our organization and everybody else up here has been getting pretty uptight because nothing's been going on, and the pipeline's just about finished."

"Yes, I know. That's the problem. I don't know who's doing the bombing, and I don't suppose you do either, but I imagine you can find out if you have to, since you're the head man in the Mackenzie area. Somehow I've got to get a message to those people and let them know that we're in a crisis and it's imperative that they stop the sabotage immediately.

"I want you to pass the word along that if the native people are really interested in having a settlement, then they're going to have to help me maintain the strongest possible bargaining position with the President. The deadline on the ultimatum is six o'clock tomorrow night. The blowing up of the pipe has got to be stopped now. There must be no explosions during that time."

Sam's smile had long since been replaced by a frown of concentration as he sorted out the implications of what the Prime Minister was saying. "Bob," he said, "what if I can't get the message through to the right people? What if there's a blast between now and tomorrow night?"

"I don't know what the consequences will be, Sam, except that they won't be good. You know there are a lot of people in Parliament who don't agree that we should settle with the Indian and Eskimo people. I've got to have your support to get a fair settlement through. I can tell you that it's absolutely crucial to your people that these bombings be stopped."

Sam turned away from the window and sat down on a rickety office chair.

"I'll have to leave that one with you," said the Prime Minister, "and I can't give you much time to do something about it, because I need you here in Ottawa immediately to begin settlement talks. I'll be asking the Minister of Indian Affairs and the Secretary of State to begin meetings with you and the heads of the Yukon and Northwest Territories Indian Brotherhoods starting tomorrow morning. There's an Armed Forces Hercules on its way now to pick you up. It should be there by eleven o'clock your time. Then it will go over to Whitehorse to pick up Chief Abner and back to Yellowknife to pick up the new President of the N.W.T. Indian Brotherhood. What's his name?"

"Peter Firth. He's a Dog Rib Indian."

"Well, Sam, I hope you're prepared to come to Ottawa."

"I sure am, Bob, even though I hate the lousy place. But, look, if I can make contact with the people who've been blowing up the pipe and get them to stop, can I promise them amnesty? Maybe they've already planted some bombs. If so, they'll have to go out and defuse them and perhaps get some help. What if they're caught while they're doing that?"

There was a pause while the Prime Minister considered what Sam had said and the way in which he'd said it. He replied, "You've got a good point. I'll see to it that the Attorney General and the RCMP lay no charges against anyone who co-operates in finding and defusing any explosive charges on the pipeline. In fact I'll see that the RCMP are instructed to do everything they can to assist in getting to the locations and getting the bombs defused."

Sam looked down at his elaborately beaded and embroidered mukluks and said slowly, "Will the amnesty be extended to anyone who has had a part in the blowing up of the pipes to this point?"

The Prime Minister's voice said firmly, "Yes. My secretary's here with me. She's been taking down what I've said about the amnesty and a telegram will go out to you immediately and to the RCMP to confirm."

Sam turned around in his chair to face Ray and said, "Bob, I've got Staff Sergeant Ray of the RCMP here with me. If you'll tell him what you've just told me about the amnesty for everybody, then I think we can get this whole thing going pretty quickly."

"O.K. Put him on."

Sam handed the telephone to Ray, who identified himself and listened quietly to the Prime Minister as he repeated what he had said to Sam. Porter went on, "You people have a Twin Otter up there, haven't you?"

"Yes, sir, we have."

"Well, if Sam puts you in contact with people who know where the bombs are, I suggest you use that plane to get out to the pipe. From what I can gather from Sam, there are bombs there right now. You'll have to act quickly, because the Herc. that's being sent up for Sam and the people from Whitehorse and Yellowknife will be into Inuvik by eleven o'clock tonight."

"We'll do our best, sir."

"Good, now will you put me back to Sam, please?"

Sam took the telephone from the Staff Sergeant and said, "I'll look after everything here, Bob. Now that we've got the amnesty thing going I guess I should tell you it's Bessie and I who've been setting the bombs."

"I had that figured out five minutes ago, Sam."

Staff Sergeant Ray shook his head slowly from side to side, as much in gesture of disappointment as in disgust. In his book Sam and Bessie had committed a serious crime, and he really wouldn't have expected it of them, though he had to admit that if they wanted to draw attention to the wrongs of their people they couldn't have picked a more dramatic way to achieve it.

The telephone discussion with the Prime Minister over, Sam hung up. He turned to Ray and with a small-boy grin on his face said, "Did you have any idea it was us, Jim?"

The Staff Sergeant shifted slightly, pulled at his moustache, and looked uncomfortable. "As a matter of fact, no, Sam. I thought you'd be too smart to do it yourself. I suspected you knew who was doing it, and maybe even you were planning it, but I had nothing to go on. I certainly didn't think it was you and Bessie. But the main thing now is, how the hell are we going to get those bombs defused? You've got to leave almost at once for Ottawa, so someone else is going to have to do the work."

Sam bent down by the desk and picked up the green knapsack. Flipping it open, he took out the explosive charge and timing mechanism. That brought Ray to his feet quickly.

"Where on earth did you get that?" he asked.

Sam laughed and responded, "No names, Jim. Pretty good-looking stuff, isn't it?" He laid the package on the desk.

Ray was astonished. "It sure is."

Sam went on. "Bessie knows exactly where all the bombs are located. You should be able to land the Twin Otter close to all of them. They're at river crossings. The charges are set to go off in a series over the next twelve days. The first one is set for 7:30 tomorrow morning, so you're going to have to get going as soon as it's light."

"I've taken a fair amount of training in explosives," Ray said, "but you're going to have to go through it pretty carefully for me."

Sam explained the working mechanism and timing device, and the sequence of steps to disable it. "If you turn that wheel the wrong way, Jim, you've got four seconds before it blows."

"Four seconds," thought the Staff Sergeant. "With snowshoes on, that won't get you very far."

Ottawa / 9:40 p.m., EDT

The Prime Minister was looking into the baleful, inanimate eye of the television camera focused on him. His half-hour address was almost finished, and had gone well. He had begun with a review of the terms of the ultimatum and described the meetings he had held during the day and the plans for the briefing in the House of Commons the next morning, followed by the full session of Parliament.

Then he had discussed in depth the American energy crisis, explaining why it was natural gas that was the precious commodity for the United States rather than oil. He had spoken with great sympathy and understanding for the American position, and he had renewed his plea for a calm and controlled response to the United States' action rather than the stirring up of anti-American demonstrations. Finally, he spoke forcefully of the decision to resist the sanctions which had been imposed, and reported on the decision to threaten a counter-sanction and the gains which had thus been won. Then he continued:

"The President now knows, and I hope that the American people will shortly know, that Canadians will not meekly give in to threats and intimidation.

"As we move toward the moment of decision when the Commons and the Senate sit tomorrow afternoon, it becomes more and more important to me that some mechanism be established through which as many Canadians as possible can communicate their views on the ultimatum.

"With the co-operation of the Trans Canada Telephone System, the television networks, and all private TV and radio stations across the country, we have set up a system which will enable any of you who wish to let me know directly whether you think Canada should accept or reject the ultimatum. Simply telephone any of the stations broadcasting in your local area. Switchboards are open and staff are ready to receive calls. When you are connected, do not discuss the situation; merely say 'accept' or 'reject' and then hang up. Please get off the line as quickly as possible so that others can have their opinions recorded. And of course I ask you to make only one such call.

"I ask all of the radio, television and news people in the country not to attempt to influence the poll. It would be in the best interests of Canada if the news media devoted their full attention to reporting the facts. In this way, I hope that as many people as possible will have an opportunity to make their opinions known to Parliament.

"The radio and television stations will receive calls until twelve noon tomorrow, Ottawa time. The results will then be tabulated and passed to me in the House at about three o'clock, before the close of debate, and I will be able to advise the House of the result.

"And so I urge every Canadian citizen who can do so to telephone and pass on his opinion about the ultimatum, saying either 'accept' or 'reject'.

"Thank you and good-night."

Day Two

The telephone was ringing. Porter struggled awake and reached out for it, almost rolling off the narrow couch in the process.

It was Tom Scott's voice. "It's seven o'clock, Prime Minister. You asked me to give you a call."

"Thank you, Tom. I'll get going right away."

Still fogged with sleep, the Prime Minister sat up and tried to collect his wits. God, what a night! It was late when he'd got to bed. The television address had taken much longer than he'd expected — almost an hour — and after that there had been several important telephone calls. He had talked with the Canadian Ambassador in Washington, the Canadian High Commissioner in London, whom he had routed out of bed at 3:30 in the morning, and with several of the Cabinet ministers who wanted clarification and direction regarding the morning briefing.

About midnight Tom Scott had poured a drink for Porter, Thomas and himself, and the three of them sat and talked for a while, speculating about what action the United States would take should Parliament refuse the ultimatum. Finally the other two left and Porter had stretched out on the couch, completely exhausted.

He slept fitfully. Twice he was awakened with reports from the Chief of the Defence Staff, and then by a call from George Townsend, Prime Minister of the United Kingdom, which had come through at 4 a.m. Townsend wanted the Prime Minister to know that Great Britain would stand behind Canada whatever the decision on the ultimatum. If it was rejected, the United Kingdom would do its best to support the economic structure of Canada in the face of the sanctions which the United States would undoubtedly impose, and would attempt to give the country preferential treatment in terms of trade. However, because of the tight restrictions imposed by membership in the Common Market, such preferences would have to be limited. But, as much as anything, Townsend wanted to offer his moral support.

Porter thanked him for the encouragement, and the two men went on to an extensive discussion of military support. Certain emergency measures were agreed on.

After speaking to Townsend, the Prime Minister called the Chief of the Defence Staff to inform him of the military arrangements he had made and to give him further instructions.

And now, just as he had got back to sleep, it was time to get going again.

The Prime Minister got up stiffly, showered and dressed quickly in the dark blue suit Mike Cranston had brought in the night before. After that he sat down to the light breakfast that was waiting for him on his desk and opened the Toronto *Globe and Mail.*

He saw at once that the *Globe* had done exactly what he had pleaded with the press not to do. Across the front page was the enormous headline, "U.S. Threatens Canada." Underneath was an editorial by the editor-in-chief and a full report of the ultimatum and the actions of the government. The editorial was strongly anti-American, and called for demonstrations.

Porter was furious. His first thought was to get the publisher and the editor-in-chief on the line and raise hell with them. But he had tangled with both of these men before and he knew that it would be of little value to talk to them. There was never any question that they would change their position, no matter what the facts were, and it was clear to Porter that any call from him would only encourage them to take a more extreme view.

What he did do, however, was to get in touch with his long-time friend, the editor-in-chief of *The Toronto Star* and a bright and dynamic young man who shared many of Porter's views. They discussed the approach the *Globe and Mail* had taken and ways in which the *Star* might treat the situation to counteract the dangerous effect of the morning paper. He also reported on his assessment of feelings of people in the Toronto area, where opinion was running high in favour of rejecting the ultimatum. Anti-Americanism was being expressed everywhere, and parades and demonstrations were already being organized.

At this point, off the record, the Prime Minister said that he had ordered the Chief of the Defence Staff to move regular-force troops into the city during the night. They were now secretly stationed, with their vehicles and equipment, at the Fort York and Moss Park armouries, and also at the Canadian Forces Base at Downsview. The CDS and his staff were in close co-operation with the Metropolitan Toronto Police and the Ontario Provincial Police. Similar action had been taken in Montreal, Windsor, Winnipeg, Calgary, Vancouver and Edmonton. Military forces were available to provide "aid to the civil power" if called upon by the local authorities.

When he had finished his conversation, John Thomas entered the office. He sat and listened while Tom Scott briefed the Prime Minister on the success of the parliamentary airlift and on general editorial reaction in the Canadian and American newspapers.

Scott reported that the leaders of the opposition parties had accepted the proposed motion on the ultimatum with only minor revisions. They had also wanted to know when the Prime Minister would have ready the preliminary remarks he would make in introducing the motion in the House.

"That's right!" Porter said. "I promised to let them have a look at what I intended to say in advance. Could you draft out something, John? It should be very brief."

"Glad to. I'll have it for you in fifteen minutes."

Thomas went off to another office to begin work on the draft, and after some more instructions, Tom Scott left the office. The Prime Minister called in his secretary to dictate notes on some of the points he wanted to make in closing the debate in the House.

It was soon time to leave for the Commons Chamber and the briefing. Before leaving, Porter called Scott on the intercom. "Tom, I'm leaving now. Would you hold the fort here and send down messages only if they are of the utmost urgency? The RCMP are standing by to get me through the mob of reporters that I'm sure are just outside the door."

"Yes, sir, they're there, all right, only this time there must be twice as many as yesterday."

"Good Lord!"

Bracing himself, the Prime Minister picked up his black loose-leaf notebook and went out to the reception area to pick up the RCMP escort.

A mob scene it was. Clearly, the emotions aroused by the bluntness of the ultimatum were reaching a high pitch. There was a tremendous milling about and shouting as the reporters attempted to put their questions to him.

The Prime Minister grabbed the sleeve of the RCMP Staff Sergeant, senior man in the group, and shouted something in his ear. The Sergeant disappeared back into the reception room and reappeared immediately with a chair. Porter climbed onto it so that he could look over the crowd and speak. He raised his arms to signal for quiet. Gradually the babble of talk died down.

There was an air of tension and expectancy. This was *the* event and this was the man at the centre.

The Prime Minister smiled as he began to speak. "Good morning, ladies and gentlemen."

There was much clapping and cheering.

"There is very little new for me to report to you this morning. Not a great deal has transpired since my television address last night.

"As you know, an extensive briefing of all the Members of Parliament is to begin in the Commons Chamber in three or four minutes' time. I want that meeting to get under way promptly because there is so much to cover in the three-hour period available.

"The Press Gallery will of course be open during the briefing, and we have arranged for television coverage in the Commons, so the people of Canada will be getting the same information and background as their elected representatives and the Senate. The debate this afternoon will also be televised across the country."

A shouted question. "What position are you going to take on the vote on the ultimatum?" It was the same question he had declined the day before.

"That is not a question I wish to answer at this time. When I come to wind up the debate in the Commons this afternoon I shall make my position absolutely clear. By then, too, we should have the results of the national telephone poll that is now going on. Before I state my position, I want to know what response there has been from the people."

"It's been fantastic," a reporter shouted.

"Good!" said the Prime Minister. "Now if you will all be kind enough to let me and my football team through, I'll get the briefing under way."

The crowd of reporters opened up easily to let Robert Porter and his escort through. When they reached the foyer to the House of Commons the Prime Minister left the escort behind and proceeded directly into the government lobby. It was crowded with members of his party hurrying to their seats. Porter acknowledged the greetings as he walked down the long room towards the curtained entrance to the aisle which led directly to his place on the front bench.

As the curtain fell behind him and he started down the incline of steps towards his seat, he was startled by a thundering noise, a tremendous pounding of the desks by members of every party and a burst of applause from the galleries and from the senators seated on the floor of the House. It was an unusual sound, and the Prime Minister was profoundly moved by it.

As he walked slowly down the steps toward his seat, his eyes swept across the vast chamber from left to right. They took in an impressive and most unusual sight, one that he would never forget. Nor would he forget the atmosphere of apprehension and excitement that would inevitably mount as the events of that day moved inexorably forward, building up wave upon wave to the crest of decision which was to come shortly after five o'clock.

He stopped halfway down the aisle to acknowledge the rare tribute being paid to him. He knew that actually the applause was not for him but for the position he held as the First Minister of Canada. Nevertheless, he was deeply impressed by this sign that all present were united in a strong feeling for their country.

158

He turned to the left and saw the faces of his own members, sitting at their seats thumping away vigorously. He could see the vacant Speaker's Chair, that small elegant throne from which the "chairman" of Parliament presided over the battles and debates, an ornate, carved dais which the Speaker would ascend that afternoon after the Speech from the Throne had been read in the Senate Chamber.

Overhead, the Press Gallery was crowded with the men and women who reported to the nation the happenings in the House. In the Visitors' Gallery immediately opposite were many familiar faces — ambassadors, friends — and in a special section the provincial premiers, together with the two Commissioners of the territories, Jones of the Yukon and Nellie Vladm of the Northwest Territories.

The Spectators' Gallery was jammed. Everyone who could possibly be squeezed in was there. There were even people sitting in the aisles. At the opposite end of the chamber, two television cameras which were now fixtures in the Commons Chamber, were trained on him.

This was Canada. Canada was in this room, and the eyes of all Canadians were upon Parliament and upon him.

As he resumed his walk down the aisle to his seat, he reminded himself that this was not a session of Parliament but only a briefing. Informality would have to prevail. The Speaker would not be in the chair. He himself would be chairman and general controller of the session.

In front of the Speaker's Chair a large projection screen had been placed. To the left of the screen was a long table on which sat a lectern with a set of microphones mounted on it. The Prime Minister could see the Minister for External Affairs, his deputy and two other staff members seated at the table, ready to begin the briefing.

The Prime Minister arrived at his seat and remained

standing. He nodded and half bowed to the Leader of the Opposition and to all sides of the House, while the banging of desks and applause kept on. Finally, with a gesture he had had to use twice with the press in the last few hours, he raised his hands to ask that the meeting might come to order and the proceedings begin.

As the din began to subside, he took out his glasses and ran his eyes over the points he had prepared in his notebook.

The Chamber had fallen silent. There was the odd cough and clearing of throat here and there and some activity in the Press Gallery. As the Prime Minister began to speak, even the small noises died down and his voice filled the vast chamber.

"Ladies and gentlemen," he began, "we are at the opening of what may well be the most important and momentous day of decision in the history of Canada."

Byam Channel / 5:59 a.m., CDT

The Polar Gas helicopter levelled off at two hundred feet as it moved away from the base camp bound for the main dome in mid-channel between Melville and Byam Martin Islands. Across the twelve-mile stretch of snow, bathed in the Arctic dawn sunlight, the President could make out patches of turquoise-coloured ice — pure, hard, deep ice. Stretched out across the channel like beads on an invisible thread were the beet-red domes that covered each of the sealhole stations over the pipelines.

Magnusson, sitting behind the President, tapped him on the shoulder and pointed to the right. "That's the pumping station, sir. The compressors will start at 6:10 sharp. We'll be at the master sealhole in about three minutes, about two minutes after six, which will give us just enough time."

Ahead of the aircraft the President saw the broad sweep of Byam Martin Island, a brownish, treeless tundra, rising to heights above the level of the swift-moving helicopter. Then out to his right beyond the southern tips of both Melville and Byam Martin, the broad expanse of whiteness disappeared into the horizon. High above, his eye caught the vapour trail of a high-flying jet leaving its impermanent white mark on the crystal blue of the cloudless Arctic sky.

The President turned to Magnusson and asked above the

noise of the helicopter, "Get any polar bears in these parts?"

"Sure do, Mr. President. We don't let our people get away from the domes on the ice any distance at all. The bears are mean creatures and, man, are they fast! Had a fellow killed over at Panarctic's base camp last year, so we treat them with great respect."

The helicopter pilot set the small machine down gently just a few feet from the red dome of the master sealhole and cut off his power. He would wait to fly the President back to the Polar Gas base camp and the Hercules transport which would take him to Resolute.

The President and Magnusson entered the dome through the entrance chamber which trapped the cold air like an igloo and then through another door into the dome itself. In the centre was the 10-foot wide sealhole that Magnusson had described to him, the water sitting just about two feet below the level of the ice. The ice surface inside the dome had been covered with plastic material to give a secure footing and also to minimize the heating required to maintain the interior of the dome at an acceptable working temperature of 60°.

In the sealhole a ladder had been attached to the lip of the ice so the divers could get in and out of the water. Mounted on a double A-frame rig directly over the hole was a cable drum carrying the cables from the television sets and pressure gauges mounted on the main control console to the cameras and sensors underwater. One of Magnusson's men was at the pressure gauges checking them for readings prior to the start-up of pressurization. Magnusson introduced him to the President.

Near the sealhole was a rack from which two heavily-insulated diving wetsuits hung. Oxygen tanks, masks,

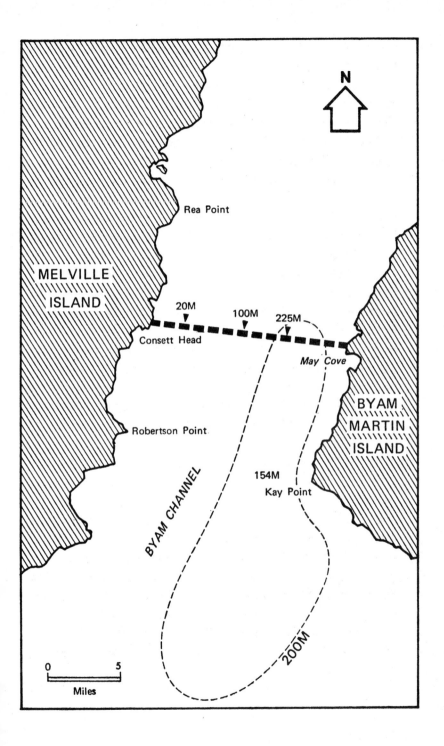

N

MELVILLE
ISLAND

Rea Point

20M   100M   225M

Consett Head

May Cove

Robertson Point

BYAM
MARTIN
ISLAND

154M
Kay Point

BYAM CHANNEL

200M

0   5
Miles

flippers and gloves were neatly piled on the floor next to the rack.

The interior of the dome was bathed in a soft white light from the brilliant, rapidly rising sun, which filtered through two opaque panels in the centre of the dome.

Magnusson moved toward the hole, and the President followed him. They stood at the edge and looked down into the water.

"Because of the possibility one of the pipelines may fail, we've put this dome about a quarter of a mile away," Magnusson said. "The ice here is about eight feet thick. You can see down quite a distance because the water's perfectly clear and the ice lets a good deal of sunlight through. Just below the level of the ice you can see one of the control buoys for the television cable. We've run the cable just under the ice from here across to a point just above the pipes, then down to pipe level. Our divers have been checking the cable buoys and the control buoys for the tower system. In fact, you can just see one of the divers checking the cable buoy immediately under this hole. We also supply power from here to lights down at pipe level for the divers and the TV cameras. We get our electricity from portable generators. You can hear the one for this sealhole chugging away outside."

Magnusson and the President moved to the television sets and the pressure gauges. Magnusson said to the technician, "How does it look, Oscar?"

"Everything checks O.K., Harold. The TV sets and cameras and everything are functioning well, as you can see from the pictures on the screens."

The wide angle television cameras had been lowered until each was directly opposite the pipelines at mid-point of the twenty-yard distance between the two systems.

A 30-foot section of the "tower" pipeline was displayed

164

on the left screen in colour. The right screen showed the "concrete" system.

The President said, "The insides of the pipes look as though they're squashed."

Magnusson responded, "They are, Mr. President. At a depth of 600 feet the water pressure — about 290 pounds per square inch — is sufficient to cause the neoprene pipe to collapse. The steel mesh sheath retains its shape. When the pressure is applied internally and the gas is fed in, the pipe will come out to its normal shape."

He picked up the small phone on the console. "Compressor Station!"

A voice came back, "Go ahead, Harold."

"Bill, have you confirmation that the checks have been done on all the buoys?"

"Yeah, everybody has reported in that everything is O.K. — that is, everybody except Joe Henderson, who should be at your sealhole."

Magnusson turned toward the sealhole and the sound of splashing. He replied, "Just a minute. He's coming out of the hole now."

A black figure emerged from the water and climbed up the ladder. The diver turned toward Magnusson and gave him a thumbs-up sign. Magnusson continued: "Everything's O.K. here, so we're all set to go. Have you confirmed that the valves at the Byam Martin end are open for the blowout of water and set to shut off external venting when the water and the oil plugs have gone through?"

"I have."

Magnusson said, "O.K., Bill. Turn her on and keep your fingers crossed."

Henderson, the diver, had taken off his wet suit and put on his parka. He was introduced and joined the President, Magnusson and Oscar at the instrument table.

As Magnusson busied himself with the instruments and the television set, the President asked Henderson, "What's it like working under ice? Is it uncomfortable? Do you feel trapped with all that mass of ice over you?"

"Not a bit, sir," Henderson replied. "It's the most interesting work I've ever done. I'm not really a diver by profession, but like the rest of the gang I took special training, not only in diving but on pipelines and all the new fangled equipment we've got here."

"You mean you didn't do any diving before you started this job?"

"Yes, sir, that's correct," replied Henderson.

"And how long have you been at it now?"

"Just a little over six months. That's how long it's taken us to get these two pipeline systems organized and put together in position. When you first start at this business it's difficult to get used to the weightlessness condition under which we have to work, but once you get used to it, there's no problem. One of the things that really helps us is the sub-igloo. I don't really know how to describe it except that it's a big plastic ball into which a diver can go to rest at fifty or a hundred or two hundred feet down and get a new supply of oxygen rather than having to come up all the way to the surface. It's an invention of Dr. Joe MacInnis. He's one of the world's leading underwater scientists — a Canadian."

"What about underwater wildlife around here?" the President said. "I'd guess there really isn't anything."

"That isn't the case at all, Mr. President. I've seen all kinds of seals, walrus and whales, particularly the beluga whale and the narwhal — that's a small whale with a great spear on its nose. The water is as clear as a bell, and with the strong sunlight even through the ice you can see for a long distance. It's really something to be working just a

166

few feet under water and see these great beasts swimming by. As a matter of fact, this whole area is just teeming with wildlife. It's incredible."

Magnusson interrupted. "Pressurization has started!"

Pressurization began at 6:10 exactly, with the flow of gas following a 50-gallon oil plug through each of the pipes. All of them had immediately resumed their normal circular shape.

By 6:20 the instruments indicated that gas now filled each of the pipes 50 per cent of the way across, by 6:25 three-quarters of the way.

On the left-hand television screen the tower line sat stable.

On the right-hand screen the pipeline of the concrete system started to move. Slowly at first, then more and more rapidly it twisted and tugged at the cable locking it to the channel floor.

The four men watched the screen in fascination. Magnusson muttered, "Christ, I hope the cable holds."

At that very instant the winch lock on the ballast block was ripped apart by a mighty upward pull. Unleashed, the pipe gathered speed and instantly disappeared from the view of the television camera. Magnusson's computer-like mind told him that the loosened pipe would surface at almost 150 miles an hour, and would take only six or seven seconds before it smashed against the bottom of the ice with incredible force.

He shouted at the President, "Let's get out of here fast!" All four men made a rush for the entrance of the dome. In a near-panic they broke from it into the crisp sun-filled cold of the Arctic morning. The ice beneath their feet shook, vibrated and lifted. Four hundred yards to the south the frozen white surface under the long line of red plastic domes exploded upwards, lifting and showering cascades of shattered ice high into the air, spinning domes off in every direction. The noise was like a massive clap of rolling, unceasing thunder, deafening and continuing as the huge pipeline, moving with the force and speed of a projectile, burst through the ice, still whipping and thrashing about like a reptile gone mad.

As the thick ice rose in front of them, the President stood transfixed by the fantastic sight.

As the ice rose to its peak and the pipeline broke past it into the air, fissures began to race outward from the point of impact.

The President could see the crack coming, but it was moving so rapidly he had no time to move. In an instant it was by him. The ice almost under his right foot opened to a fissure about a yard wide. As he turned, startled, to look into the frigid water which had suddenly appeared, his right foot slipped. Thrashing wildly to regain his balance the President of the United States of America fell toward the crevasse.

Magnusson, standing just to his left, using all his power — and using it roughly — caught the President's parka. With a mighty heave he pulled the President back from the edge just as he was going to fall into the water.

As the President hit the ice flat on his back, the crevasse slammed closed as quickly as it had opened.

The writhing pipeline had broken clear of the ice and rose about a hundred feet in the air, where it hung momentarily. The thundering noise of the cascade of ice falling back to the surface was joined by a piercing, whistling sound like a balloon deflating, as the holes in the pipe ripped by the ice allowed the natural gas to escape. The enormous pressure in the pipes was gradually relieved. The rampaging snake slowly fell back onto the water and its fractured cover of ice fragments, then disappeared through it. As the pipe, still hissing and losing pressure, sank beneath the surface, the massive upheaval totally subsided.

Magnusson helped the President to his feet. His face was white. "Are you O.K.? I didn't think I'd be able to grab you."

The President took a deep breath. "God Almighty, what a sight! Son, I haven't been so close since the war. You saved my life for sure. You shook me up some, but I'm all right now. Let's go and have a look."

The four men ran quickly back into the dome. On the television monitor the tower pipe was still where it had been. Magnusson hurriedly scanned the gauges. "Sir, it's looking good. The towers are rock-solid on the bottom and the pipe is up to full pressure. We've got a pipeline!"

The President shook his hand and placed his arm on Magnusson's shoulder. "Harold, you and your team have really done a job up here. A whole lot of people are going to know about it before I'm through."

The hush in the House of Commons was complete. The Prime Minister was speaking.

"This may well be the single most urgent and direct crisis, apart from war, which Canada has ever had to face. The United States has not only given us a three-pronged ultimatum, but has specified that the answer to that ultimatum must be given by six o'clock this evening. I have asked the President to extend that time, but he has flatly refused. Therefore, the Commons and the Senate must deal with the ultimatum within the time left to us.

"At twelve noon emergency sessions of the House and Senate will begin. At that time, appropriate resolutions will be placed before both bodies. The form of the resolution has already been made known to all of you.

"From the very beginning, I have thought it absolutely essential that an opportunity be given to every member of Parliament to be informed as thoroughly as possible on the general background of this crisis. I have therefore asked the ministries most directly concerned to prepare a presentation. In this way, you will be informed of the events which have led up to the current situation, Canada's relationship with the United States and the status of the government's dealings with the native people of the Northwest Territories and the Yukon. You will also receive reports on the Mackenzie Valley pipeline, the Arctic Islands gas reserves, the question of ownership of the natural gas resources, and the transportation systems being considered with a view to getting the gas out.

"Each minister has been asked to limit his presentation to twenty-five minutes. Fifteen minutes will be devoted to a point-by-point briefing. Ten minutes will be set aside for questions and answers. Questions are to be submitted in writing and given to the pages, who will deliver them to the Speaker.

"We have a lot of ground to cover. This is no time to be attaching blame to any ministry of the past or of the present. Further to this end, I have instructed the ministers and their staffs that in the presentations to be made to you this morning I do not want any opinions given; I just want the facts.

"All parties have proposed that I chair this session. I have agreed to do so, and I have made it clear that I will insist on the time limits being strictly adhered to, both in the presentations and in the question-and-answer periods.

"I would be obliged if the Minister for External Affairs would lead off."

As Porter sat down he suddenly became conscious of the deep, attentive silence filling the Commons Chamber. This was the moment at which the burden of carrying the full responsibility shifted from his shoulders alone, to be shared by the men and women who crowded that vast hall. They sensed this, they knew it, they accepted the responsibility. And with that responsibility came apprehension and the stimulation of knowing that they themselves were participating in this most difficult of all Canadian crises.

The Minister for External Affairs was on his feet at the lectern.

"Prime Minister," Robert Gendron began, "Honourable Members, Honourable Members of the Senate, Honourable Premiers, ladies and gentlemen. . . ."

After reviewing the history of the Arctic resource development, the Minister continued, "Negotiations with the Americans for the acquisition and transportation of natural gas have been going on for years. At the beginning of the seventies we held a series of discussions with them regarding a trans-Canada route for movement of the Prudhoe Bay and Mackenzie Delta gas into the Midwestern States. This resulted in the Mackenzie Valley pipeline which is now undergoing tests.

"But in other areas we have failed to come to an agreement. As far back as the days of Mr. Walter Hickel, the Secretary of the Interior, and his successor, Mr. Rogers Morton, the concept of a continental energy policy between the United States and Canada began to take shape. The Americans clearly wanted to have full access to all Canadian fossil fuels just as if Canada were part of the United States. The effect would be that Canada would share its fuel resources with the United States and take on the U.S. energy shortages in return.

"The Americans have doggedly pursued their attempts to negotiate such a continental energy policy with us. Just as doggedly, Canada has refused, with the result that no agreement exists for the transfer of the natural gas which lies in the Canadian Arctic archipelago.

"If the Americans had been prepared to negotiate with us for the natural gas alone, without attempting to wrap the whole thing up in one continental policy, it is very likely that they would have been given access to one-third of the reserves now proven in the Arctic Islands, and the transportation system would have been in preparation.

"I turn now to consideration of the American attitude toward Canada so that you may conclude what the Americans would be prepared to do to enforce the ultimatum. But first, a few remarks about the American presence in the world scene.

"During the 1950's, the United States, under President Eisenhower and the Secretary of State, John Foster Dulles, accepted the so-called domino theory of communist expansion. Dulles reasoned that if one country in Southeast Asia was to fall to the communists, then the country next to it would fall, and so on until all the nations had fallen into communist hands. This he conceived to be a direct threat to the United States and to the freedom of the world. On the basis of this theory, the United States had a right, indeed even a responsibility, to intervene militarily wherever a communist takeover seemed possible. Thus when the French were driven out of Vietnam in 1954, the United States refused to sign the Geneva armistice, the only western nation to do so. Ultimately the Americans moved to thwart the general election which was planned in that country. It did so on the ground that it was clear that Hanoi forces would win. As a result, the Americans became involved in a direct military intervention on an enormous scale which lasted for a period of nineteen years.

"The point I want to make is that in the case of Vietnam, and before that in Korea and elsewhere in the world, the United States has never hesitated to use, or to threaten to use, military force if it felt that its own national interests or security were threatened.

"The U.S. continues to maintain strategic bases in various parts of the world — air bases, radar sites, submarines and surface vessels, together with a vast armory of sophisticated missiles.

"Granted, then, that the United States has the power and is prepared to use it, what support would Canada have in its struggle with that giant? Very little. Under President Nixon, many of the tensions between the United States and the Soviet Union, on the one hand, and the United States and China on the other, were substantially eased, with the result that the relationship of the United

States to both these countries is on a stable level. Therefore, it would be impossible to expect that in this crisis Canada could depend on any diplomatic or other support from the Soviet Union, and certainly not from China.

"Probably the best we could expect would be the support of world opinion against the action taken by the President. Frankly, I do not expect world criticism to have any effect whatsoever on the President. Canada stands alone, without any hope of defending itself militarily.

"On the other hand, I do not think the President would be prepared to take Canada by force, thereby risking the confidence of all the major powers and indeed of the world. The spectacle of the United States seizing an ally, its major trading partner, is one which I cannot visualize. Furthermore, there is little doubt in my mind that the President can achieve most of his objectives by hard bargaining now that he has stressed that the United States needs the fossil fuels immediately and that he is not prepared to accept any further delays.

"Let us for the moment assume that the United States will act against Canada by way of sanctions should we fail to accede to the ultimatum. There is no doubt that this is in the President's mind. As we all know, he imposed an embargo yesterday at noon against the flow of investment capital into Canada, though he later withdrew that sanction when we countered with the threat to cut off all exports of oil and gas.

"Sanctions have undoubtedly been the United States' prime weapon against its trading partners who have gained an economic advantage. The States first employed such measures in earnest a decade ago when, as a result of a deficit in world trade, it began to take steps to protect its dollar and to support its work force. As foreign goods became competitive in quality as well as price, and as the

174

outflow of American dollars around the world continued to exceed inflow of capital, it became apparent that the American dollar could not withstand world competition. It began to fall in value, a reflection of the fall in relative productivity of the United States' industrial complex.

"Finally, in 1971, as a reaction to the thrust of foreign products into the American market, President Nixon imposed a 10 per cent surcharge on all imports of manufactured goods. It is significant that he very carefully excluded from this category the natural resources necessary to keep the U.S. industrial machine in operation. Canada was caught in that net, despite the fact that we were the major trading partner of the United States. After some revaluations of foreign currencies, President Nixon withdrew the impost. Nevertheless, shortly after, the United States government created the Domestic Incentive Sales Corporation program. DISC was designed to attract American manufacturing capital back to the United States, to induce American corporations which had manufacturing subsidiaries in foreign countries such as Canada to shut those subsidiaries down and return the jobs to the U.S. The device was, and still is, a very simple one, and while the DISC program cannot be classified technically as a sanction, it nevertheless demonstrates the type of America-first action which that country is prepared to take, regardless of its trading partners or neighbouring countries.

"In 1975, the United States enacted the Burke-Hartke Act, which provides even more protection by making it possible to put a ceiling on the import of any given commodity into the United States. As you well know, this has worked a serious hardship on Canadian industries, the majority of which are subsidiaries of United States firms, and has created an enormous impediment to the sale of

Canadian-manufactured goods in the United States, Canada's biggest market.

"Thus there is little doubt in my mind that the United States will not hesitate to impose economic sanctions to achieve the aims of the ultimatum.

"That concludes my brief, Prime Minister. Now if I may, I will deal with the questions in the order in which they have been delivered."

Gendron stopped and turned to speak to his deputy, Max Peterson, sitting on his right. Peterson had been collecting and making notes on the question papers. He gathered them together and handed them all to the Minister.

Gendron put the stack of papers on the lectern and said, "Ladies and gentlemen, I have about nine minutes left of my time allocation. I'll try to get through as many of these questions as I can.

"The first question is, 'Is there any evidence of troop movement in Detroit or Buffalo, or in any of the northern American cities?'

"The answer is, 'No, there is not, although as of yesterday morning at nine o'clock there was a sharp increase in the number of bomber and fighter flights over Canadian territory by the USAF. We regard these overflights as merely a form of intimidation rather than any preparation for military action.'

"The next question is, 'If the flow of United States investment capital to Canada is cut off, what are the chances of getting an increased volume from Western Europe, and especially from the Middle East members of the Organization of Petroleum Exporting Countries?'

"That is an excellent question. As you know, the members of OPEC — which includes Saudi Arabia, Iran, Iraq, Kuwait, Venezuela, Libya, Algeria, and others — are tremendously wealthy as a result of their sale of oil to the

United States. They export 80 per cent of the petroleum on the international market and control 70 per cent of the world's oil reserves. They are therefore very powerful.

"It is regrettable, perhaps, that Canada does not belong to OPEC. We were invited to join two years ago, but when pressure was put on by the United States to decline, we did so. Nevertheless, I have instructed our ambassadors at Beirut and Teheran to set up emergency meetings today with the heads of government of all the OPEC countries in the Middle East. Our Ambassador in Italy is in Libya and will also go on to Algeria. The Ambassador will explain the nature of the emergency and seek immediate investment support in the event that sanctions are imposed.

"At this point we don't know what the response of the government leaders of the OPEC countries will be. I believe there is an enormous base of sympathy on their part for Canada. They realize that our relationship with the United States has slowly become more difficult over the years. I can assure you if the OPEC countries do support Canada with investment funds, it will be on the condition that we join their organization. One of OPEC's reasons for existence is that, since its members control so much of the world's supply of oil, they can apply pressure on the United States, which now must buy over 60 per cent of its oil and energy supply from foreign sources.

"There is one further point. . . . Excuse me for just a moment." The Minister for External Affairs hesitated, then left the lectern and walked around the end of the table to his right to where the Prime Minister sat. The two whispered together briefly, and then Gendron returned to the lectern.

"I thought I should check with the Prime Minister on what I am going to tell you next. As you know, the Prime Minister secured the lifting of the American investment

177

embargo by threatening to cut off exports of oil and gas to the United States. He had hoped that the threat would be strong enough to cause the President to lift the ultimatum altogether, but it was not. What the Prime Minister has now agreed that I may reveal to you is that our ambassadors have been instructed to say that if Canada is forced to apply such a counter-sanction, we will join OPEC provided the OPEC countries agree to institute a similar embargo and cut off all supplies of oil to the United States."

At that, the silence of the audience was broken. There were gasps, and people turned to each other, first with looks of astonishment and then with smiles of approval as the full implications of this move became evident.

When the buzz of conversation had diminished, Gendron went on.

"Unfortunately I have no idea whether we can have an answer from all these countries within the time limit given to us. We have sent a message to every head of state in OPEC outlining our position and asking for support, but it will be the attendance of the appropriate Canadian ambassador that will be important in securing a commitment. With good luck, we may have some answers by the time the vote is taken at five o'clock this evening."

Gendron's assistant, to his left, plucked at his sleeve, and pointed to his watch. Gendron concluded, "Prime Minister, ladies and gentlemen, I have used up my time allocation. I now turn you over to the Honourable Otto Gunther, Minister of Energy, Mines and Resources, and his Deputy Minister, Claude Lafrance."

The Twin Otter was circling over Placer Lake thirty-five miles southwest of Aklavik. This was the spot marked Number Two on Sam's map, the site of the bomb that was due to explode first in sequence.

They had worked late the night before, after Sam's departure on the government Hercules, going over the map and rechecking carefully the locations and the planned explosion times. Bessie peered intently as the plane passed over the point where the pipeline crossed the stream feeding the lake. "This is it," she said.

Ray turned and shouted to the pilot, "O.K., Sandy, you can put her down on the lake."

They still had lots of time. If they could find this bomb and get it safely defused without unexpected problems, they'd likely get to the rest of the bombs all right.

The pilot completed his turn and headed northeast to touch down on the lake about half a mile from the pipe crossing. He landed in the soft snow and taxied back to get as close to the pipeline as he could. Then he shut down the engines.

Bessie and the Staff Sergeant collected their gear — snowshoes, a shovel and a small tool kit containing a set of screwdrivers, a pair of pliers and insulating tape. Then Ray opened the rear passenger door, sat down on the aircraft floor with his feet outboard and put on his snowshoes before jumping onto the snow-covered surface of the lake. Bessie followed.

Pulling their parka hoods up over their heads, they set off at a fast pace with the Staff Sergeant leading. They crossed the shore of the lake, passed through a heavy stand of jackpine, and broke into the pipeline clearing a few feet away from where the pipe crossed the stream and Sam had planted the explosive charge. When they entered the clearing, Bessie moved ahead of the Staff Sergeant, taking the small shovel from his hand as she passed him. She led the way to the pipe and located the spot where she thought the bomb was buried. Even though Sam and she had been there only two days earlier, the windblown snow had obliterated any tracks they had left, and all evidence of their tampering was gone. Gently she began to scrape away the top layer of snow with a sideways motion of the shovel, but then she stopped and handed it back to the Staff Sergeant saying, "Maybe I shouldn't use the shovel. If I hit the timing mechanism I might set it off."

She began to scoop the snow away with her fur-mittened hands, slowly and cautiously. Finally she touched something hard. She said, "I've got it."

The Staff Sergeant said, "O.K., Bessie, I'll handle it now."

He took Bessie's place. He could see the corner of the blue plastic bag at the bottom of the hole, about a foot down, and he scraped away some more snow until he could see clearly the entire top of the package. Using both hands, he pulled it up towards him. It came easily, for the snow had not been packed down. Moving very carefully, he backed away from the pipe for a distance of about ten feet, and laid the package gently in the snow. Because of its weight, it sank several inches into the surface. It was going to be difficult to work on.

Ray said, "Bessie, if you'd come around facing me and bring the front of one of your snowshoes in between mine, the three together should give me a flat surface I can work on."

Gingerly Ray lifted the package out of the snow and laid it on the snowshoes. He pulled off his fur mitts and undid the twist fastener around the neck of the bag. With his left hand he held the bottom of the bag and attempted to reach inside to grasp the timer and detonator. "It won't work. I'll have to cut the bag open. I don't want to pull on the wires to get the explosives out."

He took out a short, extremely sharp knife and slit the plastic bag from end to end, revealing the entire explosive apparatus. Quickly he checked the timer. Correct, as listed. It had been set to go off forty-three hours from the time the bomb was laid. Just an hour to go. Then he examined the detonator carefully. The arming device was in and set, the all-important defusing wheel had its white marker in the correct position. Cautiously Ray placed the index finger and thumb of his left hand on the edge of the arming device to steady it, then slowly he rotated the wheel clockwise until the marker disappeared and it came to a full stop.

It was twenty degrees below zero, but the Staff Sergeant was soaking wet with perspiration. While, as he had said, he knew something about explosives, he was far from being an expert, and here he was, deep in the bush, relying totally on a quick briefing given to him by Sam Allen. If that briefing had been wrong... !

Now that the timer had been disarmed, Ray picked up the pair of pliers and quickly cut the connection between the plastic explosives and the arming device. He got stiffly up from his crouched position, looked down at Bessie from his great height and said quietly, "Bessie, I can understand that you people feel strongly about what the white man is doing to you, but to play around with this stuff you and Sam must be right out of your goddam minds." Then he bent over and picked up the explosive, stuffed it in his left pocket and took the small tool kit, arming device and timer. Bessie didn't reply, but her eyes showed the strain. She picked up the shovel and fell quietly in behind Ray as he headed back toward the aircraft. As they emerged from the jackpines at the edge of the lake, Sandy started up the engines. As they climbed on board, he said, "Everything O.K.?"

Ray nodded. "Everything's O.K., but this is the best way I know of to get a heart attack. Let's hit Number One next. That's up to the northwest. We'll do it, and then come straight back south, doing the rest of them in the series. We've got the tough one out of the way now."

The pilot nodded, did his pre-takeoff check, and shoved the throttle forward. The aircraft skied a few feet down the track and was almost immediately airborne. In five minutes they reached Number One point.

Ottawa / 8:30 a.m., EDT

As the Minister for External Affairs was returning to his seat next to the Prime Minister, he passed Otto Gunther and his deputy on their way to the front of the Chamber. There was a general rustle in the audience as people shuffled papers and shifted positions, but by the time the Minister of Energy, Mines and Resources was established behind the lectern with his notes before him, the room was silent once again.

Gunther's bald head reflected the lights of the Chamber and the television spotlights. Already a few tiny beads of perspiration were appearing. He was not a good speaker, and it was a strain for him to address this kind of audience, or any kind of audience, for that matter. With a final nervous clearing of his throat, he began, his flat, Newfoundland accent more pronounced than usual. "Prime Minister, ladies and gentlemen ... I mean Prime Minister, Members of the Senate, Members of the House, Premiers, ladies and gentlemen: From the viewpoint of my department — I am sorry — my ministry, Energy, Mines and Resources — if I may I will refer to it as EMR — we have been ... rather, we are responsible ... that is to say, I am the minister to whom the National Energy Board reports, so we have a major interest in the amount of gas and oil which is surplus to Canada, whether it should ... whether it is sufficient to sell it to the United States. We are also interested in the financing and construction of the pipelines and other kinds of transportation methods used to get the gas out. So, for that matter, of course, are Northern Affairs and the Ministry of the Environment and the Ministry of Transport. We don't always see eye to eye, but we try." He coughed and wiped his head. "Also there are some questions between us in the various ministries as to who is responsible for what.

"I want to deal first with the Arctic Islands. I brought some slides along to show you the places I want to talk about." He turned and said to Lafrance, "Claude, will you put the slides on for me? And you'd better run the machine also, if you don't mind."

Lafrance went around the table and dropped a tray of slides into the projector. He switched on the machine and flicked to the first picture, a map of the Arctic Islands from Banks across to Ellesmere, and from the Boothia Peninsula and Northwest Passage to the North Pole. Gunther proceeded.

"On this map you can see Melville Island at the bottom left-hand corner. The area between Melville Island on the southwest and the Eureka area of Ellesmere Island to the northeast is known as the Sverdrup Basin, and these islands are called the Sverdrup Islands. Starting in 1970, with the first strike at Drake Point on Melville Island, successful exploration work has been going on here. There are now fifty drilling rigs on the islands, and gas finds have been made on Melville, King Christian, Thor, Ellef Ringnes, Axel Heiberg and Ellesmere. There have also been four oil finds, one on Banks Island to the southwest of Melville, another on Thor, and a third on Ellesmere and a major new discovery on Melville.

"Our best estimate on the gas reserves in the Islands is now approximately 60-trillion cubic feet, which is about three times the amount necessary to justify the cost of

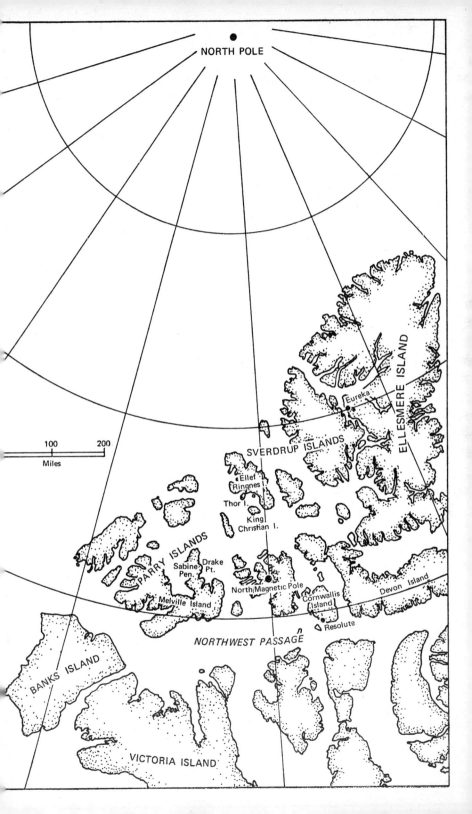

construction of a transportation system to deliver 1½-trillion cubic feet a year to the market in the United States. On the basis of a thirty-year projection, Canada needs 35-trillion cubic feet to meet its future requirements. This leaves a surplus of 25-trillion cubic feet which could be exported."

Gunther paused a moment, took out his handkerchief again and wiped his face and bald head. He was now perspiring profusely, but he struggled on, reading from his notes.

"Most of the gas reserves are held by Panarctic, which is a Canadian-controlled company, as I am sure you are all aware. It was formed in 1968 because the Canadian government was afraid that exploration wouldn't go forward in the Arctic without some incentives. It is 45 per cent owned by the government of Canada, 10 per cent by Canadian corporations such as Canadian Pacific Investment, and 45 per cent by foreign corporations. At no time have any shares of Panarctic been made available for purchase by the Canadian public — unfortunately.

"When Panarctic started to hit in 1970 with its first discovery well at Drake Point on Melville, and a later find on King Christian Island, American interests quickly appeared on the scene. Gas distribution firms in the U.S. quickly saw there was going to be a major supply on the Arctic Islands and they wanted to be there for a piece of the action. It was clear there was going to be an enormous shortage of natural gas, and they were anxious to advance exploration money to Panarctic in return for the right to purchase the gas when it was discovered. And that's what they've done. Tenneco of Houston, Columbia Natural Gas and other gas distributors have advanced Panarctic interest-free money repayable only in the event that gas is produced. Within three years of the first discoveries, the

Panarctic shareholders had put up $101-million, while the American group had invested over $75-million. Since that time, the capital input by Panarctic has remained at $101-million, but now the American investment is over $500-million.

"It can be said that because Tenneco and its associates have the first right to negotiate for the gas discovered by Panarctic, and because they have put up the lion's share of the capital . . . it can be said the American firms in effect own the gas in the ground. They own it, but they have to get permission to take it out and transport it to market.

"Now I'd like to return to the question of a continental energy policy, touched on by the Minister of External Affairs. During the Nixon administration, the Americans decided that an over-all policy concerned with all available forms of energy was essential throughout North America. They pointed out that since the United States and Canada occupy the same continent, and since the United States had in effect paid for the discoveries made in the Canadian Archipelago, it made sense to have an agreement regarding the distribution of the products resulting from those discoveries.

"For the Americans, a continental energy policy meant that Canada would share all of its energy resources with the United States, which in turn meant that we would have to share the shortages as well. When the President says that Canada has refused to agree to make available to the United States the Arctic Islands gas, he is not correct. What we have refused to do is enter into a continental energy policy agreement, of which gas would only be a part. I am of the firm view that if negotiations had proceeded on the basis of gas alone, the Americans could have had a commitment for the Arctic reserves long ago, and the transportation system would have been well on its way by now.

"In a way, Canada has been fortunate that an agreement wasn't reached. Up until the middle of the last decade, we were practically giving our gas and oil away. To obtain exploration rights in the Mackenzie Delta and the Arctic Islands, a company was only required to put down a deposit of between 5 cents and 25 cents per acre. Then, if drilling was successful, it would pay a royalty of 5 per cent on all production for the first five years (if the find was north of latitude 70 degrees) and 10 per cent thereafter, or (if the find was below latitude 70 degrees) 5 per cent for the first three years and 10 per cent thereafter. Anyone can see that this works out at not much more than bank interest on the capital which had been given away in the ground. Thus Canada stood to gain practically nothing from the sale of oil and gas.

"Compare that kind of giveaway with what the Middle East countries have done and are now doing in terms of retaining ownership of the fossil fuels in the ground and taxing the product. With royalties, taxes and payment money, they get a return of between five and six dollars a barrel for oil which costs twenty cents to produce. It's little wonder that the Middle East and Mediterranean members of OPEC have become among the richest nations in the world with very little effort. In fact, the control of billions upon billions of American dollars, in the hands of the leaders of these countries, has enabled them to manipulate the American dollar in world markets and cause serious changes in the value of the dollar from time to time.

"Fortunately Canada has smartened up a bit in its dealings. We have issued new leases covering the drilled acreage in the North. Under the new terms, a fair share of the proceeds of the sale at well-head will go to the Canadian people, in export taxes and a royalty of 25 per cent on all production in the Islands and the Delta. The U.S. oil and gas companies have been extremely annoyed at the new terms, but for Canadians they could provide a return of 50 per cent of the market price of the gas, and in effect a yearly income equivalent to all federal expenditures. Thus it is certainly in Canada's interests to arrange for the export of these resources, provided Canada's future needs are protected.

"Now I see my time has just about run out. Perhaps I can answer one question."

Gunther took one of the notes which had been left beside the lectern on the table. "Why shouldn't Canada enter into a continental energy agreement with the United States?"

"Well, I can't answer for the previous administrations, and I may not be able to answer for this one. . . ." He glanced down toward the Prime Minister.

Robert Porter stood up. "If I may, I'll answer that question for Mr. Gunther. It is a most difficult one. I don't want him to bear a responsibility which he should not have.

"It boils down quite simply to a question of sovereignty. If Canada is to remain an independent nation with its own goals and objectives and a political and judicial system quite different from that of the United States, then it is clear that we must be as free as possible to plan our own economic development and in particular the use to which our natural resources, especially those which are non-renewable, are put. It is apparent to all of us that we already live in the economic and cultural shadow of the United States. As a result, it is most difficult at times to maintain a position of independence.

"If we should agree to a continental policy on all sources of energy, it is clear that we would then have to share the United States' shortages. The Americans are dependent now on foreign imports for 60 per cent of their energy. Canada is self-sufficient. If the two countries were to merge their interests in energy, Canada would join the United States in being largely dependent on offshore suppliers. This would undoubtedly make us even more vulnerable to economic domination from abroad, and we would find it almost impossible to maintain our independence. For these reasons, Canada has taken its present position, and I can see no reason for changing at this moment, although I must confess that with the ultimatum now handed to us by the President, it is very likely that we can expect other pressure to be applied.

"Clearly, what is at issue is not so much the access to the energy reserves of the Canadian Arctic as the whole question of an independent future for Canadians."

Air Force One / (Resolute Bay)
7:57 a.m., CDT

The President settled down in his favourite spot, the captain's seat in the Boeing 747, Air Force One. He had just taken off from Resolute Bay for Washington.

Things were moving on schedule. This early morning start should get him back into the White House before three o'clock in the afternoon. It was not to be a direct trip, however. He had one more visit in mind.

They were climbing sharply, headed south over the Northwest Passage. Suddenly the President pulled back the power and levelled off at 2,000 feet. And then, smiling to himself at the startled glance Colonel Mike Wypich threw his way, he turned the big bird in a slow arc to proceed east down the Passage.

Answering the captain's unspoken question he said, "Don't panic, Mike. We're going to inspect the newest, toughest ice-breaker in the world. You don't know it, the Canadians don't know it — yet — but the *Polar Star* is in the Northwest Passage, and she should steam by Resolute Bay in about an hour and a half! This is her first shakedown voyage, and we're going to drop by."

Wypich asked, "How did she get up here so fast, Mr. President?"

"Very simple, Mike. She was in Baffin Bay last week, pretty close to Lancaster Sound, the eastern entrance of the Northwest Passage. I thought it might be useful to show the flag this morning, so I instructed the captain to take her past Resolute Bay as close to shore as he could safely go, and then head east toward McClure Strait. That's where the *Manhattan* got stuck in 1972. I'd like the captain to go right through McClure Strait. The underwater ice formations they call pingoes may make it difficult, but the *Polar Star* has two pretty sophisticated sets of sonar sounding gear which should make it possible for her to get through all right. The United States claims that the Northwest Passage is high seas, Mike, and I want to show Canada we mean what we say."

"There she is, sir," Mike exclaimed. "Twelve o'clock and about five miles coming straight at us."

"Beautiful!" said the President. "Beautiful! Let's have a good look."

As Air Force One approached the *Polar Star* from the west, the President let down to 1,000 feet and turned slightly to the south so he could pass by the ship and have a good view of her.

"Beautiful" he said once again. "Mike, see if you can crank up the captain on the blower. His name is Anderson. You can probably get him on the emergency frequency."

Within forty-five seconds Mike had the captain on the radio. The President said, "Captain Anderson, this is the President. I want to congratulate you on a first-class job in getting that beautiful big ship into the Northwest Passage and over here as quickly as you have. Try to get in as close to Resolute Bay as you can when you go by. I don't want anybody to miss the fact you're here carrying the flag. I know you should probably keep twelve miles offshore to stay clear of Canadian waters, but I think you ought to bend it a little this morning. Do you think you can get the *Polar Star* through McClure Strait?"

Anderson came back, "Yes, sir, no question about it. The pingoes have been charted and I have a channel through them, so that shouldn't be any problem. And with my 75,000 horsepower, I'm sure I can get through that ice whether it's ten feet or fourteen feet thick."

"Fine," the President said. "Mighty fine. Now remember, Captain, it's important to the United States that the *Polar Star* get through McClure Strait. It's also important that she doesn't sink, of course."

"Yes, sir."

"I'll be keeping an eye on you once you get into the McClure, Captain. Good luck."

"Thank you, sir," said Anderson.

The President did one more circle around his prize polar ice-breaker — 14,000 tons of super-hard, ice-fortified steel.

As the President watched, the gray-painted hull of the *Polar Star* sliced neatly through a three-foot pan of ice as if it wasn't there. The President guessed she was steaming about 20 knots. He could see the two helicopters which she carried on board to the rear of the great funnel. The high bridge, located just slightly ahead of midships, was strewn with electronic gear and wires. Otherwise the great ship was completely uncluttered. Despite her vast bulk and weight, the *Polar Star* was as trim and sleek as a racer. She had an appearance of grace, lightness, and speed which belied her function as a floating battering-ram.

As he finished his last circling turn over the bow, the President said, "She's the best in the world, Mike. For the United States, that's the way it should be."

With that, he put Air Force One on its course for Washington, and poured climbing power into the engines. "You have control, Mike. Head her for the barn; I've got work to do."

The Minister of Indian Affairs and Northern Development, Pierre Allard from Northern Manitoba, a tall, thin man with a long, sharp-featured face and grey-streaked straight hair, strode briskly to the lectern. On his way, he set his tray of slides on the projector and switched immediately to a map of Canada on which had been outlined the Mackenzie Valley Corridor.

Obviously not a man to waste time, he began as soon as he reached the microphone. "Like the minister who preceded me, I have not held this portfolio very long — only about seven weeks — but I feel confident that the background knowledge I acquired before taking office, added to what I have learned since, will enable me to make clear the situation as it exists in the Mackenzie Valley Corridor, particularly as it relates to the rights of the native people.

"The Mackenzie River, as you can see from the map, flows north from Great Slave Lake to the Mackenzie Delta, where it spreads and enters the Arctic Ocean. The wide river valley, called the Corridor, is a relatively habitable area as opposed to the barren Arctic tundra. That is because the river itself softens the climate, permitting trees to grow and providing food and shelter for men and animals. For centuries, Indians have lived in the treed area and Eskimos in the tundra at the north end of the river and to the east toward Hudson Bay. In ancient times, the Indian and Eskimo were mortal enemies. There were many

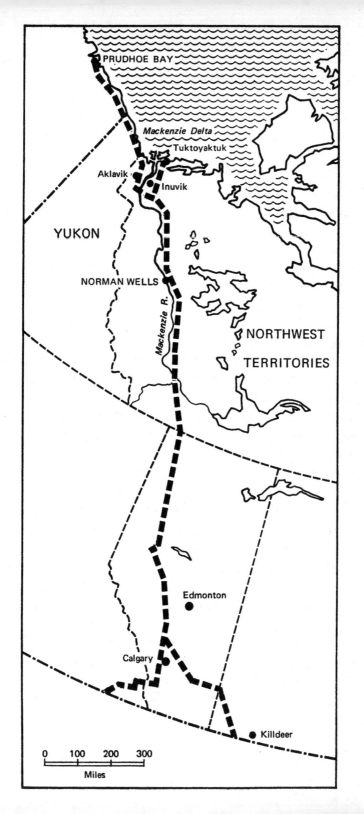

PRUDHOE BAY

Mackenzie Delta

Tuktoyaktuk

Aklavik

Inuvik

YUKON

NORMAN WELLS

Mackenzie R.

NORTHWEST

TERRITORIES

Edmonton

Calgary

Killdeer

0   100   200   300

Miles

bloody battles waged between the two races.

"The Mackenzie River has been the prime route into the Western Arctic since its discovery by Alexander Mackenzie in 1789. In the early days, canoes carried trading goods and furs along its waters. In modern times, barges transport products north to Norman Wells and Tuktoyaktuk. Recently the aircraft has begun to play a major role in the Corridor as well as throughout the entire Arctic. During the 1960's and into the 70's, Pacific Western, a regional air carrier was securely established, running from Edmonton to Yellowknife and Inuvik. And Inuvik, a relatively new town situated to the east of Aklavik in the Mackenzie Delta, is now the regional centre for that entire area.

"After 1968, when the Prudhoe Bay discovery was announced, the pace of exploration in the Mackenzie Delta region quickened. Then, with the first discovery of oil at Atkinson Point on the Tuktoyaktuk Peninsula in January 1970, the importance of the area as a source of hydrocarbons, both gas and oil, was firmly established, and drilling rigs really began to get to work. By the winter of 1972, there were thirteen rigs in operation in the Delta. Major finds had been made on Richards Island as well as on the Tuktoyaktuk Peninsula, and natural gas was being found in increasing amounts. By 1974 there were sufficient reserves to meet the minimum requirements for the creation of a pipeline from the Mackenzie Delta to the American market even without the Prudhoe Bay flow.

"Air transport moved regularly and by charter down the Corridor from Edmonton and Yellowknife into the Delta. Barge traffic increased to such an extent that by 1974 the Northern Transportation Company, a CNR subsidiary, was carrying 500,000 tons of goods annually. So even then the Corridor was very much alive.

"In 1972 a decision was made to build a highway from

196

Yellowknife to Inuvik and Tuktoyaktuk. Construction was begun, but it soon ground to a halt because of a lack of government co-ordination. The enterprise was revived and set on course again, however, after the Prime Minister had intervened, and a reasonable degree of inter-departmental liaison had been established. Eventually the highway, which paralleled the route for the gas pipeline, was completed, and has been extensively used in the pipeline construction.

"The next element of transportation to appear in the Mackenzie Valley Corridor was the pipeline itself, forty-eight inches in diameter, and laid underground or in mounds called berms.

"Now, as you are all aware, what is happening is that in the Northwest Territories and the Yukon, where the pipe is most remote from points of service and repair, explosions are now regularly taking place, destroying segments of the pipe. It is believed that the sabotage is the work of certain native groups, but since no one has been caught in the act and no one has been charged, it's impossible to say. Nevertheless, the native peoples have made no secret of the fact that they are prepared to take such action if their rights to the land in the Northwest Territories are not recognized.

"There has been no such recognition. It was not until 1973, as a result of the findings of the Supreme Court of Canada in the Nishga Indians' case, that Prime Minister Trudeau was forced to agree to negotiate. Talks did begin, but collapsed almost immediately. The result is that there is no agreement with the native people.

"The Indians, Eskimos, and Métis of the Northwest Territories and the Yukon claim that they have the rights to the land as the original inhabitants. By far the greater part of the Corridor is occupied by Indians and Eskimos with whom no treaty has ever been signed. Some of the Indians in the Lower Mackenzie Valley signed treaties during the 1800's, and the native people point to these as evidence that the white man recognized their original rights.

"They have naturally been angered to see drilling rigs appear on their lands at Tuktoyaktuk, on Cape Bathurst, on Banks Island, and in the Mackenzie Delta, without their permission. They have watched while the white man destroyed their hunting grounds and the terrain and has pierced the permafrost with his rigs to drill down and secure rich deposits of gas and oil without paying them any compensation.

"And so they began, ten years ago, to gather together in groups such as the Committee for Original Peoples' Entitlement at Inuvik, the Indian Brotherhood of the Northwest Territories, the Indian Brotherhood of the Yukon, the Inuit Tapirisat, and others. They have rallied their people and have presented their claims to the white man. They said, 'Look, you are doing everything you can to help the foreign oil companies come into our lands and rip up our ground and put in drilling rigs to take out oil and gas, but you have given us no sign that you are prepared to settle as the government of the United States settled with the native people of Alaska when it came time to take the oil and gas from Prudhoe Bay and build a pipeline across to Valdez. Why are we, the native people in Canada, different from the native people in Alaska? We want not only the jobs that go with pipeline construction, but we want more than anything else to have a fair settlement for our lands and for the rich minerals that lie under them.'

"So we who live in the rest of Canada, and the government, have only ourselves to blame for the bombings. We have been too cheap and too short-sighted, at least until this time, to settle fairly with our native people and to bring the American and French oil and gas owners in the Mackenzie Delta into the settlement. After all, even a poor Métis like myself can understand the frustration of the native people when they see themselves being defrauded.

"One further point is this. There has been much agitation in the North because they have not been permitted their own elected representative government. I have been instructed by the Prime Minister to advise this meeting that it is the intention of this government to place legislation before this Parliament very shortly to give self-government, in a modified provincial form, to both territories. When that occurs, the archaic system of government by the Minister or the Deputy Minister or the Assistant Deputy Minister in Ottawa will come to a long-overdue end.

"That concludes my statement, and now I will proceed to the questions."

The pages had brought only three pieces of paper to Allard as he was speaking. He glanced quickly over the top one and said, "The first question is double-barrelled. It asks which of the ministries has been responsible for negotiating with the United States on the Arctic natural gas and oil, and whether the American complaint about dealing with Ottawa is justified."

Allard paused a moment, ran a hand through his thick hair, and shifted uncomfortably from one foot to the other. "This is a very difficult question. The answer to the first part is that it has been mainly the responsibility of the Minister of Energy, Mines and Resources. However, because the natural gas and oil lie within the Northwest Territories and the Yukon, my ministry has historically felt that it, and not EMR, controlled the resources. My people feel that they should have just as much say in the matter as the EMR people do, not only in dealing with the Americans, but also in the setting of policy on royalties and the rules and regulations governing the drilling and exploration activities in the Arctic.

"Quite frankly, we've been involved in a leadership brawl over the work of the Advisory Committee on Northern Development. This committee, made up of senior civil servants from all the ministries with responsibilities in the Territories, makes recommendations to the various ministers. In the past, the committee has been so strong and the ministers so weak that virtually all the recommendations have been accepted without question. As a result, we have had policy-making, in fact, government, by a committee of civil servants.

"Each of the ministries responsible for the Territories is jealous of the others. Thus, there is little communication between them, even at the advisory committee, and there is example after example of overlapping of activity in the departments because of a failure to communicate. What has been truly lacking has been a committee at the ministerial level, with a strong leader who can cut across the decisions of all the ministries. It is also deplorable that we have not had, up until this time, a clearcut statement of national goals and objectives for the Canadian North.

"Therefore, the answer to the second part of the question, Do the Americans have a valid complaint? must be Yes, because if Canadians themselves find it difficult to deal with bureaucracy, to get decisions, then the Americans must find it a hundred times more difficult and frustrating.

"As you are all aware, the Prime Minister has already announced a major reorganization of the civil service and a radical change in the government's approach to the Northwest Territories and the Yukon. He has already declared that he will create a Ministry of State for the

Arctic under his personal leadership to which all the ministries which are now involved in the Advisory Committee will be responsible.

"Also, my ministry will soon be split, with the Indian Affairs section going to Secretary of State and the Northern Development branch to Energy, Mines and Resources. These two areas of responsibility have been conflicting. On the one hand we deal with and protect people, and on the other encourage and assist development. That situation has not made sense, and the results have been easy to see."

At this point the Prime Minister caught Allard's eye and motioned to his watch. He responded by saying, "The Prime Minister has informed me my time is up. Thank you."

Porter rose and said, "Thank you, Pierre. I have just had word that the Minister of Defence has been held up and will not be able to make his presentation, so perhaps I can substitute for him. What I'll attempt to do is give you a status report on the Canadian armed forces so that you can weigh their role and possible effectiveness in this crisis. The regular force establishment is 55,000, and we are up to full strength. This government is in the process of withdrawing the 5,000 troops that have been on NATO duty in Europe, together with the air squadrons which support them, although we are maintaining our commitment to NATO to keep them completely air mobile so that they can be relied upon as available reserves in the event of an armed confrontation in Europe.

"In Canada, under Mobile Command, we have three CF5 fighter squadrons, and approximately 3,000 combat-ready troops.

"The reserves, that is to say the Militia, the Air Reserve, and the Naval Reserve, have been increased in strength in recent years to a present level of 30,000 men, and we are working up to an establishment of 40,000.

"I have instructed the Chief of the Defence Staff to put all his troops at full alert during this crisis, not because we anticipate an attack from the United States — that would be unthinkable — but to support the civil authorities in case there are anti-American demonstrations.

"This has been a very brief statement. I don't think I need cover any more points on the military side. The next report will come from the Ministry of Transport."

Ottawa / 9:56 a.m., EDT

The Minister of Transport, Leonard Watts, began by out-lining the problems inherent in transporting the natural gas from the Arctic Islands by undersea pipe. He then went on, "If this is the way the United States and its buyers, such as Tenneco, choose to go, they will obviously want access to the Islands and other parts of the North-west Territories, and they will want the authority to set the standards for environmental protection so that con-struction is not hampered by regulations which are too stringent. My colleague, the Minister of the Environment, will undoubtedly have a few words to say on this subject.

"The next form of transportation is the tanker. Speci-ally-built ice-strengthened ships equipped with massive tanks designed to carry liquefied natural gas do not exist today. Such ships would have to be at least 250,000 tons dead weight, and they would have to have special tanks for ballast so that they could cut through the permanent ice on their way into the Islands.

"There's a very serious question in my mind as to whether the ships would be able to navigate in the heavy pack ice which surrounds the Islands. There are some who believe they could, but there has been no proof as yet. If a tanker fleet were used, it would need the support of ice-breakers.

"When the first *Manhattan* experiment took place, the United States Coastguard ice-breaker, the *North Wind*, a small ship, failed miserably, and the Canadian ice-breaker, the *John A. Macdonald*, had to come to the rescue several times. Stung by this failure, the U.S. government quickly approved the construction of an ice-breaker, the *Polar Star*, at 14,000 tons and 75,000 h.p.

"Once again the Americans took the initiative.

"Canada had the opportunity to build a polar ice-breaker at the beginning of this decade. Hearings were held by the Standing Committee on Northern Development in 1972, and Wartsila, a Finnish firm, reported that they had been retained by Humble Oil of the U.S. to do preliminary work on an icebreaker — 50,000 tons and 140,000 h.p. A similar ship could have been built by Canada at a cost of approximately $90-million, but the Ministry of Transport was not prepared to recommend the construction of such a ship unless major finds of resources were discovered in the Arctic Islands. Such discoveries in the form of natural gas had already been made, but this fact was ignored, and Canada took no steps to equip itself with an adequate ice-breaker fleet.

"Now I have some news for you, ladies and gentlemen. Just before I left my office to come to this briefing, I was informed that the *Polar Star* had been sighted this morning in the Northwest Passage off Resolute Bay."

The Chamber was filled with gasps of astonishment, followed by a burst of conversation. Even the Prime Minister had not heard the news, and immediately plunged into discussion with Robert Gendron on his right. Watts waited patiently, and as soon as the discussion petered out, proceeded.

"The ship is steaming westbound. It is very likely that her destination is Melville Island and the forcing of the McClure Strait ice which stopped the *Manhattan* in 1969. Obviously the President has directed the experimental trip to show the flag and to see how the vessel copes with the heavy ice. For your information, the United States has not asked for permission to sail through the Northwest Passage, because they maintain the position that these are high seas and not Canadian waters."

At this point the Prime Minister scribbled a note and had it delivered to Watts. He stopped, read the note, and said, " I have been informed by the Prime Minister that although my time is now officially up, I can use up the balance of the time allotted to the Minister of Defence and carry on with my presentation.

"I should also advise you that the Americans have been considering a submarine-tanker to carry crude oil or liquid natural gas from the Arctic. This is a proposal which was originally put forward by General Dynamics ten years ago. They have done a great deal of experimental work since, and are satisfied that a system could be built to pump liquefied gas into a submarine which could be docked at special under-water berths offshore. A fleet of thirty or forty of these craft could move about three billion cubic feet of gas a day from the Islands to the eastern seaboard of the United States. But once again, such a fleet does not exist, and the time factor is critically urgent for the Americans."

Watts then pushed the remote control and a new slide appeared on the screen. It was a photograph of the Resources Carrier aircraft. He went on to give details of the relationship of the Great Plains Project with Boeing, and information concerning the specifications and operational capabilities of the aircraft. He explained Canada's former control over the rights to the aircraft and its failure to participate in the research, development and construction.

"In my opinion," said Watts, "the RCA is by far the most practical way to take natural gas off the Islands. It

LARGE RESOURCE TRANSPORT AIRPLANE

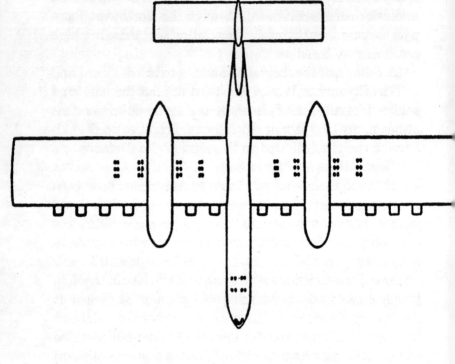

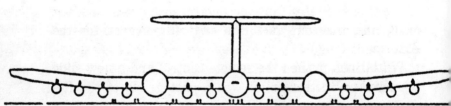

MAX GROSS WEIGHT (LB)	3,500,000
MAX PAYLOAD (LB)	2,300,000 AT 500 N.MI. RA
WING SPAN (FT)	478
POWER PLANT	(12) 50,000 LB SLST THRUST FANS

THE *BOEING* COMP
RC-0128

flies over all the difficult tundra, permafrost and mountainous terrain, and can operate in any weather. It's safe and reliable. Calculations, based on Boeing's experience with large aircraft, are that at the outside there'll be one crash per million operations, and with a single-purpose use for the craft the frequency could be even less.

"The Resources Carrier will burn natural gas, the least polluting of all fossil fuels. Landing fields will present no problem. All the Arctic Islands on which gas has been found have excellent airfield locations and approaches.

"Indications are that the aircraft can be operated for about 1½ to 2 cents per ton mile, which makes it competitive to a pipe even if a pipe could be built from the Islands. With today's prices for natural gas running at $1.25 per thousand cubic feet, there's no doubt the aircraft would be economical."

"Thirty-six Resources Aircraft would be required to transport two billion cubic feet of gas per day between the Arctic Islands and Cochrane, site of the northern end of a new LNG pipe system to New York State. If, on the other hand, Canada agrees to the United States' ultimatum and allows the Americans to come in to create their own transportation system, it is very likely that the United States will completely bypass southern Canada and move the gas directly from the Arctic Islands to key terminal points in the United States.

"It is my strong belief that the RCA system provides the United States with a practical means which is close to being operational."

Watts concluded his presentation and answered a number of questions. When he was through, he turned the lectern over to Arthur Green, Minister of the Environment.

The white and blue RCMP Twin Otter touched down softly in the blowing, light snow which blanketed the pipeline corridor between the scrawny jackpines. The wind was now gusting up to thirty and forty miles an hour, lifting the snow and making it difficult for the pilot to see ahead in the last few feet of his descent. But he brought it down perfectly.

They were at Rat River, the final pipeline water-crossing on Sam Allen's list.

It was near the lake where Freddie Armstrong had picked up Sam and Bessie the night before.

This would be the final defusing ordeal. By this time, having successfully completed nine attempts, Staff Sergeant Ray was relaxed and confident. As they were landing, he looked back over his long career with the RCMP.

Nothing he had ever done would compare with this. He could sure tell his boys quite a story: direct orders from the P.M., defuse the bombs, save the pipeline, save the country! They'd probably never believe him! Ray was proud. Not many men could see their whole career justified in one job.

But God! Was he tired!

Just one more of those bloody bombs and the whole thing would be finished.

He and Bessie had the defusing procedure down pat by now.

Bessie would find the package, Ray would lift it out of its hiding-place in the snow, they would lock their snowshoes together head on, then Ray would defuse the bomb.

It really was quite simple.

As the Twin Otter came to a halt, the pilot immediately put power to the engines to move it forward just slightly. He did this several times to get rid of the heat which had built up in the skis because of the friction with the snow. Otherwise, the skis would melt the snow and then freeze in, locking the aircraft solid.

Once again Ray and Bessie went through the ritual of strapping on snowshoes, getting their parkas snug to be ready to leave the aircraft.

As they made their final preparations, it was clear that Bessie, for all her strength and youth, was beginning to wilt under the strain. Ray could see it in her face and in the slow way she was moving — she was exhausted. During the entire morning she had said next to nothing, even during the tense moments of the first defusing or when it was apparent that they had successfully brought it off.

The aircraft came to a stop facing directly into the wind which was fortunately blowing straight down the Corridor from the southeast. The pilot shut the engines down.

Ray and Bessie climbed out. They were met by the high wind and blinding snow. Ray led the way, pushed along by the wind, his parka up tightly over his head. Bessie followed him closely.

They had gone only a few yards towards the watercrossing where the last bomb lay hidden in the snow when the Staff Sergeant heard Bessie moan close behind him. He turned just as she stumbled and fell into the snow. As he struggled back to her with the driven snow whipping viciously into his face, Bessie got to her knees. Then she retched and vomited.

Ray bent down, put his hands under her arms to steady her, and shouted above the wind, "Bessie, come on, I'll get you back to the aircraft."

He tried to lift her, but Bessie resisted. "No, I'll be O.K. in a minute." Her retching stopped.

Gently the Staff Sergeant helped her to stand.

He said, "Look, I can find this one by myself. You've got to get back in the aircraft where it's warm. Come on."

Bessie turned to look up at him, the snow lining her parka hood and beginning to sting her face. "Look, Jim, there's nothing wrong with me except that I'm a little bit pregnant. That's all. I'm O.K. now. Let's get this over with."

Ray gave up. He moved past Bessie and snowshoed toward the water-crossing of the Rat River where the last explosive package was to be found just at the point the enormous pipe entered the mound at the edge of the water.

Now the familiar defusing pattern began.

Bessie went up to the pipe, crouched down on her snowshoes, and gently pushed the snow from side to side until she exposed the top of a blue plastic bag. Ray lifted it out of the snow, backed off with the package until he was about ten feet from the pipe. Bessie came round in front of him, put her snowshoe in between his to form the working platform.

The two of them opened the package. Tired as he was, Ray was quite sure of himself.

Quickly he checked the timer and saw that it was O.K. They had plenty of time. He took the arming device in his left hand, then reached with the index finger of his right and firmly pushed the arming wheel away from him. At that instant he realized that he had the arming device upside down. He had twisted the arming wheel counterclockwise to detonate!

The bomb would blow in four seconds!

He shouted, "Run!" as he sprang to his feet, dropping the bomb beside him. Bessie turned and fled, snowshoes flailing — Ray about ten feet behind her.

Suddenly the snow-filled air was shattered by a pillar of flame and a blast that rocked and almost lifted the Twin Otter sitting a hundred yards away.

In the aircraft, with its tail toward the explosion, the young pilots could see nothing but instantly knew what had happened when the shockwave and noise of the blast hit them.

"My God! They've had it!" Sandy shouted.

Frantically, he whipped off his seatbelt, threw on his parka, opened the back door, got his snowshoes on, leaped out and raced toward the pipe — his co-pilot a few yards behind. As he reached the point of the blast, Sandy could smell, almost taste, the acrid fumes of the explosive material which still hung over the blast site despite the strong wind. Ahead of them as he raced toward the water-crossing, he could see the Staff Sergeant flat on his back with his arms outspread, and just in front of him, the figure of Bessie, face down in the snow.

He stopped and shouted to the co-pilot, "Get back to the aircraft, bring the medical kit and the stretcher. Also see if you can reach the Inuvik tower to notify headquarters. Hurry!"

The pilot went quickly over to Bessie and crouched down beside her on her right side. Very gently he lifted her head and turned it to the side, facing away from him and away from the howling wind.

Gently he brushed the snow off her face, and could see that it was unmarked. There was no evidence of blood, but under the parka and heavy trousers it could be possible she was bleeding or that her limbs were broken.

To check her pulse, the young constable placed his fingers on her neck. He could feel her heart beating. It was a strong beat.

As soon as the co-pilot came with the stretcher they would strap her arms to her side and lash her to two rough poles they would have to cut from the jackpines. That way, they could make sure her back was rigid when they lifted her onto the stretcher. Perhaps with any luck she might regain consciousness before they had to move her, so she could tell them if she had any pain in any particular part of her body. Already the pilot's mind was reaching back into his memory to recall the vigorous St. John Ambulance training he had been through.

Then he went over to Ray. Again there was no blood visible, but the familiar face was an ashen gray. Ray's blue eyes were wide open, vacantly staring. As the Captain put his hand under the Staff Sergeant's parka, reaching for the rib-cage immediately over the heart, he had a strong sense that he would find no trace of the pulse of life.

Ottawa / 10:40 a.m., EDT

Clarkson, the Minister of Finance, was a little man, but he had a great deal of presence and a booming voice, so he had no trouble in holding the attention of those in the House.

He got through the usual preliminaries without delay, and then plunged immediately into facts and figures, using a chart to clarify his points. He explained that legislation enacted by the federal government to regulate the financing of the Mackenzie Valley pipeline had specified that not less than two-thirds of the ownership be in Canadian hands, while not more than 10 per cent of the funds for financing the pipe were to be obtained in Canada. "This system has worked," he said, "and the major oil purchasers of the gas in the United States, together with the U.S. government, quickly made the money available without interest until the gas started to flow through the pipe." He pointed out, however, that this deferral of interest made the investors in the United States doubly concerned when the native people began blowing up the pipeline. Undoubtedly the President was under enormous pressure from the holders of the debt to do everything in his power to force Canada to make a settlement with the native people.

Clarkson then reviewed the possible economic and trade sanctions which the United States might invoke against Canada and the counter-sanctions which Canada might employ. "Ladies and gentlemen, there is no doubt that the sanctions which can be applied against us will have disastrous short-term effects upon every individual in this country.

"I can visualize industries being shut down from coast to coast, resources extraction and processing coming to an abrupt halt and imports of foodstuffs and supplies from the United States being cut off. We would immediately have to impose rationing and price controls and establish an emergency system to feed and house thousands of people who would be without jobs.

"On the other hand, there is no doubt that the United States would suffer as well, because by counter-sanction we would cut off the 1½-million barrels of oil and the two billion cubic feet of gas per day that we supply. Furthermore, the U.S. industries which depend on our natural resources, particularly the basic minerals such as iron, nickel and copper, would be shut down until new sources of supply from offshore could be arranged, so the United States would also experience massive short-term unemployment.

"In other words, the sanctions and counter-sanctions would be harmful to the economy of both countries and would cause massive unemployment on both sides of the border. And of course, to impose drastic sanctions on Canada would be damaging to the U.S. subsidiaries in this country. I'm sure the President has considered this, but apparently he's prepared to sacrifice their interests in order to gain his objective.

"I believe that the darkest period for Canada would be the first six months after the imposition of the sanctions. By the end of that time, world opinion and world support in terms of trade and investment, and the opening of foreign markets to Canadian goods, would have taken effect and the new supply of investment capital that could be obtained from Japan, the Soviet Union, Western Europe, and from OPEC would improve conditions. Nevertheless, the Canadian economy would undoubtedly have suffered a blow from which it could take us a generation to recover.

"On the other hand, if the ultimatum is accepted by Canada, no such sanctions will be imposed and no such hardships will be endured, at least so we are led to believe. Employment will be sustained, shipment of finished goods and raw materials to the United States will continue, as will the export of our precious natural gas in quantities without regard to what Canada may need for its own requirements."

Clarkson turned to his right to face the Prime Minister. "Prime Minister, strangely enough there appear to be no questions. It's now one minute to eleven. Thank you."

As Clarkson sat down, Porter rose to his feet. "Ladies and gentlemen," he said, "the special sitting of Parliament will commence at noon. His Excellency the Governor-General will open Parliament with a brief Speech from the Throne in the Senate Chamber.

"This briefing is concluded."

Immediately following the briefing, the Prime Minister
went directly to his office in the Main Block. He was joined
by Robert Gendron, John Thomas and Tom Scott, all of
whom assisted him in working out the rough draft for a
brief Speech from the Throne. When they were satisfied,
Porter phoned the Governor-General and discussed the
speech with him. In the light of his comments, the draft
was revised and the final typescript despatched by special
courier to Government House. Gendron got up and prepared to leave for his own office.

"Stay and have a bite of lunch, Bob," the Prime Minister said. "Tom has ordered sandwiches and coffee for all
of us."

"Thanks, but I'd better not. My name was drawn as one
of those to speak in the debate this afternoon, and I've got
a little over half an hour to get my thoughts on paper. I'll
see you in the House."

As he left, Scott, who had gone into the outer office to
pick up the lunch, came in. His face was very grave. "I
have some bad news, Prime Minister. Bessie Tobac and
Staff Sergeant Ray of the RCMP went out early this morning to defuse the bombs that had beet set.

"Well, sir, I don't know exactly what went wrong, but
Ray must have made a slip, because the last bomb exploded
on them. They seem to have known it was going to go,
because they were both running, if you can run in snow-

shoes, but it all happened too fast. Bessie was knocked out and suffered concussion, but she seems to be O.K. She was farther away from the blast than Ray, and her heavy clothing helped protect her.

"Ray bought it immediately. He must have been crouching down to work on the bomb, because he didn't get very far. The blast broke his neck."

Porter was stunned. "Good God! Just think of the hell he must have gone through with each one of those bombs, and then to have the last one blow when he was almost home free. That's what I call a brave, brave man. I must phone his wife. I knew them when I was in Inuvik. This will be terrible for her, and they've got two teen-age boys.

"Let me know what the word is about Bessie as soon as you hear. I can tell you I'm mighty thankful she wasn't killed. She'd be a real martyr to the native people.

"Would you get a telegram off to her, Tom? Tell her how grateful we are for the risk she took and how thankful that she survived. Let me see it before you send it. Does Sam know yet?"

"No, sir. I thought it would be better if the word came from you."

"You're right. Get him on the phone for me, will you? Have the newspapers got wind of it yet?"

"Not so far as I know. The messages have come through the National Defence net by way of Inuvik Base. May I use your intercom, sir? I think I can get Sam Allen quite quickly."

The Prime Minister said, "Go ahead." Then he went back to reviewing his notes as Scott leaned across the desk and flipped the intercom switch.

"Joan, would you please get Sam Allen for me? He's at a meeting with the Deputy Minister of Indian Affairs and his Assistant."

"Yes, sir," she responded. In about two minutes the word came back. "Sam Allen on line 1, sir."

The Prime Minister picked up the phone. "Sam?"

"Yes, Bob."

The Prime Minister said, "First let me thank you for responding so quickly in coming down to start the negotiations. It's going to be tough and it's going to take time to work out, but I know I can count on you."

"I'll do my best, Bob, you know that. We've all worked hard to get to the point where our rights are recognized and an agreement can be reached. It looks to me as though we're nearly there."

"Well, stay with it. We're counting on you.

"Now, Sam, there's something else I have to tell you. I've got some bad news. Evidently Bessie and Staff Sergeant Ray got all the explosive charges defused except the last one. Something went wrong — we're not sure what exactly. Anyway it blew.

"Bessie's O.K., she's going to be fine, but Ray was killed instantly. They must have realized the explosion was coming because they'd managed to get a few feet away from the thing before it went off. Bessie got a little farther away than Ray. She was knocked out and suffered concussion, but he didn't have a chance."

Sam broke in. "Bessie's O.K.?"

"Yes, Sam, she's O.K."

"Let me tell you this, Bob. If anything had happened to her, there's no way that the native people would have settled with you or anybody else. If you think you've got problems with the Americans, I can tell you they are nothing to the problems you would have had with us if anything had happened to Bessie. Where is she?"

"She's in the hospital in Inuvik. My people will help you get through so you can talk to the doctors."

"Thanks. Bob, it seems to me if they were both trying to get away, Ray must have moved the defusing switch the wrong way. They would have had only four seconds. It's a miracle that Bessie came through. I'm sorry about Jim Ray. He was a first-rate person and a really great policeman. He did a hell of a lot for Inuvik and as much as he could for the Indians and Eskimos. I hope you can do something for his family, Bob."

"I will, Sam. I've got to get into the House shortly, so I must get back to my preparation. I just wanted to tell you myself what happened and to let you know how much I appreciate your co-operation and help."

The Prime Minister spent the rest of the hour going over the notes he had prepared earlier for his own address to the House. He jotted down the individual points on separate sheets of paper, and after he had reviewed each one passed it on to Thomas. By 11:45 he was finished. He asked his secretary to duplicate the notes on the copier and send a set to each of the other party leaders as promised.

"Send along my set of notes directly to my desk in the Commons. I've got to leave now to meet the Governor-General."

At that point Thomas said, "Bob, I've gone over all those points with you and it seems to me you've covered all the bases, but I haven't seen anything which indicates which way you're going to vote on the motion."

The Prime Minister chuckled. "I wondered when you'd ask. I've pretty well made up my mind which way I'm going to vote, John, but I decided yesterday I would give no clue in anything I wrote so that no one working with me would know and perhaps let it slip.

"Also I'm very anxious to get the results of the television and radio poll, which should be finished in just a few minutes. I'd appreciate it if you'd get hold of the President of

219

the CBC, tell him how important it is that the information from the survey get to me in the House not later than four o'clock."

Porter held out his hand. "Thanks, John. I couldn't have got through everything without your help."

Thomas took the outstretched hand in both of his and said, "Good luck, Bob. I know the House will be behind you all the way."

The RCMP escort was waiting for the Prime Minister outside his office. They took up their position around him and once again pushed and shoved their way through the throng in the corridor. As a body they moved down to the Commons Chamber and there the escort was left behind. The Prime Minister proceeded alone, down the long centre aisle of the Chamber and then along the corridor leading to the office of the Speaker of the Senate, where he had arranged to meet the Governor-General to escort him into the Senate Chamber where the Speech from the Throne would be read.

When he arrived, the Governor-General was already in the office with the Speaker.

They shook hands, and with his usual warm smile His Excellency said, "Well, Bob, this is the moment of truth. Things have been pretty hectic. Have you been able to get as much done as you'd like?"

"Well, I think things are about as ready as I could have expected. We'll just have to hope everything goes smoothly from here on," the Prime Minister replied. Then he added, "Your Excellency, I'd be grateful if you'd stay here in the Speaker's office after you deliver the Speech from the Throne. You can watch the debate on television here. I'd like to know you're nearby while the debate is going on, so that if you have some advice to give me, all you'll have to do is send in a note. Frankly, I'd like to be able to get your opinion quickly, too."

"I'd be delighted to do that, Bob. You flatter an old man by such an expression of confidence. I'll stay here until the vote is finished and then return at once to Government House. I'll be there if you need me after that."

The two men excused themselves from the presence of the Speaker and left his Chambers. In the corridor they were met by the escort.

As they reached the Senate Chamber they were met by Senator Anderson, the Government Leader in the Senate. Everyone rose as the Governor-General entered the hall and was escorted to the Speaker's dais.

In the traditional ritual His Excellency raised his hat briefly in salute and sat down. When his audience was seated he removed the hat and handed it to the page standing behind his chair on the right.

Each time the Prime Minister had been in the Senate Chamber he had been struck by the difference between it and the House of Commons. The huge hall had a warm glow, and its handsome carpets enhanced the elaborate walnut-carved panelling of the walls. On this occasion, the room was jammed with the senators, judges of the Supreme Court of Canada and all the members of the Commons. Many of the faces of the senators were old, since the Chamber was peopled to a large extent by members of former cabinets. Other appointments were made from time to time from among outstanding Canadians, but it was an older and more august body than the Prime Minister usually faced in the Commons.

The Governor-General unrolled the scroll on which the Speech from the Throne was inscribed and began to read.

"Prime Minister, Honourable Members of the Senate, I bring you greetings from Her Most Gracious Majesty...."

In a little more than a minute, he had finished. He rose to his feet, as did everyone in the Chamber, and, accompanied by the Prime Minister who had been standing at his right, moved quickly out by the Speaker's Door.

After Porter had escorted the Governor-General back to the Speaker's Chambers and the two had exchanged a brief few words, he hurried on down the hall towards the entrance to the House of Commons. As he reached the chamber, the last of the members were making their way quickly to their seats. The premiers were in their appointed place in the Spectators' Gallery, and the balance of the Gallery was crammed with viewers.

The Prime Minister took his place. Sealed in a plastic folder on the desk were the notes that he had made earlier. As he sat down beside Gendron he asked, "Are you all set, Robert?"

"All set, Bob. Are you?"

"Oh, we Inuvikers are always ready."

The two men smiled. Except during Pierre Johnston's humorous yet convincing speech later in the afternoon, it was the last time these two men were to smile during the remainder of the day.

The room was suddenly quiet. Everyone stood as Black Rod, carrying the Mace, entered the Chamber ahead of the Speaker of the House. The Speaker mounted the dais, the Mace was placed on the table in the centre of the floor, and this most important session of the House of Commons of Canada began.

The Speaker doffed his hat to the members of the House and took his seat. Everyone sat down except the Prime Minister, who remained standing at his desk.

The Speaker recognized Robert Porter by saying, "The Right Honourable Prime Minister."

"Mr. Speaker, I have the honour to present to the House

a motion jointly put forward by the Leader of the Opposition, Mr. George Foot, the Leader of the New Democratic Party, Mr. Donald Walker, the Leader of the Social Credit Party, Mr. Pierre Johnson, and myself. It is understood, Mr. Speaker, that the motion is a formality which does not bind the movers themselves to support or reject it. It is further understood that the vote of all members shall be a free vote, so that each Honourable Member may express his opinion as his conscience dictates.

"Because of the limited time available, the leaders of the parties, other than myself, have agreed to speak on the motion for a period of twenty minutes at the opening of the debate. Each party has prepared a list — which has been placed in your hands — of those who will be entitled to speak for ten minutes each. I am quite sure, Mr. Speaker, that in the presence of this grave crisis all will adhere strictly to the time limits imposed.

"It has been agreed that, as First Minister, I shall be permitted to wind up the debate, and for that purpose will have a period of thirty minutes commencing at 4:30. The vote on the question should commence immediately after I conclude at five o'clock.

"Mr. Speaker, before I present the motion, I wish to say in your presence and in the presence of all the people of Canada who are watching or hearing these proceedings through television or radio, how profoundly grateful I am to the Honourable Leader of the Opposition and to the leaders of the New Democratic and the Social Credit parties for the non-partisan, statesmanlike attitude which each of them has demonstrated during this crisis. They have shown themselves to be true Canadians and patriots whose interest in their country and the Canadian people transcends partisan concerns in this time of emergency."

There was a burst of desk pounding in support of this tribute. When the din had subsided, the Prime Minister put on his glasses, picked up the sheet of paper upon which the motion was written, and said, "Mr. Speaker, with your permission I shall read the motion and then jointly move it with my honourable colleagues. It is as follows:

"Whereas the Government of the United States has issued and given to the Government of Canada an ultimatum which requires —

"(a) That the Government of Canada shall unconditionally undertake to commence negotiations toward an agreement with the native people of the Yukon and the Northwest Territories for a settlement of their aboriginal rights in terms and amounts comparable to the settlement made by the Government of the United States with the people of Alaska, and;

"(b) That the Government of Canada shall conditionally agree to grant to the Government of the United States or its designated nationals full access to the natural gas reserve discovered in the Arctic Islands, without any reservation for the future use and requirements of Canada, and;

"(c) That the Government of Canada shall unconditionally grant permission to the Government of the United States of America or its designated nationals to enter into and upon and across such Canadian territory as the Government of the United States may deem appropriate for the purpose of constructing or mounting a transportation system to carry the aforesaid natural gas from the Canadian Arctic Islands to any designated sector of the United States;

"And whereas the Government of the United States has required that an answer be given by the Parliament of

225

Canada to the aforesaid ultimatum by or before the hour of six o'clock in the evening on the date of the moving of this motion —

"Therefore this House resolves as follows:

"(1) That the aforesaid ultimatum be rejected and refused; and (2) that the Government of Canada be authorized by this Parliament to commence negotiations with the native people of the Yukon and Northwest Territories immediately to effect an equitable settlement with them in compensation for the taking of their aboriginal rights, using as a model the settlement effected between the native people of Alaska and the Government of the United States of America; and (3) that the Prime Minister of Canada be requested by Parliament to attend upon the President of the United States in Washington forthwith to open negotiations for the immediate provision to the United States of America of a sufficient quantity of natural gas from the Canadian Arctic Islands to meet both the short- and long-term requirements of the United States, subject first to the future needs of Canada, and to make arrangements for the construction and establishment of a transportation system which will make possible the movement of the aforesaid natural gas from the Canadian Arctic Islands to the United States at the earliest possible time."

The Prime Minister put down the paper from which he had been reading, slowly took off his glasses and turned to the Speaker, saying, "Mr. Speaker, that is the motion. I move its adoption."

Across the floor immediately opposite the Prime Minister, the Leader of the Opposition rose to be recognized by the Speaker. He said, "Mr. Speaker, I join in moving the motion, and to the extent that formality requires, I also second it."

He was immediately followed by the leaders of the New

Democratic Party and the Social Credit Party, each of whom confirmed their joint participation in the motion. When this was done, George Foot again rose and was recognized by the Speaker. He began, "Mr. Speaker, as Leader of the Opposition, and as a joint mover of the resolution, I have the privilege of leading off this debate. While the Prime Minister has made it clear that the participation of each of us in moving the motion in no way binds any one of us to support or reject it, I would like it made perfectly clear at the outset that I, as an individual Canadian, will take the position and vote in regard to the motion in the following way...."

The President was in the communications cabin of Air Force One. He was facing a television set, sitting on the edge of his chair watching closely as Robert Porter read the motion in the House of Commons. When the reading was finished, he slumped back, tugged on his chin, then turned to Irving Wolf. "Irving, I've had to act the role of the tough son-of-a-bitch for the last day and a half. I'm really not very happy about it. I've a soft spot in my heart for the Canadians. They're really a mighty fine people. There's nothing sneaky about them. Whether they know it or not they're proud of their country and they've got a lot to be proud of."

He turned back to the TV set. "I really don't like putting a gun to their heads, but you and my Cabinet have advised me that this is what we should be doing and I've gone along with it."

Irving Wolf peered at the President through his black horn-rimmed glasses and said, "Mr. President, I know this is very difficult for you. Right at this moment we're at the crunch. If the Parliament of Canada accepts the motion the Prime Minister has just placed before the House then you'll have to make the next move and pronounce the sanctions which have already been agreed upon with the Cabinet and the House Leaders."

"It's those sanctions and the counter-sanctions that worry the hell out of me, Irving. We just can't afford to have the western Canadian oil and gas turned off. In the Chicago/Detroit area the energy shortage is bad enough

as it is without that. And you know if we impose investment sanctions and cut off trade to Canada, we're just
going to knock the hell out of billions of dollars' worth of
Canadian resources and manufacturing firms which are
subsidiaries of American corporations.

"It seems to me to be just too big a price to pay to get the
Canadians to come across with their natural gas. But
we've gone too far. There's no easy way back, Irving. If
they stand firm, we're all going to suffer."

Irving Wolf sat with his long nose between his two
index fingers as he thought out the President's dilemma.
Finally he said, "Mr. President, if you feel you must take
another course of action to avoid the counter-sanctions,
and at the same time save face, while ending up with an
assured supply of Arctic natural gas, I think you've no
choice but to take a hard look at the alternative plan which
you and I discussed on the weekend. I know it's perfectly
clear, but it might be helpful to you to go over the pros and
cons of it once again.

"If you decide to use it, you may wish to have it en-
dorsed by the Cabinet and government leaders when they
meet in your office at five o'clock to hear the Canadians'
decision."

Wolf dropped his hands from his face. "This is how I
think you might put the alternative plan into effect...."

The President leaned back in his chair, half-closed his
eyes, and listened to Irving Wolf's line of reasoning, nod-
ding affirmatively from time to time.

As Wolf finished, the President opened his eyes and
turned to look out at the Canadian CF5's still sitting in
battle formation about a hundred yards out, watched for
a moment, then slowly turned and said, "Irving, I've no
choice but to go with the alternative."

Air Force One was high over James Bay southbound for
Washington when the decision was taken.

"I now recognize the Right Honourable the Prime Minister of Canada."

It was 4:30. The Speaker of the House had brought the long debate to a close and turned the floor over to Robert Porter. As he slowly stood up, the vast room, jammed to capacity, had a stillness as if it were empty.

"Mr. Speaker, I will be brief. I am indeed obliged to all the Honourable Members who have spoken so eloquently this afternoon. Through all their words I have detected a strong thread of sympathy and understanding for the plight of the people of the United States as they face the suffering of an energy shortage unparalleled in their history. You have witnessed this afternoon, Mr. Speaker, a most profound and understanding analysis of the bonds, the relationships, the ties which exist between our great neighbour and ourselves.

"I think it can be said, Mr. Speaker, that there has been expressed here today a fundamental recognition that Canada has a moral obligation to permit the United States reasonable access to the natural gas in the Arctic Islands and full co-operation to create a transportation system which can deliver that precious commodity to them at the earliest possible moment.

"I have said many times before, and I say again, to you this afternoon, that I share the great sympathy for the American people. And yet we must all recognize, Mr.

Speaker, the cause underlying this current crisis. The United States has permitted dangerous and unrestrained expansion of its population and its industrial complex. Per capita, the American people are by far the most prolific consumers in the world, as well as the most undisciplined. If Canada must provide the people of the United States with vast and increasing quantities of our non-renewable resources, these resources will soon be exhausted. We have every right, and indeed a profound responsibility, to demand that they take strong and far-reaching measures to conserve these resources, to place constraints upon their voracious appetite for new consumer products, and to curb the unfettered expansion of industry and market which has brought them to their current state.

"There has been a broad range of opinion expressed here today. Some members are obviously and rightly upset by the ultimatum and are clearly prepared to vote for the motion before the House. There are others who, because of the enormous sympathy they have for the people of the United States, and because they are critical of our governmental ineptitude, seem inclined to vote against the motion, but I have detected in the speches of even those members an unwillingness to give into the ultimatum without reservation.

"And so, Mr. Speaker, as I read the mood of the House, it is that the ultimatum given to Parliament by the Government of the United States should be rejected.

"Now let me turn to what the public have said about the ultimatum. As you are aware, Mr. Speaker, with the cooperation of the radio and television stations, we have been able to give the people of Canada an opportunity to express themselves for or against acceptance.

"The survey terminated at twelve o'clock noon today. At four o'clock this afternoon the President of the Canadian Broadcasting Corporation, who was charged with the responsibility of collecting the results, delivered the final report to me. During the survey period there were 5,335,000 telephone calls. Of this number, 4,269,000 or 80 per cent, were for rejecting the ultimatum."

This announcement sparked immediate response in the audience. There was a buzz of conversation and shouts of "Hear, hear!" The Prime Minister went on.

For myself, Mr. Speaker, there is no doubt that Canada should do everything in its power at this time to assist the United States. On the other hand, I find totally unacceptable the tactics of the Government of the United States of America in forcing an ultimatum upon Canada, its largest trading partner, its closest ally, and its primary source of natural resources and raw material. Such a course is unworthy of the fundamental precepts of freedom, justice and liberty upon which that country was founded.

"Mr. Speaker, Canada must always be prepared and willing to sit down and negotiate face to face with the United States. I am ready now to go to Washington, but not under the compulsion of an ultimatum.

"Therefore, Mr. Speaker, while I fully comprehend the energy dilemma of the United States, I have no choice but to follow the lead of the members of this House and the clear indication which the people of Canada have given. I must vote in support of the motion to reject the ultimatum and to stand firm with all Canadians whatever the consequences."

Ottawa / 4:47 p.m., EDT

For a moment after the Prime Minister sat down, the House was silent. Then there was a burst of applause. Across the aisle the leaders of the opposition parties pounded their desks in approval. In the Spectators' Galleries there was shouting and cheering.

As the Speaker called for order, the tension and expectancy of the House, which had been there unbroken throughout the afternoon, reached a new height.

"It has been agreed that there should be a recorded vote. I point out to all Honourable Members that we are somewhat ahead of schedule, as the Prime Minister has not spoken for his full allotted time. Nevertheless, I believe it is the mood of the House that we should proceed with the vote-taking immediately. Unless I receive a motion to the contrary, I shall begin.

"Mr. Clerk of the House, will you please proceed with a call of the roll."

The Clerk began, calling on each member alphabetically, without reference to party, to give his vote — yea or nay. By the time thirty members had been polled, not one vote against the motion had been recorded. At the halfway point, still no negative vote had been recorded.

As the roll call proceeded rapidly, the excited murmur became a roar. When the final vote was taken, the decision had been unanimous. The House was bedlam. The Prime Minister broke through the crush of supporters who

233

had rushed to shake his hand or pound him on the back, and strode quickly across the floor to the Leader of the Opposition. The two embraced, and were immediately swamped by their followers.

In the Senate, a page handed a note to Senator Martinson. He signalled to the Speaker, who at once brought the debate to a close and called for a vote. When it was over, without waiting for the formality of the retirement of the Speaker, Senator Martinson rushed from the Chamber to the House of Commons to convey to the Prime Minister the unanimous support of the Senate.

Robert Porter was back in his Main Block office. With him were Gendron of External Affairs, the leaders of the opposition parties, and John Thomas. He had asked them all to join him when he informed the President formally of the decision.

While Tom Scott was placing the call, drinks were passed around. When he got through to the President's aide, he waved everyone in the room silent, and handed the telephone to the Prime Minister. "The President will be on the line in a moment, sir."

"Mr. President?"

"Yes, Mr. Prime Minister, I watched your debate on television and I know exactly what you're going to tell me. You know, we Americans think our country is mighty fine, and I must admit I admire other people who are proud of theirs. On the other hand, I think you people are a bunch of damn fools for not being prepared to do right by us at this time."

The Texas drawl became even more pronounced as the President went on. "All I can say to you, Mr. Prime Minister, is that I sure wish you'd given in, because what I must do next I don't like to have to do, but I haven't any choice now."

Porter asked quickly, "What do you propose to do, Mr. President?"

"I'm not about to tell you, son, except that I'm meeting

with my Cabinet, the leaders of the Senate and the House, and the Chief Justice and the National Security Council at 5:45. I've cleared all television and radio air time for a statement to the American people at 6:30. My suggestion, Prime Minister, is that you tune in to any television station on the Canadian network, because I'm sure they'll all pick up what I've got to say.

"There's one thing I can tell you for certain. You people aren't at a Texas tea party. You're in a Texas barroom, boy, and you'd better believe it. You'll know what I'm going to do when I speak at 6:30.

"Thank you for calling, Mr. Prime Minister. Good-bye." He hung up.

Porter had decided that the best possible place for him to be when the decision of the United States was made known at 6:30 would be Government House, so he soon made his excuses to the people in his office and went immediately to Rideau Hall. Alexander Simpson met him himself and congratulated him warmly. Then the two men went directly to the Governor-General's drawing room and settled down to watch the President's speech.

The President spoke slowly and deliberately. His face was drawn, and for the first time, he seemed tense. "My fellow Americans: Shortly after five o'clock this afternoon, little more than an hour ago, the Parliament of Canada unanimously rejected the ultimatum which I as President of the United States of America presented to the Prime Minister of Canada yesterday morning.

"Despite a full recognition by the government and the people of Canada that there is a critical energy shortage facing the United States this coming winter, and notwithstanding the fact that they know many of our hospitals, schools and factories will be shut down and many homes and apartments without electricity and heat, the Canadian government still refuses to let us have the natural gas which belongs to the American people by right of investment.

"I must point out that in rejecting the ultimatum the Canadian Parliament did make a commitment to comply with one of our demands and agreed to negotiate with the native people of the Northwest Territories and the Yukon in order to effect a settlement with them as soon as possible. I am pleased to see that the government will respond to this at least.

"Also, it is to be noted that Parliament authorized the Prime Minister to open negotiations directly with me for the purpose of ensuring that the United States obtains an adequate supply of natural gas from the Arctic Islands.

"However, in spite of the pious expression of willingness to co-operate, the rejection of our ultimatum is totally unacceptable to the United States. My administration has been dealing with the Canadians for many years now in an attempt to establish an over-all continental policy.

"These extensive negotiations have proved to be fruitless and valueless because of the inability of the government of Canada to come to a decision or to make a commitment. An undertaking to keep on negotiating, even at the highest level, is merely an undertaking to further postpone a decision.

"Time has run out. The ultimatum has been rejected, and now I have no alternative but to take a course of action which will ensure that we obtain access to the Canadian Arctic Islands gas.

"My advisers and I have been discussing the possibility of a series of economic sanctions against Canada. These can take many forms. For example, as you know, yesterday at noon I imposed an embargo on the flow of all investment funds. In addition, we can close the border to the movement of all manufactured goods and natural resource materials from Canada into the United States, with the exception of electricity, natural gas and crude oil, of course.

"It is within my power to terminate all defence-spending contracts which are now in the hands of Canadian manufacturers, and to cut off the shipment of all Canadian agricultural and food products into the American market. It is within my power to cancel the long-standing automotive free trade pact between the two countries, and there are many other sanctions which the United States could impose which would bring the Canadian economy to a halt.

"But to invoke such harsh measures would be harmful to the individual Canadian. It would be vindictive and completely out of character for the United States to take such ruthless steps. After all, we are a nation of people who cherish liberty and justice, and welcome free trade and competition. During this century we have gone to the succour and aid of people all over the world especially for the purpose of preserving the freedom of mankind against the threat of communism.

"We bear no man or nation ill, provided that nation treats our interests and our needs with honesty and fairness. But the need of the people of the United States, the need of individual American citizens for Canadian energy is imperative. It is critical, it is absolute. Canadians have a moral obligation, as our neighbours on this continent, to make this resource, which is totally surplus to Canada's own foreseeable requirements, available to us at the earliest possible moment. And yet their government will not yield.

"I cannot expect the citizens of Canada, the individual Canadian worker and his family, to suffer as a result of the selfish decision taken today by the Parliament of Canada. I cannot bring myself to impose sanctions, not only for the reason that I do not wish to see the people of Canada suffer, but also because I do not wish to see the hundreds of major Canadian subsidiaries of United States corporations shut down. Nor do I wish to see the flow of natural resources, iron ore, copper, nickel, pulp and paper, from the Western Provinces cut off from the mighty American industrial complex.

"Instead, I have decided on a completely different course of action, one which will avoid the effects of a disastrous confrontation by sanction and counter-sanction. It is a course of action which should be of direct and welcome benefit to all Canadians.

"My decision has been made with the concurrence of all the members of my Cabinet and that of the leaders of both parties in the Senate and the House of Representatives. It will provide all the Canadian people with a better opportunity to share their massive resources with us, and in exchange to participate directly in the high standard of living and superior citizenship enjoyed by the people of the United States.

"As of this moment, Canada will become part of the United States of America. The Government of Canada is hereby dissolved. The provinces will become full member states of the Union. All necessary legislation will be presented to Congress to implement this decision.

"To ensure that this transfer of power takes place smoothly and without incident, transport aircraft and helicopters of the United States Air Force carrying troops and equipment are now landing at airports in all major Canadian cities and at all Canadian Armed Forces bases.

"I hereby instruct the Governor-General of Canada, as Commander-in-Chief of the Canadian Armed Forces, to instruct the Chief of the Defence Staff to order his forces to lay down their arms and to co-operate fully with our troops.

"The citizens of Canada are now citizens of the proudest, finest, greatest nation in the world. To all of you we give the gift of citizenship in the United States of America. I want every one of you to be proud of this new gift, and I bid each of you welcome, my fellow Americans."

The Governor-General reached over and lightly touched Robert Porter on the arm.

"Well, Bob, it appears we have no choice. We fought for our independence as long as possible, but it couldn't last. My last act as Governor-General must be to follow the instructions of the President."

EXXONERATION

Special thanks to
John A. MacNaughton of Fry Mills Spence
for his technical advice

**To my mother
and my father**

October 6 & 7, 1980

On Monday morning, October 6, 1980, the President of the United States—a tough Texan fighting for re-election the next month—telephoned the new Prime Minister of Canada, Robert Porter, to deliver a harsh, unexpected set of demands for access to Canada's Arctic natural gas.

The conclusion of their one-sided discussion had led to the President's ultimatum.

After explaining that the United States was heading for a national disaster as a result of natural gas shortages, the President demanded three unconditional commitments from the Parliament of Canada. First, Canada had to settle the problem of aboriginal rights which had been holding up the pipeline construction. The President's model for such a settlement was the one the United States had worked out with the native people of Alaska.

Second, the President demanded that Canada grant the United States full access to all the natural gas in the Arctic Islands without reference to Canada's future needs.

And third, he requested a commitment that the United States be allowed to construct a transportation system as quickly as possible from the Arctic Islands to the United States.

"I want these commitments by six o'clock tomorrow night," the President told Porter, "and they must be given by the Parliament of Canada, not simply the government."

The Prime Minister acted quickly. Parliament was called for an emergency session, and by 5:00 P.M., October 7, both the House of Commons and the Senate had unanimously rejected the ultimatum. Instead, they proposed a conciliatory resolution, expressing a desire to negotiate with the native peoples of the Yukon and the Northwest Territories and with the government of the United States, but not without taking into account the future needs and requirements of Canada.

At 5:25 P.M., in the afternoon of October 7, 1980, just slightly more than a half hour before the expiry of the President's ultimatum, the Prime Minister officially informed the President of Parliament's decision. The President refused to tell the Prime Minister what his next step would be. The Prime Minister would have to wait until 6:30 that evening, he said, when he would advise the American people of the action of the Canadian Parliament and his decision on the matter.

The Prime Minister then went to Government House to be with his friend and longtime mentor and now Governor-General, Alexander Sinclair, to await the President's television statement.

The two of them watched and heard the President with apprehension. As he drew to the end of his speech, the President explained that he did not want the Canadian people to suffer as a result of the Canadian government's selfish decision, and wished to avoid the confrontation that would result if economic sanctions and counter-sanctions were put into force.

"As of this moment," he announced, "Canada will become a part of the United States of America." The government of Canada was to be dissolved, and the provinces to become states of the Union. After explaining that to ensure this annexation he had ordered transport aircraft and helicopters of the United States Air Force to all major Canadian cities and Armed Forces bases, he went on to bestow upon the people of Canada citizenship in the "proudest, finest, greatest nation in the world"–the United States.

The Governor-General and Prime Minister Porter had sat in stunned silence throughout this speech.

"Well, Bob," the Governor-General sighed, touching Porter lightly on the arm, "it appears we have no choice. We fought for our independence as long as possible, but it couldn't last. My last act as Governor-General must be to follow the instructions of the President."

Ottawa
Tuesday, October 7, 1980, 6:38 P.M.

The Prime Minister leaped to his feet. "No! There is no goddamn way we're going to surrender, sir." He walked quickly to the telephone which was already ringing. Before he picked it up, he turned to the Governor-General and said, "This is exactly what we expected them to do if they were going to do anything military, and we're ready for them."

Before the Governor-General could express his surprise, Porter picked up the telephone and said, "Porter here."

At the other end was the Chief of Defence Staff, General Adamson.

"Sir, the Americans are committed to land. Their lead aircraft are on their final landing approaches right across the country – Dorval, Toronto, Vancouver, Edmonton, Halifax – the whole bit."

The Prime Minister's response was instant. "Okay, General, Operation Reception Party is GO."

Toronto
Tuesday, October 7, 1980, 5:15 P.M.

Colonel Pierre de Gaspé, commander of the Toronto District of the Canadian Reserves land forces, reached quickly for the ringing phone on his Fort York Armouries desk as it rang. He was expecting this call.

"De Gaspé here."

It was, as he expected, the commander of the Mobile Command, Lieutenant General Christie, at the Canadian Forces Base, St. Hubert, Quebec.

"Pierre, it's Christie. As briefed, Operation Reception Party will be mounted immediately. Parliament has just rejected the American ultimatum, so God knows what's going to happen next. I hope Reception Party turns out to be an academic exercise for all of us."

"So do I, sir," de Gaspé responded. "I might tell you that the response of the Reservists of the Toronto garrison has been incredible. We have every man and woman out who can move, and the British troops are just as up as we are."

"I'm not surprised," said Christie. "As you know, the Prime Minister must give the President Canada's answer by six o'clock. If the Americans take the military action against us, we calculate they'll start at us some time this evening. I can't believe they will, but they might. The Prime Minister and the Chief of the Defence Staff both are of the strong opinion that the Americans will go for economic sanctions but the possibility of an attack is obviously one we have to be prepared for. It's now seventeen fifteen hours. What's the status of your deployment."

De Gaspé's response was immediate. "We're set to go, sir. We've been in position at the airport since four-thirty. We moved our vans and jeeps independently, rather than in convoy, so we wouldn't get the public panicking. My artillery people have done an excellent job picking out the hidden locations for their guns around the edge of the airfield, and the ground-to-air missile people are deployed so they have clear shots at aircraft on the ground or in the air. Everybody's in place and my chopper's across the street waiting for me."

"Great stuff, Pierre. Our communications net is now locked in so you and I can be in constant touch. If you need decisions, you can get me instantly. Away you go."

As he put the receiver down, Pierre de Gaspé's mind went back to the staggering briefing he and the other district commanders from across Canada had received that morning in Ottawa where they had all been summoned on an emergency call from the Chief of the Defence Staff.

As a Reservist and as the man responsible for the Toronto Militia District, Colonel de Gaspé had moved into full-time command the day before, immediately the news was out that the President of the United States had given the ultimatum to the Prime Minister. Even before the mobilization signal had been received from National Defence Headquarters, de Gaspé had left his comfortable office in the new Metro Centre complex. In his civilian capacity as president of Petro-Canada and one of the most experienced and knowledgeable petroleum industry executives in Canada, he had been expecting an ultimatum to be delivered by the United States as its natural gas shortages escalated to crisis proportions. Now his fears had been realized in a scale and with a ruthlessness no one could have expected from, of all nations, the United States.

The briefing had taken place at 9:15 A.M. on the second day of the ultimatum period. It was held in an auditorium in National Defence Headquarters and had been given by the Chief of the Defence Staff himself.

The entire room had stood as General Adamson, an athletic-looking man of medium height, entered and proceeded to his position in front of the projection screen. He placed his papers on the lectern and asked the assembly to be seated.

He scanned the auditorium, filled with senior Regular Force and Reserve officers brought in overnight from across the country. He proceeded directly to the point.

"Gentlemen, as you are all aware, the President of the United States has delivered a three-part ultimatum to the Prime Minister of Canada. That ultimatum must be answered by the Parliament of Canada by six o'clock this evening.

"Just before noon yesterday I was instructed by the Prime Minister to call out the Reserves and to mobilize the Canadian Armed Forces to the fullest possible degree. This has been done, as is evidenced by the presence here of the Reserve District Militia commanders from all the major cities across Canada—and by the Air Reserve and Naval Reserve commanders.

"The government has directed that the Canadian Armed Forces be mobilized for two reasons. The first is that should there be raids or demonstrations which are anti-American and which might turn into physical violence requiring control, then the military will be available to aid the civil power, that is to say, the police, in containing such action. At the same time, the government is anxious that the military presence not be shown to the public unless and until absolutely necessary. Therefore, I have instructed all of you by signal, and I repeat it now, that all troops must be lodged inside the local armouries. They are not to venture out unless and until ordered.

"The second but most important purpose for mobilization is that the Prime Minister has instructed me that the Canadian Armed Forces must be prepared to meet any attack mounted by the United States against Canada, should the Parliament of Canada refuse the ultimatum."

With that there was much scuffling in the audience, the passing of whispered comments, and the rolling of eyeballs upwards.

General Adamson had expected this sort of reaction and waited a moment till his people settled down. He ran his hand through his thick greying hair. Then he took both sides of the lectern in his hands and continued.

"Gentlemen, let me tell you something. This Prime Minister of ours is one tough son-of-a-bitch. His instructions to me are very simple. There is no goddamn way the Americans are going to take over Canada without one hell of a fight!"

With that the room burst into spontaneous applause. The CDS beamed with pleasure at the response and went on. "The Prime Minister expects that if the ultimatum is rejected, the Americans will resort to economic sanctions rather than military force. On the other hand, the Americans look on our resources as being their own. They've put their money into them. They look on us as being weak-kneed, grey-faced people and they see our country as a colony of the States. Their attitude will probably be, 'Why not just take over Canada. After all, they've only got 50,000 people in the Regular Force and 35,000 in the Reserves. That should be peanuts so far as the giant American military machine is concerned.' They can see us sitting here with only five fighter squadrons, no bombers, no rockets, no ballistic missiles, no nuclear warheads. Nothing. A half-assed military force. At least that's what they think.

"Well, let's look at the facts. Our Regular Force is far too small. Our hardware—aircraft, tanks, guns, anti-tank and anti-aircraft weapons—are about one-tenth of what we should have. We're in that position because the Canadian people and their leaders decided and they decided some time ago, that this is the way it was going to be and that military expenditures were to be reduced and kept small.

"At the beginning of the 1970's almost all risk of war had disappeared, at least as between the major powers. People in government had no background in war or the military and were mainly concerned with social and cultural problems. They had little time or money for the military. They were brassed off with the Vietnam thing and what they saw there, even though that was strictly an American show.

"Well, the result is that if we have to take on the Americans, we haven't got much to do it with. In fact, we've got damn little."

His hand went through his hair again.

"Now, the fact that we've got little and the Americans recognize it, is the basis for our strategy and tactics in meeting this potential threat. And I can tell you, gentlemen, that it is my considered opinion as a military person that the Americans are going to bite the bullet and go for taking over Canada."

The CDS waved his hand toward the collection of sitting generals to his left and right.

"The Defence Staff and I have kicked this whole thing around from top to bottom. We think the Americans are going to take a look at us and say, 'There's no way these people are going to fight. They've got nothing to fight with, they're just a grey-faced bunch of people with a banana-republic military force. If we tell them to lay down their arms, that's exactly what they're going to do. So there's not going to be any need to send fighter or bomber aircraft to whip the hell out of them, or to bomb their cities. Furthermore, if we bomb or strafe, we'll probably be destroying U.S.-owned factories, office buildings, oil refineries – you name it. So we'll just tell the Canadians we're coming and then we'll walk in.'

"In fact, for the last twelve hours that's exactly the message we've been giving the Americans, just to lead them into the position of thinking we're going to be patsies. If they thought for one second we were going to take them on, they'd set up their strategy and tactics quite differently.

"Our analysis goes this way. If the Americans attack us in force with fighters, bombers, and troops shooting from the hip, we're going to be in real trouble because we just haven't got the capability of meeting them. On the other hand, if they are sensitive to world opinion – God knows whether they are or not – and if they think we're going to be pushovers and they can move in without firing a shot, then we've got a real chance to catch them by the shorts.

"Therefore, we've built our operational plan, called 'Operation Reception Party,' on the thesis that the Americans are going to think they can walk, ride, and fly in.

"If my analysis is correct, then how will they do it?

"First, they will mount an air assault by lifting in their men by using Starlifters, Hercules, and other large troop-transport aircraft, including helicopters. They will land at all major Canadian civilian and military airports, and they will be expecting absolutely no military resistance for the reasons I've given you. Also, they'll expect to take us by surprise.

"Second, no bombing or strafing will take place because of the likelihood of damage to American investments in Canada and possible injury or death for American nationals resident in or visiting this country.

"Third, there will be no advance attack by paratroopers

256

because that effort will be judged unnecessary by the politicians, even though their use will be recommended the the Pentagon.

"Fourth, ground troops, personnel carriers, and tanks will simultaneously attempt to move across the border.

"Gentlemen, if I were the Chairman of the United States Joint Chiefs of Staff this is how I'd read Canada, and this is how I would obey the President's instruction to invade.

"Each of you will now be handed a copy of the operation order for Operation Reception Party. The first thing you'll note is that I've decided to leave the Reserve District commanders in charge of the operation at Montreal, Toronto, and Winnipeg. It's too late to try to plug Regular Force people in. And the District commanders will report directly to the Commander of Mobile Command." He pointed toward the hefty, dark-haired Lieutenant General Christie on his immediate left.

"As you read the order one of the things you should add is that 1,200 British troops–two battalions–of the 15th Parabrigade will be arriving early this afternoon from the U.K. by arrangements made between our Prime Minister and the British Prime Minister last night. They'll be going into Canadian Forces Base, St. Hubert–just southeast of Montreal–CFB Downsview at Toronto, and at London, Ontario. Some of them will be moved into the Windsor sector. They will be under the command and control of the local District commanders.

"And now to the mechanics of Operation Reception Party."

Pierre Thomas de Gaspé

Colonel Pierre Thomas de Gaspé, a tall man with an easy smile and a domineering, forceful presence, was well suited to his temporary role of a military commander placed in a position of enormous emergent responsibility.

His father, Simon de Gaspé, had been a well-to-do Montreal lawyer, from an élite Quebec family. In 1941, shortly before his son's birth he had gone overseas as a captain of Lęs Fusiliers Mont-Royal Regiment, the FMR's. On August 19, 1942, he died on the beach of Dieppe, without ever seeing his son.

Simon's legacy of military and legal aspirations and examples had been strong motivating forces in the shaping of the life and career of his son. Pierre's mother, a delicate but strong-willed little woman from the wealthy, influential Thomas family of London, Ontario, had remained in Montreal until 1952, during which time Pierre received his education in French at the hands of excellent Jesuit teachers.

That year his mother had married a Toronto consulting economist and academic. This union brought her and Pierre to Toronto where the young boy continued his secondary school education with priests, this time with the Basilian Fathers at St. Michael's College.

He was raised with mother tongues of both French and English and with a soul and spirit saturated with each of the founding cultures and languages of Canada.

In 1960, at age eighteen, he entered the Royal Military College at Kingston, where he excelled in all aspects of his military and university training, graduating at the top of his class in engineering with sufficient economics credits from Queen's University to allow him to go on to obtain his Masters in Economics at that university, then to Harvard for his doctorate.

Early in his university studies, de Gaspé became intrigued by the relationship and importance of energy to the existence and maintenance of civilization. Eventually he concentrated on energy with particular reference to fossil fuels—crude oil and natural gas with their multitude of derivatives.

His masters thesis, written in 1963, on "Canada's Trade Prospects in the World Energy Shortage Crisis of the late 1970's" had shaken the Dean of the School of Economics, who found it impossible to believe that there could be such a thing as a world energy shortage, let alone one that would hit Canada. Nevertheless, the Dean recognized de Gaspé's brilliance as a student and envied his ability to deal with forward-looking concepts.

He had been so impressed that he sent the paper to the business editor of the Toronto *Globe and Mail*. The editor was also impressed and published major sections of Pierre de Gaspé's work in series form.

These articles caused an enormous amount of discussion at the Petroleum Club in Calgary. Many heated debates over de Gaspé's opinions took place over long liquid lunches and strenuous dinners. Thus at the age of twenty-two, de Gaspé was already causing controversy in the oil and gas industry in Canada. It was only the beginning of such disturbances.

At Harvard, he produced his doctoral thesis on "The Fossil Fuel Vulnerability of the United States and the

Urgent Requirement for Plans for Energy Self-Sufficiency," a paper which found its way in part into pages of the *New York Times* Sunday edition. With the publication of his work in that prestigious newspaper, Pierre de Gaspé established the beginnings of his credentials as a knowledgeable commentator on the economics of oil and natural gas in relation to the future requirements of the North American continent.

When he completed his work at Harvard in 1966, he was approached by several American oil corporations. The best offer was from Standard Oil of New Jersey, later known as Exxon. De Gaspé was at the top of their selection list from among all the bright young Ph.Ds emerging from American universities that year. But he was uncertain as to whether he should go directly into the oil industry. What he had in his mind was a law degree, not only because of his desire to follow in the path of the legendary father he had never known, but also because he could see that members of the legal profession occupied most of the chairs of power in big business in America and that lawyers generally had an enormous amount of flexibility. When he had talked about going on to law, his mother had chided him in a joking way about becoming a "professional" student.

In the end, after much discussion with and solicitation by the Standard Oil people, de Gaspé joined their corporate planning division as an economist. At the head office in New York, he spent the most intensive year of his life examining, probing, forecasting, analyzing, guessing, prophesying, and above all, learning about the intricate, complex, globe-encircling network of power that rested with a handful of the top executives of this largest of multinational oil companies, a firm of staggering wealth, virtually a nation unto itself.

De Gaspé soon became the protégé of the senior vice-president, George Shaw, and his wife Janet. They were both originally Canadians, and felt a kinship for this young man, even though they had long since become United States citizens. Through their almost parental interest in him, Pierre had been invited to many cocktail parties and dinners. In this way he had quickly broadened his association with both the young and the senior executives in the head office group.

Within a few months, de Gaspé had become a protégé part of the executive "family" of Standard Oil of New Jersey. The brilliance of his work was the cause of mounting admiration and respect for him. Promotion within his section came and with it a substantial raise.

But he was a man who kept looking ahead – where was he going, what was he doing, what were the prospects?

Within a year after he had joined Standard Oil, de Gaspé had made up his mind that, even though the attractions at Standard were enormous and the future looked to be incredibly good for him, he should take his law degree – but in Canada, not in the United States. He discussed the situation with Shaw in order to seek his advice and also to assess what the prospects would be for his return to Standard Oil when the law degree was behind him. Shaw tried to dissuade him, telling him what the future could hold if he stayed inside Standard. But Shaw's discouragement was only half-hearted because he knew if Pierre had his law degree that that professional qualification, combined with this young man's superior ability in economics, would enable him to call his own shots if he wished to return to Standard. He was frank and direct with de Gaspé. By the end of their talk, he had reversed himself.

In the late summer of 1968, de Gaspé packed his bags and, after a round of farewell parties and dinners, departed the head office of Standard Oil of New Jersey and headed for Montreal and the McGill University. The next three academic years were heavy with study of both Common Law and the Civil Code and in both French and English, with some of his courses being taken at Laval University. De Gaspé had headed his class and at the conclusion of the intensive law course was awarded the Gold Medal for academic achievement.

During his law studies, he spent his summer months in Toronto in the economic planning division of the head office of Imperial Oil, the Canadian subsidiary of Standard Oil of New Jersey. Working with Imperial did two things for him: it provided him with sufficient money to carry through the next academic year, and it allowed him to up-date his knowledge of the world oil, natural gas, and energy scene. He was also able to maintain his public visibility by continuing to write incisive, important papers which were published and commented upon in the petroleum industry's magazines and periodicals. These publications earned him some extra money, as did the occasional speaking engagements at various conferences and meetings. He had, however, no urgent need of money; he had been the beneficiary of two substantial bequests, one from his father's mother, who had died in 1959, and another from his father's own estate, the capital of which came to him when he turned twenty-one.

After graduating from McGill Law School and completing his Bar Admission course in Ontario in 1972, Pierre de Gaspé once again received several offers, but only two interested him. The first was from Shaw of Standard Oil of New Jersey which had changed its name to Exxon Corporation on January 1 of that year. Shaw, who had moved up to the position of executive vice-president and the number two man in the entire organization, wanted de Gaspé to be his executive assistant. He would be with him right at the top of Exxon and he would be paid accordingly. The opportunities for the future were unlimited. Pierre was mightily tempted, but he was certain that he did not want to live in the United States, nor would he give up his Canadian citizenship. He was apprehensive about the racial strife in the United States and the growing decadence of the once great American cities. Watergate was yet to be heard from but its roots had been silently planted and were flourishing.

The other offer – the one he accepted – was from Panarctic Oils Limited, then in its formative stages. Panarctic was a corporation put together in 1967 by the federal government of Canada, which took 45 per cent of its shares, offering the balance to Canadian and American oil corporations. The government had found that the oil companies operating in Canada were reluctant to make the high-risk and high-cost investment in exploration in the Arctic Islands, particularly in the Sverdrup Basin from Melville Island northeast to the Eureka area of Ellesmere Island.

When de Gaspé was approached by Panarctic, the company was at the beginning of a massive exploration program which was to prove enormously successful over the years, especially in the finds of natural gas on Melville at Drake Point at the beginning of 1970, King Christian Island later that year, then a whole series, not only on Melville and King Christian, also on Ellef Ringnes, Thor, Ellesmere, and other locations.

The money offered by Panarctic to join them as vice-president of economic planning and legal services was just slightly more than half of the Exxon bid, but de Gaspé was enthusiastic about the Panarctic's prospects in the Canadian Arctic Islands and about its ultimate potential as the national petroleum company. He could clearly foresee that such a company would be necessary if Canada was to deal with the Arabs, the South Americans, and other oil-producing countries around the world – nations that traditionally preferred to deal with governments or government companies. He could see Panarctic as the basic formation block for the future national petroleum company of Canada, provided it was successful in its exploration work in the Arctic. This condition was amply met within a short time after de Gaspé joined the firm at its head offices in Calgary in 1969.

In Calgary, Pierre had met and courted Ann Samson, a vivacious, petite medical doctor just finishing her internship at the Calgary General Hospital. Their marriage in 1970 was followed in 1971 by the birth of their son, Mark. Mark's godfather, George Shaw of Exxon, was thus on hand to celebrate another occasion in Pierre's life, when he was appointed senior vice-president of Panarctic, with a hefty salary increase and enlarged responsibilities in the exploration end of the firm's operation as well as in long-range planning and legal services.

During the mid-seventies, de Gaspé found himself in the middle of the escalating controversial debate between the federal government and the government of Alberta. He was seconded to Ottawa for a period of six months during the winter of 1974/75 to head up a team which would be responsible for laying out the ground rules and format for a continuing locked-in-until-it-was-finished conference between the federal government and the oil-producing and -exporting provinces. De Gaspé and other influential people in the oil industry had protested quietly but effectively to the federal government that a two-day first ministers "on camera" type of conference which had been held in January of 1974 was no answer whatsoever to the urgent need to resolve a whole series of questions related to what a national oil and natural gas policy should be. It was de

Gaspé's opinion that there should be a conference held on neutral ground away from Ottawa and that the participants should stay at it for weeks, if necessary, until they hammered out an overall set of principles under which the federal and provincial governments could operate in co-operation rather than confrontation. In early 1974, de Gaspé wrote a draft paper, "A National Energy Policy for Canada," in which he set out his policy proposals and his design for a Canada Energy Corporation.

Later in the year, the then Prime Minister read de Gaspé's paper, and he and the first ministers of the western oil and gas provinces agreed to use it as the starting point of the discussions in the conference.*

The great National Energy Conference, which took place in Winnipeg in the spring of 1975, went on for five weeks until all the major issues were resolved and new working arrangements were established under heads of agreement which were still effective and operative in 1980.

Immediately after the energy conference, the government had proceeded with the creation of a national petroleum corporation, which they called Petro-Canada. The corporation then acquired the government's interest in Panarctic and with it all its experienced personnel and all its wells, exploration rights, and know-how. De Gaspé was gratified to have his proposal put into action, but was appalled by the name Petro-Canada, which he detested.

The president of Panarctic, who had nurtured that firm from its beginning days and had done what was by and large regarded as an excellent job, was anxious to move away from the heavy responsibilities and constant travelling which he was finding exceedingly difficult to maintain.

And so, on the formation of Petro-Canada, Pierre

*Appendix I, page 444

Thomas de Gaspé became its first president and executive officer, and Panarctic's former president became chairman of the board. The head office of Petro-Canada was established in Toronto on an interim basis.

After his return to Toronto, the demands on de Gaspé's time almost doubled. He put his entire heart and soul into creating, shaping, and moulding this new national corporation. During the next five years, he spent a great deal of time travelling throughout Canada, the United States, Europe, and the Middle East. His wife Ann began to complain bitterly about his lack of time for his family. A strong-willed person, who by this time was having problems with her own identity, she began to spend more and more time in London, Ontario, with her mother.

By the summer of 1980, the relationship between Ann and Pierre had become distant, strained, and unhappy. Without consulting her husband, Ann made plans to take up her medical practice again, but this time in parternship with a young doctor with whom she had interned in Calgary. De Gaspé was furious when he found out, but powerless to do anything about it. When he met Ann's partner for the first time, he was even more upset. Dr. Rease was a strikingly handsome man, and a bachelor.

Notwithstanding this growing marital difficulty, de Gaspé's remarkable organizational ability, leadership, and intelligence had made Petro-Canada flourish as a combined free-enterprise/government undertaking, with de Gaspé marshalling new acquisitions and financings as he quickly spread the broad base of the new corporation to make it truly a national petroleum company.

But by the fall of 1980, he still had not been able to get Petro-Canada into the refining of crude oil and the wholesale and retail distribution of gasoline, fuel oil, and other petroleum products. For him, this was both a major objective and a source of frustration.

The fall of 1980 also provided Pierre Thomas de Gaspé with the most senior appointment of his military career, that of commander of the Toronto District of the land element of the Canadian Armed Forces Reserve, more easily recognized in Canada as the Militia.

When he had brought his family back to Toronto from Calgary in 1975, de Gaspé had accepted an invitation to return to his old Reserve unit, the Queen's York Rangers (1st American Regiment), as second in command with the rank of major.

He enjoyed his military hobby enormously. It gave him a much-needed recreational outlet and, at the same time, provided him a sense of satisfaction and fulfilment of the duty strongly embedded in his nature and background. By 1976 he had become commanding officer of the regiment with the rank of lieutenant-colonel, moving in 1979 as a full colonel to take the post of Toronto District Commander with all the Reserve regiments and other Militia units in the area under his command and control.

Thus, on the day of the President's ultimatum to the new Prime Minister of Canada, Pierre Thomas de Gaspé was wearing two hats, each of significant importance to Canada at that moment: the one as president of Petro-Canada which controlled and owned most of the natural gas in the Canadian Arctic Islands so desperately needed and coveted by the President of the United States; and the other as commander of the Toronto Militia District in a focal position of military responsibility. The hat of the energy executive had high public visibility, but that of the military commander, as is traditional in Canada in time of peace, was of little prestige or importance in a smug society which placed little value on its military establishment – except in an emergency.

On October 6, 1980, the emergency arrived.

Toronto
Tuesday, October 7, 1980, 6:10 P.M.

At noon, the Canadian government had closed the Canadian/U.S. border at all points where it physically could do so: these being the main points of traffic entry in the western provinces, the bridges at Sault Ste. Marie and Windsor/Detroit, and the tunnel there, the Peace Bridge at Fort Erie/Buffalo, the bridges at Niagara Falls and across the St. Lawrence.

Explosive charges were set in all of these structures so that a section but not all of the bridge or tunnel could be blown at the first sign of a military crossing from the American side.

At the same time, the Ministry of Transport ordered the closing down of all air traffic between the United States and Canada. By 6:00 in the evening when Operation Reception Party was in total readiness, there was absolutely no traffic into or out of any Canadian airport, big or small, except for military aircraft.

Telephone, telex, telegram, radio, and all other communications links with the United States were cut off at 3:00 P.M. The communications systems between the two nations had, however, been built without any planning for a shutdown situation, and considerable difficulties were encountered in this procedure.

All operatives of the CIA working in Canada were unobtrusively collected and taken to police or military headquarters for protective questioning.

Thus, while the House of Commons was in the last stages of its deliberation on the ultimatum question, an effective emergency shut-down of communications and transportation between Canada and the United States was being carried off as part of the plan of Operation Reception Party.

At the border-crossing points along the Great Lakes system, troops with machine guns, anti-tank weapons, and light artillery were in position in strategic locations overlooking the approaches to the lofting bridges. On a normal day they carried thousands of people, automobiles, buses, and trucks between two nations which, up to this moment, had lived side by side, divided only by an imaginary line – the longest, unprotected boundary between two nations in the Western world.

To the west of the Great Lakes, Operation Reception Party did not call for protection of the border crossings but the setting up of heavy roadblocks on each of the main highways between the border and the first major Canadian city to which each highway led. The roadblocks were approximately ten miles south of each urban objective. The Chief of the Defence Staff had calculated it would take the U.S. ground troops, personnel carriers, and tanks between one and two hours to reach the western roadblocks. By that time, the airports phase of Reception Party should be finished.

The scene at Toronto International Airport was typical of all major Canadian airfields. Air traffic had totally stopped by mid-afternoon following the Ministry of Transport order at noon. Both terminal buildings had been cleared of passengers and the lengthy ramps around the huge buildings were deserted of people and vehicles although jammed with parked aircraft.

Dispersed around the perimeter of the airport but in

locations that could not be seen by low-flying reconnaissance aircraft, troops equipped with missiles, machine guns, and artillery were in camouflaged positions at points overlooking the runways. Special priority had been given to the positioning of the light anti-tank TOW* missiles, the hand-held, short-range, surface-to-air Blowpipe missiles, and sophisticated British Rapiers, which were also surface-to-air missiles. They were to have a maximum opportunity for clear shots at incoming aircraft, both on the ground and in the air. It was these versatile weapons that would either make or break Operation Reception Party, if indeed the Americans decided to take the unthinkable military step.

Colonel de Gaspé's Kiowa helicopter hovered behind the control tower on the west side of the Toronto International, then gently touched down. His camouflage-net-covered command post vehicles were set up to the west of the control tower structure so that anyone in the air terminal building on the east side of the airfield would not be able to see them.

As the pilot eased the helicopter to the ground, de Gaspé pushed the VHF transmitter button on the control column in front of him and spoke into the microphone on his crash helmet.

"Toronto Tower. This is Reception leader. Over."

Toronto Tower came back, "Reception leader, Toronto Tower. Go."

"Right, Toronto Tower. Are you people all set as briefed?"

"Yes, sir, we sure are. If they come, we don't expect them to get any clearances from us until they're about twenty miles out. I don't expect they'll be getting air traffic control clearances, but we'll have no trouble painting them on our radar screens."

*TOW – tube-launched, optically tracked, wire-guided.

"Okay, Toronto Tower. We'll monitor your VHF control channels, and our communications net will monitor all normal military channels. We don't expect they'll have a communications security blackout. We think they'll do it wide open. Be with you in a couple of minutes."

"Roger. All your people are here waiting for you."

As de Gaspé swung himself out of the helicopter, he was met just outside the arc of the lift blades by his Regular Force staff officer, Lieutenant-Colonel Peter Armstrong, a tall, bear of a man for whom de Gaspé had developed an enormous respect since Armstrong had joined his staff that summer. De Gaspé regarded him as an enormously efficient soldier. He had graduated at the top of his class at Canadian Forces Staff College, commanded a section of the Canadian Airborne Regiment, seen combat service in Korea, and had taken part in the Canadian peace-keeping efforts in Cypress. What's more, Armstrong could drink even Pierre de Gaspé under the table, as he had proved on more than one occasion in mess dinners held from time to time by the various regiments and other units in the Toronto area.

Armstrong's hulking figure loomed even larger in his dark green camouflaged battle gear. His carbon blackened face completed his camouflage dress but looked a little amusing to de Gaspé who, as he returned Armstrong's salute, said, "Christ, Peter, you look like a goddamn grizzly bear."

Armstrong's great white teeth showed in a wide smile. "Thank you, sir. I thought you'd never notice."

As the two of them moved towards the control tower building and the command post truck parked directly to the west side of it, de Gaspé said, "Okay, Peter, give me a status report."

The sound of the helicopter engine died as the pilot cut off the power behind them. Men began to move toward the aircraft with camouflage nets.

271

"Yes, sir," Armstrong responded, "everything's in good shape. All units are in position. But I'd like to wait till we get up to the tower so I can point out to you where everyone is. The COs of all the regiments are there waiting for us. I thought if we had everybody together I could bring you up to date and then you could give us our final instructions."

Colonel de Gaspé took the stairs up to the control tower two at a time with Armstrong following close behind. As he entered the glass-walled control area, the battle-uniformed men, who seemed to fill the room with activity, chatting, and noise, came to military attention. Those with their helmets on saluted. De Gaspé returned the salute.

"Thank you, gentlemen," he said. "Stand easy."

His eyes swept across his team, making a fast inventory of who was there. Holoduke, commanding officer of the Queen's York Rangers; Purdy of the Queen's Own Rifles; Foy of the 48th Highlanders; Esplen of the Toronto Scottish; and Shepherd, the CO of the battalion of the crack British Parabrigade assigned to Toronto. The Brits, all 315 of them, had arrived an hour before in Hercules aircraft of the Royal Air Force Transport Command. They brought with them thirty-six of their new, highly accurate surface-to-air Rapier missile projectors with a supply of over five hundred missiles, a formidable arsenal to meet any air attack.

De Gaspé had been informed during the CDS's morning briefing that, because of the lack of time for preparation and also because of the need to spread them across the border-crossing roadblocks and the commercial and military airports in western Canada, the Alberta-based Canadian Airborne Regiment—the only available combat-ready mobile Regular Force unit—would have to be assigned exclusively to the western task. Therefore, virtually the entire defence of eastern Canada would be the responsibility of the Reserves, supported by whatever British troops would be shipped across in time.

De Gaspé introduced himself to Lieutenant Colonel Michael Shepherd, commander of the British unit.

"I can tell you, Colonel Shepherd, that I'm delighted to have you and your people on board."

Shepherd, a stocky, red-cheeked man in his early thirties, looked up at the much taller de Gaspé and smiled. "I think you're just interested in having our bloody Rapier missiles, sir."

De Gaspé laughed. "Now that you mention it . . . I haven't seen one in operation but I understand they're fantastically accurate, even on high-speed supersonic aircraft."

"That's right, sir. And on top of that, they have an excellent range. If we can see the target, we can hit it, whether it is one mile away or ten."

De Gaspé was impressed. "I understand Colonel Armstrong briefed you when you arrived?"

"Yes, sir. He brought me up to speed on the whole bit: what was happening in Parliament, the briefing you gave him and the Regimental commanders earlier this afternoon, the Defence Staff's analysis, the general strategy and tactics."

"Good," de Gaspé said. "I want to have a word with the air traffic controllers now, and then we'll get on with the final briefing." He smiled and put his hand on Shepherd's shoulder. "I'm delighted you're here, believe me."

Then he turned and introduced himself to the two air traffic controllers who identified themselves as Ray Walnek and Tom Spence. Both of them were obviously senior and highly experienced. Walnek was in charge.

"With the airfield shut down, I don't suppose you fellows have had it so quiet since your last strike." All three laughed together.

"I know Colonel Armstrong has briefed you, but I'd like to go over the plan with you myself, since you," de Gaspé nodded toward Walnek, "and I will be the main actors in receiving our American friends if, in fact, they do arrive."

With that, de Gaspé, Walnek, and Spence spent five minutes meticulously going over the role each would play should an American landing be in fact attempted. Walnek explained the functional workings of the VHF* radio equipment with which he controlled inbound and outbound aircraft and what de Gaspé was to do when it was time for him to interject as Walnek was dealing with the hypothetical incoming Americans.

In turn, de Gaspé made sure that Walnek and Spence knew how to use the military radio and communications equipment that had been set up in the tower.

"As Armstrong has told you, I plan to use the control tower as my command post," he said. "I want you to understand that all three of us will be highly vulnerable, because once I get on the air with my instructions to the lead American aircraft, the pilots will know I'm in the tower with you. Unless they have explicit instructions not to fire, they'll probably come in and attempt to take us out." Walnek and Spence looked at each other nervously. "I hope you're still game?"

"Sure, Colonel," Walnek responded. "Frankly, I don't think it's going to come off the way you think. I just can't see the Americans attacking us."

Spence nodded in agreement.

"I can't either," said de Gaspé. "But we've got to be prepared for the worst."

He then turned to Peter Armstrong. "Okay, Peter, let's get into the final briefing." Then, raising his voice, he

*VHF – very high frequency.

274

addressed the assembled men. "Gentlemen, we'll get on with the final briefing. Colonel Armstrong will brief me as to the deployment of your units. Don't hesitate to break in at any point with suggestions and questions. When he's finished, I will have a word or two, then you can get back to your people." He looked at his watch. "We haven't much time left. It's just after six. The President is scheduled to speak at six-thirty. My guess is if they're going to come after us, they're in their aircraft right now."

The men looked uneasily at each other. It was hard for any one of them to believe that this could be so.

"Okay, Peter. It's all yours."

Lieutenant Colonel Peter Armstrong began. "Right, sir. I've stuck up on the north window," he pointed, "a map of the airport. I will refer to it and indicate where our people are on the ground. Obviously, this control tower is perfect because we can see any part of the airfield from here.

"I'm only going to say, 'if they come' just this once, because the rest of my briefing will assume that they are coming. If they come, they'll be coming from the south, across the lake, probably from the southeast, south and southwest. The wind at this time is zero two zero at fifteen miles an hour and gusting, so they'll probably use the Runway 32–the longest. We don't know how many of them there'll be, but let's assume there are at least fifty. They'll want to get on the ground as quickly as possible and start unloading their troops as soon as they can get clear of the runway. The first aircraft will have to get quite a distance off before it stops, in order to let the incoming aircraft behind it have enough turnoff room."

He waved his right hand toward the Terminal One building, about half a mile to the east of the control tower.

"This airfield is designed so that aircraft landing on the north-south runway move easterly toward the terminal

Toronto International Airport

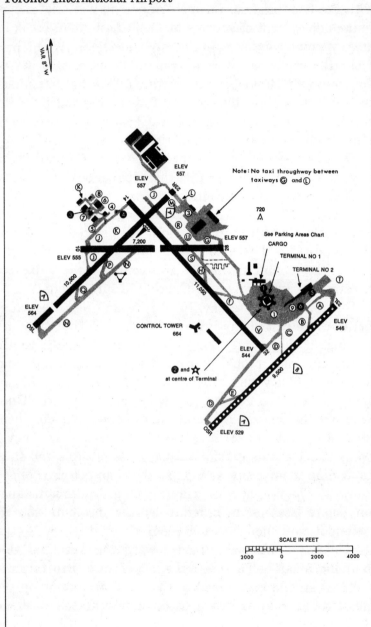

buildings. So we can expect that the first aircraft–really all of them–will head in that direction once they're on the ground."

Armstrong pointed toward the north.

"At the north end of the north-south runway we've got the Toronto Scottish dug in on each side of the runway facing south. The ground is lower there than it is at the south end of the airfield, so they'll have a good shot with their TOW and Blowpipe missiles."

He turned to face east toward the huge Terminal One structure with the eight stories of parking garage sitting on top of it.

"We've used the open parking levels of Terminal One almost like an ancient man-of-war. We've got the Queen's York Rangers and the artillery regiment with twenty-five pounders and TOW missiles and machine guns on every floor except the roof. They have a commanding view of the entire airfield. My only concern is that if they have to fire, they know exactly where the Toronto Scottish, the 48th Highlanders–I'll come to them in a minute–and the Brits are, so they don't take our own people out."

Then Armstrong turned and walked to the south window of the control tower and pointed to the west end of Runway 5 Right.

"The 48th Highlanders are at the west end of Runway 5 Right. The button of 5 Right is lower than the eastern end of the runway, so they get a good view should the Americans come in from either direction on it. Also, the 48th are equipped with the TOW missile as well as the Blowpipe. They have five Rapiers as have the Toronto Scottish up at the north end. Each Rapier has at least fifteen missiles. Each of the TOW units–and there are thirty-two of those on the airfield, the Toronto Scottish have ten, Queen's York Rangers in Terminal One have twelve, and the other ten are with the 48th–each of them has five missiles."

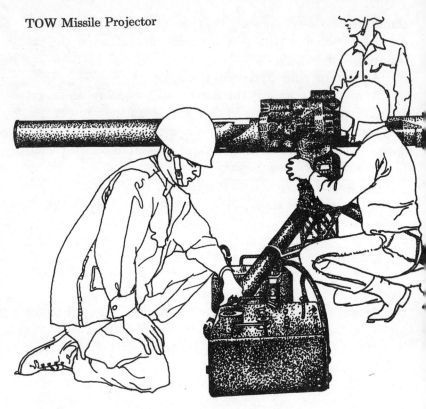

He turned back to face south again.

"Now our friends, the Brits, with their magic Rapier missiles are divided. South of the airfield at Centennial Park–that's the ski hill made out of garbage many years ago–they have twenty-one Rapiers with the Queen's Own Rifles who also have twenty Blowpipes. The Brits and the Queen's Own are on top of the hill, which gives them a superb shot at any inbound or circling aircraft. Then they have another five Rapiers with Colonel Foy and his 48th Highlanders at the west of Runway 5 Right and another five with Colonel Esplen and the Torscots to the north."

Armstrong now faced Colonel de Gaspé. "That's the deployment, sir."

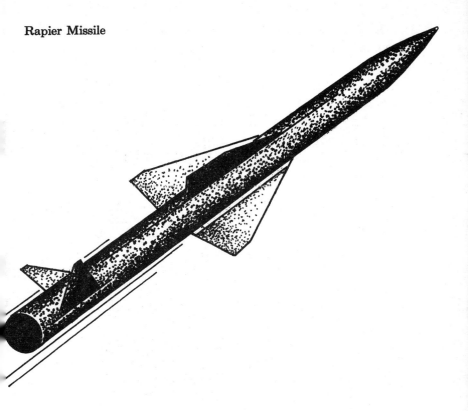

"Thank you, Colonel. Now give me your communications net again, please," de Gaspé said.

"Your command channel is number three, sir, with a backup channel number five. Only the commanding officers are on that net. They have their own channels to their own people, so there won't be any overlap."

"Good." De Gaspé looked around at his commanding officers and said, "Any questions?"

Colonel Holoduke of the Queen's York Rangers spoke up. "Sir, in the event we have to fire on one or all of the aircraft, what's the procedure? We've been briefed, but could we just go over it again, please."

Colonel de Gaspé nodded. "Okay. This is the way it goes.

If they come in on the north-south runway, the prime responsibility for aircraft on the ground will be the Toronto Scottish. You've got your TOW missiles numbered one to ten. As they land, your number one unit should pick up number one aircraft and keep trained on it. Number two should do the same with number two aircraft, and so forth, until the tenth aircraft is down. Then the Queen's York Rangers with their twelve TOW missiles numbered in sequence, should pick up the eleventh aircraft, twelfth, and so forth. The twenty-third should be picked up by the 48th and followed through. Holoduke, you're in Terminal One. You and your people have got to remember that the 48th are at the west end of Runway 5 Right. You can't fire in their direction, nor can you fire at the Toronto Scottish at the north end. Let me put it another way, if you're firing in their direction, you must do so with extreme caution.

"We will not fire at any aircraft unless the troops in it attempt to disembark contrary to my instructions. If they start to disembark, it will be my command—and my command only—upon which you are permitted to fire. The command will be, 'hit number . . . fire.' I will give you the number of the aircraft. So if it's the fourth aircraft on the ground, and it starts to disgorge people, my command will be 'hit number four, fire.' That will be your TOW missile unit number four, Esplen, which should be tracking number four airplane, and should launch on it immediately my order is passed to you."

Shepherd of the British unit asked, "And aircraft still airborne, sir?"

"Right. You will fire with your Rapier weapons only at my command. Your targets will be airborne aircraft that attempt to turn and head back for the United States. I will use the Blowpipe and Rapier in reserve. If the fighters attack us, then we'll go for them too."

280

De Gaspé paused, then said, "Whatever we do, gentlemen, must be done with the greatest discretion. Ideally, we will not fire at all. I'm sure that none of us has any desire whatsoever to kill or injure any of our American friends, and I have a feeling they feel the same way about us. Let's hope they do anyhow.

"One final thing. I'll be in the tower with the air traffic controllers, brave souls that they are. Colonel Armstrong will be in the backup control unit in the vehicles to the west of the tower." De Gaspé smiled at Walnek and Spence, who returned the smile rather self-consciously.

"Any further questions?" he asked as he looked around the glass-walled room. The light of the sun disappearing below the horizon in the clear sky to the west silhouetted his commanders against the terminal buildings, hangars, and runways of the vast Toronto International Airport. There were no questions.

Suddenly they were startled by the loud voice from the traffic controllers loudspeaker system. "Tower, this is radar. I'm getting a formation of unidentified aircraft at the outer limit of my range at a bearing of about one six zero. Looks to me like about thirty aircraft. They appear to be tracking on a heading of three four zero, which should put them over Rochester in five, their speed and altitude unknown at this time."

Walnek was at his microphone immediately. "Okay, radar, give me your speed on those aircraft as quickly as you can, and an estimate as to what time they might arrive here, assuming they're coming here."

The voice came back, "Will do, Tower . . . good God, I'm just picking up another gaggle. Looks to me like perhaps fifty of them strung out. They're on a bearing of about two zero five, their track also looks like Rochester!"

Walnek was calm. "Yeah. Looks like they're going to rendezvous across the lake. Have you got an ETA for me yet?"

With a slight pause, radar came back. "Looks like eighteen forty-five, about twenty minutes from now."

Colonel de Gaspé, his voice raised with excitement, shouted to his commanders, "All right, chaps, get moving."

As they rushed out, he turned to Walnek. "Get a red alert signal out immediately." Walnek nodded and reached for his telephone. De Gaspé grabbed the one next to it and quickly dialled the direct line to the Commander of Mobile Command at St. Hubert. A soft voice. "Christie here."

"Sir, it's de Gaspé in the control tower at Toronto. They're on their way. We've picked up about eighty of them. Apparently they're going to rendezvous at Rochester. Assuming they're coming here, they'll arrive about eighteen forty-five hours."

Lieutenant-General Christie did not respond for a moment, then said, "That's just about when the President will finish his television address. Keep me posted. I'm in my battle command room at this time. I'll report immediately to the Vice-Chief in Ottawa."

Ottawa
Tuesday, October 7, 1980, 6:26 P.M.

The Vice-Chief of the Defence Staff, General White, turned
to the CDS in the battle operations room of the Alternate
Command Centre near Ottawa and gave him Christie's
report on de Gaspé's information, then asked, "What about
the Prime Minister, sir."

The CDS ran his hand through his thick hair and looked
up at the wall clock. Eighteen twenty-six hours. Robert Porter would just be driving through the gates of the long
driveway into Government House, where he was to meet
the Governor-General.

As the CDS dialled the Government House number, he
glanced around the operations room at the green-uniformed
Canadian Armed Forces men and women receiving reports
from across Canada on the status of Operation Reception
Party. They posted the incoming information on boards,
maps, and charts so the CDS and his staff could monitor
quickly the input which was now flowing rapidly.

When the switchboard operator came on at Government
House, the CDS gave her terse instructions that the line
was to be left clear for him on an emergency basis so he
could communicate with the Prime Minister at will. The
operator found the Governor-General's executive assistant
in the front lobby of Government House waiting for the
arrival of the Prime Minister. The CDS waited. Within two
minutes Porter was on the line.

When he had received the CDS's report, he said, calmly, "Well, we still can't be exactly certain what their intent is. The main thing is we're ready. I'm just going to join the Governor-General. I don't propose to tell him about this until I have to. It may be a bluff, but we'll soon find out. Call me as soon as they've committed to landing."

The CDS's call back to the Prime Minister coincided with the final words of the President's invasion announcement ten minutes later at eighteen thirty-nine hours, 6:39 P.M., when, without any knowledge of the existence of the plans for Operation Reception Party, the Governor-General thought he had no choice but to follow the instructions of the President.

Toronto
Tuesday, October 7, 1980, 6:41 P.M.

De Gaspé's body tensed as he heard the first southern-accented words of the American leader through the control tower loudspeaker. "Toronto Arrival, this is USAF Blueforce leader. Over."

Toronto Arrival's voice came back instantly, as briefed. "USAF Blueforce leader, Toronto Arrival. Go."

The American leader read his message, which was as much an announcement: "Toronto Arrival, Blueforce leader. I am Major-General Dudley Smith, personally appointed by the President of the United States to lead the USAF Blueforce to land at Toronto International Airport and Downsview Canadian Forces Base for the purpose of taking over military occupancy and government of the Metropolitan Toronto area and southern Ontario in accordance with the President's decree that Canada should become and is now part of the United States of America."

Toronto Arrival broke in. "We have monitored the President's statement, sir."

"Okay, Toronto Arrival, since this is a peaceful invasion exercise, please be advised of my requirements. They are as follows: A normal straight-in approach clearance is requested for all Blueforce aircraft into Toronto International. I have sixty Hercules and Starlifters with me for Toronto International and twenty-one into Downsview. For Toronto International I request, as I said, straight-in

approach on Runway 32 for all my aircraft. We will be landing in close sequence. After landing, you will marshall us to
positions on the ramps of both Terminals One and Two.
You will instruct your ground-handling people to open all
doors and gates leading into both terminals. Also instruct
your ground-handling people to marshall all buses and
trucks in the airfield area and have them stand by. We have
our own vehicles on board but we will need extras. And we
have helicopters following us in with an ETA of twenty
minutes from now."

Toronto Arrival replied, "Roger, Blueforce leader. Will
you require fuel?"

"Negative," came the Blueforce leader's voice.

"Okay, Blueforce leader. Go to Toronto Tower on 118.0
now."

In the control tower, there was a silence for a few seconds. Then it came.

"Toronto Tower, this is USAF Blueforce leader, ten miles
back at five thousand feet, clear for straight-in approach on
32. I have sixty–six zero–aircraft with me, and this call is
for clearance for all to land. Over."

De Gaspé stood looking out the southern glass wall of
the control tower beside Walnek, who put his microphone
to his mouth and said, "Roger, Blueforce leader. This is
Toronto Tower. Do not have you visual yet. We have a lot
of haze this evening. Have been monitoring your discussion
with Toronto Arrival. You're cleared for a straight-in
approach on 32 with the sixty–six zero–aircraft with you.
The twenty-one aircraft bound for Downsview should go to
126.2 at this time. The wind is zero two zero at fifteen to
twenty, the altimeter is twenty-nine decimal nine two.
Over."

"Blueforce leader," the acknowledgement came back.

With those words, de Gaspé saw the first flickering of

landing lights over the lake. He turned to Walnek and pointing said excitedly, "There they are."

As he watched, the first signs of the lead aircraft were quickly followed by the emergence of another, then another, until a small section of the darkened sky over Lake Ontario appeared to be filled with the twinkling lights of fireflies.

Walnek spoke into the microphone.

"Blueforce leader, Toronto Tower. Suggest you land long and exit on the right on Runway 5 Left at the north end. What will be the landing interval between your aircraft?"

"About twenty seconds, I reckon," an answer came back. "I know you civilian controllers don't like to have but one airplane on the runway. But this is a military operation and we'd like to get all our airplanes down as fast as we can. So when I'm turning right off onto Runway 5 Left, number two and three aircraft'll be on the ground behind me, and four and five should just be ready to touch down, and so on."

"Roger, Blueforce leader. When you're on the ground, do not switch to Toronto ground control. I will maintain control of all aircraft from the tower position."

"Roger, Toronto Tower."

Then "Blueforce leader to Blueforce, I am selecting gear down, selecting gear down now!"

The voice of Toronto radar came over the loudspeaker. "Tower, I'm painting a gaggle of fast-moving aircraft coming in from the Buffalo sector. They're just crossing the smokestacks now. They're probably at low level."

De Gaspé saw Walnek's eyes shift from watching the ever brighter landing lights of the inbound transports toward the position of the four hydro electric power station smokestacks on the shore of Lake Ontario to the southwest of the airport. As de Gaspé followed his gaze, he could see about three miles away, almost at treetop level, the clus-tered snouts of a dozen fighter aircraft, with missiles and bombs drooping under their wings, hurtling straight at them.

"This is it," said de Gaspé as he waited, transfixed, expecting to see missiles or bombs leave the fighters. He was absolutely helpless. There was no protection at all.

But the jets were by in two seconds as the formation thundered across the airfield with no attempt to attack.

Radar was on again. "Tower, I have three more fast-moving gaggles, one from the west at about thirty miles, another from the southeast at eighteen, and the third from the southwest, also at eighteen."

"Yeah, radar," said Walnek, "fighter squadrons – they're covering the landings of the big birds. Stand by, one."

Walnek picked up his microphone, "Toronto Tower to USAF fighter squadron leader, do you read. Over."

Silence.

"Toronto Tower to USAF fighter leader. Over."

Still no response.

"Blueforce leader is clear final," came the American's call for the final clearance to land.

De Gaspé turned away from the northeast where he had been watching the fighter squadron turning in a wide arc westerly toward Bramalea, swinging around to come back across the airfield again. His eyes went back to the long line of huge transport aircraft stretching for miles behind the leader, like a flock of geese strung out and up into the dis-tance.

Again Walnek spoke into his microphone. "Blueforce leader is clear to land. Check gear down and locked. Wind is zero two five at fifteen."

"Blueforce leader."

Walnek muttered to de Gaspé. "The lead craft is a C141

Starlifter, the one behind it is a Hercules and most of the rest appear to be Hercs."

De Gaspé moved over to the east wall of the glass control tower and picked up the microphone Walnek had assigned to him. He watched, fascinated, as the huge leading Starlifter aircraft, appearing to be barely moving at all, almost hanging in the sky, completed its flareout well down the runway, tail down, its tires smoking as they touched. A short distance behind was the second aircraft, then the third, and the rest strung out almost as far as the eye could see.

Overhead, de Gaspé caught the flash of a turning squadron of American fighter aircraft. Walnek saw him look up and said, "We now have four fighter squadrons with us. Let's hope they've been instructed not to attack. I don't know what frequency they're on yet."

De Gaspé merely nodded.

The second USAF transport aircraft had touched down. The third was about to put its wheels on the runway. Blueforce leader was reaching the end of his landing run and beginning his turnoff onto Runway 5 Left. Then he was clear and number four and number five aircraft were on the runway.

Now de Gaspé spoke into his microphone; his voice was calm, but his hand shaking. "Blueforce leader, this is the Canadian military commander at Toronto International. For communication purposes, I will be called Reception leader. Do you read?"

"Blueforce leader, go."

"Okay, Blueforce leader, this message should be copied by all of your aircraft and passed on to your fighters. Each of your aircraft on the ground is covered by a TOW missile and each of your aircraft in the air is covered by a surface-to-air missile. In addition, the entire airfield is covered by light artillery and machine guns. You are to carry out the following instructions. In the event you fail or refuse to follow these orders, I will destroy your entire fleet and can do so instantly.

"Blueforce leader, you are to continue taxiing along taxiway Romeo toward Terminal One and all aircraft on the ground or airborne are to continue to land as originally planned. No aircraft commander is to permit troops or personnel to disembark and no aircraft still airborne is to attempt to make a run for the United States. Any aircraft that permits troops to disembark or, if airborne, turns for the United States, will be immediately destroyed. Do you copy, Blueforce leader."

De Gaspé's eyes were on the huge lead aircraft taxiing southeasterly toward Terminal One, followed fifty yards behind by Blueforce number two, and then by number three, which was just turning right onto Runway 5 Left. There were another four aircraft on Runway 32 at this time.

Blueforce leader's voice had evidence of shock.

"Who the hell do you think you are! This was supposed to be a peaceful landing! You haven't got all that fire power. You're bluffing, man, you're bluffing!"

De Gaspé's voice was cold and firm. "Blueforce leader, I am not bluffing."

Suddenly a new voice. "Blueforce leader, this is Blueforce two. He's goddamn well bluffing and these goddamn Canadians haven't got anything. I've got a planeful of Green Berets. I'm going to call the bluff right now!"

The number two aircraft, a Hercules, then swung sharply to the west on Taxiway Sierra where it came to an abrupt stop. The side entrance doors flew open and the tail loading ramp began to lower. De Gaspé had his command microphone in his left hand. Into it he shouted, "Hit number two–fire! Hit number two–fire!" He could hear Foy's voice feed back. "Hit number two–fire! Hit number two–fire!" De Gaspé automatically counted the seconds. "A thousand and one, a thousand and two." The ramp of the Herc was still lowering. In the gathering dusk, men were leaping out of the doors . . . "a thousand and three" . . . then in one instant the entire aircraft became a huge ball of orange-yellow flame enveloping the green, running bodies around it. In a split second, the fuselage expanded like a toy balloon, then exploded, spewing out pieces of equipment, bodies, and more fire. The force of the blast shook the control tower glass, almost shattering it.

Into the microphone in his right hand, de Gaspé said, still with a cool unbroken voice, "Reception leader to all Blueforce aircraft. I repeat, you are not to disembark any troops, and all aircraft still airborne are to land. Aircraft on the ground are to keep rolling toward the parking ramps at Terminals One and Two. Follow the 'Follow Me' vehicle in front of you, Blueforce leader. You will be marshalled by ground personnel when you get there."

The American leader did not acknowledge de Gaspé. Instead his agitated voice was heard calling, "Blueforce leader to all helicopters–turn back, turn back."

Toronto radar's voice again. "I'm tracking one aircraft about three miles south doing a 180 degree turn toward the lake."

De Gaspé rushed to the south window and tried to find the turning aircraft, but couldn't. Back to his communications microphone, he barked, "Shepherd, one of them is doing a 180 toward the lake. He should be just to the south of you."

Shepherd was back immediately. "I've got him, sir."

"Then fire! Fire!"

"Firing, sir! Firing!" Shepherd acknowledged.

Walnek protested. "Shouldn't you have given them another warning?"

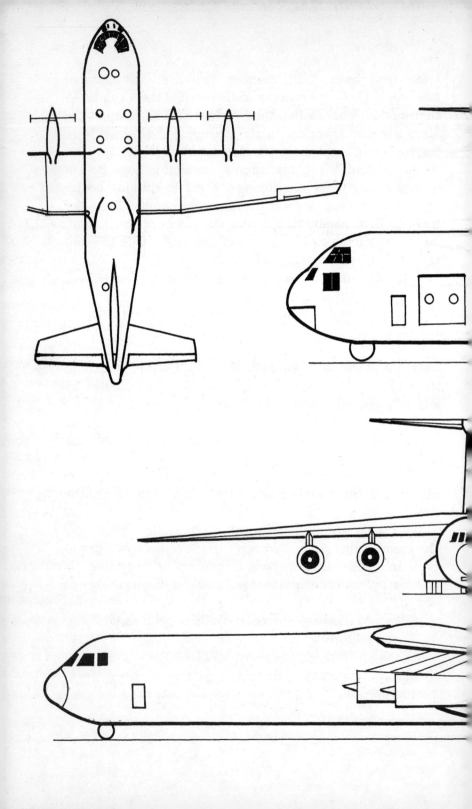

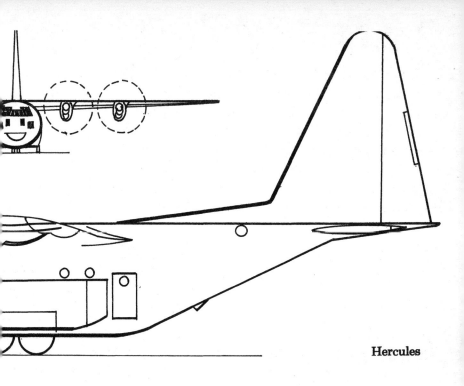

Hercules

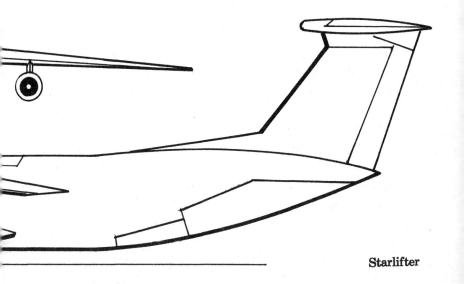

Starlifter

De Gaspé shook his head. "No way. They've had their warning. Things are moving too fast."

Again de Gaspé was back to the American leader. "Blueleader, this is Reception leader. Will you please give me the frequency your fighter squadrons are on? We've been trying to pick it up and can't."

At that instant–just as the words "They're on emergency radar frequency 121.5" came back–the darkening sky to the south of the airport lit up like instant sunlight as the massive warhead of Shepherd's Rapier missile detonated on contact with the inboard port engine of the enormous fuel-, man-, and equipment-laden Hercules. The explosives in the warhead, coupled with the thousands of gallons of jetfuel ignited by the blast, created an enormous orange meteor of flame, spreading a trail of engines, bodies, and pieces of the aircraft as it disintegrated in the centre core of the inferno.

Walnek watched with disbelief, shaking his head from side to side. But de Gaspé was concentrating on his next critical move.

"Mr. Walnek, give me 121.5 as quickly as you can."

Walnek reached out to the selector switch on his panel, turned to the 121.5 frequency and gave de Gaspé a quick thumbs-up signal.

De Gaspé looked out the control tower windows through 360 degrees, looking hard for the fighter squadrons. He said tersely to Walnek, "I'm going to talk to the fighters. While I'm doing that, ask radar to tell you where they are. I can't see them."

Then he spoke into his tower microphone. "USAF fighter squadron leaders, this is the Canadian military commander at Toronto International–Reception leader. I will not ask you to acknowledge until I am finished. All of your transport aircraft assigned to Toronto International have landed or are in the process of landing. As at this moment,

F4 Phantom

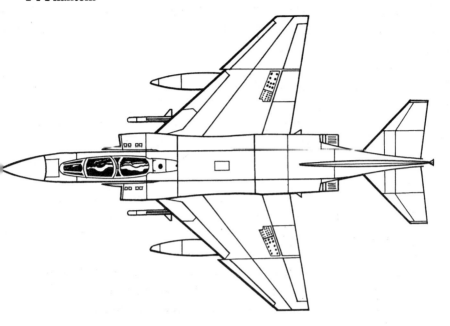

they are not yet prisoners of war and are still open to attack by my forces in the event they commit any further hostile actions contrary to my instructions.

"I have already been forced to destroy two of them. I do not know what your instructions are about strafing or bombing in support of your troops or transport aircraft, but I will tell you this . . . the moment you commence an attack on any one of my ground positions, I will immediately order my missile people to destroy you and every one of your transport aircraft, whether in the air or on the ground."

Walnek had shoved a sketch in front of him showing the location of the four fighter squadrons—about forty-eight aircraft. The diagram hastily drawn by Walnek showed that the four squadrons had apparently made a rendezvous at the Kleinberg VOR* station fifteen miles north of the

*VOR – VHF omni-directional Range.

Toronto International Airport, and the lead squadron had just left that location headed directly for the airport, with the second, third, and fourth squadrons following with two-mile intervals between them. It was obvious to de Gaspé that this formation was set up for strafing and bombing so that the first squadron could make its attack and clear before the next wave came in. Another minute and a half and the first wave would be on top of them.

Back to the microphone. "Reception leader to the lead USAF fighter squadron commander. Have you copied my message?"

The response was immediate. The voice coming through the loudspeaker was angry and venomous, "Yes, I have, you blackmailing bastard."

De Gaspé half shouted into his microphone, "My instructions to you are to break off immediately and to return to your bases. I give you ten seconds to acknowledge in the affirmative and to commence your break-off by a turn to the starboard."

De Gaspé barked into his command communications microphone in his left hand, still pressing the switch on his tower transmitter so the fighters could hear, "All missile commanders, standby, standby! There are four fighter squadrons approaching from the north at low level. If the fighter squadrons do not break off in ten seconds, I will give the order to fire on all aircraft on the ground and in the air. All Rapiers track the fighters. Standby one!"

De Gaspé's eyes went to the huge second sweeping clock in the control tower as he measured the last five seconds of the response time he had given the lead American squadron commander.

On the ninth second, it came. "Number one squadron is breaking off and returning to base. Turning starboard now."

Then a new voice. "Number two squadron following."

Then another. "Number three squadron following."

And the final. "Number four squadron following."

Radar's voice came through strong and clear. "All squadrons are turning west, turning west."

De Gaspé could see them now, very low, as the lead squadron was part way through its turn to the west. It was no more than half a mile to the north of the Toronto International Airport, just beyond Malton, the swept back wings of its twelve F4 Phantom aircraft glitteringly etched against the crimson sky and the sun just disappearing below the horizon.

De Gaspé's shoulders seemed to sag slightly as the high pressure of that moment of tension was eased.

'Reception leader to missile commanders. The fighter squadrons have broken off. Maintain watch on all aircraft on the ground and inbound."

Walnek turned to him and said, "We have thirty-eight aircraft on the ground, two destroyed, and radar informs we've got another twenty inbound."

De Gaspé looked at his watch. "Could you split them and bring half in on Runway 5 Right and the other half on Runway 5 Left? If you could do that we could speed up the landing time considerably."

Walnek checked the wind direction and speed, and replied. "Yeah. The wind is now zero three zero at about twelve, so these big birds should have no problem."

Into his microphone Walnek said, "The three USAF aircraft on final for 32 below seventeen hundred feet indicated are to continue on final for 32 and land. The remaining aircraft above seventeen hundred feet indicated will turn port downwind for landings on Runway 5 Right and Runway 5 Left. The number one aircraft will take 5 Left, the number two aircraft 5 Right, and the remaining aircraft will alternate accordingly. It is not necessary to acknowledge this transmission except if you have any questions or difficulty."

Silence followed Walnek's instructions, and de Gaspé could see the fourth aircraft in the landing line begin a slow turn to its left toward the west. The landing lights of the aircraft following it began the westward turn almost in unison.

Walnek nodded affirmatively. "They've got it."

De Gaspé paused for a moment to take a look at the incredible sight spread out in front of him. At the far eastern end of the Terminal Two ramp, he could see the flashing navigation lights of Blueforce leader's aircraft becoming brighter as darkness descended. He could still see the aircraft clearly as it was being led to its parking position by the ground control vehicle, the red signal light on its roof flashing insistently.

Strung out behind the leader in an unending line from Terminal Two westerly around the Terminal One ramp, and north along Taxiway Romeo to the exit points from the northerly end of 32, stretched the long line of the huge Starlifters and Hercules moved slowly. Their green and red navigation lights and flashing white strobes looked to de Gaspé like a string of Christmas lights as they passed by the darkened Terminal One. He wondered whether the crews on board the American transports could see the muzzles of the guns and missiles trained on them from the parking levels above the terminal.

"Reception leader to Blueforce leader."

"Blueforce leader, go," came the American General's response.

"When you have been marshalled and parked, sir, and this applies to all Blueforce aircraft, you are to remain inside your aircraft. No one, I repeat, no one, is to open a door, lower a ramp, or in any way attempt to disembark from any of your aircraft. When you have shut down, you will continue to monitor Toronto Tower for further instructions."

Blueforce leader repeated the instructions de Gaspé had given him, and then proceeded to get a copy check from all his aircraft by asking them to acknowledge by their numbers in sequence. He knew that the Canadian military commander's instructions were crucial for the safety of each aircraft and its crew and passengers, so no chance could be taken that one of the crews had missed the instructions.

While this check was going on, Colonel de Gaspé reported to the commander at Mobile Command at the operations room at St. Hubert.

General Christie was delighted. "Excellent, Pierre, excellent. We've got them at Downsview, and here at St. Hubert, and at Dorval and right across the country, but yours is the only place that had to take a shot at them. American troops and vehicles started to move across the bridges along the Great Lakes system, so we blew sections of them as planned. That stopped them right in their tracks. They didn't try to come through the tunnel at Windsor though. Guess they knew that if it was blown, it would be a real deathtrap.

"So we've stopped them for the moment in the East. Reception Party has worked right across the board. Winnipeg, Edmonton, Calgary, Vancouver, Cold Lake, everywhere. They made their landings simultaneously almost to the minute. If they had staggered their timing, then the first ones in could have warned the others across the country, but they didn't plan it that way. Strange."

De Gaspé asked, "What about their ground movements in the West, sir?"

"I haven't got a reading on that yet. They should be hitting our roadblocks starting in about twenty minutes. The air landings began twenty-four minutes ago, so it will be pretty close to an hour before they reach our people in Manitoba, Saskatchewan, and Alberta. Intelligence informs us they're on the move there, but apparently no attempt has been made to move in by land into British Columbia."

Christie broke off, "Sorry. Must go, Pierre. The CDS wants me to give him my report so he can brief the Prime Minister. Keep up the good work."

The atmosphere in the Oval Office of the White House was tense. The President, white hair dishevelled, suit-coat off, tie unloosened at the neck, sat at his desk. He was reading a report which had just been brought to him and at the same time keeping his ear tuned to the television set, listening to the news reports and commentary on his speech and the progress of the annexation of Canada.

Sitting on the edge of the couch to the right of the President's desk was Irving Wolf, his Secretary of State, the man whose advice and strategies had brought him to this moment of confrontation with the Canadians. Wolf had drafted the original ultimatum and had convinced the reluctant President of its value. Wolf sat now, head down, gaze on the floor, his nose between his two index fingers, as he listened to the television announcer.

Pacing back and forth, but out of the President's and Wolf's line of sight, was the Secretary of Defence, J. William Crisp, a round man of medium height and age. Crisp had been a naval hero during the Korean War, and had caught the President's eye many years ago. The financial support he had provided had greatly helped the President during his campaign.

As an industrialist from the Midwest, Crisp knew nothing at all about Canada, except that it lay to the north of the United States and had a lot of oil and natural gas–gas that was desperately needed by the United States. Mostly it was American money that had discovered it. The country, so far as he knew, was still run by England and the Queen. It had no defence force except a Regular Force of 50,000, of which maybe 5,000 at the outside might be combat trained, and a nondescript Reserve Force of about 30,000, most of whom were militia troops, with about 1,200 Air Reservists made up of eight squadrons, flying—and Crisp wouldn't believe it when he was briefed—single-engine Otters, an antique light transport aircraft produced in Canada in the 1950's, and a handful of Second World War DC3s.

When Crisp had received the recommendation of the Joint Chiefs of Staff for Operation Northland, he was forced by his own ignorance of Canada to rely totally on the battle plan they submitted. Unfortunately for Crisp, while the Joint Chiefs of Staff and their immediate staff had the military and logistic statistics on Canada, their general attitude toward Canada and their knowledge of the country, its people, its government, and its background were similar to those of Crisp himself.

Operation Northland had been based on the thesis that the Canadians had no real defence force and that, in any event, Canada would welcome the Americans and capitulate immediately without a fight.

Since the President was right in the middle of a heavy campaign for re-election, he was also concerned about the reaction of American multi-national corporations to any destruction of their Canadian investments. This factor weighed heavily on Crisp's thinking when he approved the walk-ride-fly-in approach submitted by the Joint Chiefs of Staff, and rejected their proposal for an all-out paratroop and "Heliborne" assault for openers.

So, if Operation Northland failed, J. William Crisp, as Secretary of Defence, would be the first one to carry the can and be fired, but it would be the President, the Commander-in-Chief of all United States forces, who would take the responsibility.

By 7:12, the three men in the Oval Office of the White House knew they had failed, that the Canadians had been totally misjudged, and that all 228 Starlifters and Hercules and the over 15,000 men on board this great air armada were at this moment trapped in their aircraft on airfields all across Canada.

News of their capture had not yet reached the media and had not come across in the television bulletins, but the President and the two men in the room with him knew, and they knew it was total disaster for them.

The conversations between the military commanders at all Canadian commercial and military bases and the air commander assigned to each had been fully monitored by the U.S. Federal Aeronautics Authority and military controllers. The sequence of the landing actions had been reported by the commanders of the covering fighter squadrons. All of them had been ordered not to strafe, bomb, or use their missiles except in the event of Canadian attack on the transport aircraft, which was the situation at Toronto.

Using these monitored reports, the chairman of the Joint Chiefs of Staff (JCS) had kept the President informed on open line from the Pentagon. A final call from the JCS Chairman confirmed the worst. All aircraft and airtroops had been captured. Only the following helicopters had been able to turn back before they came into missile range. The bridges on the Great Lakes system had been blown. The only possible hope was that the tank and armoured car columns which had crossed the western U.S./Canadian border east of the Rockies might achieve their objectives and take the major Canadian cities there.

As he listened to the chairman of the JCS certifying the Canadian coup, the President shook his head in disbelief.

"General, how in God's name could you have misread the situation so badly?" With that he transfixed Crisp with a look that stopped him right in his tracks. "Do you realize we'll be the laughing stock of the world? Now listen to this one carefully, General. I want the answer in ten minutes, and it had better be good. The question is simple. What do we do next?" He slammed on the phone, and looked again at Crisp.

The President shouted a fast resumé of the disastrous news from the chairman of the Joint Chiefs of Staff. His voice rising, he shouted even louder.

"For Christ sake, how could you people have been so stupid? Sure, the Canadians have a small force. It's next to nothing. Sure, our forefathers all got off the same boat. Sure, we speak the same language, and sure, the United States owns most of the country. But those people have a fighting record in the First World War and the Second World War like you wouldn't believe. Crisp, why the hell didn't you have our fighters clean out the airfields with bombs and rockets before transports went in? And what happened to our intelligence people? Didn't they report any troop movements? And how in God's name did we fail to track the RAF transport aircraft bringing the commandos and paratroopers across? Your people in the Pentagon are stupid beyond belief!"

The President turned in his chair and stabbed his left hand toward a map of Canada that had been hastily draped over a briefing board brought into the office. "And what about our troops moving across the border into the Canadian West?" he shouted, "I know what's going to happen to them and I know what's going to happen to us. The Canadians are going to stop us cold. Not by troops, not by weapons, but by the Prime Minister calling me on that goddamn phone, that red phone right there. Look at it! He's going to

304

call me, and he's going to say, if your tanks, armoured vehicles, personnel carriers, anything–if they go beyond point X, you can kiss your troops sitting in their metal capsules at airports all across Canada GOODBYE!" The President pounded the desk with his fist in total anger.

Suddenly the red telephone rang. It rang again.

The President stood up, looking at it incredulously, then slowly picked it up.

The President put the phone to his ear–it was only the second time he had used it in almost four years.

"Hello."

"Mr. President," said a female voice. The President thought he caught a slight Slavic accent.

"Yes."

"The Chairman of the Supreme Soviet wishes to speak with you, Mr. President, and I will interpret for him. Would you speak with him, Mr. President?"

"Of course, put him on."

The President clapped his hand over the telephone mouthpiece and said to Wolf and Crisp with a lift of his eyebrows, "It's Yaroslav."

The saying of Yaroslov's name brought a quick vision to the President's mind. When the two leaders had met a year earlier during the President's only visit to the Soviet Union, he had been mightily impressed by this clever man who was from the same region as Stalin. Only in his early fifties, he was highly educated and totally dedicated to Communism and the cause of the Soviet Union. Yet his knowledge about world affairs was really better than the President's. The President well remembered his easy smile, and icy blue eyes which pierced as well as perceived.

As the Chairman of the Supreme Soviet began to speak, the translation immediately and disconcertingly overrode his voice. It would be the same when the President replied.

There was a brief exchange of pleasantries during which the Chairman pointed out that the President's activities had caused him to be wakened at 2:00 A.M. in Moscow time, that it was now 4:15 A.M. there, and that the Chairman was still in his night clothes. The President chuckled. "Sorry about that," he said.

Then the Chairman went straight to the purpose of his unusual telephone call.

"For the past two days, the Soviet Union has been closely monitoring the position you have taken against Canada, Mr. President. We understand the position in which the United States finds itself and we can understand very well the reasons why you decided to give Canada an ultimatum, an ultimatum that could have been enforced by economic sanctions which would have brought Canada to her knees very quickly.

"Instead, you have moved to take over Canada by force, and to annex it to the United States. Unfortunately, Mr. President, this is a course of action which the Soviet Union finds totally unacceptable. Under no circumstances can we tolerate the sovereign presence of the United States in the Canadian Arctic Islands. To have your military installations in Alaska is bad enough, but to find you in a strategic position from which you can hit easily at the vital parts of the Soviet Union across the polar icecap from Ellesmere or the other Arctic Islands by aircraft or by ballistic missiles, this represents a power shift and a threat to the security of the Soviet Union which, as I have said, Mr. President, we find totally unacceptable."

The President broke in. "Mr. Chairman, we have no intention whatsoever of using the Canadian Arctic Islands for military purposes. All we want is the gas."

"That may be your intention at this instant, Mr. President, but your intentions can change at any time – to say nothing of the intentions of your successor, whoever he may be and whenever that event might occur." This last shaft was designed to let the President know the Chairman was aware of his precarious re-election position.

"To occupy Canada militarily for a short period of time is one thing, but to annex Canada and to make it part of the United States is quite another. No, Mr. President, your action against Canada is one the Soviet Union cannot live with, even though my intelligence people inform me that the Canadians, by ingenious planning and by out-thinking your military people, have led your flies into a net of spider's webs.

"I would guess that at this very moment you and your advisors are grappling with the elusive problem of what you should do next. I am sure the Canadian Prime Minister will have a suggestion or two for you in that regard, and that you will hear from him very soon, if you have not already done so. But the Soviet Union has a suggestion for you, Mr. President, and I put it forward in the strongest possible terms. On behalf of the Soviet Union, I suggest that you forthwith agree to stop the movement of your ground troops and to remove your military aircraft from Canada. I ask that I might have your response to this suggestion within the next fifteen minutes, Mr. President. I know you will wish to consult with your advisors and the time I have given you is short, but you have put me in an untenable position. Your ultimatum to the Canadians and your action to enforce their refusal to comply has left me with no choice but to give *you* an ultimatum.

"To demonstrate that the Soviet Union is serious about this course of action, Soviet submarines from the best and largest fleet in the world, equipped with long-range nuclear warhead rockets, are at this time surfacing just beyond the twelve-mile limit offshore from every major American city on both the eastern and western seaboards, and there are others with them which will not surface.

"This is a confrontation, Mr. President, but it is not of our making. We did not expect that the United States would take a military action against Canada, but nevertheless, like the Canadians, we planned for that eventuality. Therefore, our submarines are in position."

The Chairman paused, waiting for a response from the President. It came. "I don't believe you'd start a nuclear war over this, Mr. Chairman. I think you're bluffing."

"I can assure you, Mr. President, that I, like the Canadians, am not bluffing. And also, please carefully note that I have not yet said that my submarines *will* attack, nor have I threatened you with war. What I have demonstrated to you is that the Soviet Union is totally ready for this crisis. Not only is the United States not ready, but you have suffered a humiliating defeat and loss of face at the hands of the Canadians. As I have said, I wish to have the courtesy of a response to my suggestion of withdrawal within fifteen minutes. May I have your assurance that I will hear from you in that time?"

The President responded reluctantly. "You'll hear from me," he said.

As he hung up the President looked at Crisp and rasped, "Go tell the Pentagon to halt our troops in western Canada immediately. If they have engaged the Canadians, have them disengage. They are to withdraw to the United States as quickly as possible."

Irving Wolf interjected. "Surely you're not going to capitulate so quickly. We can do a massive para-drop and really go into Canada with full air support this time . . ."

"That's the way we should have done it in the first place," the President retorted, "and now we've got the Soviet Union on our backs. No, Irving, I've made up my mind. We have no choice but to pull out. I'm going to salvage those men and planes sitting on Canadian airfields."

The hot line telephone rang again. Reaching for it, the President muttered, "It's got to be Porter this time." It was.

There were no pleasantries or formalities.

"Mr. President, Porter here. I now have all your transport aircraft and your airborne troops. I regard them as hostages, not prisoners of war. If you mount a further attack on us, I will have no choice but to destroy them where they sit. I can assure you that's the last thing I want to do, but if I have to, I will.

"If you agree to stop and withdraw your ground troops in western Canada and not to mount a further attack, then on those conditions I am prepared to negotiate with you for the natural gas you need. I can do that under the mandate of the resolution the House of Commons passed this afternoon."

The President asked, "And if I agree not to attack again, what then?"

"If you are prepared to negotiate, and not to attack again, then I propose a meeting on neutral ground, commencing next Monday. The neutral ground will be the French islands of St-Pierre et Miquelon in the Gulf of St. Lawrence, which will be handy for both of us – that is, if the French government will agree to play host and I believe they will."

The President, who had been standing from the beginning of his conversation with the Chairman of the Soviet Union, sat down heavily on his swivel chair, leaned back, and looked up at the ceiling, not seeing it.

"Okay, so if I agree not to mount a further attack, and agree to immediately stop and withdraw my ground troops in the West, and if I agree to negotiate, what about my men and aircraft on your airports – your hostages as you call them?"

"Simple," the Prime Minister replied. "If you agree to these conditions–and I am prepared to accept your word for it now–then immediately I am advised by my Chief of the Defence Staff that all of your ground troops have crossed back into the United States, I will release your transport aircraft and your men with them."

The President leaned forward in his chair. His Texas drawl became pronounced and his voice relaxed slightly. "Well, Prime Minister, we Texans sure know an ace when we see one. And you've got it. In fact, so far as I can see, you're holding all the cards. Okay, I'll agree to negotiate on the terms and conditions you've stated."

Robert Porter was delighted, and his voice showed it. "Good. I'll get in touch with the President of France immediately, and my External Affairs Minister will be in touch with Mr. Wolf to work out details for the St-Pierre et Miquelon meeting.

"And by the way, the Chairman of the Soviet Union called to confirm what was going on and to tell me he was going to have a word with you about sovereignty, security, and submarines. It sounds as though you got his message. When you call him in the next few minutes, Mr. President, please tell him how much I appreciate his intervention."

The President slammed down the receiver.

Ottawa
Tuesday, October 7, 1980, 10:09 P.M.

The Prime Minister was in his office in the East Block of the Parliament Buildings. The military had tried to persuade him and his government to take up quarters and administration in the war emergency underground building, but Porter had emphatically declined. Events had moved far too rapidly from the first sign of American military action for him to be any other place than in his East Block office, next to his red hot line telephone and his direct line from the Chief of Defence Staff. The same facilities existed in the emergency war building, but the Prime Minister would have no part of it. The military were operating from that location. That was good enough for him.

It was 10:09 and he was alone in his office stretched out on the sofa where he had been for about half an hour. He had suddenly felt extremely fatigued and decided that he should put his head down for a few minutes. He had asked his close friend, Senator John Thomas, and his Defence Minister if they wouldn't mind setting up shop in the outside office where they could take all incoming calls for him, with the exception of calls on the hot line or from the CDS. He had turned out the lights in the office except for a small lamp on his desk. A pillow and blanket had been produced by his secretary. He was asleep as soon as his head hit the pillow. He hadn't moved.

The first ring of the telephone brought him up to his feet

312

and striding quickly toward his desk. It was the direct line from the Chief of the Defence Staff. Adamson launched right in. "Sir, the last of the United States ground forces in the West have crossed back over the border as of this moment."

The Prime Minister had still been a bit groggy during the CDS's first words, but now his mind was totally alert. "Excellent, General, excellent!" he exclaimed. "Now I authorize you to release all the American transport aircraft to return direct to their home bases . . . and General I'll have more to say about this later on, but I can't tell you how grateful I am to you and your team for pulling off this incredible miracle. It's nothing short of fantastic."

Adamson's response was a quiet "Thank you, sir."

The Prime Minister went on. "Now, one final thing. I've got to get in touch with Pierre de Gaspé. I need him at the St-Pierre et Miquelon negotiations. When I started to gather my negotiating team for that one earlier this evening, I discovered that de Gaspé, as well as being the president of Petro-Canada, is also your Toronto District commander and is running Operation Reception Party at the Toronto International Airport."

The CDS responded, "He's an exceptional man, Prime Minister, there's no question about that. I'll find out where he is at this moment. He's somewhere at Toronto International and is in touch with the commander at Mobile Command at all times. Somebody from my staff will get back to you shortly."

De Gaspé left the control tower for a quick tour of the hulking United States airfleet strung out along the entire outside perimeter of the parking ramps of both Terminals One and Two. The monster craft were outlined vaguely by the distant floodlights from the terminal buildings. Their service engines whined away providing electrical and other control facilities in each aircraft and enabling radio contact to be maintained at all times. Lights were on in the fuselage and as well in the flight deck of each aircraft, but all navigation and landing lights had been extinguished.

As he drove up to the aircraft of Blueforce leader, de Gaspé could not overcome the urge to stop, see, and exchange words with the American General. He pulled his VHF radio-equipped Ministry of Transport car up in front of the leader's aircraft, stopped, and got out, with the car's radio microphone in his hand. He was on tower frequency. Looking up – he guessed probably about three stories in height – to the lighted cockpit where he could see the sitting, waiting figures of men. De Gaspé spoke into the microphone.

"Blueforce leader, this is Reception leader. Do you read? Over."

He could see movement from the captain's seat.

"Blueforce leader, go."

"Good evening, General Smith. I've just done a tour of

314

the airfield to visit my commanders and thought I should come by and pay my respects while we wait for our governments to make up their minds about what they're going to do next."

A startled de Gaspé was instantly bathed in a blinding white light which took him a few seconds to adjust to. The General opened his side cockpit window and stuck his head out. Against the strong landing lights de Gaspé couldn't see him all that well, but well enough.

The crew-cut American General looked grim as he said through his radio transmitter in his now unprofessional southern accent, "Ah didn't know you Canadians had that much gumption, but ah sure know it now."

Even though he was the victor, the responsibility for the death of two hundred of the General's men weighed heavily on de Gaspé. "Perhaps when this skit's finished," he said, "and you're all safe and sound back in your big bird's nest—maybe we can have a drink together sometime and figure out what *really* happened tonight."

The General's reply was blocked out by an urgent transmission from Walnek in the tower.

"Reception leader, General Christie is standing by waiting for your return call. He would not give me the message but says it is most urgent, most urgent. Over."

"I'll be there in five," de Gaspé responded crisply.

With a wave to the American General, de Gaspé climbed back into the car and was off at high speed, lights flashing, bound for the control tower on the far side of the airport.

As he bounded into the control room, Walnek handed him the telephone, "General Christie's on the line."

De Gaspé was slightly short of breath from the climb up the stairs and paused briefly before he said, "Yes, sir."

"Pierre, the Americans have completed their end of the deal and have pulled out their people in the West. The

Prime Minister has authorized the immediate release of all USAF transport aircraft, their crews, and passengers."

De Gaspé beamed into the telephone. "That's fantastic. I'll inform my captive southern General, Blueforce leader, and turn him loose right away."

"Right. A signal has gone out to all our other commanders across the country so all the Americans will be heading out at the same time. I wanted to call you personally Pierre, because you're the only commander who was forced into taking a shot at them. I wanted to give you the word myself, and also to let you know how pleased I am with the way you handled things. It took a lot of guts, and believe me, the unanimous opinion around here is that you've got them."

Christie did not give him a chance to respond.

"One final thing, the P.M. was astonished to find that a) you're in the Reserves, and b) that you're the military commander at Toronto International. He thinks you're supposed to be riding an oil or gas pipe somewhere as president of PetroCan. I think it was an awful shock for him when he found out where you were and what you were doing. Evidently he wants you on an emergency basis to talk about the arrangements for the meeting with the U.S. President and his staff at St-Pierre et Miquelon."

"Yes, I heard about that part of the deal."

Christie closed off. "He'll be calling you about ten-thirty. Keep the line clear. Again, great work, Pierre!"

De Gaspé hung up and immediately reached for the VHF microphone.

"Blueforce leader, this is Reception leader. Over."

"Blueforce leader, go."

"I have some news, Blueforce leader. The Prime Minister has just authorized the release of your aircraft and passengers. My instructions are that you are to be airborne as quickly as possible and you are to return directly, repeat, directly, to your bases or to the original point of pickup of your passengers or cargo."

The pleasant southern voice came back immediately, "Roger, Wilco, Reception leader."

A further caution from de Gaspé. "And my troops will maintain their alert and weapons coverage of you until you are airborne and out of range."

"Roger." A pause. "Blueforce leader to all Blueforce aircraft. Start engines, start engines – go. I will call for a start-up check in five. Out."

It was Walnek's turn. "Toronto Tower to all Blueforce aircraft, after your start-up is completed and you have been checked in with your leader, stand by, stand by for taxi instructions. Do not acknowledge at this time."

As the start-up procedures began, the twinkling, flashing green and red navigation lights came on once again. The pulsating strobe lights and red beacons atop all aircraft appeared, flashing their special signal that each aircraft was coming alive. Then as the huge engines of the aircraft started up, de Gaspé could see one, then another, then another of the angry yellow-bluish-green exhaust flames emerging from the jet exhausts then disappearing to a quiet bluish light as the engines settled down to an idle burn. And as the engines started up, the initial whine turned into a vibrating, thunderlike noise.

"Blueforce leader to Blueforce, check in, check in. Go."

De Gaspé and Walnek could hear the aircraft check in in sequence. They all reported start-up.

When the last one had called, Walnek was ready.

"Toronto Tower to all Blueforce aircraft. All aircraft parked to the east of the easterly edge of Terminal One will use Runway 23 Left for take-off. All aircraft to the west of that line will use Runway 32. Proceed to taxi in your own

317

sequence and take off at your own intervals when ready. After take-off, maintain visual watch for other aircraft–there are too many of you for Toronto departure or radar to handle. Normal ATC* clearance is waived. On take-off go to Rochester Approach Control, on 119.55. I will repeat, I will repeat, because I cannot ask acknowledgements from you."

With that, Walnek repeated his entire message, at the end of which the southern voice returned.

"Toronto Tower, this is Blueforce leader, we copy your instructions which are . . ." And he then repeated them, giving Walnek confirmation that the leader had it right and giving the aircraft commanders a third opportunity to hear.

"Blueforce leader moving out now, moving out now."

Slowly and deliberately, the mass of air machinery –dull, almost invisible objects in the darkness but illuminated partly by their own lights–began to move in two solemn processions along the ramps and the taxiways toward the runways assigned to them.

Another instruction from the General: "Blueforce leader to all Blueforce aircraft. Once airborne, you will proceed independently to the point of original pickup of your passengers or load."

As the General's aircraft approached the button of Runway 23 Left on Taxiway Alpha, Walnek transmitted to him.

"Toronto Tower to Blueforce leader, you're cleared for take-off. The wind is slightly on your tail at zero two five at fifteen. You're cleared for a left turn out on course. The lead aircraft on Taxiway Delta for Runway 32, you also are cleared for take-off and for left turn out on course. All aircraft following in sequence are clear to go without any further clearance from this tower."

*ATC – Air Traffic Control.

Through the clear windows of the control tower, completely dark except for the dim blue illuminating lights, de Gaspé could hear and feel the thunder of the massive jet engines as they went to full thrust and power. Blueforce leader's troop-loaded Starlifter moved ever faster down the runway to its rotation speed, then lifted off the ground smoothly, gracefully, just opposite the button of Runway 32, where Blueforce 28 was swinging onto the runway, landing lights switched on, then rolling for take-off.

For the next twelve minutes, the clear night air for miles around the Toronto International Airport was filled with the continuous vibrating roar from the huge jet engines of the Starlifters and the screaming turboprop power plants of the Hercules as they rushed like a flock of frightened big birds to escape from a place of sudden danger.

As the last aircraft was rotating on liftoff from Runway 32, Walnek answered the telephone, then handed it without a word to de Gaspé.

His eyes still following the lights of the climbing machines, he said, "De Gaspé here."

It was a familiar voice. "Pierre, it's Tom Scott. The P.M. wants to have a word with you. Hang on."

In a moment Robert Porter came on. His voice was that of a happy, confident man.

He opened good naturedly. "Pierre, for God's sake, how many hats do you wear? I go looking for the president of Petro-Canada to tell him I need him immediately to start organizing the meeting with the President, and where do I find him? He's my military commander at Toronto and the key man in the success of Operation Reception Party!

"Even though I've known you for years, Pierre, I had no idea you were involved in the military, but I can tell you that tonight I'm delighted you are. You know, if it hadn't been for the Reserves, we would never have done it."

"May be, sir," de Gaspé replied. "But on the other hand, let's face it, it's the Regular Force, small in number as they are, who've kept it all together since Korea. We've worked Reception Party as a team with them and with the Brits."

"True, true," the Prime Minister agreed, then changed his tone. "I want to talk with you about the meeting at St-Pierre et Miquelon, Pierre, but before we get into that, what's going on at Toronto International? Are there still American aircraft on the ground there?"

"No, sir. The last one was airborne just as you called. I can still see him." As he talked, de Gaspé turned to look out the control room windows to the north, then to the west and south. "I can still see him and the nav lights of – I guess maybe twenty of his buddies, all hightailing it in different directions back south of the border."

The Prime Minister's voice sounded subdued for a moment. "I still can't believe they attacked us. It's just incredible. What's even more incredible – in fact, it's just ridiculous – is that this sort of thing could happen at all. The Americans have taken us for granted for so long – their Presidents never come here, their Secretaries of State rarely come here. They really don't know anything about Canada. It's a goddamn shame. However, they did it. The thing I really regret is that you had to destroy those two aircraft."

De Gaspé was on the defensive immediately. "I had no choice, sir."

"Pierre, I know that. I wasn't being critical. I was just saying that I regret it had to be done. I agree with you. You had absolutely no choice whatsoever. Were there any survivors?"

"None, not even from the one on the ground. We'll start the cleanup operation right away."

They had arrived at the reason for the Prime Minister's call.

"Well, I'm afraid you're going to have to leave that for somebody else to handle, Pierre, because I want you up here in Ottawa right away. We've got only four days to get ready for the St-Pierre et Miquelon meeting with the President. When we meet with that bastard, we've got to be prepared.

"I want you here in my East Block office at eight o'clock in the morning. I've instructed the Chief of the Defence Staff to release you from your command. There'll be a Jet Star in at Downsview at six in the morning to pick you up."

In the now quiet darkness of the control tower, de Gaspé could see the lights of vehicles converging on the area of the blown-up transport aircraft, but his mind was still totally on the conversation with his Prime Minister.

"I'll be there, sir."

"And Pierre, I've got one final thing to say to you. It may sound somewhat un-Canadian."

De Gaspé was startled. "What's that, sir?"

"I'm goddamn proud of you."

Hôtel Île-de-France, St-Pierre et Miquelon
Tuesday, October 14, 1980, 10:00 A.M.

It took a lot to get Pierre de Gaspé nervous. At this moment, he was.

The Prime Minister had asked de Gaspé to backstop him in presenting Canada's position on the various transportation modes which would have to be considered before deciding which one or which combination would carry the urgently needed natural gas from the Canadian Arctic Islands to the energy-short American market.

Part of his mind recorded the sight as he looked around the vast new dining chamber of the Hôtel Île-de-France now being used as the conference room for this historic confrontation, while the other part of his mind worked over the facts, figures, and approach he and his assistants had prepared and the Prime Minister had approved.

The huge chamber was of typical Norman-French design, solid stone and mortar laced with wooden beams against a high white ceiling, elaborately carved heavy doors, and a highly polished wooden floor. At the end of the room, at de Gaspé's left, just behind the seat of the chairman at the head of the U-formed conference table, an elegant, superbly carved stone fireplace dancing with flame threw its welcome into the chilled room, a place which would become much warmer as the negotiations progressed.

The chairman had not yet entered the room, but three of his staff of four were already seated at their places on each side of his chair. Nor had the Prime Minister of Canada or the President of the United States arrived.

The seat to de Gaspé's immediate right was empty, waiting for the Prime Minister. The remainder of the chairs on the Canadian side were filled by the Minister of Energy, Mines and Resources on the Prime Minister's immediate right, then the Minister of External Affairs. On de Gaspé's left was the chairman of the National Energy Board, Kenneth Atrill, who had been appointed by the Prime Minister only six weeks before. His background as Deputy Minister of Energy in Alberta had failed to prepare him for the major burden of carrying out the preparation and conduct of these most difficult negotiations with the Americans. The Prime Minister had seen that his most reliable advice would have to come from Pierre de Gaspé, and that the new NEB chairman would not resent that confidence.

De Gaspé made an observation to Atrill, "Thank God there are no press permitted at this meeting." He got an agreeing nod from Atrill, then looked across to the men seated at the opposite wing of the conference table.

To right of the still-vacant chair of the President sat Irving Wolf, elbows on the table, nose between the index fingers. On Wolf's right, the heavy-jowled, rotund head of the U.S. Federal Power Commission, a man who had said absolutely nothing on the first day of the conference but had chosen to scribble notes and pass them through the Secretary of State to the President–if Wolf thought they were worthy of passing.

On the left of the President's place was his energy czar and then the Secretary of the Interior.

Sitting to the immediate rear of each of the negotiating teams were their staff people, ready to provide their masters with instant statistics, information, charts, maps, photo-

St-Pierre et Miquelon

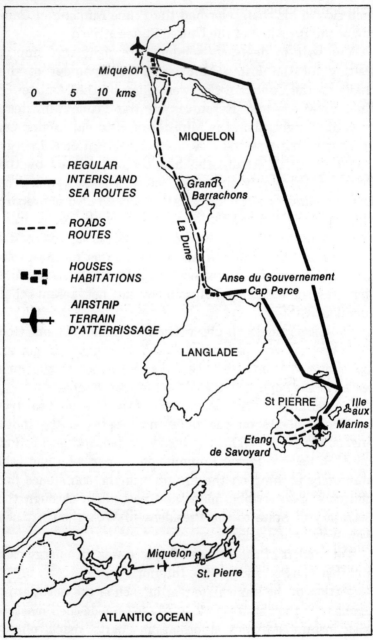

324

graphs, and sometimes their opinions–whether they were asked or not.

It was cold in the dining chamber of the Hôtel Île-de-France on October 14, 1980, the second day of this crucial conference. The question for the day was the building, location, and financing of a transportation system to carry natural gas to the United States from the Canadian Arctic Islands.

The proceedings of the first day had been chaired by the Foreign Minister of France. During that opening session, both the Canadian and United States leaders had been cool and almost hostile toward each other, but during the give and take of debate a new, well-founded regard for each other's ability had developed.

The first subject matter of the negotiations had been resolved by the end of the opening day. The United States would have access to 50 per cent of the natural gas discoveries in the Canadian Arctic Islands at a wellhead price of slightly under $1.00 U.S. per a thousand cubic feet. This was an effective Canadian price of $.89 C. because by the fall of 1980 the Canadian dollar had risen 11 per cent in value above the U.S. dollar.

Suddenly the talking among the waiting conference participants abruptly ceased as all eyes turned toward the double-doored entrance to the room. Immediately there was the sound of scraping chairs as to a man they stood as three men entered the chamber together. As he ushered them forward toward the conference table, the man in the centre held with his left hand the arm of the President of the United States, and with his right hand the arm of the Prime Minister of Canada. To the surprise of Pierre de Gaspé and all except the French participants, the man in the centre was not the Foreign Minister of France, but the enormously successful President of France, who was just finishing his first term of seven years and who soon would begin his campaign for re-election.

The President of France, Valéry Giscard d'Estaing, tall, elegant, and still young at fifty-five, released his two colleagues as they approached the conference table. Each went to his designated seat and sat down. The second day of the conference got under way. The French Foreign Minister, who had followed the three into the room, took the chair immediately on the right of his President.

When everyone in the room had settled down, the President of France began.

"Monsieur le Président, Monsieur le Premier Ministre, there is no doubt that I have caught both of you off guard by arriving just a half hour ago without notice. As I have already explained to you and will now say to all members of the conference so they will understand, I thought it my high personal duty and responsibility to each of your magnificent countries, Canada and the United States, and to their people with whom the people of France have historically had the closest of connections and good relationships, both in peace and in war, in times of plenty and in times of adversity, that I should attend."

In his deliberate and forceful way, President Giscard d'Estaing alternated his gaze from the Prime Minister to the President as he spoke.

"Much of France dwells in Canada, not only in la belle province de Québec, but throughout the rest of the nation as well, where there are now some seven million French-Canadians of descent from stock which came from Normandy, Brittany, and the Basque country at the very time that these islands, St-Pierre et Miquelon, were first inhabited in the days of Jacques Cartier. That these two small islands are a part of France and not a part of Canada is almost a miracle and is a source of joy to all of France."

326

Then a wry smile. "On the other hand, the fact that these two islands exist in this location and are part of France within the North American complex will come as a matter of complete and total surprise to the close to 250 million people who populate your two magnificent countries." Knowing smiles from all in the chamber greeted that remark.

"Gentlemen, the nature of the dispute between your two nations, the military methods that have been used, the ramifications of those actions, and the results of this conference are of enormous importance to the Western world and its stability, both political and economic. They are of such consequence that I personally deem it of the highest order of importance that the matters between you be amicably resolved. This is why I immediately agreed with your request, Mr. Prime Minister, that this conference might he held on these islands, on neutral ground, even though the notice could scarcely have been shorter. It is for the same reason that I have put aside all other business of state and have come here to participate in this the second day of this meeting."

The long solemn face of President Valéry Giscard d'Estaing broke into a smile as he said, "Well now, gentlemen . . ." Out and on came his glasses as he picked up the sheet of paper in front of him.

He proceeded.

"The prime matter for discussion today is the transportation mode for the movement of the natural gas from the Canadian Arctic Islands to the United States market between the Boston/New York sector of the eastern seaboard and the Detroit/Chicago sector of the Midwest."

The white-haired President from Texas turned to have a brief whispered conversation with Irving Wolf on his right, then, looking at President Giscard d'Estaing, said, "Monsieur le Président, I would like to speak to this matter and outline the position of the United States if I may?"

The President of France looked to the Prime Minister, who nodded his head in assent.

"Please go ahead, Mr. President," said d'Estaing.

The President did not read but referred to his notes as he went on.

"What we're talking about here is the movement of natural gas in large quantities over a straight-line distance between 2,500 and 3,000 miles, over some of the worst terrain, most difficult climate conditions, and most prohibitive water and ice crossings to be encountered on the face of this earth. The need of the United States for this precious commodity is beyond question. The shortage of it even at this point in time has been of disastrous consequences for my country, so bad that they were able to move me and my administration toward an attempted annexation of Canada, an action which has brought us to this table. I might say Monsieur le Président, that it was an action I did not want to take against our good friends, the Canadians, but under the circumstances I felt, as President of the United States, that I had no choice. My attitude is reflected in the fact that our military action against Canada was probably one of the least warlike demonstrations of an invasion ever recorded in the books of history!"

The Prime Minister sat back and smiled.

The President was obviously ill at ease. "The United States must have that natural gas as quickly as we can get our hands on it. On the other hand, we must balance the time requirements against the cost of delivery. If we build a pipeline system – and as you know, Monsieur le Président, I've just been up to the Arctic Islands and I have seen a new method of laying large natural gas pipelines in the water under the thick ice that exists there – then it's going

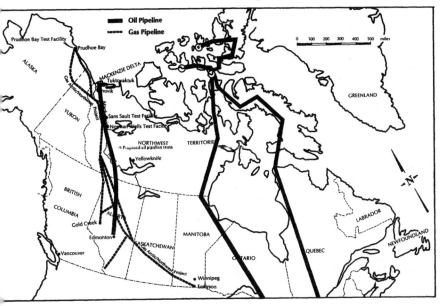

to take us another three years to lay pipe. It will have to go from the principal source of supply, Melville Island, east to Cornwallis Island, and then south through Somerset Island and the Boothia Peninsula, and either down the west coast of Hudson Bay through Manitoba and Ontario into the United States, or, in the alternative, east from the Boothia Peninsula, through Baffin Island and down through the province of Quebec and then into the United States.

"There may be some alternative methods of moving the natural gas sooner, but those methods, all of them, are very costly and their economics can't even touch a pipeline once you get it laid."

The President laid down his notes, took off his glasses. "On the basis of the advice of my experts, Monsieur le Président"—he looked to those seated on his left and then to those on his right and smiled—"and I could tell you sometimes I wish I didn't have any experts and I wish I hadn't taken their advice ... anyway, my experts advise me that on the basis of the success of the under-ice experiments in the Byam Channel between Byam Martin Island and Melville, and on the basis of long-term economics, we will support the building of a pipeline from the Canadian Arctic Islands to the United States.

"While the pipeline is under construction, we'll just have to suffer as we have in the past. And I have to say this, if the Canadians had responded earlier by three or four years, the American people wouldn't be in this terrible crisis, we wouldn't have people freezing in the cold, we wouldn't have factories shutting down!"

Robert Porter bristled, colour coming immediately to his face. De Gaspé thought he was going to go after the President.

Instead, the Prime Minister kept his temper and conciliatory position. He said, "Monsieur le Président, as the President very well knows, my party and my government have been in power for only a short period of time. I understand his feelings of frustration in having to deal with the former government of Canada. But I must say I resent his trying to put on my shoulders the responsibility for negligence, default, or failure to give the United States what it needs in natural gas. If we're going to get anywhere in this bargaining, Monsieur le Président, I would respectfully suggest through you to the President that, before he starts another battle, he must understand he has just lost a war."

The President rose to the bait. "Now see here, Porter! Goddamn it . . ." He shook his fist in Porter's direction.

President Giscard d'Estaing intervened immediately. "Now gentlemen, please. I understand all the issues, all the emotions, but the question is what shall the transportation mode be? Mr. President, you have stated your choice in no uncertain terms." D'Estaing turned to Porter. "And what does the Prime Minister have to say in response?"

Robert Porter leaned forward on the conference table, left his operating file closed and referred to no notes. He looked at Giscard d'Estaing during his first few words, then turned to look the President of the United States in the eye. "Monsieur le Président, let me say that from the very beginning of the energy shortages in America, we in Canada have been and are very sympathetic to the crisis in which the people of the United States find themselves. The fact that the President as Commander-in-Chief of the United States Forces attempted a military annexation of Canada, failure though it was, has profoundly impressed me and my Cabinet and everyone in my nation. Fortunately, the people of Canada look upon that action as the act of one man, in isolation from the reality of the wishes, desires, and aspirations of the great people of the United States." Porter addressed the next remark to the President. "One would have thought, Mr. President, that the example of your immediate predecessor who took that kind of remote position might have been enough to stop you from taking military action against us."

Now it was time to be conciliatory.

The Prime Minister turned his head to address his remarks to the Chair. "Monsieur le Président, having said those things, let me say to you that not only do I understand fully the urgent need of the United States to have an enormous new supply of natural gas at the earliest possible moment, I also comprehend the American and, in particular, the Texas oil and gas people's love affair with the pipeline. All of them in the oil business, every one of them, is so enchanted with the pipe you'd think it had hair around it!"

There were a few snorts around the table at that remark. Porter paused for a moment.

"There are other methods of moving natural gas from the Arctic Islands. I'd like to review them very quickly before I state Canada's position on the President's proposal."

The President of France nodded his head in agreement, at which point Porter, for the first time opened his file and referred to his notes.

The American President leaned back in his chair, his hostile attitude somewhat diminished by Porter's apparent softening of attitude.

Wolf was taking notes.

Glasses now in place, Robert Porter said, "Monsieur le Président, I shall be very brief for the simple reason that the President and his advisors are fully aware of what the alternatives are. But it is necessary to state them for the record.

"If a pipeline is not used, then the alternative must be either submarine, aircraft, the lighter-than-air craft, or the tanker. Using any one of these four modes or any combination of them requires that the gas be liquified, that is to say, be reduced to 260 degrees below zero Fahrenheit. The liquid gas then must be placed in special, uncontaminated containers which also hold the cold. It is in these tanks that the commodity is transported.

"The lighter-than-air craft has many grave shortcomings as a long-distance or, for that matter, even short-distance hauler of bulk commodities especially in the Arctic where ice can be easily picked up on the surface of the craft."

The President of the United States, a skilled, experienced airman, nodded his agreement to that remark.

"In addition, they have relatively small payload and handle poorly in substantial winds. Nevertheless, a great deal of research has been going on with the dirigible particularly in the Soviet Union and in the United Kingdom. Even so, I would discount this vehicle for a high-volume, twenty-four-hours-a-day, reliable movement."

He waited for an objection from the President. There was none.

"The next is the submarine. General Dynamics Corporation of the U.S. have had on the drawing boards and in the experimental works for many years now a system of submarines of about 150,000 tons deadweight which could operate under the icepack in the Canadian Arctic Islands. They would take on their LNG* loads at special stations under water and under the ice, moving them out to open water ports at the eastern end of the Northwest passage, to ordinary LNG tankers which would take the commodity to designated American ports where it would be offloaded, gasified, and fed into normal domestic pipeline transmission systems.

"The next mode is the aircraft. Boeing has in production the huge resources carrier aircraft which is now committed to moving crude oil from Melville Island across to Prudhoe Bay where it is fed into the enlarged pipeline transmission system from Prudhoe Bay to Valdez, then into tankers for trans-shipment to the western seaboard of the lower United States. That aircraft, which has a pay load of over 2.3 million pounds, could also be readily adapted to a liquid natural gas movement following the same route."

President d'Estaing interrupted Prime Minister Porter. "You speak of a route which is not across or through Canada. I should have thought that you would want to utilize your own land mass for such a system?"

"Your point is well taken, Monsieur le Président. If I may, I will come back to it in a moment.

"There is already in existence a new but relatively small fleet of special Boeing 747s, which are freighters designed

*LNG – liquid natural gas.

333

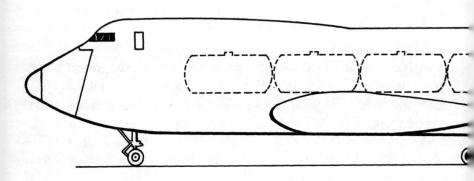

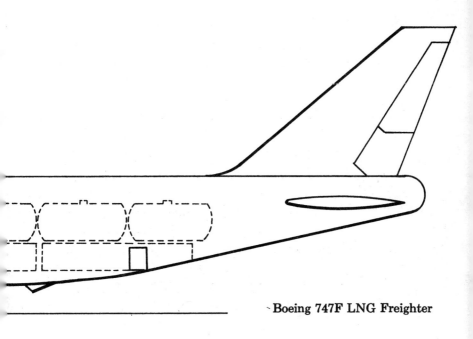

Boeing 747F LNG Freighter

specifically to carry liquid natural gas. These units are committed to a domestic Canadian movement of gas from King Christian Island where it is liquified and flown to an open water port on Devon Island at the east end of the Northwest Passage. There is is transferred into Class 10 ice-strengthened liquid-natural-gas tankers and then carried south through the Hudson Strait into Hudson Bay and James Bay, where it is discharged at a new deepwater harbour called Jamesport on the west coast of James Bay about thirty-five miles north of a place called Moosonee in northern Ontario. There the LNG is gasified, stripped of feedstock ingredients–there is a new petrochemical plant at Moosonee for that purpose–and the gas put into the normal distribution system for the southern Ontario/Quebec markets.

"The 747s operate in the system for the five winter months of the year when ice conditions in the Canadian Arctic Islands are such that not even Class 10 strengthened freighters can get through. The ice conditions coupled with total darkness make ship navigation impossible. There are six Class 10 LNG tankers in this system. The shipyards of the United States, France, the United Kingdom, and Japan could turn out many more in quick order.

"At King Christian Island, the gas liquefaction plant in operation there was constructed in the United States, assembled at Newport News on a specially designed series of barges and was successfully towed into the Arctic Islands and into position a year ago last summer–1979."

The U.S. President's patience was beginning to wear a little thin. "What are you going through this long shopping list for? We're prepared to build and pay for a pipeline system direct from the Arctic Islands. We'll do it ourselves. All *you* have to do is give us the right-of-way."

The Prime Minister shook his head in disagreement. "If

it were to be a pipeline, Mr. President, that pipeline would have to be owned and controlled in Canada and its construction and financing would have to be done by Canada. That would mean using your money and other world money in debt form. We'd have to bring it into Canada. And if we go for the pipeline, we have several other basic problems. The first is another settlement with the native people whose lands lie in its path. Then we would have another confrontation with those concerned about the damage to the ecology. And then there is the competition between Quebec, on the one hand, and Manitoba, on the other, for the pipe to come through their territories. In other words, a pipeline would be a divisive interest in a country which is already hanging together by its fingernails ... although I must say, Mr. President, that your unhappy attempt to annex us last week has done wonders for national unity."

The Prime Minister turned and addressed his remarks to President Giscard d'Estaing. "Monsieur le Président, the reason that I have been going through the shopping list, as the President puts it, of alternative modes of transportation of natural gas from the Canadian Arctic Islands to the lower United States is simply that Canada cannot tolerate any further upward pressure on its dollar. That dollar has already been driven to $1.11 against U.S. currency, largely because of the infusion of foreign capital into Canada for the purpose of building the Mackenzie Valley pipeline. Of the $10 billion total capital requirement for that venture, $6.72 billion was spent in Canada for goods and services.

"In addition, over $8 billion has been spent on the James Bay project in the province of Quebec since 1973; some $12 billion for synthetic oil plants in the Athabaska Tar Sands in Alberta; and, in that same period of time, approximately $9 billion for nuclear generating plants for electricity and

337

the heavy-water plants that go with them.

"The financing of this enormous capital investment has been through the money markets of the world. This input of foreign capital into Canada, when taken together with a continuing substantial trade surplus brought about by our sale of raw natural resources, has put our dollar in a high position. As a result, our secondary industries, our manufacturing firms whose goods must now be bought in the world market place at $1.11 U.S., when the same product can be bought from the United States for $1.00, are now priced right out of the market. We've faced with the shutting down of plants across Canada and unemployment in large scale at a time when our economy ought to be booming."

Robert Porter was speaking calmly, confidently.

"My advisors tell me that, in their opinion, if a pipeline is built from the Canadian Arctic Islands to the American border, the cost of it has got to be somewhere in the neighborhood of $12 billion and that the resultant strain on manpower, equipment, services, and supplies would drive prices even higher in Canada in a period of continuing escalation. But even more important, our dollar would very likely rise to $1.25 U.S. within the next two years. This would be totally unacceptable for Canada and would bring about the collapse of the industrial and manufacturing segment of our economy and destroy our grain and agricultural export markets.

"I'm sure the President and *his* enormously skilled advisors know exactly what I'm talking about."

The President remained silent.

The Prime Minister continued. "For all of these reasons, Monsieur le Président, the position of Canada is straightforward and simple. The United States can and will have access to the natural gas in the Canadian Arctic Islands, but the transportation system designed and built to carry it out of that region must be one built and paid for outside of Canada, whether that transportation system takes the form of submarines, aircraft, liquid natural gas tankers, or a combination of all of those modes.

"Furthermore, the gas liquefaction plants must also be built in some country other than Canada. The money for the capital expenditures for this transportation system, whatever form it takes, must be foreign capital and it must be expended in countries other than Canada.

"Tankers, aircraft, and submarines can be brought on stream and put into operation much quicker than the pipelines. Since time is of the essence for the people of the United States, who so desperately need the natural gas, I would have thought that the modes other than pipelines would have been highly attractive to the President."

The Prime Minister concluded. "For these reasons, Monsieur le Président, it is the position of Canada that a pipeline to deliver natural gas from the Canadian Arctic Islands to the lower United States cannot be permitted. On the other hand, we will do everything in our power to facilitate the development of port, navigation, air, and other facilities necessary to assist the United States to mount and operate a sea/air transportation system."

Robert Porter sat back in his chair, leaned toward Pierre de Gaspé, and asked if there was anything that he should add. In de Gaspé's opinion there was not.

The President of the United States remained silent for a few moments, contemplating the astute young Canadian Prime Minister across the table from him. This was not the time for a snap response.

The President did not ask advice of his people.

Finally he turned to Giscard d'Estaing and said, in his slowest Texas drawl, "Monsieur le Président, as I told you before this meeting started, I am in the middle of my re-election campaign and I must get away from here as fast as I can. I'm committed for a big kickoff dinner in Houston tonight, and I've got to stop at the White House on the way through to deal with urgent business."

The President of France nodded his head knowingly, a man in complete sympathy whose own re-election campaign days were not too far away.

"Yes, I could sit here and wrangle with you, Prime Minister, over these issues for the next two or three days, but I just haven't got the time and also it doesn't make sense. What does make sense is for me to recognize Canada's economic position and the danger of further erosion of its economy by driving the Canadian dollar up further. I can see that clear as a bell.

"And you're right. The oil company people do look at pipelines as if they had hair around them. It's time they changed their thinking and their pressure on people like me.

"Well, you've given us access to the natural gas up there in the Arctic, and you've set a reasonable wellhead price, and I think it's only fair that we go along with your transportation position."

Irving Wolf pulled at the President's sleeve, but was waved off. The President wished to conclude.

"The United States is most grateful to you, Monsieur le Président, for your most helpful, soothing presence at these important proceedings and for making this neutral meeting place available on such short notice. The friendship of the great people of France has always been and will continue to be treasured by the United States."

Then facing Prime Minister Robert Porter and at the same time standing up, the President said, "And Prime Minister, I would be less than honest if I didn't say to you that you have my admiration and respect, the respect of a

Texan, for the way you've handled yourself, not only today, but also during the events of last week. I only regret that I fell into the trap of all my predecessors in taking you and Canada for granted and not making a real effort to come to you and talk before I acted."

The United States
October/November, 1980

Immediately after leaving the St-Pierre et Miquelon conference on October 14, 1980, the President of the United States
had gone back to the campaign trail, travelling throughout
America claiming he had solved the natural gas shortage by
putting the Canadians over the barrel.

His challenger was the bright, articulate Senator from
Michigan, David Dennis, whose political base was in the
membership of the United Auto Workers of America. He
had served the interests of the auto workers as a hard-
bargaining labour lawyer during all of his remarkable professional career until politics – first as the Mayor of Detroit
and then as Senator – had taken him out of the practice of
law.

Dennis had taken the other side of the energy issue and
the confrontation with the Canadians, saying that the President got no more out of the Canadians by attacking them
than he Dennis could have done by accepting their perfectly reasonable offer to negotiate; the President had
humiliated America in the eyes of its own people and in the
eyes of the world by attempting to take Canada by force
and – what was worse – by failing.

David Dennis won the election.

Like the man he defeated, Dennis was tough and a hard
negotiator. A lean, lightly-built person of medium height,
the new President moved with agility and quickness. His

appearance and presence were commanding. His long, narrow face was dominated by deep-set almost grayish eyes and a head of black fringe-graying hair. His swarthy complexion provided a background to the magnificent white teeth which were often displayed by a man who smiled a great deal and enjoyed doing so.

David Dennis was a superb orator and a man who came across extremely effectively on television.

Dennis, the experienced politician, accepted as his political Golden Rule the principle attributed to Mahatma Ghandi. Ghandi's statement—and he used it often—was "There go my people. I must follow them for I am their leader."

David Dennis was indeed the new leader of the people of the United States of America.

He was also their first Jewish President.

The negotiations with the native people had gone well, a
money settlement being arrived at similar to that of the
U.S. government with the native people in Alaska, but in
higher amounts. They would get $750 million in cash, sixty
million acres of land in the Mackenzie Valley corridor, the
Mackenzie Delta, and the Yukon; and a further $750 mil-
lion to be paid out at the rate of a 2 per cent per annum royalty on gas and oil production from the area over a period of
years. The money would go to co-operative corporations,
owned and controlled by the native people according to
their regions, with the proceeds to be used as they saw fit.
The land would have to be selected by each co-operative
group but could not include the pipeline rights-of-way or
any roads or railway lines routes currently planned for the
future. Any lands designated by the native people would be
subject to expropriation by the Crown for the purpose of
constructing roads, railways, or other transportation or
communication facilities as are all other land holdings in
the rest of Canada. These negotiations had been successfully completed by mid-January, 1981.

It was at this time, with the native settlement question
out of the way and off the Prime Minister's mind, that
Pierre de Gaspé decided it was the moment to approach
him with the proposal for the take-over of Exxon.

The time was right.

The Americans had been sent home with their tails between their legs. The Canadian people were on top of the world and ready to take on anybody. The economy was booming. Substantial new crude oil discoveries continued to be made in both the Canadian Arctic Islands and the Mackenzie delta. Petro-Canada was expanding its exploration activities, but still had not been able to get into the business of refining and marketing petroleum products. De Gaspé desperately wanted to have refineries for the crude oil that Petro-Canada was producing as well as buying from off shore. But all such facilities in Canada were in the hands of the Big Six.*

If Petro-Canada could get into the retailing of fuel oil and gasoline, it could act as a competitive Canadian force to hold prices down. There was mounting public concern that the oil companies were ripping off the consumer. Gasoline in Ontario had gone from 69/70¢ a gallon in 1974 to $1.05 in 1981.

The next step in de Gaspé's thinking was rather than build a vertically integrated oil company, why not buy one. What better candidate for purchase than his old alma mater, Exxon Corporation, the biggest, the largest, the most powerful, and one which he knew well—the people at the top, the method and style of operation, its holdings throughout the world. His prime objective was to get his hands on Imperial Oil Limited, Exxon's Canadian subsidiary. Imperial was the major integrated oil corporation in Canada. It would be the ideal vehicle for Petro-Canada to control, but, in de Gaspé's judgment, the only way to get at Imperial Oil was for Petro-Canada to marry and carry off Imperial's parent, Exxon.

In the late afternoon on January 23, 1981, de Gaspé had

*Imperial (Exxon), Gulf, Texaco, Sun Oil, BP, and Shell.

345

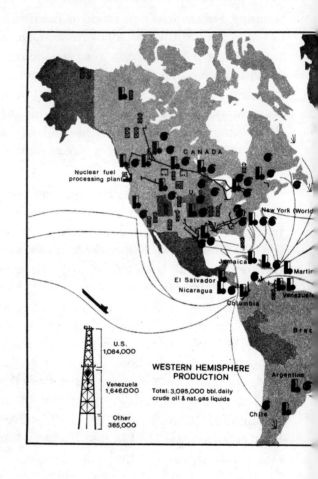

Nuclear fuel
processing plant

CANADA

U.S.

New York (World

Jamaica

Martir

El Salvador
Nicaragua

Venezuel

Columbia

Braz

Argentina

Chile

U.S.
1,084,000

Venezuela
1,646,000

Other
365,000

WESTERN HEMISPHERE
PRODUCTION

Total: 3,095,000 bbl. daily
crude oil & nat. gas liquids

346

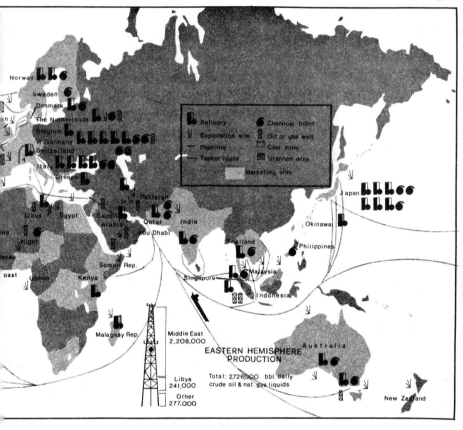

EASTERN HEMISPHERE
PRODUCTION

Middle East
2,208,000

Libya
241,000

Other
277,000

Total: 2,726,000 bbl. daily
crude oil & nat. gas liquids

347

met with the Prime Minister in his office in the East Block of the Parliament Buildings. De Gaspé had opened by saying, "Prime Minister, I propose that Petro-Canada do a take-over bid on Exxon."

The Prime Minister, totally astonished, had responded, "Exxon? Pierre, you must be out of your mind."

"Maybe I am, but let me put my case to you, then make your decision."

The Prime Minister laughed, "Go ahead, but I think I should have a sedative before you start."

De Gaspé took from his briefcase two copies of his memorandum on Exxon. He handed one to the Prime Minister, who said, "I don't want to look at this. You tell me what the deal is and if I'm interested, I'll read it."

Porter leaned over, flicked on his intercom switch, and said, "Joan, hold my calls for the next few minutes, please. Okay, Pierre, now tell me all about Exxon. Exxon?!"

Pierre de Gaspé was very relaxed with the Prime Minister. Their friendship, which began at the time Porter first entered Parliament, had grown during Porter's time as Prime Minister. They had continued to see a great deal of each other, since certain major elements of Petro-Canada's policy-making process were in the hands of the Cabinet.

De Gaspé began. "First, let's look at why we should buy. Ever since the October war between the Egyptians and the Israelis back in 1973 and the resulting crude oil embargo, crude oil prices on the world market have gone up to fourteen dollars a barrel. The corporate profits of all of the major oil companies have escalated enormously. Sure, they'd had periods of low return, but the high prices of gasoline against enormous profits all combined to put the oil companies in a pretty bad light. And instead of holding the line, they've continued to jack up their prices, despite the fact that the cost of product in Canada has not escalated.

"Now, as you know, all of the vertically integrated major retailing oil companies in Canada are foreign owned. Five are owned in the United States and the sixth, BP, is owned in the United Kingdom. That means that the major policy decisions of all of these companies, including Imperial Oil which is Exxon, are taken at the foreign head office. I know the protests we get when we say this, but it's a fact. The major decisions of Imperial are made at the Exxon building in New York, including the appointment of Imperial's chairman and president.

"If Petro-Canada is to be an effective arm of government policy in keeping gasoline and fuel oil prices competitive, then we've got to have control in Canada of one of the major retailers. If oil company prices get out of line, we can put our product on the market at levels that will force the others down, but at the same time allow them a reasonable profit.

"So, my first reason is that PetroCan and Canada need to own or control one of the major gasoline and fuel oil retail companies.

"If the principle is accepted, then we've got two ways to go. One is to build and develop our own marketing company. That would entail buying service station sites, building our own stations, and developing the entire infrastructure. It would take an enormous effort and a long period of time.

"The other route is to take over one of the existing majors. I've examined the availability of the Canadian operation of all of them and, short of expropriation or nationalization—which you have said is unacceptable—the only way to go is by take-over bid on a foreign parent.

"Another reason for PetroCan's acquisition of a major Canadian oil company—let's call it Canadian at this time even though it's American owned—is that almost all of them are engaged in exploration work in the Mackenzie Delta, the Canadian Arctic Islands, Alberta, and offshore on the east coast. They're either alone or in partnership or in farm-out arrangements. PetroCan's exploration program, which is a development of Panarctic's original position, is doing very well, with continuing major gas discoveries and, more recently, the oil on Melville. But to have ownership of the wells and the exploration work and techniques of Imperial would be of enormous domestic assistance to Petro-Canada's objectives. And of course, Imperial is the largest retailer of petroleum products in Canada. If it were controlled by PetroCan, its marketing would have a profound influence on pricing practices throughout Canada."

The Prime Minister nodded in agreement. "Yes, the points you make are good ones, not bad at all. But what about Exxon itself? Why should we get involved in a worldwide operation such as theirs? . . . I think I know the reasons myself, and they already sound attractive to me, but let me hear what you think, Pierre."

"All right. If Canada buys Exxon, you automatically have control of an oil and chemical company that trades around the world from the position of an empire unto itself. Exxon has, in effect, a diplomatic interface with practically every country on this planet. It uses that interface for its own corporate purposes and also to further the interests of the United States. Clearly, that's the name of the game everywhere. In my opinion . . ."

The Prime Minister broke in. "It's your opinion I want, Pierre."

". . . Exxon, as a multi-national worldwide Canadian corporation would enhance our prestige everywhere. It would give us contact points in countries where even our External Affairs people aren't represented. And speaking of the External Affairs department, to have the Exxon trade-mark with a maple leaf in the centre of the "O" spread out throughout the United States, Europe, the Far East, and everywhere else Exxon operates would probably make them pick up their socks–and God knows they need it. I can remember back at the beginning of the seventies trying to get External Affairs to put an ambassador into Kuwait and one into Saudi Arabia and the rest of the Middle East countries. But no, they accredited our ambassador to Tehran to those countries much to the anger of the Arabs, who couldn't understand why Canada didn't know that the Iranians were not Arabs. For them the fact that our Ambassador to Tehran was also accredited to the adjacent Arab countries was a terrible insult. It still is."

De Gaspé checked with his memorandum. On to the next point. "On a worldwide basis, the cash flow from Exxon will be sufficient to do a pay-out of the acquisition cost plus carrying charges in less than ten years."

The Prime Minister stood up, turned, and looked out the window behind his desk, with his hands shoved in his pockets, he thought about the matter for a few moments.

Then he turned to face Pierre de Gaspé and said, slowly, "You know, Pierre, that's quite an idea. But tell me, how much is it going to cost?"

"We're going to have to find $20.5 billion to get 50.1 per cent. We'll have to borrow $14.5 billion of that outside Canada."

The Prime Minister was aghast. "My God, where can we find money like that?"

Pierre de Gaspé was ready. "I have a plan, sir. It's in the memorandum, and if you'll give me a minute, I'll go over it with you."

De Gaspé went over the figures carefully with the Prime Minister. When they were finished, Porter looked up and said, "I like it, Pierre, but there's no way I'm going to make a decision on that one all by myself. Give me a shorter memorandum—even a handwritten one. Security on this will have to be tight. Don't make it any more than two pages if you can help it. Let me have it. I'll get my key people in Finance; Treasury Board; Energy, Mines and Resources; Industry, Trade and Commerce; and the Bank of Canada. I want you here, too. We'll sit down and kick it around." He checked his diary and with Tom Scott. "Right. We'll meet tomorrow morning at eleven o'clock—here."

De Gaspé had prepared his memorandum. The meeting had been pulled together as promised. He had been grilled for three hours. The result was unanimous: an enthusiastic approval of his scheme for the financing and execution of the Exxon take-over bid.

With the go-ahead approval wrapped up, de Gaspé moved quickly.

Obviously, financing was his first problem. There was no way he could look south across the border into the United States for that commodity. He had to go east, across the Atlantic to Switzerland and do business with the gnomes of Zurich.

Zurich
Thursday, March 12, 1981, 3:15 P.M.

By mid-afternoon on Thursday, March 12, 1981, a typical, misty drizzle had settled over Zurich.

Pierre de Gaspé looked out from his high hotel window across this grey, sombre city, the legendary home of the bankers known around the world as the "gnomes of Zurich." He was waiting impatiently for the international operator to report on his urgent telephone call to Canada.

During the past week, he had been negotiating with Swiss bankers on a continuing, almost around-the-clock basis. As the days had moved along, he had finally narrowed his discussions down to one, Credit Swiss, an ancient, conservative banking institution with enormous reserves and ready access to U.S. dollars.

This was not a conventional attempt to borrow. As president of Petro-Canada, his task was to arrange firm banking commitments to lend funds to Petro-Canada with its principal shareholder, the government of Canada, as guarantor.

At two o'clock that afternoon in the elegant, walnut-panelled office suite of Kurt Reimer, the president of Credit Swiss, the negotiations had been successfully completed with the signing of a memorandum outlining the basic terms of the deal that would give Petro-Canada and de Gaspé access to more than enough capital to finance the Canadian take-over of Exxon, the largest multi-national oil corporation in the world.

Immediately after the signing of the memorandum of agreement and a jovial celebration drink and toast with Kurt Reimer and his banking colleagues, de Gaspé had hurried to the privacy of his hotel room so he could report by telephone to the man who was his main supporter in the execution of this most grandiose of all take-over schemes.

De Gaspé had had several discussions with Robert Porter during the past few days when he needed instructions and advice. Because of the absolute need for maximum security, de Gaspé had taken on the negotiations single-handedly and, for the time being, had by-passed his own board of directors to deal directly with the Prime Minister.

At this moment, his jubilant euphoria at having pulled off this enormous financing deal made him tense and fidgety as he waited for the Prime Minister to call back. When the phone finally rang, de Gaspé leaped for it.

"We are ready with your call to Prime Minister Porter in Edmonton, Canada," the operator reported.

"How are you making out, Pierre?" came the clear, strong voice of the Prime Minister.

De Gaspé's response was loud and enthusiastic. "Terrific, Prime Minister. We've got a deal! It's done! We've just signed the memorandum of agreement."

The Prime Minister was delighted. "Congratulations, Pierre. Frankly I didn't think you'd be able to do it. You've been working against some of the best negotiators in the world for what has to be the biggest amount of money ever borrowed in one package. Now, if you can pull the rest of this deal off, it will be the greatest coup in financial history. It will be marvellous for Canada. Just incredible. What are your plans now?"

"I have to be back here in a week, next Thursday. The formal documentation will be ready for checking and signature by then. That'll give me time to get back to Canada to report in detail to you—"

Porter broke in, "And my Cabinet committee—"

"... and your Cabinet committee and to my own board of directors. My target is to be in Edmonton by Sunday night. I'd like to see you first thing Monday morning, sir. Is that possible?"

"I'm not sure, Pierre. I'll leave word for you at your hotel. Where will you be staying?"

"At the Château La Combe."

"Okay. Now, what does your timing look like on the take-over bid?"

"Well, the funds will be available to us whenever we're ready to go—that looks to me like a target date of the first of May. I'll need that kind of time to organize my legal documentation, set up both my Canadian and U.S. fiscal agents, prepare the documents for filing with the Securities Exchange Commission, and also finalize with the Canadian bankers."

The Prime Minister agreed. "You'll need that kind of time—no doubt about it. The House of Commons will be back in Ottawa by then. Just as well, because there'll be a hell of a commotion when we let this one go."

"You better believe it!" de Gaspé laughed. "I'm off to London now. I just might do a little celebrating tonight."

"Why not," said Robert Porter. "After all, it isn't every day that a fellow arranges to borrow $14.5 billion. Your pals at Exxon are going to go right out of their minds the day Canada bids to take them over. See you here Monday morning."

Pierre de Gaspé knocked gently on the door of the Prime
Minister's suite in the Macdonald Hotel in Edmonton. Rob-
ert Porter had arranged to see him after breakfast at 9:30.
He would be able to see de Gaspé for an hour.

The door was opened by Tom Scott, the Prime
Minister's principal secretary. The two men exchanged
familiar greetings as Scott took de Gaspé's coat. They
moved into the suite's main sitting room which had been
turned into an office area with desks, filing cabinets, telephones, stacks of files and papers, and three secretaries, two
of whom were attractive young things, a fact not missed by
Pierre de Gaspé as he took in the scene. The third was a
rather senior lady, grey-haired, glasses, plump, with a pleasant warm face, Joan Michaels, the Prime Minister's long-
time secretary who had been with him through thick and
thin. After de Gaspé's words of greeting with her, Tom
Scott explained the set-up.

"The P.M. is using the bedroom over on the right as his
private office. We've had the bed taken out, and a desk and
telephone and all the other good things installed temporarily. His own personal suite is the Royal Suite at the end of
the hall on this floor. As you can see, we've got teletype, television on a closed circuit with Ottawa through the satellite
Anik IV, and in his office we've got the red hot line telephone which puts him in touch with the usual people on the
international map."

Scott checked his watch. "He should be along in about ten minutes, Pierre. He's meeting with the Cabinet in the sitting room of his own suite which is doubling as the Cabinet room. We've got a long table set up. It's working very well. He didn't tell me what you're seeing him about. Sounds to me like a deep, dark secret."

De Gaspé smiled lightly, "Yes, it sure is a deep, dark secret and I hope to hell it stays that way until we have a chance to put it all together."

He waved his hand in a circular motion, around the room, and asked, "Tell me, Tom, how is this concept of a mobile House of Commons working out in practice?"

Scott's head nodded positively. "It's going very well. Much better than I thought it would and I think a lot better than the P.M. had hoped for." He took de Gaspé by the arm, "Come on, let's go into his office, we can sit and have a chat for a minute before he gets here."

Scott led the way, asking one of the younger secretaries for coffee, which was quickly produced for them after they had settled down in Porter's office.

De Gaspé was well versed on the theory which brought the House of Commons to Edmonton for the first of many sittings at major regional cities across Canada. Porter had persuaded the Commons that 114 years after Confederation it was time to make some drastic changes in the form and style of Parliament without going through tedious efforts to obtain amendments to the British North America Act.* It seemed that changes in the B.N.A. Act could never be brought about because of a continuing inability to get the provincial governments together on a common ground with the federal government.

Porter's "Mobile House of Commons" concept did not

*Appendix II, page 451

require any change to the constitution. What it needed to bring it off was a little imagination, some inconvenience, and the unlocking of the House of Commons from the hallowed and never-challenged belief that it should sit only in Ottawa.

Tom Scott continued. "As I said, it's going very well. There've been some communications gaps but nothing really serious. The ministers and deputies can keep in constant touch with their offices in Ottawa and their staffs there. We have a closed-circuit television net which allows them to deal directly with their own people virtually face to face. The telecommunications system is good and so are the telephones, obviously. So they've been able to keep up and keep on doing business with no problem at all. In fact, I think they're having a ball."

De Gaspé was curious. "And what about the press reaction?"

"Well, by and large, an excellent reception." Scott had a pleased smile on his face. "And the people of Alberta seem to think it's great. We've also got many Members of the House, particularly those from Ontario, Quebec, and the Maritimes, who've never been to the West. I can tell you they're getting their eyes opened in this city and in the surrounding region. They've been out looking at the gas and oil fields. They've been into the Rockies. They've talked to people. It's been quite an experience and I think one hell of a good one."

Without warning, the Prime Minister entered the office, moving quickly, as usual. Pierre de Gaspé jumped to his feet as the two men greeted each other warmly, the Prime Minister enthusiastically patting de Gaspé on the shoulder while shaking his hand.

"It's great to see you, Pierre, or maybe I should call you moneybags."

He laughed, "Not yet, Prime Minister. We've got the money but we haven't bought anything."

"Well," said the Prime Minister, directing de Gaspé to a chair opposite his desk, as he went around it to take up his own seat, "there's only one person in Canada who can put this deal together. You're it. And frankly, I'd have been damned disappointed if you hadn't pulled it off in Europe."

The Prime Minister turned to Scott who was still standing and said, "Tom, I wonder if you'd leave Pierre and me alone. We've got one or two important things to discuss that I don't want to bother you about at this time."

Scott smiled, said, "Yes, sir," and promptly left the room, shutting the door quietly behind him.

The Prime Minister leaned back in his leather swivel chair and said, "Well now, Pierre, I want to hear all about the Zurich exercise and your big deal there." A knock on the door signalled the production of coffee.

De Gaspé gave Porter a comprehensive detailed report on the negotiations, the memorandum which had been signed, and an outline of the next steps and the pattern toward launching the take-over bid on Friday the first of May.

When Pierre was finished, Porter said, "All right, I want you to be prepared to make a presentation to the . . . what I call the 'take-over' committee of the Cabinet. I don't want any more than the gang you met with earlier to have any knowledge of what's going on. That's the Ministers of Finance; Energy, Mines and Resources; Trade and Commerce; President of the Treasury Board; Governor of the Bank of Canada. And again, nothing in writing.

"I suggest you give us this briefing immediately after you've settled your arrangements with both your Canadian and American fiscal agents. You'll need their opinions on the bid price and the layout of the finalized scheme. When you have that information, that'll be the time to talk with us and we'll give you a final 'go' or 'no go.'"

The Prime Minister took a sip of coffee. "When do you think you'll be back to me?" he asked.

De Gaspé thought for a minute, pulled out his diary, stuck on his glasses, plowed through the pages, and announced, "The twenty-sixth–ten days from now. It won't take too long to get both the Canadian and U.S. fiscal agents organized. I've laid out a plan of action I think they'll probably buy anyhow."

The Prime Minister snorted. "Knowing you, I'm sure you've got the whole thing set up in a way that they'll be happy to follow."

"I do my best," de Gaspé replied. "If you can give me a time during the twenty-sixth, I'll set up my own PetroCan board for a meeting in the afternoon or immediately following your Cabinet meeting."

The Prime Minister reached over to flick his intercom button and said, "Tom, March twenty-sixth–what does ten A.M. look like for a one-hour meeting."

The response was immediate. "It's okay, sir."

"Good. Line up Finance, Energy, Treasury Board, Trade and Commerce, Bank of Canada–just the Ministers and the Governor of the Bank. No one else, please."

"Yes, sir."

Porter turned back to de Gaspé. "That's it, Pierre, you're on. It's organized."

"One final thing, Prime Minister, the Canadian agent I propose is Fry Mills Spence Limited. If you have no objection, I'd like to use them."

The Prime Minister smiled, "You have my blessing. The Fry Mills firm, like all financial houses in Canada, is politically acceptable if you understand what I mean."

De Gaspé returned the smile. "I knew they were when I

asked them if they'd be prepared to take part in a large deal – subject to your approval.

"And in the States, Morgan Stanley has been the fiscal agent for both the government of Canada and Exxon Corporation so they couldn't act because of a conflict. In my view, there's only one logical candidate and that's Merrill, Lynch, Pierce, Fenner and Smith. They've got the background and institutional contacts; they're spread right across the country, and they're international."

"Press on, Pierre, the Canadian oil industry needs some Exxoneration," he laughed, "if I may be permitted the privilege of coining a word."

Toronto
Tuesday, March 17, 1981 8:00 P.M.

De Gaspé shut the door of his Royal York Hotel suite behind the first of his two visitors. As Paul Zimet was hanging his coat in the hall closet, de Gaspé apologized to him. "Sorry to drag you out for one of these long evening meetings, Paul, but I have no choice as you'll soon find out. I've got one more person coming I didn't tell you about—Hubert Peters of Merrill Lynch."

Paul Zimet's eyebrows lifted in an involuntary show of surprise. In the investment fraternity the best know the best, and as a senior vice-president of Fry, Mills, Spence Limited and one of Canada's top oil investment experts, Zimet knew them all.

"Good Christ, Pierre, you must really have something hot going for you to bring Peters to Toronto," he said. "He's got to be top dog in the United States in oil securities. Why the hell would you have him here?"

De Gaspé chortled, "Eat your heart out, Zimet. You don't know what I've got up my sleeve, and neither does Peters. But when I'm finished with you people tonight, you'll have been through one of the great evenings of your lifetime. I guarantee you'll be in a state of shock."

"Try me," quipped Zimet, as he made his way to the conference table temporarily set up in the middle of the sitting room.

At that point, the legendary Hubert Peters arrived to be greeted by de Gaspé who then introduced him to Zimet.

The balding Peters, with his portly contours and hanging jowls, presented quite a contrast to the youthful Zimet, whose reddish-blond hair was stylishly cut and whose eyes were clear and alert. Peters, in his late fifties, looked a mess, but his facile, experienced brain was in fine shape.

"I can see you're wondering what Zimet is doing here, Hubert," de Gaspé said to him. "Well, I can tell you he was wondering the same thing about you. I have an idea you're going to see quite a bit of each other in the next few weeks, if what I have in mind is acceptable to both of you. Well, gentlemen, shall we sit down and get going."

De Gaspé took the head of the table. To his right he had a blackboard set up so any of them could explain a point graphically but without leaving any record.

"Now then gentlemen, in the folders I have here," and de Gaspé patted the stack by his right hand, "I have all the basic information on the world's largest multi-national American controlled oil company – Exxon.

"I have carefully checked out both of your firms, and I am satisfied that there is not conflict of interest which could be raised if you agree tonight to act as agents for Petro-Canada, backed by the government of Canada, in a take-over bid on Exxon. That is why I have brought you here – to ask if you will act as our agents. You've already taken a pledge to secrecy. What I want to ask you now is whether either one of you is aware of any impediment which would prevent your firm from acting."

Zimet asked in an astonished tone, "Exxon? Are you sure you don't mean Imperial Oil?"

"No way," de Gaspé replied. "I mean Exxon – which obviously includes its 70 per cent interest in Imperial Oil."

Hubert Peters was stunned. He said, "I know the Exxon situation inside out. Do you have any idea what a take-over bid would cost? How much of the stock are you looking for?"

"I'll come to those questions when we've got the answer to the question I put to both of you. I'll put it another way. Is there any reason why you could not act as agents, and if there is not, are your prepared to act? What about it, Paul?"

Paul Zimet had regained some of his cool. "The answer, Pierre, is there is no impediment to our acting. We would be privileged to be a part of the deal."

De Gaspé was pleased. "Excellent," he said. Then he turned to Peters. "And what about Merrill Lynch?"

Hubert Peters looked uncomfortable. He hesitated, then said quietly, "We are prepared to act as your agent in the United States. There is no impediment I'm aware of that would prevent us from doing so, but—I've got to say this—as an American I believe in my country. I think it's the finest in the world. I think Exxon is the finest oil company in the world. It's American, even though it's multinational and operates in virtually every country of the globe. So I've got to tell you in my gut I feel like a traitor to my country when I say 'yes,' but I say yes anyhow." He raised his right hand slightly in a cautionary way. "And frankly, Pierre, just another gut reaction. I think you're going to have a hell of a fight on your hands from the Exxon board—and from every goddamn politician in the United States. Well, anyhow, Merrill Lynch will act as your agent in the United States subject, of course, to knowing what the proposal is and whether we think it's a workable deal."

De Gaspé smiled with satisfaction. "I'm delighted, Hubert, and I agree with you. I think we're going to have one hell of a fight on our hands, but in my view it's going to be worth it."

Hubert Peters came right back at him, "Yeah, but why take on the whole Exxon thing? Why not just go after Imperial Oil?"

"Simple. Exxon's not about to sell its 70 per cent interest in Imperial, and the government of Canada is not about to expropriate the 70 per cent interest. Yet we want Imperial and we also want access to the world's markets for our surplus oil. With the enormous finds in the high Arctic we have an opportunity to export to western Europe, Japan, anywhere we can find a market. And the government believes that it is in the best interest of the people of Canada to have a Canadian oil-based multi-national corporation interfacing with as much of the world as possible.

"Because Exxon is so large in Canada–it predominates in our domestic market and in exploration and discoveries –it's the logical choice to go after. But again, not by expropriation or nationalization. We have to use the take-over route."

De Gaspé was emphatic. "The decision has been made to go. We've done all our homework."

Peters shrugged his shoulders, "Okay. So we go."

De Gaspé passed around the thick folders. "At the top of each of these you'll find a two-page memorandum which sets out the basic parameters of the proposal. The rest of the stuff is background material which each of you has in your own research files anyhow. What I want to do is review this memorandum with you, answer your basic questions, then give the two of you forty-eight hours to come back to me with your suggested modifications to this plan and your joint proposals as to how the bid can be successfully engineered."

Zimet and Peters extracted the material. De Gaspé waited until they were organized.

"Let me run through this memorandum quickly with you. The bid will be for 50.1 per cent of the outstanding shares of Exxon. There are presently 236,643,000 shares issued and outstanding. The bid should be at a 10 per cent premium at current market values. That puts the bid price at $170 a share. I think 10 per cent is sufficient to flush out 50.1 per cent.

"At $170 a share, 50.1 per cent will cost us $20,325,224,310 rounded to $20.5 billion plus your commissions."

Zimet exclaimed, "Jesus Christ! Where in the hell are you going to find that kind of money? That's impossible!"

De Gaspé smiled, but his voice was slightly hard as he shot back, "It's not impossible. I've got it all arranged. If I didn't have it all arranged, I wouldn't have you here.

"Petro-Canada is in for two billion; the government will put in another two; the Canadian banks will advance two; and the balance has been negotiated with the Credit Swiss Bank in Zurich and will be available in U.S. dollars as required. The background material in the file provides that information and all details sufficient for both of you to be able to assess the viability of the proposal and for your lawyers to be able to put together the necessary documents for filing with the Securities and Exchange Commission."

Hubert Peters shook his head in amazement and then turned to de Gaspé and said, "If your bid is successful, what happens to the Exxon management?"

"Good question. Again, you'll find the answer in the supporting material, but it goes this way. The existing management, top to bottom, will be invited to continue, including the current chairman. I would become the vice-chairman and the majority of the board of directors would be carefully selected Canadians. I have a slate in mind that the Prime Minister has already approved. There would be an executive committee of the board made up of five people, two Canadians, two Americans and myself. The Americans would, of course, represent the interests of the 49.9 per cent of the shareholdings that we did not take out."

Peters nodded silently in agreement.

"Over a period of time, the head office of the company would be moved to Canada. I have in mind Calgary. The current head office building in New York would become the main operations office. Through the natural growth of Exxon it would take up the sectors of the building vacated by the executive and administrative move to Calgary. It follows that the head office of PetroCan will also be moved to Calgary and be on the same site as the Exxon head office.

"But let me make it perfectly clear, this acquisition of Exxon is much more than just an investment such as the Canada Development Corporation made in Texasgulf back in 1973. If we get control of Exxon, it will mean policy-making control, control over management, and putting the corporation on a worldwide direction which will benefit Canada, the country that controls it."

General discussion went on for another two hours, during which strategy, tactics, fees, the take-over bid chain of command, banking, preparation of material for filing, lawyers and who they were to be, date of the making of the bid, acquisition of Exxon shares on the market in advance of the bid, and other questions were raised and settled.

A major decision was taken to set up a take-over bid headquarters in New York inside the Merrill Lynch office. Hubert Peters of Merrill Lynch would mastermind the preparation of the scheme and its execution in the United States; and Fry Mills Spence, while they were performing the same function for the Canadian operation, would use the New York headquarters for the co-ordination and liason necessary to bring the take-over to a successful conclusion.

"Well, gentlemen," de Gaspé said at the end of the two hours, "we're just about finished for this opening session, but remember we've got, or at least I have, a critical deadline which all of us have to meet. Nine days from now, I have to report to the Prime Minister and his take-over bid committee of Ministers to get their approval of what you people and I, the three of us, are going to put together for the mechanics of the take-over bid. And immediately following that meeting, assuming we get approval, I have to face my own board of directors.

"Now how long will it take you two to put a comprehensive plan together?"

Peters responded, "Well, I don't know about Paul, but if I can get my butt back to New York, get my hands on my research people and a computer, I can be back to you within seventy-two hours with a comprehensive plan. In fact, I don't see any reason why Paul and I can't have our joint plan ready within that period of time. What do you think, Paul?"

Zimet agreed. "From my end, the deal won't be nearly so complicated because of the few shares of Exxon held in Canada. I'll get together with our research people first thing tomorrow morning, spend the day at it, and then go down to New York tomorrow night. Then I'll move in with Merrill Lynch and Hubert."

De Gaspé was happy. "Sounds good, gentlemen. Sounds good. Let's set a time to meet back here. Say ten in the morning on Saturday, four days from now?"

"God, Saturday again," Zimet remarked. "My wife will kill me. Don't you ever spend any time at home, Pierre?"

"As a matter of fact very little these days," he said.

There was an uncomfortable pause until de Gaspé, pulling his thoughts together, said, "Now the final thing is this! Security is an absolute essential. My question is going to be, Hubert, how can we cover up or disguise the work that's going on in your offices and this whole scheme. For example, could you appear to be examining a take-over of Shell Canada which is 85 per cent held in New York, and appear to be using Exxon information for comparison purposes? Think about it."

"Sounds feasible," Peters agreed.

"If you have to have anything typed, refer to Exxon as Company Y, or for that matter, just leave the name blank. Even secretaries have big mouths. I don't have to remind you that if this deal blows because somebody in one of your firms leaks it, or no matter where the leak comes from, you people will lose out on the biggest commission ever paid for a single transaction."

As Pierre de Gaspé stood up to conclude the meeting, Hubert Peters had the parting shot, "Even brokers sometimes make a living by keeping their mouths shut. Our business is built on it."

Pierre de Gaspé looked down the long table past the faces of the full board of Petro-Canada to his chairman at the far end. All twenty-one faces showed that de Gaspé had their complete and undivided attention. He could see they had been knocked out by his request for approval of the Exxon bid, which the Prime Minister and his Cabinet committee had approved that morning in Ottawa.

This emergency meeting of the Petro-Canada board was held in a special room of the Royal York Hotel in Toronto. It was much more convenient for the board members who had to fly in from all over Canada to come to Toronto rather than out-of-the-way Ottawa. De Gaspé had come directly from his meeting in Ottawa in ample time for the board meeting which had started at 2:30 P.M.

He had first outlined to his board the arrangements made for Swiss bank financing, the participation of the government, and the take-over bid scheme (which de Gaspé now referred to as the Merrill-Fry proposal).

There had been questions—the most pointed of them coming from Senator Margaret Cameron. He now moved to the conclusion of his presentation.

"Mr. Chairman, ladies and gentlemen of the board, I've attempted in a fairly short period of time to place before you all of the background and all of the facts behind the proposed take-over bid of Exxon by Petro-Canada. This is, as I have said, the largest take-over bid in history, and it's bound to have an enormous impact, politically and publicly, in the United States. That country is especially sensitive since their humiliation by Canada last October.

"If you do approve of the proposition, the take-over bid date will begin on Friday, May first. We will need every moment of the month in between to prepare the bid documents, the filings with the Securities and Exchange Commission, and an effective public-relations program which will be launched at the same time as the take-over bid. Of course, the main focus of that program will be in the United States.

"So what I am asking for, Mr. Chairman, is approval to proceed with the take-over bid on Exxon as proposed in the material which has been submitted to you. I also ask, by the way, that none of this documentation be taken away."

The chairman nodded and said, "Thank you, Pierre." Then to the board. "Are there any further questions."

De Gaspé sat back in his chair and waited.

Senator Margaret Cameron's hand was raised instantly and recognized by the chair. She had only recently been appointed to the Senate, after her party had been defeated in the provincial election in Nova Scotia where she had been deputy premier. Not only had her party lost but she had lost her seat in the legislature as well. Rumour had it, and Pierre de Gaspé had good access to rumours in the Ottawa mill, that the widower Prime Minister, Robert Porter, had been seeing a great deal of her–some people thought in more ways than one–after they first met during the ultimatum crisis, when Margaret Cameron had represented the absent Premier of Nova Scotia at the emergency meetings with the Prime Minister.

Some people were sure that the two of them were spending weekends together, but de Gaspé didn't think that was possible. Robert Porter, while a very discreet man, was totally in the public eye and thus had no privacy at all. And if they had shacked up together, at least for any period of time, the press would have been on to it in an instant.

It had also not escaped de Gaspé's notice that Margaret Cameron was a good-looking woman, with her flashing green eyes, red hair, and pink, smooth complexion–a real Scottish beauty. "If the P.M. had privileges with her, well, good luck to him," he thought as she began to speak.

Her soft but authoritative voice brought him back from his speculation, but not before he agreed with himself on a plan. She was staying in the hotel on the same floor as he. De Gaspé had booked in for the night. Maybe she would have a drink with him . . .

The meeting had been adjourned with approval to proceed, unanimously granted by the board. Even Margaret Cameron had voted in favour, notwithstanding her cross-examination of de Gaspé as to why the take-over of Exxon would be in the public interest for Canada. Immediately the meeting broke up, de Gaspé moved as quickly as he politely could to intercept her before she left the room.

Margaret Cameron was moving toward the door by herself when he touched her arm from behind. She turned, looked up at him, gave him a broad smile, "I hope you didn't mind my going after you."

De Gaspé looked down at her handsome face and returned the smile. "Senator Cameron, you asked a lot of questions which I'm sure I didn't answer fully, or to your total satisfaction. I'd like to pursue them a little further. Having made that statement, my question is whether you would join me for a drink in the Library Bar in about half an hour."

His mock, tongue-in-cheek seriousness and formality amused her.

"Pierre, I'd be glad to take you on – if you would pardon the expression. See you in the lobby in half an hour."

Each was prompt. They went in to the darkened Library Bar where Pierre's good friend, the maitre d', Caesar, placed them in a corner side-by-side table in the softly lighted room. Two gentleman-sized martinis relaxed them. It became increasingly clear to both of them that their obvious mutual attraction was not limited to their wide-ranging intellects and common interests.

As they started on their third round of martinis, Margaret touched de Gaspé's arm gently with her right hand, then left it there as she spoke to him.

He was acutely aware of that touch. It carried a message.

"Pierre, we've talked about the Exxon bid, and we've talked about all the good things it will do for Canada, and we've talked about the future of PetroCan. But you haven't asked me how I got on the board, although you probably have guessed . . ."

Pierre's shoulders lifted slightly as he interjected. "Well, the word around is that the Prime Minister has a soft spot in his heart for you, and when you lost your seat in Nova Scotia – you know which seat I'm talking about – two of the things he was able to do for you, and one hears there might have been other things as well, were to appoint you to the Senate and to the board of PetroCan. I might say that that was one of his better movements on the day he did it, or perhaps I should say actions. Anyhow, I'm delighted because you're here and I'm more relaxed than I've been in weeks."

There was a gentle squeeze on his arm as she said, "And I'm delighted to be here also. You know, there are some rumours about you also. But what really interests me is how you got involved in this whole thing. Here you are, thirty-nine years old, tall, dark and handsome, and enormously intelligent and well educated. What made you start on this project? What is it that drives you to put together the biggest take-over deal ever?"

De Gaspé picked up his martini glass in his right hand and looked into it with a long gaze.

"I can't tell you, Margaret. It's just my nature. I can see things that have to be done, at least I think they have to be done. There are opportunities to do things, concepts which emerge, needs that have to be filled, so I go and do the things I can. It's my nature, I guess. The way my genes are put together. But I often get the feeling when I see something that should be done – something that should be built, deals that should be made – if I don't do it no one's going to do it. So I get the bug and there's nothing I can do to turn it off. I just have to do it, or at least try to do it, because I fail as often as I succeed."

He turned to look at her for a moment, and took her hand in his. "There's another thing too. As you go through life you collect certain experiences, a certain education, a certain background, and each of these things is a sort of block on which your ability to conceive or accomplish things builds. I have a hell of a lot more building blocks now than I had ten years ago and certainly fifteen years ago. I just have to use them, that's all. I just can't throw them away, or let them go to waste."

"Keep going," she said, "I'm interested. There are certain personal questions I won't ask you. But I'm interested in you and what makes you tick." She had not tried to withdraw her hand from his. As she spoke, he looked into her green eyes which danced brightly even in the semidarkness. He nodded and took a sip from his martini glass.

"I suppose as much as anything I'm interested in influencing the course of events, whatever that means. How can I have a hand in, or influence on where this country – or the world, for that matter – is going? To me that's most important. Can I do something in my work or in my profession that will be significant, that will help the people of my country, maybe even get me a little recognition or prestige in passing?"

Margaret broke in. "And to do what you've done, are doing, or what I'm doing, requires perhaps just a little bit more than a small ego, or translated another way, a small belief in one's own self and one's confidence and capability. What the hell, you've got to have confidence in yourself."

Pierre responded. "Absolutely. I want to be where the action is. I want to be in the centre of things, and why? Well, because there is satisfaction, a personal satisfaction in achieving an objective whether it's thinking up an idea or building something. It's the whole business of saying, 'My God, here's an idea – let's look at the idea. It's a good idea. And now, having had the idea, let's do it. Let's execute it.'"

Another sip of the martini.

"You know, Margaret, there are goddamn few people who have an idea and then put the idea into being, or into practice. Damn few. I've heard hundreds of people say, 'You know, I had that idea once, but I never did anything about it.' Sure, there are lots of ideas I have that I never get around to executing. One of my drives, one of the monkeys on my back, is that I'm a compulsive doer of things. If I have an idea I've got to try to carry it out. Not all of them, but most of them if they're any good at all."

Margaret squeezed the hand holding hers. "Speaking of ideas, you mentioned dinner. I think it would be a marvellous idea if we executed that one right now."

They both laughed. "Great idea," said Pierre, finishing off his martini.

An effusive Caesar escorted them the few steps to the

entrance of the Imperial Room where he delivered them into the hands of Louis, the famous maitre d' of the most elegant eating and entertainment place in Canada. Louis, an astute, discreet man, sized up the appearance of his valued client, Pierre de Gaspé, cast his eye around his vast room, then led the couple, as had Caesar, to a side-by-side table in the corner, not too far from the stage area. He seated them with the caution that he would return to make sure the service was to their satisfaction.

During the dinner, Pierre said to Margaret, "Look, I'm being personal, but one hears that your relationship with the Prime Minister is really very close. I mean there's nothing wrong with that, but if it is close—how can I put it—if it is close, is it also exclusive?"

She laughed and took his hand again under the table. "How sweet of you to ask. My relationship with the Prime Minister is a nice, comfortable one. We like each other a great deal and enjoy each other's company. It's a close relationship, but it is neither intimate nor exclusive." She paused. "Does that please you?"

He smiled. "Very much."

She went on, "And please understand that I know a lot about you. About your personal life, about your background. I've made it a point to find out, so I don't have to ask you any questions, nor do I intend to. I like you as you are, as you can tell."

After the floor show, they danced and talked about themselves.

Later as they moved from the elevator toward the door of her suite, Margaret looked up Pierre and said, "I'd like you to join me for a night cap, would you?"

"Well . . ."

"Come on now. I know you have a big day ahead of you in New York, but it's only eleven o'clock."

De Gaspé looked down into the green eyes of this most attractive woman. "What I was going to say before you interrupted me was that there is no way I would refuse your offer."

She had a fresh bottle of Courvoisier cognac, a favourite of Pierre's. There was more talk and more brandy.

He finally stood up and said, "Margaret, I really must go, it's after midnight. I have to be up at six to catch the plane for New York."

As she stood up beside him, he bent down and kissed her.

"Pierre, stay with me," she whispered.

New York City
Friday, May 1, 1981, 3:10 P.M.

It was 3:10 on Friday, May 1, 1981, as Pierre de Gaspé and his American agent, Hubert Peters, got out of their cab at the entrance to the tall, linear Exxon building on the Avenue of the Americas in New York City. De Gaspé stopped to look up along the pronounced vertical lines of the beautiful structure which housed the corporate headquarters of the most powerful, most productive, multi-national oil corporation in the world.

It was a warm, pleasant spring afternoon with an unusually clear sky above Manhattan, letting in sunlight unhampered by either cloud or smog. The glare from the windows of the top of the building where he would soon be meeting with George Shaw made de Gaspé squint his eyes.

He wondered, as he had many times before this day, what the reaction of his old mentor and now chairman of Exxon, George Shaw, would be when de Gaspé dropped his take-over bomb shell.

As he and Peters walked quickly towards the main entrance, their briefcases in hand, de Gaspé said nothing but his mind was racing with anxiety. He was, in fact, nervous. If he hadn't known George Shaw so well, and had such a close relationship with him, Pierre would have been his normal self, but Shaw's response was too important to him for too many reasons. And he knew that he was about to give the chairman of Exxon probably the biggest surprise of his life.

Having gone through two security checks and a final clearance to the executive suite on the top floor, de Gaspé and Peters were met by Shaw's secretary. She had been with him for over twenty years and was obviously, as was her boss, fond of Pierre de Gaspé. She escorted them directly to George Shaw's office where Shaw greeted de Gaspé affectionately and Peters, whom he had met during several negotiating sessions in the past, cordially.

After a discussion between Shaw and de Gaspé about their respective wives and de Gaspé's children, it was time for business. Shaw led them to the lounge area of the office rather than to his desk.

As he sat back in his special easy chair, he said, "Well now, Pierre, three-fifteen on a Friday afternoon is a bad time for an appointment, but I know that if you wanted to see me it had to be important. How can I help you?"

Pierre de Gaspé was sitting nervously on the edge of the sofa.

"George," he replied, "I want to come directly to the point. At five minutes past three, Petro-Canada, with Merrill Lynch as its American fiscal agent, launched a bid for 50.1 per cent of the outstanding shares of Exxon."

The colour quickly drained from George Shaw's face as a look of complete astonishment took over the comfortable, pleased countenance he'd worn just a second or two before. He gripped the arms of his chair and hauled himself to his full height.

He gasped, "You must be joking."

De Gaspé stood up to face him. "I'm not joking, George. A circular letter of offering has just been mailed to every shareholder of record. I'm here to inform you of the situation and to say to you that I hope that your board will regard this as a friendly take-over bid, because, George, we want your whole team to stay on. We have no intention of changing management."

Shaw walked over to his desk where he sat heavily in his chair, reached for the intercom button for his secretary and said, "Dorothy, ask Robertson to come in, please, as quickly as possible. Have him drop anything he's doing. I need him right now." Craig Robertson, another of Shaw's protégés, was now his president. They shared adjoining office suites. In a matter of a few seconds Robertson arrived and was perfunctorily introduced to de Gaspé, whom he had met years before, and to Peters.

"I thought you should hear this with me, Craig. I've just been informed by Pierre that Petro-Canada with the backing of the Canadian government has just launched a take-over bid on Exxon." Like Shaw, Robertson was practically overcome with appalled astonishment. For the moment he was speechless.

Shaw turned to de Gaspé and said, "All right, Pierre, you've told me that you want this to be a friendly take-over and you want management to stay on, but before we get into those details do you expect me to believe that Petro-Canada and the government of Canada are going to be able to find enough money to buy over 50 per cent of Exxon? I don't believe you."

De Gaspé responded quickly, as he fished into his briefcase. "The financing I completed on March tenth." He handed Shaw a document. "This is the offer which has been mailed to all of the shareholders of record. And, as you know, in accordance with the requirements of the Securities and Exchange Commission, we've had to make full and complete disclosure on all points. The offer expires at the close of business Monday, the eighteenth of May." He handed another copy to Robertson.

"Exxon has an authorized capital of 250 million common shares of which you now have 238,643,000 outstanding. In order to get 50.1 per cent, I have to buy 119,560,143. In the past week the market range has been around $155 so we're offering $170 a share. Exxon stock performance has been poor in the past two years and a lot of people will want to get out. We believe that a 10 per cent premium will be sufficient to get the offering of shares that we want. The way I see it that will cost us about $20.5 billion."

Shaw broke in, "Okay. Now, I see from the financing statement that you've got two billion from the government of Canada, two billion from the sale of shares of PetroCan and a further two billion from the Canadian chartered banks on a two-year term, and the balance of 14.5 billion from the Credit Swiss Bank in Zurich. God knows whose money *that* is."

"Maybe only God knows, George, but I've got it against the guarantee of the government of Canada and I've got it for ten years at 10 per cent. That will be bringing home a lot of American dollars."

Robertson snorted, "That's about the only good thing I can see about it." He continued, "Listen, Mr. de Gaspé, perhaps I should, but I really don't know very much about Petro-Canada, not in depth anyhow. But doesn't the government of Canada own 45 per cent of its capital stock? In other words, isn't Petro-Canada a vehicle of the Canadian government? And if that's true, isn't this really a take-over of Exxon by the Canadian government? I'm going to tell you one thing, Mr. de Gaspe,"–de Gaspé could hear the hard ring of Robertson's Boston accent–"as the president of the world's largest oil and chemical complex, an American company through and through, which has done great service to the United States, to Canada, and to the entire world, and as an American citizen, I find it totally unacceptable and completely contrary to the national interest that Exxon should be controlled by foreign nationals, let alone by a foreign government and especially the government of

Canada, a country which is very little more than an economic colony of the United States."

Robertson was hurt, angry, and insulted. He stood up. "And let me say one thing more, Mr. de Gaspé, while I appreciate the courtesy of your coming here to tell us of this take-over bid, I for one am going to call an emergency meeting of the board of directors for tomorrow morning. I don't know what George is going to do, but I can tell you what I'm going to do. I'm going to ask the board to join me in fighting this take-over bid in every way we can—in the courts and in the Congress, if necessary."

New York City
Sunday, May 3, 1981, 2:00 P.M.

The news of the Canadian take-over bid on Exxon spread across the world almost instantly, stunning financial houses, enraging the corporate élite of the United States, and titillating millions of American citizens who had grown to despise the oil companies, good or bad. The news made proud, and perhaps a little bewildered, the people of Canada. Much like the woman who thinks she has a tumor but suddenly winds up giving birth to a child, Canadians were by and large enormously pleased.

And in Exxon countries around the world, where the friendly Canadians were applauded for having vanquished the Americans in the brief but stupid military incursion into Canada the prior October, there was even more delight in seeing the Canadian David once again taking on the U.S. Goliath with every possibility of success.

This was the largest take-over bid ever attempted. Its potential ramifications, the speculation as to the reasons behind Canada's move, the effects on Exxon management, the impact on the United States and its national interests, became instant newspaper fodder and headlines.

Throughout the United States, the editorial theme was consistent from New York to Los Angeles. The Canadian take-over bid on Exxon must be stopped at all costs because it would be against the national and international interests of the United States to have a foreign government in control of Exxon. Canada's use of Exxon would be in the national interests of Canada, not that of the shareholders. Furthermore, they feared Canada would cause the company to take steps that would further the interests of the Canadian nation rather than of the United States. In the presence of the increasing reliance on foreign crude oil and the continuing massive natural gas shortages, it would be critical for Exxon and the other major American-based, multinational oil corporations to do everything in their joint power to ensure the maintenance of an adequate supply of crude oil from the Middle East, Venezuela, and other sectors of the world. It was absolutely essential to the American national interest that the United States' share of Exxon's daily world production of 7.5 million barrels of crude oil not be diverted to Canada or be under the control of Canada to be diverted as it might direct.

A major sector of the Prudhoe Bay field in Alaska was owned by Exxon as well as major finds of oil and gas in the Mackenzie delta. The latter were under the name of Imperial Oil Limited, the Canadian subsidiary of Exxon. In order not to attract the attention of the average Canadian by reminding him that the largest, vertically integrated oil company in Canada was United States-controlled rather than Canadian, a decision had been made in 1972 not to change the name of Imperial to Exxon, although that change took place virtually everywhere else in the world.

Craig Robertson, president of Exxon Corporation, stepped out from the stage wings of the Exxon building screening room which sometimes, as on this occasion, doubled as the location for a press conference. He moved quickly to the lectern at the centre of the stage where he placed the statement from which he would read.

The room was jammed with people, taping machines,

television cameras, lights. This was an important moment for Robertson, who was about to announce the position of the board of directors and management on the Petro-Canada take-over bid.

Robertson was a diminutive man, with a round face and receding brown hair. Behind his black horn-rimmed glasses, his intense, piercing brown eyes gave some indication of his quick intellect. While small of stature, he possessed a presence and self-confidence which often bordered on arrogance. The product of a well-to-do Boston family, he had never known the sting of poverty nor the cut of failure. Throughout his years in school, culminating in a doctorate in chemical engineering, he was consistently at the top of his class. During his career with Standard Oil of New Jersey, later to become Exxon, Robertson had moved from position to position within the organization leaving a superior record of achievement and accomplishment behind him. As president of Exxon Chemical Company, while also serving as a vice-president of Exxon Corporation, he had overseen the development of many new plastics and had supervised improving the quality of Exxon's worldwide chemical business.

In 1978, George Shaw, as the new chairman of the board, had reached down the line beyond his senior vice-presidents to pick Robertson to be one of his two executive vice-presidents. Then in July, 1980, when the then president of Exxon had died suddenly of a heart attack at sixty-two, Shaw had moved up Robertson to succeed him.

The two of them, Shaw and Robertson, worked extremely well as a team, but there was no question that it was Shaw who was the chairman and chief executive officer of Exxon.

As Robertson walked onto the stage, his appearance caused some chattering among the reporters, most of whom had expected to see Shaw. But Shaw, although he was now a United States citizen, had been born and raised a Canadian and so felt that Robertson should handle the press conference.

Robertson peered against the lights into the faces of the men and women, who sat poised with their pencils, pens, pads, cameras, and recorders ready. He waited a moment until the noise of discussion stopped and then began in his deep, strong voice, an unusual voice for such a small man.

"Ladies and gentlemen, on behalf of the board of directors and the senior executive group of the Exxon Corporation, I want to thank you for coming here on a Sunday afternoon when you could be out playing golf or," this with a devilish smile, "be in bed."

After the laughter had died down, Robertson went on. "The board and executive group of Exxon met in an emergency session yesterday morning and afternoon, and again this morning to work out a response to the Canadian takeover bid which was announced after the stock exchange closed on Friday afternoon. The board has authorized me to present this statement to you so the public can understand as quickly as possible, and before the stock market opens tomorrow morning, exactly where Exxon stands."

A voice from the audience to Robertson's left: "You mean, where the board of directors and the management group stand, don't you?"

Robertson tried to pick out the face that went with the voice, but couldn't do so in the smoke and lights. He replied, "Yes, that's true, but in a critical, urgent matter of this kind we have to manage in the best interests of the company just as we have to manage its day-to-day operations.

"Now if I can deal with the statement. Copies of it have been distributed. What I propose to do is go through it quickly and answer any questions."

Robertson read the statement rapidly, dealing first with

Petro-Canada's announcement on Friday and the visit of the president of PetroCan to Exxon to advise that the bid was on and that the intent was that management should remain. He then described the take-over bid as outlined in the stock offer documents filed with the United States Security and Exchange Commission. The offer was open until the close of trading on Monday, May 18, 1981, for 119,561,-000 common shares at $170 each. When he got to the meat of the statement, Robertson slowed his pace so the television and radio people could get a better audio coverage and impact. Robertson was an excellent speaker, well practiced and versed in appearing before television cameras and on the banquet circuit.

"The Exxon board and executive group are fully aware of, and in sympathy with, the national aspirations of Canada as it grows and develops and attempts to seek its rightful place as a major nation at the bargaining tables of the world. It is a country in which Exxon, through its subsidiary Imperial Oil Limited, has done business for many decades. Indeed, Imperial is the largest of all the integrated oil companies operating in Canada.

"If control of Exxon were to be taken over by an agency of a foreign government, Canada would have been our first choice because of the continued good relations between the two countries, notwithstanding the abortive and in our opinion ill-conceived attempt on the part of the former administration to forcibly annex Canada to the United States."

Robertson's voice rose as he put more emotion into his reading. "On the other hand, as the largest American-based multi-national oil corporation in the world, we believe that Exxon has a duty to more than just its shareholders. In our opinion, Exxon has a duty to the United States of America to do everything in its power to maintain ownership and control in this country so that Exxon can continue to serve the goals, objectives, and interests of the people of the United States and not be diverted from that course by the assumption of control of Exxon by a foreign government, let alone by foreign nationals."

Robertson paused for effect. "What we are concerned with is a conflict of interest between the public policy and national interests of the United States and that of Canada, the foreign nation which would control the policies and indeed the management of Exxon for its own interests and purposes. In Canada's assumption of control of Exxon, we can see a real and direct threat to the continued supply of crude oil from our fields in Prudhoe Bay in Alaska and a real threat of diversion of a fundamental source of supply in Venezuela and as well the Middle East. Exxon now has a gross production of crude oil and natural gas liquids–together with crude oil off-take under special arrangements with other producers–which averages 7,500,-000 barrels a day. Refinery runs by Exxon and its affiliates average 6,400,000 barrels daily.

"The United States is an energy-starved nation, which depends heavily upon imported crude oil and petroleum products for its existence. To have the control of Exxon's massive, daily production in the hands of a foreign government constitutes, in our opinion," Robertson's right hand, index finger pointing Kennedy style, punched toward his audience for emphasis, "a threat to the national security of the United States.

"Exxon is not above the law, yet in many respects it is comparable to a nation unto itself with responsibilities which cross borders and are carried on the seas and in the air. Our total revenues last year were in excess of $30 billion–more than the revenues of the government which wishes to take us over.

"At this time, our attorneys are examining the offering circular. There are certain representations made in that document which may be worthy of challenge on behalf of the shareholders.

"In any event, we have instructed our attorneys to make application to the appropriate United States Federal District Court for a temporary order restraining Petro-Canada from proceeding with its take-over bid on the grounds that such take-over would be contrary to public policy and the national interest. If we are successful in that application, then a further application will be brought within a few days to continue that injunction and to ask for a preliminary injunction which would last until the trial of the issue. This application will be launched tomorrow morning."

Robertson noted with satisfaction that at least three reporters had gotten up to file hot copy.

"In addition, the management of Exxon will be sending a letter to all shareholders of record advising them not to tender their shares to Petro-Canada. That letter is in preparation and will be sent immediately.

"The third step that Exxon is taking relates to the fact that the courts of the United States have historically refused to prohibit the take-over of American-based multinational corporations largely on the grounds that it would be inequitable for the United States to exclude a foreign corporation from taking over in the United States when United States corporations are doing exactly that abroad.

"The most recent example of a foreign take-over of a major United States multi-national corporation was a case not dissimilar to PetroCan's take-over bid on Exxon. This was the successful attempt of the Canada Development Corporation, a cousin of PetroCan, to buy 35 per cent of the issued stock in Texasgulf Inc., in the latter part of 1973. In that instance, the Canada Development Corporation sought to acquire about ten million shares which would have given the CDC an effective controlling interest if management had viewed the bid as friendly. Management did not so view the bid and fought the take-over in the Federal District Court at Houston, Texas. In that application, the question of a possible conflict of interest on the part of the government of Canada and the Canada Development Corporation was raised and dealt with by the judge and upheld by an appeal court. The court held that the particular acquisition of Texasgulf by CDC was not contrary to the public policy of the United States nor against the national interest."

Robertson's mouth was getting dry. A sip of water. An adjustment of the glasses.

"Since the Texasgulf case there has been much discussion about the enactment of protective legislation to prevent take-over bids against the major or giant U.S. multinationals. No such legislation has been passed. The directors and executive group of Exxon corporation and countless others across the country believe that the time has now come when it is urgent and necessary in the public interest that prohibitive legislation be enacted by the Congress.

"In the interests of time, Exxon believes that if any legislation is to be passed, it should specifically deal with this crisis and not the whole general field of take-over bids against major firms.

"To this end, the chairman of Exxon corporation is meeting this afternoon with both the majority and minority leaders of the Senate and the House of Representatives.

"You should also know that our chairman and I will attend upon the President of the United States on Tuesday morning immediately after his return from his State visit to Israel. We have reason to believe that the President will support our request for prohibitive legislation."

The President of the United States greeted George Shaw and Craig Robertson cordially and motioned them to chairs in front of his desk in the famous Oval Office of the White House.

When they were all seated, the President said, "I understand you gentlemen have been in this room many times before doing business with the President of the United States, and I'm honoured to have you here on the occasion of your first visit with me."

Shaw responded, "We are obliged to you for seeing us so soon after your return from Israel, Mr. President. I gather your State visit went well?"

The President leaned back in his chair, smiling broadly. "Yes, indeed it went well. As you know I'm not an orthodox Jew – in fact a lot of people think I'm very unorthodox." His flat, nasal Detroit accent grated on Robertson's refined Harvard ears. "But for a Jewish boy from Detroit, a boy who's come up the hard way, to arrive in Israel as President of the most powerful democratic country in the world! Such a welcome! It was almost embarrassing. And I can tell you, gentlemen, I loved it."

The smile disappeared as the President leaned forward in his chair. "Mr. Shaw," he said, "you've asked to see me about Petro-Canada's take-over bid on Exxon. My staff have kept me abreast of the events that have occurred starting with last Friday when the bid was announced, but perhaps you can bring me up to date on what it is you want of me, although I assume you want my support for the prohibitive legislation you've already asked the leaders of the Senate and House of Representatives for.

"And if you do want my support, in all fairness, I think you ought to be prepared to make a very good case as to why I should give it, because I'm not at all sure I should."

Both Shaw and Robertson were considerably taken aback by the President's attitude. They had expected him to rally to the nationalistic cause and emphatically assert his support for their proposal.

It was Robertson who reacted first. "But Mr. President, perhaps you don't understand. Petro-Canada's take-over bid is in fact a take-over bid by the government of Canada. In other words, Exxon would come under the direct policy control of foreign government, which would clearly be in a position of acting contrary to the interests of the United States. Since Exxon is the largest oil company in the world and the United States relies on our crude oil production and refining capacity – I mean, Mr. President, it is in the national interest . . ."

The President held up his hand gesturing as if to slow down Robertson. "I understand the thesis you're putting forward, Mr. Robertson. Now I'm going to play the devil's advocate, but before I do so, you must remember that I personally am going to look at the situation through a different window than you two. First of all, both of you are at the top of the world's largest oil company. You're rich multimillionaires who are responsible to the shareholders of Exxon for managing the day-to-day affairs of the company subject to policy made by the board of your firm. You're well-educated gentlemen. You've lived in the almost royal milieu of the corporate élite of the United States for more than two decades, each of you. Your responsibility is, as I said, to your shareholders, not to the people of the United States, although you are now attempting to create a responsibility to the American people in order to preserve your own management position, your own freedom of operation. In the United States you are not subject to direction or policy control by government, but you would be if the Canadians were successful in their take-over bid. You wouldn't like that and I don't blame you.

"On the other hand, that's a matter of corporate concern, not of public policy.

"The window from which I look at this scene has a different view. As you know, I'm a labour lawyer. For all of my professional career I have acted as counsel for labour unions, not for management but for labour unions in the toughest area of all, Detroit–and for the United Auto Workers in particular. My prime focus in life has been for the rights of the worker against corporate management–for the worker fighting for every buck and every privilege he can get out of the corporate élite. And so you must understand that my basic sympathies lie with the people, the workers of this country, and not with the handful of the citizenry who through private ownership or through corporations own the outstanding shares of Exxon."

The President caught Robertson's nervous look toward Shaw. "To gain my support, you will have to convince me that it is contrary to public policy and contrary to the national interest–that is to say, the interests of the people, not just the interest of Exxon and its shareholders–for the Canadians to be allowed to take control of Exxon.

"After all, Exxon and all the giant American corporations operate in virtually every country in the world. They have not been shut out except in certain places which have become violently anti-American or totally nationalistic.

Except for the Middle East—where the oil-producing countries have nationalized and taken over the oil companies' interests, including yours—you've had a pretty free hand all over the world as have all American based multi-national corporations.

"You know, if the Canadians *did* control Exxon, perhaps they'd keep their prices and profits down to a reasonable limit. A lot of Americans think the oil companies have been ripping off the public for years and that you've been working with other oil companies to control supplies and create shortages when shortages don't really exist. You know your credibility with the public is pretty low. As I say, maybe it would be a good idea to have the Canadians control one of our major oil companies. After all, every integrated oil company in Canada is American owned, except BP."

Shaw, who was becoming increasingly concerned that the President might argue himself into a negative corner, decided to attempt to change the line of discussion. He interjected, "Mr. President, it's quite clear that we've got some homework to do to convince you to support the prohibitive legislation. What we'd like to do is to come back in about a week's time and make a presentation to you and your advisors. Would you be prepared to give us this opportunity?"

David Dennis, the lawyer, skilled negotiator, and President, smiled. "Of course I would, Mr. Shaw. What I've attempted to do is to give you some insight into the kind of questions that are in my mind, not only questions, but attitudes. I think that my attitudes may well reflect those of a majority of the people in the United States.

"But instead of a week from now, why don't we leave it until the Federal Court has disposed of your application for a preliminary injunction. As I understand it, you're going to fight for the injunction on just about the same grounds you want to convince me of. So if we leave your presentation until after the court has disposed of that application, I'll have the benefit not only of your proposals to me but of the thinking of the court as well. In fact, the court might uphold your position, in which event legislation might be unnecessary, although Congress may still think it desirable."

Shaw looked at Robertson, then turned to the President and said, "That would be acceptable, Mr. President, and makes good sense."

The President looked pleased. "Good," he said. "Now, before you leave, can you tell me what steps you've taken? I know that yesterday you got a temporary order restraining PetroCan from proceeding with its take-over bid, and that the court has set next Monday, the eleventh, for the commencement of the hearing for the preliminary injunction."

Robertson said, "That's correct, sir. We expect the hearing to last ten days to two weeks. We'll be calling expert witnesses, including some government people on the constitutional issues, on the question of national security and the national interest, and on public policy. I expect that Petro-Can will be doing the same thing. In the meantime, shareholders of record are still able to tender their stock. Even though the temporary order is in effect, it does not stop the tendering of shares in response to PetroCan's offer. At this point we've found no serious defects in the representation made by PetroCan in the offering circular, so we're going to go strictly on the national interests and national security grounds.

"We have, however, sent out a letter to our shareholders advising them against tendering their shares to Petro-Canada. We've told them that we believe the current record price of Exxon shares is not realistic in view of the growing strength of the corporation and its diversified operations. We've made some new crude oil discoveries in the Mackenzie Delta which have yet to be proved up but our preliminary information indicates that our finds are going to be greater even than at Prudhoe Bay.

"We have pointed out the conflict of interest which we've discussed here this morning and have advised all of our shareholders–and most of them are American–that they should consider in their own conscience whether or not the tendering of their shares to PetroCan is unAmerican. We have advised that the board and management have concluded that the PetroCan offer is inadequate and not in the best interests of Exxon and its stock holders or in the best interests of the United States."

The President snorted, "That'll certainly make them think, but I'll make a bet with you, Mr. Robertson. My guess is that 50.1 per cent of the Exxon shares will have been tendered long before the expiry date. I hope you've been thinking about what you will do if my guess is right. Will you still proceed with the court action? Of course, the better question is, will you still want the prohibitive legislation when a majority of your shareholders are prepared to sell?"

Shaw concluded the discussion by saying, "Mr. President, we're considering those questions as any prudent businessmen would do. When we have to answer them, we will. Thank you for seeing us, Mr. President."

New York City
Monday, May 18, 1981, 12:24 P.M.

Judge Rupert Amory sat forward in his chair and tugged at his black gown. "Mr. Petroff," he said, you have informed me that your next witness will be the last one you will call for the applicant Exxon. Since it's almost twelve-thirty, I suggest the court might adjourn for lunch to reconvene at two o'clock. But before we do that there are certain matters that I would like to know about.

"First, how long do you think this next witness will take, Mr. Petroff? We've been at this for a week and I'd like to have some idea of how much longer we have to go on."

John Petroff, counsel for Exxon, rose to reply. "Your Honour, my last witness will be the president of Exxon, Mr. Craig Robertson. My estimate is that I will require this afternoon and most of tomorrow morning for my examination in-chief. My friend will probably require as much time for cross-examination but he can speak to that question."

Petroff sat down.

"Thank you, Mr. Petroff, and now, Mr. Day, how many witnesses will you call?"

Ambrose Day, the attorney for Petro-Canada, stood and replied, "Just one, Your Honour, the president of Petro-Canada who will give evidence on the background of the offer and the intent of Petro-Canada and the government of Canada in making the bid for control of Exxon. I will not call any witnesses in relation to the question of the United

States' national interest or conflict of interest or public policy because my client has instructed me that it does not wish to presume through witnesses or otherwise to argue as to the position that this court should take or indeed the government of this country should take in determining what is or is not contrary to the national interest or contrary to public policy of the United States."

Judge Amory nodded his approval, "I commend your client, Mr. Day, for a decision that is both wise and diplomatic."

The judge watched with some amusement the rapid scribbling of the host of reporters in the court room. This was news indeed.

"Well, gentlemen, it seems to me that with two more witnesses we should be able to complete this hearing by Thursday. If it is of any assistance to you, because of the importance of this matter and the urgency that a decision be handed down, I propose to have my judgment ready within five days after whatever day it is we conclude on.

"Also, I am aware of certain expressions of intention on the part of certain members of the Senate and the House of Representatives to put forward and support prohibitive legislation should the courts—that is to say, this court or any court above—fail or refuse to grant the injunction that the board of directors and management of Exxon seek. I can assure counsel that the possibility of the creation of such legislation will in no way affect my approach to the decision that I give, whatever it is."

Judge Amory paused for a moment, slipped on his glasses, took up his pen, and addressed himself to Ambrose Day. "Mr. Day, there is a matter of statistical information which is of interest to me. I do not propose that the information I wish should be placed on the record through a witness, but I'm prepared to accept it from counsel, although if pressed by the other side, I'm prepared to entertain the evidence coming through a witness. But what I want to know is this–today is Monday, May eighteenth, the day on which Petro-Canada's offer to the shareholders of record of Exxon terminates. Quite apart from the matter of an extension of the time of the offer–and clearly because this application for an injunction has not yet been disposed of, there must be an extension offer by Petro-Canada–how many shares have been tendered so far? If I miss my guess, Mr. de Gaspé, whom I recognize as being in the courtroom, will probably have this figure up-to-date within the last half hour.

"If Mr. Petroff does not object, would you please inform yourself through Mr. de Gaspé as to the number of shares tendered to this time." Petroff, without getting up, shook his head in a negative way, indicating that he had no objection. "For the record, Mr. Petroff indicates he has no objection."

Ambrose Day, who had been standing during the judge's question, turned, looked into the audience, found Pierre de Gaspé in the second row, two seats removed from the centre aisle, went through the gate of the bar separating the audience from the attorneys, and met de Gaspé in the aisle where the two had a brief whispered conference. Then Day returned to the counsel table and still standing, said, "Your Honour, I'm informed by my client that at noon today, there have been tendered to the United States fiscal agents of my client 122,531,201 common shares of Exxon, which is substantially in excess of the 50.1 per cent. My client will, of course, acquire on a first-come, first-served basis the number of common shares of Exxon required to give Petro-Canada 50.1 per cent of all of the issued and outstanding common shares of Exxon. We anticipate late offerings which will, of course, be of interest to Petro-Canada."

Day turned for an instant to look back at Pierre de Gaspé who nodded his approval from the audience.

Day went on, "It follows, Your Honour, that an extension of the offer to purchase must be made by Petro-Canada to a date when it can be reasonably expected that these proceedings might be completed and your decision rendered and the matter of an appeal considered by each side, then launched or not launched. Also, in this case, each party must have an eye to what the Congress may do in terms of prohibitive legislation.

"Under the circumstances, my client considers it appropriate to extend the date of the offering to the shareholders of record on the same terms and conditions as heretofore have applied to be open until Monday, the first day of June. That extension means, of course, that those who have tendered their shares to this point are free to withdraw them up until June first. So therefore, Your Honour, while the figure I've given you is a valid one today, on June first it could well be that the number of common shares of Exxon then outstanding as tendered might be more or might be less."

The judge continued to make notes for a moment, then looking up toward Day, he remarked, "Quite right, Mr. Day."

"But from what you have told me it is apparent that the shareholders of Exxon, which are largely United States corporations and citizens, have decided that it is in their interests and–to the extent that one can interpret that decision–in the interests of the corporation that Petro-Canada's proposal should be accepted.

"That evidence should be of great significance to the board of directors and the executive group of Exxon and is of substantial importance to this court.

"This court is adjourned until two o'clock."

New York City
Tuesday, May 26, 1981, 7:22 A.M.

Pierre de Gaspé lay staring at the ceiling of his New York hotel room, eyes wide, but seeing nothing as the room slowly filled with brilliant morning light. His mind was racing, his body relaxed and comfortable with the warmth of the smooth, soft body of the sleeping Margaret Cameron nestled close up against him. But his mind was not on her. Instead, he was recapping, going back and forth over the quickly changing series of events of the past few days.

De Gaspé had come down to New York from Toronto on Wednesday, May 6, to be formally questioned in discovery proceedings by the attorneys for Exxon in preparation for the hearing in the Federal Court before Judge Rupert Amory which began in May 11. De Gaspé had intended to return to Canada immediately, but on the advice of Ambrose Day, Petro-Canada's New York attorney, he had decided to stay. It was just as well that he had. The need to make decisions and judgments, not only on the mounting pressure of the Exxon application for an injunction but on the acquisition of Exxon shares as well, had increased rapidly. He was the only one who could make those decisions and give instructions, either to the attorney, Day, or to Hubert Peters of Merrill Lynch.

As the emotional and nationalistic reactions to Petro-Canada's take-over bid on Exxon accelerated during the first few days after the bid was announced, de Gaspé had taken Peters' advice and accompanied him on quick visits to major holders of blocks of Exxon stock to assure them that PetroCan and the government of Canada would not attempt to cause Exxon to operate in any way detrimental to the interests of the United States, pointing out that the United States had so many opportunities for economic leverage and reprisals against Canada that it would be foolish for Canada to cut off crude oil or divert world supplies away from the United States or do anything that would be harmful to the American economy.

When the first of these major shareholders had tendered its stock, the event was widely publicized and encouraged other holders to put their shares forward.

By May 18, de Gaspé's maximum effort had paid off. Ambrose Day was able to advise Judge Amory that the number of shares tendered exceeded the required 50.1 per cent and tenders were still being received.

On the morning of Wednesday, May 20, Exxon had completed its case before Judge Amory. At that point Day had put de Gaspé, his only witness, in the box to outline the position of the government of Canada and Petro-Canada. In his examination-in-chief of de Gaspé, Ambrose Day limited his questions to Canada's objectives and took care not to ask any questions that would elicit from de Gaspé any opinion concerning the national interests of the United States or whether, in his opinion, control of Exxon by a foreign government could be detrimental to the national security of the United States.

However, John Petroff, counsel for Exxon, coursed back and forth over the difference in national interests of the government of Canada and that of the United States, citing Canada's early willingness to trade with Cuba and with Red China during the period when the United States had sealed off all doors to those countries, even though in 1981 the doors were wide open.

As a lawyer himself, de Gaspé had felt uncomfortable in the witness box. Petroff's questions were incisive and showed his intelligence and knowledge of his subject. De Gaspé could not help but admire the man.

De Gaspé had been the last witness. Petroff had called no evidence in reply. And so the case concluded late on Thursday, May 21, after both counsel had made argument.

In his concluding remarks Judge Amory stated that he would give his decision in writing at 10:00 A.M. on Tuesday, May 26.

The weekend had been hectic.

Late Thursday, Prime Minister Porter had sent a Canadian Forces Jet Star to pick up de Gaspé at La Guardia and take him directly to Ottawa where the House of Commons was again sitting. On Friday morning, he had met with the Prime Minister and his Cabinet committee and at the same time, with the executive committee of the board of directors of Petro-Canada which again included Senator Margaret Cameron.

His briefing of the group had been exhaustive.

On the question of which way Judge Amory would go, de Gaspé refused to give an opinion. He had great respect for the judge's background in corporate and constitutional law. In de Gaspé's view, he was an ideal choice to hear the case. There was, of course, an appeal to the appellate division of the U.S. Federal Court which could be taken by either side. It was likely if Exxon lost before Judge Amory, Exxon would appeal, which, of course, would further delay the completion of the take-over bid because undoubtedly the appeal court would continue the order restraining Petro-Canada from taking up and paying for the shares tendered.

De Gaspé's main concern was that even if Judge Amory's decision was favourable to PetroCan and the injunction was refused, the Congress might well enact specific prohibitive legislation. Some powerful members of both the Senate and the House of Representatives from both parties were making strong nationalistic and anti-Canadian speeches and promising support of a prohibitive bill.

But what was much more serious than mere talk was the fact that he had been informed, just before leaving New York that morning, that Senator Jacob Weinstein of New York, the Democratic majority leader in the Senate, and Congressman Albert Foss of Louisiana, the majority leader in the House of Representatives (the majority in both Houses being Democratic with a Democratic President in the White House) had announced that they would jointly sponsor an emergency bill to prevent the take-over of Exxon Corporation by Petro-Canada. It would be introduced in the House of Representatives, on May 27, the day after Judge Amory's decision, if that decision was against Exxon.

The Prime Minister remarked that it appeared to him that the Americans were almost panicking.

After answering a series of questions from the group, the Prime Minister closed off the meeting, saying he had to get into the House. However, he thought that it would be helpful to the committee of Cabinet and to the executive committee of Petro-Canada and to Pierre de Gaspé if de Gaspé had a liaison person from the joint group to work closely with him in New York in the last stages of the take-over operation. Porter had suggested Senator Margaret Cameron as the ideal person for the job and for obvious reasons he didn't think that Pierre would object to her presence. This with a smile.

De Gaspé had no idea whether the Prime Minister had any inkling of his relationship with Margaret Cameron, but

404

he certainly did not object to the suggestion nor did Margaret Cameron.

Friday afternoon de Gaspé spent at his offices in Toronto. At home, Friday night, he had a flat-out fight with Ann, in which the names of Margaret Cameron and Dr. Rease, Ann's partner, were mentioned many times. Ann's new-found independence in her growing medical partnership and Pierre's indifference had brought both of them to the point of separation. De Gaspé packed and left that night. In fact, he had joined Margaret Cameron at the Royal York.

She had accompanied him back to New York on Saturday afternoon. Sunday morning they met with Hubert Peters and Paul Zimet at the PetroCan temporary headquarters in the Merrill, Lynch, Pierce, Fenner and Smith offices where Peters and Zimet of the Fry Mills Spence firm and their staffs were updating their statistics on shares tendered and certificates delivered. Only one block of 100,-000 shares had been withdrawn since the original closing date of May 1, while an additional 1,273,565 shares had been tendered after that date making a total offered of 59.3 per cent of the issued shares of Exxon.

From the viewpoint of an operation designed to gain control of the world's largest multi-national oil corporation without warning and by complete surprise, the exercise had gone perfectly, without a hitch.

Monday morning, May 25, de Gaspé had spent preparing for a press conference scheduled for 12:15 in a meeting room at his hotel. Lunch and drinks were served to the press before the one-hour conference had gotten under way at 12:45. De Gaspé and his advisors had felt it essential to make public for the benefit of the members of Congress the number of shares which had been tendered by the Exxon shareholders. They felt that the figure 59.3 per cent would have an effect on the thinking of the members of Congress and on the board of directors and executive group of Exxon. This impressive tendering of shares would be a crucial factor for consideration by Exxon management if they had to make a decision to appeal from the as-yet undelivered judgment of Judge Rupert Amory. For clearly, by fighting the injunction, the management were no longer speaking for a majority of the shareholders of Exxon. If they were to win in their plea for an injunction, either at Judge Amory's level or in the appeal court, the take-over bid would be destroyed and very likely their future prospects with Exxon.

On Monday, May 25, the proceedings of Congress had opened against a background of television, radio, and press statements by Senator Weinstein and Representative Foss decrying Petro-Canada's take-over bid as being against the national interest of the United States and saying that they were prepared to put forward the Weinstein/Foss bill on Wednesday, May 27, if the decision of the court made it necessary that legislation be passed.

Senator Weinstein was a powerful figure in American politics and a highly respected senior member of the Senate. His reputation as a hard bargainer gave added force to his proposal. He made it clear on Monday that the Weinstein/Foss proposal was in two stages. The first stage would be a bill specifically designed to intercept and cut off the Petro-Canada take-over bid on Exxon. This was the key gut issue for the country and he felt that the bill would easily carry the House and the Senate. The bill would be short and sweet. Non-residents or foreign nationals—whether corporations, individuals, or foreign-controlled U.S. corporations—would be prohibited from voting or holding either directly or indirectly in the aggregate more than 25 per cent of the issued and outstanding voting shares of Exxon Corporation.

The second stage of the Weinstein/Foss plan was another bill to be introduced later in the Congressional session, but after the Exxon/PetroCan matter had been disposed of. This bill would similarly prevent the foreign acquisition of more than 25 per cent of the voting shares of any U.S. national or multi-national corporation with assets of over $5 billion as at December 31, 1980.

Weinstein and Foss, both of them old pros, could see that the second bill could get bogged down in debate, protracted committee hearings, and intense lobbying. That bill was for the long haul. The key political issue for the moment was Exxon and so they chose to cut their cloth to suit the occasion.

A major figure was yet to be heard from. The President of the United States, a Democratic President, a Jew from Detroit, sitting in the White House with a Democratic Congress, had not yet said what he would do with any bill, whether the Weinstein/Foss bill or any other legislation, that might be enacted by the Congress on the issue and placed before him for approval or veto.

As Pierre de Gaspé lay starting at the hotel room ceiling, his body breathing quickly but lightly, his brain focused on this question, what would the President do? What could he be expected to do, looking at his track record: labour lawyer for the United Auto Workers; a man always fighting against the big corporations and for the workers; and not known to be beholden to any major corporation at any time in any of his political career as Mayor of Detroit, Senator and now President?

During his election campaign, the President had pledged to the American people that he would conduct an open, aboveboard and public administration. He felt a strong obligation to keep the people of America informed as to his actions and had pledged that he would do so during his campaign.

Now that the Weinstein/Foss proposals for prohibitive legislation had been made public, speculation as to what the President would do was rising rapidly.

Pierre de Gaspé's mind was distracted momentarily by Margaret Cameron turning over in her sleep, intuitively moving her warm back into the curve of his body.

But speculation about what the President would do would be academic if Judge Rupert Amory came down against Petro-Canada and granted the injunction to the management of Exxon. Sure PetroCan could appeal, but that would take one, possibly two months, or even longer. A negative judgment by Amory, a distinguished, experienced jurist, skilled in corporate and constitutional law, would be end of the matter. No doubt about it. Pierre de Gaspé would soon have the answer to that question because at 10:00, in a little more than two and a half hours, Judge Amory would be entering his court room to deliver his decision. . . .

The telephone rang shrilly, startling de Gaspé and waking Margaret Cameron.

He lunged for the phone which was on his side of the bed.

"Yes?"

"Mr. de Gaspé?"

"Yes."

"Mr. de Gaspé, I'm sorry to call you so early in the morning. I hope you don't mind. You and I haven't met."

De Gaspé had already twigged to the voice.

"My name is Senator Weinstein."

"I recognized your voice, Senator. I've seen you on television a great deal in the last couple of days."

The Senator chuckled. "Good, good. Now, the reason I called is I think you and I should get together."

De Gaspé was startled. "Okay. When and where?"

"Your suite. Eight o'clock. What's that? I guess half and hour from now. Order me Sanka and a fruit cup. Gotta watch my weight."

Margaret Cameron had hurriedly dressed and gone to her own suite two floors below while Pierre de Gaspé ordered breakfast for Weinstein and himself, showered, shaved, and dressed.

The Senator arrived at 8:00 sharp, just as the breakfast appeared. While they were exchanging pleasantries, de Gaspé was impressed by the aura of confidence and power which literally exuded from this rotund New Yorker. A New Yorker he was, complete with the city's own accent. De Gaspé knew he was in his early sixties. He looked it, although he appeared fit, tanned, and well preserved.

When they had finished their meal, Weinstein pulled out a long, elegant cigar and said, "Hope you don't mind?"

"Not at all."

Weinstein lit it, sucking vigorously to get it going. "Yeah. Well, I guess we should get down to the short strokes. Today we hear what the court is going to say. If the Exxon management get their injunction, you're finished. You're out and Foss and I will not present the bill. I can't see you going for an appeal, or Exxon for that matter."

De Gaspé remained expressionless.

"Now if the court refuses the Exxon injunction, then Foss and I will introduce our bill tomorrow. It's sure to go through. As majority leader of the Senate, I guarantee it, and if Foss was here he'd say the same about the House. Okay?"

There was still no expression on de Gaspé's face.

The Senator went on. "So if the judge refuses the injunction, you look good, PetroCan looks good, and the Canadian government looks good–and the United States and Exxon lose face. And so, Foss and I introduce our bill. It goes through. The United States looks good. Exxon is preserved as it should be, as an American company, the largest oil company in the world. Canada and the Canadian government look bad; the relationship between the two countries, bad enough as it is now with that shambles last fall, will be in terrible condition again. Reprisals you know, the whole thing. Bad for both countries–very bad."

A long suck on the cigar, a great cloud of smoke billowing around de Gaspé, a non-smoker. Still no evidence of any emotion, or reaction.

"So what I'm saying is this–a deal." He spoke slowly now. "If the court refuses the Exxon application for an injunction, then Foss and I will not put forward our Exxon legislation if you agree to withdraw your offer to the shareholders. That way we can all back off and go home, and there won't be any confrontation between the two countries. God knows we've had enough of that."

Pierre de Gaspé coughed lightly from the cigar smoke, reached forward, and picked up the coffee pot. "More Sanka, Senator?"

"No thank you, Pierre." For the Senator everybody should be on a first-name basis, except when addressing the Senator.

"Senator," de Gaspé looked him squarely in the eye, "I've anticipated the proposition that you've just put to me so I got instructions from my government and from my board of directors on this very question last Friday. It might be an attractive proposition except for one thing."

"And what's that, Pierre?"

411

"You've got a President . . ."

The Senator broke in, "A fine President, a fine President, the best we've ever had. Fabulous guy and a Democrat and a Jew. My God, man, are we ever proud of him. He's honest and straight and free and not tied to anybody. A great man, a big man."

Pierre de Gaspé smiled, "Yes he is. And you've hit the nail right on the head. He's honest and he's not tied to anybody. He's the kind of guy who can make up his own mind, and he hasn't yet made up his mind as to whether he will veto or approve your bill. I don't care what leverage you've got on him, he's going to call the shot the way he sees it and he hasn't called it yet. Until he does, Senator, and until he calls it your way—"

The Senator's benign face hardened. He spat out with pure venom. "He'll call it our way or the son of a bitch will never get a goddamn proposal from the White House through the Senate again."

Suddenly the Senator's eyes shifted. His cigar turned slightly up as he kept it between his teeth. Then he took it from his mouth and smiled.

"On the other hand, Pierre baby, you may well be right. If you are, and he goes with you, there are a lot of us in Congress who owe a great deal to the oil companies in more ways than one, if you get what I mean, Pierre."

Yes, he knew what he meant, but said nothing.

The Senator went on, the smile still showing but the eyes ice-hard. "Now Pierre, there are two ways of getting at a young guy like you. One way is to use a little . . . how shall I put it . . . not blackmail, but a little bit of persuasion. Like, for example, a file on your relationship with Senator Margaret Cameron—complete with photographs—delivered to your wife." A puff on the cigar.

De Gaspé looked him right in the eye and said, "You rotten bastard."

The Senator tapped the ash off his cigar and said, "Relax, Pierre, relax. My personal file on you tells me two things. From your background, from the way you do business and from the way you handle yourself, you'd probably tell me to go to hell, and to send it to your wife anyway. The stakes are just too big.

"But my file also tells me that your wife already knows and that while you were in Toronto on the weekend, you and your wife called it quits. As a matter of fact, there has been a lot of screwing around–if you'll pardon the expression–on both sides."

De Gaspé's face was white with astonishment. "How in hell do you know? That was only last Friday."

The Senator chuckled, "Pierre baby, you're talking to the powerful Senator from New York. The Petro-Canada bid on Exxon is a matter of national security. You ever heard of the CIA, Pierre? They've got more stuff on their computer about you than you know yourself."

With that the Senator stood up, belched, walked to the closet, took out his tailored top coat and pearl grey homberg, and, with the cigar still clenched in mouth, put his hat on and said, "No, Pierre, that's not the way to deal with you. There's only one possible way I can get at you. I'm only going to say this once, so I want you to listen hard."

Weinstein's coat was on by this time. De Gaspé sat fixed in his chair.

The Senator said quietly, "You're the guy in the driver's seat. That's where you like to be and that's why I'm making this proposal. You make a formal request to come and see me and that dumb bastard Foss in the open–there will be press coverage–and you say that you've assessed the anti-take-over feeling in the Congress and you're certain that the bill is going to pass, and that the President will have no choice but to go along with the bill. You with me so far?

Then you say that in the interests of the relationship between two great countries – you know what to say, all that crap – Canada is going to withdraw its bid.

"Then if you do this, Pierre – and you've got to do it after the House has passed the bill but before it hits the Senate – then if you do this, Pierre baby, then there is two million dollars sitting for you in a numbered Swiss bank account. I'll give you the number after you've done your part of the deal. Think about it, Pierre baby. Think about it."

The Senator opened the door to leave and turned to de Gaspé for a final remark. "By the way, don't worry about this frank talk of ours. I took the precaution of having this place cased for bugs and taping equipment about two this morning. My people tell me that you and Maggie were so busy in bed you had no idea you had visitors.

"See ya, Pierre baby."

New York City
Tuesday, May 26, 1981, 11:00 A.M.

Judge Rupert Amory entered the courtroom directly from
his chambers. Black robes flowing, he walked briskly to the
steps leading to the dias and to his chair where, before being
seated, he nodded to the counsel and audience who had
risen on his entrance. He could see that the courtroom was
jampacked again mainly with press people, their notebooks
in hand. Television and other cameras were not permitted
in this court, nor were recording machines.

The judge looked at the counsel tables in front of him.
On his left was John Petroff, lead attorney for Exxon Corporation, who had with him today George Shaw and Craig
Robertson of Exxon Corporation. The judge reflected that
the presence of these two men showed that the Exxon management were taking this moment seriously, as indeed they
should. At the counsel table on his right were Petro-
Canada's attorney, Ambrose Day, and Pierre de Gaspé, the
president of the corporation.

As Judge Amory sat down, and the people in the courtroom with him, he withdrew some papers from the large
brown envelope he had carried into the courtroom with
him.

The clerk of the court had called out the usual formal
greeting, bringing the court into session.

Judge Amory waited for the people in the courtroom to
settle down and then, glasses in hand, he made some preliminary remarks.

"Last Thursday, at the completion of the evidence and argument in the case of Exxon Corporation versus Petro-Canada, I stated that I would deliver my judgment this morning. I am now prepared to do so, but before I proceed further, I wish to compliment counsel on both sides for their superlative preparation and presentation of the evidence and their arguments. Their efforts have been of enormous value to me in the writing of this judgment, a judgment which will undoubtedly be the most important that I will be called upon to deliver during my career on the bench. The issue at stake, and the results of the determination of that issue, could have far-reaching effects relative to the ownership and control of American multi-national corporations which carry on business not only in the United States, which is their home country, but in one or more other nations throughout the world as well."

With this, Judge Rupert Amory put on his glasses, took up the text of his judgment, and began to read.

He dealt first with the background of the take-over offer, the financing of it, its compliance with the rules and regulations of the Securities and Exchange Commission, and the technical features of the circular in which the offer was made to the shareholders of record of Exxon. Then he dealt with the evidence of the expert witnesses for Exxon on the constitutional and corporate law of the United States, and as well the evidence of the president of Exxon, Craig Robertson. Next he dealt with the evidence of Pierre de Gaspé and with the arguments of counsel.

Judge Amory noted the percentage of the common stock, 59.3 per cent, which had been tendered to Petro-Canada by Exxon shareholders and he stressed his awareness of the expressed intent of the majority leaders of the Senate and House of Representatives to introduce prohibitive legislation should the court fail to allow the injunction applied for.

At this point in his judgment he said, "At no time should a court in the United States of America be put in a position by the legislative or executive branch of government where a decision of the court, or the judge making that decision, is publicly intimidated by a proposed legislative course of action. I wish to make it perfectly clear that I am not intimidated. On the other hand, as will appear from the reasons which I provide later in this judgment, it may well be appropriate that legislation is being contemplated."

This was a clue, rather a vague one, but sufficient to set up a slight chattering among the audience and between counsel and their clients.

The judge paused and waited for the discussion to subside. He used his gavel only on the rarest of occasions.

"As I perceive it, the real question before this court is what should the national policy be in protecting the national interests of the United States from the intrusion of a foreign multi-national corporation, owned or controlled by a foreign government, through its acquisition of an American multi-national corporation.

"To put the proposition another way, the question is whether the acquisition of control of Exxon, an American-based multi-national corporation and the world's largest oil corporation, by Petro-Canada is contrary to public policy and the national interest of the United States. The management of Exxon brought their application for a preliminary injunction on this sole, but enormously important point."

There was a distracting, short-lived commotion at the back of the courtroom. Judge Amory stopped, waited patiently until it subsided, then went on.

"Those who gave expert evidence for Exxon and especially Mr. McGarvey, a senior official of the State Department, who is particularly knowledgeable concerning the Middle East, were particularly informative. He said that through its arrangements with the various members of the Organization of Petroleum Exporting Countries, (such as Venezuela, Saudi Arabia, Libya, Kuwait, and others), and through its exploration work around the world, Exxon now controls the production of approximately 7,500,000 barrels of crude oil a day, a large proportion of which is shipped into the United States for consumption here. Also, the reliance of the United States on imported crude oil has risen from approximately 25 per cent of all crude oil consumed in this nation in 1973 to over 60 per cent today. It was his firm opinion, therefore, that any diversion to foreign markets, such as western Europe or Japan of crude oil now flowing under the Exxon banner into the United States could cause critical shortages of petroleum, fuel oil, and petroleum derivatives. He reasoned that if control of Exxon were to fall into the hands of a foreign government that government would likely use its control of Exxon to serve its own national interests in priority to the interests of the United States and that, accordingly, the acquisition of control of Exxon Corporation by Petro-Canada would be contrary to the public interest.

"I found Mr. McGarvey to be a strong and persuasive witness and I can find no reason to reject his cogent testimony."

Judge Amory paused for a moment, looked up and saw Petroff turn from his note-taking to whisper with a smile to George Shaw.

Judge Amory continued. "On the other hand, there is the real question of whether the issue of public policy and national interest as to the role of the multi-nationals should be decided by Congress, by legislation, and not by the court.

"To this date, the Congress of the United States has failed to enact legislation that gives guidance to the courts by settling in legislative form what is public policy and what is, or is not, in the national interest.

"This is so, notwithstanding the judgment of Judge Woodrow Seals in the case of Texasgulf Inc. vs Canada Development Corporation which was decided by the learned judge at Houston on September 5, 1973 and later confirmed by the Fifth U.S. Circuit Court of Appeals. The citation is 366F. Supp. 374 (1973).

"That case was not dissimilar to the one before me. As a result of a bid for 35 per cent of the issued and outstanding shares of Texasgulf Inc., made by the Canada Development Corporation, which historically is the corporate relation of the present respondent, Petro-Canada, the management of Texasgulf, a major multi-national mining firm with then approximately 65 per cent of its assets in Canada, applied to the court for an injunction restraining the Canada Development Corporation from proceeding with and completing its take-over bid.

"There were several grounds put forward in support of the application for the injunction, but in the result all of them were rejected and the application refused.

"One of the grounds relied upon by Texasgulf was the very question which confronts this court, that of public policy and the national interest. I quote from the lucid and well-reasoned judgment of Judge Seals which, in that it was upheld by the Circuit Court of Appeals, I consider to be binding upon me as a precedent. At page 418 he says this:

The court is aware that the issue of a possible conflict of interest also must be considered in a larger and broader context of public policy and national interest. That is, what should our national policy be in protecting the national interest of the American people from a real or an imaginary threat of the multi-national corporation, regardless if it is a private foreign corporation or one that is ostensibly a private corporation but nevertheless

419

is an instrument, directly or indirectly, of a foreign nation-state, such as the Japanese corporations who are now buying tracts of timber land and cotton fields in this country, or one such as Canada Development Corp. (which will sell to the Canadian public all but 10% of its common stock in the near future) and British Petroleum which is almost 50% owned by the government of Great Britain and has recently been reported to want to increase its ownership of Standard Oil of Ohio from a 25% interest to a 50% interest?

It seems to this court that if the threat is real, it makes little difference if the foreign multi-national is government owned and controlled or not. If it is government controlled, at least we will know 'our enemy' and to whom it owes this allegiance and through diplomacy and treaties could balance their political influence and their economic power....

Perhaps these defenders of the multi-nationals are correct; that the entire world will benefit from an economic integration.

Be that as it may, we must realize that it is our [U.S.] multi-nationals who are the real giants–ITT, Xerox, Standard Oil, General Motors, Singer, Goodyear, IBM, Colgate-Palmolive, National Cash Register, Eastman Kodak, Minnesota Mining and Manufacturing, International Harvester, and many others.

Should we expect to operate freely around the world and exclude a foreign corporation such as CDC?

The answer of this court *in this case* is no. This particular acquisition is not a threat to the U.S. In fact, it might be, that if their acquisition is thwarted, our long-time friend, neighbour and ally, who we all know is now experiencing an increasing feeling of economic nationalism, might look to other methods of expressing this growing sense of economic nationalism.

It is an issue of public policy and national interest as to the role multi-nationals will play in the future, but this court cannot decide generally in the context of this case what this role may be. It belongs in the legislative and executive branches of government. This broad issue is too fraught with economic subtleties and questions of delicate balances of trade, as well as problems of economic reciprocity. Remember, turn about is fair play.

Suffice to say this case is not the vehicle to wander into this bog of uncertainty.

Of course, what makes this problem so pertinent now is the constant and continuous devaluation of the U.S. dollar, the depressed stock prices of many U.S. companies and the long period of unfavourable balances of trade. These factors emphasize and multiply this whole issue.

There are many good buys today in the U.S. by foreign-held American dollars as well as by foreign currencies. This acquisition, eventually successful or not, will not be the last one and especially from Canada where it is said that the U.S. controls 60% of their mining industry and 80% of their smelting and refining capacity. The CDC emphasizes that this acquisition would help our balance of trade to the extent of $290 million.

How can a court of law or equity even consider a problem so complex, hard and difficult? Only the Congress or the executive branch has the resources to determine what is in the best interest of this country in the increasing problems of multi-nationals.

Judge Amory hitched up his gown again, paused, took a sip of water, and looked around the courtroom at the furiously scribbling reporters.

"I have no choice but to agree with the reasons set forth

by Judge Seals when he says, 'Only the Congress or the executive branch has the resources to determine what is in the best interest of this country in the increasing problems of multi-nationals.'

"If I were to decide that the acquisition of control of Exxon by Petro-Canada is contrary to the national interest, or contrary to the national policy, I would be making a decision on a question of fact and not of law because neither the Congress nor the executive branch has enunciated the law. In this court, the law is interpreted, not made."

The judge could feel and hear the increasing tension in the court. He read quickly now.

"For the above reasons my decision in this case is as follows: the original temporary restraining order I granted on May 4, which allowed depositaries to continue to receive stock but has restrained Petro-Canada from further solicitation or taking up and paying for stock tendered pending outcome of this case, will continue for ten days to allow the applicant, if it so chooses to launch an appeal.

He paused for a moment. "The application by Exxon Corporation for a preliminary injunction against Petro-Canada is refused."

A stunned silence filled the courtroom for a moment – then bedlam.

**New York City
Tuesday, May 26, 1981, 11:33 A.M.**

Pierre de Gaspé was still at the counsel table with his attorney when he was interrupted by Hubert Peters. "Congratulations, Pierre, you must be really pleased."

"Congratulations to you, Hubert. You've done a fantastic job for us."

"Yes, but we're a long way from finished yet. We still have the Congress and the President ahead of us. Pierre, the president of the Credit Swiss Bank wants to speak with you urgently. They gave me the message when I called the office just a couple of minutes ago. Let's go to my office; you can call him from there."

When Kurt Reimer came on the line from Zurich, de Gaspé could hear him clearly. "First, how did the injunction go, Pierre?"

"Perfectly. The application was dismissed."

"Excellent! Excellent! Well done. You and your people have done a superb job." He paused. "But we have a problem."

With those words Pierre de Gaspé's victory euphoria suddenly faded. Reimer went on. "My principals are very much concerned that the Congress will pass prohibitive legislation and that the President will approve of it. It may be late in the day, but my people want to renegotiate one or two major points. They think their proposals will provide the final leverage you need to get by the President. They can meet you in London. Can you come over immediately?"

De Gaspé's reply was instantaneous. "Of course I can, Kurt. I'll catch a flight this evening."

"I've already made your hotel booking–at the Stafford, of course."

"Good. I hope we can get this over with quickly. I want to have a meeting with Weinstein at his Senate office first thing Thursday morning before the Weinstein/Foss bill is introduced in the Senate. I expect the bill will go to the House of Representatives tomorrow for emergency debate. It should pass. Then it goes to the Senate the next morning and quite possibly to the President that afternoon. The President still hasn't declared himself and he won't until he sees what Congress is going to do with it. And he's promised the Exxon people another shot at him to convince him as to why he should approve the bill, assuming it gets through Congress."

Reimer responded. "Well, there's still a chance. As I say, I think you and your corporation and your government will find the new proposals acceptable. While Canada might wind up in a different position in this deal, I'm confident its basic objectives can be satisfactorily met. See you tomorrow."

De Gaspé broke in quickly, "Kurt, before you go–I want to bring Senator Margaret Cameron with me. She's the liaison person for the Cabinet and executive committee of the board of PetroCan." In his mind's eye de Gaspé could see Reimer smiling.

"I'll book a separate room for her, Pierre."

"Thanks a lot. One final thing Kurt. Could you check through your old-boys bankers net to see if there's been a numbered account set up in Zurich in the last seven days. I don't want to know who or any details. I just want to know if it's been set up. The amount is two million . . ."

London, England
Wednesday, May 27, 1981, 12:45 P.M.

Margaret Cameron and de Gaspé had caught an overnight Pan Am 747 which put them into London shortly after 8:00 the next morning. They went directly to the Stafford Hotel on St. James Place, just behind the Ritz and just a short distance away from Buckingham Palance. The Stafford, a small elegant establishment, was, as usual, fully booked, but Simon Broome, the managing director and long-time friend of Pierre de Gaspé, had given up his own bedroom to de Gaspé and a last-minute cancellation had opened up space for Margaret Cameron.

After the commotion of their arrival – de Gaspé, the big Canadian, was a special favourite of the concierge, the porters, and especially of Louis and Charles, the French barmen in the delightful little room at the rear of the building on Blueball Yard – de Gaspé had checked with Kurt Reimer, who was at the Dorchester. He had agreed that they would have lunch at the Stafford with Reimer and his as-yet undisclosed principal. After agreeing to meet for a drink at 12:45, Senator Cameron and de Gaspé went to their respective bedrooms for some much needed sleep.

They met at the appointed hour in Louis' and Charles' small, very English bar, both of them much refreshed. A fast Vodka martini for Margaret and a gin and tonic for de Gaspé were ordered as they perched on stools at the bar.

"I suggested to Kurt that we could use your room for our discussions. Hope you don't mind, Margaret."

She laughed. "Not at all. I don't remember the last time I had three men in my bedroom at once, but I think I can cope."

De Gaspé gave her his best leer. "You don't need three, sweetheart, I can take care of you all by myself." At that moment he caught Charles totally absorbed in their conversation, taking in every look, gesture, and word. Charles knew Mrs. de Gaspé well, and he couldn't put these goings on with Margaret Cameron together at all.

"Charles, I'll explain all to you later," whispered Pierre.

Charles, embarrassed, looked away just as Douglas, the hotel valet-porter entered the bar, approached de Gaspé and said, "Mr. Reimer and another gentleman are waiting for you in the sitting room, Mr. de Gaspé! Cor, you ought to see the chap with 'im. Gor blimey." Then, with that a lift of his eyebrows and a twitch of his military moustache, he was gone.

"Let's go," said Pierre, gulping down the last of his gin and tonic.

As they went through the corridor from the bar into the sitting room, Kurt Reimer and his man were standing with their backs to de Gaspé and Margaret Cameron, but the new man's profile could be seen as he spoke to Reimer.

Margaret Cameron stopped in her tracks. "My God, you know who that is, don't you?" She was shocked.

So was de Gaspé. "I sure do. Every oil man in the world knows him." He took her by the arm saying, "I'll have to get out my pocket computer when we're dealing with this guy. He's incredible."

With that they went on to meet their new companions.

The luncheon went extremely well. As the luxurious food and wine were discreetly served and consumed, the new deal was presented to de Gaspé in a very British, gentlemanly fashion, adjusted on a few minor points, and agreed to by him, with Senator Cameron saying she was prepared to support the proposals.

At 2:20, de Gaspé excused himself from the table and went to his room where he placed a call to and reached first the Prime Minister in Ottawa and then the chairman of the board of Petro-Canada, whom he found this day in Winnipeg. Both men agreed to the new deal. The chairman said he would do a telephone canvas of the board and then get back to de Gaspé within two or three hours.

De Gaspé returned to the luncheon table within twenty minutes of his departure and produced the news of the Prime Minister's and chairman's reaction. There was a happy clinking of glasses in an informal spontaneous expression of delight at the new accord.

The luncheon party broke up shortly after three, with Reimer and his principal making their way back to the Dorchester, while Senator Cameron and Pierre de Gaspé returned to her room in the Stafford Hotel where, for a long, languorous hour, they "made up for lost time," as Margaret put it.

At 4:00, they were interrupted by a call from the Petro-Can's chairman of the board, who stated that the board was unanimously behind the new proposal, and in fact were quite relieved by it.

By 6:00 that evening, they were hurtling down a runway of London's Heathrow Airport in another Pan Am 747 bound for Washington and de Gaspé's meeting with Senator Weinstein in his Senate chambers. De Gaspé was well prepared for this meeting. Kurt Reimer had confirmed to him that there had indeed been two million deposited in a new numbered bank account in Switzerland.

When the steward served them their first first-class drink of the flight, Pierre turned to Margaret and said, "I think I . . . well, in all fairness, I ought to tell you about a deal that Senator Weinstein has offered me if I would back-off on the Exxon takeover. When I've told you what it is, you'll know why I'm meeting him in the morning and you can tell me what you would do under the circumstances."

"Try me," replied a willing Margaret.

Senator Weinstein's attractive secretary took de Gaspé into the Senator's office, telling him that the Senator was going to be a bit late, but coffee would probably help the waiting period.

As he sipped his coffee, he took in this elegant Victorian office which was Weinstein's lair of power. The room was not large, but its richness was striking. The walls were panelled in dark, superbly crafted walnut put in place by the hands of some long-gone artisan. Books filled the shelves behind the Senator's polished mid-1800's carved desk. The brown leather covering of the chairs and chesterfield and the deep-piled rust rug blended with the reddish tone of the panelling. Not much light came in from the narrow curtained windows, but the light from a polished brass chandelier provided a sedate luster to the entire room.

The smell of cigar smoke pervaded the office, as did pictures of Senator Weinstein with famous world figures reaching back over the past twenty-five years.

This suite was indeed appropriate for a holder of one of the highest offices in the United States of America.

De Gaspé could hear the commotion in the outer office as Senator Weinstein arrived, barking orders and being asked obsequiously for instructions. Through the door of the office he came, striding quickly toward de Gaspé, a new cigar clenched firmly in his teeth. De Gaspé rose to his feet as the Senator reached for his right hand and patted him on the shoulder. "Pierre boy, it's good to see you, real good to see you. You've come just in time."

The Senator dropped de Gaspé's hand, raised his right index finger to his lips and put the tip of his left index finger to his left ear. De Gaspé got the message that the place was or might be bugged, and that extreme caution should be taken in whatever was said.

The Senator stood back and looked him in the eye. "I assume you wanted to make a statement to the press," he asked.

"I don't want to, Senator, but I think I really have no choice."

The Senator pulled his cigar out of his mouth, took de Gaspé's shoulders in both of his hands, and beamed at him, "Excellent, Pierre baby, excellent. And knowing you, I assume that you've checked on that information I gave you the other day."

De Gaspé smiled. "As your operatives have undoubtedly told you, I've just come back from Europe and, yes, I have checked, and what you told me is there, is there."

"Excellent," the Senator repeated again. He lowered his voice. "I don't think I should ask you what it is you intend to say about the situation, but I told my friends in the press you would be here this morning, and that undoubtedly you would have something important to say to them after our meeting."

With that the Senator took de Gaspé by the arm, pulled him through the office door, the outer office, and along the corridor to the Senate press conference room where it seemed to de Gaspé half the world's television cameras and reporters were waiting.

This was an environment the Senator knew and enjoyed. He left de Gaspé at the edge of the rostrum which he mounted, cigar in hand. He started immediately, "Ladies and gentlemen of the press, we haven't much time because the morning session of the Senate is scheduled to begin in just a few minutes.

"As you know, Congressman Foss and I have jointly sponsored a bill to prohibit the acquisition of control of Exxon by Petro-Canada. The Weinstein/Foss bill was passed yesterday by the House of Representatives and as majority leader of the Senate, I will be introducing the Weinstein/Foss bill," he liked to hear his own name, "this morning, subject, of course, to any material change of position on the part of the Canadian government."

He waved his left arm in Pierre de Gaspé's direction. "I want to introduce to you this morning, the president of Petro-Canada. As you know, we have had discussions on this critical and serious problem of Exxon. Mr. de Gaspé has indicated to me that he has a few words to say to the press before this morning's session of the Senate. Mr. de Gaspé."

The Senator retreated from the rostrum and de Gaspé took his place, taking from his pocket a long card on which he had made some notes of the points he wanted to cover. He began quickly, the cameras whirring, microphones stacked in front of him, and eager reporters writing at full speed.

"Ladies and gentlemen," he began, "I want to say to you that in my meetings with Senator Weinstein he has been very direct and forceful in pressing his position that it is contrary to the national interest and public policy of the United States for the government of Canada or any other foreign government to gain control of Exxon Corporation or any other major American multi-national corporation. He has made it clear that he will do everything in his power to have the Weinstein/Foss bill to prohibit Petro-Canada's take-over of Exxon passed by the Senate. Having dealt with this man, I am sure that he will convince his colleagues in the Senate that the bill should be passed.

"On the other hand, we in Canada have long been concerned that all of the vertically integrated oil companies operating in Canada are American owned, except BP Canada Limited, which is British owned. We believe that one of those companies should be owned by Canada, and operated in the interests of Canada. And it has been our belief that rather than nationalize, expropriate, or in some other way forcibly take over ownership or control of such a corporation in Canada, it would be more in keeping with the spirit of the way business is done on this continent, and in particular the United States, that we should attempt to buy control of such an oil corporation on the open market, thereby doing two things: number one, getting control of that corporation's operations within Canada, and number two, through the multi-national activities of the corporation, buying for ourselves a new trading, marketing, and business position in the world's markets.

"Canada's relationship with the United States, at least up until last October, has been a peaceful one, marred only by economic pushing and shoving from time to time when the great leverage and weight of the United States has been used where required to put Canada in its place."

De Gaspé turned to look at Senator Weinstein standing behind him and to his right, then back to his audience.

"Senator Weinstein has suggested to me in the most forcible of terms that Canada should withdraw its take-over bid on Exxon before he introduces his bill in the Senate, because if that bill passes, and if the President ratifies it, not only will the proposal be killed, the relationship between our two great countries will be once again greatly strained.

"He has offered that if Canada is prepared to withdraw

its take-over bid, then he will not introduce the Weinstein/Foss bill in the Senate this morning. I have discussed the Senator's proposal with my principals in Canada and, of course, with the Prime Minister. I am not at liberty to disclose the nature and details of those discussions except to say that the entire status of the Exxon take-over bid has been reviewed, as has been the proposal of Senator Weinstein.

"Having some idea of the Senator's belief in his own power, including his power of persuasion, there is little doubt in my mind that he now expects me to say that. I have advised the Prime Minister and my principals to withdraw the Exxon bid.

"That is not what I have advised them, and therefore, that is not what I am going to say will happen.

"On the contrary, my instructions are that, subject to one material change in the offer to the shareholders of record, which change will be disclosed this afternoon, the take-over bid on Exxon is to continue."

Those words were barely out of de Gaspé's mouth when the Senator grabbed him from behind, twirled him around, stuck his face up below de Gaspé's chin and hissed, "You double-crossing bastard. I'll have you and your banana republic country for bookends."

With that Senator Jacob Weinstein of New York stormed out of the press conference.

The President greeted the two men at the door of his Oval Office full of apologies. "I'm sorry to have kept you waiting, Your Excellency, but sometimes one's luncheon guests stay a little longer than anticipated – especially if they're from Exxon."

"Please, it is of no concern, Mr. President," replied the Canadian Ambassador to the United States. "It is a privilege to attend upon you on such short notice. May I introduce Pierre de Gaspé, the president of Petro-Canada."

As they shook hands, the President said, "I've certainly heard a great deal about you, Mr. de Gaspé. You've shaken the hell out of Exxon – and the whole of the United States for that matter." Then he turned, went behind his desk and motioned to his guests to be seated. As they did so, the Ambassador, Georges Charbonneau, said, "There is one other person to join us, Mr. President. He has come a long way to be here and unfortunately he has not yet arrived."

The President waved his hand, "That's all right. After all, I was good and late myself. As a matter of fact, I'm expecting Senator Weinstein and Congressman Foss any moment now. They're bringing their bill which was passed by the Senate this morning, as I'm sure you know. It's now up to me to decide what to do with it."

It was de Gaspé who spoke up. "That's the reason for the request for our meeting with you. You haven't publicly disclosed your position on the Weinstein/Foss bill. We know you gave the Exxon people another chance to convince you to sign it. And then there are some new factors –"

The President broke in, "I've been on the horns of a dilemma with this one, let me assure you. As I told the Exxon people, my whole background is with the labouring class, the workers. For me to have to approve of a bill which in the long run will prevent a willing shareholder from selling his shares to a willing buyer, a bill which serves mainly to preserve the position of the Exxon management group – frankly, gentlemen, I find it damn difficult."

He shrugged. "On the other hand, here I am, a Democratic President, with a Democratic Senate and a Democratic House. Between us we're supposed to represent the will of the great American people. The Congress has spoken clearly and with a substantial majority in both houses. The Congress considers it to be contrary to the national interest and public policy that control of Exxon Corporation fall into the hands of a foreign government."

The President leaned back in his chair, "Gentlemen, reluctant as I might be in my own conscience, I'm afraid I'm going to have to approve the Weinstein/Foss bill."

As he was speaking the last few words, his intercom bell sounded and his secretary advised that the third visitor with the Canadian party had arrived. "Send him in, please," the President instructed.

The door opened instantly. President Dennis rose to move to greet the tall young man who swept elegantly into the room.

The Canadian Ambassador introduced him. "Mr. President, I have the honour to present to you another man about whom you have undoubtedly heard a great deal, His Excellency Sheik Kamel Abdul Rahman, the Minister of Oil for the Kingdom of Saudi Arabia."

The President stopped in his tracks but quickly recovered. The Sheik bowed to the President and the two men lightly shook hands.

It was an emotional moment for both, each a powerful leader among races of men who had known hatred for one another for centuries. But there would be no show, no outward trace of animosity or ingrained emotion displayed by these two men, each of them highly cultured within his own society and environment.

When they were all seated again around the desk, the President leaned forward on the edge of his chair. He was an experienced bargainer, who could sense that the crunch was coming.

He said crisply, "Well, gentlemen . . .?"

The Sheik looked at the Ambassador and then at Pierre de Gaspé. They were waiting for him to lead. "If I may, Mr. President, perhaps I can explain. I'm sure that His Excellency the Ambassador or Mr. de Gaspé will break in at any time to amplify or correct anything I have to say. I speak with the full authority of my most revered King, who as you know, Mr. President, has always held the people of the United States of America in the highest regard."

The President nodded.

"At the end of February of this year, our principal banker in Switzerland, Credit Swiss, approached my government and me concerning a request made by the Canadian government and Petro-Canada to borrow $14.5 billion for the purpose of acquiring control of Exxon Corporation. My country has had dealing for many many many years with Standard Oil of New Jersey—that is, Exxon through Aramco, the enormously profitable oil-producing firm which Exxon originally owned with others and now is mainly held by Saudi Arabia.

"The Arab oil-exporting countries such as Kuwait, Libya,

Qatar, and Abhu Dhabi and, of course, Saudi Arabia now have massive holdings of American dollars. But as a race, our characteristic is to invest those dollars as debt rather than as equity.

"The opportunity to invest $14.5 billion as debt with the security of the guarantee of the government of Canada, together with the pledge of the shares of Exxon acquired on the take-over bid as collateral – it was a unique investment opportunity for us. Therefore, without disclosing our identity, we instructed our bank to complete the negotiations and to agree to advance the required funds."

The Minister drew out a long cigarette case and said to the President, "Do you mind, sir?"

The President indicated that he did not, and in a few seconds the Sheik was puffing away, apparently relaxed and confident.

The President had not moved.

"Quite naturally we monitored closely every move made by the Canadian government and by Petro-Canada during the take-over bid. By Monday of this week it became apparent to us that the Weinstein/Foss bill would be approved by the Congress in the event that the court refused to grant the injunction that the Exxon management had applied for.

"Also, at this time, my government—that is to say, the King and his advisors—had decided that perhaps over all these years we had been too conservative, investing only in debt opportunities rather than equity. As you know, Mr. President, it is very difficult to invest large sums with reasonable security, especially when the sums I am talking of are surpluses which we now have available of at least $100 billion U.S.

"Well, we could see that one way or the other the Canadian bid would be destroyed, either by the court or in the alternative by the Congress. As we all know, the court did

437

not uphold Exxon and therefore it was left to the Congress to act, which it has done in passing the Weinstein/Foss bill. In all this process, Mr. President, there was one unknown, or at least one unstated position, and that was yours."

The President nodded but remained silent.

"In our analysis, the Canadian proposal was doomed for failure. We felt that you, sir, would be reluctant to approve of the bill, but that for political reasons you would be forced to do so – forced unless there was some new ingredient, some new leverage, which would make it compellingly attractive for you to veto the Weinstein/Foss bill."

The Minister's monologue was interrupted by the President's intercom bell. His secretary informed him that Senator Weinstein and Representative Foss were waiting. "I'll see them shortly" was the President's terse response.

"Go on, Mr. Minister."

"Saudi Arabia and the other oil-exporting countries are now supplying the United States with about 60 per cent of its overall crude oil requirements. To have our co-operation in continuing the security of that supply, the government of the United States has in the past indicated a willingness to compromise in many areas of the relationship between the United States and the Organization of Arab Petroleum Exporting Countries.

"Perhaps it would have been enough for me to appear before you today to say that it is Saudi Arabia which is the heretofore-undisclosed financier of the main sector of the Canadian take-over bid on Exxon. Perhaps you would have decided to veto the bill on the basis of our request, and our involvement as lenders. But my King and I were of the considered view that our presence merely as disclosed lenders might not be sufficient. Accordingly, we have taken steps to put ourselves in a new position which we believe deserves your support."

Again the intercom bell. "Senator Weinstein says its urgent, Mr. President."

David Dennis sighed. "Tell him I'm aware of that and I'll be with him as quickly as I can. Please continue, Mr. Minister."

Sheik Kamel Abdul Rahman went on. "The great American oil companies, of which Exxon is but one, have been extracting and selling Saudi Arabia's crude oil throughout the world. For example, Exxon, Texaco and Standard of California are partners with my country in Aramco, the Arabian American Oil Company, and each year make huge profits from their investment. We feel that it is now time for Saudi Arabia to take the other side of the coin and do business in the United States, and to return, by way of investment, some of the enormous number of dollars that your country has been good enough to pay us for our precious oil."

The President caustically remarked, "I am also well aware that Saudia Arabia now owns 60 per cent of Aramco–35 per cent more than it did at the beginning of 1974."

The Minister was somewhat shaken by the President's knowledge of the numbers.

"Yes, well, the day before yesterday, before Judge Amory had given his decision, I requested our bankers in Switzerland to have Mr. de Gaspé come to London to meet with me. To this point the presence of Saudi Arabia had not been disclosed to de Gaspé. I was in Geneva, at OPEC headquarters when the decision was made, so it was convenient for me to go to London." Rahman smiled, "London is a marvellous place. Such beautiful women ...

"In any event, as a result of meetings which we held yesterday, the results of which have been confirmed by my King and our government–"

De Gaspé interjected, "And by the government of Canada as well."

The Minister carried on. "A new agreement has been entered into. Of course, these new arrangements can be circulated among the shareholders of record of Exxon as an amending circular to Petro-Canada's original offer which is open until June first. So I can see no problem in dealing with your Securities and Exchange Commission rules." He tamped out his cigarette butt in the ashtray on the President's desk.

"Now, Mr. President, the new arrangement is this: First, Saudi Arabia will take the place of Petro-Canada as the buyer of the shares tendered to date and will take all 59.3 per cent, which as I understand it is the amount offered as of last Sunday.

"Secondly, Saudi Arabia will continue to buy shares of Exxon Corporation on the open market until it achieves a holding of 67 per cent of all of the issued and outstanding common shares, thereby giving it total control.

"Thirdly, on the completion of the Saudi Arabian take-over of Exxon, it has been agreed that Canada will purchase from Exxon all of its issued and outstanding shares in Imperial Oil Limited, the Canadian subsidiary of Exxon Corporation, 70 per cent of the shares of which are in Exxon's hands, the balance being owned by the public."

"In this way, Canada can achieve a major national objective by owning and controlling a vertically integrated oil company which is devoted to exploration, production, refining, and merchandising petroleum products and chemicals."

President Dennis looked at de Gaspé, "This is quite a comedown for Canada, isn't it, just getting Imperial and not Exxon itself?"

The reply was quick and enthusiastic. "Not really, Mr.

440

President, the Exxon deal was an enormous financial commitment for the Canadian government. There is no doubt it would have strained the country's capabilities to the limit. And you may have heard that the Prime Minister has been getting a lot of flack from the Opposition and the press.

"Most of the people who have opposed the take-over bid on Exxon agree with the proposition that Petro-Canada should own and control Imperial Oil. No question about that. The financing of the acquisition is something that PetroCan itself can take care of without getting the government and the banks involved. No, Canada will be quite happy, Mr. President, to wind up in this deal with ownership of Imperial Oil, and if we can do that, the exercise of a take-over bid will have been extremely worth while. Through Imperial we can put gasoline and fuel oil on the market at low, more competitive prices and force the other majors down to a reasonable profit position which allows them an adequate return for their investors and enough money to maintain their much needed exploration programs. Speaking for Petro-Canada, I will be delighted to have Imperial's new gas and oil wells in the Mackenzie Delta as well as in the Canadian Arctic Islands and Alberta in our inventory.

"No, Mr. President, I think that, politically, the Prime Minister is absolutely delighted with the result and is really far more comfortable with the Imperial acquisition than he was with the Exxon deal."

The President nodded. "I can believe that. Also, Canada, through its deal with Saudi Arabia will have made a friend in the Arab world finally. Yes, your Prime Minister's got a good deal."

The Sheik pressed the point further. "Insofar as Saudi Arabia is concerned, Mr. President, for the first time we will be in a position to do business in your country in the same way your companies have been doing business in ours for many decades. Furthermore, this cross-fertilization of the economies of the Middle East and the United States can only serve to benefit the mutual understanding and co-operation which ought to exist between the Arab nations and the United States.

"Such new close economic ties should make it easier for both of us to strive unceasingly to maintain peace in the Middle East and to settle the Palestinian matter in an equitable and just fashion. That would be a sign of a new era, would it not, Mr. President?"

President Dennis, taut on the edge of his chair, put the question, "I hear what you're saying, Mr. Minister, and it sounds to me like either I go along with you or you and the other Arab oil countries will cut us off again just as you did after the October war in 1973!"

Rahman agreed. "That is a fair analysis, except that our cut off this time will be strictly enforced. There will be no leaks. And the interests of all of your American companies in the Middle East, including Exxon's, will be seized."

"And what if I say the United States will cut off the Arab nations in reprisal—food, machinery, medical supplies?" the President countered.

The Sheik smiled, "My dear President, cut us off if you will. We Arabs lived in the desert for 6,000 years before you people—I'm sorry—the Americans descended upon us and we can live there for another 6,000 without you. But in any event we now have a new trade relationship not only with Western Europe where you still retain a modicum of influence, but also with Japan, whose ties with us have become close and tight since the October war.

"No, Mr. President, I think this is not a time for reprisals. It is a time for doing business with your friends the Arabs who wish to have done unto them only what you have done unto yourselves."

The President stood up slowly. He paused for a moment, looked at de Gaspé and Charbonneau, then back at Sheik Kamel Abdul Rahman. The meeting was over. The President said softly, "Gentlemen, I am grateful to you for the important intelligence you have brought to me. I would appreciate it if you might leave by the side door, over to my right. Senator Weinstein and Representative Foss are waiting in the office you came through and I would like at this point to avoid a confrontation."

As his visitors stood to make their departure, the President said, "And one final thing. You should be aware that all conversations in this office are taped automatically, and that what we have said in these last few minutes is on record. I intend to play back this conversation for Weinstein and Foss before I tell them"–the President stopped and looked down at his hands which were trembling–" that I have no choice but to veto their bill."

Appendix I
A National Energy Policy for Canada

THE GOALS

It is in the interests of the people of Canada and urgent that a comprehensive national policy for energy be forthwith created so that the goals and objectives of Canada are clearly established and that:

Such policy should deal first with crude oil, natural gas, coal and their derivatives;

It should be designed to ensure that for the foreseeable future every Canadian citizen is assured of an adequate supply of fuel oil, gasoline, and other fossil fuel products which are required to maintain the standard of living which this nation has achieved;

The national energy policy should ensure that the people of Canada have a maximum participation in the ownership of the crude oil, natural gas, coal, and their derivatives produced in Canada and that there is a maximum return to the people of Canada either through their governments or through private enterprise endeavours;

Upon the sale of the fossil fuel commodities either domestically or internationally, opportunities for Canadians to share in the proceeds be maximized through royalties, export taxes, and Canadian ownership of all unexplored gas and oil acreage in the Yukon and Northwest Territories.

In order to transport to domestic markets any and all crude oil, natural gas, coal, or other energy resources, transmission and transportation systems should be constructed in such a manner as to ensure that Canada can achieve energy self-sufficiency, while at the same time retaining the opportunity to import these vital fossil commodities should market and geopolitical conditions make it desirable to do so;

Surpluses of energy commodities should be made available to the United States;

Immediate assistance should be given to the United States in building the transportation system to move its massive volumes of natural gas from Prudhoe Bay and Alaska across Canada into the United States of America for its Midwest market.

In order to implement the national energy policy the government of Canada should work closely with an in cooperation and equality with the oil-producing and -exporting provinces of Canada rather than by confrontation and with attitudes of superiority so that the interest and positions of those provinces as clearly defined under the British North America act are respected and given full weight.

NATIONAL POLICY

1) It is the national policy that all sources of energy available within Canada are to be identified, evaluated, and estimated as to potential capacity and proven reserves.

2) The energy resources of Canada shall be conserved and shall be dedicated first to the needs and requirements of the Canadian people, provided that those amounts of energy forms which are calculated to be surplus to the needs of the Canadians within the foreseeable future may be committed for export to foreign markets.

3) Canada must achieve total energy self-sufficency at the earliest possible time and must give urgent priority and encouragement to exploration and development of its crude oil and natural gas resources including the Athabasca tarsands.

4) Canada must forthwith create transportation systems

which ensure the movement of sufficient quantities of energy in whatever form from the place or origin within Canada to the domestic market of need.

5) The national energy policy shall be both created and implemented by consultative, co-operative, joint procedures among the energy-producing governments (federal and provincial), it being the intent that both levels of government should work together as equals provided that the principles established under the British North America Act as to the resource or other jurisdictions of each level of government shall be totally respected provided further that, those rights and privileges shall be mixed and blended where it is in the interests of the people of Canada.

6) It is national policy for Canada that there be established a Canada Energy Corporation (CEC) which will work in co-operation with the National Energy Board. The purposes of the Canada Energy Corporation, which will not be a Crown corporation but which will offer shares to the Canadian public and to the provincial and federal governments, will be, among other things, as follows:

a) CEC would undertake all crude oil and natural gas exploration in the Yukon and Northwest Territories provided that CEC will be entitled to raise exploration funds against "first rights to negotiate" for gas or oil discovered (Panarctic now has this arrangement with Tenneco and Columbia of the U.S.).

b) CEC would finance and undertake the construction of the Mackenzie Valley Corridor natural gas pipeline from the Yukon-Alaska border and the Mackenzie Delta through to the U.S. border and to connect with TransCanada Pipelines for distribution throughout Canada. If no Alaska gas is committed, then a smaller line should be built to bring Mackenzie Valley gas to Canada South.

c) CEC would undertake the Mackenzie Valley Corridor pipeline construction through a wholly owned subsidiary which would raise the required construction funds 10 per cent by equity and the balance by debt financing. The division of financing would be legislated and would require a low equity input for the reason that the owners of the natural gas in the Arctic, which are all large, well-funded, U.S. multi-national corporations, and the buyers of the commodity in the United States, all have access to substantial quantities of funds and credit. Therefore the funding of construction would not be the usual "market" situation. With a $6 billion construction cost the Canadian equity required ($600 million) would be raised by public subscription and by governmental participation: no dividends would be declared nor would any interest be payable on the debt financing until such time as the gas from Prudhoe Bay and the Mackenzie Delta began to flow in the pipe.

d) CEC would be responsible for the production and sale of all crude oil and gas within its holdings and the development of systems to transport its commodities to market.

e) CEC would be empowered to undertake with the government of Alberta the creation of synthetic oil production plants in the Athabasca tarsands or to undertake such development with private enterprise.

f) CEC would be empowered to market petroleum products on a retail or wholesale basis, refine and process petroleum products. CEC would not enter the hydro electric power field except as a financing participant but would be allowed to engage with Atomic Energy of Canada Limited in the production of electricity by nuclear power.

g) CEC would undertake research and development in the search for new forms of energy.

7) It is national policy that in the Yukon and the Northwest Territories the privilege of exploring for crude oil and natural gas be the exclusive right of Canadians and the Canada Energy Corporation and that all exploration permits for acreage in the territories which has not yet been drilled will be revoked and the deposit monies returned to the foreign or foreign-controlled exploration companies which now hold them and all such rights shall be granted to CEC by the government of Canada.

8) It is the national policy of Canada that all steps be taken to assist the United States in obtaining access to its Prudhoe Bay and other Alaskan natural gas by the creation of a transCanada pipeline system. Commencement of construction must be early because when the crude oil pipeline from Prudhoe Bay to Valdez in Alaska is completed, the natural gas generated by the oil production at Prudhoe Bay will require that a natural gas transmission system to the United States be built within two years.

9) It is national policy that the government of Canada recognizes the rights of the native people of the Yukon and Northwest Territories and that before commencement of construction of the Mackenzie Valley natural gas pipeline a settlement should be negotiated with them.

10) It is national energy policy that the pipeline transmission corporations, being Canadian-owned regulated common carriers, be given statutory power to engage in and finance petroleum exploration and development within Canada.

11) It is national policy that exhaustive research be mounted into all possible modes of transporting fossil fuels from the Canadian Arctic Islands having due regard to the delicate eco-system of that region.

12) It is the national policy of Canada that there be established an authority to have power to exercise an over-

view of the domestic and international marketing, distribution, and pricing for all crude oil and natural gas and their derivatives produced in Canada; and that the members of such authority be comprised of nominees of the oil- and gas-producing governments (federal and provincial); and that such body be named the Canadian Organization of Petroleum Exporting Governments (COPEG).

13) The price to be paid by Canadians for their domestic forms of energy shall be related to the cost of production of those resources within Canada and shall not be related to world market prices: provided that energy forms for export shall be priced in accordance with the world market. The share of the people of Canada of the price paid for energy commodities shall be maximized by means of ownership, royalties, and taxes.

14) COPEG would be responsible for creating and implementing such programs as may be necessary for the allocation, distribution, pricing, and rationing of gasoline and fuel oil.

15) The National Energy Board would retain its historic role and powers except where such powers are provided to COPEG: and the NEB shall be advisory to COPEG.

IMPLEMENTING POLICIES

1) A pipeline to deliver western crude oil to Montreal refineries should be built forthwith by Canada using government funds; and a transportation system for western crude oil and refined products to the Maritime provinces should be designed and built.

2) Emergency plans should be prepared to move gasoline and fuel oil from Ontario refineries into Quebec and the Maritimes.

3) The price of western crude should be allowed to rise

when the federal export impost is removed provided that the price to which it is permitted to rise for domestic consumption is limited to an amount which reflects the Canadian oil industry's stated need for funds to enable it to continue its exploration and development (the industry says that western crude production will cease by 1984 unless new finds are made); and provided further that the oil industry gives a firm commitment that the funds obtained by the price rise will be used for exploration and development.

4) Special tax incentives should be provided immediately for the development of the Athabasca tarsands.

5) Comprehensive steps be taken on a nationwide basis to encourage and, if necessary, direct that the consumption of fossil fuels be reduced, especially by automobile users.

6) A national energy conference of first ministers should be held immediately to:

a) resolve energy disputes between the federal and provincial governments.

b) negotiate and create a national energy policy for Canada.

c) resolve the matter of domestic and export pricing of crude oil and natural gas

d) establish the Canadian Organization of Petroleum Exporting Governments and to provide COPEG with terms of reference and such legislated authority as may be necessary.

e) prepare short- and long-term goals and strategy to ensure that Canada's energy relationship with the United States is responsive to the escalating energy crisis in that nation.

Appendix II
Hansard, Thursday, November 20, 1980

THE PRIME MINISTER'S SPEECH OUTLINING THE CONCEPT OF A
MOBILE HOUSE OF COMMONS.

Mr. Speaker, when this nation was created and this Confederation established in 1867, it was appropriate and indeed it was mandatory that there be a capital. That capital was Ottawa, and it was mandatory and appropriate for all Honourable Members of this House in that day to proceed to Ottawa from their constituencies for the sittings of this House, knowing full well that apart from the benefit of communications by post, carried from their homes and the ridings which they represented to Ottawa by horse, carriage, rail, and often by vessel, there would be no opportunity to communicate with the home riding or other parts of Canada as it then was, and there would be little or no way of returning quickly to one's home area for a short visit.

Therefore, for all Members and Senators the Parliament Buildings at Ottawa were the one and only place in which it was practical for the House of Commons to meet. And so it has remained over the past one hundred and fourteen years a requirement that all who have business to do with Parliament whether from the Pacific Coast, the Atlantic Coast, or indeed, from the shores of the Arctic Ocean, they must come to Ottawa. Decisions are made by the House of Commons affecting all of those places by men and women of this House, many of whom have never seen those regions, or been among the people who populate them.

Mr. Speaker, in the almost twelve decades since Confederation there have been changes in the world the like of which mankind has never before seen.

451

We now have the magic of television, of computers, of the telephone, of the telex system. We can transmit pictures and pages of print electronically. We can communicate with all parts of the world by fantastic space satellites. We can move in massive jet aircraft from place to place throughout this country in short, almost magically short, periods of time. We have automobiles which carry us from place to place as matters of mecessity. We have radio, trucks, and a host of other transportation and communications devices which have made this country small, reachable – a place in which close contact can be maintained at all times.

While I do not propose that what I am about to say should be actually done, I do say to you, Mr. Speaker, that theoretically – I am sure it would never be done for obvious reasons – we could take every Member of this House and every Deputy Minister and put them all in one huge Boeing 747 and transport all of them to any major city in Canada within a matter of four hours at the outside.

Mr. Speaker, I am not proposing that the House of Commons move across Canada as a single unit, first of all because we would be fighting over which direction in which to fly and, secondly, if the aircraft were to crash, there would be a slight vacuum created.

One of the prime concerns of this government is to maintain every possible strength of national unity which can be achieved. We have been racked in this country by regional stresses and claims by the rising power of the provinces in their confrontations with the Federal Government, matters of regional disparity and some issues which from time to time, Mr. Speaker, have made it a real question as to whether or not Canada in its current form of Confederation would be able to survive.

Mr. Speaker, the time has come when the House of Commons, with all of the transportation and communications facilities available to it, ought properly to sit and do business for short periods of time in the major regional cities of Canada.

In this way, all Members of the House will demonstrate to the people of the local area in which the House is sitting that they have an interest in the people of that region and their problems and that the Members of Parliament are available to those people. Furthermore, it may well be that for many Members of this House a visit to a given city of Canada might well be that Member's first visit to that region.

For these reasons, Mr. Speaker, I propose that the House of Commons sit in Edmonton, the capital city of the Province of Alberta, for the period commencing Tuesday, March 3rd, 1981, and for a six-week period thereafter, and that the House should sit at Quebec City for a similar period in the fall of 1981 and in Yellowknife in the spring of 1982 and in other cities in the spring and fall of each following year.

This proposal has been reviewed and approved by a committee comprised of all parties which has worked out the arrangements for accommodation and for conversion of an appropriate arena or other structure in Edmonton into a temporary House of Commons.

PERISCOPE RED

1

9 March   7:05 A.M.

Beirut, Lebanon

A dense night fog had enveloped the silent port and its mutilated city, shrouding the shattered buildings and gutted streets. Now in the early light of dawn, the fog lifted to reveal the rubble of brick, concrete, and glass that spilled from the ruined towers. A light mist still swirled over the undulating sea. Through it, Said caught sight of the Beirut skyline as he sat hunched in the bow of the long, narrow rowboat, which decades ago must have been a lifeboat on some large, long-forgotten ship. As the craft moved slowly away from the shore, he shivered in the penetrating cold of the moisture-laden air which surrounded him and his companions. The thin material of his long black gown, his *aba*, offered little protection against the unaccustomed chill of the air.

As the shapes of the blackened, desolate buildings emerged from the misty darkness, their rectangular forms thrusting up from the bowels of the earth, Said's mind focused on the plan. It was his plan—all the details, all the training, all the scheming, the arrangements, the negotiations, and the objective. The goal, that was his, too. If he was successful—and he knew unquestionably that he would be—he, Said, would surely deal the mightiest, most powerful blow ever struck for his oppressed Palestinian brothers still in the refugee camps, those putrid, cancerous places in Lebanon where hundreds of thousands of nationless Palestinian Arabs had dwelt for decade after decade.

He praised Allah for giving him the genius, and with it the responsibility, to create and deliver this most massive revolutionary victory, one that would stun the world, rivet the attention of people everywhere on the plight of the Palestinians. His plan would make those indifferent, bloodsucking leeches of the Western world—especially the Jewish-Americans and that detested country that they controlled—take notice; it would compel them finally, once and for all, to recognize the Palestinian nation. Those Jewish-American imperialists would have no choice. None. They and their Western European comrades in oppression would have no alternative but to force the Israelis to give back every hectare of land, every building, every city, every port, all that they had stolen from the Palestinian Arabs in 1948, the year that he, Said Kassem, had been born in Haifa. Just one week after his birth he and his young mother and her parents were driven from their home by the British-backed Israelis.

Said's gaze rested on the black wool jacket of the man rowing the boat. The oarsman's back moved regularly as he skilfully lifted the oars out of the sea and swung them back and down in again, running the small, decrepit craft through the black, rolling water toward an as yet unseen destination.

When Said had gone to the harbor's edge the previous afternoon to hire a boat, he found this swarthy, squat and, like his vessel, unkempt boatman sitting on his beached craft waiting for business. A quick scan of the water revealed the nondescript coastal freighter Said had pointed out. It was standing about a mile offshore. The oarsman knew her well. Her owners were a group of Palestinian Arabs who had come to Beirut many years before. Unlike him they had prospered. Instead he, a native-born

Lebanese, a Christian Arab, had spent a lifetime working his father's boat—which was now his boat—off the Beirut beach and around the port. After one look at the anchored ship, he told Said he could take him there blindfolded, let alone in fog or a heavy mist.

Aft of the indifferent rower were three more passengers. Like Said they were dressed in dark, flowing robes. One of them was sitting on the seat immediately in front of the oarsman with his back to him. Hassan, too, hunched forward, his hands thrust through the sides of his gown in an attempt to hold in the heat of his own body.

The other two were crowded together in the stern seat. Their freezing legs and arms were pressed against each others' for warmth; their hands were hidden in folds of their gowns. In whispers they cursed the cold and their shared discomfort.

The larger of the two men at the far end of the boat lit a cigarette. The unexpected yellow burst of flame accosted Said's vision like a golden beacon in the lessening darkness, bringing his thoughts back to his surroundings. In the instant that the firelight played upon the angular, dark face of the thick-browed colossus of a man, Said wondered for the thousandth time how Ahmed and, for that matter, the other two, Hassan and Maan, the happy-witted soul pressed against Ahmed, would perform under the enormous stress of the high dangers to come and the risks he had promised them they would have to take in the name of the revolution and of the Palestinian Liberation Organization. They were PLO people, Arab freedom fighters. The task they were to perform was a PLO plan hatched from the fertile brain of a member of the PLO's Executive Council, Said himself, the right-hand man of the chief of the PLO. Said, it was rumored, might well succeed the chief if, Allah forbid, the leader were lost to the cause of the liberation.

For the past three months Said had trained these three men. Taught them everything he knew. Given them discipline and hard daily physical workouts, both in and out of the sea in which the final part of the plan would be performed.

In the main PLO camp, to the south of Beirut and some ten miles north of the Israeli-held Palestinian lands, Said had coached and instructed his recruits in everything he knew about the handling of automatic guns and knives and in the many ways of killing an enemy in close combat with no warning or noise. The ancient and refined commando tactics of hand garrote and other methods of silent murder were honed. Over the ninety-day training period, Said had run them countless miles, put them through hours upon endless hours of calisthenics, and kept them on a strict diet. The result was that at the end of the period, each of his men was lean and muscular. Even Maan, the roly-poly one of the trio, was slim and fit, although none of his jesting good humor had been lost in the process.

There had been extensive, thorough instruction in the handling of explosives, including their detonation by various means. Plastic explosives had been exhaustively covered, but no more so than the use of the special, incredibly powerful and sensitive device that they would use on their targets. It was not possible to teach them anything but the rudiments of radio electronics, the method that would be used to detonate their special explosive devices. Nor was it necessary, because Hassan was an expert. He had been selected as a member of the team because he was a communications specialist, with a Ph.D. in electronics from the Massachusetts Institute of Technology. However, as a precautionary measure, in case something happened to Hassan during the operation, Said had taught the other two the basics of the operation of the radio mechanisms that would be used to detonate the explosives at the right time.

It was the underwater work that in the beginning gave the three recruits the most difficulty. After long hours of working in the ocean, when they had become confident of themselves in their special gear, they found great pleasure in the new skills. Day after day, they had done classroom work on the handling of oxygen bottles, masks, and all the paraphernalia associated with scuba diving, although the task was made easier by the knowledge that during the operation they would not have to go to a depth greater than

460

one hundred feet. After the blackboard sessions they would put their diving gear, with the inflatable speedboat and its motors, into the huge van that had been allocated to them for the training period. Then they would bounce off across the rough roads westward from the camp to the wintry shores of the Mediterranean.

During their training months of December through to the end of February, that sea of ancient history would greet them in varied colors—sometimes azure blue, or turquoise, or gray or, at the time of storms, black-gray with towering, crushing waves whose crests foamed white as they thundered into the isolated sandy cove Said used as their launching base. As the colors of the ocean were varied, so were the weather conditions and the surface of the sea. In the first two weeks of the training the elements had been ideal. The Mediterranean rolled with a calm surface under blue skies sometimes dotted with lumpy white cumulus clouds. The winds were light and the temperature in the middle sixties, excellent conditions under which to introduce three men, all skilled swimmers, to the demanding challenges of underwater living, where preparation, safety checks, top-notch equipment, and rigid maintenance can provide the difference between a safe operation and death; and where the margin for disaster by error is minimal when handling sophisticated explosives and their delicate electronic trips.

When, however, the winter winds and storms produced a cold and heavy sea condition, Said canceled further underwater training, explaining to his students that the place where they were going to carry out the operation never had below-freezing temperatures or high waves. There was no need to expose themselves to unnecessary risks.

No one argued with his decision. For that matter, none of the trio ever argued with Said. Intelligent and well educated, all three had quickly taken stock of the man who had selected them from more than two hundred applicants. Each knew that when he was with Said he was in the company of a man he would naturally follow. Said, whom they guessed to be in his early thirties, while they themselves ranged from twenty-two to twenty-five years of age, had an impressive range of experience and knowledge of the fields and he quickly won their total confidence and respect. They had speculated about where he came from, his background; but he gave them no clues, and they accepted him for what he was—headstrong, intelligent, articulate; and quick witted, inventive, and impatient with anyone who could not understand what he thought was a clearly explained, easily comprehensible proposition.

Said was in excellent physical condition. He had to be, in order to lead them in rigorous calisthenics or take them into and under the sea for long periods. And his dedication to the revolutionary cause of the liberation of the Palestinian nation, its recognition by the world powers and the return of its land, was absolutely and totally unswerving—as was his dedication to carrying out the plan that he fully believed would fulfill the dreams and gain all the objectives of the PLO for the liberation of the Palestinian Arab people.

As the small boat carried them silently through the early morning Beirut mist to begin the first phase of their operation, his three companions knew little more about Said's background than they did when they first met him. He was an enigma. The only hint they received had come when Said was in an unguarded and relaxed mood as they sat around their campfire after supper one night. There had been much talk about many things—families, the future of Palestine, the inequities of the past, and women. None of them was married. Said would not have chosen a married man to be on his team. During the conversation that evening, friendly arguments flared over Maan's provocative opinions. Said had remained silent until Hassan spoke of his university life in the United States and how much living in the midst of rich Americans had changed his outlook. He had been shocked by their wanton wastefulness and by the way they looked upon the rest of the world, especially Arabs and Blacks, as grossly inferior and unintelligent. Hassan's story had struck a responsive chord with Said, who acknowledged that he had found similar attitudes in England while attending the London School of Economics. His three companions were able to take from what he had said no more than the fact that he had been a student at the university. There was nothing about the nature of his studies or whether he had a degree. No one dared ask questions.

One question they longed to ask concerned Said's appearance. His burnt brown Arabic face, enhanced by a heavy black mustache, bushy eyebrows, jet-black, wavy hair already flecked with gray, framed a pair of stunningly incongruous eyes that set him apart from his Palestinian brothers. For those eyes were blue—not an ordinary shade of blue but clear and bright, sometimes like the color of the daytime sky, sometimes like the crystal turquoise of Arctic ice. They were eyes transplanted from some northern race, perhaps Scandinavian, maybe English. Could they be Russian? About their origin, Hassan, Ahmed, and Maan had speculated countless times after they had first been exposed to them. That had happened the first time Said had removed his protective sunglasses in order to put on his scuba diving face mask. Said knew that they had been startled by what they had seen. He expected they would be. It was customary. But he had said nothing to them about it nor did he to anyone, ever. Nor did anyone ever ask.

Said's eyes were his father's. He knew his father well, respected him, loved and admired him. As a child he had spent several summers with him at his home in another seaport far to the north in a land where towering white-capped mountains, a forest of tall evergreen trees, snow, ice, rock and long, sinuous, cliff-edged estuaries leading to the bordering sea were the pattern of the terrain. It was a hard country which produced hardy, tough, intelligent, industrious people, people with blue eyes, turquoise like the brilliant ice off their winter shores.

Notwithstanding the Nordic strain, Said was a Palestinian through and through. His Arab inheritance was nurtured by the experience of being raised in the poverty and deprivation of a Palestinian refugee camp. He was immersed in the life, language, culture and society of his mother and her parents, whose tent they had shared from the time of Said's first memories. He used his mother's surname, Kassem. In that atmosphere his growing mind had been filled with the bitter rantings and invectives of a subjugated and forgotten race, in a camp teeming with unproductive people whose only thoughts were for the injustices heaped upon them, who yearned for freedom, and for the restoration of their lands and their dignity.

Thus Said was a Palestinian Arab. And yet he also carried an unusual genetic strain of which his blue eyes were the manifestation. It was this combination that set him apart and provided for him the special initiatives. He thought as did his Arab fellows but unlike them he did not rant, rave and merely talk. He could act. It was because of his inborn reticence, combined with a compulsive need to perform, to do, to execute, that Said was in that boat being rowed, to nowhere it seemed, his eyes and mind now focused on the huge brown face of Ahmed, bathed in the yellow light of the cupped flame as the big man lit his cigarette. Then the flame was gone and Ahmed's face was a dark blurred background for the glowing tip of the sucked cigarette.

Ahmed will be as a rock, Said reflected. I only wish he didn't smoke those damned cigarettes. Such poison. Even so, like me he is nervous, and there is nothing wrong with that. If we get into difficulty, if there is shooting or something goes wrong underwater, if something happens to me—and of course nothing ever will—it will be Ahmed who will remain calm, will think things out. He is the cool one, perhaps even more than I. I envy him his strength. And Maan, the puppy dog, bright, funny. But he has just a slight tendency to panic if things aren't going right. Like the time when his oxygen flow was cut off. It was a good thing we were only about twenty feet down and I was there with him, watching. I made sure he got it fixed all right and quickly. But the wild thrashing about and the popping eyes behind the mask: he panicked. So I'll have to keep an eye on him. Apart from that he is good. Very good. And I

464

guess being a schoolteacher helps you to learn. In fact he's almost as bright as Hassan.

Said's eyes shifted from the dim countenance of Maan to the back of Hassan's head, visible over the right shoulder of the pumping oarsman. He has to have one of the finest brains I've ever run across, thought Said. He contemplated the tall, thin, athletic body, which he sometimes thought resembled an elongated crab, particularly when Hassan was working underwater, huge flippers on his feet thrusting and propelling him through the sea. If we have any kind of a problem I'm certain Hassan can cope. He doesn't panic. No problem with him. He isn't physically as strong as the rest of us but he shouldn't have any problem handling what we have to do when we get there. He really pressed me last night to tell them the plan—where we're going, what we're going to do when we get there. I could tell he was annoyed when I refused. Do they have a right to know? Hassan thinks they do and I think they do too. But Yassir thinks not. He is the chief and so that's it. We have such a long way to sail; many things could go wrong. If one of them fell into the hands of unfriendly interrogators, the whole operation might be blown. I can't quarrel too much with Arafat's thinking. Not knowing the plan just makes it that much more difficult for my team. Anyway they'll know soon enough.

Said's train of thought was interrupted when the boatman leaned on his oars, turning his head round to the right so he could look forward and past Said. He was searching the mist for the anchored ship. It should not be too much farther. The light was improving rapidly and with it the mist was dissipating.

"There she is, dead ahead!" he announced triumphantly. All eyes in the rowboat squinted as they peered at the vessel waiting to receive them. She was about a hundred yards away, her bow pointing out to sea, meeting the incoming roll of the waves.

Across her stern, just below the deck level, her name was emblazoned in flaked, dirt-streaked white against rust-pocked black paint that had long ago been slapped over her

300-foot-long hull. She was the *Mecca*. The word appeared in both English and Arabic script, as was appropriate for a homeless coaster that traveled the length and breadth of the Mediterranean, putting into small ports and large, serving particularly the fishing villages and shallow harbors denied the larger freighters.

When briefed about his team's travel arrangements, and the supply of its weapons and equipment, Said was informed that arrangements had been made with the Beirut owners of the *Mecca*—all of them dedicated Palestinian Arabs except for a convenient Egyptian partner. The old vessel would pick up a full cargo at Piraeus, the bustling major Greek port near Athens. Her cargo was to be a mix of foodstuffs, bagged grain, six four-wheel-drive motor vehicles, oil exploration equipment, and ten large wood-crated compressors for a natural gas installation being built in Kuwait.

The *Mecca*'s first stop out of Piraeus would be Beirut where she would put ashore two of the motor vehicles, using her own crane to off-load them into lightering craft as she stood at anchor offshore. She would then take on board four large wooden crates which would be stacked for convenience next to the German manufactured compressors.

She would arrive off Beirut at about three in the afternoon of March 8 and complete her unloading. Her captain would go ashore to complete his paper work with the port authorities and check in with the Lloyd's of London agent to confirm his voyage intentions. Then he would get back to his ship as quickly as possible.

In the old days, Captain Rashid loved Beirut. He would go hundreds of miles out of his way to get his anchor into the waters off the craggy shore so he could spend the night at the fabulous gambling casino that sat at cliff's edge overlooking the Mediterranean, just a few miles north of the city. He swore that the Beirut casino presented the most spectacular floor shows in the entire world, with the most beautiful of all European women, long legged and bare breasted, on the stage. Back in those days he would take a shower before he went ashore because, more often than not, he was able to make arrangements for a little after-the-

466

show association with one of the casino's gorgeous creatures —he being a regular and recognized customer, well able to afford the substantial fee.

But those days were long gone. Now Beirut was completely ravaged from within. Its religious factions were still fighting and killing each other. To be in a place where shooting was going on was not in the least attractive to Captain Rashid, a man who placed the highest value on his own hide. Furthermore, the glamorous casino, like the center of the city of which it was a satellite, was dead. Its slot machines and games rooms stood silent, its choice, high-stepping European beauties long since back in Hamburg and Paris and London. It was all very sad.

Thus Captain Rashid was on board his ship rather than bedded in Beirut when the rowboat carrying the four black-robed men and their hand luggage pulled alongside the *Mecca*'s battered hull shortly after 7:20 on the morning of March 8. Indeed, the captain was on deck waiting for his passengers. He had climbed out of his large bed shortly after six. After a leisurely breakfast, he completed his morning ablutions which concluded with a careful combing of his short beard, a gray and white one as befitted a man with sixty-five lustily lived years. In the scratched mahogany paneled bedroom of the master's cabin, which ran almost the width of the vessel under its bridge, he had dressed in his usual gear: a dirty rolled-neck wool pullover; heavy, navy-blue, unpressed trousers and jacket of the same material. The last thing on was his scruffy captain's flat cap, its peak sporting tattered, salt-tarnished gold braid. The cap sat squarely on a head of thinning white hair trimmed at collar level. Captain Rashid was pleased with what he saw in the mirror. He fluffed the underside of his beard with the back of his hand. Smiling at himself with gold-mottled teeth, he smoothed back the strands of hair pushed down and out by the cap in front of his ears. Satisfied, he stepped out the cabin door to stand at the top of the gangway on the starboard side of the craft, moments before Said's boat bumped to a halt against the gangway's landing platform.

At the railing, Rashid watched the movement of the

467

boat some ten feet below. He uttered no greeting as he looked down in the morning light into the strange faces peering up at him. He would watch to see who moved first or gave an order. That man would be the leader of the group. No order was given.

The boatman reached out from his seat to grab and hang on to the gangway platform, steadying the small craft against it. Without a word, Said lifted himself up from the seat in the bow and picked up his dunnage bag from the boards at his feet. Effortlessly he flung it over his left shoulder and stepped lightly past the oarsman's horizontal right arm, up and over it and onto the platform. With a nod of appreciation to the boatman, he lifted the hem of his robe to avoid tripping as he took the gangway steps three at a time.

At the deck he was greeted with a welcoming smile by Captain Rashid.

"God be with you."

"And with you, captain. I am . . ."

"Yes, I know. You are Said. You are the leader." It was a statement, not a question. The two men shook hands briefly as the captain went on.

"Welcome to my ship. I hope you and your companions enjoy the trip. You will be with us . . ."

Said nodded. "Yes, we'll be with you for a long time. Too long, I'm afraid."

Out of the corner of his eye he could see the rowboat pulling away and could feel the weight of his three colleagues on the gangway behind him. Stepping aside to allow them to go by, he introduced each man as he stepped onto the deck. The greetings out of the way, the captain walked aft, beckoning the group to follow him.

"I have accommodation for you on the poop in the crew area just up there on the second deck." He pointed upward toward the stern of the craft.

On the deck level on which they were standing there were hatches leading to the cargo hold. To each side of those hatches, both fore and aft of the bridge, ten huge crates with German markings on them were lashed to the deck. Those would be the compressors. Six were between the bridge and the crew's quarters. The other four were between the bridge and the fo'c'sle. Four smaller wooden crates, brought on board the day before, were also lashed on the afterdeck in the space between the compressor cargo and the bridge. This was as planned. Said was pleased to note that, so far, everything was in accordance with the arrangements. As he understood it, Captain Rashid had not been informed of the true contents of the crates boarded at Beirut. According to the bill of lading, they each contained one hundred subsoil very high frequency [VHF] electronic transmitter-receivers. The papers declared that, like the compressors next to them, the electronic devices had been manufactured in and were shipped from West Germany. It also showed that, having been picked up at Naples, they had arrived at Beirut one week earlier in another coaster for transfer to the *Mecca* and furtherance to their final destination, Kuwait. The consignee for the electronic communication devices was the same as for the compressors, the Kuwaiti National Oil Company.

Said was pleased. The positioning of the smaller cases was perfect for a quick transfer of their contents to the compressor boxes, if need be.

Captain Rashid spoke as he continued to walk along the cargo deck toward the steps up to the cabin deck.

"Unfortunately it is not possible to provide you with single cabin accommodation. There are only eight crew members other than myself and the first mate—his cabin is back here also—but this vessel was not built for people or comfort. The best I could do is to put you two to a cabin." He shrugged his shoulders and turned both his hands palms upwards in a gesture of regret.

"Where is the crew?" Ahmed asked. He had not seen a soul on the deck save the captain.

"The deck hands are still sleeping. They had a big night in Beirut—with permission of course, even though I personally avoid the place. They're sleeping it off. That includes the first mate. He has a—how should I put it?—a close friend in Beirut. He has an interest in her business.

469

You do understand. And whenever he's here,"—the captain's eyebrows arched and his mouth twisted slightly into a leer—"it is essential for the two of them to have a business conference."

Maan could not resist interjecting. "Which of course lasts all night?"

"But of course. And why not? As for Nabil, the first mate, you can be sure he's back on board. He arrived just a few minutes ahead of you. My two engine room men are down below getting ready for our departure."

"What time are you planning on leaving, captain?"

"We will up-anchor in an hour, at 8:30. That will be enough time to get my crew back on their feet."

At the ladder the captain appeared to shed his years. With the agility of an old sailor he hoisted himself up the near-vertical steps to the cabin deck.

Said stood at the bottom of the ladder and assessed the situation for a moment. It was almost impossible for him to raise his gown with one hand, balance his huge dunnage bag on his shoulder with the other, and get up those steps. He guessed there were perhaps ten or twelve. Without a word he eased the bag to the deck, undid the buttons down the front of his gown and pulled the garment away from his shoulders. With a quick movement he lowered it to his feet and stepped out, transforming himself instantly into a military figure. Under his gown he wore a light olive-green, short-sleeved shirt, open at the neck, with buttoned epaulets on each shoulder and trim, tight-fitting, light material trousers of the same color tucked into the tops of tan, calf-length combat boots. His shirt bore no markings or insignia of any kind. Nevertheless, with his headband holding the cloth piece on his head at a slight angle—as his chief always wore his—the trim, heavily muscled Said looked every inch a well-trained soldier, which indeed he was. Said's men followed their leader's example. In a few seconds their gowns were off, revealing that all of them were in the uniform of the Palestinian Liberation Organization.

Captain Rashid's bearded jaw sagged in surprise as he

watched the silent stripping on the deck below. He knew that the men coming on board were PLO soldiers. That had been made perfectly clear to him by the owners' agent in Piraeus. He had no problem accepting their presence because he was a Palestinian Arab himself but, fortunately for him, one who was already free from the shackles of refugee camps and out in the open world. Nevertheless Rashid was apprehensive about these men. Furthermore he detested the kind of reflecting sunglasses Said was wearing because you can't read the man's eyes, you can't see who he is or how he is reacting to what you're saying or doing. But there was no reason to believe that Said would be anything but friendly and cooperative. After all, they were in the same cause, Palestinian Arabs together in support of the PLO and freedom for the Palestinian people and the recapture of their lands. No . . . there was no reason to be alarmed.

Even so an alarm had sounded in Captain Rashid's head. He had often had to handle unusual, sometimes mysterious, passengers whom the owners had forced upon him; or for that matter whom he himself had secretly allowed on board in exchange for an appropriate package of money.

I'm sure I have nothing to fear from them, thought the captain as he watched the four lithe men bound up the ladder. But I must handle them with care. Yes, great care. Those packing cases that came on board yesterday. I wonder . . .

The captain led the group along the open starboard passageway to the door of the first cabin which he shoved open but did not enter. Walking straight on, he similarly opened a second door. Then he turned to face Said. "There you are." Rashid waved his left arm toward the two open doorways inviting entrance. "The best rooms in the house."

Said, his dunnage bag still on his left shoulder, stuck his head in the cabin door and took a quick look around the cramped compartment. He saw two bunks, each with a mattress but no sheets or pillows, a chair, two tables under the porthole, a light over each of the bunks, dirty gray-painted walls. On the floor was a filthy, once-green carpet. A pair of cockroaches scuttled across it. The place stank of a hundred bodies that had lived in that cubicle and the thousands of pungent Arabian cigarettes they had smoked. Said's first thought was that he would throw out the mattresses, hose the place down, disinfect it somehow.

He backed out into the passageway. Looking at the captain, he said in a subdued voice, "They'll do. We'll clean them out. We won't use the mattresses. Do you want to store them or should we just pitch them overboard?"

Rashid smiled and shook his head "No, young man. I make it a practice to keep everything I can . . ." he couldn't resist a slight twist, "even my patience with members of the PLO." He paused to wait for a reaction from Said but he was frustrated. He could not see the eyes behind the mirrored glasses. The face remained expressionless.

"You can take the mattresses and store them in the paint locker aft beside the heads. One of my men will show you where it is later." He made to move by Said and his men, saying, "Now, if you'll excuse me, I must get this ship under way." He started to move back down the companionway past the men, but Said stood firm. He did not step aside to let the ship's master pass. His voice was cold. His words were delivered in a monotone. "We are not on your ship to try your patience, captain. We are here because we have no choice. We have a mission to carry out in the revolutionary cause of the Palestinian people. The only way we can get to our objective is on this stinking, filthy ship. You have been well paid to carry us and that includes the price of your patience. Get your ship under way, captain, and I will see you in your cabin at ten o'clock. There are some things you and I must settle."

The captain was incensed. He drew himself up to his full height, his white beard quivering with rage. "You cannot give me orders on my own ship!"

"I'm not giving you an order, captain. Not yet, anyway. I will be at your cabin at ten o'clock."

Those words spoken, Said turned abruptly and went into the first cabin while his team stood aside, their backs against the railing, to allow the indignant captain to storm past toward the first mate's cabin on the port side of that same deck.

In the next half hour the ship came to life. The angry Rashid rooted Nabil, the still half-inebriated first mate, out of his bunk, shouting at him to get the ill-begotten crew on deck, and get the ship under way. Nabil, the nephew of the Egyptian partner in the *Mecca*, was a scrawny twenty-nine-year-old with bulging eyes and matted, unkempt black hair, a pencil-thin mustache, and huge ears which he was partly able to hide by covering them with greasy strands of hair. The captain was forced to accept him, like it or not. The slovenly young man at first scarcely knew the ship's stem from its stern, but in the past three months he had learned quickly under the shouting, snarling direction of the normally calm Rashid.

Shaken out of his drunken sleep by his irate captain, the first mate stumbled around his cabin dressing, struggling into his long-soiled clothes, trying to pull himself together before he half fell out the door. The brilliant light of the morning sun was a shock to his bloodshot eyes. Steadying himself, he made his way aft to the heads, the communal toilets. Having relieved himself, he staggered along the starboard passageway, making for the ladder that Said and his men had ascended just a short time before. Nabil was startled and puzzled to find four bareheaded, bare-chested, and shoeless strangers in scruffy blue jeans, spraying high-velocity water from the starboard firehose into one cabin, and in another using scrub brushes on the walls, ceiling, and floor.

The first mate's eyes bugged even more than normally when they ran over the size of the enormous man handling the hose. Ahmed, the nozzle in his two hands, stood with feet planted wide apart just outside the second cabin door. His face was split by an ear-to-ear grin of enjoyment as the powerful jet of water screamed from the nozzle, hammering against the layers of dirt on the grime-encrusted walls. Just to make sure his comrades were doing their share of the work, he had let all three of them have an accidental short burst on the backsides as they scrubbed away in the water-soaked first cabin. Roaring with laughter, they cursed and shook their fists at him. Within a dozen paces of this wild scene, the first mate quickly sized up the situation and made the right decision. Back aft he went to scuttle across toward the deck ladder on the port side and down. Suddenly he remembered what the captain had ordered him to do before he went to the bridge. In two minutes he had opened every cabin door, shouting at the besotted deckhands to report to their assigned departure stations immediately.

Half an hour later, Captain Rashid, standing on the starboard flying wing of his bridge, shouted the order to the three weaving deck hands assembled on the fo'c'sle deck, "Up anchor!" Turning to his left he growled at the first mate standing in the center of the bridgehouse by the wheelsman, "Slow ahead to take the slack off the anchor chain."

"Aye, aye, sir." The first mate moved the engine telegraph levers to slow ahead. He knew that in the bowels of the engine room aft, the so-called chief engineer would hear the signal bell and move the throttles of the two diesels to the slow ahead position. Then he would wait for the stop signal to come. This was the usual pattern in lifting anchor. A relatively simple one in a calm sea, much more difficult in heavy weather.

On the fo'c'sle, the three deck hands, still debilitated by the previous night's carousing, gritted their teeth and leaned into the arms of the capstan to begin the rounds that drew up the anchor chain like a gigantic bobbin taking up thread.

As soon as the ship's propeller began to bite into the sea, moving the craft slowly forward, the captain ordered, "Stop engines." Power off, the *Mecca* coasted toward the anchor while the laboring deck hands ran their capstan arms in a wide circle, picking up the chain slack as quickly as they could; they slowed as the ship's bow passed over the anchor and the taut chain picked up its full weight from the rocky bottom a hundred feet below. Fifteen minutes later, after countless back-wrenching revolutions of the capstan, the *Mecca*'s anchor was up and on the fo'c'sle.

As soon as he was satisfied that it was securely on board, the captain ordered, "Full speed ahead!" and the *Mecca* was under way out of Beirut. Her hoary diesels thundered in the hot, fume-filled engine room cavern, while black smoke belched from the spindly stack that pierced the center of the crew's quarters. With the smoke began the reassuring thumping of the drive shaft and the huge single screw that pushed the *Mecca* through the waveless blue waters of the eastern Mediterranean under a cloudless sky.

When Said had decided to scour the cabins, he and his men had made a fast change from their olive-green uniforms into well-worn blue jeans. Ahmed found the firehose and Maan discovered four long-unused scrub brushes and one serviceable mop, complete with bucket and some soap, stored in the corner of the paintless paint locker. Those weapons of cleanliness had been out of favor for years on the *Mecca*. The use of them involved work which any right-minded crew member of a decrepit Middle Eastern coastal freighter would avoid like the worst kind of plague.

By ten o'clock they had finished their cleaning chore. The soiled, foul-smelling mattresses had been shoved into the paint locker. Every inch of the small cubicles had been hosed and scrubbed with brushes and soap, then hosed again. The wooden bunks, tables, and chairs received the same treatment. Cleansed, they were placed along the forward edge of the cabin deck to dry in the lifting sun and light breeze that flowed along the *Mecca*'s decks. Their four dunnage bags had been left on the open passageway, well away from the flow of the cleansing stream of water from the firehose.

Said and his men changed back into their olive-green uniforms, Arab headdresses, and combat boots. Said had decided that he would be properly dressed for his confrontation with the old man. He intended to take a soft-line approach to Rashid, at least until the first part of their mission had been completed. That should be in two weeks and a day, Allah being with them.

Said had given much thought to his upcoming meeting with the captain, in his own way a rather intimidating man. It would not do to appear in scruffy work pants for this first formal discussion when an understanding would have to be reached between the two of them as equals. And equals they would have to be, whether the captain liked it or not, notwithstanding the substantial age difference between them. Said had years ago perceived that the social structure of each country of the world, whatever its politics or race, had as its skeleton a sharply-defined pecking order, pervasive even in its lowest extremities. And that in all business, governmental, diplomatic, academic, and other institutionalized relationships, certain outward manifestations were necessary to mark, sometimes dramatically, sometimes subliminally, the station of the person in that pecking order. Of these manifestations, the manner and style of dress was of the utmost importance. This was particularly so during the opening engagement, the initial sparring round with a stranger with whom business had to be done, negotiations undertaken, and arrangements made on a level of equality.

Equality was especially difficult to achieve when the youthfulness, and therefore apparent inexperience, of a younger person was enhanced by the older person's lack of knowledge of the younger's background and credentials, his authority, or his intelligence. It was in this kind of encounter that Said recognized he was naturally disadvantaged at the outset. That impediment would be increased if he failed to present himself to the captain in his PLO garb. The uniform of the PLO army clothed him with dignity and prestige, made him a recognizable symbol of the power and authority of the PLO army, its chief and the Palestinian people.

Said shaved before he changed into his uniform. There was no sink in the cabins assigned to them so he had to do his shaving in the heads on the cabin deck, aft near the stern. Like the rest of the ship, the place was filthy and stinking. They would have to hose it down too. Barely able to breathe the stench, he shaved as quickly as his heavy black stubble would permit. When he returned to his nearly dry cabin he changed into his uniform. He was ready for Captain Rashid. As he walked to the steps to the cargo deck and the captain's cabin, he gave instructions to his three companions. Following his orders, they dispersed as Said went gingerly down the still-unfamiliar steep steps.

Rashid was standing on the starboard wing of his bridge, watching him. There was no way the captain would be waiting in his cabin at ten o'clock. That would have been an acknowledgment of Said's authority. No, he would watch for him, then leave his bridge to go down to the cabin when Said arrived at its door.

"Keep her steady as she goes." With a perfunctory, unnecessary order to the suffering first mate whose red, bulging eyes could barely focus on the bow of the *Mecca*, thumping steadily along at its cruising speed of twelve knots, Rashid went to his cabin down steps leading directly into it from the bridge.

As he opened the door to allow Said to enter he noted that the young man was freshly shaved and carefully dressed. Motioning him in with a cordial smile, he offered Said a seat at the long, pock-marked table that doubled as a desk and an eating place. Papers, maps, and charts were stacked untidily at each end but the working space in the middle was clear except for a pot of Arabian coffee and two cups brought in by the ship's cook just a few minutes before. The cups were small, the coffee thick and strong. The captain sat in his own chair opposite Said, offered the coffee, which was accepted, then a cigarette, which was declined. When his cigarette was lit, the captain took off his ever-present cap and threw it on the closest pile of papers, picked up his cup and leaned back in his high-backed, threadbare upholstered chair. He was ready.

"Well now, what am I permitted to call you?"

"Said."

"And no military rank?"

Said shook his head.

"But I was informed that you were a lieutenant-colonel in the PLO army." He wanted the young man to believe that he knew quite a bit about him, although, in fact, he knew almost nothing.

"My rank is not important. On this ship I simply want to be known as Said."

The captain shrugged. "Very well. Now, you wanted to talk with me."

"I'm not sure how much you have been told about us."

"Not very much. Simply that the four of you are members of the PLO army and that I'm to take you to Kuwait. Beyond that I know nothing except that having you on board has its risks."

Said did not believe that this was all the captain knew. But he was certain that he had no knowledge of the operation to be carried out and in which the *Mecca*, its captain, and its crew would have a part. "What risks? We are signed on as part of the ship's crew. Our papers are in order. What risks could there be?"

Rashid took a deep drag on his cigarette and a sip of the powerful coffee. "You know as well as I do, Said, that in Egypt—and we have to go through the Suez Canal—in Egypt the PLO is as welcome as a snake in a whore's bed. And in Aden, well, maybe not so much there, but in Kuwait, it's the same as Egypt. They're scared to death of the PLO. After all, most of the population is Palestinian, brought in to do the work. To the Kuwaiti, you PLO people, particularly the revolutionary wing, *you* people are unwanted enemies of the state . . . even though they support the right of all Palestinians to have their own land. So I can tell you, as far as I'm concerned, having you on board involves risks. The last thing I want is to have my ship impounded or get into any kind of trouble with the port authorities. As it is, I'm well received wherever this ship goes."

"I assure you the last thing I want to do is cause any trouble for you. We want to get to Kuwait just as badly as you want to avoid any trouble. So I'm here to tell you, captain, that my group and I are prepared to cooperate with you in every way. We're supposed to be part of the crew."

Rashid leaned forward, his face and eyes showing the hardness of his voice. "Then you'd better start by understanding that I am the captain of this ship, not you; that you and your people are signed on as deck hands and you'd better start behaving like deck hands. I told my crew you are deck hands. And what do you do as soon as you get on board? You strip down to your uniforms for all the world to see. Fortunately I was the only one on deck at the time, but here you are again. You just let my whole crew see you in this regalia. Maybe they won't know what the uniform is, but I can tell you, Said, it won't be long before they start asking questions."

No reaction from Said.

"I don't want to see those uniforms again. Before you leave this cabin I'll have one of your men bring your work clothes so you can change." The captain did not wait for Said's agreement. "What about weapons, guns, knives? I assume you've got those things in your bags?"

Said shifted in his chair to pick up the coffee pot. He would not wait for the captain to pour for him. Rashid had said all that Said had expected he would. Now it was time to respond.

"You worry unduly about uniforms, captain. So far as I'm concerned it could not matter less who sees us in our uniforms. There are how many people on this ship other than yourself? Nine?"

Rashid nodded his agreement.

"I would expect that out of that nine, you personally would trust not one. Correct?"

The captain snorted. "Correct."

Said hesitated. "The point is this, captain: you don't trust your crew. I certainly don't trust them. I don't even know them. Furthermore I have no reason to trust you, either. I'm quite sure that if you thought it was to your advantage you would sell us to the highest bidder."

The captain made as if to protest but Said waved him down. "Don't be insulted. Please. In my profession, if I am to survive, I can trust no one except my own people. You ask about guns, weapons. Sure we have them. You wouldn't expect us to come aboard your vessel unarmed. As a matter of fact, at this very moment one of my men is on your bridge and another is standing beside the cabin door." His right hand lifted to point to the entrance to the captain's cabin through which he had walked just a few minutes before, "and the third man is on the cabin deck where he can see any of your crew members moving to or from that area. My people are in uniform, captain, whether you like it or not. Furthermore, they're armed to the teeth. Each man has an automatic weapon that he can fire with great skill. And each man has a pistol that he can use with equal skill. They also all carry knives, which they can throw into your heart from thirty feet."

Captain Rashid's face was white with shock. His vein-laced hands gripped the arms of his chair. His lips blurted out the word "Hijack!"

Said's head shook once again. "No, no, captain, I'm not hijacking your ship. Not at all. What I'm doing—how should I put it?—is for security purposes and to ensure the ultimate success of our operation. In fact, for the safety of your own crew, we're going to impose military—perhaps you would call it naval—discipline." He made a conciliatory gesture with the hint of a smile. "But not over you."

Rashid's voice was filled with sarcasm. "That's extremely decent of you."

"This is your ship, captain. You know how to run it, navigate it, handle it . . ."

"And I know how to handle my crew."

"With kid gloves. Obviously you have about as much control over them as an old dog over a pack of thirsty camels. Letting them carouse all night in Beirut . . . And the condition of this ship. It's filthy. And it's badly maintained."

The PLO leader nudged his mirror sunglasses, pushing them back on the ridge of his nose. For one second, Rashid thought he was going to take them off. Finally he would be able to see those hidden eyes. Said had no such intention. He went on: "From now on my men and I are in charge of this ship. I want that understood clearly. On the other hand, so long as I know you are sailing it competently and in accordance with your instructions from the owners, I will not interfere with its operation. I want life on the ship to go on normally. But I want the crew to understand without a doubt that they are responsible to both of us. Any orders I give them will have to do with how they handle themselves when we're in a port and when we get to Kuwait. The ship will load and unload its cargo. You will do your business and we will sail as quickly as possible. As soon as you and I are finished here I will confiscate all the weapons you and your crew have. And when that's done I want everybody on the afterdeck. Everybody. That includes the people in the engine room. I want to talk to them and tell them what's going on."

As Said was speaking the wily old captain was assessing his own situation and that of his ship. He could not have cared less about the crew. To a man, they were a soulless lot, the dregs of Mediterranean ports. They had no loyalty to him nor he to them. The only thing that mattered was that he and his ship had to survive. The *Mecca* was his life. He could not quarrel with the young Palestinian's description of it. Maybe Said and his people could force some work out of the lazy crew members. While he was running those thoughts through his mind he was paying close attention to everything Said was saying.

"I want to stress this, captain. I wish in no way to interfere with the operation of your ship. On the other hand, there may be some way I can help you. That's up to you. But our objective is far more important than this putrid ship or its crew."

"Including me?"

"Yes, including you and, for that matter, including me."

The old man stubbed out his cigarette. "If you're looking for my cooperation you're certainly going about it the wrong way." He did not wait for a response from Said. "What about those packing cases?"

"What do you mean?" Said sounded puzzled.

"They came on board last evening. They're sitting on

481

the deck. You saw them. The smaller ones. There are four. I'm sure you saw them."

"What does the bill of lading say? You've got the papers. How should I know?"

The captain leaned forward and to his right to leaf through the pile of papers on the table. He pulled one out and placed it down in front of him. He read aloud, "Cargo—four packing cases each containing fifty subsoil electronic transmitter-receivers. The consignor is a company in Germany. I can't pronounce the name. The consignee is the Kuwait National Oil Company.

Said added, "The same consignee as the big crates on the deck. The compressors."

"How did you know that?" He was startled.

The Palestinian smiled. "It is printed on the side of the crates—and I happen to be fluent in German."

The document was thrown back on the pile from which it had come. The captain persisted, "Do you mean to tell me you don't know what's in those cases?"

Said ignored the note of incredulity. "Look, if you really want to find out what's in them why don't you open them up and take a look."

That produced a reaction he had not expected.

"Perhaps I don't want to know after all."

"Why not?"

The captain pulled out another cigarette and lit it quickly, blowing a cloud toward the ceiling of the cabin. "You can't or won't tell me. Either way I will leave it at that. As to opening them up to take a look—really I can't do that."

"Why not?"

"Well, the customs people, particularly at Port Said, have eyes like hawks. If goods are traveling in bond as these are,"—his right hand waved vaguely at the bill of lading back on the pile—"and if there is any evidence that the crate has been opened, they will be sure to catch it. Then the trouble begins. They will insist on opening it themselves to make sure that the contents do in fact match the manifest. And if they were to find what I think they might find, then I am in very serious difficulty, my friend. My ship can be impounded, I can be fined, even imprisoned—again if those crates contain what I think they might contain."

He shrugged, puffed on the cigarette, and continued to talk. "On the other hand, if those crates are untouched, and if for whatever reason the customs people decide to open them for inspection, then I have a complete defense. I know only what the bill of lading, the manifest, tells me." He butted his cigarette in a small tin ashtray. "So I think not, Said, I think not. You don't want to tell me what's in those crates. Perhaps you don't know. That's fine. But open them? Never. You were asking about my cooperation. Before I answer, let me ask you a question. It's a question I ask often. What's in it for me? You do understand, young man?"

Between the two Palestinian Arabs, whose ancestors from time immemorial had been traders, the meaning of the question was perfectly clear. Said had anticipated it. He would indeed make it worth Captain Rashid's while to cooperate. The worth was in cash, half of which Said produced then and there. The remainder would be handed to the captain when the *Mecca* next anchored off Beirut, whenever that might be.

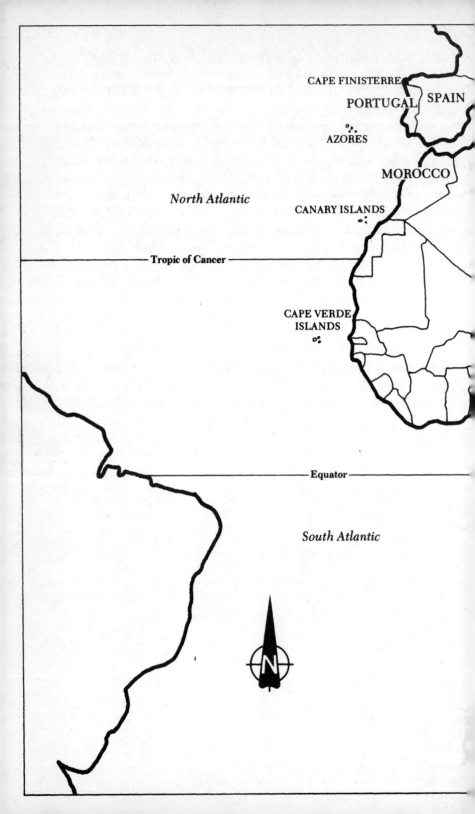

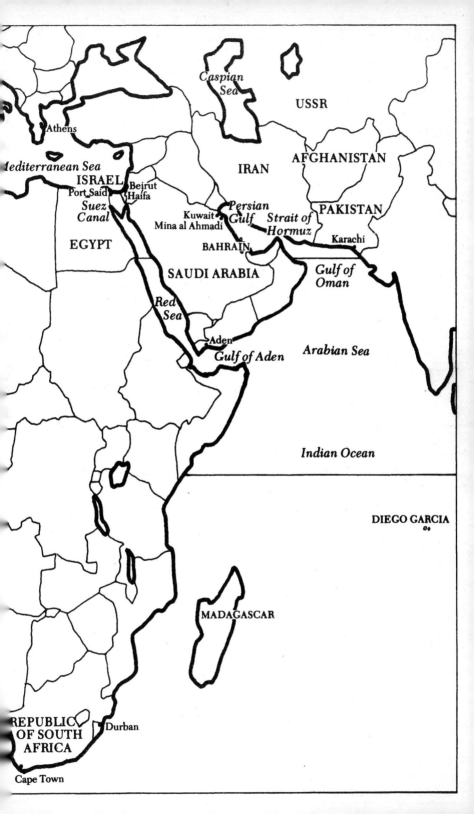

2

9 March

Atlantic Ocean, off Spain

"Up search periscope," the captain called.

When the eye pieces were in front of him at the right level, he said, "Stop." The periscope shaft halted. Commander Marcus Leach, RN, snapped the handles down, put his face to the eye pieces, and, slowly turning the periscope, searched across the rolling surface of the Atlantic eastward in the evening darkness for the familiar Cape Finisterre light. Some day he would go to Spain to see Finisterre, to go up the steep circular steps to the top of that ancient lighthouse. He would touch the tall cone of circling glass that blasted out its coded light across countless miles of the Atlantic. Outside, the sea was whipped up by winds of fifteen knots laced by squalls of heavy rain under low, black scudding clouds. But inside the control room of the Royal Navy fleet submarine, the nuclear-powered attack vessel H.M.S. *Splendid*, riding rock-solid and stable, her tower fifty feet below the churning water surface, the weather above was merely a statistic.

"Stand by bearings."

"Stand by bearings, sir." The messenger of the watch, Able Seaman Tom Smith, moved behind the captain, ready to read off the bearing from the periscope compass ring on the shaft above Leach's hatless head.

Leach kept turning the periscope slowly, intently searching through the dark night, concentrating on the area due east to the port of *Splendid*. She was cruising southbound out of her home base of Faslane in the Firth of Clyde. According to the navigating officer, they were abeam the Finisterre light and 26.2 miles due west of it. There was no real need to use the periscope to check on the Finisterre light, because with the submarine's vast array of computers and electronic gear and her inertial navigation system—the same device that guided jet aircraft from continent to continent with perfect precision—the navigating officer, Pilot as he was traditionally called, knew the exact location of his ship.

It had been six months since the most senior of the fleet submarine captains had been to sea, except for the working up trials of *Splendid*, so Leach was keen to get hands on his above-surface eye, the only visual contact with the upper world that the ship would have for the eight weeks—perhaps longer—she would remain submerged.

His orders were to take *Splendid* south in the Atlantic past the Tropic of Cancer, the self-imposed southern boundary of the North Atlantic Treaty Organization's jurisdiction, under the sea lanes of the huge supertankers running between the Persian Gulf and Western Europe past Cape Town and the Cape of Good Hope at the southern tip of Africa. Then north up the Indian Ocean to the east of the Island of Madagascar, north beyond the Seychelles into the Arabian Sea to join the British Second Flotilla cruising those waters in a joint show of strength with the American Fifth Fleet. *Splendid* would have to sail for 12,000 miles just to get to her station. It would take her sixteen days.

A flicker of light in the distant darkness. Leach steadied the periscope "Bearing is . . ."

"Zero-eight-nine, sir," Smith read off the compass ring.

"Just where you said it would be, Pilot."

The navigating officer was pleased. "Yes, sir."

Leach stepped back from the eye piece and snapped the handles up, ordering, "Down search." The device began to move silently down into its well. "Keep two hundred feet." The planesman responded as he pushed forward on the ship's control wheel, easing it toward the ordered depth.

Leach stood for a moment looking around his control room, bathed in its dull red night lights. The navigation officer was busy at his chart table. Peter Pritchard, the torpedo and sonar officer and officer of the watch, was perched in his chair behind the two-man team steering the submarine with control wheels that looked as if they had been taken from an aircraft. When the wheel was pushed forward or pulled back, it would cause the hydroplanes at the stern and those forward near the nose to move, pitching the vessel down or up. A roll of the wheel would cause the submarine to bank into a turn. In front of the two control positions the "blind flying panel" with its instruments and electronic inertial attitude displays was being carefully watched. The radar watchkeeper was in his place. Everything appeared to be in order and functioning smoothly.

A few steps took the captain into the small sonar room which opened off the control room. At the far end of the room sat the sonar's huge electronic screen, on which white blips of light showed the reflections of the sounds produced in the waters for several miles around the submarine, creating patterns that provided an image not unlike a map. At the center of the screen was a bright dot, *Splendid*'s position as it moved down the Spanish coast at a comfortable rate of thirty knots.

As the captain poked his head in the door, he nodded to his communications officer, Lieutenant Peter Pritchard, but asked his question of the sonar watchkeeper, Petty Officer Pratt: "Any joy?"

"Yes, sir. I was just going to report. You can see it on the edge of the screen."

Yes, there it was, a blip at the top right-hand edge of the screen.

"Green four – zero, range 11,000 yards. Sound signature

on the computer says she's a single-screw tanker, a super-tanker judging by the cavitation noise." A computer check had been made against the noise created by the engines of the craft and the sound caused by drops of water falling off its screw—the cavitation noise. While *Splendid*'s computer did not contain the sound signatures of the world's mercantile fleet, it had in its brain every class of warship in every navy. Of these, the most important were accurate readings on all classes of vessels in the American, Soviet, and British fleets.

"I had a look at the NATO log this afternoon," the captain told the sonar watchkeeper. "The Soviets have an unusual number of submarines in the Atlantic at this time. It's put the wind up for the people at NATO headquarters. But it's the usual Russian pattern when there's a world crisis on like the one at the moment. It seems there are over a hundred bandits at sea out of the Kola Peninsula and the Baltic. They're of all classes—everything they have, the SSBNs to the SSs."

In naval jargon the SSBNs were nuclear-powered submarines of the ballistic missile class, while the SSs were patrol submarines, diesel powered. The NATO log had also confirmed that the operational strength of the Red Navy's submarine fleet was an astounding 426, with ten abuilding. The log contained a series of signals that set out the Admiralty's estimates of the location and numbers of the Soviet warships around the world. In the area of interest to Leach, the Atlantic and the Indian Oceans, over two hundred ships were listed, including two aircraft carriers, the *Kiev* and the *Minsk*. There were two helicopter cruisers, the *Moskva* and the *Leningrad*. A substantial number of these ships were deployed in the Arabian Sea, where *Splendid* had been ordered to join the small British flotilla made up of the helicopter cruiser H. M. S. *Tiger*; the Rothesay class, antisubmarine frigate H. M. S. *Rhyl*; and their supporting provisioning vessels.

The NATO log cursorily assessed the strategic military situation as it was developing in the Middle East. The Soviets were continuing to build up their ground forces in

Afghanistan and had been observed by satellite to be massing at least ten divisions of troops, tanks, artillery and their supporting tactical air squadrons at several marshalling points along the mountainous, thousand-mile northern border of Iran, both to the west and east of the Caspian Sea.

The Soviets had planned to conduct their five-yearly, Moscow coordinated and controlled naval and air exercise, code-named OKEAN, commencing April 1. It would last for one month, with attack and defense naval forces deployed in the Atlantic, Indian, and Pacific Oceans. The plans for OKEAN had long been in preparation.

The captain explained none of those factors to the sonar watchkeeper. He was simply alerting him. "You'll have to keep a sharp watch, unusually sharp. Not only are the Russian submarines out in force, the Americans have almost every one of their Atlantic attack submarines, everything that's serviceable, at sea."

"How many do you estimate that to be, sir?"

"In the Atlantic, it has to be fifty-five."

The young petty officer's head had moved incredulously from side to side as he muttered, "Christ!"

Turning his head toward Pritchard, who was standing just in front of the sonar screen and watching it, but listening to the conversation, the captain said, "So, Peter, I want you to have all your watchkeepers on alert. I don't want any goddamn Russian, or any American for that matter, up our ass on the sneak!"

3

9 March   Evening
Mediterranean Sea, off Haifa

Said stood by the railing outside the galley where he and his men had just finished their first evening meal on board the *Mecca*. He was watching the far distant shore to the east on the horizon edge, the land where he and all Palestinian Arabs yearned to be, their land, now called Israel. Was that Haifa? He could barely see, in the far distance, the hills and tall buildings of the city of his birth, the place to which he was dedicated to return. His mind could picture the house of his grandparents where he had been born, the house that had been stolen from them by the Israelis. He had only seen photographs of it, but one day the Palestinian Liberation army would win the battle, and Haifa would again be theirs.

As he was contemplating, picking scraps of fish from between his brilliant white teeth, his eyes caught sight of a slash of white foam made by a fast-moving boat cutting through the calm, darkening sea. The sun was still above the cloudless horizon behind him in the west. Squinting to focus, assessing what he was seeing, Said quickly confirmed his first suspicion. Shouting to his team, who were chatting just a few feet aft of him, Ahmed having his after-dinner cigarette, Said pointed toward the oncoming craft.

"It's an Israeli patrol boat. Get to your stations!" The sharp bow of the patrol ship was clearly visible. She was about three miles off, closing rapidly, doing about twenty-five knots. As he sprinted toward the bridge to warn the captain, Said sized up the approaching warship. About eighty feet long, with two torpedo tubes plus two missile launchers. He could not yet see a gun. Most likely she carried two twenty-millimeter cannons, a brace of .5-inch machine guns and some depth charges. The speeding craft was still too far away for him to see any of the crew on deck, or behind the glass of the wheelhouse or the canvas of the flying bridge. Said took the steps to the *Mecca*'s bridge two at a time. There he found the captain, binoculars in his hands, calmly watching the fast-approaching Israeli gunboat.

Rashid saw Said out of the corner of his eye. Without a word, the captain lifted the powerful binoculars over his head, and handed them to Said, saying, "This often happens."

Momentarily turning his back to Rashid, Said slipped off his sunglasses and put the binoculars to his eyes. "But why? We're in international waters."

"Not as far as the Israelis are concerned. They think they own this part of the Mediterranean and to hell with boundary lines. They're afraid of commando attacks from you people."

The point was acknowledged with a curt nod by Said.

"And they will confiscate any armaments, weapons, shells, rockets, vehicles being shipped to a destination country that they think might be capable of using the stuff against them."

"That's piracy," Said objected.

"Not according to Israel's rules. They're at war with the entire Arab world—except Egypt. And Allah only knows how long that peace will last. In the rules of war, you're entitled to capture, seize—whatever you want to call it—the enemy's supplies."

The Israeli warship was less than a mile away and still closing rapidly. The captain thought of calling Nabil to the bridge. The Egyptian was off watch and sleeping. Rashid decided to leave him be.

Through the powerful glasses, Said could see every detail of the low-lying, lethal warship: the twin 17.7-inch torpedo tubes straddling the wheelhouse; the gray bulk of the surface-to-surface rocket launcher on the foredeck near the bow. Just ahead of the glinting glass of the wheelhouse, twin twenty-millimeter cannons, manned by two white-uniformed sailors, were pointed directly at the *Mecca*'s bridge. He still could not see inside the glass-enclosed wheelhouse, but above it and behind the shield of canvas on the flying bridge, he could see half a dozen white-capped men. The one with binoculars trained back on him had gold braid on the peak of his hat. As Said watched, two crew members moved smartly to their stations next to the torpedo tubes on each side of the vessel. She was at full attack readiness.

His head turned away so that his unprotected eyes could not be seen, Said handed the binoculars back to the captain and put his sunglasses back on.

Rashid slipped the strap around his neck but did not use the glasses. His eyes were riveted on the sleek, gray ship as she corrected her converging heading to run parallel to the *Mecca*, abreast of her a hundred yards to port. The thundering roar of the warship's engines, clearly audible on the larger ship, suddenly abated. Her speed dropped to match the ten-knot progress of the weatherbeaten, ancient freighter.

Without looking at Said, the captain told him, "I think you should get off the bridge. They'll be suspicious, wondering what you're doing up here. At least you're not wearing those damn uniforms. Where are your men?"

"One is up near the bow. One is just under the bridge, and one is at the stern. Like all good deck hands, they're leaning on the railing watching what's going on."

"They're not armed?"

"Of course not."

"What have you done with your weapons, the stuff you brought on board?"

"We've hidden them under the junk in the paint locker."

The captain was satisfied. He had last taken a look in the paint locker about six weeks before and was appalled by what was piled in that small cubicle—mops, brushes, cans of paint, rope, buckets, heavy sea gear, and soiled rags. It was a mess. He had left it that way. If the PLO people stashed their weapons in there, an Israeli search party would never find them.

But Said lied. After he had had his meeting with the captain, Said and his team talked to the crew members one at a time. All four of them clustered around each intimidated sailor while Said explained that they were members of the PLO army; that they were on a special mission; that they would be serving as deck hands with the other members of the crew; that they didn't want any trouble; that they would take care of anybody who gave them trouble or tipped off port authorities that they were on board. A direct threat to each man was essential. It was the only code those riffraff sailors would understand. In his own way, each told Said not to worry about him.

That job done, the PLO men had changed from their uniforms into faded blue denim working clothes and set about making a thorough inspection of the ship from one grime-covered, stinking end of it to the other. Said wanted to find out whether, in the fo'c'sle or under the cabin level aft, there was a compartment that they could clean out and use as a secure workshop for the last two days of the voyage when the final preparations for their operation had to be made. Said had not asked the captain for permission to take a look around his ship, or whether there was a suitable space available. He intended to find out himself.

There was no space in the fo'c'sle. The entire cargo area had been filled with some sort of bagged commodity. But in the engineer's compartment Maan had discovered a spacious area where the engineer kept his tools, machinery, and other equipment necessary to repair and maintain the humping, ancient diesel engines that drove the *Mecca*. The compartment was just forward of the engine room on the lower deck level, where the noise from the laboring engines was only slightly dampened by a heavy separating bulkhead. A door led to the engine room. A second door opened onto the passageway and steps led up to the cabin deck level. The ten- by twenty-foot space had two portholes almost at ceiling level. Left open, those two windows in the wall of the ship vented part of the overpowering heat and fumes from the *Mecca*'s engine room. Said was well pleased with Maan's find. He would make a deal with the chief engineer at the right time.

During their inspection, they had also been looking for places on the upper deck where they could hide their automatic weapons, but at the same time get at them easily. They had to have three such locations. Each would become a fighting station in the event of an emergency. Ahmed would be aft, Maan amidship on the port side, and Hassan in the fo'c'sle. With their hidden automatic weapons a step away, within seconds the three men could be armed and able to sweep the ship's deck with a withering crossfire. They could take on an attacking boarding party or any craft within reasonable range. In the bow, Hassan's weapon was on the deck covered by a heavy coil of rope. Amidships on the port side, the corner of the canvas covering the aft cargo hold concealed Maan's gun. The starboard lifeboat on the cabin deck received Ahmed's automatic weapon under its protective tarpaulin. Said's instructions were that if the threat came from the port side, then Ahmed would move his gun to the port lifeboat. If it came from the starboard, Maan would move with his weapon across to that side.

As the Israeli gunboat cut its speed to run parallel to the *Mecca*, Said shoved his automatic pistol between his flat stomach and his trouser belt under the tails of his untucked blue denim shirt. He stood at the port rail with Maan. Ahmed was aft by the port lifeboat. Hassan was on the fo'c'sle. At their assigned stations, all four PLO soldiers looked for all the world like simple, slovenly, lazy, harmless Arab deck hands.

The gold braid on the peak of his white cap sparkling

in the evening sun, the Israeli captain moved to the starboard side of his bridge. Lifting a bullhorn to his mouth, he shouted up to the bridge of the plodding, old rust bucket, speaking in English, "Where are you bound, *Mecca*?"

Having been through this routine before, Rashid was ready with his own bullhorn. "Port Said and Kuwait."

"What do you have in those crates?"

"The big ones have natural gas compressors, and the smaller ones have transmitters—some kind of electronic devices."

Rashid's explanation did not satisfy the Israeli captain, who could be seen in discussion with one of the other men on his flying bridge. The bullhorn went up to his face again. His words were distinct. They were clearly understood by Said and Hassan, the only two of the PLO team who could understand English. The amplified words put an extra charge of adrenalin through Said's body.

"Heave to, *Mecca*! Stand by to receive a boarding party!"

From the port wing of his bridge, Rashid responded, "I'll lower the gangway on the starboard side. You can come alongside there." Turning to Nabil, he quietly ordered, "Full stop." The Egyptian promptly moved the telegraph lever back to the stop position. The unexpected ringing of the order bells startled the chief engineer in the bowels of the engine room. He immediately complied, then called the bridge on the ship's loudspeaker system to ask what was going on. Nabil's brief explanation was sufficient.

The warship's captain declined the offer to come alongside. To put his ship next to an unknown ship would be courting disaster. He would be vulnerable, totally open to attack from the deck above.

Even so, the old decrepit coastal freighter looked harmless enough. For a moment, the Israeli pondered the situation. He wanted to get back to Haifa as quickly as possible. He had a date with a woman he had been eyeing for weeks, Rachel, a gorgeous creature, the secretary of the harbormaster at Haifa. The captain's wife was in Tel Aviv visiting her parents. He was to meet Rachel at eight at her apartment for a drink and then they would go to dinner. With luck they would go back to her apartment. He was sure he would score that night. She had given him such a come-on during his last visit to the harbormaster's office. He looked at his watch: 6:35. If he got this boarding over with quickly, he could be back in Haifa just in time to be at Rachel's at eight. Maybe five or ten minutes late. But if he put his boarding party on board the *Mecca* in his boat's small dinghy, he would be the better part of an hour late, and she might not wait. The decision was made. He would throw caution to the winds and save time. He would take his vessel alongside and do the boarding himself. He could feel Rachel's large, firm young breasts under his hands.

Over his left shoulder, the Israeli captain ordered his helmsman, "Hard aport and half power. Take her around the freighter's stern to the starboard side. We'll see what his gangway looks like when we get there." As his twin diesels roared to half power, he turned back to the *Mecca* and raised the bullhorn: "Lower your gangway, *Mecca*. We will come alongside. Have your papers ready for inspection!"

Said turned to Maan standing to his left. "Walk slowly with me back to our cabin and don't ask any questions. Just do as I tell you." A once-in-a-lifetime opportunity was being handed to Said. He had to seize it.

The Israeli patrol boat turned abruptly to the left, swinging in a tight, white-foamed arc behind the *Mecca*, still moving slowly. At quarter power, the chine of her bow did not lift out of the water.

Said judged it would take the gunboat about four minutes to get to the landing platform of the *Mecca*'s lowered gangway. Maan, who could not understand what was being said by the Israeli captain, was startled by Said's unexpected order, but immediately complied. The two of them ambled aft up the steps to the cabin deck, Said leading. The patrol boat had rounded the stern of the *Mecca* and passed out of their line of sight when they reached the cabin deck. With Maan following, Said raced down the port passageway, swinging left into the cross-ship corridor where the crowded paint locker was located. When he reached its door, Said hauled it open.

"Scuba gear and make it fast," he shouted to Maan.

Maan flicked on the weak light and fiercely shoved aside the mix of brooms, buckets, cans, and brushes. In a few seconds he had his hands on two flippers, an oxygen bottle with its shoulder and belly straps and its tubes to mouthpiece and face mask in place. He thrust the gear out through the door to Said, who spoke quickly.

"I'll get this on while you find the limpet." Again, Maan routed under the pile of junk. In short order his sensitive hands felt the smooth surface of the white, molded plastic package. It contained a radio-operated, explosive-packed limpet mine. Said had intended to use it as a practice device to maintain their standard of training during this long three-week voyage to their first destination.

Said pulled off his shirt and shoved his mirror sunglasses into his trouser pocket. By the time Maan had pulled the mine out from under the junk and turned to step outside the door, Said had strapped the oxygen bottle on his back and pulled on his face mask. His penetrating, cold blue eyes leaped through the glass of his face mask as he barked at Maan. "Take it out of the packing case and set it to frequency 3."

Bending over, Maan set the white package on the deck. It was about a foot square and nine inches deep. Gingerly, he lifted off the top section of the plastic container. Lodged in the protection of the white styrofoam, like an oyster snug in a safe, sandy seabed, sat a shiny, gray, thick, circular metal device. In its center was a dial with the numbers 1 through 10 stamped on its face like those on a combination lock. Maan's nimble fingers turned the dial setting until the 3 lay against the red line. Before he lifted the limpet device out of its protective package, he looked up at Said. "What about arming it?"

Said shook his head. "I'll do it when I'm in the water."

Closing the door on the paint locker, the two men dashed down the corridor to the port side of the ship. At the railing they glanced quickly around; then Said pulled on his flippers and swung his legs over the side, planting his feet on the outside edge of the deck. Hanging on to the railing with his left hand, he activated his oxygen bottle with his right. Then he shoved the mouthpiece between his teeth and nodded to Maan, who carefully handed him the deadly magnetic mine. Clutching it to his breast with all the strength of his powerful arms, Said jumped. Thirty feet below the deck he hit the surface cleanly. The impact from that height tore his mouthpiece away, but as soon as the cushioning water stopped his downward descent, he stuffed it back into his mouth. The buoyant salt water lessened the weight of the mine but still he clutched it tightly. Orienting himself, he looked up through the pale blue water. The bottom side of the stern of the old *Mecca*, its propeller stopped, sat in the water like a barnacle-covered black whale. Kicking his flippered feet, Said swam to the rounded edge of the freighter's hull, just forward of the propeller shaft, then down under the sharp edge of the keel to the ship's starboard side. There above him, nestled against the ponderous bulk of the *Mecca*, sat the Israeli patrol boat, its shiny twin propellers turning ever so slowly. Said could hear its engines quietly rumbling at idle and the popping of the exhaust from the pipes at the stern of the powerful craft.

His target area was the stern plate near the surface. It would have to be metal for the limpet mine's magnetic clamp mechanism to hold fast to the hull. The stern plate was ideal because it was out of the main pull of the flow of the sea water. On the underside of a hull, moving at twenty-five to thirty miles an hour, the force of the surging water might rip the explosive device away from the ship's surface, even though the mine was contoured to lie flush like a leech against the body of a boat.

To avoid detection by one of the warship's crew who might see the bubbles from his oxygen system, Said swam quickly out from under the hull of the freighter to a position about ten feet directly under the idling propellers of the Israeli vessel. There his bubbles would mix with the turbulence caused by the propellers and the burbling exhaust pipes. At that point, he paused to assess the situation before beginning his contact maneuver.

On the *Mecca*'s cargo deck, thirty feet above him, the

youthful Israeli patrol boat captain, a lieutenant-commander by rank, stood beside one of the large packing cases containing, as its manifest papers stated, a natural gas compressor. Behind him as he faced aft were two of his seamen, dressed like their captain in spotless white from their caps to their shoes. Each carried a stubby automatic weapon at the ready, its safety catch off. Standing at the top of the gangway, one of the strapping young Israeli sailors stood scanning the deck of the forward part of the ship, watching for any suspicious or hostile movement.

On the bridge above him, he could see a gaunt Arab face under an officer's cap, peering down but making no move. On the fo'c'sle, sitting on the capstan, was a deck hand—an Arab, judging by his unkempt clothing and his *khafia* headdress. There was no one else to be seen. The other Israeli soldier covered his captain, the *Mecca*'s cargo, and cabin deck aft. At that level, he could see a huge, dirty-looking—weren't they all?—Arab deck hand casually leaning against the starboard lifeboat puffing on a cigarette. He looked harmless enough. Between the bridge and the smaller crates immediately aft of it, he could see another Arab sailor squatting on the deck. His back was to the railing, arms folded, apparently trying to keep out of the way while watching what was going on.

In his hand, the Israeli captain held the sheaf of bills of lading that Rashid handed to him as soon as he stepped on board. The top bills covered the natural gas compressors consigned to Kuwait. With an expert eye, the Israeli checked the information on the document against the markings stenciled on the crate. He was satisfied that they tallied. He then flipped through the papers to the bills for the smaller crates. Again the information stenciled on them was satisfactory. Nevertheless, it was his responsibility to open one of the crates to confirm the contents by visual inspection. Rashid's experienced eyes watched the patrol boat captain carefully. He knew that a look-inside examination was part of the routine. What would be found in the smaller crates, the *Mecca*'s captain did not know. But he expected the worst.

As the Israeli moved toward the closest small crate on the starboard side, Ahmed at his vantage point aft flicked his cigarette overboard. He moved casually to the lifeboat where his automatic gun was stowed. He knew he could have it in his hand within seconds. In the fo'c'sle, Hassan slipped off the capstan to sit on the large coil of rope on the deck. He was ready to reach for the gun concealed under it, close to his right hand. Amidships Maan remained where he was. The activity on the far side of the vessel was out of his line of vision. Any move that he might make could cause suspicion. So he just sat, his eyes on Hassan.

The patrol boat captain, still checking the markings on the small crate, turned to Rashid. "A crowbar, captain."

Without a word, Rashid walked past the Israeli and his two guards toward the forward side of the bridge, where crowbars and other deck handling tools were stowed. As he did so, the gunboat officer's left wrist twisted so that he could see his watch.

"Never mind, I haven't got enough time." Rachel was at the front of his mind. If he opened this crate he would lose another ten minutes, and he was going to be late enough as it was. Anyway, the bills of lading and the information on the crates cross-checked. The motor vehicles lashed down on the deck were obviously nonmilitary.

Relieved, Rashid stopped and turned back to face the Israeli, who asked, "What's below in the holds?"

"Bagged stuff, grain and cement. You have the manifests. If you'd like to take a look . . ?"

The Israeli shook his head. It was clear that he wanted to get off the *Mecca* and get going. "No, that won't be necessary." He thrust the wad of papers into Rashid's hands, declaring, "You are cleared to go, captain."

He threw Rashid a hasty salute, which the startled Rashid returned. The Israeli trio scrambled down the gangway into their waiting craft, its engines still rumbling at the idle. Climbing the ladder to his bridge, the Israeli captain shouted his orders to cast off. Immediately the lines were clear, the warship's engines thundered to full power, driving the craft rapidly away from the *Mecca*, a billowing rooster-tail plume of white foam and spray in its trail. Its sharp bow lifted out of the water, its hull planing along the smooth Mediterranean surface at high speed toward Haifa and the waiting arms and—the expectant Israeli captain hoped—the waiting breasts and open thighs of Rachel.

As soon as the Israelis left the deck of the *Mecca*, Maan seized the length of rope he had brought from the paint locker when he returned to his station after Said had leaped into the sea. He tied one end of it securely to the railing and threw the other over the side into the water. Peering down over the railing, he was relieved to see Said's masked head surface just a few yards aft. Spitting out his mouthpiece, his face split in a wide grin of triumph, Said lifted both arms out of the water, his fists clenched, the thumb of each pointing rigidly up. He had done it!

Swimming easily to the rope, Said quickly hand-hauled himself up to the level of the deck where Ahmed, flanked by Maan and Hassan, reached over the railing to lift him by the armpits. They shouted with joy as the big man lifted their leader as lightly as a small child and set him gently on the deck. There was much back-slapping, laughing, and hooting as Said, still too excited himself to think of slipping off the oxygen bottle, let alone getting out of the flippers and face mask, explained every last detail of what he had done. The limpet mine, fully armed, was securely attached to the Israeli patrol boat's stern plate just above the rudder, about two feet below the water line. The mine's telescopic radio antenna was fully extended, waiting only for the detonation signal.

Caught up in the euphoria of the moment, none of them noticed the *Mecca* get under way almost at the same time that Ahmed was lifting Said over the railing. They did notice, however, when the booming voice of an incredulous Captain Rashid came down upon them from the bridge immediately over their heads.

"Said!"

At the sound of the captain's commanding voice, all four faces turned up to look at the bridge. For a moment Rashid was speechless, for at that instant he saw Said's unguarded, crystal-blue eyes shining at him through the glass of the diving mask. No Arab could have eyes like that! Yet, no one was more an Arab than this young man.

"Said! What in the name of Allah is going on?"

From the look of astonishment on the captain's face, Said realized that the old man had seen his eyes. Slowly and deliberately, Said removed his face mask and reached into the pocket of his wet trousers for his mirror sunglasses, which he wiped dry on Ahmed's shirttail and put on. He looked up again at Rashid, who inexplicably felt relieved that he did not have to look into those astounding blue eyes again.

"My dear captain, we have been undertaking some operational practice. That's all, just some operational practice." The three heads surrounding him, faces at full grin, vigorously nodded their agreement.

The captain could not contain his curiosity any longer, but he did not want any member of his crew to hear the explanation if, indeed, he was to get one. His face disappeared from the bridge opening. They could hear him noisily clambering down the metal steps. In a moment, breathless, he was standing nose to nose with Said. By this time the PLO leader had unbuckled the oxygen canister which Ahmed tucked protectively under his muscular arm.

"What have you been doing?" Rashid demanded. "I'm the captain of this ship, and I have a right to know."

The smile disappeared from Said's face. It was replaced by a look of grim satisfaction. "The Israeli patrol boat . . ."

"Yes, what about it?"

"Attached to its ass-end, clamped on like a bloodsucker, is a beautiful metal mechanism, packed, my dear captain, with enough high-power explosive to blast it and anything close to it to a million pieces."

The old man's teeth sucked air. "A mine!"

"A mine."

Rashid's eyes opened wide with astonishment mixed with fear. "You fool. When that thing goes off, the Israelis will be out after us like a pack of bloodhounds."

"They will not. I can assure you, captain, they will not. If I had thought otherwise, I wouldn't have done it. I don't want to foul up our main mission—or this boat."

The captain was adamant. His right arm lifted to point over Said's shoulder toward Haifa. "I tell you, if that damn thing goes off between here and Haifa, we'll have the whole Israeli navy after us!"

"There's no way it can go off between here and Haifa. It can't explode unless I set it off myself."

"And how can you do that?" There was a tone of disbelief in the captain's voice.

"By radio signal."

The nonplussed Rashid contemplated the consequences of that information until its significance dawned on him. His voice rose in a hiss of protest, "You are not going to . . . You can't. In the name of Allah, no!"

"I not only can, but I will. They'll never know what hit them. Don't worry. There won't be any evidence to tie this old rust bucket with what's going to happen."

Hassan, the radio expert, added, "Because it's going to happen right in the harbor at Haifa." He repeated what Said had said. "They'll never know what hit them."

"And," Said went on, "with any luck we'll destroy any other ships close to it."

That was the end of the explanation. It was time to get on with the business of finishing the first operational exercise. Said bent down to take off his flippers. As he stood up, he asked the shocked captain, "Give me your best estimate on how long it will take them to get back into port at Haifa and tie up. And remember, captain, it's in your best interest as well as mine to have them in the port, well inside it."

Rashid looked at his watch. "I checked our position on the chart just before they came on board. We have just gotten under way. We're about thirty-six miles off Haifa, and it's ten to seven now. They should be in the harbor by five after eight, ten after, at the outside."

Said turned to Hassan, "Get the transmitter out. Test to make sure it's working properly. We go at quarter past eight."

The captain protested, "But the crew will still be on board."

If Rashid could have seen Said's eyes through the sunglasses, he would have caught the cold determination that filled them. "Precisely. The destruction must be maximum. The Israelis are our enemies to the death."

The conversation with Rashid was at an end. Telling Maan and Hassan to bring his gear, Said walked aft, his bare feet padding against the metal deck, his mind rejoicing with his success, yet impatient for the next step. Would the mine go off in response to the radio signal? Detonating the deadly device on the tail of the Israeli patrol boat would be crucial to the chance of success in the big operation to come.

By eight o'clock, Hassan had completed his meticulous testing of the radio transmitter-receiver. He was satisfied. The portable, battery-operated unit was a compact high-powered HF (high frequency) radio with a designed transmission range of up to 4,000 miles. Ingenious Japanese miniaturization had produced a radio that weighed less than three pounds, a black box of the most sophisticated type. Hassan was confident that it would not fail.

He had set up the radio on a wooden table that Ahmed had appropriated from the galley of the protesting cook and placed on the open passageway on the port side of the *Mecca*. That position provided a clear line of sight to the area where they estimated Haifa, now well over the horizon, to be. The sea was still calm, but with a gentle roll from the west to which the ship responded as it plowed on. The table on which the radio rested was solid and stable, a good base for the testing equipment as well as Hassan's tool kit. Now all they could do was wait in the gathering darkness. The sun had gone down at 7:15. By eight the darkness was virtually complete. The sky was crystal clear. A rising half-moon split the horizon to the southeast. The running lights of the *Mecca* were not matched by those of any other ship as the old freighter thumped along its lonely course to Port Said, drawing farther and farther away from the menace of Haifa.

At ten past eight, all four PLO soldiers were near the precious radio. Ahmed and Maan squatted a few feet forward of it in the passageway, talking as Ahmed sucked on a cigarette. Hassan sat at the table on a chair he had brought from his cabin. He wore earphones as he twisted the radio's receiver dial in the futile hope that he might pick up some message from the Israeli patrol boat as it approached and entered Haifa harbor. It was doubly futile in that, had he been lucky enough to pick up their operating frequency, he did not understand the language. Even so, there was an off-chance.

At two minutes past eight the Israeli boat was in the entrance of Haifa harbor, moving fast past Bat Galim. The twinkling lights of the city glittered close by on the starboard side, rising up in the distance to the heights of central Carmel, some 600 feet above the sea. At half speed, the warship moved past the long pier that stretches eastward for almost a mile from Bat Galim and protects the main harbor from the onslaughts of the Mediterranean. The anxious Israeli captain picked his way slowly through the ships anchored in the main harbor at the agonizing speed of eight knots, steering for the pier lights that mark the narrow entrance to the inner Kishon harbor, where his craft and the six others of the patrol squadron were berthed.

At 8:10 he cut his speed back even further in the darkness. With his searchlight on, the commander ordered hard to starboard to round the northern end of the western jetty forming the Kishon harbor. Ahead he could see the long forms of the other five patrol boats of his squadron crowded along the U-shaped dock. His boat's berth was in the middle, right at the bottom of the U. Towering floodlights bathed the area with glaring white light. In a few minutes he would be docked. Then he would turn over the ship to his second-in-command to secure for the night. The filing of his report on the boarding of the *Mecca* could wait until the morning. At 8:12 the starboard side of the patrol boat touched gently against the protective rubber bumpers lining the pier wall. Reversed engines brought the craft to a full stop. He gave instructions to his first lieutenant as hands secured the mooring lines fore and aft. He tried to control his impatience, but the need to get to Rachel was compelling. He was already ten minutes late. By the time he got into his car at the end of the pier, it would be another fifteen minutes before he was at her apartment in the Kiryat Hatechnion area of the city to the south.

At 8:15, the captain of the patrol boat stepped from the gangplank to the pier. He took one quick step southward toward his car, looking to his left with pleasure and pride at his magnificent boat. At that instant, the Israeli captain, his splendid craft and crew, were no more. They dissolved, totally disintegrating in the vortex of the thundering, flaming blast as its devastating shock waves hammered out in all directions, filling the air. A rolling mass of fire and smoke, torn, shredded, broken bits of metal, plastic, glass and human flesh burst up and out in a black, red, and white ball mixed with steaming harbor water sucked from the spot where the patrol boat had sat only a second before.

Within the trapped confines of the small naval basin, the reverberating waves rammed out against the fetid salt water, shoving it over the confining piers and lifting the five other patrol boats into the air with the outward thrust of the blast. They shattered like toys as they smashed against the unbending concrete of the dock. Secondary explosions burst from their splitting fuel tanks as they opened to spill thousands of volatile gallons of diesel fuel into the already raging inferno.

Far out to sea, to the southwest, on a weatherbeaten, derelict old freighter, four young Arabs clustered in the darkness watching in silent awe as the tip of a gigantic, orange fireball lifted above the eastern horizon like a new sun. The pressure of Hassan's index finger on the radio's detonate button, orange and circular like the fireball it had created, was all it had taken to cause death and destruction in the harbor of Said's birthplace.

The four uttered no sounds of jubilation, made no signs of the lifting emotions of victory. Rather, it was a moment of sober assessment of the scale of the power that was in their hands. It was a mammoth power. Brutal. Instantaneous. A power of mass destruction that could annihilate a target-object a hundred, hundreds, or even thousands of miles distant. All that was needed was the pressure of a single finger on the small orange button on a black box.

In Haifa the woman named Rachel would never know that she had influenced the course of events that would soon turn the direction of the world.

4

9 March   10:00 A.M.

Cabinet Room, the White House

"To sum up the main points of the briefing, Mr. President . . ."

John Hansen, the forty-first president of the United States of America, moved his eyes away from the Pentagon briefing officer standing at the lectern on his right at the end of the cabinet room conference table. He looked across the table at his secretary of defense, Robert Levy. On Levy's right was the chairman of the Joint Chiefs of Staff, a five-star air force general, Glen Young. To the president's immediate left was his secretary of state, John Eaton; on his right, Vice-President Mark James; and immediately beyond him, his National Security Council special adviser, Walter Kruger. This group comprised the executive committee of the National Security Council. It was this team the new president would rely upon for assistance and advice in dealing with foreign crises.

Before his installation two months before, Senator John Hansen, as he then was, did not have a full appreciation of the amount of time and attention the president must give to foreign affairs. It seemed to him he was spending at least half his waking hours considering how to deal with problems in South America, how to handle Cuba, and the intrusions of the Cubans in Africa with their mentors the Soviets, how to cope with the sensitive Western Europeans, and the problems in NATO, the North Atlantic Treaty Organization. Then there was the subject matter of this meeting on the morning of March 9—the buildup of Soviet forces, not only in Afghanistan, but also along the Soviet-Iran border both east and west of the Caspian Sea.

The briefing was almost finished: "Six new infantry divisions and two armored have been identified along the Soviet-Iran border. In Afghanistan, indications are that another 20,000 troops with supporting equipment have been deployed with concentrations in the area of Herat, a major Afghanistan city in the northwest sector of the country, near the border with Iran. The estimated number of Soviet troops in Afghanistan now is 130,000, supported by tanks and aircraft. All the increases in strength in Afghanistan and along the Soviet-Iran border have occurred in the last seven days and are significant in terms of a potential Soviet move against Iran. That is the end of the briefing, sir."

The president looked to the other men around the table and at the one man he had not appointed, General Glen Young. He wasn't sure about Young. In the meetings they'd had in the two months since Hansen took office, he had had difficulty in drawing the general out. Perhaps it was that, having been appointed by Hansen's predecessor, a man quite different from Hansen and of another party, Young simply did not like the president and his politics. In Young, Hansen found a degree of truculence as well as condescension. He was no expert in military matters; the general had made that very clear several times in the patronizing way he answered the president's questions. It was quite obvious that General Young considered himself to be superior, even perhaps to the president himself.

Hansen spoke to the heavyset air force general. "What do you and your people make of this?"

Young was ready with his reply. "We think they're

about to make a move on Iran, Mr. President. We don't know when it's going to come. It could be within the next week or ten days. Or they may wait until the weather is better, say the beginning of May. That's what we think they'll do, wait for good weather. The highway net into Iran from the north is good. They'd have a straight run in unless the Iranians were able to mount a defense. The Iranian army is in a shambles, as is the country. Their defense is nonexistent. As we see it, the Russian troops in Afghanistan would have difficulty crossing the mountain range on the east side of Iran, but we think they would try it, at the same time the main force was moving down from the north."

Secretary of State John Eaton asked, "What about Pakistan?"

The general nodded: "We think that when the Russians move against Iran, they'll also go for Pakistan. They invaded Afghanistan for the weak reason that they wanted to protect their influence there. They have a far more compelling reason to invade Pakistan: they want the warm water port at Karachi for the Red Navy."

"I'm interested in compelling reasons." The president turned to his Secretary of State. "John, if you were Grigori Romanov in the Kremlin, what would be your compelling reason to move into Iran?"

Eaton opened the leather file folder he had placed on the conference table in front of him at the beginning of the meeting. He ruffled through the papers and found the one he wanted. He scanned it for a moment, then lifted his head to reply.

"There's more than one compelling reason, Mr. President. The first is an oil shortage. As you know, at the end of the seventies the Soviets were net exporters of crude oil, about one million barrels a day. Today, we estimate they have a shortfall of half a million barrels a day and their shortages are escalating rapidly. In fact, we may be conservative in our estimates, but that's the best number I have at the moment. The fact is that the Soviets desperately need oil. They haven't had any big finds of their own in recent years. The place to make up that shortfall is Iran, which is capable of producing about four-and-a-half million barrels a day, even though recently they've only been producing one-and-a-half and that's falling. All of their production equipment is American and since our hassle over the hostages with the Ayatollah Khomaini, it's a wonder they're producing anything. So that's compelling reason number one."

The secretary checked his notes.

"The second is to maintain the Soviet Union's fulfillment of the ideological doctrine of world domination. You may not think that's compelling, Mr. President, but it is. Iran is in a shambles, in virtual anarchy. With the counterrevolutionary activity that has been going on, it's in a state of civil war. If the call for help came from one side or the other in Iran, that would be the pretext for the Soviets to enter to stabilize the country. The same justification was used for the first incursions into Afghanistan, long before they went in in the last days of 1979. In keeping with the Marxist-Leninist ideology of world domination, Iran is an ideal objective.

"The third compelling reason is the one General Young has outlined. It goes along with the taking of Iran. The Russians desperately need that warm water port in the Indian Ocean, one they can put money and equipment into and know they're not going to lose it, as they lost the Port of Berbera in Somalia. If they had Karachi, no one would take it away from them. While the invasion of Pakistan is not the same as an invasion of Iran—which is your question, Mr. President—I agree with General Young. The two things would be done together."

The president went back to the chairman of the Joint Chiefs of Staff, "What can we do if we have to stop them, General Young?"

"In Iran or Pakistan, Mr. President?"

The president thought his question was perfectly plain. He was tempted to answer, "In the whole of the Persian Gulf," but said instead, "Both—Iran and Pakistan."

The general examined his fingernails, then looked up at the president.

"Not as much as I'd like to," he said finally. "You're

512

aware of these things, Mr. President, from the briefings we've given you over the last two months."

That was designed to put me in place, the president thought.

"I'll review the situation for you. In the whole of the Persian Gulf area, the Arabian Sea, and the Indian Ocean we have only one base available to us. That's Diego Garcia.

"Diego Garcia is a British island, one thousand nautical miles south of the tip of India. We made a deal with the Brits back in the middle seventies and took the island over. It has a good anchorage. We've put in everything that's needed for a complete support base for a full fleet. There's a runway 12,000 feet long which can handle anything we put in the area, even a C-5. The Soviets countered us by doing a deal recently with the Maldivian government—the Maldive Islands are about 450 miles north of Diego Garcia. They've taken over abandoned British military installations, airport, harbor, the whole works.

"The only other place where we can use facilities is Bahrain in the Persian Gulf. We can do bunkering and reprovisioning there. They have one of the biggest dry docks in the world. Beyond those two places, Mr. President, we have nothing. As you know, the previous administration was negotiating with Oman for the use of their facilities at Muscat and Masirah Island; with Somalia for Mogadishu and Berbera. The Russians had Berbera for quite a while and put in excellent facilities, but got kicked out when they sided with Ethiopia in its war with Somalia. And there have been negotiations for Mombasa in Kenya. But negotiations are negotiations, Mr. President. Nothing's been finalized yet in any of those places."

The president acknowledged, "I'm aware of that. State," he nodded to the left toward Eaton, "has been instructed to carry on with those negotiations with the highest priority and urgency." He paused to let Young continue.

"That's all we have, Mr. President. We're in an extremely weak position. The only operating base we can use is Diego Garcia."

"What about Pakistan?" Vice-President James asked.

"You didn't mention that. We've been in negotiation with their new president since he took over ten days ago."

General Young was startled, "I knew that Zia had been ousted by a coup of his own generals, but I haven't heard about any negotiations with the new man—what's his name?"

"General Mujeeb-Ul-Rehman," James replied. "In all fairness, you didn't know this, but immediately after the coup that put Mujeeb in power, President Hansen instructed the secretary of state and me to open negotiations with Mujeeb for the use of the port and airfield at Karachi. We've been dealing with the Pakistani ambassador here. With things so unsettled after the coup, we haven't made much progress. And from what you and the briefing have told us this morning, it appears that the Soviets are building up their forces to take Iran or Pakistan or both. In other words, we're heading for a direct confrontation with the Soviets, but with no foothold in the area we're virtually powerless to stop them."

General Young agreed. "The best we could do would be to get in by air the 82nd Airborne Regiment and perhaps two marine battalions. We could do that within two weeks. That would be 20,000 men and a handful of reconnaissance tanks and helicopters. With aircraft from the Fifth Fleet and with what the British have in the area at the moment . . ."

"But the Russians could take the whole of the Persian Gulf in two weeks, long before you got there. Right?"

The general glumly nodded in agreement, as the vice-president went on, "It seems to me, Mr. President, that we should expand the scope of our negotiations with the Pakistanis for not simply Karachi and the airport there, but for a full-scale positioning of our troops, equipment, and aircraft in Pakistan. In other words, a matching force to what the Russians have in Afghanistan: 120,000 men, fully equipped, tanks, fighter attack aircraft, the whole thing. After all, we have an obligation. There's a 1959 security accord between the United States and Pakistan. What do you think, general?"

The president broke in, "I'll answer that question. I think it's one hell of a suggestion, and I think we ought to do something about it right now." To the group at large he put the question, "What do we know about General Mujeeb?"

It was his National Security Council adviser, Walter Kruger, who responded. "I have a complete file on him, Mr. President. I'm sure State does too." Eaton nodded that he had. "Believe it or not, he is very pro-American. He took his helicopter training in Key West. He's more likely to accept an offer from us than General Zia was. You may remember that Zia turned down President Carter's offer of 400 million dollars back in 1980, saying it was 'peanuts'."

The others around the table nodded.

Eaton added, "Mujeeb says that he will have free elections within the year, but then Zia had been saying that for years. As you know, Mr. President, the generals are still in tight control of the government of the country."

"I know that. In this particular instance, it might be good because in a dictatorship the head man can make a decision on the spot. In a democracy like ours, I have to get permission from Congress practically every time I want to go to the john."

Smiles appeared all around, but disappeared quickly when General Young spoke up.

"I'm sorry, Mr. President, but from a military point of view, from a logistics point of view, a 13,000-mile line of supply, highly vulnerable to submarines and surface ships . . . Well, I just don't have the resources. I haven't got the ships, haven't got the budget, haven't got the men."

Hansen's voice had the hard edge of determination. "We'll find you the ships, we'll find you the money, we'll find you the men, we'll call up the reserves."

The general shook his head. "Even if I had everything I needed, from a military point of view lugging 120,000 Americans to some godforsaken place like Pakistan where the full weight of the Soviet army and air force can be thrown at us from their home ground, would be disastrous, Mr. President. I'm sorry, I have some real reservations about this. Maybe we can do it. Yes, we can do it if you give me the men and the ships and the money, but I say from a military point of view, it's dangerous. And the logistics are next to impossible."

Hansen did not answer immediately. He was angry, but hid his emotions. "But from my perspective, from my viewpoint, general, I must take into consideration not only the military, but all the other factors in deciding whether we do or do not act in the presence of obvious Soviet initiatives. I must take into account the grand strategies of the Soviet Union—their economic strategies, their geopolitical strategies, their goal of world domination by peaceful means if they can achieve it that way. And God knows they've been successful since World War II in doing just that. What I have to do is to develop strategies to counterbalance the ever increasing Soviet aggression. I'm talking about economic and political as well as military aggression. Soviet agression in the Persian Gulf is a threat to the lifestyle of the United States and the free world. If they interfere with our oil supplies it could mean the end of our way of life. I have to take your objections into account. But I cannot allow the military point of view to be the only consideration. If I took your advice and yours alone then I would probably decide against going to Pakistan."

John Hansen was not going to let that caustic bastard off the hook yet. "You may be surprised to know, general, that I not only have sympathy with the deplorable state of the American military, I also understand something about it. I know that since 1968 our military manpower has declined by more than one-and-a-half million men. Right now it's about 600,000 below the pre-Vietnam level. Just look at our navy. In 1968, the navy had 976 ships, now it's down to 472. Whereas the Red Navy, in the days of the Kennedy-Khrushchev confrontation, was nothing more than a coastal offense and interdiction force, now it is the strongest, most formidable blue-water navy in the world.

"Since 1960, Soviet military manpower has grown from approximately three million to 4.5 million, more than twice the size of our military organization. In every class of military hardware, even helicopters, the Russians are producing far more than we are. In ground forces equipment, their output ratio is about six to one, particularly in tanks. They're producing fighter aircraft at rates that exceed ours by a factor of four. The CIA tells me that the Soviets outspend us on defense by about forty-five percent in dollar equivalence. A pretty bad scenario, general. It reflects, I think, the military turn-off of the American people that flowed out of Vietnam. That also comes from our not being a militaristic people. The fact is, the Russian military machine has it all over ours like a tent. Just look at that submarine fleet of theirs, almost 400 in service. What do we have? One hundred and forty."

Although Hansen was directing his remarks to Young, the general sat with his hands clasped, his eyes looking down at the table. He did not like being lectured to by a politician on the state of America's military, a matter about which he was the most knowledgeable of all Americans. Furthermore, going into Pakistan with a task force, however big it was, was military madness.

"I'll tell you this, general, if I can work a deal with Pakistan, I'll guarantee you the men, the money, and the equipment to do the job."

Jim Crane, the president's chief of staff, came into the meeting. Before sitting down next to Levy, he handed a note to Secretary Eaton. As he read its contents, Eaton's eyebrows lifted and he shook his head. Hansen stopped and asked, "Anything important, John?"

"Nothing of earth-shattering consequence. Perhaps that's a bad way of putting it. Six Israeli ships have been blown up in the harbor at Haifa. Fifty people killed. Probably a PLO raid."

Eaton was right. The item was not earth-shattering, but it was a link in the chain of events that would follow the decisions that were being taken around the Cabinet conference table that morning.

Hansen had made up his mind what he wanted to do. "Gentlemen, it's obvious to me that we're getting down to the short strokes with the Russians in the Middle East. Under no circumstances can the United States afford to lose Persian Gulf oil, and for Western Europe the situation is even more critical. It is apparent to me that it is vital to the interests of the United States and the Western world that we get forces into the Middle East to counterbalance the Soviets. There is only one place we can do that—Pakistan. The vice-president is right on. We should expand our negotiations. We should go for putting in as many troops as you, General Young, and your staff might advise: *a*, that are needed to produce an effective balancing force—it might be 120,000 more or less, that's up to you to advise on, general; and *b*, a force that we can afford to take out of our existing troop and equipment resources, having in mind all our commitments around the world. To put such a force in place, will we have to call up the reserves? These are questions you'll have to answer, General Young. What I want you to do is to put together immediately a Pakistan Task Force Plan. I want that draft plan by Monday noon, two or three pages with all the meat in it. You can expand it later on. I want to know how many troops for Pakistan, how we'll get them there, your best estimate on an arrival date. I know this is Saturday, general, and a bad day to try to collect people, but I have to move quickly." The president was pleased to see that the general himself was taking notes.

"As to Pakistan and General Mujeeb, it is imperative that we make a maximum effort to negotiate an agreement that will let our forces into Pakistan and in strength. Furthermore, it is of the utmost urgency that the agreement be negotiated forthwith. There is only one person in the United States of America who can do the negotiating." The President broke his line of thought. He turned to Crane. "Jim, ask the energy secretary to have his people produce an aide memoire for me, or maybe it should be some economist in the General Accounting Office. Yes, I think you better ask GAO. I want something on the economic and other ramifications for the United States if the Persian Gulf oil is cut off. Do the same for Western Europe. And I want a second aide memoire covering both the United

States and Western Europe: what happens if *all* the OPEC oil is cut off?"

"Do you mean *all*, sir?" Crane asked in astonishment. The other faces around the table reflected the same emotion.

The president was emphatic. "I sure as hell do!"

General Young wanted to quarrel with that request. "That just couldn't happen, Mr. President. Anyway, we're only dealing here with the Middle East, the Persian Gulf, not with Malaysia or Venezuela or Mexico."

Hansen, who was six-foot five when he stood up, looked down across the table at the chairman of the Joint Chiefs of Staff. "General Young, such a study may not be relevant to the military mind, but it sure as hell is to mine."

5

10 March   6:00 P.M.
Port Said, Egypt

The coastal approach to Egypt's ancient, timeless Port Said must be navigated with considerable care. On each side of the constantly dredged channel, which weaves inward from the Mediterranean past the port's protective western pier into the harbor basin, lurks a shallow, muddy bottom. The harbor of Port Said is the northern gateway to the Suez Canal, a hundred-mile-long finger of lockless water that can take ships of up to 45,000 tons, small vessels in comparison to the mammoth crude-oil tankers that range up to half a million tons. Those tankers must round the southern tip of Africa to deliver their cargos from the Persian Gulf to Western Europe and America.

On the west bank of the 570-acre harbor sits a tumble of docks and warehouses through which the goods of Egyptian trade and commerce have moved over the centuries. Beyond the dock area, to the west, lies the city in which over a quarter of a million Egyptians live and work, their existence tied to the fortunes of the port and the Suez Canal.

On the eastern side of the harbor are antiquated shipbuilding and repair yards, which look more like cemeteries for the rusted hulls and skeletons of ships that litter the channel-webbed, flat landscape. In the prolific smuggling trade, goods of all kinds, including opium, cocaine, and marijuana, pass over the labyrinth of waterways of the east bank.

At Port Said, all loading and discharging of freighters is done by lighters, small craft which carry cargos to and from shore. Vessels are prohibited from coming alongside the quays. Fuel, water, and provisions are readily available.

Whenever he went south through the Suez Canal, it was Captain Rashid's practice to make sure that his bunker fuel and water tanks were topped up, and that he had ample food supplies on board. To satisfy his taste for good wine, illegal in many of the Muslim ports he visited, he would also indulge himself by buying several cases of acceptable French white and red wines. These he would store in a secret compartment in the ship's hold beneath his quarters. So expertly had the compartment and its hidden entrance been built that even the most skilful customs inspectors had not found them. A curious inspector would only see, at the forward end of the aft cargo hold, a solid stress-carrying bulkhead. Conversely, when he entered the forward cargo hold, he would perceive, at the aft end of it, the other side of the bulkhead he had seen in the first compartment. The only entrance to the covert compartment was located in the captain's bathroom at the port end of his suite. In order to gain access to the trap door on the bathroom floor, a concealed lever allowed the entire shower stall to swing away from the wall. Under it was the ladder down into the hold.

Only Rashid knew of the existence of the secret compartment. To have shared that knowledge with any of his itinerant first officers or crew would have been to share it with the world. The customs people in every port he called at would have known that the innocent-looking old *Mecca* had a clandestine hot spot. They would investigate it as a matter of routine.

There were severe limitations to what the captain

could do with his smuggling hold. He could only put cargo in it that he could load himself without the assistance of any of his crew. If he was carrying armaments, weapons, marijuana, opium, whatever the contraband goods, they had to be packaged so that one person could handle them. At the pick-up port, he would send his entire crew ashore for a night on the town, as he had at Beirut. It was usually during the period between the fall of darkness and midnight that a small craft, its running lights dark, would pull up to the lowered gangway platform. In short order its cargo would be deposited on the floor of the captain's cabin, just inside the doorway.

Rashid would then go to work. The shower stall would be moved to one side, the hatch below it lifted. A heavy pulley would be screwed into a hole in the ceiling above the hatch. A rope would be fed through it and tied to a small cargo net, which Rashid would use to lower the goods through the hatch down to the deck of the compartment, or to lift the stuff out at its destination.

As old as he was, the captain was still in excellent condition. He was a powerful man, thick chested, carrying heavy muscular arms developed from a lifetime of hard physical work in the tough business of being a Mediterranean sailor. For survival, Rashid had to be strong. He had to be able to lift cargo or take on the world in a bar-room brawl. He prided himself on still being able to handle up to a hundred pounds, a lot less than he used to lift, but, at his age, not bad. In an hour, perhaps an hour-and-a-half, of work, he could get any incoming cargo neatly stowed below, the hatch back in place, the pulley out of the ceiling and the shower stall returned.

From time to time, Rashid took on board another kind of cargo. Human cargo. Many times he had been sought out in the favorite bars of sea captains in Alexandria, Piraeus, or Marseilles by some desperate soul seeking escape to another country. When the compartment had been built, its use as living quarters had been anticipated. A toilet and a sink were installed at the starboard end. Primitive and filthy, but practical. There were no bunks, chairs, furniture of any kind—not even a porthole for air.

On this voyage, the captain's special compartment had a cargo. It, too, had come on board at Beirut: a thousand pounds of opium for shipment to Kuwait. It was packaged in thirty-pound plastic bags enclosed in ordinary-looking burlap sacks. Rashid guessed that when it was off-loaded the stuff would find its way onto one of the tankers waiting to be loaded with crude oil. The white treasure would then be carried to Europe or North America. Where the opium came from he did not know and cared less. Probably Afghanistan or Pakistan. All that mattered was that he and the ship's owners were paid handsomely and in cash for carrying the contraband.

While the captain was satisfied that no customs inspector would be able to discover the existence of the compartment or the entrance to it, nevertheless he was always apprehensive when he was anchored in a harbor such as Port Said, which teemed with other freighters, tankers, customs boats, and prowling Egyptian naval vessels. There was always the chance that something could go wrong.

The *Mecca* had arrived at the entrance to Port Said just before ten o'clock on the evening of March 10. Since she was not on a tight schedule, the captain elected to wait until morning before proceeding into harbor. He picked out the familiar light of the Fairway buoy, the main channel marker outside the port's entrance. He then steamed two miles west of it, where he dropped anchor to spend the night. During that day, he had been following the news reports from Beirut, Cairo, and the BBC about the massive explosion in Haifa harbor that killed fifty-three naval personnel, destroyed six of the Israelis' best, most modern high-speed patrol boats, and leveled three warehouses. The Israelis were still uncertain about the cause of the blast, but officials believed it was the work of PLO terrorists. Did that mean that they suspected the *Mecca*? Rashid had agreed with Said that the Israeli officials would not be able to find any evidence to tie the two together. On the other hand, the patrol boat that had stopped them had been dispatched by staff at the Haifa naval control of shipping office. They would know that the *Mecca* had been stopped and boarded and that it was that particular patrol craft that had taken the full brunt of the blast.

So far Said was right in one respect. In the destruction, chaos, and ensuing panic, no one would think of chasing after the *Mecca*. Indeed, there would be nothing in Haifa to chase her with. A patrol boat could have been sent out from Tel Aviv to intercept her. It wasn't. But Rashid turned the situation over in his mind as he monitored the radio news reports. He was becoming convinced that, in the light of day, the Israelis might connect the boarding of the *Mecca* with the harbor explosion. Possibly it was only because by late morning after the blast his ship was not only well into international waters, but also well out of range, that she had not been pursued and brought back into an Israeli port to face investigation.

It was the six o'clock BBC evening news that jolted Rashid as he sat in his cabin eating his supper. It also disturbed Said, sitting in his cabin listening to the same newscast coming from Hassan's black box. In his droll English accent the BBC reporter added to the information about the explosion that had been repeated during the day:

"Israeli officials have now determined that the cause of the blast was a radio-activated Russian mine planted on the hull of one of their patrol boats in the harbor. As yet they are not certain how the mine was planted, but they are sure it was the work of PLO terrorists."

The captain immediately phoned up to the bridge, instructing Nabil to send for Said. "I want to see him immediately. Now!"

Rashid was certain Nabil had slept through the Israeli boarding and that none of the deck hands had seen Said climb back on board the ship after the mine planting. They were too busy gawking at the patrol boat on the other side of the *Mecca*'s packing-case-filled cargo deck. Undoubtedly Nabil and the rest of the crew had heard the news reports during the day about the explosion on Haifa, but would not connect them with their own ship.

In short order, bareheaded, barefooted, and dressed in his blue denim work clothes, Said was standing in front of the captain's table, looking down at the agitated old man puffing furiously on a mutilated cigarette.

"You wanted to see me?"

"Did you hear the BBC news report just now?"

With a curt nod of his head, the young Arab acknowledged that he had.

"A Russian mine. Is it true? Was it a Russian mine?"

There was no answer. The furious Rashid stubbed out his cigarette, leaned forward, the palms of his hands planted on the table, and growled at Said, "I want you to understand one thing, you young idiot. If what you planted on that Israeli boat was a Russian mine, and if what you've got in those ill-begotten packing cases out there," his right hand rose to point over Said's shoulder, "are Russian mines, and if you think I am going to take this ship into Port Said with those things sitting on my deck, you must be out of your mind!"

Still no response from the PLO leader.

"The Israelis and Egyptians are bedfellows now. Even the Egyptians hate the PLO. When we go in that harbor, the police, the navy, somebody will swarm all over this ship." The captain drew himself up to his full height. He had to be strong. "Those packing cases will have to go overboard."

With a slow, deliberate motion, Said removed his mirrored sunglasses. His crystal blue eyes were ice, as his voice hissed through clenched teeth. "Touch those crates and I'll kill you."

The cut of the words made the captain flinch inside. "But in the name of Allah, we can't go into the port with that stuff on deck—Russian mines!"

The sunglasses went back on again. Said was not about to admit what was in those crates. However, the captain had a point. As a matter of diplomatic courtesy, the Egyptians would have nothing to lose and much cooperation to gain by responding to an urgent Israeli request to go over the *Mecca* and her crew with a fine-tooth comb. He could not understand how the Israelis had found out that it was a

Russian-made mine or, for that matter, that it was a mine at all. Said had thought that the blast would wipe out any trace. He realized he ought to have known better. He had made a mistake. He recanted. "You're right. I've been through this ship from one end to the other looking for a place to . . ."

It was against Rashid's better judgment but . . . He held up the palm of his right hand and said, "I have the place for the stuff."

"And what about us?"

The beleaguered captain managed a weak smile. "And for the four of you, too."

He slumped back in his chair, waved Said into the chair opposite, pulled out a cigarette and lit it with a trembling match. Blowing out the first cloud of smoke he told Said, "This is what we'll do. I'll break out some Italian wine for the whole crew. By midnight, they'll all be drunk, and when this lot drinks, they're right out of it."

"Including Nabil?"

The captain guffawed, "Nabil? He'll be the first one under the table. Now this is what I want you and your people to do. We can start say at one o'clock, not any earlier . . ."

The *Mecca* arrived at her anchorage in the darkness at about 8:30 that evening. When the captain was satisfied that the anchor was down and the ship was secure, he announced over the loudspeaker system that because they had to stand offshore and couldn't get into port that night so the crew could get ashore, on behalf of the owners he was opening the wine locker at two liters per man, red or white. He could hear cheers from cabin deck. Both Nabil and the helmsman with him on the bridge gave the captain happy salutes and disappeared toward the galley. There the cook was already dispensing bottles and glasses amid laughter and the popping of corks. Among the nine crew members were two men with guitars who knew every foul song sung by Mediterranean sailors.

As predicted, by midnight all the wine was gone. Every man of the crew, all nine of them, had passed out.

Some had made it to their bunks, others just collapsed where they were. Their evening of revelry had taken place on the fantail of the ship, with singing, shouting, cursing, and one short fist fight which wound up with the participants amicably throwing their arms around each other after not a single drunken blow was landed.

At one o'clock, the captain made a tour of inspection of the cabin deck. As a precaution, he nudged or pushed each man with his foot, watching for a reaction. Not one of them responded.

Satisfied, he went to Said's darkened cabin, tapped on the door, opened it a crack and said, "Let's go."

The four PLO men were ready in their blue work clothes. This would be their job, not the captain's. Crowbars were removed from their stowed position, one for each man. In the dim light cast by the red, green, and white running lights, they began prying open the tops of the small crates, one at a time. When the first came off, Captain Rashid had no idea what to expect. Gray shining objects perhaps. Guns. He didn't know, but he was expecting the worst. He was disappointed when all he could see were the tops of what appeared to be styrofoam squares tightly packed together. Putting his crowbar down, Said lifted out the first white package. It was heavy, awkward to remove. The rest would be easier. He looked at the captain who turned, opened his cabin door, and led Said through to the washroom. There the shower stall had already been moved aside. The hatch was open and the pulley, rope, and net were in place.

Said asked, "Spread the net out for me, please." Rashid quickly flattened the net out on the floor, pulling the corners taut to make it square. Said put his heavy, white package in the center. It was quickly joined by three more, carried in by the team close behind. When eight were on the pile, Said decided that was enough weight for the first lift.

He ordered Ahmed, "You go down into the hold. We'll lower them down to you. Stack them . . ."

The captain broke in. "Stack them against the forward

bulkhead over toward the toilet. Just keep away from the sacks. I'll turn the light on."

"What's in the sacks?" Ahmed asked.

"Seed," was the partly true reply.

Satisfied, Ahmed lowered his enormous bulk gingerly down the vertical steps into the dimly lit compartment. When he reached the floor, his head almost touched the ceiling. To his left, about ten feet toward the bow of the boat, was a solid bulkhead that ran the width of the ship. To his right was an identical bulkhead about three feet away. At each end of the compartment were the steel ribs and curved plates of the hull. Ahmed was satisfied that there was plenty of room for their weapons and equipment, and, for that matter, themselves.

"It looks good," he whispered up the hatchway to Said. "Lower away whenever you're ready."

Standing outside the washroom, the captain watched as Said and Maan hauled on the rope, pulling up the four corners of the net. The square white packs were firmly in the pocket of the net which swung over the hatch as soon as it cleared the deck. Maan steadied the net as it swung back and forth like a pendulum. Gently, they lowered it through the hatch into the waiting hands of Ahmed, who guided it to the floor. Working quickly, he lifted each piece out, setting it down carefully. When the net was empty he called, "Take it up for the next load." Then he began stacking them against the forward bulkhead, keeping well clear of the sacks of seed which filled the room with a peculiar odor, almost a perfume. Ahmed didn't know what it was, but he could smell it when he first came down the steps.

Nine loads later, three of the packing cases had been cleared of their contents. It was the fourth one that caught Captain Rashid's imagination. From it, Said, Maan and Hassan extracted two forty-horsepower outboard motors and gasoline tanks; a pair of large, noiseless, electric outboard motors and their wet-cell batteries; two sets of plastic oars in sections; two large dunnage bags, each filled with a large rolled-up object; and four oxygen bottles, face masks and sets of flippers.

When those items were stowed, the next things to put into the compartment were the sleeping bags off their bunks, all their personal gear and sufficient canned food from the galley to last them a week. They expected to be confined for a much shorter period than that, but the captain had cautioned Said to be on the safe side.

Finally they broke up the wooden packing crates and threw the debris overboard. The one-and-one-half-knot current flowing across the entrance to Port Said would take the pieces of wood many miles to the east by dawn.

At seven the next morning the captain did a repeat of his Beirut wake-up rounds to get his crew and his ship going. He routed the still half-drunk Nabil out of his bunk, shouting at him to get the rest of the crew up and moving. The ship had to get under way as soon as possible.

The captain returned to his quarters and waited for about ten minutes until he heard footsteps on the bridge above. That was the signal that Nabil and the helmsman had finally pulled themselves together. When he heard the groaning chatter of the deck hands, moving forward to the fo'c'sle to bring up the anchor, he knew it was time to go up top.

As he stepped on the bridge, the brilliant rays of the early morning sun shining through the streaked forward glass of the wheelhouse made him squint. It would be another hot, humid, windless day.

Nabil's eyes were twitching from his hangover. Nevertheless, he was perceptive enough to realize that something was missing.

"What happened to the crates, the four small crates that came out of Beirut?"

The captain ignored him. He flicked the speaker switch to the engine room, shouting, "Engine room, are you ready to get under way?" There was a long pause as the wine-soaked chief engineer hauled himself within range of his speaker and summoned enough precision to find the transmitting switch.

"Engine room ready, sir."

"Slow ahead" was the order to Nabil.

It was only after the anchor was up, the fo'c'sle secured, and the order "full ahead" given, that the captain chose to answer.

"Our PLO friends disembarked last night and took the packing cases with them."

Nabil scratched his forehead, lifting the peak of his cap. "Last night? I didn't hear anything."

Rashid roared, "Hear anything! You were dead drunk. A lighter came by shortly after midnight and took them off. I was happy to see the last of them."

"They must have used the crane to get those crates off . . ."

"The big one, Ahmed, had the crane motor going in no time. Must be an expert. He had the crates on the lighter in ten minutes."

Shaking his head in bewilderment the Egyptian mused, "I wonder if they had anything to do with that big explosion in Haifa."

Busying himself with the navigation of the ship, the captain made no response. "Starboard ninety" was his order to the helmsman, as the *Mecca* passed the Fairway buoy. The captain's next order was to bring the ship directly into the channel line "*Yaminak shwayya*, starboard a bit." The new heading would take them straight into the harbor channel of Port Said. Half an hour later, the *Mecca* dropped anchor once again, this time at the south end of Port Said harbor, in the lee of a large luxury passenger ship. To the north of the freighter *Mecca* stood a crude oil tanker in ballast, to the south another freighter, and beyond it a second tanker. If he could get his port clearances finished in time, the *Mecca* would join those ships in the afternoon southbound convoy down the Suez Canal.

Because the procedures were complex, Captain Rashid normally went ashore to pay the canal transit dues. But he was uneasy about the Haifa incident. He had a feeling in his bones that something was going to happen, that he should stay on his ship. If the authorities came aboard while he was away and Nabil was in charge, only Allah knew what would happen. No, he would send Nabil ashore. Anyway, an Egyptian could deal best with an Egyptian. He thought of all Egyptians with condescending disdain and about Nabil with disdain without condescension. Furthermore, Nabil could use the experience and undoubtedly somewhere in the city he had a little woman he could spend a fast hour in bed with.

When the anchoring procedures were finished, Rashid turned to the sallow-faced young officer.

"Go and shave. Get cleaned up. I want you to go to the transit office for me and get our clearances. And I want you to look respectable when you go ashore." The captain added with a tone of sarcasm, "You might take a shower, even if it's the only one this trip. When you're ready to go, report back to my cabin. I'll give you some money and instructions as to what has to be done."

When Nabil reported to the captain half an hour later, Rashid was astonished. The first officer had indeed shaved and showered. His wet, black hair was plastered down and neatly combed. Instead of the usual scruffy brass-buttoned jacket and dirty gray turtleneck pullover he wore ashore, he had on a clean, neatly pressed uniform, two stripes of gold braid gleaming on the sleeve. A spotless white shirt sported a black tie. Even his shoes were polished and—the last straw—his fingernails were clean.

"Allah be praised! I should bring you to Port Said more often!" Rashid couldn't believe the transformation. "She must really be something."

The clean first officer smiled, his crooked, shiny white teeth showing his anticipated pleasure. "She's gorgeous." His hands made an arcing motion out in front at chest level. "She has the biggest, hardest . . ." Then his hands dropped to his crotch. "And the tightest, wettest black . . ." His bloodshot eyes rolled upward towards the ceiling as he ran his tongue back and forth across his mustached upper lip.

It was almost too much for the old seaman, "In the name of heaven get a grip on yourself, Nabil. She might not be at home."

"I have worthy alternatives, captain."

It was time to get down to business. "This is what I

want you to do. Go to the transit office. Here's the money for the transit dues and a list of the information you have to give, and here's the Suez Canal special tonnage certificate. Anything else?"

"What time do you want me back?"

Never, if I had my choice, the captain thought, but the words he spoke were "Twelve o'clock. That's noon today, Nabil, noon. It's coming up to nine now. Do you think you can get everything done and be back here by noon?"

There was a pleading look on the first officer's face. "One o'clock would be much better, much, much better."

"All right, one o'clock, but not one minute after. The convoy moves out of the harbor at three, and we have to move with it. Understand?"

Nabil was surprisingly deferential. "Yes, sir. One o'clock, sir. I'm very grateful, sir."

"Get going!" the captain growled. He wanted Nabil off the ship as quickly as possible. If there was going to be any trouble with the port police or the navy over the Haifa affair, the last person he wanted to have on board while inspection and interrogation was going on was Nabil. The Egyptian scuttled out of the captain's cabin, ran down the gangway steps and into the waiting, leaky lifeboat to be rowed by a sullen deck hand westward to the transit office dock. The deck hand was annoyed because the captain refused him permission to stay ashore to wait for the first officer's return. The ship's master knew better than to allow two of his crew ashore at Port Said when he needed both of them back in time for departure and at least one of them sober.

Rashid's plan for the rest of the morning was to keep his crew, other than the cook and the two engineers, busy on deck scraping and painting. It was time to start cleaning up the grimy old ship, reluctant as the crew might be. Furthermore, he wanted to be on deck himself or on the bridge to keep an eye open for any approaching official Egyptian craft. By nine o'clock he had organized all hands, including the one who had taken Nabil ashore. All five were busy scraping on the fo'c'sle, having started their chore by cleaning up the paint locker which in the last two days had received more attention than it had in years. All of the PLO team's gear had been removed during the darkness a few hours earlier. The captain calculated that if he had his men working at the bow of the ship, they would be out of the way in the event of a boarding. They would, of course, be available for questioning, but at least they wouldn't be immediately underfoot or within earshot. Having assigned each man a specific area of the deck for its scrape down preparatory to painting, Rashid called to the cook for coffee and went up to the bridge to escape the increasing morning heat.

When the coffee was brought to him on the bridge, he took a cigarette from the pocket of his open-necked, white, short-sleeved shirt on which he had put his captain's epaulets. He was in his best white tropical uniform. When he had awakened that morning he had decided he should be properly dressed to greet any boarding party that might appear. Puffing contentedly on his cigarette and sipping the thick coffee, he looked out, past the work party at the bow, toward the city's docks and buildings to the west. As his eyes scanned, he noticed the gray, rakish, swept-back bow of a small vessel as it moved out from a hidden jetty in the area where he knew the customs offices to be. The craft, however, was no customs boat. Rather it was another of those cursed naval patrol boats. This time, however, it was Egyptian and not nearly so heavily armed as the Israelis'. She carried torpedo tubes but no surface-to-surface missile launchers. A pair of machine guns was mounted on the forward deck, unmanned as she turned the jetty corner heading out into the harbor. What would she do? It was unusual to see a naval patrol boat in the Port Said harbor. And since it was putting out from the customs docks, most peculiar.

Rashid kept his eyes fixed on her as he alternately sipped his coffee and pulled on his cigarette. Across the water came the booming roar of her engines as they were thrust up to full power, driving the bow of the whippet-like vessel up out of the water and then down as it gained high speed on the smooth harbor surface. Rashid was relieved when she turned north toward the harbor mouth, disappearing behind the huge bulk of the passenger ship lying between the *Mecca* and the western edge of the port. Moments later his heart sank when she reemerged heading east and close in behind the cruise ship. The boat was no more than a hundred yards to the north of the *Mecca*. It was then that he could see that all the faces of the sailors on board the patrol craft were looking at his ship, at him. There were eight white-uniformed men in the wheelhouse. All of them were armed. At least four of them had stubby automatic rifles. Wherever they were going, they meant business—and trouble. Perhaps they were headed for the labyrinth of channels of the eastern side of the harbor, smugglers' haven. The captain's wishful hope was not to be.

As the Egyptian gunboat passed a point just a few yards beyond the stern of the *Mecca* and still to the north of her, it swung south in a tight arc to come in on the freighter's starboard side from astern. They were coming aboard.

The old captain's heart raced with apprehension as he moved quickly down to the head of the gangway to receive his unwanted visitors. Her engines cut to an idle, the war boat was brought skilfully alongside and made fast. Rashid read the boarding party leader's rank on his shoulders as he mounted the gangway steps, followed by six armed sailors. The peak of the man's cap and his epaulets told Rashid that he was a commander in the Egyptian navy, an unusually senior rank for an officer leading a boarding party, even though he was assisted by a much younger lieutenant-commander who followed immediately behind.

When the commander stepped on the *Mecca*'s deck, the greeting formalities were quickly disposed of.

The naval commander, gray haired, had a narrow, angular, and weather-creased face. He was a slim, erect man but a head shorter than the *Mecca*'s captain. He quickly got down to business as his people fanned out along the ship's railing on each side of him.

"I am Commander Faher. I am in charge of the Port

Said naval district. I have been personally instructed by the president . . ." He paused, relishing the importance of being able to drop that exalted name, "by the president himself to do a thorough inspection of this . . ." He looked up and down the length of the unkempt vessel with disdain, "this ship."

Rashid began his side of the game. "Why does the president so honor the *Mecca*?"

Commander Faher gave a hint that he was an impatient man, particularly when dealing with inferiors. "Come now, captain. Surely you heard on the news about the big explosion at Haifa. Six patrol boats destroyed and over fifty people killed?"

The captain shrugged, "Yes, but what's that got to do with me?"

"You were boarded by an Israeli gunboat two days ago?"

"Yes. Off Haifa and in international waters. I intend to file a protest."

Commander Faher was sympathetic. Even though there was a peace between their countries, the hatred of the individual Egyptian for the Israelis continued unabated. Here he was acting as agent for the Israeli navy. It was a matter of extreme distaste for the commander. Had it not been for the direct order of his beloved president . . .

"Typical of the Israelis. They think they own the world," he sniffed. "What the Israelis say is that there is a possibility that while their boarding party was on your ship, someone somehow planted a mine on their patrol boat."

Rashid protested. "That's ridiculous. They were on board ten, maybe fifteen minutes. We were minding our own business, making for Port Said when they stopped us. How in heaven's name could anybody plant a mine in that kind of a situation? We had no notice. And furthermore, you can talk to my crew. There isn't one of them who would know what a mine looks like."

The naval commander folded his arms in front of him. "Come now, captain. You had four PLO soldiers on board." The Egyptian was smug, knowing that the information would catch the *Mecca*'s captain by surprise. He watched Rashid's face carefully for a reaction that did not come. He would try again. "They left your ship last night when you were anchored outside the harbor."

Outwardly Rashid gave no indication of surprise, but inwardly he was taken aback. Clever little bastard, the commander. "Where did you get that information?"

Again a smug look on the commander's face. "We've been watching your ship since dawn. When your first officer came ashore, we intercepted him. He and I had a nice chat over coffee. Being a true and loyal Egyptian, he wanted to get about his business as quickly as possible, so he told me everything he knew. Four PLO soldiers led by a man called Said who wears sunglasses night and day. They got on board at Beirut. Also four packing cases came on board there. When it was apparent that the Israelis were going to board you, the PLO man warned the crew that his team would kill all of them if they tipped off the Israelis. When the Israelis were on board, the PLO men were located in the bow, amidships and at the stern. But your man Nabil could not account for their leader."

"He was off watch, in his cabin at the time."

"Yes. He said that. But the crewmen on deck at the time told him they didn't see the leader. So, perhaps he got overboard and planted a mine."

The captain shook his head. "Impossible!"

"Maybe." The commander shrugged. "My instructions are to search this ship thoroughly. Your first officer didn't see the PLO men get off last night and he didn't see the packing cases being transferred to a lighter. If they're still on board this ship, I intend to find them." He paused, seeming to be uncomfortable about his actions. "You must understand, captain. I am under the personal instructions of the president. I am not an Israeli sympathizer."

Captain Rashid thought he might like this little man. "When you have finished your search, commander, I will have coffee ready for you in my cabin."

Within twenty minutes, Commander Faher and his

men had been through every part of the *Mecca* from the engine room and the cabins and lockers at the stern to the hold under the fo'c'sle. They had been into both the forward and aft cargo holds. The four motor vehicles lashed in the forward deck had been carefully scrutinized. The tops had been pried off all six of the huge compressor packing cases, their contents checked out and the lids nailed back again. Faher was satisfied that there was not a square foot of the boat which had not been accounted for.

When the inspection was finished, the commander accepted the captain's invitation to coffee. The two men chatted politely about ships and politics. When it was time to leave, the commander asked permission to use the captain's washroom. The apprehensive Rashid could only agree. It seemed to him that Faher was secluded in that room for an inordinate length of time, even though it was perhaps no more than four minutes. The Egyptian finally emerged. He picked up his hat to leave. Holding out his hand to Captain Rashid, Commander Faher said, "It would have gone well on my record to have found what I was looking for. But I must tell you, captain, as an Arab and an Egyptian and as a naval officer, I was delighted with what happened at Haifa. And so I would have been most unhappy, most disappointed if I had found the PLO men. Frankly, I have the fullest sympathy for the Palestinian people. So, captain, I am pleased to have failed. By the way, the latch that moves your shower stall away from the hatch should be oiled. It is a little sticky."

Rashid was caught by surprise and showed it. His jaw fell open with astonishment as the sprightly commander stepped out of the cabin and disappeared with his men down the gangway steps.

6

11 March   6:00 P.M.

Atlantic Ocean

By 1800 hours on the evening of March 11, H.M.S. *Splendid*, holding at 500 feet, was midway between the island of Santa Maria, at the eastern end of the Azores, and Madeira, coming up on its port side. From the time it had passed the Finisterre light, the moving panorama of the sonar screen picked up the blips of forty surface vessels. As the plot record showed, all but seven were tankers carrying their precious crude oil, without which Western Europe could not survive, north to waiting ports, or steaming south in ballast toward the Cape of Good Hope still some 6,000 miles ahead. There they would gradually turn eastward and then north up the Indian Ocean toward the Strait of Hormuz and the Persian Gulf or, as it was known by the Arabs of the area, the Arabian Gulf.

The captain was in his cabin on number one deck, just forward of the control room. He had chosen to have supper by himself in his tiny cubicle, cramped by its bunk, desk, cupboards, lockers, a pair of chairs, and a wash basin. On the desk was a telephone and above it shelves holding official publications, charts, and a clutch of the newest paperback books to come out of London. Above the shelves was a depth gauge and beside it a clock and barometer, the most basic of all nautical instruments.

He had eaten in a leisurely fashion. The dish was curried shrimp which the senior of the wardroom's two stewards, Petty Officer Robert Joyce, a squat, short, kindly Glaswegian, had served with dexterity after covering the desk with a stiff linen tablecloth and setting out shiny new silverware, each piece bearing the name *Splendid* along its handle. His final touch was a sparkling silver tankard into which, before the food was served, Joyce had poured a pint of lager beer.

"Is there something significant about having Indian curry?" Leach had jokingly asked Joyce.

The reply came with almost a giggle, "After all, sir, we are going to the . . ."

"Yes. I know, the Indian Ocean."

The telephone, stark black against the white tablecloth, rang sharply.

"Pritchard in the control room, sir. I have a sonar contact. Looks like a bogey."

Brushing past his startled steward, the captain was in the sonar department in a few rapid strides. Pritchard was there, standing behind Petty Officer Pratt and his assistant, both seated and wearing earphones. All eyes were glued on the sonar screen.

Their heads turned momentarily as the captain entered the tiny space, asking, "Where is it?"

Pritchard pointed to the right-hand bottom corner of the screen. "There it is, abeam of us and closing on a parallel course about a mile to starboard."

The captain was astonished. "Closing? Cor' crikey. We're going thirty knots and she's closing?"

"Yes, sir." Petty Officer Pratt checked at the red numbers coming up in his computer readout faces. "At ten knots."

"What depth?"

"Eight hundred feet. Range 9,500 yards."

She had to be either an American or a Russian. With

that speed she had to be an attack vessel like *Splendid* herself.

The sonar watchkeeper's voice was calm. "I'll have the answer on her signature in a minute, sir. It's in the computer now."

The identification came up in red digits against the black face of the computer glass, in the large electronic machine sitting against the aft bulkhead of the sonar room. It was one word: *Alfa*.

Leach knew the Alfa class Soviet submarines. There were only four of them in service. A downstream generation of the Novembers of the early sixties and later the Victors, her ship's complement was only fifty against that of his twelve officers and eighty-five men. Smaller than the *Splendid*, the Alfa was 260 feet against the *Splendid*'s 272. Her displacement was 3,300 tons deadweight against the 4,500 of Leach's boat. Her advertised speed was thirty-two knots plus, against the *Splendid*'s thirty. With her lesser weight and bulk, she had much greater power, 24,000 shaft horsepower from her nuclear reactor and steam turbine as against the 15,000 of *Splendid*. No wonder she was overtaking at ten knots.

"Has she got us? Has she been pinging?"

If the answer was yes, that meant that the "bogey" (now transformed through its Soviet identity to a "bandit") was on active sonar, sending out enormous belts of energy into the surrounding waters to bounce back from any object coursing through the depths of the ocean. On passive sonar, the huge hydrophones of the boat's sonar system sent out no energy pulse but would simply take in and record the noises it picked up.

Earphones in place but able to hear the words from the captain as well as the electronic sounds, Pratt, his eyes moving from his control panel to the huge screen, nodded vigorously. "Aye, sir. No doubt about it. She started pinging just as she came on the screen."

"We've got her and she's got us," Pritchard added.

"But she'll soon be long gone unless she wants to play silly bugger with us."

Suddenly the huge gray map of the sonar screen flickered, interference lines running up and down its face like a television set.

"What in hell is that?" the captain half shouted.

"Damned if I know, sir," Pritchard replied. "I've never seen anything like that before and it's not in any of the textbooks."

For a moment, the full sweeping image of the screen was restored. With it came another shock. Marcus Leach could scarcely believe what he saw. "Hell's teeth. There's another bloody sub."

There on the screen, about a mile behind the first bandit but slightly off to port, steering exactly the same course, was the blip of the second submarine. Was it another Alfa? Or was it a shadowing American?

"What's the second one?" Leach's voice had a note of urgency.

Pratt was furiously punching buttons on his console, trying to capture the signature and feed it into the computer, when the screen again lost its image and showed only horizontal rolling lines.

More furious button punching, switch flicking, dial twisting by the sonar watchkeeper. Suddenly he took the phones away from his ears. He turned to his right, handing the earphones past Pritchard to the captain. "Listen to that, sir. Gorblimey, I've never heard anything like that in my bleedin' life."

Leach clamped one of the phones to his left ear. What he heard was an undulating signal, a sound curiously similar to the range of white noise in the relatively narrow band of frequencies emitted by the engines, machinery and propellers of submarines but at a much higher, more penetrating volume.

"What do you think it is, sir?" Pratt had swiveled around in his seat to watch the captain as he listened to the peculiar sound.

Leach kept the phone to his ear for a few more seconds before saying, "I haven't a clue. I've never heard anything like that before either."

He handed the head set back to the petty officer and spoke to Pritchard. "There may be something wrong with our own sonar gear. Better check it out, chop, chop. I'll take over the watch while you're doing it."

"Aye, aye, sir."

Back in the control room, Leach dispatched the messenger of the watch, Smith, to fetch the first lieutenant. As he waited for Lieutenant-Commander Paul Tait to appear, he settled into the chair between the two watchkeepers on the steering and hydroplane controls, his eyes expertly reading the instruments in front of them.

When his tall, ungainly first lieutenant burst into the control room, sandals flapping, Leach told him to go into the sonar room, take a look at the screen and listen to the sound on the earphones. Tait promptly disappeared.

In a few minutes he was back, the forehead below his long, stringy, brown hair furrowed.

"What do you make of it, Paul?"

Tait's puzzled eyes contemplated the deck, unseeing, as he puzzled over what he had heard. Then they lifted to look at Leach. "I really don't know, sir. It's a new one on me. There's probably something wrong in our own gear."

A clue crossed Leach's mind. He got up and stepped forward through the doorway to stick his head in the sonar room again, where Pritchard and the two watchkeepers were busy running through the standard test checks.

"Is that Alfa still pinging us?"

"No, sir," Petty Officer Pratt replied, the earphones back on his head. "They stopped just after the big sound started, just before I gave the earphones to you."

"But you could hear the pinging over the big sound. It didn't blank out the pinging."

"That's right, sir."

"What about our back-up sonar?"

Pritchard shrugged. "We've tried it, sir. We get the same thing. The big noise, as Pratt calls it."

Back again in the control room the captain leaned against the periscope shaft as he turned this new information over in his mind. Either there was something wrong with their own sonar gear or there was some strong external force out there producing an overpowering, overriding noise on the white sound frequencies. His memory told him that he had seen an intelligence report some months back. How did it go? The Soviets had been trying out some sort of a noise-generating device in their "race track" testing area in the Barents Sea north of the Kola Peninsula. Intelligence had made no judgment on what the device was for. Just that the defensive hydrophone chain across the Iceland Gap to Norway had picked up short bursts of its sound.

Whether the interference was from an internal fault in the boat's gear or an external source, way below periscope depth, which was also radar depth, *Splendid* was blind. Then what about the ship's inertial navigation system?

"Pilot, is SINS functioning all right?"

The navigation officer appeared startled by the question, even though he had heard the commotion going on about the sonar. "No problem, sir."

So the navigation system was not affected. But without the sonar, *Splendid* was not only blind but, as an attack vessel, useless. With its sonar eyes in operation, the attack submarine could do many things. It could act unsupported against surface ships. It was complementary to aircraft and antisubmarine operations in that the long range patrol aircraft "located" the enemy ship, the ship-borne helicopter "pinpointed" and the submarine "destroyed." By itself the attack submarine was also an extremely good antisubmarine vessel, greatly aided by its ability to carry the biggest and best sonar—because of its size, its powerful nuclear reactor, and its ability to stay submerged for weeks on end. It was capable of firing a variety of weapons from its torpedo tubes in support of a task force such as the flotilla that *Splendid* was on its way to join in the Arabian Sea. But without the sonar, she could perform none of the functions for which she was built.

Pritchard appeared in the door behind the captain. "Sir, we've completed all the checks."

Leach was certain of what his sonar officer was going to tell him. "And?"

"There's nothing wrong with the main sonar or the back-up. We're getting interference from an outside source."

"That's probably why the Alfa stopped pinging at us. She's undoubtedly getting the same big noise. It would blanket her active sonar reception."

"That's right, sir," Pritchard agreed.

"Have your watchkeepers let me know the minute that damn noise disappears—if it does, that is—or if there's any other change in the situation. You can take back the watch."

"Aye, aye, sir."

To his first lieutenant, the captain extended an invitation, "Buy you a beer." Without waiting for Tait's acceptance, Leach went down the passageway toward the front of the ship to the cramped but comfortable wardroom. It was empty. All the officers not standing watch were down on the deck below in the Junior Ranks' Mess watching a movie from the ship's ample library of first-run films. The steward, Joyce, was hovering as soon as they entered his domain. He took their order and immediately produced two lagers. Leach slumped in the corner of the settee that ran along the curve of the ship's hull. His first lieutenant perched on a small padded chair, his long legs and big feet propped up on another.

"Well, what do you make of it, Paul?" Leach asked.

"Blessed if I know. It must be some diabolical device the Russkis dreamt up."

"Or the Americans, or for that matter our own research people."

Tait smiled, "Perhaps. What do you propose to do, sir?" There was no first-name familiarity permitted the first lieutenant. The captain was far senior to Tait. They had never served together in equal ranks and Leach never gave the first name invitation, nor would he.

"I think we should either surface or go to periscope depth, and I think we should do it immediately." The captain had come to that conclusion before they left the control room, but he wanted to try it on for size with the first lieutenant, out of earshot of the rest of the crew.

Tait was alarmed. "But, sir, going to the surface at night in one of the busiest sea lanes in the world and with no sonar. The chance of collision . . ."

The captain finished the sentence: "Is very high, I agree. But there's a chance of collision down here, too. Maybe not as great. We know that there were two subs. The other's probably an Alfa too, about six miles behind us and closing when the sonar went off. Right now, they're probably just as blind as we are and they can be right up our jaxy. As long as we're below periscope depth we have a collision risk. Sure, it may be small, but it's there. On the other hand, if we run close to the surface, we'll be able to use our eyes and our radar. The risk of collision will be practically nil."

"Except when we're on our way up."

"That's right," Leach acknowledged, "Furthermore, I want to make a signal to Admiralty as soon as possible, telling them what's happened and asking for instructions." Leach could not transmit while *Splendid* was completely submerged. He could only do so if he surfaced or was running at periscope depth with his aerial exposed.

The first lieutenant was still not convinced. "Shouldn't you wait until first light, sir?"

"I think not." The captain had made up his mind. He had had only one sip of beer. He put his glass down, reached over his head to the switch on the speaker on the forward bulkhead immediately above him. Turning his face toward the speaker, he pulled down on the switch, saying, "Pilot, this is the captain."

From the control room, the navigating officer's voice crackled through the box, "Pilot here, go ahead, sir."

"What are the surface conditions?"

All ears in the control room listened with curiosity. Why was the old man asking about surface conditions?

"The latest weather report, sir, at 16:00 Zulu [Greenwich mean time]: We're in a high pressure area. Winds five to six knots from 085 degrees. No cloud cover reported. Sea rolling, almost calm."

"What's the temperature?"

"Seventy-eight degrees, sir."

As he stood up to leave the wardroom, Leach turned to Tait and said, "Good show. It's a pleasant night up top, Paul. Let's hope there aren't any great goddamn tankers up there."

He was followed into the control room by the first lieutenant. Leach picked up the broadcast microphone and clicked the button twice to test it. He heard the clicking echo throughout the ship, alerting the entire crew that something was coming. Even those who were sleeping wakened, their ears sensitive to the signs of an imminent announcement.

"This is the captain speaking. We will be going to periscope depth in a few minutes and I want to tell you why. Our sonar is unserviceable. It has experienced a most unusual interference from outside the ship in the form of a big noise on the range of frequencies that it's designed to operate in. The result is that our boat is now blind in the water. By not hearing we can't see a thing." He thought he put that fairly well.

He then explained his line of reasoning, as he had to the first lieutenant in the wardroom.

"Everyone should realize there is a risk of collision when we go up blind, at least until we get up to periscope level. At fifty feet, we can take a look around to make sure no bloody tanker is bearing down on us. Most tankers don't have a draft of fifty feet, so they would pass over us. But these days some of the loaded big ones reach down ninety feet and more. If we have trouble, it will be from one of those. But I'm quite certain nothing's going to happen. I'm sure that when we get the periscope up I won't find a ship anywhere. So we're going to go to periscope depth so we can take a look around and use our radar for anticollision purposes. As soon as the sonar interference is cleared, we'll dive and go back to normal running procedures." He concluded by giving them a report on the weather up top. "That's all. Carry on please."

He put the microphone back on its storage holder.

Splendid was still running at 500 feet.

"Keep 150 feet."

"One hundred and fifty feet, sir," the planesman reported the order pulling gently back on his wheel. The cant of the deck tilted upwards while the blowing of the ballast tanks began. *Splendid* was headed for the surface.

At the systems console, the first lieutenant, who had taken over from Pritchard, gave a flow of running orders to the watchkeeper controlling the blowing, flooding, and topping of the trim tanks and the blowing of the main ballast tank.

Splendid was rising rapidly.

Leach sat in his chair, listening to the chatter of orders and responses around the control room.

"Two hundred feet, sir."

His eyes confirmed the figure on the depth gauges.

Slightly nervous, he got up to stand beside the periscope. Time to cut back the speed. If they were going to hit another ship, no sense doing it at full bore. "Half ahead."

"Half ahead, sir."

He could feel the propellers and the ship itself slowing down.

"One hundred and fifty feet, sir. Keeping 150 feet, sir."

He would keep it there for a few moments, making sure that the first lieutenant had the trim and was able to keep her level close to the hard-to-achieve neutral point of buoyancy that would allow her to sit at the desired periscope level so the ship would not pop out of the water. He wanted the glass eye at the top of the periscope to emerge cleanly and stop just about a foot above the surface. In the red glow of the control room, darkened to allow the captain to maximize his night vision, he called, "Keep fifty feet!"

"Keep fifty feet, sir." A gentle easing back on the control wheel. A shade of ballast blowing.

"Up search periscope!"

Instantly, the thick shaft standing vertical in the middle of the control room responded. Oil pressure rams forced down the unseen wire pulleys that silently moved the binocular and bifocal, high-powered periscope, able to see and search for many miles, upward in a shaft until its eye pieces stopped in front of the waiting face of the captain.

"One hundred feet, sir."

Leach moved the periscope handles out and down from their stored position. A question went through his mind. Would it be best to stop engines so that *Splendid* had no forward motion? Would that minimize damage in the event of a collision? He had thought of those questions before and decided against stopping. He reasoned that if his boat was making way at, say, fifteen knots when the periscope first cut the surface of the water, and some great bloody monster of a tanker was bearing down on him, his hydroplanes at fifteen knots would have sufficient bite to bunt the *Splendid* down the additional fifty feet to get under the biggest tanker's hull. He would stay with the fifteen knots option.

"Seventy-five feet, sir."

Leach grabbed the periscope handles turning the shaft until it pointed dead ahead. Then his face clamped into the eye piece.

His voice ranged out through the control room, "Be prepared for emergency dive. If I give the order to dive, just shove the goddamn wheel right through the front!"

"Aye, aye, sir!" came the sharp response from the planesman.

Through the flat, glass eye of the extended periscope, Leach could see nothing but smooth blackness.

"Coming up to fifty feet, sir."

"Up radar."

There it was, just a slight tone change in the blackness.

A streak of white foam, and phosphorescence, then a new, lighter blackness. The periscope had surfaced, cutting cleanly.

Dead ahead—nothing. A fast turn of the periscope to starboard, sweeping the horizon to ninety degrees. There in the distance, green and white twinkling running lights. No problem.

A quick wheel back to begin a sweep of the port side. He had moved the periscope no more than twenty degrees to port off the bow when he caught the first blazing running light. It was red and close. A swing further to port. A green light!

"Christ, she's coming right at us!" The words ripped through Leach's brain. Range? In the darkness and in a split second guess maybe 300 yards.

Leach could hear himself screaming, "Dive! Dive! Dive!"

He felt the boat lurch forward as he slammed up the periscope handle, shouting, "Down periscope! Down radar! Full speed ahead!"

By this time the submarine was approaching the maximum downward dive angle that the riding control systems would permit. In the stern, *Splendid*'s propeller spun furiously, pushing her faster and faster. The periscope slammed down into its well.

All that could be done was to wait. Wait.

"Sixty feet, sir." Yes, he knew it was sixty feet. His eyes were glued on the depth gauges, as they moved slower than he had ever seen them before. Seconds clicked by. Sixty-five feet. More seconds. Seventy feet. More seconds. Eighty feet.

He could hear the thumping of the churning screw of the gargantuan tanker, its booming noise reverberating through the hull of the plunging *Splendid*. Closer and louder came the petrifying, ominous pounding.

More seconds.

Ninety feet. The crescendo of deafening propeller noise shook *Splendid* from stem to stern. Its thumping beat was the signal of death and disaster for every man of the *Splendid*'s crew. At the peak of the devastating noise, a long screaming sound could be heard above like the screech of reluctant chalk drawn across a blackboard. That penetrating din lasted for two seconds. Then as quickly as it had started it was gone. Immediately the deafening thunder of the tanker's engine and screw began to diminish. Slowly, then more rapidly, their throbbing noise disappeared to the north as the distance between the two vessels rapidly increased.

Splendid's crew, many of them buffeted about by the harsh handling of their boat, knew what had happened, what the brutal noise immediately above them meant, and in fear of their own lives began pulling themselves together. The captain, steadying himself and gathering his wits after that closest of calls, ordered in a calm business-like voice, "Keep 125 feet!"

"Keep 125 feet, sir."

As the boat's descent stopped and she leveled off, Commander Leach picked up the broadcast microphone once again. After his usual testing and alerting clicks on the speak button, he said into it, "This is the captain. I think it is obvious to everybody that we've just had a narrow escape."

He heard the words muttered from the planesman, "By a bleeding snatch hair!"

"What I plan to do is this. The area to the west is clear. I checked it first just before I caught the tanker coming in on top of us. We'll sail west for ten minutes, then surface. There may have been some damage. However, I'm quite certain there are no ships in the area where we're going to surface next."

He released the microphone button, shouting forward toward the sonar room, "Any joy on the sonar yet, Pritchard?"

The young officer's head popped around the doorway. "No, sir, it's still duff."

Back into the microphone, "There's still no joy on the

sonar, so we're going to run on the surface as I earlier advised. Carry on please."

Ten minutes later, Leach brought his vessel to periscope level. Up went the search periscope. The horizon was clean and clear except for the port and aft running lights of the retreating tanker that had almost killed them.

To the first lieutenant went the order, "Clear. Take her up. Down periscope. Telegraph to stop. Wheel amidships. Planes amidships!"

Splendid was sitting comfortably on the surface of the South Atlantic, rolling gently with the swell. Orders were given to raise and drain the snort mast, to open the lower hatch of the tower and switch on the power and lighting. Before he climbed the rungs of the ladder into the tower, Leach planted his gold-braided hat squarely on his head, telling the messenger of the watch to get him a flashlight. There was something he would have to inspect in the darkness of the tiny bridge, high up the top of the tower. Young Smith was back within twenty seconds.

"Stick it in your shirt and follow me up the ladder."

The young lad, no more than seventeen, was thrilled to have the privilege of following his captain and to be the first one after him to be up on the bridge. "Aye, aye, sir."

The call came, "Lights switched on in the tower, sir."

"How's the pressure in the boat?"

"No pressure in the boat, sir."

Smith followed him up the ladder to the top.

"Shine the torch up here, lad."

In the wavering, strong light Leach took out the two upper hatch hooks and undid both. The hatch swung upward and back easily under the pressure of his right hand.

The captain hauled himself quickly up onto the deck of the small bridge. The steel of the vessel glistened as the sea water ran off through the perforated lattice work of the deck. Leach strained to adjust his eyes to the total darkness, moving rapidly in a 360-degree turn to scan the ebony sea for running lights. There were none except those of their near nemesis, now some miles to the north, its stern superstructure and port lights showing themselves to the master of *Splendid*.

Leaning down, Leach gave a hand to the young seaman scrambling up behind with the much-needed torch. Behind Smith, whose unsure feet were now solidly on the tower deck, came the first lieutenant with the portable voice pipe and the broadcast extension. Both communications instruments were essential to the sailing of the ship on the surface.

Leach stepped to the rear of the bridge, waiting until Tait was on the deck. He stood in darkness illuminated only by the internal tower lights shining up through the open hatch.

Ordinarily, the captain would have called for running lights by that time, but he was so preoccupied with the urgent need to examine the top side of the boat that the routine order had gone out of his mind.

When the first lieutenant was at his side at the aft end of the bridge, Leach looked back toward the stern. The cylindrical shape of the boat's black hull was outlined in phosphorescent foam where it met the lapping sea water. Leach switched on the torch, directing its penetrating beam along the flat top side of the tower to the point some twenty feet aft through which the attack and search periscopes and radar mast emerged. As Leach shone his torch across that section of the tower, he could see that the tops of all the retracted instruments were flush with the surface and undamaged.

The tower's topside should have been gunmetal gray in color, dull with its protective coats of heavily leaded paint. Instead, the entire surface shone with the bright glint of unpainted steel. There were no gouging lines, just the smooth, bare metal surface, gleaming as if newly polished. Wheeling to his right, Leach shone the torch beam along the port edge of the bridge, following its shining lip to the middle of the curve that formed the front of the tower. The paintless surface stopped abruptly in a line that ran roughly twenty degrees off the ship's bow to port. That demarcation line appeared again under Leach's torch on the starboard side of the tower's surface aft the bridge and on a reciprocal line 160 degrees off the ship's bow.

The captain involuntarily sucked air through his teeth as the full impact of what he had seen hit him. His first lieutenant gasped in astonishment, "Christ, the keel of that goddamn tanker . . ."

Leach, incredulous but happy to be alive, couldn't resist, "Almost polished us off."

His mind's eye saw the wide keel of the monster tanker gently contacting and screeching its way along the tower top, meeting *Splendid* almost head on and pushing the submarine down ever so slightly as the tanker's keel ran smoothly along the tower's surface from mid-bridge aft like a gigantic buffing tool.

"Another foot or two and she would have had us," Tait said.

The captain disagreed, "Try six inches."

Leach went to the portable voice pipe and shouted into it, "Control room, do you read me?"

The voice that came back was that of the ship's coxswain, Chief Petty Officer Richards. "You're a little muffled, but I can hear you all right, sir."

"Report telegraph when ready."

"Telegraph to stop, wheel's amidships, sir."

"Navigation lights on the bridge. Officer of the watch and lookouts on the bridge. Test raise and lower both periscopes and all masts and get an inspection party on deck with torches to take a look for any damage!"

The coxswain automatically responded, "Aye, aye, sir."

Leach watched the periscopes and masts go up and down. He was satisfied that they were functioning properly. The officer of the watch and two hands to serve as lookouts came up through the hatch to the bridge. The captain then clambered down the ladder rungs to the control room, followed by the first lieutenant and the messenger of the watch, who was still carrying the torch.

All faces in the rosy glow of the control room were turned expectantly toward the captain.

"Get her under way, Paul. As soon as the damage inspection party reports back, take her to periscope level. I'm sure they won't find anything. Pick up the same course we were following when we were so rudely interrupted. Have the watch on the bridge and the radar keep a sharp eye. I've got to start the bloody paper war."

In the event of any accident or incident it was mandatory that full written reports be made and recorded. Every detail would be scrutinized by the Admiralty. If the ship's captain was seen to be at fault, a court martial could follow. "But first I have to prepare my signal to the Admiralty. Tell Pots to stand by. It will take me about fifteen minutes to put it together." Petty officer telegraphists were now titled radio supervisors but the name "Pots" had survived for the senior rating in the ship's communications center.

At his desk in the privacy of his cabin, Commander Marcus Leach laboriously wrote out his reporting signal to the Admiralty in his strong vertical handwriting. He described the sonar interference situation, asking for an explanation and instructions if any. Then followed the preliminary report on the near miss with the tanker, the latitude and longitude of the spot where the incident occurred and a request that the identity of the ship be obtained and passed back to *Splendid*. Back at Faslane and then Whitehall the signal would send staff officers scurrying. The tanker's identity would easily be found, both from satellite photographs and from Lloyd's of London. Among other things, it would be interesting to know which ship almost did them in.

Within an hour after his signal was sent, the first of a series of responses arrived. The slip of paper was delivered by Pots to the captain, still at his desk writing the preliminary report on the tanker incident. The message read, "Your visitor was *Esso Atlantic*, owner Exxon Corporation. Built Japan 1977; deadweight tons 509,000, speed 15 knots; registry Liberia; length 1,334 feet, draft loaded 91 feet; sails mainly from Persian Gulf to Ports in northern Europe. Also lighters in Gulf of Mexico."

"Draft ninety-one feet!" Leach thought, "No bloody wonder I've got a polished tower top."

That was the first of two meetings between H.M.S. *Splendid* and the mighty Exxon Corporation's mammoth *Esso Atlantic*. The second would be more than a month and a half later on the first day of May, off Cape Town, South Africa.

7

11-13 March

Camp David   Diego Garcia

On Sunday, March 10, the presidential schedule for the following week was altered. The published version stated that John Hansen had canceled all appointments until next Friday to allow him four days of complete rest and seclusion at Camp David. He had long since decided that, while at the age of sixty-one he was in excellent health and quite capable of working eighteen hours a day, seven days a week, he had no intention of working himself to death. He recognized that his responsibilities were so heavy, covered such a broad range of domestic and international matters, that it was now an office that was too much for one man, that the overpowering pressure could kill, and that he, John Hansen, would not let that happen to him. So he had let it be widely known that from time to time he would retreat to the privacy of Camp David with minimum time notice to his staff and to the public and, for that matter, to his young wife, Judith Hansen.

The president and his wife arrived at Camp David shortly before five in the afternoon of Monday, March 11. Their arrival was duly noted by a covey of reporters and photographers. During the evening of the eleventh and on into the night, helicopters were heard banging their way in and out of Camp David. In all, four trips were made. Not an unusual number when the president was there. None of them had been the enormous Marine Corps chopper that usually carried the president. The helicopter that landed at two in the morning of March 12 was much smaller, a single-rotor, twin-engined aircraft. Precisely on time, it had picked up its four passengers: two secret service men, Judith Hansen, and the president. They carried no luggage. It was already on Air Force One waiting for them at Andrews Air Force Base.

At 4:01 A.M., Tuesday, March 12, the captain of the glistening Boeing 707, Air Force One, received his air traffic control clearance as he taxied to the end of the runway, navigation lights blazing, landing lights cutting the darkness ahead, the brilliant blips of strobe lights flashing from its wing tips. At 4:06, Air Force One was airborne, climbing steeply up from Andrews to turn east. The captain had punched into the inertial navigation system his ultimate destination over seventeen hours flying time away. Other adjustments were made in the aircraft's complex electronic navigation and control system. The president's aircraft would fly without the touch of the captain or his copilot on the controls during the entire 10,200 miles to its destination, a mere speck of an island in the Indian Ocean. On board were the president and his wife, Secretary of State Eaton, Secretary of Defense Robert Levy, the president's national security adviser, Walter Kruger, and President Hansen's chief of staff, Jim Crane. In addition, there were four secret service men, part of the highly trained Washington team whose principal function was to protect the president, the vice-president, and all those members of the administration who were by law entitled to security.

President Hansen spent the first hours of the flight with his cabinet members and Kruger. Judith was by his side listening to everything being said. From time to time she put in a question or a relevant comment. She was as much a part of her husband's team as were any of the men.

Crane sat within easy earshot of the conversation and took notes. The secret service quartet sat in the forward section of the aircraft near the flight deck, in a separate compartment. They chatted, read, played cards, and slept.

By the time Air Force One crossed the shores of northwest Africa, dinner had been served and the president and his lady had retired to their private quarters at the rear of the aircraft for some sleep. As it hurtled eastward in the clear, black, star-dotted night sky over Niger in central Africa, John Hansen, the president of the United States of America, lay naked on his side under silk sheets, his huge right hand cupping the firm breasts of his young wife, the skin of her back and round bottom tucked against his chest and his satisfied thighs.

At 07:10 local time on Wednesday morning, Air Force One gently touched down on Diego Garcia, a miniscule island in the Indian Ocean a thousand nautical miles south of the southern tip of India, and some 2,200 miles, five days' sail, away from the shores of Pakistan. Diego Garcia had no inhabitants except for the U.S. Navy personnel stationed there to operate the base, and a handful of British naval personnel who worked in a communications center which the Americans and British jointly ran.

Diego Garcia was part of the British Indian Ocean Territory (BIOT), created in 1965 to provide sites for joint U.K./U.S. military facilities. In the mid 1970s the U.S. government negotiated an agreement with the United Kingdom for the use of Diego Garcia as a permanent naval base. From that time, the U.S. Navy had continued to improve the naval and air facilities on the island. The original 8,000-foot runway on the west arm of the atoll was extended to 12,000 feet. The lagoon, which was twelve miles wide at its broadest point and twenty-four miles long, was dredged for anchorages that would accept the heaviest of the American aircraft carriers. Docks were built, fuel storage capacity was substantially increased, aircraft hangars and buildings for personnel accommodation were constructed. Marine maintenance shops were placed near the dry dock that was built in Japan in 1980 and installed inside Diego Garcia's lagoon just to the north of the air strip.

At President Hansen's request, the captain of Air Force One made a broad sweeping circle over the island before landing, so the president and his party could get a good look at the crystal clear water, and the multi-shaded coral reefs around the flat island's edge. That morning, as on most mornings on an island that received up to 145 inches annually, sheets of rain gusted across the atoll.

Hansen's spirits were lifted when he caught sight of the majestic flat-topped aircraft carrier, the *Dwight D. Eisenhower*, riding at anchor in the Diego Garcia lagoon, her vast gray bulk surrounded by a cluster of five destroyers and a cruiser. He was always thrilled by the raw power that huge warships exuded, particularly those of his own country. As he circled the remote island of Diego Garcia that morning, the president felt a strong surge of pride for his navy and his country. It was his responsibility to keep both of them strong.

On the rain-soaked ramp of the airstrip at Diego Garcia, the president and his wife, both dressed in their lightest white summer clothes, were received by the flag officer from the *Dwight D. Eisenhower*, followed by her captain, and the local base commander. The rain stopped momentarily as the president inspected the drenched honor guard of a hundred men from the *Eisenhower* before being lifted with his party by helicopters to the carrier's deck. As they stepped out of the helicopter onto the sunlit flight deck, Hansen could see a gray sheet of rain moving toward the ship across the airstrip. Fortunately the ceremony welcoming him on board was short. When it was over, he and Judith were escorted inside the towering superstructure of the *Eisenhower*, just as the next flood of rain enveloped the ship.

General Mujeeb-Ul-Rehman, the recently appointed president of Pakistan, had arrived at Diego Garcia in his own small jet aircraft forty-five minutes earlier and had been brought to the *Eisenhower*. With the two other Pakistani generals who had accompanied him, he had awaited President Hansen's arrival in the ship's aircrew briefing room. It was there that, amidst much formality, the two men met for the first time. When the captain of the *Eisenhower* and Judith left the conference room for a tour of the carrier, the two negotiating groups seated themselves opposite each other at the long table.

Hansen had not had much time to size up Mujeeb. Although he knew a great deal about him from the files that Kruger and State had produced, it was the actual presence of the man that had to be assessed. Mujeeb was of medium height, fifty years of age and looked it. His jet-black straight hair was combed directly back from a high forehead. His eyes were deepset, ringed with dark marks of fatigue. As did his colleagues, he sported a trimmed, black mustache. His even, unblemished teeth were often framed in a ready smile. His swarthy face was almost the same color as his light khaki, high-collared uniform. Mujeeb appeared affable enough, although he was obviously nervous in the presence of such power.

President Hansen opened the proceedings with an elaborate explanation of how the United States viewed the current buildup of the Soviet forces in Afghanistan and along the Soviet-Iran border. He stressed the growing probability of a Soviet move against Pakistan, Iran, and the Persian Gulf countries. He explained the American difficulty in not having an operating base from which it could quickly deploy forces to protect the Persian Gulf countries or to defend Pakistan under the terms of the 1959 agreement that obliged the United States to come to the aid of Pakistan against any attacker.

"I want to confirm to you, President Mujeeb, that the United States of America regards that 1959 agreement as still valid and binding."

Mujeeb smiled. "My government reciprocates, Mr. President. In fact we think that the existence of that agreement has been instrumental in deterring the Soviet Union from driving on into our country with its Afghanistan forces, at least to this date. But we share your concern. The buildup of Soviet forces in Afghanistan is—how shall I put it?—ominous indeed. We in Pakistan are virtually defenseless, as you well know. My predecessor never could bring himself to work out a deal with the United States for much-needed equipment."

"Perhaps he was afraid that if he made a deal with us he would incur the wrath of India, as well as the Soviet Union?" the President suggested.

"Perhaps," Mujeeb allowed. "I happen to know what was in his mind on those questions, but he is gone and the Soviets are threatening as never before. My country is in economic difficulty and we need help in defending ourselves. Nevertheless, Mr. President, I must not mislead you into thinking that we are so desperate that we are prepared to 'give the store away' as you might put it." Again Mujeeb smiled.

Hansen returned the smile, shaking his head in protest, "No, Mr. President, I don't think you're going to give us the store, nor would my government want you to."

One thing Hansen knew was that, like most Pakistanis, Mujeeb was a good haggler, a trader, a bargainer.

It was time for him to play his opening card. "As a matter of fact our price for what you want will be high, extremely high. That should be understood from the outset. Mind you, you haven't yet told me what it is you want of us. But I can guess that it's far more than just access to the Port of Karachi and the airport there."

"It is."

"Of course it must be, for the president of the United States himself to come this far to meet with a small, insignificant person such as myself."

Hansen was tempted to protest the Pakistani's self-demeaning remark, but resisted.

Mujeeb did not smile when he said, "My colleagues and I believe that you wish to put American troops and equipment on Pakistani soil; that is why you have come here. Is that correct, Mr. President?"

"Yes, it is."

"As I have said, the price will be high. Very high."

It was John Hansen's turn to smile. "If you're prepared to talk price, President Mujeeb, you're prepared to let us in. I'll tell you what we want. You tell me the price."

8

15 March   11:01 A.M.
Washington, D.C.

On Thursday, March 14, Air Force One had touched down at Andrews Air Force Base, where a small Marine helicopter sat waiting on the ramp for the trip to Camp David. Shortly after four that afternoon, the presidential limousine was bound for the White House. Ever mindful of the need for good relations with the press, the president stopped the car at the Camp David gate to get out and talk to the reporters and photographers waiting for him. Had the president had a good three-day rest? When did the president think that gas rationing would be lifted? Did he think that legislative steps should be taken to hold the price of gasoline at three dollars a gallon? Would the United States take any action as a result of the Soviet buildup on the Iran border?

The president parried all the questions with the expertise of a long-time politician. The experienced reporters quickly understood that any answer they got that day would have little meat. So when, after ten minutes of talk, he made to get back into the limousine, no one was pressing him with further questions.

At a presidential press conference in the East Room of the White House, there was never an empty seat. The president's decision to meet with the press the next day was made as soon as he arrived back at Camp David. The announcement did not specify the reason for the meeting with the nation's top journalists, a fact which piqued their curiosity. Hansen had considered asking for network time to speak to the people, but decided against it. The press coverage of the conference would be sufficient.

At the stroke of ten, on the morning of March 15, President John Hansen entered the packed East Room to stride briskly to the lectern. Everyone in the room stood up as he mounted the dais and looked down at the sea of faces.

"Good morning, ladies and gentlemen," he said, and then waited until everyone was again seated. "As you all know, my wife and I went to Camp David on Monday. My press secretary said that I was going because I needed a rest. Well, I needed a rest all right, but I didn't get one. Judith and I went to Camp David as advertised but we didn't stop there. We left by helicopter at two in the morning on Tuesday for Andrews Air Force Base where we collected the secretary of state, the secretary of defense, the national security adviser and Jim Crane, my chief of staff. From Andrews, which we left at four in the morning in Air Force One, we flew almost due east for seventeen hours to an island in the Indian Ocean called Diego Garcia."

The room buzzed as the press people asked each other. "Where the hell is Diego Garcia?" Some of the more knowledgeable, however, nodded as they took their notes. They knew where it was. But what the hell was the president of the United States doing at Diego Garcia?

"The reason for my trip was to meet in total secrecy with the president of a nation whose future is critical to the best interests of the United States. My meeting was with General Mujeeb-Ul-Rehman, the president of Pakistan."

As tape recorders and TV cameras recorded the scene and pens and pencils flew furiously, there was a buzz of side talk from his audience. A few faces looked up from their writing to stare at Hansen in astonishment. The room seemed to flow with tension as the minds of the top journalists from America instantly began to analyze what they were hearing. This was news, big news. Some wished they could bolt through the door to get to a telephone, but that was against the rules of presidential press conferences.

Hansen then listed the reasons why he was compelled to go. In the presence of the escalating Soviet military threat, it was imperative that a new understanding be reached with Pakistan and it had to be done quickly. It had to be done in secret and it had to be done head of state to head of state.

With the preamble out of the way, the president slipped on his bifocal glasses and read from his prepared text:

I am pleased to announce that at 10 A.M. local time yesterday at Diego Garcia, the President of Pakistan, General Mujeeb-Ul-Rehman, on behalf of his government, and I on behalf of the government of the United States, signed an agreement which will permit the entry into Pakistan of United States land, sea, and air forces in such numbers and on whatever scale the Government of the United States feels appropriate under the circumstances. The agreement does not permit the entry of any nuclear weapons. The American forces so deployed in Pakistan will be solely for the purpose of the defense of Pakistan against attack, although that limitation will not prevail in the event of any military action in the Middle East that might threaten the vital interests of the United States.

In consideration for the entry of U.S. forces to Pakistan, the United States will provide to the government of Pakistan up to two billion dollars' worth of fighter aircraft, tanks, surface-to-air missiles, and other weaponry designed to strengthen the ability of the Pakistan forces to defend their nation. The delivery of these armaments will begin on May the seventh, which is the day American forces will first be permitted to land. It will take that long to assemble our task force and transport it by ship to Pakistan. Furthermore, this agreement will require the ratification of Congress before it can be implemented. In this connection, I have been assured by the majority and minority leaders, both in the Senate and the House of Representatives, that they will support the accord with Pakistan. Therefore, I look for an early ratification by Congress.

In addition to the military aid package, the United States will provide Pakistan with four billion dollars in economic aid over the next three years. That money will be used for the purchase of food, the building of housing, the creation of new industry, and the general welfare of the Pakistani people. Almost all the foreign purchases to be made by Pakistan under this program will be from the United States. In addition, the United States will assist Pakistan in refinancing its extensive foreign debt.

The positioning of American forces in Pakistan will serve notice to the Soviet Union that it cannot have a free hand in the Middle East, that it cannot seize Pakistan or Iran as it took Afghanistan. It will serve notice to the Soviet Union that the United States intends to use its full might and power to preserve the integrity and sovereignty of the Arab and Persian nations upon which the Western world and Japan depend for their supplies of crude oil. Sixty-one percent of all the crude oil imported into Western Europe—ninety-six percent of its oil is imported—comes from the Persian Gulf. For Japan, which imports all of its oil, seventy-two percent is from the Persian Gulf. For the United States, which now imports forty-nine percent of the crude oil it consumes, some thirty-four percent of that quantity is from the Persian Gulf. Those supplies cannot be halted, they cannot be tampered with. The countries which provide them to us must be assured by the United States that they will not come under the heel of the Soviets.

The time has come when the United States must draw a line in the Middle East across which the Soviets shall not pass. Having drawn that line, we must be able to demonstrate that we can enforce it by having a military force in place on the ground, in the air, and on the sea, a force that can repel any Soviet incursion.

This agreement with Pakistan is a major step in achieving those objectives, all of which are designed to preserve world peace and stability.

The president left his text and slipped off his glasses. "That's the end of my formal statement for this morning, ladies and gentlemen. Are there any questions?"

Eleven people stood waving their hands for attention. The president selected the *New York Times* correspondent. The rest sat down. They would try again. Her question was, "Mr. President, what do you think the Soviet reaction will be to this agreement?"

"The Soviets are used to having a free hand in Africa and the Middle East. They are hypersensitive about the areas around their own borders. Therefore, I think we can expect a strong propaganda campaign to be mounted. Tass, *Pravda*, and *Izvestia* will undoubtedly be screaming about an American imperialist capitalist invasion of the Middle East. The Soviets will probably take action against us in the United Nations. So the answer is, I expect their reaction to be violent."

He turned to look across the audience. It was the signal that that answer was finished and he would accept another question. From the group who leaped to their feet he selected the correspondent from the *Chicago Tribune* whose question was, "Mr. President, do you think the Soviets would regard the entry of the United States into Pakistan as an act of aggression that they would go to war over?"

"In a word, no. They'll make threats. There's no question about that. But in the assessment of my advisors, they will not risk a direct shooting confrontation with us."

The next correspondent to ask a question was from the *Washington Post*. "Mr. President, there's been much speculation that Pakistan has developed a nuclear bomb.

India in particular is worried about that and about any strengthening of Pakistan, because she regards that country as a threat. Do you have any comment?"

Hansen nodded.

"It is part of the agreement with Pakistan that while we are in their country, they will not deploy or threaten to use or indeed use any nuclear weapon; and that any development of such a weapon—which they deny—will be stopped. They said that since they're not developing a nuclear weapon, they would not have any hesitation in agreeing to such a clause. As to India, I understand the concerns of their prime minister. They've always looked upon Pakistan as a threat and have complained every time weapons or aircraft have been provided to that country. However, our direct presence in Pakistan should provide a stabilizing atmosphere and ease India's concern. On the other hand, our 1959 Defense Pact with Pakistan, of which this new agreement is an extension, says that we will assist Pakistan no matter who attacks her. India was not happy about that agreement in 1959 and it won't be about this one."

The reporter from the *Wall Street Journal* asked, "Sir, have you had consultation with our NATO allies about this agreement or your intention to put troops into Pakistan?"

"No, I have not. There hasn't been time. Pakistan and the Persian Gulf are well outside the chosen jurisdiction of the North Atlantic Treaty Organization. The European NATO members don't want to get involved in the Middle East, although I have great difficulty in understanding why, because their interest in a continuing crude oil supply is far greater than ours. The fact is, they've chosen not to do so, except for the British. They've assigned a flotilla to work with our Fifth Fleet in the Arabian Sea, the approach to the Persian Gulf. In fact I talked to the prime minister late yesterday afternoon when I arrived back in Camp David. As to the rest of our NATO allies, no, I've had no consultation with them. This is a unilateral action on the part of the United States. If our NATO allies want to support us, they can do so by removing the boundary line at the Tropic of Cancer beyond which the NATO naval forces cannot operate, something I think they should have done years ago."

The next would be the final question. It was from the Associated Press. "This is slightly off the subject, Mr. President. The Soviets activated a sonar interference mechanism in the Atlantic on March eleventh. This is the first time it's been used. What is the purpose behind it?"

"Obviously, the sonar interference system is designed to make inoperative all the passive and active sonar systems that sit on the bed of the Atlantic Ocean. It also makes inoperative the sonar systems on all surface ships and submarines, whether they're ours or theirs. The best intelligence information indicates that the main purpose of the system is to prevent the hearing or tracking of their submarines when they move out of their bases in the Kola Peninsula or the Baltic or elsewhere. It also makes it impossible for us to know where their ballistic missile submarines are located in the Atlantic, and their numbers. However, we can tell how many submarines are at sea, because we do a regular satellite inventory of the Soviet submarine bases. Where they are when at sea can only be determined by sonar. Current satellite photographs show that there are an unusual number of submarines at sea, about a hundred out of the Soviet's 426-boat fleet. We are concerned about that, but we believe they've left to take part in the upcoming Soviet exercise. It's called OKEAN. If there was a mass movement of Soviet submarines out of port, that would be a significant danger signal to us. In fact we'd mobilize, go to a state of war readiness, if that happened. In any event, we're monitoring the sonar interference carefully. We don't know how long it's going to last. One of the devices has been found. It appears to be radio-activated and runs for a fixed period of time. We don't know how long that is. At this time we think they're just giving it a practice run. Whatever they're doing, it's very effective."

Hansen thought he'd take one more question. The man from Reuters: "Do you intend to talk to Chairman Romanov on the hot line about the Pakistan agreement, Mr. President?"

"We haven't had to use the hot line yet. The answer is, no, I don't intend to talk with him about it. But if he calls me, I'll be pleased to discuss it with him. One thing is certain, one way or the other, I'll hear from him, either by the hot line or by a formal note or letter."

9

17 March   8:50 A.M.

Moscow

The polished black ZIL limousine of Fleet Admiral of the Soviet Union Nikolai Ivanovich Smirnov, moved at high speed down the center lane of Kutozovsky Prospekt, slowing as it crossed the wet cobblestones of Red Square. It was ten minutes to nine on March 17. Smirnov reclined in the back seat, feeling splendid in his gold-embroidered admiral's uniform. His medals—Order of Lenin and Hero of the Soviet Union—gleamed on both sides of his chest. He had received the summons to the Kremlin in midafternoon the day before. Chairman Romanov himself had called, saying that a matter of the utmost importance had arisen upon which he required the admiral's advice.

As commander in chief of the Soviet navy and worthy successor to its principal creator, Admiral Gorshkov, under whom Smirnov had served as first deputy, he had found it annoying to be summoned without being told the nature of the meeting. On the other hand, he comforted himself by the fact that only two men in the Soviet Union, other than the chief of the General Staff, had the power to summon him. The chairman himself was the first. The second was the minister of defense. He had known them both for years. He had first met the new chairman of the Supreme Soviet Presidium when Grigori Romanov came to Moscow in September of 1970 as the Leningrad Oblast first secretary. Later he saw much more of him when Romanov became the youngest voting member of the Politburo in 1976. He had always liked the chairman. The younger man was courteous and amiable but could also be tough minded. He was a party man who enjoyed power and could make a show of it. Smirnov had been surprised when, on the demise of Brezhnev, the thirteen surviving members of the Politburo had elected the youngest member of their group to ascend to the pinnacle of power in the Soviet Union, the chairmanship of the Politburo and of the Supreme Soviet Presidium. He had been surprised because Romanov, not yet sixty, had been elected by a group of old men whose average age was at least seventy, men who did not like change and wished at all times to preserve the status quo, something that a younger man would not guarantee to do.

As to Marshal Ustinov, the minister of defense, he had been primarily responsible for the appointment of Smirnov first as Gorshkov's first deputy and then as commander in chief. Smirnov had a great affection for Ustinov. As matters stood, he, Smirnov, had a good chance, when the time came, of succeeding to the post of minister of defense. He had thought about that many times. And if he played his cards right . . .

He was speculating about why he had been summoned as he approached the door of the chairman's office at one minute to nine. He handed his cap to his aide and took from him his ever-present briefcase. The door was ceremoniously opened by the major of the Kremlin guard who had escorted Smirnov from his ZIL.

When the admiral stepped into Romanov's impressive office, it was immediately apparent to him that this was to be a meeting of the utmost importance. At the end of the long, green, baize-covered conference table with its eighteen leather chairs, which accommodated the executive membership of the Politburo when it was in full session, sat

Minister of Defense Ustinov, the perennial minister of foreign affairs, Andrei Gromyko, and army General Yu Andropov, like the others a voting member of the Central Committee of the Politburo and chairman of the Committee for State Security, the infamous KGB. One other man was seated at the table. He was Smirnov's immediate superior, the chief of the General Staff of the Armed Forces, Marshal of the Soviet Union Mikhail Kozlov. In the corner of the office to the right, Chairman Romanov sat at his working desk, speaking into one of the three white telephones that sat on a table at its side.

Smirnov was always impressed when he walked into this imposing room in which he had spent many long hours over the years, first when Leonid Brezhnev was its occupant and now under the forceful Romanov. The chairman's office, although big, was sparse in its furnishings. The off-white silk walls, their monotony broken by rectangular strips of mahogany molding, displayed two portraits, those of Karl Marx and Vladimir Lenin. At the end of the room opposite its main entrance were curtained double doors leading to a private study which the chairman used from time to time as a bedroom and dining room.

Smirnov made the ritual, punctilious, formal greetings to each of the men at the table. Although they knew each other well and most were on a first-name basis, it was the protocol that when in the office of the chairman and, in particular, when seated at the long Politburo conference table, formality was the order. The pecking order of position and seniority was strictly observed.

Smirnov seated himself at the conference table to the left of his superior, Marshal Kozlov. To Kozlov's right sat Ustinov. At the end of the table was the empty place that the chairman would occupy. Opposite the military trio sat Gromyko and, on his right, Andropov, their backs to the working desk of the chairman some thirty feet away.

When the chairman put down the receiver into which he had been speaking quietly and began to walk across the room to the conference table, Smirnov's eyes fastened on the younger man. Of medium height, heavy-set with a rounded Slavic face and pale-blue, Great Russian eyes and a full head of straight brown hair graying at the temples, Romanov looked much younger than his near sixty years. Like his predecessor, he was known as one of the best-dressed men in Russia, favoring finely cut dark suits and elegant shirts. Even though he had been installed in office for only a short period of time, he had already been recognized as an outstanding politician, a disciplined executive and a respected, if not feared, force in the quick-shifting sands of world power. He was seen as honest and straightforward in his dealings with the party, supportive of his political colleagues, conservative in his approach to policy making and, so far, resistant to any inclination toward purging among his associates. Like Brezhnev, he enjoyed widespread popularity among the countless Communist party bureaucrats who saw him as a centrist and an able administrator, to whom they willingly gave their all-important support. As with Brezhnev, his penchant for yachts, foreign cars, and luxurious living was both well-known and accepted. That penchant also enabled him to move comfortably not only among the leaders of the Warsaw Pact countries but among those of the North Atlantic Treaty Organization and, for that matter, the rest of the world.

Quite a man. An excellent choice for the old men of the Politburo to make, thought Smirnov as Romanov took his seat at the head of the conference table, apologizing for the delay.

"That was Kuznetsov." All knew he meant Vasili Kuznetsov, the Soviet ambassador to the United States. "I wanted to talk with him before we began this meeting. I had a couple of points to clarify about his conversation with President Hansen last night. As Comrade Gromyko knows, as soon as I learned yesterday that those fools, the Pakistanis, had agreed to let American troops enter the country, I instructed Kuznetsov to lodge a formal protest directly with the president. He saw Comrade Kuznetsov at ten o'clock."

"Did he deliver a note, sir?" Ustinov asked.

"Yes, a note. Comrade Gromyko and I put it together. It's short. I'll read it to you."

He opened the leather folder he had brought from his desk. Reading the note addressed to the president of the United States, he spoke slowly, his well-modulated, deep voice pronouncing each word carefully as was his practice:

The Soviet Union considers the agreement made between the United States and Pakistan for the movement of American military forces in strength into Pakistan as an explicit threat to the territorial integrity and the security of the Soviet Union. This threat to peace is a deliberately provocative and unjustified change in the status quo which the Soviet Union finds totally unacceptable.

Romanov looked up at the men sitting on each side of the table. "It is necessary for the Russian Bear to draw a line across which the American Eagle must neither step nor fly. In these words you will find the line." His eyes went back to the paper as he continued to read:

If the United States implements this despicable agreement either in whole or in part it will be regarded as an act of aggression which will require a full retaliatory response from the Soviet Union.

Gromyko, his face showing no emotion, added, "In the world of diplomacy the words 'full retaliatory response' leave us with all our options open."

"You mean economic . . ?" Andropov asked.

Gromyko nodded. "As well as military. Including nuclear if we have to go that far."

Romanov agreed. "If we have to go that far, and so far as I'm concerned, we will if the American imperialists push us there."

There was no voice of protest against that statement. Instead, the KGB head, Andropov, put a question. "Do you think the Americans understand we would be prepared to consider going nuclear?"

"We would be more than prepared, but the answer is no. They don't understand."

Gromyko, with his long experience in dealing with the Americans, silently nodded his agreement with the chairman's position.

"They cannot get it through their heads that our doctrine vigorously states that while we recognize that a nuclear war, an all-out nuclear war, would be extremely destructive to both sides, its outcome would not be mutual genocide . . . mutual suicide. The nation best prepared for it and with a superior strategy could win and survive with a functional society. The Americans cannot understand, cannot believe, that there would be a victor in a thermonuclear world war."

"Exactly," Gromyko agreed. "The Americans believe in the principle of mutual deterrent and have for decades. By themselves the words 'mutual deterrent' imply a reciprocal attitude on our part. They imply that we wouldn't be the first to strike and they certainly wouldn't be the first to strike. So neither side goes nuclear because both have the capability."

Andropov asked, "What was Hansen's reaction to the note?"

"Evidently he was taken aback. He said that if we were concerned about his action then we should take the matter to the United Nations."

"*Nyet*," Gromyko exclaimed.

"He said that we had no right to complain because we had invaded Afghanistan."

"Not true!" Gromyko spoke again.

"I know it's not true, Comrade Gromyko. We were invited in by the government of Afghanistan to stabilize a destabilized political and religious revolutionary situation. Hansen says that the United States too has been invited in by a country needing help, economic and military help. He claims that we and the Afghans are making incursions into Pakistan, that the Pakistanis are expecting a full-scale invasion from us."

"What did Kuznetsov say to that?"

"He said that that was a lie. The Soviet Union has no intention of moving against Pakistan—unless it commits an act of aggression against Afghanistan."

"That's a good answer."

Romanov smiled. "It's good enough for the moment." The chairman decided to get to the point of the meeting. "Gentlemen, the time has come for some hard decisions. The goal of the Soviet Union is world domination by the socialist order. We must continue to conduct a resolute struggle against American imperialism and to rebuff the evil designs and subversions of the American aggressors. We have drawn the line over which they may not cross. And now it is up to us to decide what retaliatory steps and what options are open to us if the Americans do, in fact, go into Pakistan on May 7. But even before that, we must decide what steps we can take to prevent them from moving into Pakistan.

"Before I ask you to give me your ideas, I must tell you that I think that whatever preventative action we take must be strong. It must be forceful. And because we have very little economic leverage, the kind of retaliatory pressure the Americans like to use on us whenever they can . . ."

Marshal Kozlov snorted his first entry into the discussion. "Like an Olympic boycott."

That brought laughter all around.

Romanov went on. "What we should look for is some sort of military or naval prophylactic action." Looking at Kozlov and Smirnov, the chairman said, "Which is why I have invited you gentlemen to this meeting and, of course, my colleague the minister of defense."

His left hand gently touched the sleeve of Marshal Ustinov's uniform.

It was the brilliant General Andropov, the head of the KGB, who made the initial response to Romanov's request for ideas. Looking more like a scholarly academic than the head of one of the world's most respected and feared security and intelligence agencies, he said, "Comrade Chairman, the KGB has been supporting the PLO in the mounting of a most unusual operation that I think will be of interest to you. It could be an excellent smokescreen for us."

The discussion at the end of the long green-baize conference table lasted another hour and twenty minutes. As Andropov outlined his proposal and a consensus appeared to be developing early in the meeting, Romanov realized he would need advice from the economic administration of the Politburo on two counts. The first had to do with the basic figures and statistics in the crude oil segment of the Soviet economy. All of them knew the shortages would soon become crippling. A full paper on that subject would be necessary immediately. The second was an immediate study on the ramifications for the Western world if the plan they were developing around the table was, in fact, carried out. While the others talked, he quietly sent for the man who would be responsible for the preparation of the required studies. This was Aliyev, a man only three years younger than Romanov. He had been appointed only recently to succeed Tikhonov as first deputy premier, and was responsible for economic administration and industry. Aliyev was immediately available.

When the matter was settled to the chairman's satisfaction, he concluded the session by saying, "Gentlemen, this has been most productive. Because of the scale and consequences of the course of action we have agreed upon and are driven to by the imperialist Americans in our own defense, I feel I must have the approval of a plenary meeting of the Politburo. However, with four members of the fourteen being here present and in support . . ." Gromyko, Andropov, and Ustinov nodded their heads in agreement. "I think our decision will be supported."

The plenary Politburo session that approved the Andropov Plan took place in Chairman Romanov's office on the morning of March 20. The chairman himself had laid out the proposal in detail, using as presentation aids, photographic slides of charts from the comprehensive report that Comrade Aliyev's staff had produced on the current, short-term and long-range shortages of domestic production of crude oil, the commodity central to the sustenance of the economies of the Soviet Union and her Eastern Bloc satellites. Aliyev's report was also covered by Romanov in his presentation. By itself, the report was sufficient to justify in the minds of all Politburo members the drastic plan of action in the Andropov proposal. Now was the time. All of the factors at play pointed in only one direction—action immediately if a drastic shortage of crude was to be avoided.

The second report that was to be prepared by Aliyev's

people had not yet been completed. It was a new region of research that would require much more than two days to prepare. Furthermore, it would involve much supposition and speculation. However, when the Politburo meeting was informed of its nature, told that it would be presented to them in due course, and when its terms of reference were described, each man was able to conjure up in his own mind an image of the economic and cultural state of the society of the Western world that would result if the last and ultimate phase of the Andropov Plan was put into effect.

After a lengthy discussion, during which many members raised serious reservations about the wisdom of "going that far," the persuasive chairman convinced them that the actions of the United States in entering Pakistan would, in fact, be equivalent to an act of aggression, indeed, virtually an act of war against the Mother Country. At the end of his monologue, Chairman Romanov had pounded the table saying, "*Mir, mir, i yeshche raz mir*; peace, peace, peace, that is all we want for our people, but the imperialist American aggressor wants war! We must be determined not to let him have it, not to let him have his war but, at the same time, we must demonstrate to him all the consequences to his nation of the war he wishes to start. We are at the point of a showdown between capitalism and communism. It is not a time to be vacillating or sentimental. On the contrary, we may be on the threshold of permanent peace through a communist victory. Remember what Lenin said about the issue between capitalism and communism: 'Until the final issue is decided, the state of awful war will continue . . . sentimentality is no less a crime than cowardice in war.' Gentlemen, I ask your support for the Andropov Plan."

There was no need for a vote. Clearly there was a consensus among the Politburo members as they sat silent after the chairman's urging flow of compelling rhetoric ceased.

The Andropov Plan was approved.

10

22 March   12:00 Noon
Atlantic Ocean, off Cape Town

On the morning of March 22, *Splendid* received a message from the Admiralty to all Royal Navy ships at sea:

Urgent nonstop investigation of source of sonar interference in all areas North and South Atlantic and Arctic Ocean resulted in discovery March 14 of the Soviet-made, seabed-stationed noise generator. The device functions on principle similar to that of active sonar making constant rather than pulsing emissions in a band of transmission frequencies covering a full spectrum of known ship machinery, propeller and cavitation noises. The sonar interference device (SONINT) has high-volume sonar-interrupting range of up to one hundred miles. It can be deployed by aircraft or ship.

First device retrieved yesterday by U.S. Navy bathysphere from ocean floor one hundred miles off Maine coast. It is an electronic transmitter equipped with power package capable of estimated one-year operation, contained in rigid pressure-resistant plastic ball, color white, approximately two feet diameter;

appropriate weights attached to deliver to desired depths.

As it descends SONINT automatically deploys a ball-shaped antenna buoy six inches diameter, positioned six feet below water surface with quarter-inch plastic aerial rod appearing above surface making radar pick-up almost impossible; antenna buoy is connected to SONINT by a small diameter conductor cable which carries activating message received via satellite.

Estimate deployment of SONINTs commenced approximately nine months ago carried out by all transportation modes including Soviet fishing fleets and merchant marine vessels augmented by aircraft.

Also believe that, once activated, all SONINTs programed to produce transmissions for a set period of time thus cannot be halted by electronic countermeasures. It appears that Soviet surface and submarine fleets' sonars are not immune to SONINT.

Intelligence opinion is that Soviet activation of SONINT this time associated with opening of Red Navy's OKEAN operation.

The message underscored in the mind of Commander Marcus Leach the urgent need to allow NATO naval forces to operate below the Tropic of Cancer. South of that imaginary line the politicians of NATO would not go, although their naval and military commander wanted to extend their area of jurisdiction not only into the South Atlantic but around the Cape of Good Hope into the Indian Ocean and the Arabian Sea, thereby straddling with strong naval protection the sea lanes along which moved the crude oil and petroleum products necessary to sustain the civilization and economy of Western Europe. In those same sea lanes a substantial part of the daily oil consumption of the United States and Canada was carried. However, their political masters in Western Europe were intimidated by the presence of the ever-threatening Russians. They were dedicated to maintaining détente at all costs.

Furthermore, they did not want to prejudice the rich flow of their manufactured goods across the Iron Curtain into Eastern Bloc countries and the Soviet Union itself. Consequently, Western Europe had vacillated and continually demurred at removing from NATO the naval boundary line of the Tropic of Cancer. They were fearful of disturbing the status quo, notwithstanding the real possibility that their failure to protect their vital crude oil sources in the Middle East, and the equally important tanker transportation system, might lead to an interdiction of both.

The Royal Navy's captains knew that NATO's widespread sonar arrays throughout the North Atlantic were particularly heavy through the Denmark Strait, the gap between Iceland and Norway, and across the Skagerrak exit to the North Sea from the Soviet naval strongholds in the Baltic. The main fixed system was known as SOSUS. Those concentrated nets of hydrophones which were connected by seabed cable to computer and communications centers ashore, were in place for the purpose of monitoring and detecting the movement of any Soviet submarines from their major bases in the Kola Peninsula, abutting Finland and Norway high in the Arctic, and from the Baltic. The sound of any submarine—except the most silent moving at no more than one or two knots to negate any cavitation noise—would be picked up by the huge hydrophones mounted on their vast tripods standing on the seabeds of the North Atlantic even in the Newfoundland and Labrador basins.

During World War II, bombers of the Allied air forces were able to baffle the German radar by dropping clouds of tiny strips of aluminum foil which threw off the scanning enemy radar, preventing it from giving direction to their night fighters and aircraft guns. If a similar method could be found to baffle those sonars, then the Soviets would have a cover under which they could move their entire submarine fleet out into the Atlantic. The ability of NATO to discover the location and tracks of the lethal Soviet underwater fleet would be nullified. NATO's military satellites in space could keep count of the Soviet submarines at their Baltic and other northern bases, but the whereabouts of the Red Navy's submarine fleet at sea would be unknown.

It was, therefore, apparent to all ship commanders of the Royal Navy that should the Soviets come up with an answer to North Atlantic sonar arrays, they would have won a tremendous tactical advantage, one that would be particularly valuable during a prehostility buildup and deployment of forces in any escalating crisis.

At 1200 hours GMT on March 22, a full eleven days after the sonar interference began and two hours after Leach received the Admiralty signal, the interference stopped. It did so abruptly, just as if someone had flicked a switch.

At that moment, *Splendid* was still just below the surface in the Atlantic, abeam of Cape Town. The news of the rebirth of their sonar brought hoots of joy throughout the boat. Leach immediately dived·his ship down into the sanctuary of the deep, warm sea over the continental shelf of Africa.

As *Splendid* descended, Leach reflected on the Admiralty signal and on the sonar interference capability of the Soviets. That goddamn SONINT thing wasn't just a toy the Soviets would use in an exercise, in a month of war games. If SONINT was as effective as he knew it to be—it had almost cost him his brand new ship, let alone his life—why in hell would the Red Navy let the whole world know they had the damn thing by turning it on just so that they could use it at OKEAN? The isolated captain had little information with which to make an accurate judgment.

What he did know, however, was that the Americans and the Soviets were eyeball to eyeball over the Middle East. The Red Navy had more ships at sea than it had ever had at any one time. Sure, the Soviets were mounting OKEAN, but OKEAN wasn't sufficient reason to trigger the use of SONINT. No, those bastards were definitely up to something. He'd bet his last pound on it.

Commander Marcus Leach was right.

11

25 March   4:00 P.M.

The White House

Washington, D.C.

Across the polished, historic desk of the Oval Office over which so many decisions had been taken and upon which so many documents had been signed, President Hansen watched the lined, pitted face and red, watery eyes of Vasili Kuznetsov, the likeable old Soviet ambassador to the United States, a man who had represented his country on the Washington scene for over two decades. He had been summoned by the president through the office of the secretary of state, John Eaton, who sat next to Kuznetsov.

Kuznetsov spoke excellent English, but with a heavy Russian accent. At this morning meeting with the new president, he was clearly unhappy that events had taken a turn for the worse between the United States and his nation. He felt responsible for maintaining good relations between the two giants of the world and took it as a personal failure that things had gone awry.

On the desk in front of Hansen was an envelope bearing the presidential seal. In it was President Hansen's reply to Romanov's harsh note, which Ambassador Kuznetsov had handed to him on March 16, the day following the president's announcement of the Pakistan agreement. Next to that envelope was a duplicate addressed to Kuznetsov. The president knew Kuznotsov well, having met the ancient ambassador countless times at cocktail parties during most of the twenty years he had been in the Senate. Kuznetsov, the gregarious, friendly, round bear, as he used to be, was now thin and emaciated with the advent of his eightieth year. He was a man whose open personality invited his American friends to loosen their tongues over drinks on the cocktail party circuit. He would pick up snippets of information from this one and that one from which he would put together relatively accurate scenarios of what was going on behind closed government doors at the highest level. The one thing Hansen knew about the old man was that he was totally loyal, completely dedicated to the cause of his Mother Country and to the principles of hard-line, Marxist-Leninist communist ideology.

This meeting, however, was no cocktail party. For all their long acquaintance and affection for each other, Hansen and Kuznetsov represented the full power of their respective nations. Each country was angry with and suspicious of the other. They were like two ancient medieval warriors, shield on one arm, sword in the other hand, circling each other and looking for the opening to strike the first blow.

Kuznetsov had been in the Oval Office many times before, delivering or receiving official notes to or from his masters in the Kremlin. He had been there with Kennedy, Johnson, Nixon, Ford, Carter, and the man who followed him. None of them had been as tough as he knew Hansen would be. He had told Gromyko many times that Hansen was tough-minded, hard-nosed, ideologically certain, and ruthless enough to be a member of the Politburo. Sitting across from the big man in the president's chair and listening to his words, Kuznetsov was disconcerted by the accuracy of his description of Hansen, for the man was now much harder, much tougher than he had been before he took office. He was a leader with power whose attitude spoke to his firm intention to lead his nation through adversity. In fact, Kuznetsov thought, in dedication, determination of spirit, aggressiveness and the willingness to fight for what he believed to be right and in his country's interest, President Hansen was the equal of Chairman Romanov. In the old ambassador's judgment, so strong was each man, so determined, that at a critical moment when compromise might deflect them from a shooting war, neither would back off.

"Your Excellency, please be good enough to deliver this official note to Chairman Romanov." The diplomat reached out with shaking hands to accept the envelope addressed to Chairman Romanov.

Hansen then gave him the second one. "This envelope contains a copy for your eyes." Providing the ambassador with a duplicate would enable him to telephone the contents of the note to the Kremlin well in advance of the delivery of the unopened original by courier.

When Kuznetsov had the second envelope in his hands, President Hansen said, "Please tell Chairman Romanov I regret that it took so long to prepare the reply. On the other hand the strident and, indeed, belligerent tone of his note was such that I wished to be as prudent, conservative, and unemotional as I could be in phrasing my response." The lawyer-president chose his words carefully and spoke them formally. "In short, my note says," his long right index finger pointed toward the two envelopes, "that the United States will not back off. We are going to put a task force of 120,000 men into Pakistan in order to protect our vital interests in the Middle East. We believe that the Soviet Union is building up its forces in Afghanistan and on the Soviet-Iran border to mount a strike against Pakistan and Iran. When we enter Pakistan, it will not be an invasion as the entry of the Soviet Union into Afghanistan was, but rather one country helping another under a long-standing agreement. We will be coming to their aid militarily strictly for the purpose of defense and we will be providing them with massive economic aid.

"Please tell the chairman, Your Excellency, that this is a situation of the Soviet Union's own making. On the other hand, I want you to assure Chairman Romanov that I am not inflexible, that I would be prepared to consider any quid pro quo that might relieve me of the necessity of dispatching my task force to Pakistan."

Ambassador Kuznetsov's normally benign eyes narrowed to slits. "The nature of my instructions, Mr. President, is such that I can tell you that if any quid pro quo is offered by Chairman Romanov, it will be in the form of an ultimatum that you will find difficult to refuse." His face suddenly changed, eyes opening wide. He smiled, displaying his well-known silver-filled teeth. "On the other hand, Mr. President, we both know that my government wishes to continue our peaceful coexistence. Perhaps there can be compromise. Perhaps. But I daresay the answer largely depends on the contents and tone of your note." His finger tapped the envelope addressed to Romanov.

The emaciated ambassador leaned on his cane and began to struggle to his feet. Hansen and Eaton stood as the old man pulled himself erect. He looked up at the president with a gaze that showed his personal affection. "You should know, my friend, just before I came to your office I was notified by Comrade Gromyko that I was being recalled to Moscow—for consultations of course. That is the sure sign that the relations between our two countries are indeed precarious. Perhaps more so at this moment than at any time since World War II. And you should also know that our ambassador to the United Nations has been instructed today to seek support for a motion of censure against the United States." The ambassador lowered his head momentarily, shaking it slowly. "A pity that we should come to this point. It is rather reminiscent of the Khrushchev-Kennedy confrontation over Cuba."

"In which you played such an important part."

"Yes, in which I played a part."

Ambassador Kuznetsov held out his wavering hand to his friend, John Hansen, who took it as the old man spoke. "History repeats itself, Mr. President. Let us hope that it will do so and that this confrontation can also be resolved."

"It can be—if your chairman is prepared to compromise."

12

25 March   Midnight
Moscow

The reply of the president of the United States to the stiff note from Chairman Romanov of the Soviet Union was handed to Ambassador Kuznetsov on March 21. Intensive diplomatic preparations went into the development of the reply. It was essential to secure the support, or at least the acceptance, of America's principal allies for the action Hansen intended to take. Romanov and his Politburo colleagues had monitored the strong efforts of the Americans to secure support by keeping close watch on their diplomatic activities in the capitals of Western Europe and North America and Japan. This was done through the Soviet Union's normal channels of surveillance, their worldwide net of embassies and consulates in which KGB agents, both men and women, functioned as important cogs in the worldwide Russian espionage machine, operating under the protective blanket of diplomatic immunity.

Great Britain had leaped in to support Hansen from the outset. But West Germany and France were reluctant. They were concerned with maintaining the last vestiges of détente in order to protect their valuable flow of trade with the Soviet Union and its Eastern Bloc satellites. Romanov knew that, under pressure from him, both the West German and French governments would waiver. West Germany, in particular, would vacillate, and if the right leverage was applied, he might force the West Germans to withhold their support for the United States in its proposed entry into Pakistan. At best, he could pressure them into denouncing the move. The chairman understood well the West German government's weaknesses. Germany was divided. The Red Army occupied East Germany, its government under the Soviet heel. The position of Berlin was still insecure. The value of West Germany's exports to the Soviet Union was greater than American sales to the USSR.

At the same time the West Germans relied even more heavily on Persian Gulf oil than the United States. That they were not equally concerned and willing to act against the Soviet Union baffled the American administration. It failed to understand the priorities and attitudes of a European nation that lived next to and had close economic ties to the Soviet Union and its Eastern Bloc satellites.

On the other hand, Chairman Romanov understood those attitudes and economic ties very well. He watched them resurface immediately. The American president began his diplomatic campaign in Western Europe for support for his plan to enter Pakistan. Romanov and Gromyko used every diplomatic weapon in their arsenal to dissuade West Germany and France from backing the American initiative, knowing that if those two major countries withheld their endorsement, it would severely blunt the willingness of the United States to risk a unilateral war with the Soviet Union. At the same time, it would drive a wedge into the U.S./West German heart of the NATO alliance, a body which the Soviet leaders regarded as an offensive rather than a defensive organization.

As Romanov saw it, by taking the initiative without first consulting their allies—it was an historically common fault of all American presidents and administrations to act without consulting allies—the Americans had put themselves on the horns of a diplomatic dilemma: to go or not to go into Pakistan if they could not get the support of their principal West European NATO allies. Worse, if even one of those principal allies denounced the American initiative in Pakistan, what then?

Romanov was at his desk in the Kremlin when Kuznetsov called from Washington at midnight, immediately after being handed President Hansen's reply in midafternoon of March 25. When Kuznetsov finished reading the note to him, Romanov did not respond immediately but sat silently contemplating what he had heard. Alone in his vast office of power, Romanov spoke into the white telephone to his apprehensive ambassador to the imperialist aggressor enemy. "Just as I expected."

"What will you do next, Comrade Chairman?" The security-unscrambled voice sounded as if it were coming from the depths of a well.

"I'm not sure yet. We will have to talk about it here. But I think . . . As you know we are going to the United Nations. This time it will be the United States' turn to be censured. And pressure, Comrade Kuznetsov, pressure. We will throw in the full weight of our propaganda machine. Tass, *Pravda*, and *Izvestia* will mount a worldwide campaign. We will harass the Americans everywhere. We will really put pressure on Hansen between now and the seventh of May!"

"And if that doesn't work?"

Chairman Romanov smiled. "Then we will put the boots to him, heavy Russian combat boots right where it hurts the most!"

13

28-30 March

Mecca, Suez to Aden

It seemed to Said that he had been on board the *Mecca* for an eternity. It was almost three weeks since their narrow escape at Port Said. The long voyage on the plodding *Mecca* had seemed interminable.

Said and his men had been let out of their hidden sanctuary by the captain at about three the next morning, when he was satisfied that his first officer and all his deck hands were asleep and that he, Rashid, the helmsman, whose eyes were fixed on the lights of the ship ahead of him in the convoy, and the engineer below were the only people awake on the *Mecca*.

While the crew was startled to find the PLO team again with them the next morning, no one questioned where they had come from, although Nabil had hoped never to see them again. He, who had talked so freely to Commander Faher, was startled to see them emerge from their customary cabins for breakfast. How did they get back on board? Or is there a secret compartment on this old tub? These questions went through Nabil's mind. But being a fatalist and being able to do nothing about their presence on board, he promptly forgot about them and their strange reappearance. What did it matter anyway?

At the tail of the long afternoon convoy, the *Mecca* had serenely steamed down the Suez Canal, past the battered relics of guns and tanks resting on the eastern sandbanks of the old waterway, souvenirs of the 1973 Egyptian thrust that had caught the Israelis by surprise; past the tall, tan-colored main building of the all-watching Suez Canal authority at the west bank of the president of Egypt's favorite city of Ismailia; by Port Tewfik at the entrance to the Red Sea and a gathering of ships waiting to take their convoy turn northward; then on into the long, dull 1,700-mile stretch of the Red Sea, down to the Gulf of Aden and east into the Port of Aden to take on fuel and food. The crew would have their night on the port's town of Tawahi. There was no cargo to be either off-loaded or taken on.

They had stayed in Aden overnight, snug in a slip which provided them with bunkering, supplies, and fresh water. After clearing customs, completing his arrangements with the port authorities, checking with the local Lloyd's agent, the National Insurance and Reinsurance Company, Captain Rashid turned his crew loose for the night. Said volunteered that he and his team would remain on board to keep security watch on the ship. When the crew had gone ashore, Said relented to Maan's pleas and allowed his three colleagues to go ashore with strict orders: no bars, no fights, no women. His men left the ship at seven but were back and in their bunks by ten, all perfectly sober and delighted with having seen the town. On the other hand, the crew's behavior was completely consistent with past performances. They began appearing in ones and twos after midnight, staggering up the gangplank, operating on homing instinct alone. The last to return were the captain and his first officer. Both were roaring drunk, but still able to navigate. They had become good temporary friends during the course of the evening, a relationship which would terminate in the sober light of the next morning.

Another nine days of sailing in windy, stormy weather

and heavy, uncomfortable seas had taken them east-northeast along the coast of south Yemen, past Oman, north past Muscat into the Gulf of Oman where they first caught sight of the never-ending outbound line of loaded crude oil and petroleum tankers, the decks of their enormous hulls down almost to the level of the sea, moving one after the other like a parade of plodding elephants; and the inbound line funneling into the Gulf of Oman from Japan, Europe and North America, riding high in the water in ballast, making for their assigned loading ports at Saudi Arabia, Qatar, the United Arab Emirates, Bahrain, Iran, Iraq, and Kuwait.

Turning west into the Gulf of Oman, Rashid had gingerly crossed the lines of tankers to take up a course for the Strait of Hormuz. That position put the *Mecca* to the north of the main line of fast-moving tanker traffic. In ballast, without cargo, the mammoth ships traveled at a much greater speed than the old *Mecca* could muster. For safety's sake it was wise to be well out of their way.

Late in the afternoon of March 28, three weeks after they had departed Beirut, the *Mecca* sailed into the Strait of Hormuz, the most traveled strait in the world, a narrow gut of water twenty-four miles across, containing a navigable channel about twelve miles in width.

The rising burnt hills on each side served to accentuate the narrowness of the water passage through which hundreds of huge tankers passed each month. This was the strait that the PLO's leader Arafat had often talked of blocking in order to publicize the urgency of the plight of the Palestinian people. He had spoken of sinking some large ships, but in running his eyes over the crowded strait that afternoon, Said could not visualize how it could be done. The ships that would have to be sunk in one place to provide a barrier would have to number perhaps a hundred, maybe two. Impossible. Mines could be laid but they could be cleaned out quickly. No, the plan that he had presented and Arafat and the council had accepted was by far the best solution.

As the *Mecca* left the Strait of Hormuz astern and

night fell, Said joined the captain on the bridge to chat with the old man and watch the mammoth tankers go by: the Ultra Large Crude Carriers (ULCCs), anything over 300,000 tons; the Very Large Crude Carriers (VLCCs), those in the range of 200,000 to 300,000 tons, and several smaller tankers, all of them large in their own right and huge in comparison with the *Mecca*.

"When will we be at Kuwait?" Said asked.

"We'll be there in two days. We still have about five hundred miles to go."

"We should talk soon about a plan of action when we get there."

The captain looked toward Nabil—who had not missed a word of what was being said on the bridge—and at the wheelsman. It would not do to talk about plans in front of those two.

"In the morning, Said. In the morning. Come to my cabin, say at eight."

At that time the next day, Said appeared at Rashid's quarters. He was surprised to find the captain's table cleared of its piles of papers. There was the usual pot of coffee and waiting small cups sitting at the port end, but in the center and at the starboard end of the table, Rashid had spread out two charts. One was of the channel approaches to the city of Kuwait and Shuwaikh port at its northern edge. The second was of the oil terminal at Mina-al-Ahmadi, on the coast some fifty miles southeast of Kuwait city.

The two men stood shoulder to shoulder at the table as the captain, having poured the coffee and lit a cigarette, began. "Let me tell you what I have to do first and then you can tell me what you have in mind."

Said nodded his head in agreement.

"All of my cargo, everything—except the special cargo—you know the stuff I mean . . ."

Another nod from Said. Rashid meant the opium of course.

"Everything goes off at Shuwaikh. I want to enter the harbor in daylight. I've only been there once, so it's best not to go in at night. The approach is too tricky." With a finger he traced a line from out to sea, west into the harbor mouth. "We have to go in through a channel. It's marked by dolphins and buoys. It's about four and a half miles long. Wide enough, 500 feet. With all the building that's going on in Kuwait, this port is quite often badly congested, another reason I don't want to go in at night. I have no idea where the harbormaster will put us, but it will probably be at the northwest corner. There are quays up there that can handle a small ship like this very easily. When we go by Bahrain in the morning, I'll radio in to the harbormaster there and ask him to notify Shuwaikh of our arrival intentions. According to the book, I have to give him my estimated time of arrival, the draft of the ship, state that the Kuwait cargo is clear, that my ship's discharging gear is in order, and since I can do it with my own crane, that all my cargo can be handled by the ship's own gear. The point is, once I give them an estimated time of arrival, I have to stick to that. So when I find out from you what you want to do, we can settle on an ETA."

The PLO leader was thinking ahead. "What about fuel, water and provisions at Shuwaikh?"

"Obviously, bunker fuel oil is not a problem in Kuwait. If they put us alongside deep-water berths numbers one through seven, we can take on fuel through hoses that are right there. Otherwise we might have to move to pick it up, but fuel is not a problem. We can get fresh water. The Kuwaitis are well organized. All you need is money."

The captain shifted his weight, reached across in front of Said and pulled the Mina-al-Ahmadi chart across so that it sat in front of them on top of the Kuwait map.

"At Mina-al-Ahmadi, there are two loading piers and a sea terminal. The south pier here has six tanker berths and depth alongside up to fifty feet. The north pier has five tanker berths, and depth alongside to sixty feet. The sea terminal has seven berths. For the big tankers, the VLCCs and ULCCs, there is a special offshore terminal that has two berths with a depth alongside of ninety-five feet. It can take just about anything that floats. The Kuwaitis operate their big refinery here. It processes about 800,000 barrels of oil a day, refines it that is . . . That's out of an overall production in the country of about a million and a half a day. They've cut back their production recently because they think it's better to keep the oil in the ground.

"So when we get to Mina-al-Ahmadi, we'll undoubtedly find all the tanker berths filled, that's about twenty ships. They'll mostly be VLCCs and larger. We'll find another twenty anchored, waiting their turn. They'll be in this area." He pointed to an area two to three miles out to sea from the piers and sea terminal.

Rashid walked around to the far side of the table, opened its small drawer in front of his chair, pulled out a sheet of paper and went back to stand beside Said again.

"The instructions for my special cargo are . . ." He read from the piece of paper, "Rendezvous at midnight of first night after entry Shuwaikh. Rendezvous point: five miles northeast off north pier of Mina-al-Ahmadi. Torch code: three long, two short." He folded the paper and stuffed it in a trouser pocket, then jabbed his right index finger at the chart saying, "That's where I have to be, five miles northeast of the north pier and well away from the tanker waiting area. The Kuwaitis used to keep a fairly tight security patrol around the tankers, but I hear they're lax now. Anyway, we'll keep well away from them."

Said repeated, "At midnight of the first night."

"Correct. Now what do you want to do? What's your plan?"

To that very moment in the long voyage, Said had not discussed his operation with the captain, although by that time the older man had some idea of what their objective was. Even so, Rashid was not sure.

For a moment Said contemplated the chart. "Will you anchor her at that point?"

"Yes, I'd like to be there early some time between ten and eleven. Yes, we'll anchor."

"As we go by Mina-al-Ahmadi on our way to Shuwaikh, can we run in close to the anchored tankers, the ones waiting to load? I'd like to have a good look at them."

"Yes, no problem."

"Will it be daylight?"

"Daylight. It should be between three and four o'clock tomorrow afternoon."

"Perfect."

The captain was perplexed. "Well, what about your plan? What do you want to do?"

Said shrugged, saying, "I can fit into your plan of action without any changes at all. If we're anchored five miles off the north pier by ten or eleven o'clock as you said . . . What time do you want to up anchor and leave?"

Rashid was emphatic. "Midnight. As soon as I get rid of the stuff."

"And get your money."

"Exactly!"

Said thought for a moment and asked, "I might need an hour or two beyond that. If we could anchor at ten, I'd like to have four hours, say until two o'clock. It's important to have that much time. I don't want to be rushed. My men and I will have to work in the dark. It'll be difficult enough as it is."

The captain was reluctant, but he understood the young man's concern. Furthermore, he had become quite fond of Said in the past three weeks, developed a kind of fatherly affection for him. He could bend a little bit. "All right, two o'clock it is. But no later, mind you. If the people who take the stuff off get caught and we're still sitting there . . ." He shook his head.

"I understand," Said acknowledged. "We're both taking risks, big ones. Those extra two hours could make the difference between success and failure."

The frustrated Rashid, still not knowing what Said and his team were going to do, broke in, "Whatever that is you're doing. You still haven't told me."

"That's right. I haven't."

14

30 March   5:04 P.M.
Mina-al-Ahmadi,
Kuwait

A few minutes after five on the afternoon of March 30, the *Mecca* was abeam the south pier of Mina-al-Ahmadi. She was running at half speed at the request of Said. The old freighter made its way slowly past the gargantuan tankers sitting at their maximum height out of the water, ballast tanks emptied, each patiently waiting its call to proceed into its assigned berth for loading. The wait might be a few hours, at most not more than two or three days. The PLO team, armed with binoculars, plotted the location of each vessel on charts Captain Rashid had provided. To Said it was of greatest importance to record the name of each ship, for he was under the strictest instructions to avoid dealing with any tanker carrying the flag of a NATO country or France. To the captain's amazement, Hassan produced a Polaroid camera and took a picture of each vessel they passed. As they left the flock of giant craft, all at anchor with their noses pointed into the stiff wind from the east like a herd of cattle, Said mounted the steps to the bridge.

"Can you show me where will you be anchoring when we come back tomorrow night?" he asked the captain.

The old man's eyes squinted as he looked westerly toward the long piers filled with loading ships and beyond them the towers and tanks of the enormous refinery. He had his bearings. He was just to the north of the north pier, about four miles out.

He turned to face north toward the bow. "Dead ahead about a mile. We'll be about two miles north of the last tanker we passed."

"The *Esso Madrid*." Said was pleased. "Excellent." He opened the book he was carrying, saying facetiously, "You will be pleased to know, captain, that according to this publication of the U.S. Department of Commerce— *Foreign Flag Merchant Ships Owned by U.S. Parent Companies*—the *Esso Madrid* is owned by Esso Tankers Inc. It was built in Japan in 1976. It is 380,000 deadweight tons, has a speed of sixteen knots, and its country of registry is Liberia."

Rashid was amazed. "Where did you get that?" he demanded, pointing to the book.

"Oh, I just happened to find it in my kit when I left Beirut. I also have a copy of the Lloyd's of London Shipping Register which told me that all those ships would be here. It also tells me where they're going next."

Perhaps now Said would let Rashid in on his plan. But there was no need to ask. Not really, because the scheme of the PLO operation had become perfectly clear to the shrewd old sailor, although he guessed there would still be a few surprises in store for him before he saw the last of Said and his people.

He was right.

15

31 March   12:35 A.M.

Indian Ocean

On March 31, just before 10:35 P.M. Zulu, 12:35 A.M. local, the captain of *Splendid* called his communication center from the control room.

"Pots, this is the captain."

"Pots here. Go ahead, sir."

"We're approaching the flotilla. At least we're in VHF range. I'll be bringing her up to periscope depth so we can take a look around and also transmit. Stand by to take a message to the flag officer, Second Flotilla. He's aboard the *Tiger*."

The *Tiger* was the Royal Navy's famous helicopter cruiser. Rear-Admiral Rex Ward, the flotilla commander, had gone aboard her a week earlier to assume effective control of the British navy's show of force to the Soviets. With his flagship were his third and eighth squadrons of the Second Flotilla. The third was led by the frigate *Arethusa*, who had with her one destroyer and five other frigates. The other squadron, the eighth, was led by the frigate *Ajax* and with her were one destroyer and three frigates. To cap off this strongest show of naval force the British had put into the Indian Ocean in decades, the flotilla had, as its center-piece, the Royal Navy's most recently commissioned ship, the light aircraft carrier *Illustrious*, with its squadron of VTOL (Vertical Take-Off and Landing) Sea Harriers and ten Sea King helicopters, the workhorses of the British Fleet Air Arm.

The British flotilla joined the American Fifth Fleet, which had been formed and committed to permanent sta-tion in the Indian Ocean in response to the Soviet initiatives in the Middle East. Central to that fleet was the aircraft carrier *Coral Sea*, the only flat top the U.S. Navy could spare out of its total of seventeen aircraft carriers, twelve of which were assigned to the Atlantic and Mediterranean and five to the Pacific. For some years the *Coral Sea* had carried no air wing, but in the crisis of 1980 she had taken one on, assembled from squadrons assigned to carriers in overhaul and other sources. The Fifth Fleet, complete with two cruisers, five destroyers, and six frigates taken from both the Atlantic and Pacific fleets, had steamed into the Indian Ocean in late February. Coincidentally it became the visi-ble enhancement of the president's bargaining power in dealing with Pakistan. Like the British flotilla, which had joined the American force in entering the Arabian Sea in mid-March, the Fifth Fleet was supported by several un-seen attack submarines. They were there for the purpose of fending off any enemy surface or subsurface naval forces that might approach.

It had earlier been intended that the American and British naval forces would undertake joint exercises in the Indian Ocean and the Arabian Sea in advance of the Soviet's operation, OKEAN, which was believed to be scheduled to commence in the Atlantic, Pacific, and Indian Oceans sometime between April 1 and April 15. Elements of the American and British forces were assigned to monitor and watch the Soviet naval and air forces during the exer-cise. Their task was to observe the Russian maneuvering and tactical methods and, at the same time, make them as uncomfortable as possible. Shadowing was harassing activ-ity at which the Russians themselves had become experts.

For years their naval and merchant-marine craft had shadowed and spied on virtually every Allied naval operation, exercise, or experiment such as the launching of submarine-carried ballistic missiles. The Soviets had even gone so far as to play chicken with American destroyers and frigates in international waters. It was time to give the Soviets some of their own medicine.

As it happened, the timing of the planned U.S./U.K. Indian Ocean exercise could not have better suited the Pakistan objectives of President Hansen. Furthermore, as the Soviet reaction to his successful negotiations with Pakistan grew more violent, the presence of the powerful combined naval forces in that flashpoint sector of the world had a salutary effect on the shrill Soviet propaganda machine as it lashed out against the imperialistic intentions of the "warmongering" U.S. president, as the Russians were labeling him. On the other hand, it had a sobering effect on the Soviet military strategists and planners plotting their short- and long-term moves in Moscow. For them and their political masters, the unswerving Marxist-Leninist goal was world domination. They were at undeclared ideological and physical war with the West. The rhetoric was left to the Politburo and the propagandists. The use of force and the Soviet's military, naval, and air power belonged to the admirals and generals. All of them understood and had the greatest respect for the single tool of their own profession—physical force. They were experts in the use or threatened use of powerful sea, land, and air forces anywhere at any time. Behind their planning was the recognized ability of the Soviet Union to deliver intercontinental or tactical nuclear weapons. Therefore, the presence of American and British armadas in the Arabian Sea simultaneously with the preparations for the movement of large-scale American military forces to Pakistan had caused the Kremlin's military brains to pause.

From his control room in the *Splendid*, its captain spoke slowly into the telephone, choosing his words carefully. At the other end, in his communications center domain, Pots scribbled furiously. "Make a signal to flag officer, Second Flotilla, aboard the *Arethusa* . . ." Years ago, as a young lieutenant-commander, Leach had worked for then Captain, now Rear-Admiral Ward when he was Captain, Sea Training at Faslane. Leach was in that part of Ward's shop responsible for working up new submarines and new crews. He could remember the face of the banty admiral, a gray-haired, balding, little man, his gimlet eyes dancing with nervous energy. Ward was a man well able to carry his high rank and responsibility. Too bad he wouldn't be able to visit the old boy on board the *Arethusa*. If he even had a chance to see the British flotilla he would be lucky. The admiral would probably station *Splendid* on patrol, perhaps fifty or hundred miles away from his group of ships. Apparently, the Russians were beginning to rendezvous at the western end of the Gulf of Aden, in and around the port of Aden where they had access to bunkering and provisioning facilities.

In addition to the gathering fleet, satellite photographs had shown the presence of several fuel-carrying tenders for Soviet diesel submarines. Tenders were also found operating out of the ports of Soviet client states on both the east and west coasts of Africa. Almost half of its submarine fleet, some 160 boats, were diesel powered rather than nuclear. It was essential, therefore, for the Soviets to have anchoring, provisioning, and docking facilities in as many foreign ports, in strategically important areas, as could be arranged. Throughout Africa, in the shifting sands of ruthless politics, many nations had forced the Soviets to keep negotiating for access to new ports. Several times, in recent years, facilities they had built or had been using for long periods were denied to them by new, unsympathetic governments. Their successful drive for an increased number of ports of access on both the Atlantic and Indian Ocean coasts of the continent was motivated by the continuing thrust, begun in 1962, to become the world's dominant naval power, an objective completely consonant with the USSR's overall goal of world domination.

Leach had paused as some of those factors ran through

his mind. He began again, "*Splendid* is presently at 60° 5'
12" east, 13° 8' 3" north and reporting for tasking. Happy
to be working for you again. It's a long way from Faslane."

Once more the captain paused. He was satisfied.
"That's it. Make the signal as soon as we're at periscope
depth. Should be about five minutes."

"Aye, aye, sir."

Within Leach's estimated time his search periscope
was up, the radar mast and its radio antenna with it. Just as
he clamped his face to the periscope, the captain checked
his watch: 10:42 P.M. Zulu. Old Ward would soon be
reading his signal. Admiral Ward was not old in the conventional sense, only forty-nine as against Leach's thirty-
four years. But it seemed that all admirals were referred to
as "old men" regardless of their ages.

Scanning the horizon, he called out to the radar
watchkeeper, "Anything, radar?"

"Yes, sir. Contact. Surface vessel. Bearing 030, range
thirty-two miles."

Leach swung the periscope to that heading. Yes, there
she was. It looked like a freighter, its bridge amidships,
crane masts reaching skyward like fingers. "Have you got
him, sonar?"

Petty Officer Pratt's voice was loud and clear. "Aye,
sir, and I just got something else. Contact. Bearing 185,
classified submarine, range 1,500 yards . . ."

The reaction of the captain was instantaneous. "Two
thousand yards!" he exclaimed, pulling his eyes away from
the periscope and turning to shout in the direction of the
sonar compartment. "Jesus Christ, Pratt! Have you been
asleep! Is that your first contact?" Pratt should have picked
up the bogey miles out . . . Unless. The captain realized
that he had been feeling a little edgy that morning. Perhaps
he had reacted too quickly. He left the periscope to go to the
sonar room. He stood at the door looking in at the screen.
There was the submarine, its blip shining white just where
Pratt said it was, sitting there in a constant, unmoving position. No doubt about it. They had picked up a shadow.

Out of the corner of his eye, Petty Officer Pratt caught

the figure of the captain standing in the doorway looking at the screen. His own face turned again toward the bright sonar images. In a voice which showed his unhappiness at being shouted at when he was not at fault, he said, "I think we've passed over her, sir. She was probably sitting silent waiting for us and started up when we were about fifteen hundred yards past her. That's when I first got her. Now she's sitting where you see her, about two thousand back." The young petty officer was one of the best sonar men in the fleet. And he was right. Leach was wrong to have shouted at him.

"You're absolutely right, Pratt. Sorry. I shouldn't have raised my voice."

Pratt still hadn't turned to look at him, but his right hand lifted and partly turned as he said, "Not a problem, sir." Turning toward his console of electronic gear he added, "The signature's coming up now, sir. It's a Victor II."

Bloody Russian bastard, was Leach's first thought. If he missed his guess, that goddamn submarine would be glued to his tail so long as *Splendid* was in the Indian Ocean. He knew the Victor II class. They were a match any day for the Swiftsure class of British attack submarine to which *Splendid* belonged. The Victor II had an advertised speed of thirty-one knots dived, but he thought it would be far greater. She was bigger than *Splendid*, at 323 feet in length with a displacement of 5,700 deadweight tons as against his boat's length of 272 feet and 4,500 tons. But the Soviet craft's nuclear power plant delivered twice the power of *Splendid*, 30,000 shaft horsepower against his ship's 15,000.

The Victor II was a long way from home. Most of them were based with the Soviet northern fleet operating out of the Kola Peninsula, although some were positioned in the Pacific. Built at the admiralty yard in Leningrad, the big, fast antisubmarine and antiship vessel had eight torpedo tubes in its bow and carried twenty-one of those ship-destroying devices. In addition, it carried a SUBROC type of weapon, probably ten of them, an underwater-launched missile carrying a depth charge which could be nuclear. Like *Splendid*, the trailing Victor could stay

604

submerged for weeks on end, putting as much as 40,000 nautical miles past her keel in a single voyage.

"What's her depth?"

"Looks like 300 feet, sir."

There was nothing the captain could do about it. The Russki would sit there, watching his every move. Even so, it would be no more than a bothersome worry. Not a real threat unless some idiot started a war while they were playing tag in the Indian Ocean. If the captain of the Victor heard about it before he did, *Splendid* would be the first submarine sunk in World War III. But surely no one in his right mind on either side would start a war, Leach reassured himself, as he often had in the past when the possibility of war came into his mind. But in his heart Leach knew he did not believe that no one would start a war. If he had believed it, he would not have been in *Splendid* as its captain on that morning of March 31.

He could sense someone behind him in the passageway. He turned. It was Pots with a message.

"From the admiral, sir."

Back beside the periscope, Leach read, "To the man who sticks to everything, welcome." That was how the admiral used to refer to him in the old days. A play on Leach's name, it used to amuse the old man. Obviously it still did.

"*Splendid* will proceed to take up patrol station across eastern Gulf of Aden, generally in a line running north from Cape Guardafui. Soviet fleet is assembling to the west in area of Aden preparatory to OKEAN. Report when on station, then every six hours from the exact minute of your first on-station transmission. Emergency watch will be kept on assigned frequencies. Use caution. Russian bear is baring teeth at Yanks over Pakistan. Give a wag of *Splendid*'s tail to your dog Victor. We have a whole pack with us."

Leach laughed out loud. Leave it to the old man. He thought, I'll bet the Sea Kings off the *Tiger* are working their butts off, plopping their sonars into the drink for miles around the flotilla. Between him and the Americans, they'll know by this time exactly what the Russkis have under the water up there.

He walked over to the chart table. Putting both hands

on it, he leaned across to look at his navigating officer who was busily tracking the course of *Splendid* and its position. Pilot looked up. "Sir?"

"Fish out your charts for the Gulf of Aden."

Pilot's hands reached out to the bottom of his stack of long drawers. In an instant the marine chart covering the entire gulf was spread smoothly on the table.

Leach looked southward on the map's face. His right index finger traced a line from Cape Guardafui north across the mouth of the Gulf to the shore of South Yemen, another client state of the Russians.

"We're going to take up station there, roughly on that line," he said. "Calculate the course to get there and, when you have a chance, set up a good line for station holding. You know, find some high landmarks on both shores so I can pick them up easily on the periscope."

"I can give you a preliminary course to the Gulf right now, sir," Pilot advised, rolling out his parallel ruler from the side of the chart table. "Try 278 degrees, that will put us into the slot just north of Socotra, the Island of Socotra, here." He pointed to a large island about one hundred miles to the east of Cape Guardafui.

"Good."

Straightening up, Leach returned to the search periscope and had a look around the horizon. The only thing to be seen was the freighter, now slightly closer. Satisfied, he brought the periscope down and gave the order to dive to 500 feet. Once the diving procedures were finished and the ship was on its way down to its ordered level, he gave the change of course that would take them from their northbound track almost due west into the Gulf of Aden.

When *Splendid* was well into her long, banking left turn for her new course, Leach called to the sonar room, "What's our Russian doing?"

Pratt had been expecting the question. "She's turning right with us, sir."

Moments after, when *Splendid* had come straight and level on her course for Aden, the voice of the sonar watchkeeper came again. "Contact. Bearing red 030, classified submarine, range thirty-five miles, speed estimated thirty-five knots, estimated course 355."

Whoever she was, she was not headed for the same place as *Splendid*: the Gulf of Aden. Pratt's reply to the captain's question about her signature was totally anticipated. "She's Russian, sir. Another Victor II." That explained her high speed.

Lowering himself into his chair, he muttered out loud to himself, "Christ, the whole bloody world is filled with Russian submarines!"

16

31 March

Kuwait

As you approach the city of Kuwait from the sea, there is an impression of total flatness. The usually calm waters of the Arabian Gulf blend toward the endless desert sand that holds the streets, buildings, and people within the ancient city. In recent times, tall, sparkling office buildings and hotels have sprung up, crude-oil nurtured, from the sand, in Kuwait's rush to modernity and prosperity. Moving northwest along the channel into Shuwaikh port, an inbound ship passes Ras Jouza Point on the left, the Kuwait Towers on its shores, by the Dasman and Sief palaces, and the Sheraton Hotel. At the entrance to the port area sit the embassies of East Germany, Somalia, and Morocco. In the southern section of the city, near the tall Hilton Hotel, stands the American Embassy, just off First Ring Road. At the Ras Jouza Point, a stone's throw north of the Kuwait Towers, the embassies of the Soviet Union and the United Kingdom stand almost cheek by jowl, just a few yards from the Afghanistan embassy and its easterly neighbor, the People's Republic of China.

The skyline is broken not only by the new buildings,

but by the traditional minarets whose shape has been copied by the designers of two tall water towers, their concrete forms thrusting up hundreds of feet into the air, each with enormous tanks like balls bulging out at midpoint to hold hundreds of thousands of gallons of desalinated drinking water from the plant at their feet, a short distance from the port entrance.

The early morning sun rose out of the waters of the gulf behind them as the *Mecca* made its way up the channel. By eight o'clock the *Mecca* was berthed, customs clearances had been completed and registration procedures had been cleared up by Rashid with the port authority. Trucks and men of the Kuwait Stevedoring Company had appeared at dockside to assist the crew of the *Mecca* in unloading her mixed cargo.

Shortly after, the PLO team walked down the gangplank to the pier. Once again, their long black *abas* covered their uniforms. Clean *khafias* were on their heads, their plain black *guptas* (headbands) squarely in place. They headed for the Sheraton Hotel. As they were coming into port, Said had spotted the attractive, tall building, its sign prominently displayed at roof level. He had to do some telephoning. The Sheraton, catering as it did to Americans and the flood of Europeans doing business in Kuwait, would be able to cope with his overseas telephone calls without any difficulty. In preparation for this eventuality, he had obtained in Beirut a supply of Kuwait dinars; enough, he estimated, for a good meal and one long distance call to Beirut.

Inside the air-conditioned, marble-floored foyer, Said bought two street maps of the city at the news kiosk. One he handed to Ahmed with a wad of money, telling the three of them to make a tour of the city and meet him back at the hotel at twelve noon for lunch. The second map he would keep for himself. When his telephone calls were finished, he would take a walk around the city.

When they had departed, he talked with the concierge, gave him a Beirut telephone number and a hastening tip of dinars. The concierge said he would let him know when the call was ready. In the meantime if he would take a seat in the lobby, a man would be by with coffee shortly, as was the practice.

It was almost an hour later, shortly after ten, that he was summoned to the telephone. His leader, Arafat, was at his headquarters. He was expecting Said's call, anxious to know about the Haifa affair and the prospects for the success of the Kuwait operation. Said hurried to the booth and gave his mentor a complete report, promising that the first phase would be completed that night. If something went wrong, he would report by a cable he would send when the *Mecca* stopped at Bahrain.

Arafat listened without interrupting. The line was good. No need to shout. When his lieutenant was finished, Arafat complimented him. "You have done well, Said, very well indeed. The Haifa operation was superb, absolutely superb. I'm confident you're going to have great success tonight. May Allah be with you. But let me go back to Haifa. The Israelis are furious. They've attacked our refugee camps by air in retaliation, as you might have expected."

In his telephone booth far away from Beirut, Said nodded silently. He had heard the news reports on the radio. Revenge, and who could blame them. That was the normal pattern between blood enemies. But it was what his chief said next that filled the young man's soul with apprehension.

"However, there is one thing I must warn you about. Our intelligence people tell me that the Israelis know that you and your team were on the *Mecca*. They're convinced that you did the job. They're sending out their best hit team to find you. As far as I know, they don't know where the *Mecca* is yet and right now even if they did, it wouldn't do them any good because they wouldn't be able to get into Kuwait . . . Said, are you still there?"

There was a pause. "Yes, sir, I'm still here. What you are telling me is no surprise."

"All I am saying is be careful!"

"Don't worry. My team is as good as any they have."

"You have to be better, my son."

When their conversation was finished, the line went dead. Said hung up with a vacant stare on his face, turning over in his mind Arafat's words of warning. He would cross that bridge when he came to it. There were many other things to do first. The first phase had to be finished. There would be another long voyage, one that Captain Rashid did not know about yet. And then the final phase at that far distant port.

He straightened up. His team could handle any Israeli hit squad, out-think them, out-fight them, out-kill them.

There was one more telephone call to be made. It was a local call to a number in the city of Kuwait. Once again he went to the concierge, who gave him his bill for the Beirut call. That was paid. There would be no charge for the local call. He could put it through directly. When the connection was made, he asked the embassy receptionist for the military attaché. Said identified himself to that officer's secretary, using the Arabic language. The military attaché, ostensibly a lieutenant-colonel in the army, in reality was a high-ranking officer of the infamous KGB. When he came on the line, Said spoke with him eloquently, fluently, and without accent in the language of his Russian father, a sea captain of the northern city of Murmansk, nestled in a deep and narrow fjord of the frigid Barents Sea in the Arctic Ocean. When Said spoke to the colonel it was as an equal. For not only was Said a lieutenant-colonel in the Palestinian Liberation Army, as Captain Rashid knew him to be, he was also a member of the KGB, the world-grasping octopus of intrigue, intelligence, counterintelligence, and espionage. Said worked to further the world domination objectives of the Supreme Soviet, goals that were consistent with those of the Palestinian Liberation movement.

Lieutenant-Colonel Said of the KGB provided essentially the same report he had given to Yassir Arafat, including the date and time of the execution of the Phase II, 1300 hours Greenwich Mean Time (GMT) on April 26.

The *Mecca*'s crew cast off her lines from the Shuwaikh docks shortly after five that afternoon. Without a cargo, the old boat rode high out of the water. But she would be without freight only until she reached Bahrain, the highly industrialized Arab island nation a day's sail away on the *Mecca*'s route back to the Mediterranean. Her owner's Bahrain agents had contracted for the carriage of two thousand tons of aluminum ingots from Bahrain to Aden.

Rashid had informed Said of the Bahrain stop when he and his team returned to the freighter.

"How long will we be at Bahrain?" Said asked.

"The stuff's sitting on the dock. It shouldn't take us any more than three or four hours to get it on board." The captain thought it was time to raise the question. "Bahrain might be a good place for you people to leave the *Mecca*. It has one of the best-served airports in the Middle East. You can fly direct to Beirut from there. I can bring home any gear you don't want to carry on the aircraft."

"In your special compartment?"

Rashid smiled. "If need be."

"I'll think about it," was Said's evasive response.

He would not think about it at all. He would wait until the *Mecca* was two days out of Aden before he told Captain Rashid that instead of heading back up the Red Sea to the Suez and the Mediterranean, the *Mecca* would be sailing south down the coast of Africa. The two days' warning would give Rashid time to get on the radio and attempt to arrange a southbound cargo out of Aden. If he couldn't, the *Mecca* would have to sail south in ballast. The captain and owners would be fully compensated. That would be made perfectly clear.

Said returned to the bridge as Captain Rashid was getting the *Mecca* under way. They left Shuwaikh harbor, running out the channel past the water towers and the Sheraton Hotel bathed in the golden glow of the setting sun.

The captain had confirmed that the *Mecca* would be dropping anchor off Mina-al-Ahmadi around ten o'clock, as originally planned. From the time the *Mecca* left the Shuwaikh harbor astern, there was little more than four hours for the PLO team to get ready. The cook served them supper at 6:30. By the time that meal was finished, the *Mecca* was steaming slowly southward in total darkness except for her running lights and the faint glow of the flaring natural gas from the Kuwait oil fields far to the west. The four Arabs had to get their gear and weapons out of the captain's secret compartment without disclosing to the crew where they had hidden the material during the long voyage. The captain's men had been surprised enough when they found the PLO four back on board after the *Mecca* had left Port Said.

This time the scenario was different. The move had to be done under cover of darkness. Other than Nabil and the wheelsman engaged on the bridge, the crew would have to be occupied on some part of the ship that would keep them away from the deck. The solution was simple. While the cook had served the PLO group their supper at 6:30, Rashid ordered that the crew would be fed at seven. Furthermore, they would have the best food in the cook's larder and once again some wine, but this time only a liter per man.

With Maan standing guard at the head of the steps on the port side of the cabin deck, the lift-out operation began as soon as he was satisfied that all the crew were seated in the galley and digging into their special dinner. Working furiously, Said, Hassan, and Ahmed had their cache of equipment and Rashid's unmarked sacks of opium up and out of the secret compartment and on the deck immediately aft of the master's quarters. On the bridge above, Captain Rashid kept Nabil occupied during the critical period, going over charts of the approaches to Mina-al-Ahmadi.

Once their equipment was on deck, the need for cover and secrecy no longer existed. They would complete their preparations in the open with the curious crew as spectators. Curious they were. When they began straggling out of the galley, smoking and talking in the darkness, one of the deck hands sauntered up to the forward railing of the cabin deck to look into the black night to see what was ahead of the *Mecca*. As his eyes adjusted to the darkness, they opened wide with astonishment when he saw dark figures moving on the deck below, vague silhouettes against the dim grayness of the wall of the master's cabin. It was those damn PLO people. What were they doing? Calling to his companions to join him, the deck hand and the rest of the crew, including the cook, surrounded the Palestinians. They were amazed at what they saw.

On the starboard side of the deck, Said and Hassan were gently lifting from their styrofoam packages, gray, metallic objects about as big around as a large dinner plate. Their bottoms were flat but the tops domelike. In the center was a dial. To the right of the dial was a thick metal tube some six inches long attached to the surface by a universal swivel. To the left of the dial was a hinged ring just big enough for a large index finger.

The ring was attached to an arming pin which, when pulled out, permitted two internal spring-loaded wires to make contact, thereby activating a high-powered, electric-battery-generated charge which did two things. First, it set up a strong magnetic field in the base of the device, a field that would last indefinitely after the electrical power source terminated. Second, it completed the circuit that activated a tiny radio receiver preset to the frequency selected on the dial face. When the radio received the master signal on the selected frequency, it would trip the detonating circuit. At that instant the device, packed with immensely powerful material, would explode. The thick tube was a telescopic aerial that would extend to a distance of twenty feet.

The metal objects were deadly limpet mines, one of which could shatter the whole of a ship like the *Mecca* and send her to the bottom in seconds. Or it could destroy six Israeli gunboats. Ten of them strategically planted along the hull of a VLCC or ULCC supertanker could turn it into a blazing mass of wreckage in a split second, to sink in a matter of minutes if the ship was loaded and in a matter of seconds if it was in ballast.

On the port side of the deck, Ahmed and Maan took the two inflatable speedboats out of their container bags, unrolled them and inflated them using CO_2 bottles to bring them up to maximum and rigidity pressure. The gasoline-driven outboard motors had to be test run. They were clamped to the wooden shaft of the old ship's railing. The tubes from the red gasoline tanks were inserted into the front of each motor and the gasoline lines energized. With a strong pull on the starter rope by Ahmed, the motors roared into life, billowing huge clouds of blue smoke which disappeared as soon as the engines settled into a steady run.

Satisfied with the performance of the motors, Ahmed shut them off, lifted them off the railing and secured one on the back of each of the speedboats. He set the gas tanks on the floor amidships for balance.

The next test was of the quiet electric motors, the ones they would use throughout the entire operation. The gasoline engines were for emergency getaway purposes only, or if the batteries lost power. The railing was used again as a base on which to clamp the electric motors for testing. Their power lines ran to two wet batteries sitting on the deck in separate metal cases with a leather handle strap for easy carrying. Both electric motors worked perfectly, emitting almost no noise as their propellers spun freely in the night air. But it was apparent that the batteries needed a fast charge in order to bring them up to full power.

After transferring the electric motors to the back of the boats to sit next to their gasoline-driven counterparts, Ahmed and Maan took the batteries and their electrical charge machine down to the chief engineer's workshop. They hooked the charger into the ship's electrical supply, then clamped the positive and negative claws of the charger's wires onto the poles of the first set of batteries. By the time they were ready to launch the operation at ten that night, all four batteries would be up to their full power.

The two of them returned to their speedboats to begin assembling the oars and installing the ropes by which the boats would be lifted by the ship's crane over the side and gently lowered to the water. Up to that point, the crew members had simply stood and gawked at what was going on. Now they started to ask some questions. Said freely answered almost all. There was no need for them not to know. In any event, he would make sure they could not use the information until both phases of the operation had been completed. After that it wouldn't matter. He explained to them how the mines worked; how they clung to the metal surface of the hull of a ship with such a force that it was almost impossible to pry them off; how they were armed and the method of detonation by radio over long distances.

When asked, however, why they were going to mine the tankers, all he would say was, "In the cause of the liberation of the Palestinian people." And to the question of which ships he was going to mine, he would only say, "Those carrying the right flag."

Kneeling on the deck working on the last of the one hundred mines, Said had not noticed that the captain had joined the little group in the darkness as he gave those answers. Rashid was appalled by the lethal power that lay glinting on the deck, with flashes of the red, green, and white running lights reflecting off their shiny surfaces.

"Said, you could blow up the whole world with these!"

"That's exactly what I intend to do, captain, at least come as close to it as I possibly can."

Rashid shook his head. "All in the name of the liberation of the Palestinian people. There must be an easier way."

Said's voice, calm and soft in the balmy night air, was barely audible over the roar of the old *Mecca*'s engines and the thumping of her screw.

The far twinkling lights of the huge refinery at Mina-al-Ahmadi, and the flickering flames of gas from the multitude of its chimneys, appeared on the horizon ahead of the *Mecca* shortly after nine. Then came the first signs of the running lights of the empty supertankers clustered seaward, waiting at anchor. Against the web of loading piers, a multitude of tiny, red, green, and white beams showed the presence of about twenty vessels taking on their loads of heavy black crude or processed liquid petroleum from the pipes of the refinery.

A few minutes before ten, the *Mecca* was coming up to her agreed anchorage station, five miles northeast of the northern pier, about two miles from the northernmost waiting tanker. Captain Rashid had returned to his bridge after taking a look at the mines and the fully rigged speed-boats. Nabil was already on the bridge, pacing back and forth behind the helmsman, fearful for his own safety after seeing those dreadful mines for the first time. He was conjuring up in his mind all manner of scenarios for the ships that would have them clamped to their bottoms. Were those wild men actually going to put those mines on those tankers out there? He couldn't believe it. Why? Were they going to blow them up right then and there? If they did, the whole place would blow up: the refinery, the piers, the storage tanks. He could see the entire area going up like an atomic bomb.

As soon as the captain came back on the bridge, Nabil began pleading with him to get the *Mecca* going as soon as the special cargo sacks had been picked up. Leave the Palestinians behind if they weren't back by then, he urged. Nabil was close to panic as he saw Said in a black wetsuit coming up the steps from the port wing of the bridge, an apparition that served to escalate the fear in Nabil's gut. The Egyptian withdrew to the far end of the bridge's starboard wing to get as far away from the PLO leader as he could.

The captain asked for "slow ahead." In the blackness he could barely see the deck hands in the fo'c'sle, ready at their anchor positions. He estimated another three or four minutes before he ordered the engines stopped.

He turned to face Said as he padded toward him. "Are you ready to go?"

Said nodded. "Everything's set, just waiting for the last battery. It should be up any minute."

Suddenly Rashid noticed in the dim light from the engine instruments that Said did not have on his perpetual sunglasses. It was one of those rare moments when he could see, but only barely, into the young man's eyes. He thought he saw a glimmer of affection.

"Rashid," Said said, "this is going to be a dangerous operation. Something might go wrong. I am sure it won't. But I want you to know how much . . . how grateful I am to you. Do you understand?"

617

The captain's creased face broke into a smile as he laid a hand on Said's black shoulder. "Of course I do. Of course, and may Allah be with you, Said."

Said's eyes dropped away from the old man's for a moment just as Rashid removed his hand. Then those incongruous blue eyes were fixed again on Rashid's. "There is something you must know. I have had to take a precaution. I thought about doing it at Port Said, but it wasn't necessary as you had the opium on board, but now I have to do it. I have to be absolutely sure that the *Mecca* will still be here when we're finished. Once you get rid of your special cargo there will be nothing to keep you here, nothing to make you wait for us."

"But you have my word!" Rashid protested.

"And I accept it." He looked in the distance toward Nabil and judged that he could hear none of the conversation. He lifted his voice so the first officer could get every word. "But there may be others on this ship who will think differently. You're only one man against nine, captain. So to make sure the *Mecca* is still here when I get back, I have planted one of the mines. It's activated. There's the safety pin." He held up the right hand and opened it palm down. Around his index finger was a steel ring. Attached to it and hanging down was the safety pin of the hidden mine. The captain looked at it without emotion, but Nabil, his bulging eyes wide with fear, gasped, "You're mad! You'll kill us all!"

"If the *Mecca* stays here, you have nothing to worry about. If you leave, you're dead. Our transmitter is in my boat. It doesn't matter where you are. All we have to do is push a button." Those words were directed to the trembling Nabil. Said had taken one further precaution. "And we've put your radio transmitter out of commission."

Said turned to Captain Rashid. "I'm sorry," he said.

The black figure disappeared down the steps. Rashid sized up his position and ordered, "Stop engines."

In a state of near mental collapse, the petrified Nabil did not respond. Pushing him aside, the captain pulled back on the telegraph levers to the "stop" position. Im-

618

mediately he could hear the roar of the engines die as the chief engineer, in his private hell of an engine room below, moved the throttles to idle.

On the cargo deck aft, Ahmed started up the crane motor. When it had settled down, he skilfully moved the levers, swinging its cable and hook over the waiting speedboats. Ahmed stopped it about five feet above the first craft to be lifted. Immediately, three black-suited figures slipped the loops of the boat's lifting ropes—one at the bow, two from each corner of the stern, two from each gunwale, just forward of the middle of the boat—over the sharp tip of the waiting hook. Said raised his right hand palm up, the signal to Ahmed. With the surging sound of the crane motor, the cable began to lift, pulling the ropes taut. Slowly the speedboat with its two motors moved up and away from the deck. At head height, Ahmed stopped the lift without any instructions from Said and pulled the right directional lever on the crane. He swung the boat slowly over the starboard railing to a point about ten feet beyond. Gingerly, he pushed on the lowering lever, watching the speedboat disappear below the deck level and out of sight.

Ahmed's eyes were on Said's hands. The PLO leader leaned over the railing, his black form barely visible to Ahmed in the darkness, but he could pick up the white-brown hands, both of which Said had moved over to his right side, holding them vertically apart and as wide as he could. Below him was Maan standing on the lowered gangway platform, his hands similarly extended. When Maan calculated that the bottom of the inflated craft was about three feet from the surface of the calm, millpond-like black water—it was hard to judge the height in the blackness of the night—he began to move his hands slowly together to indicate the diminishing height of the speedboat. His gesture was copied by Said and seen by Ahmed. Finally the palms of the two outstretched pairs of hands were only a foot apart, then they were together as the bottom of the boat touched the water.

On the gangway platform, Maan was ready. Immediately the boat was in the water, no more than two feet beyond the platform, he leaped into it to take the boat ropes off the cable's lift hook. Those ropes would be left in place but coiled on the floor of the boat for the haul back onto the *Mecca*'s deck when they returned. Maan signaled to Said above him that the hook was clear, sat on the middle seat between the oarlocks, seized the handles of the oars and rowed toward the stern of the freighter to clear the touchdown area for the second boat. It appeared a few moments later, riding over the rail to meet the water gently. Hassan guided it down as Maan had done.

Within ten minutes, both boats were successfully launched. Hassan jumped into the boat from the gangway platform to unhitch it and bring it alongside. This would be his and Ahmed's craft. The next step was to load it with its fifty mines. In three-man chain fashion, Ahmed lifted each one off the deck and handed it to Said halfway down the steps, who carried it the rest of the way to the platform and then to Hassan. Then followed the radio transmitter, their oxygen bottles, masks, flippers, and black gloves. Boat number one was ready.

Hassan rowed it a few strokes away from the *Mecca* to allow Maan to come in with boat number two. In short order it received the remaining forty-nine limpet mines, Said and Maan's diving gear, then Said himself. Maan moved to the bow of the craft, while Said sat in the rear seat to operate the motor and steer. There was no need for them to wait for the other boat. They knew exactly where they had to go, what they had to do. Said moved the throttle on the electric motor to full speed. He looked up toward the *Mecca*'s railing where the entire ship's crew stood watching them, their figures barely visible in the murk. He could distinguish Rashid's broad figure, standing apart from the rest at the head of the gangway. He waved to the old captain, but in the darkness the gesture was not returned.

Silently the black, heavy-laden boat blended into the enveloping night, leaving only a pencil-like trace of white glowing water in its wake which pointed to the lights of the anchored leviathans to the south.

Hassan moved his craft back to the gangway platform where Ahmed stood waiting. When his huge bulk was on board, settled in the stern position, the second boat moved soundlessly into the darkness.

Said had briefed his team thoroughly when they returned to the *Mecca* that afternoon. On the back of one of his maps he had carefully plotted the location of the supertankers as they had been anchored the day before. Of the twenty anchored ships, he estimated between eight and ten would have moved into the piers of Mina-al-Ahmadi to take on their loads. The remainder would still be at anchor and in exactly the same locations. Every one of the ships was registered in Liberia or Panama and therefore qualified as an acceptable target in that neither of those countries was a member of NATO. In fact, few of the more than 700 supertankers that roamed the seas of the world carried the flags of the countries of their owners. Instead they flew a flag of convenience, that of Liberia or Panama.

In his briefing, Said attempted to keep the plan of attack as simple as possible. He drew an erratic north-south line on his map, marking on it the location of each of the ten target ships. He and Maan would take the even-numbered ships in the line. Ahmed and Hassan would take the first one and after that the odd ones in the sequence. To avoid being seen, each tanker would be approached from directly on its bow. The likelihood of being spotted by a crew member was remote, in that the accommodation for the thirty or forty crew members was always at the stern of the ship, a thousand feet or more away from the bow. Furthermore, once their boats were running alongside a target ship, they would, in fact, be under the vessel. By this time, each of the tankers had pumped out its ballast and was riding high in the water. A major part of its vast body was exposed, its hull curving sharply at the water line to produce an overhang under which the two small boats would operate unseen from the deck above.

In the calm, windless night, Said could see from the jumble of running lights ahead that the tankers did not all point in the same direction as they rode at anchor. He steered the boat well to the east of the first ship. It was Hassan and Ahmed's initial target. Though Said and Maan were half a mile from it, the massive ship appeared to loom above them. The funnel at its towering stern was floodlit to display its owner's proud symbol: ESSO. They passed behind the supertanker, knowing that at that moment Ahmed and Maan would be at its nose ready to begin their task.

Beyond the Esso tanker, they turned slightly toward shore to their first target some 300 yards south of it, its bow conveniently pointing directly toward them. In the moonless night, the cloaking darkness was softened only slightly by the yellowish glow of the distant flaring at the refinery ashore. So dark was it that a pair of naked eyes on the deck of the fo'c'sle of one of the anchored supertankers high above the water would not have been able to find the black rubber boat, its passengers, or its lethal cargo. The slim line of phosphorus wake might have been visible, but nothing else.

The Esso insignia blazing proudly in the night on the first ship, combined with its peculiar superstructure, had enabled Said to identify her. From his memory of the photographs they had taken yesterday and the ship's position chart he had drawn, he knew she was the *Esso Italia*. She was in the size range of 250,000 deadweight tons and registered in Liberia. That key identification made, his memory of the chart gave him the names and details of the next nine ships in the waiting line. Any other ships would be new arrivals since the day before.

His mind quickly reviewed the ships they would visit that night. Their first target, the second ship in the line, was the *Afran Zodiac*, owned by Gulf Oil, about 227,000 tons, flag Liberia. The third was the *Fairfield Jason*, owned by Fairway Tankers, about 270,000 tons, flag Liberia. The fourth, *Conoco Europe*, about the same size as the *Fairfield Jason*, flag Liberia. He could not remember the name of the owner. The fifth, *Chevron Edinburgh*, owned by Chevron Transport, same size, flag Liberia. The sixth, *Esso Malaysia*, about 200,000 tons, owned by Esso Tankers Inc., flag Panama. The seventh, *Saint Marcet*, owner he had forgotten, about 280,000 tons, flag Liberia. Eighth, the *Mobil Magnolia*, again about 280,000 tons, the owner Mobil Oil, flag Liberia. The ninth, *Charles Pigott*, owner Bank of California National Association, about 270,000 tons, flag Liberia. And the last, the *Amoco Singapore*, owner Amoco Transport Company, about 230,000 tons, flag Liberia. Not a NATO flag in the lot.

The *Afran Zodiac*'s massive anchor chain slipped by so closely that they could have touched it. In a few seconds they bumped against the enormous hydrodynamic bulb that sat under the bow of the ship, its orange paint making it dully visible only when they were making contact. Maan cut the power immediately. The yielding surface of the rubber boat bounced gently off the ship's hull. They were ready to begin. Not a word would be spoken.

Said put on his flippers, gloves, face mask, and, with Maan's help, strapped on his black-painted oxygen bottle. He eased himself over the gunwale of the boat into the water between it and the towering bow of the *Afran Zodiac*. Oxygen tube firmly clamped in his mouth, he reached up and took from Hassan's hands the first limpet mine. He clutched it to his chest with both arms, the flat surface to be magnetized facing away from his body. Turning toward the hull he submerged to a point where he calculated he was about three feet below the water line. With both hands he shoved the mine against the hard metal of the hull. Holding it there with his left hand, he explored with his right the rounded surface of the device, found the ring of the arming pin, inserted his index finger in it and pulled. Instantaneously the mine was both magnetized and armed, clamped firmly to the underbelly of the monster ship.

Only one thing remained to be done. Deftly his hands found the telescopic aerial and pulled it out to its full length, leaving it flush against the hull pointing aft toward the stern. The "wings" at the aerial's tip would lift it to the surface once the ship was under way. Back Said went to the surface, where he hung on to the gunwale rope as the electric motor drove the boat about a hundred feet along under the curved hull toward the stern. There the mining procedure was repeated as it was at similar intervals along the water line, with the last one, the tenth, placed close to the stern under the engine room. They were finished. With Maan's help, Said climbed back into the boat. As silently as they had arrived, the small craft, its electric motor whirring noiselessly, crept back to the bow under the protective overhang of the hull, past the anchor chain and on in the darkness to the *Conoco Europe*.

Said checked his watch. It had taken him twenty-two minutes to mine the *Afran Zodiac*. The time was seven minutes to eleven. Four more ships to do, with a transit time of say ten minutes between each of them and forty minutes to get back to the *Mecca*, that would get them back to her by 01:40, long before Rashid's deadline of 02:00—if nothing went wrong. So far so good.

Guided by the running lights of the anchored ships, they moved past the third ship, the *Fairfield Jason*, both men wondering how Ahmed and Hassan were doing. They should have started on her by that time.

The approach of Said and Maan to the *Conoco Europe* was similar to their handling of the *Afran Zodiac*. The mine planting went as planned without incident, but this time it was Maan who was in the water. Then on to the *Esso Malaysia*, the *Mobil Magnolia* and finally the *Amoco Singapore*.

Said had mined both the Mobil and Esso ships, so it was Maan who was in the water to finish the operation. The eighth limpet mine had been clamped to the hull of the *Amoco Singapore*. The next one would be the last of the forty-nine mines they had brought from the *Mecca*. Said took the boat to the stern under the engine room. That position was also just ahead of the massive six blades of the ship's mighty propeller.

Just as Maan submerged with the final mine clutched to his chest, Said's ears caught the tinkle of the ship's engine telegraph bells. Immediately there was a heavy rumbling from inside the vessel as its powerful diesels accelerated, turning the propeller shaft with rapidly increasing speed. It seemed to Said no more than an instant before the water around him had turned into a churning maelstrom. The vicious blades of the mammoth screw were just below the surface twenty feet away, turning faster and faster, sucking the water ahead of the propeller into its maw with ever increasing force. Said could feel his boat being pulled toward the propeller. Reacting instantly and instinctively he rammed the throttle of his electric motor fully open, pushing its steering arm hard over to port to swing the nose of his craft to the right, away from the spreading whirlpool. But it was too late. The suction overpowered the weak motor of the light craft, even though it had managed to move out away from the ship by a yard before it was overcome by the tremendous power of the water being drawn into the thrashing blades, turning inside their protective circular shield.

The small craft was out of control. Said knew that he was being drawn inexorably into the white, foaming vortex. In one motion he was on his feet and diving out away from the tanker. But as soon as he hit the water he knew he had not escaped. He was being hauled down, tumbling. The oxygen bottle on his back was pulled violently. His arms and legs twisted as he was propelled downward and back in the churning black and white void of foaming water. The noise of the pounding screw filled his eardrums. A sharp pain shot through his left arm and shoulder as he was thrown hard against the side of the ship. Then, as quickly as he had been sucked under, he was thrown to the surface gasping for air in the churning water. He was about thirty yards behind the huge tanker, its vast bulk now beginning to move slowly forward to pick up its anchor and proceed into its assigned loading berth.

Frantically Said searched the surface for Maan. He was nowhere to be seen. But the boat was just a few feet away from him still miraculously intact except for a slash through the fabric of the starboard gunwale. The slash, however, was in only one of the many compartments of the inflated speedboat. The craft was still serviceable. He hauled himself back into it.

Where was Maan? Said did not call out. He could only look and hope. There, just to the left. There was something floating in the water about thirty feet away. Said eased on the electric power, edging the boat up to the shiny black object. As he leaned over the side to pick it up, he recoiled. It was an arm encased in the sleeve of a black wetsuit. Blood was still flowing from the stump, staining the white water. On the index finger was a black steel pull ring.

17

7 April   10:00 P.M.

Murmansk

Fleet Admiral Smirnov had been given explicit instructions by Chairman Romanov to prepare to get his entire submarine fleet to sea. The movement of the boats from their harbors should be carried out in absolute secrecy. It was imperative that no clue be found by NATO intelligence through the use of their satellites—or in any other way—that the undersea craft had left their bases. Romanov had been concerned that, either by the use of radar or infrared photography, the satellites would be able to track the submarines as they moved out. But the admiral had assured him that he could carry it off without detection. He had a special departure plan designed to fool the eyes of the enemy space vehicles.

As to the passage of the Kola Peninsula submarine fleet through the Denmark Strait between Iceland and Greenland and the gap between Iceland and Norway, Smirnov assured the chairman that the test of the sonar interference system, SONINT, from March 11 through March 22 had worked perfectly. He would use it to mask the exit of both the northern and the Baltic submarine fleets commencing April 3. Once he started the SONINT system by satellite signal, it would operate automatically for eleven days and could not be turned off. But the planned period would be more than enough to enable him to get his entire submarine fleet out to sea and for most of it to move south of the Tropic of Cancer and, therefore, out of the area covered by NATO naval forces. Furthermore, by mid-April many of the submarines, particularly the faster nuclear-powered ones, would already be at their stations, either with the Atlantic fleet for OKEAN, or at stations along the Cape tanker route in the South Atlantic and the Indian Ocean. That was as Romanov had instructed.

It was on March 17 that Smirnov had been summoned to Romanov's Kremlin office. There, in the presence of Ustinov and three other voting members of the Politburo, Kirilenko, Gromyko, and army General Yu Andropov, Romanov gave him a briefing and a set of instructions that both appalled and electrified him. The presence of the other members of the Politburo certified that Romanov's orders to him had been approved by the Politburo itself. Smirnov was to have his submarines deployed and in their required positions in the Atlantic and the Indian Ocean no later than April 20. The date of execution of the first stage of the plan, which Romanov had called the Andropov Plan, would be between April 20 and April 26. Smirnov would be informed of the precise date later on. The second and final stage was to be executed on May Day, that most significant of all days in the calendar of communist Russia.

Romanov made sure his fleet admiral understood the background and objectives the Politburo wished to achieve. There was no doubt their action would take them to the brink of a war with the Americans and their NATO allies. As the Politburo and Romanov saw it, however, the Soviet Union had no choice. The new American president and the president of Pakistan had just announced their agreement under which American troops and equipment would be moving into Pakistan beginning May 7. The presence of American imperialist forces there constituted a threat to the Soviet Union which could not be tolerated.

Romanov's first objective was to stop the Americans. If he could not do it through the United Nations or through diplomatic bargaining or by threats he would have to use force and was prepared to do so. That he made perfectly clear to Smirnov.

The second objective was to secure and control a new source of crude oil for the Soviet Union and its energy-starved Eastern Bloc countries. The Andropov Plan was bold, decisive and dramatic. There was no room for error or failure. The stakes were far too high for that. The man with full responsibility for its execution was Fleet Admiral Nikolai Ivanovich Smirnov. Smirnov would sit in his offices in Moscow, from which place he would directly control not only the OKEAN exercise but also the Andropov operation. The key people were his submarine captains. On their shoulders would fall the ultimate responsibility.

The Arctic sun had set at 9:36 on the evening of April 7. With its disappearance, the pace of activity at the Soviet Navy's submarine base in the ice-free port of Murmansk reached fever pitch as the crews of the remaining serviceable submarines prepared to take their ships to sea.

The captain of Victor II submarine 501 pulled the collar of his heavy jacket up to protect his ears from the piercing cold Murmansk night wind. Captain Second Rank Boris Chernavin barked out orders from the tiny bridge at the front of the 501's long hump of a tower, which sat slightly forward of amidships of the powerful nuclear craft. The fore and aft lines were cast off. Silently, gently, the 323-foot submarine, a black, cigar-shaped form, moved ahead and out into the darkness toward the main channel of the Kola Fjord, turning slowly starboard.

When he heard three heavy splashes in the water at the dock the 501 had just left, the captain turned to look back. In the floodlit water by the quay, three huge bundles were bobbing, each with long hoses running from them up to the dock level, where a gang of sailors was busy starting the motor of a large portable air compressor. When that machine was running satisfactorily the hose from the first bundle in the water was connected to it. In short order the bundle began to uncurl under the pressure of the compressed air being forced inside it. Quickly it snapped out to its full length, its bottom flopping with another splash as that section of 501's plastic counterpart opened fully. It was the stern section of the replica. It would take only half an hour to inflate all three sections and join them together.

This deception had been planned by Smirnov personally. During the previous year he had had inflatable plastic replicas made of all his submarines. When blown up, his flat-bottomed, round-bodied decoys presented an image to the eye of the satellite that was exactly the same as that made by the real submarine. Smirnov's departing Murmansk submarine fleet, the remaining 110 diesel and nuclear-powered vessels of the 162 based there, would be replaced immediately by their doubles. Smirnov was convinced that that action, combined with a quick dive of all boats within minutes of leaving their jetties, would fool the satellite cameras.

Chernavin was disappointed. He would have liked to have stayed to see the copy of his ship fully assembled, but in half an hour he and his submarine would be long gone. He would be five miles north up the channel with Zelenii-Mys to starboard, and preparing to follow the lights of the channel marker buoys when the 501 swung eastward toward Waenga.

Boris Chernavin anticipated that, when the OKEAN exercise was finished and the 501 was back in Murmansk, a signal would be waiting for him confirming his posting to the Marshal Grechko Naval Academy in Leningrad. If he received that posting, it meant that he was in line to move toward the top positions in the Soviet navy. His father, a retired rear-admiral, would be pleased and proud if Boris were given the honor of attending the naval academy. Undoubtedly he had been using his not inconsiderable influence among his former naval colleagues to make sure that his son was selected. A captain second rank—equivalent to an American or British naval commander—at the age of twenty-eight when he became 501's captain, Chernavin had advanced rapidly in rank. This, too, was not unusual in the elite submarine service of the 450,000-man Red Navy that he, Boris Chernavin, knew and believed was the largest, best, and most powerful navy in the world.

As the 501 approached the 150-foot deep channel, Chernavin gave the order to dive. Within eight minutes of casting off her lines, the submarine was submerged, invisible, shielded from the probing eye of any satellite by the black surface of the Kola Fjord's inpenetrable water.

Using his active sonar, attack periscope, and radar to navigate, Chernavin moved his ship into station half a mile behind 476, the Echo class submarine that had been berthed just astern of his 501. Ahead of 476 and as far as his sonar screen eyes could see were the electronic white blips of a single file line of twenty-eight submerged nuclear submarines. The unseen column moved noiselessly through the ebony water past the twinkling lights of the multitude of freighters, tankers, and bulk carriers big and small that were at Murmansk to take or deliver cargoes; past the factory ships and trawlers of the fishing fleet in port to discharge its frozen cargo; past busy shipyards. The run north from Murmansk down the Kola Fjord to the Barents Sea was forty miles, with a transit time of about five hours.

By 2 A.M. on the morning of April 8, with Victor 501 bringing up the rear, the silent line of submarines had left the port of Poliarnyi astern. An hour later, well out to sea beyond the entrance to the fjord, Chernavin took his ship down from periscope level to a running depth of 300 feet. The anticipated covering interference had hit his sonar moments after the 501 cleared the fjord. Like all his fellow submarine captains, Chernavin would have to navigate without being able to "see" until the sonar interference stopped. Furthermore, he expected he would not surface for several weeks. In fact, the 501 would never surface again.

18

8 April   6:07 P.M.

Moscow

General Andropov read the lengthy signal from his senior KGB man in Washington. There was no doubt about it. Chairman Romanov must see it immediately, first because of the urgency and importance of the contents and second, because it had demonstrated clearly the high caliber of the intelligence system that the KGB had developed in the United States. That hundreds of thousands of people in the United States at that moment were reading essentially the same information in the *New York Times* in no measure took away from Andropov's pride in the superior capability of his own agency.

The time was shortly after six in the evening in Moscow. When his aide tracked down the chairman's whereabouts, Andropov himself rang Romanov at his sumptuous riverside dacha in that special wooded area on the outskirts of Moscow reserved for high party officials. Indeed, Andropov's own dacha was in the same area. Perhaps he might stop by with the signal on his way home.

A servant answered, saying that the chairman was at dinner, but Romanov had heard the call and came on the line himself when advised that it was Andropov calling. He and Tania were just finishing dinner. Tania's name raised in Andropov's mind the image of a most beautiful woman. Some ten years younger than her husband, she bore a startling resemblance to a movie star of Andropov's youth, the exquisite Swedish beauty, Greta Garbo. Even at his advanced age, the head of the KGB had in no way lost his appraising eye for a fine-looking woman. Yes, a visit to the Romanov dacha, brief though it would be, would be well worthwhile, simply for the opportunity to be with the charming Tania before he went home to his own dumpy wife.

Twenty minutes later, he was at the white-linen-covered table of the family dining room of the Romanov dacha. It was in that richly paneled, intimate room that the Romanovs took supper together when they were not entertaining. That evening its intimacy was enhanced by glowing candles glittering off sparkling silverware, gold-encrusted plates and crystal wine goblets. The glasses were filled with Romanov's special sparkling rosé, an after-dinner delicacy that he sometimes preferred to the biting, smooth Courvoisier cognac with which he usually took his single Havana cigar of the day. Seated between the couple, twirling his goblet of wine, Andropov talked with the lovely Tania. They discussed the escalating crisis with the Americans, about which she proved fully knowledgeable, while Romanov, puffing occasionally on his cigar and taking a sip of wine, concentrated totally on the message which he read in the flickering light of the flames from the three-pointed candelabra. Perching his gold-rimmed half glasses on the bridge of his nose, his mind soaked up the KGB signal from Washington. It was dated that day, April 8:

KGB operatives report the departure of U.S.-Pakistan Task Force (PTF) sea lift. Elements comprise commandeered passenger ships carrying troops; amphibious cargo, transport dock landing, and tank landing ships; also supporting ammunition, combat stores, hospital, replenishment, and repair ships; plus recently acquired container ships. All PTF vessels left port between 0600 and 1100 hours local time departing from Mayport, Florida; Charleston, South Carolina; Norfolk, Virginia; Little Creek, Virginia; Brooklyn, New York; Newport, Rhode Island; and Boston, Massachusetts.

All elements PTF expected to rendezvous off Bermuda to proceed in convoy to Karachi, escorted by two multi-purpose and two ASW [antisubmarine warfare] aircraft carriers, ten destroyers, and ten frigates.

PTF carrying three infantry, and one armored division plus the 25th Infantry Division from Pacific Command's reserve in Hawaii, plus all tanks, vehicles, supporting equipment, and supplies. Estimate 100,000 troops in PTF sea lift. Estimated arrival time off Pakistan: May 6.

Commencing May 7 concurrent with first landings in Karachi, U.S. will also commence airlift of 82nd Airborne Division, plus two 1,800-man Marine battalions to strategic inland points along Pakistan borders with Afghanistan and Iran. 82nd Airborne has 16,000 men, 50 light reconnaissance tanks and approximately 100 helicopters, 33 of them mounting anti-tank missiles.

Twenty-six fighter/attack squadrons of Tactical Air Command (TAC) earmarked for PTF to deploy as soon as support facilities available after initial landings. Until arrival TAC squadrons aircraft from Indian Ocean Fifth Fleet augmented by convoy escort carriers will provide air support.

Detailed information on identity all units in PTF will follow.

Chairman Romanov handed the message to Andropov saying, "Let Tania take a look at that."

As the KGB chief gave the document to her, Romanov slipped off his glasses, contemplated his half-smoked cigar, and topped off the goblet of wine. "You have to hand it to the Americans, Yu. They've pulled their task force together and put it to sea in three weeks. That's not bad for an ad hoc operation."

Andropov grunted. "Ad hoc is right. The Americans never cease to amaze me with their inability to plan ahead for this sort of crisis. They seem to be completely incapable of doing any strategic long-term planning."

"Perhaps," Romanov suggested, "that is because they change their leadership every four years—or eight—and the president and his administration are always worried about the next election. Whereas our system is built for stability. The same people stay in the Politburo, some of them, such as Brezhnev and Suslov and, of course, Gromyko, for over two decades."

"Indeed that may be one of the reasons," Andropov agreed, lifting his glass to look at the perfection of the ruby colored wine against the flame of the nearest candle. "But what I'm talking about, Grigori, is that in place of intelligent long-range strategic planning they place reaction. That's the nature of the American people. It's the nature of their government, and, therefore, it's the nature of their military. In the last two and a half decades, while we were building our navy—Gorshkov was doing it—into the largest and most powerful in the world, the American navy has declined from some 900 ships to fewer than 500. Its reserve fleet is down from over two thousand ships to about 300, many of them ready for the scrapyard. If that wasn't enough, their bases around the world have gone from a hundred down to fewer than thirty."

"To our advantage," Tania commented. She had finished reading the message.

"To our advantage, indeed. And we will press that advantage at every turn. Let me give you another example. When Carter threatened to use military force to keep us out of the Persian Gulf, the American Joint Chiefs of Staff and the defence secretary told him that about the only force they could deploy quickly into the Persian Gulf was their Airborne Division, the 82nd. It's mentioned in the signal." He pointed toward the document on the table in front of

Tania. "On the recommendations of the Joint Chiefs of Staff, the secretary proposed putting together a seven-ship force loaded with combat equipment, mothballed but ready to go on short notice—tanks, trucks, guns, that sort of thing. That logistics force was to be positioned at Diego Garcia from which it could sail . . ."

"Where is Diego Garcia?" Tania asked.

"It's an American base on a British island about a thousand miles south of India. It would be about a five-day sail from there to the Persian Gulf to rendezvous with combat troops airlifted in, their so-called Rapid Deployment Force. Their target was to be able to get 13,000 men and 300 tanks into the Persian Gulf on a week's notice. What happened? They put three ships at Diego Garcia. They're still there, totally vulnerable to our submarines. And the rapid deployment force was a dream, just a dream. So, today, again to our great advantage," he acknowledged, "the Americans have had to throw together an ad hoc task force, get it to sea and spend twenty-eight days getting it to Pakistan, let alone ashore."

Romanov asked his wife, "Could I see the message again, please?"

When he had it in front of him, he checked one point on the first page and then asked Andropov, "When will our submarines start tracking them?"

"Smirnov tells me that the first contact will be made at their rendezvous point near Bermuda. The tracking process, both by submarine and satellite, will begin at that location. By the time the Americans round the Cape of Good Hope—they will stay well south of it to keep out of the tanker lanes, and going north in the Indian Ocean they will stay well to the east—by that time we should have twenty-five to thirty submarines tracking them."

The chairman nodded silent approval.

He asked, "What about the OKEAN exercise? Will Smirnov move his Atlantic fleet down to intercept?"

"No. OKEAN begins on the fifteenth of April, as you know. According to my plan," he paused to emphasize the word *my*, "all of our serviceable submarines have moved out of the Kola Peninsula between the third and the seventh under the SONINT interference cover. The last left yesterday. They should be south of the NATO coverage area, the Tropic of Cancer, by the fourteenth or fifteenth. The Atlantic OKEAN fleet will carry out its exercises in that area for the following two weeks. Smirnov wants to keep them there as a decoy to the satellites or any snooping American or British surveillance ships that cross the Tropic of Cancer on their own. In the meantime, the major part of our submarine force will deploy to their stations in the South Atlantic and the Indian Ocean. On the other hand, our Indian Ocean OKEAN attacking and defending fleets are scheduled to leave the Gulf of Aden a week from now. They will conduct coordinated naval and air exercises within seeing range of the American Fifth Fleet and the British flotilla to show them that we have powerful muscle. Then they will turn south to intercept the American task force, to give it some expert harassment during the last four or five days of its approach to Pakistan."

Romanov was pleased. He rammed his cigar butt into a silver ashtray, exclaiming, "Excellent! But if the Andropov Plan works . . ."

The KGB head preened slightly at the mention of his scheme.

"If it works, on May Day there won't be any American task force approaching Pakistan to harass, will there, Yu?"

With a smug smile General Andropov could not but agree. "No, sir, there will not!"

Her glass raised on high, Tania made a simple toast. "Let's drink to that."

Her husband, one of the two most powerful men in the world, and his proud minister enthusiastically stood, touched their glasses to each other's and hers as Grigori Romanov toasted, "To the Andropov Plan. To its glorious success!"

19

1-10 April
Port of Manama, Bahrain
and Gulf of Aden

The lethal mines of Lieutenant-Colonel Said Kassem and his PLO team had been planted on the ten hulls of the chosen supertankers of Mina-al-Ahmadi on the night of March 31. By the evening of the next day, the *Mecca* was docked in the Port of Manama, the bustling capital of the island nation of Bahrain, taking on a cargo of aluminum ingots consigned to Aden for transshipment. The Palestinians, grieving for their lost comrade and concerned that the *Mecca*'s untrustworthy crew members should not be given a chance to slip ashore to pass information about the mining to the authorities, had forbidden any of the crew to leave the ship or talk to the local stevedores loading the old freighter.

The loading had gone rapidly and the *Mecca* left Bahrain immediately after the cargo was on board, making her way out of port eastward beyond Muharraq Island and past the enormous Arab shipbuilding and repair yard with its massive dry docks, big enough to hold and repair the largest supertankers afloat.

On April 8, when the *Mecca* was three days sail away

from Aden, Said informed Captain Rashid that after she discharged her cargo at Aden, she would then have to sail back around the Horn of Africa and south down the Indian Ocean to Durban. He hastened to add that these arrangements had been made by Arafat with the ship's owners in Beirut.

Furthermore, the captain as well as the crew would be paid a substantial bonus for making the long voyage to South Africa. Captain Rashid was not disturbed by the change of plans. After all, he was in the freighter business for the purpose of making money. So long as he and his owners and crew were being paid, he would take the *Mecca* anywhere. Said had informed him of the change of plans before they arrived at Aden, so Rashid could communicate with the ship's agents at that port in order to arrange a cargo for the run down the African coast. Hassan had made the VHF radio transmitter temporarily serviceable. The message was passed to Aden through the harbormaster at Merbat on the south coast of Oman, as the *Mecca* passed abeam of that port some ten miles off shore.

Splendid had been patrolling the Gulf of Aden for nine days. When she had arrived at her station in the fifty-mile-wide stretch of the gulf between the northeast tip of Somalia and the shores of South Yemen, Commander Leach had elected to use a racetrack pattern for his patrol. The pattern changed from a port racetrack to a starboard one at the beginning of each watch.

When setting up his patrol pattern, Leach had been concerned by the fact that, while the gulf was about fifty miles wide, only twenty-six miles of it were in international waters. If he went closer than twelve miles from shore to the north or south he would be in the territorial waters of South Yemen or Somalia and would be subject to arrest or to being driven off with whatever force was available to the offended nation.

The navigating officer had also pointed out to him that the water was extremely shallow at the northern end of the proposed racetrack pattern. The depth was no more than a hundred feet. There would be little maneuvering room for a vessel as large as *Splendid*. She was some fifty-five feet high from her rounded bottom to the top of her tower. When her periscope was up, another twenty-five feet were added. In such shallow waters the submarine would be highly vulnerable.

Within twenty-four hours of taking up her slow-moving station at the mouth of the gulf, *Splendid* and her crew had settled down to a routine that was to last for days. During her ponderous moves back and forth across the gulf, Leach kept his boat at periscope level, popping his glass eye up over the surface for a good look at whatever was going by, whenever the sonar or radar watchkeepers indicated that a passing vessel was at its closest range. Occasionally, in order to take a photograph of an inbound Red Navy ship at close range, he would accelerate *Splendid* temporarily to get as close as possible to the vessel. At the right moment up would go the search periscope and the photographs would be taken quickly. Immediately the periscope would disappear below the surface, having been duly noted by the radar operators on the photographed vessel. The sonar operators of the photographed ship, their equipment having failed to pick up the *Splendid* at her slow rate of three knots, would, at the time of her acceleration, have been startled to find a target bearing down on them from nowhere, which then disappeared from their screens as quickly as it had appeared.

Thirty seconds before the exact minute assigned for *Splendid*'s reports to the admiral's flagship, her radar mast with its radio antenna would appear above the surface for the transmission to be made. At such close range to the flotilla and being under direct operational control of its flag officer, it was necessary for Pots and his team to maintain round the clock, ears-on, alert monitoring of the flotilla's operating radio frequencies. All signals made for the *Splendid* during her period on the station had to be picked up. There could be no lapses. There were only a few messages. There were no lapses.

Pots' team of watchkeepers were able to monitor all

the messages passing around the Royal Navy flotilla and its exchanges with the U.S. fleet. Leach was therefore able to keep abreast of what was going on. Every morning the captain had the communications officer brief him and the first lieutenant, and as many off-watch officers as wished to sit in, on the flotilla messages that had been monitored. Not all of them, of course, but those that the communications officer considered to be the most relevant and important.

The Victor II Soviet submarine still maintained her surveillance station on *Splendid* by pinging at her from time to time with active sonar. The Russian boat kept her position just to the west of the British ship's racetrack course. The Victor, operating at three knots, the same speed as *Splendid*, was also noiseless. The British ship reciprocated by occasionally driving her pinging active sonar waves out to bounce off the Red sub and return. It was done to confirm that the other was still there and pinpoint where she was.

Midmorning on April 9, as *Splendid* was reaching the northern turning point of one of her countless patrol runs across the Gulf of Aden, sonar reported, "Contact. 075, 11,000 yards and closing. Course 265. Making about ten knots. Sounds like some kind of a freighter." Then he added, "In forty-five minutes we should both be at the same place."

In his bunk, reading a sex-filled mystery paperback, Marcus Leach listened to the report. He decided that for amusement he would take a look at the freighter as she passed by. It would be worth a laugh to scare the hell out of her crew by sticking the periscope up right under their noses. He set the alarm on his wrist watch for forty minutes ahead and went back to his stimulating reading.

Thus at 0936 hours GMT in the sunny morning of the ninth of April, a periscope suddenly appeared about thirty degrees off the port bow and a hundred yards south of the *Mecca*.

The captain of the submarine would have been disappointed if he had realized that he had not startled the captain of the ancient freighter. The powerful magnifying lenses of the attack periscope clearly picked up the image of the weatherbeaten old captain as he stood on the port wing of his bridge, eyes focused nonchalantly on the shiny submarine eye watching him. No, he wasn't startled. A sailor who has spent a lifetime on the Mediterranean has also had a lifetime of perceiving periscopes and, in so doing, making rude gestures at them. Which is what Captain Rashid did, his hand clenched, knuckles away from his face and two fingers making a V sign as he lifted his fist upward several times, making one of the world's most universally recognized obscene gestures.

At the operating end of the periscope, Marcus Leach laughed. "Up yours too, captain!"

Watching the stern of the battered ship move westward, Leach finally caught the word painted on her fantail. So it was that the name *Mecca* was recorded in the log of the *Splendid* for the first time. She would again be recorded on the eleventh of April as she steamed out of the gulf.

What was not recorded in that log was what was not known: that the fate of the *Splendid* was linked to the nondescript *Mecca* and three of the men aboard her.

The *Mecca* put into Aden on the morning of April 10. The turnaround took a full day. The agent had obtained a cargo of baled cotton. Between the discharging of the ingots, the loading of the cotton, the bunkering to top up fuel tanks, the taking on of water and provisions, the time requirement was such that it was impossible to get under way until the morning of April 11. The departure was further delayed because Said refused to let the captain take the ship into dock. As at Bahrain, Said had to keep the crew on board and away from any opportunity to pass information about the mined tankers. So the *Mecca* was secured in the inner harbor to a buoy and dolphin berth connected to shore by submarine pipeline for bunkering purposes. A procession of vessels—a water barge and several small craft loaded with provisions—made their way to and from the *Mecca* and the shore. Included in the supplies which the captain had requisitioned through the agent was a set of marine charts that would take him south into waters he had never sailed before. They would take him safely down the steaming coast of Africa, parallel to but away from the busy shipping lanes used by the endless procession of crude oil and petroleum supertankers plying between the Arabian Gulf and ports in Western Europe and North America.

For Nabil, the prohibition against going ashore at Aden was enough, to put him over the brink. He had witnessed the launch of the PLO mining operation against the supertankers. As part of *Mecca*'s crew, was he implicated? Nabil had also been shaken by the death of Maan.

The crew had been confined to ship at Bahrain. There had been the jolting, close-in appearance of a threatening periscope. Now there was the Aden situation and on top of that the news that the PLO would force the *Mecca* to sail down to Durban. Nabil was ready to quit. He'd had enough. He told Rashid so.

"I understand, I understand." The captain was sympathetic. "But I can tell you, Nabil, Said won't let you off this ship. He can't afford to. You know too much. I haven't told you this—they're giving us a bonus to do the Durban trip."

Nabil's sullen expression vanished instantly.

"A bonus! How much?"

"How does three months' pay sound?"

A broad, toothy smile lit up the Egyptian's face.

Rashid never ceased to be amazed by what money could do.

20

8:23 GMT   12:23 P.M. Local Time
Gulf of Aden

At 0823 hours GMT on April 15, Captain Leach was in *Splendid*'s wardroom taking early breakfast when the broadcast loudspeaker on the bulkhead behind him made a clicking, scratching noise that alerted him.

"Captain, this is sonar." The excited voice of the usually placid communications officer reported, "Contact due west. I classify what looks like the whole goddamned Russian navy, range forty-five miles, closing. They're steaming eastbound in a column, sir. There are four abreast in the lead."

Leach banged down his knife and fork. In a few strides he was in the sonar room, his mouth agape at the bright white dots entering the dancing sonar screen on its left side, moving steadily in the direction of the white dot at its center—the position of *Splendid* herself as she moved northward in her patrol track.

In the control room he called for Pots on the double. A message was made to the flag officer reporting the situation. "Pilot, when will the vanguard be here, your best ETA?"

The reply was immediate. "Two hours five minutes, sir, give or take five."

"Right." Leach's eyes went up to the clock. "Estimate vanguard our position at 10:30 Zulu," he added to the message.

By 10:00 GMT the approaching Russian fleet was painted on the sonar. Their acoustic signatures had been identified by the computer. But seeing them on the sonar screen was no match for the sight of their majestic advance up the gulf under a clear blue sky across flat, azure waters chopped slightly by a spanking breeze. Leach's search periscope was up, its powerful magnifying lenses drawing the vision of the huge fleet almost on top of him. He could see the nuclear-powered aircraft carriers *Minsk* and *Kharkov*, each with its twelve STOL Forger fighters and a clutch of huge Hormone helicopters on its decks.

On each flank of the front line rode two Kashin class destroyers, the *Skory* on the port and the *Strogy* on the starboard. Out ahead of the line swarmed a dozen Hormone helicopters ranging back and forth at, Leach estimated, about 500 feet. As he watched, two of them made for *Splendid*'s location. They knew where she was. They had picked up her periscope and radar mast on their own radars. Furthermore, their crews would be able to see her black bulk outlined just below the surface of the clear Aden water.

Splendid had just completed her southbound turn at the northern end of her track. Leach had brought his craft to a halt to watch the oncoming procession. She sat in only 150 feet of water, her bottom just 70 feet off the floor of the Gulf of Aden. She had, therefore, no depth maneuvering room. On the other hand, Leach was satisfied she wouldn't need it. They were in international waters, albeit it only a few hundred yards outside Yemen's territorial waters, as Pilot confirmed. A state of hostilities did not exist between the United Kingdom and the Soviet Union. He was standing well north of the track the Soviet fleet was making. For those reasons he believed he had no cause to be concerned about being in such shallow water. On the other hand he remembered the admiral's signal that the Russian bear was showing his teeth.

It was time to let his crew share in the sight. After all they had come a long way and had endured the boring agonies of the Aden patrol.

"Coxswain?"

"Sir." It seemed that the coxswain was at his elbow in a split second.

Leach took his face away from the eye piece. "I want all the ratings to see this."

The coxswain's eyebrows shot up. "All of them, sir?"

"That's right, all eighty-four of them. And if you're quick about it, you too. You've got ten minutes to do it. Just a few seconds for each man. Then I'll run the officers through."

In eleven minutes and fifteen seconds flat every member of the crew of *Splendid* had had a short peek at the magnificent, stately line of the mighty Red Navy fleet steaming down the Gulf of Aden, an eight-mile-long column of ships gleaming gray-white in the morning sun. Behind the first line came the 30,000-ton cruiser, the *Khirov*, the Soviet's first nuclear-powered fighting surface ship. Its new generation surface-to-surface and surface-to-air missiles, its two large guns, its antiaircraft cannon submarine tracking rockets, and torpedos bristled on its decks and superstructure. At the sides of the *Khirov* were a new Kresta III cruiser, the helicopter cruiser *Leningrad*, and one of the first of the Sovietsky Soyuz class of cruiser, just commissioned. Following in the line were destroyers of the Kashin class, Krivak frigates, Tarantul missile corvettes, and several of the smaller Nanuchka missile ships. Bringing up the rear of the seemingly endless column were the replenishment and cargo vessels, among them the tanker *Boris Chilkin*.

After he had had his view through the periscope, the last man to look asked his captain, "Where do you think their attack submarines are?"

"Out in the Arabian Sea or somewhere in the Indian Ocean waiting for them. They wouldn't have come down through the Suez." Leach knew that three-quarters of the advancing Russian armada had made its way from the Soviet's northern bases south through the Atlantic, then east through the Mediterranean and down the Suez Canal. Some elements had come in from the Pacific, it was true, but the bulk had come from the Red Navy's northern and Mediterranean fleets.

Leach estimated that the northernmost of the four ships in the front line would pass about one mile immediately south of *Splendid*. He would use the ship's camera to take as many pictures as he could as the procession marched past. For a moment he toyed with the thought of surfacing but to do so would be to go against the order of the admiral. That one had come in just after they had taken up their station. It was almost as an afterthought on the flag officer's part. Leach's periscope was trained on the first line of ships, now about a mile west of his patrol line steaming at twenty knots.

A shot of adrenalin moved into Leach's system when he heard sonar watchkeeper Pratt's voice say, "Contact. Four small ships have moved out of the column at the far end of it, sir. They're moving in line astern traveling fast closing at thirty knots. They're heading directly for us, range three miles. Bearing 065."

"Have you got them, radar?"

"Aye, sir."

As he was swinging his periscope toward the oncoming craft he barked, "What are they?"

"Code signature is Grisha class."

"Christ!" exclaimed Leach. The Grishas were real trouble. The Russians called them *maly protivolodochny korabl*, meaning small antisubmarine ships. They carried four torpedo tubes with twenty-one torpedoes on board. Even though they were described as small they were, at 236 feet, almost as long as *Splendid* and, like her, fast.

What the hell were they up to? Peering through the periscope he caught the V of white foam from the lead Grisha's sharp, pitched-up bow cutting through the water, and behind it guns, rockets, and the twirling radar on the short tower bridge amidships. Behind her he could see hints of the three more following in line astern.

"Range one mile, sir."

The captain was still puzzled. Again, what were they up to? Were they going to attack with rockets or depth charges or torpedos? If so, *Splendid* was dead. But there was no war on. Killing *Splendid* would start one. They could ram her and then claim she had been in South Yemen territorial waters. But the Grishas were too small, too shallow in draft to ram his ship at periscope depth; and even if they could ram they would destroy themselves.

It had to be a practice run. It was a chance for those lethal antisubmarine craft to exercise their skills. That was it, Leach decided.

"Search periscope down. Up attack periscope and give me only two feet above the tower. Repeat—the tower. Radar mast down." He wanted to watch the Grishas from the underside on their run in. Putting the attack periscope up only two feet would still give them plenty of clearance.

"Search periscope down. Attack periscope two feet above the tower. Radar mast down, sir."

Leach could hear the rumblings of the Grishas' powerful engines growing steadily louder. Suddenly the noise dropped off almost completely. From the sonar room came the report. "They've reduced speed, sir. Five knots. They're still in line astern about a hundred feet apart. They're pinging us . . . they're dropping something off their sterns. Can't tell what it is, sir."

Strange, thought the captain. His eyes were glued to the periscope, its lens looking starboard and back to the northwest. A Soviet ship was coming in on his stern. Yes, there was the belly of the first craft.

"Range fifty yards, sir."

Leach's eyes followed the long, narrow line of the keel of the first approaching Grisha. His periscope was tilted upwards, almost vertical. As the stern and the rudder and turning twin screws passed over, Leach saw something he had never before seen. Just under the surface, the Soviet warship was towing a boom about thirty feet wide. At six-foot intervals along the boom were what looked like heavy steel cables that curved out and down like bows behind the vessel as they were being pulled through the water. Leach moved his periscope from the near-vertical to the horizontal as he tracked the cables down deeper and deeper into the darkening water. The cables were coming closer and closer to his ship. There at even level with the periscope he saw the first sharp-pointed, massive grappling hooks attached to the cables. Quickly he moved the periscope to its maximum downward facing position. Below in the murk he could see huge cement weights, six of them, holding the cables down moving at a level well below the bottom of the submarine. He could scarcely believe his eyes.

"Down periscope and be quick about it!" he shouted. "They're going to grapple us! Telegraph engines full ahead!"

The first singing of the cables against the round smooth hull of the submarine had started just as the periscope hit the bottom of its well and the first surge of *Splendid's* propeller hummed through the submarine.

The whistling of the cables rubbing against the metal was replaced by the clanging of heavy metal as the first set of grappling hooks made their way up the side of the ship at the stern. Suddenly the noise stopped. At the same instant the control wheel in the planesman's hand moved a full turn to the left and toward his chest. He was powerless to prevent the shifting of the wheel.

"The wheel, sir! The wheel!" From behind him the officer of the watch leaned forward to join him in attempting to straighten up the wheel and shove it forward. It was locked.

Christ, they've got the stern hydroplane and the rudder, Leach thought.

The thrust of the submarine's motor was beginning to move her forward when the sudden, full-power roar of the Grisha's twin engines burst through *Splendid's* hull. In an instant the drive of the Russian ship, pulling the submarine's stern to port, met the forward thrust of *Splendid* under full power, forcing the two straining vessels into a straight line, the submarine pointing south, the Grisha on the surface pointing north. Her stern was almost under water, pulled down by the weight and thrust of *Splendid* and her own propelling, powerful screws. Something had to give.

On the surface, the other three Grishas, their grappling gear at the ready, stood off to the west a hundred yards away. Their crew members gaped at the scene in front of them as their lead ship struggled to overcome the unseen submarine like a fishing vessel trying to overpower a large whale.

With a ripping, tearing sound and the screech of metal forcibly being parted from other metal, the stern davits of the ship to which the cable boom was attached gave way, taking with them the entire stern plate of the vessel. Like a surfboard flat in the water the stern plate took off in a southward direction. It disappeared under the waves as *Splendid*, loose from the clutches of her would-be captor, accelerated through the shallow water, her propeller unimpeded. She trailed behind her the prickly grappling hooks, cables, boom and the twirling stern plate of the Grisha.

In her wake on the surface, the sixty members of the damaged Grisha's crew were preparing to abandon ship as the sea flooded into her aft section. The stunned captains of the other three antisubmarine craft abandoned the chase in favor of rescuing their comrades from their sinking sister ship.

In *Splendid*, the coxswain himself was behind the control wheel. The captain and the first lieutenant hovered anxiously over him. With the wheel hard over to the left and back, the first move of the freed boat was to port. The coxswain fought to bring the wheel around to the right and forward. The captain, standing to his right, helped turn the wheel while the first lieutenant from the left and behind shoved forward on it. Under the pressure it began to turn slowly. Then in an instant the wheel was turning normally. The rudder was free and so were the hydroplanes. The coxswain shoved the wheel forward just in time to prevent the huge craft from leaping out of the water. Instead, the top of her tower porpoised a hundred yards south of the milling Grishas and disappeared again under the comforting blanket of the deepening gulf toward the last of the ships in the Soviet column. The lead ships of that mighty line steamed unwaveringly toward the entrance to the Arabian Gulf where the American Fifth Fleet and the Second British Flotilla awaited them.

21

15 April   6:45 A.M.
The White House
Washington, D.C.

Soon after he moved into the White House, John Hansen decided that he would use the president's study as his main workroom. He needed a place where he could leave files and documents, publications and books, anything he was using, on top of his desk or on the tables. He would use the Oval Office in the west wing for the never ending official and formal meetings with heads of state, cabinet members, ambassadors, congressional leaders, delegations of plain ordinary folks, and for the signing of legislation. The desk in the Oval Office was always clear, whereas the desk in the study, a similarly oval-shaped room, was always cluttered.

The president's study was conveniently situated in the family quarters of the White House on its second floor. At the southwest corner of the family quarters was the suite of bedrooms. A door led from the main bedroom directly to the east into the study. Because of its accessibility, John and Judith Hansen both used it as part of their living area as well as a work place for John. It was also a room in which he could have informal working meetings with his own staff or to have department heads in for discussions or briefings. Hansen felt more at home there than in any other part of the White House.

On Monday, April 15, when the early golden rays of the morning sun filtered through the tall, arched windows in the curved bay of the study, the president was at his desk still dressed in pajamas, dressing gown and slippers. He was sipping his first cup of decaffeinated coffee while absorbing the front page of the *New York Times*. He always believed there was no better way of staying aware of what was going on in the country than religiously reading the *Times* and the *Washington Post*. The *Post* would be next.

For the week ahead, the working hours of every day were booked. Two meetings were scheduled of the executive committee of the National Security Council, one for Tuesday and another for Friday. It was essential to keep them abreast of the developing confrontation with Romanov. The meetings provided up-to-the-minute briefings on the CIA's information and assessment of the Soviet Union's political and military activity, its Eastern Bloc satellites, the countries of the Persian Gulf and the Middle East, as well as the active hot spots in Africa where the Cubans were still playing their intervention games on behalf of their Soviet masters.

At its meeting the previous Friday, the executive committee had been briefed on several matters. The first was the progress of the huge convoy of American naval and merchant ships, the biggest assembly of American vessels to be put to sea since World War II. The main event during the week of April 8 was the departure of the task force for Pakistan. Bringing the men, equipment, ships, and supplies together over the three-week period from March 15 had been a monumental undertaking on the part of the Pentagon. The military hierarchy coordinated all the supporting government departments and the key American shipping firms that could provide the passenger ships and freighters needed to augment the navy's resources. The Pentagon people had worked day and night. Selected reserve army and air force units across the country were put on active service, some of them to participate in the task force itself and others to take the places of regular units and personnel designated to go to Pakistan. During the organization period, the president had put unrelenting pressure on the Pentagon and the secretaries of the various departments. In addition, he personally leaned on the leaders of the major industries which would provide the supply of food, fuel, ships, equipment, and transportation facilities to carry goods to the task force's embarkation points up and down the east coast.

Hansen's pursuit of support for the task force had been ruthless and relentless. The president had told the Soviets and the world that the American armed forces would be landing in Pakistan on May 7, both by sea and air. It had been decreed as a national goal and objective by the leader of the United States, the most powerful nation on earth, a nation that had rallied behind its leader's statement of a national purpose when John Kennedy said it would put a man on the moon. America would perform. That spirit was made evident, not only in editorials of the nation's media, but by the expeditious ratification by Congress of the Pakistan agreement. On March 25 it received the near unanimous approval of both the Senate and House and with little bickering over the contents of the document. Hansen had received word shortly after meeting with the Soviet ambassador, Kuznetsov, when he handed the ancient Soviet diplomat his reply to Romanov's belligerent note of March 16.

In scenes reminiscent of departures in World Wars I and II, with bands playing, flags flying, and families and friends standing on the docks waving goodbye to soldiers departing on troop ships, the warships, transports, and other vessels of the task force left the harbors along the eastern seaboard amidst the hooting signals of hundreds of craft and the dipping of flags in salute. The force was on its way exactly on schedule. It left behind a nation galvanized for the demanding, costly chore of resupplying and maintaining that force across thousands of miles of ocean infested by Soviet submarines and surface surveillance warships.

The navy could not tell the president where the Soviet submarines were located in the Atlantic because the Russians had reactivated their sonar interference system, SONINT, on April 3. SONINT had stopped operating the day before—April 14. The onshore computers, hooked by cable to the NATO and U.S. sonar nets on the bottom of the North Atlantic, quickly spewed out the location and type of the seventy-eight Russian submarines operating in that ocean. The navy could not account for the other twenty-two that were in the North Atlantic the day SONINT was reactivated. They could have returned to their bases.

"Or they could have moved into the South Atlantic beyond NATO jurisdiction, where we don't have a sonar system," the president had interjected when Defense Secretary Robert Levy called to bring him up-to-date, late in the afternoon of the fourteenth.

Levy agreed. "That's right, we really don't know where the hell they are. My guess is we'll find them shadowing the task force. We should be getting reports from the flagship of the escort anytime now. It looks as though they're set to begin their OKEAN exercise, probably on the fifteenth. As you know, they've been assembling in the South Atlantic off Senegal."

"South of the Tropic of Cancer?"

"That's right, Mr. President. And in the Indian Ocean they're assembling in the Gulf of Aden. The defending fleet there is about 300 miles southwest of Bombay. In the Pacific, their attack fleet is to the east of the Mariana Islands and the defending fleet is about one hundred miles west of Wake Island."

"Where is the defending fleet in the Atlantic?"

"It's steaming southbound off the Canary Islands. When the exercise begins, if past performances are any indication, the attack fleets, with air support from their own carriers plus big long-range antisubmarine aircraft, will launch coordinated, simultaneous attacks against the defending fleets in the Atlantic, Indian Ocean, and the Pacific. The whole thing will be run from Moscow by Admiral Smirnov himself."

"What about their submarines in port? What's the satellite count on those?"

"They tell me the satellite photographs show that everything's normal. The majority, the usual number, are tied up at their bases on the Baltic and the Kola Peninsula. Don't worry, Mr. President, we're keeping an eagle eye on that situation." He added, "But I'd hate to think what 381 of those things could do if they were turned loose."

The president agreed. "It boggles the mind. The fact is they've got them, Robert. They've built them for a reason. Some to lob nuclear ballistic missiles at us from hard-to-find moving platforms. But most of them are for destroying ships—other submarines, surface ships, freighters, anything that moves on the high seas, particularly the ones that worry me most, the tankers that carry the crude oil."

The report he had requested from GAO on the consequences of a crude oil cut-off to North American and Western Europe had been delivered to him just before he left for Camp David en route to Diego Garcia. Even though it was only a preliminary rough cut at the answer, it had shaken him badly when he read it. He was even more shaken when he went through the final in-depth report that arrived on his desk on April 11, the same day the United Nations General Assembly dealt with the Pakistan agreement. The report could not have painted a blacker picture. When he had finished reading it, he could not help but agree with the conclusion: that for Western Europe and the United States a complete cut-off of crude oil for an extended period beyond thirty days would have disastrous consequences for the economy, culture, and civilization of the Western world. It would be a calamity second only to an all-out nuclear attack. The report had only reinforced his determination to go into Pakistan. From that all-important launching area he could defend the oil-producing nations of the Persian Gulf if need be. He had ordered the final GAO crude oil cut-off report to be circulated among the members of the executive committee of the National Security Council. It was essential that every one of them should have a full understanding of what it said about the potential for catastrophe if America were once again to back down from the Soviets who threatened the Persian Gulf.

As the president had expected, the Russians were putting on diplomatic and propaganda pressures, everything in their arsenal, to force Hansen to stay out of Pakistan. On Thursday, April 11, 112 members of the General Assembly of the United Nations had voted in favor of the Soviet-sponsored resolution condemning the U.S.-Pakistan agreement on the grounds that the entry of United States forces into Pakistan would constitute a grave and unacceptable threat to world peace. In addition to the censure, the resolution demanded that the United States recall its task force. President Hansen had expected the Soviets to take their case to the United Nations. Furthermore, he expected the result. In no way did it deflect him from his determined course of action.

The president took a sip of coffee and turned to the second page of the *New York Times*, his eyes quickly running over each of the columns of interest to him. He had developed an excellent speed reading technique years before when the volume of paper he had to cope with reached the saturation point. At the bottom of the page was a small article which he almost missed. The headline was "General Critical of Pakistan Plan." Hansen couldn't believe what he was reading.

General Glen Young, chairman of the Joint Chiefs of Staff, said in a speech last night that there were high risks in sending a military task force to Pakistan. Young said that it would be impossible to support the task force for more than thirty days. The logistical problems of moving material to support a 120,000-man force 13,000 miles away from the United States could be beyond the capacity of the available American merchant fleet. Young had expressed his objections when the president decided to enter into negotiations with Pakistan.

In five minutes the president had the chairman of the Joint Chiefs of Staff on the telephone. He had found him at home.

"General Young, have you seen the *New York Times* this morning?"

"No sir, I haven't," the startled general replied.

"Let me read it to you." When the president had finished, he demanded, "Is that report correct, general?"

"It's fairly accurate, but the quote wasn't from my text, Mr. President. It was in a question-and-answer period. As you know, I put forward those objections right from the very beginning . . ."

"And I overrode them, general! I want you to understand one thing. I am the commander in chief of the armed forces of the United States of America and I'm *your* commander. I heard your opinion and I decided to take a course of action that goes against it. When I give you an order that's the end of the matter. You obey the order!"

At the other end of the line Young's voice was remarkably cool. "I did obey your order, Mr. President, even though I disagreed with it."

Young was right, he had done what he was told.

"What about your colleagues? What do they think?"

"They're with me. But we're professionals, Mr. President. We do as we're told. You also have to keep one other thing in mind. We're Americans. We're just as concerned as you are about freedom and democracy and the security and safety of the American people. Apart from yourself, Mr. President, no other four people in the country have any higher responsibility than we do in that regard."

Hansen had to agree. "I can't quarrel with that. But there's one thing you haven't mentioned, general, perhaps two. One is the matter of loyalty. That's the least I can expect, as the commander in chief, from you and the chiefs of staff, every one of them. The second is that I expect you to keep your mouth shut publicly about my decisions with which you don't agree. You know the rule better than I do, general. The elected politicians run this country, make the decisions. You in the military do what you're told. If you want to criticize me in public, particularly about a matter as important as Pakistan . . . Let me put it another way. I'll be as direct as I can. The next time you go public against me, I will expect your resignation." Hansen's voice was cold with fury.

That fury was increased by the arrogance and the tone of his chairman of the Joint Chiefs of Staff. "Next time it will be there in advance, Mr. President."

22

19 April

Diego Garcia

It had taken *Splendid* four days to reach the island of Diego Garcia after her encounter with the vicious Grisha. She arrived at the largest of the islands in the Chagos Archipelago in the late afternoon of April 18 after a submerged voyage from the Gulf of Aden.

Immediately she was clear of the Grisha, Leach had made for the lee of Socotra, at the southern edge of the approaches to the gulf. The battered submarine, trailing cables, grappling hooks, and the stern plate of the sunken Russian ship, had reached the island within a few hours. There, in calm water, the senior technical officer, the STD, and his engineering artificers had tackled the cables with blowtorches that functioned just as well in the water as out of it. It had taken them less than three hours to cut and hack their way through the tough, entwining steel cables draped over the hydroplanes and across the fin and rudder sectors.

Fortunately for *Splendid* the four hard, brass, sharp-edged blades of her propeller were turning at full revolutions when the cables from behind the Grisha swung from their line on the port side of the submarine to directly astern at the moment when the power of each ship was pitted one against the other. At that instant those blades had sliced cleanly through all of the taut cables with the exception of two that had cut through the forward edge of the ship's fin just below the top of it. Those two had trailed behind, clear of the propeller, dragging with them the boom and the stern plate of the ill-fated Russian antisubmarine craft. The stern plate, an unusual prize of hardware, was hauled aboard *Splendid* to be kept as a souvenir of the boat's first victory. It had to be cut up into sections so it could be brought inside the ship. It mattered not. It would be patched together later to hang in some place of honor back at Faslane.

Leach stood on the deck of his boat to watch the cable clearing operation and also to take a good look at the damage that had been done.

The long diagonal gash through the skin of the forward edge of the fin near its top could be easily patched, as could the cuts in the forward edge of the starboard hydroplane. What really troubled him were the deep gouges in the leading edges of each of the propeller blades. But he knew they were there the instant he felt the blades of his propeller carving through the cables when *Splendid* extricated herself from the clutches of the Russian ship. Coincidental with the cable severance, an unusual growling noise from the stern section reverberated through the boat. Experience told Leach that the cables had damaged the propeller. There would be gouges and nicks which had thrown the propeller off its delicate balance causing a constant vibration in the shaft at high revolutions. The vibration was uncomfortable at thirty knots. In fact, at that speed the captain thought it was dangerous. But at twenty knots it had diminished to the point where it was almost unnoticeable.

When the engineering crew had finished with cable clearing work, Leach signalled his report to the flagship of the second flotilla. In it he expressed his concern about the propeller and the inability of *Splendid* to operate at speeds

661

above twenty knots without causing severe damage to the bearings of her driveshaft and the gear mechanism locking it to the motor.

The response signal from the admiral congratulated him on his success, noting that "your victory over the Grisha and your escape from the clutches of the Russian fleet are in keeping with the worthy fighting traditions of Nelson and the Royal Navy. My congratulations to you and all the crew of *Splendid*. Proceed to Diego Garcia. Replacement propeller will await your arrival. Installation facilities (U.S.) available to complete screw change. Advise when change made. First Sea Lord signals: 'Pray tell *Splendid* crew proud of splendid action.'"

When *Splendid* sailed on the surface slowly southeast through the main pass to the entrance to the Diego Garcia lagoon through the hot steamy rain of the midafternoon of April 19, the American base commander and his men were ready and waiting for her. Their dry dock was flooded, its gates open. As soon as her main ballast and trim tanks were clear of the last trace of water and she was, therefore, some two hundred tons lighter than her normal diving trim, Leach moved her gradually into the dry dock. She was assisted on her tail by the gentle nudging of a small power boat that, with its heavily padded bow, pushed or pulled at the stern of the *Splendid* as she made her way into the vast rectangular box until she lay directly above the huge steel cradle upon which she would sit when the water was pumped out of the dock.

Before the sea water was drained away from the tube-like hull of the *Splendid*, a hose, carrying an inbound water supply to provide the coolant for the nuclear reactor, was put aboard. Its long line snaked out from the top of the dry dock coupled with a return pipe that would be filled with the discharging coolant water, heated as it passed through the nuclear power plant. In addition, a maze of cables, wires, hoses, and pipes were fed into the body of *Splendid*, giving her life-sustaining power like intravenous tubes implanted into the human body to sustain it against the onslaught of a major operation.

Satisfied that the submarine was properly positioned, the dock master closed the gates behind her and began his pumping procedure. By midnight the dry dock was emptied of water. Under the glare of a hundred floodlights, the *Splendid* sat high on the cradle, dry and naked as the day she was launched. Her crew began to climb down the half-dozen ladders the Americans had put in place from the floor of the dry dock as soon as the water level was low enough for them to enter. His crew following behind him, Leach was the first one down, followed by Able Seaman Smith, once again flashlight in hand, and by the rest of the crew. All were anxious to take a look at the damage those bloody Russkis had done to their ship. At the captain's order, the aft ladder was moved from its position near the tower to the stern. Its padded head rested on each side of the point of the conical cap covering the center of the propeller, where it was fitted onto the drive shaft like a spinner at the center of the propeller of an aircraft. Taking the light from the boy seaman, the captain, in his white shorts, an open, white short-sleeved shirt, white rubber-soled shoes, hatless and, like the rest of his crew, soaked to the skin in the constant, warm rain, carefully made his way up the rungs of the ladder. It was steadied at its base by the ever-present coxswain and Smith.

At the top of the ladder Marcus Leach was not prepared for what he saw. Along the sharp leading edges of each of the huge brass blades were four deep gouges at varied intervals. To him a deep gouge was anything over a quarter inch. Those were that depth if not slightly more. That was bad enough. What really gave him a jolt was that on the blade to his right and slightly above him, the four gouge marks were grouped close together, perhaps half an inch apart. From that area about five feet out from the propeller hub, a hairline crack, thin but clearly visible under the beam of his flashlight, ran diagonally upward across the shiny face of the blade toward its center. Leach was not an engineer but he guessed, and was later told he was right, that if the cable impact had been any greater, or if he had attempted to drive his ship toward Diego Garcia using his propeller at high revolutions, the enormous strain on the propeller would have caused the loss of the outer half of that massive brass blade. The result would have been catastrophic. The vibrations caused by the unbalanced propeller spinning at high speed would probably have torn the drive shaft out of its bearings, shattered the electric motors, and opened the stern of the craft to an instant flood of high-pressure ocean water. As it was, *Splendid* had survived, but only by the depth of a crack.

As promised by the admiral, *Splendid*'s new propeller was waiting for her when she arrived at Diego Garcia. The bright, polished metal masterpiece had been flown in by Royal Air Force Hercules transport that morning.

At the bottom of the ladder Leach handed the flashlight to David Scott, his senior technical officer (STO), usually referred to on British submarines as Chief. He was waiting with his clutch of officers and engineering artificers, the men who were responsible for changing the propeller and making *Splendid* seaworthy again.

"It's worse than I thought, Chief. Take a look at the top right-hand blade. It's got a nine-inch crack running back from the leading edge."

Chief was surprised. "I had a good look at the blades when we got the cables off. I didn't see anything then."

"You may have missed it. After all, when you were taking a look you were several feet under water. Or the crack might have developed during the run across. Either way it's there and we're just bloody lucky the whole god-damn thing didn't come apart."

Work began on the propeller change at first light the next morning. While the rest of the crew worked away at maintenance chores in their own shops, a gang was put to work at cleaning off the sea-green growth that had already accumulated on *Splendid*'s hull. That night Leach and his officers threw a barbecue cookout on the beach, complete with a roaring bonfire from pieces of packing crates, the only source of wood on the island. All hands got into the grog the captain supplied, but only three or four had to be assisted up the ladders back to their bunks.

On April 21, *Splendid*'s Chief pronounced her fit and ready to go. All the umbilical cords were removed with the exception of the water pipes for the nuclear reactor. They would come off as soon as she was afloat. The dry dock's seawater valves were opened to begin the flooding that would lift the boat up and out from her cradle as the level of the water in the dock rose to that of the surrounding lagoon. It was an exciting moment for all hands and especially those who were off watch and were permitted to be on deck as she was coming up, rather like the launching of a new ship. Within the hour, appropriate farewells having been said to the dry dock and base crews on that lonely island, *Splendid* was making her way out of the Diego Garcia lagoon.

At Leach's request, Chief stayed in the control room during the initial dive after leaving Diego Garcia. The captain took her down to two hundred feet, having called for revolutions to make fifteen knots. When they were settled at two hundred feet he ordered, "Telegraph full speed ahead."

"Full speed ahead, sir."

He turned to his STO, saying, "Well, Chief, this is the moment of truth."

Slowly the whispering purr of the electric motors and spinning propeller blades increased as the power moved toward full output. Suddenly they could feel it: a high frequency vibration from the stern that mounted in volume as the propeller reached its maximum revolutions per minute.

"Stop engines!" the captain ordered.

Immediately the motor was cut back, the vibrations stopped.

"Well, chief?"

Lieutenant-Commander David Scott shook his head. "It's no go, sir. There must have been some damage to the main bearings. I'm not sure what it is but obviously it's something I can't fix. It looks to me as though you can make about twenty knots but when you get your rpm's beyond that . . ." He shrugged.

"Bloody hell!" the frustrated Leach spat out. "If I can't

have full power my boat isn't operational." He leaned against the periscope drawing his hand across his forehead as he came to the only decision he could make. With a voice of resignation he said, "There's no choice. I'll have to take her home."

Chief ventured, "The admiral won't be very happy, sir."

"Up the admiral!"

23

23 April   9:00 A.M.

South Atlantic Ocean

off Cape Verde

Captain Second Rank Boris Chernavin was in a foul mood. There were three reasons. The first was that his ship and crew had not performed well during the OKEAN exercise. The second was that he was not getting along at all well with his zampolit, the ship's political officer who, unfortunately, was of equal naval rank. And the third was that he and the zampolit had been through a bottle of vodka together which had resulted in a shouting match that had ended at two o'clock in the morning when the zampolit stormed out of the captain's cabin drunk and furious. The captain had a skull-pulsing hangover.

The zampolit was a new man by the name of Vargan. Short, heavyset, about fifteen years older than Chernavin, bald, round-faced, he exuded a perpetual underarm odor which always preceded him. He had joined the 501 just a week before the Murmansk departure. In the ensuing seven days he had succeeded in causing a turmoil among the crew and much frustrating annoyance for its captain.

There was a zampolit on every Soviet warship. He directed the ideological indoctrination and monitored the political reliability of the officers and men. He directed socialist competition. He insured that party decisions were carried out. He enforced discipline—at least he was supposed to. And he acted as both "chaplain" and social worker for the crew to promote morale. The Communist party set up groups within the naval command structure, of which the captain of a ship and his line officers formed one part and the political officer and the party organizations the other. As Chernavin saw it, the system was designed to create havoc. Vargan, a man with limited naval experience, had become critical of the way he, Chernavin, was handling the crew during the OKEAN maneuvers. As a member of the party, the captain was as susceptible to its criticism and discipline as any other member. The opinionated Vargan, totally incapable of taking criticism himself, had become quite liberal with his attacks on Chernavin during their drinking bout. When the captain had protested, saying that Vargan had no naval background against which to make any valid criticisms, the zampolit had pounded the table announcing that he had had ten years at sea; that he shared with the captain the responsibility for the successful operation of the boat and its performance; that how the 501 and its crew performed was all-important to him and his career in the socialist competition by which his future would be judged.

Chernavin knew the little man was right but in his drunken state he had become angry and lost control. Matching Vargan in volume and waving his hands for effect, he told the zampolit in no uncertain terms that he, Chernavin, was the captain of the ship, he was the naval officer and he did not need some know-it-all amateur to tell him how to run his boat. From that springboard the voluble, highly heated, profane argument had proceeded until the drunken little man left the captain's cabin in a fit of fury. Chernavin would have to do something to smooth the waters, but not until he was on the other side of his hangover.

The main rankling factor was that Vargan was right about the ship's performance.

The 501 was designated as part of the attacking force in the Atlantic segment of the OKEAN exercise. Chernavin's orders were that he was to rendezvous with the attacking fleet one hundred miles west of Cape Verde off Senegal. He did not yet know where the defending fleet was. From that time he and his ship would be under the direct command of the flag officer of the attacking fleet, although subject also to direct orders from naval headquarters at Moscow. There would be similar fleets attacking and defending in the Indian and Pacific Oceans.

During the briefing that was given on OKEAN before the departure from Murmansk, he noted that there would be assigned to the exercise over two hundred surface and submarine warships, from aircraft carriers and battle cruisers to ships as small as the Grisha class corvettes, plus provisioning and at-sea maintenance and engineering vessels. Out of the 381 serviceable submarines that would be at sea during the period, only about a hundred would be used in the exercise. Their numbers would probably be known to the Americans and British, who would be shadowing them. But the rest of the submarines at sea would lie hidden, quiet in the exact locations in the Atlantic, South Atlantic, and Indian Oceans to which they had been assigned.

The 501 had been tasked to hold the attacking fleet's antisubmarine defense zone, *zona protivolodochnoy oborony*, in that instance the water expanse around the attacking fleet in which antisubmarine defense forces engage in the search for, and destruction of, enemy submarines and fulfill their mission of protecting the fleet from underwater attack. The 501 had been assigned a distant sector ahead of the attacking fleet as it advanced northward to discover and destroy the defending fleet. Somehow a defending fleet attack submarine slipped undetected through the 501's assigned area and had gone on to launch its practice torpedos against the attacking fleet's flagship. Chernavin had taken to task the sonar michman-warrant or chief petty officer who complained that he had only new, inexperienced watchkeepers on the sonar and that until they had gained more experience it was likely the same thing would happen again. No question they should have seen the incoming submarine but he was off watch when it happened. He would do his utmost to improve the capability of the sonar crew.

It was with difficulty that Chernavin explained to the exercise umpires the reason for the failure of 501. A message had been received from the flag officer himself on the afternoon of April 22 expressing his extreme displeasure at having been "sunk" and warning that he would expect face-to-face explanation from Captain Second Rank Boris Chernavin at the earliest opportunity.

For all these reasons the captain of the 501 was in a foul mood, exacerbated by the faulty focus of his eyes. To make matters worse, his orders were to open his top secret instructions this morning. At the same time, 0900 hours, all other Soviet submarine captains would be doing the same thing. The instructions were from Fleet Admiral Smirnov, the commander in chief.

Chernavin twirled the dial on his cabin safe. Twice he missed the combination setting. Finally he succeeded. His shaking hands opened the large red envelope so supremely official-looking with the commander in chief's red crest embossed on its upper left-hand corner. He extracted a two-page, neatly typed document, the admiral's orders for Operation Sink. He laid the order in front of him, put both elbows on the desk top and leaned his forehead on both hands. He began to read.

As his eyes moved slowly down the first page, he straightened his back, raising his head from his hands. The first three paragraphs were background on the escalating confrontation between the Soviet Union and the Americans, brought to a head by the planned arrival in Pakistan of the first American troops on May 7. The preamble also covered the Soviet Union's urgent need to secure a new supply of crude oil. Domestic production in the Siberian fields was falling off with no new discoveries of magnitude coming on stream, while the demands in both the USSR and her Eastern Bloc satellite countries were escalating.

The signal told Chernavin that his ship, the 501, was part of a comprehensive scheme known as the Andropov Plan through which Chairman Romanov intended to deal with both problems at the same time.

The tasks of 501, including details of how they were to be executed, were set out in precise form—the place, the date, the exact time, the direction of the approach, precautions against being observed, the aiming point for the surface-to-surface rocket and the spacing of the torpedos.

The date specified for the execution of Chernavin's task was still eight days off, on glorious May Day at precisely 1200 hours GMT.

When he had finished reading the complete message his befuddled mind reached the conclusion that Chairman Romanov was either a genius or he was mad. It did not occur to the submarine captain that Comrade Romanov, the general secretary of the Communist party and chairman of the Supreme Soviet Presidium and marshal of the Soviet Union, might be both.

24

26 April   Noon
Durban, South Africa

At noon on April 26, the *Mecca* arrived off Durban, her fuel almost exhausted. The crew had been confined to the dreadful old ship for so long without putting a foot ashore that their tempers were almost at the breaking point, their resentment of the Palestinians at a dangerous peak. Even Captain Rashid, a man of infinite patience, would be delighted when he got rid of Said and his two remaining men. He yearned for the day when the *Mecca* was back in the familiar waters of his beloved Mediterranean. Why the PLO had come this long distance he had no idea. If they had wanted to come from Bahrain to Durban, why hadn't they flown? But he thought he knew why. It was that damned transmitter they had used to blow up the Israeli gunboat in Haifa harbor. You couldn't carry it on a commercial airliner. It would be next to impossible for it to remain undetected. So what better way to get it where you want it when you want it than to take it on the *Mecca*. Was that really why they'd come all the way to Durban? Rashid was only guessing. He had no way of knowing. He would soon find out whether he was right or wrong.

By 2:45 in the afternoon (12:45 GMT), the *Mecca* was five miles to the north-northeast of Durban's harbor, the Bay of Natal, making for the entrance to the port. On the starboard wing of his bridge, the captain could see white sandy beaches, and behind them the office buildings and churches of the city center. Rising beyond were the high hills of Durban, laced with roads and expressways. He caught the glint of houses among the green of the trees. It was a big city, much bigger than he had thought. He would enjoy spending a week ashore here, for that was what he had promised himself. A full week in the best hotel. Clean clothes, good food. With luck, an amiable bedmate. Why just one? Perhaps two or three. That is, if Said would let him ashore. Surely, he would be rid of the PLOs here at Durban.

Aft in the fantail of the stern, Hassan was going through the same testing procedures on his UHF transmitter as he had off Haifa, the night they blew the Israelis to shreds. Even though the old ship was pitching in a quartering sea as she plowed toward Durban, Hassan had elected to set up his transmitter on the same wooden table he had used weeks before in calmer water. Ahmed had once again appropriated it from the galley and with great ease carried it from the port to the starboard side of the cabin deck. Hassan wanted the radio to be out in the open when he pushed the orange detonate button so that his radio transmission would reach its maximum range of a thousand miles, stretching roughly northward into the Mozambique Channel between the island of Madagascar on the east and the African mainland on the west. It would also carry southwest another thousand miles almost to the Cape of Good Hope. In that two thousand-mile expanse of Indian Ocean, scores of supertankers either filled with cargo or in ballast butted through the seas. Among them were ten which, unknown to their masters, had a common cargo other than crude oil or liquid petroleum—Russian-made, armed limpet mines waiting to be detonated by a radio signal. The first of the ten was just passing Cape Town and entering the south Atlantic. It was the *Amoco Singapore* whose propeller had claimed Maan. The last of the ten, the *Esso Malaysia*, was still in the Mozambique Channel. Each of the ships had clear horizons around them. No other tankers were in sight.

Had Captain Rashid, or for that matter, his first officer, Nabil, looked aft between 2:45 and 3 P.M. local time, they would have seen the three PLO soldiers clustered around the black box of the high-powered radio transmitter. At eleven minutes to three (12:49 GMT) Hassan had finished his testing. He was satisfied. Without looking at either Said or Ahmed he said, "We go."

Using Ahmed's accurate LCD watch which had been set against precise hour signals from the Durban radio station, Hassan began a countdown at thirty seconds before 13:00 GMT. At the instant the tiny figures 13:00 came up, Hassan's forefinger depressed the orange button on his black box. For the three PLOs on the *Mecca*, it was an anticlimactic event. If they could have seen an upward rolling ball of flame, as at Haifa, then they would know they had succeeded. But to push a button three miles off Durban with no certain knowledge of what was over the horizon? For the operation that had begun almost two months earlier on March 9—and cost so much—to end simply with the push of a button was strangely disappointing.

Hassan took off his earphones, turned to his left to look at Said, then to his right at Ahmed. He shrugged, turning the palms of his hands upwards. It was done. Was it a success or failure?

Simultaneously with his gesture there came from the southeast a rolling sound like distant thunder. It seemed to go on and on. Almost at the same time and blended with it, came another heavy drum roll sound from due east, followed by even louder rumblings from the northeast.

To those in Durban who heard the far-off noises, they were no more than the peals of remote thunder far out across the endless stretches of the Indian Ocean, not a matter for even the slightest concern.

For the PLO team, however, they were the drum rolls that signalled glorious victory, unparalleled in the history of the Palestinian nation. Among the trio on the fantail of the *Mecca* at that moment, there was elation as they embraced each other. There were tears in their eyes—tears of exaltation and joy and of grief and anguish for Maan, whose life had paid for that supreme moment of satisfying, sweet triumph.

Within the hour, the old *Mecca* was in the calm waters of Natal Bay. The captain skilfully edged her hull up to the Maydon Wharf at the west end of the port, within sight of the Congella Monument and within earshot of the heavy traffic on the southern freeway a hundred yards to the west. A steady, light drizzle had begun as they entered Durban's harbor under a low, overcast, gray sky. Said and his companions stood out of the rain on the passageway under the starboard wing of the bridge. They would be gone as soon as the gangplank was in place, on their way back to Beirut by commercial airliners as quickly as they could make reservations. Said expected they would have little difficulty in getting seats on a Lufthansa or British Airways aircraft to Frankfurt or London, then they would double back to Beirut. He would know soon enough what arrangements he could make.

Captain Rashid would take back to Beirut the team's radio transmitter, its deadly work completed at least for that mission, and the rubber boats, motors, the automatic weapons, and the scuba gear. Each man would keep his pistol in a holster inside his shirt. At the airport, the guns would be put in their dunnage bags to be checked as luggage.

Said remembered Arafat's warning about the Israeli hit squad. He cautioned Ahmed and Hassan to keep their guard up, but he really didn't believe the Israelis would try to get at them in Durban. South Africa would be offended by any attack on their soil. Furthermore, Durban was thousands of miles from Israel. The place where he, Ahmed, and Hassan would be most vulnerable was close to Israel, in Beirut itself.

They had said their farewells to the crew. It had been an especially difficult moment for Said and the old captain.

The two men had become quite close during the month-and-a-half they had been together. Rashid promised he would see Said back in Beirut, probably in a month.

The three Palestinian Arabs stood under the bridge in their freshly laundered khaki shirts and trousers. They did not wear headdresses: it would not be appropriate to wear the *khafia* in Durban. They watched the taxi they had called for on the ship's radio driving along the wharf from the north. Its lights blazed in the rain as it passed between the rows of warehouses and the freight sitting on the dock that was being loaded on or taken off the other ships alongside the Maydon Wharf. The taxi rolled cautiously by crews of stevedores, trucks, and fork lift vehicles and under the swinging cranes of that busy dock. On the wharf, also waiting for the gangplank, stood a South African customs and immigration officer looking miserable in the teeming rain. He wore plastic rain gear over his uniform and cap. The taxi stopped behind him near the open doors of the dark and empty warehouse just a few feet beyond the wharf's edge.

Finally the crew had the fore and aft lines secured to the dock. The captain left the bridge to stand beside the Palestinians as the gangplank went down. He greeted the South African officer as he came on board. Rashid invited him to his cabin to begin the inspection of the ship's papers, but asked if he would mind first clearing three members of his crew who were leaving the ship and going back to Lebanon. The affable South African inspected their passports and innoculation certificates. They were in order. He stamped the passports. They had no goods to declare, but the officer asked Ahmed to open his bag for inspection. Satisfied when that was done, he gave them permission to go ashore.

After a final handshake with Rashid, the trio began to move down the gangplank, their bags swung over their left shoulders, making for the waiting taxi. Its lights were still blazing. Its windshield wipers methodically moved back and forth, sweeping off the gray drizzle.

The gangplank was tilted down at a shallow angle

from the deck to the rain-soaked dock. The eyes of the three men were on the wet, slippery gangplank as they sought to keep their footing, steadying themselves with their right hands on its rope railing. None of them saw the movement of two shadowy figures in the dark recesses of the warehouse directly ahead. Nor did they see the glint of black gun metal.

Rashid had opened the door to his cabin and was stepping aside to allow the customs officer to go in ahead of him when he heard the first thunk. Instantly, he knew what it was. The muted sound of a rifle being fired through a silencer. As he wheeled to look for the source of the sound, there was a staccato of thunk noises. Flashes from the firing guns winked brightly against the darkness inside the warehouse. The first high power bullet smashed through Said's heart and out into Ahmed's stomach. The second entered his right eye, cutting a neat hole in the lens of the mirror sunglasses, tearing out the back of his skull. That bullet ripped through Ahmed's chest.

Rashid looked on in stunned horror. The aim of the rapidly fired bullets shifted slightly to Ahmed and, behind him, Hassan. On impact, the force of the shells propelled the victims up and backward, their arms and legs flailing in the throes of death. Ahmed lurched outward over the rope railing, then fell to the dock on his back.

Hassan was driven straight back up the gangplank, his body falling heavily against the deck and the wall of the master's cabin. His blood-stained dunnage bag fell beside him.

Said's shattered form lay askew on the gangplank, twitching convulsively. Then it was still. The blood from his wounds coursed down the gangplank, mixing silently with the soft rain water.

25

26 April   13:00 GMT

Cape of Good Hope

At 13:00 GMT on April 26, *Splendid*, bound for Faslane and home, was keeping twenty knots and 150 feet. She was 311 miles south of Cape St. Marie at the southerly tip of the island of Madagascar, steering 245 degrees, making for the Cape of Good Hope. Had *Splendid* been on the surface at that moment and her captain on the tower bridge, he might have heard rumbling explosions rolling over the horizon from ahead of his boat and along its starboard side. And moments later at those same points of the horizon he would probably have seen three or four dense black clouds of smoke creeping up into a cloud-pocked sky.

It was not, however, until 17:00 Zulu that evening that Commander Marcus Leach and his crew discovered that they were in the area of what was already being described as the worst marine disaster in history. As was his practice, Leach had the six o'clock (U.K. time) BBC world news piped through the ship's broadcast system so the entire crew could hear it.

In his cabin, working again at his paper war, the captain stopped writing in order to concentrate fully on what he was hearing as soon as the mellifluous British voice of the BBC announcer, scarred by the static of the long distance over which it was carried, began to read the first major news item:

In what is being described as the most vicious, destructive act of terrorism in history, ten of the world's largest supertankers were sunk today off the east coast of Africa, and in the Atlantic another fifteen supertankers have disappeared without trace. In Beirut early this afternoon the Palestinian Liberation Organization announced that it had carried out the sinkings, claiming that it was a blow struck for the liberation of the Palestinian people and for the return to them of their lands.

All of the ships in the Indian Ocean were in the heavily traveled Cape of Good Hope sea lane moving south out of the Persian Gulf, fully loaded with crude oil or petroleum products for destinations in Europe and North America. All were from two to five hundred miles off the African east coast and along a line between the island of Madagascar on the north and the Cape of Good Hope on the south. The explosions that destroyed the vessels caused each of them to burn sending huge pillars of smoke into the air which could be seen for miles. Ships that raced to the locations of the sinkings reported that all of the tankers sank within half an hour after the explosions had ripped through them.

In the South Atlantic, fifteen supertankers have disappeared without trace, apparently also victims of the PLO terrorists. Lloyd's of London has reported that all fifteen tankers had delivered their loads of crude oil or petroleum products to Europe and North America and were sailing back to the Persian Gulf in ballast. All the ships were in the sea lanes from the northernmost off Senegal to the southernmost off Cape Town. Lloyd's has also reported that satellite photographs taken of that part of the South Atlantic this afternoon show no traces of any one of the fifteen supertankers.

Lieutenant-Commander Paul Tait, the first lieutenant, stuck his head in the captain's doorway to make sure Leach was awake and listening to the grim BBC report. Silently Leach motioned to him to sit on the bunk.

Authorities estimate that apart from the hundreds of millions of pounds lost in ships and cargoes—a preliminary estimate puts that loss in the range of one to one-and-a-half billion pounds—there were approximately one thousand men and women on board those ships as crews.

To this moment no survivors have been reported. Lloyd's has said that there are no British crews on any of the ships, all of which carried the flags of Liberia or Panama where they are registered, although all the ships are believed to be owned by United States interests. The prime minister has denounced the action of the PLO . . .

Leach knew what the prime minister would be saying. He turned to Tait as the BBC announcer moved on to other world news.

"Well, Paul, what do you think of that?"

"Incredible. Absolutely incredible. Twenty-five tankers. What in hell is the PLO trying to prove?"

"More to the point, how did they do it? Had to be mines, radio-activated mines. Probably got them from the Russians. The Atlantic ships were in ballast. Put a hole in one of those and she'll go down in less than a minute. The oil in the loaded tankers will usually keep the hull afloat for maybe a half hour or so, depending on the type of explosion."

Tait agreed. "I saw a loaded one go down about a year ago. Some sort of big blast had hit her. Lloyd's thought it was an owner's plot to collect insurance. Anyway, she was down in forty-five minutes. Burned like hell until she went under."

Both officers talked with one ear cocked to the BBC

newscast just in case there was one other item that they might be interested in. There was.

Just as he was summing up the main points of the news, the announcer stopped momentarily and began again:

I have just been handed a bulletin. The PLO leader Yassir Arafat has denied responsibility for the fifteen tankers that have disappeared in the Atlantic, saying the PLO army was responsible for sinking only those that went down today in the Indian Ocean. This is the end of the BBC world news.

"I wonder if anybody will believe him," Leach speculated. "As I said, my guess is the tankers that went down in the Indian Ocean were mined. Limpets. Radio-activated. He could have had one team look after the ships he knew were going to be in the Indian Ocean and another to set up the mining of the tankers they knew were going to be in the South Atlantic on their way back. It takes about eighty days, almost three months, to take one of those big brutes, sail it out of the Persian Gulf, around the Cape up to Europe, unload it and get it back to the Persian Gulf. They're all on tight schedules. All you have to do is have a bright brain in London checking the daily Lloyd's Shipping Register." That unusual publication records the daily position of all ships at sea. "With a ruler, a map of the world, and a sharp pencil, it wouldn't take a genius to figure out what cluster of tankers were going to be in a particular part of the South Atlantic in ballast on a given day headed for the same Arab port in the Persian Gulf. Then you dispatch your team to that country with their mines. As long as there are ships there will be ways of smuggling men, mines, or anything else. They wait for their preselected tankers to arrive and while they're still empty waiting to be loaded, presto, the mines are planted."

The first lieutenant was still not satisfied. "But if he did it that way, why would Arafat deny it? He's accepted the blame for the ten in the Indian Ocean. Why would he say he didn't do the Atlantic job?"

Leach shook his head. "I don't know. First of all, I don't understand the Arab mind. Secondly, the pressure of negative world reaction he's undoubtedly been getting from all quarters might have made him panic. After all, who can find out the true story when the Atlantic tankers have disappeared without trace. When they're in ballast filled with water, a good explosion can send one to the bottom in forty seconds. And it's likely they're all at the bottom of the Atlantic trench where no one can get at them to see what did them in."

"But if there's one on the continental shelf in two or three hundred feet of water . . ."

The captain agreed. "He would have to take his chances on that."

Tait didn't pursue that statement. He had one of his own to make. "My guess is that the Soviets are involved on the Atlantic side."

The captain snorted his derision. "The Soviets! No bloody way. They would be risking World War III doing that." He was emphatic, shaking his head vigorously. "No bloody way. It's those goddamned Arabs, those Palestinians. It has to be!"

26

26 April   7:55 A.M.

The White House

Washington, D.C.

President Hansen had just settled in behind his desk in the study. It was five minutes to eight on the morning of Friday, April 26. Jim Crane would be along at eight with the day's agenda and some of the files for the meetings ahead. Hansen opened his file entitled *Department of Energy Proposals for Revising Gasoline Rationing Plan.* His first formal session in the Oval Office that morning, scheduled for nine o'clock, would be with Energy Secretary George Enos and his senior staff. The president had read their submission, but decided to reread the recommendations contained in the beginning of the document. He had just opened it up to the first page and started to read when Crane, who was never early, burst in waving a piece of paper.

"You should see this, sir!" he exclaimed anxiously.

As Hansen read what was printed on it, he could understand Crane's anxiety. It was a newsroom telex from Reuters reporting the tanker sinkings off Durban.

The president couldn't believe it. "Ten loaded super-tankers, all at the same time! What in hell is going on?" His rhetorical question was partly answered when a later wire report announced Arafat's claim for a PLO victory in sinking the supertankers. Within the hour word came of the disappearance of the additional fifteen vessels in the South Atlantic. Close on the heels of that news came Arafat's repudiation of responsibility for the South Atlantic sinkings. That was followed by reports of the names, ownerships, and flags of the twenty-five tankers. Every one of them was American owned. All carried the flag of Liberia with the exception of one which flew the flag of Panama. Those that were sunk in the Indian Ocean were loaded. Those in the South Atlantic were in ballast southbound for the Cape of Good Hope and round it into the Indian Ocean and the Persian Gulf. No communication or signal of any kind had been heard from any one of the twenty-five ships. The fact that all of the tankers appeared to have been hit at the same time, 1300 hours GMT, merely served to confirm Arafat's claim that it was a major PLO victory in its war for recognition, for its own land, and for the freedom of its people.

It was Arafat's denial of the PLO's involvement in the South Atlantic sinkings that sent the alarm bells through President Hansen's mind, the Pentagon, and the CIA headquarters. The "what if?" question immediately surfaced. What if Arafat was telling the truth and the PLO was not involved in the South Atlantic sinkings? What about the Japanese Red Brigade, whose wild terrorists had worked with the PLO before, dealing out murder and mayhem in airports and in hijackings throughout Europe? That was a possibility that had to be seriously considered. Perhaps it was the dreadful gang of German revolutionaries. Had they joined forces in partnership with the PLO?

As Hansen saw it, the only other possibility—if Arafat was to be believed—was totally unbelievable. It was that the Soviet navy's submarines had done it.

By late afternoon on April 26, so much more disturbing information had come in and so many puzzling questions remained unanswered that the President decided that he must have an emergency meeting of the executive committee of the National Security Council. If the worst possibility was true, that the Soviets were responsible for the deliberate sinking of fifteen American-owned super-tankers with all hands . . ! But there was no link to the Soviets, except that the PLO had used Russian-made mines. The Haifa patrol boat blast had proved that. The fifteen Atlantic ships could have been mined anywhere weeks before, in the Persian Gulf or while they were in Europort, wherever. It was apparent that each target had been carefully selected: American owned and under a foreign flag. More than that: foreign and non-NATO. Further-more, their positioning off the west coast of Africa in ballast in the time frame of one or two days could easily have been calculated weeks in advance through published schedules of the ships' movements.

While his basic logic would not let him believe that Soviet submarines were responsible—an act that could bring down retaliation and would take them to the precipice of World War III—there was, nevertheless, a nagging question in President Hansen's mind. He needed the fine brains in his National Security Council to pick over the bones of evidence with him. On the other hand, this was an overt act of aggression against United States in-terests and property. Whether it was the PLO, the Japanese Red Army, or the Soviet Union, action had to be taken. Everything possible had to be done to make sure that it did not happen again. At that point, the president had no idea what could be done.

On the other hand, all the ships were foreign flag and non-NATO. They were in international waters. They were American-owned ships, but their hulls and cargos would be covered by insurers, Lloyd's of London and the new American group that had moved into the Lloyd's field. So why should the president of the United States get involved? John Hansen couldn't fully answer that question until he and his top National Security Council people took a look at the situation. But as long as there was even the slightest possibility that the Soviets had a hand in the simultaneous sinking of the twenty-five American supertankers, the matter had to be of top priority and utmost concern to his administration.

Immediately after a luncheon he hosted for a visiting African head of state, he had words in the Oval Office with Jim Crane and Peterson, the White House press secretary, who told the President that in his judgment he had never seen such a public reaction of indignation since the hostage-taking incident in Iran. As far as the people and the press were concerned, those were American ships, regardless of the flag they flew. Their sinking, no matter who did it, called for action by the president and if necessary, the armed forces. That was Peterson's assessment of the telephone calls and telegrams that were being sent to members of Congress and were flooding into the White House. In fact, it was the same kind of reaction that John Hansen himself felt. There was no way those PLO bastards were going to get away with it. The United States would retaliate somehow.

The National Security Council executive committee met in emergency session at five o'clock that afternoon. All members were present, except General Young. The President had instructed Crane not to invite him, but to tell the chief of naval operations, Admiral Taylor, to stand by his telephone.

When the executive committee had assessed all the available information, it came to the unanimous conclusion that, in spite of Arafat's repudiation of responsibility for the Atlantic sinkings, he was probably responsible for the destruction of all twenty-five tankers as he originally had claimed. His later denial was probably the result of the hostile world reaction. It was noted that the Soviet Union had yet to make any statement condemning the action or, for that matter, approving it.

A request would be made to all NATO members with naval forces to participate in an American navy coordinated program for the mine inspection of the hulls of all the tankers operating along the Cape of Good Hope shipping route from the Persian Gulf. Examining ships in port on the American and West European coasts and in the Persian Gulf would be relatively easy to do. But the handling of those at sea would be difficult and time consuming. Of the world tanker fleet of some 3,300 vessels, only 710 were in the supertanker class of 200,000 deadweight tons or more. It was decided to concentrate first on American-owned supertankers carrying the Liberian or Panamanian flags.

The executive committee shared President Hansen's view that if Arafat's denial of responsibility for the fifteen supertankers sunk in the Atlantic was valid, it meant that some other organization was working with his on a coordinated basis. It had to be the Japanese Red Army, or the German revolutionary group, or some new revolutionary organization. The final possibility was that submarines of the Soviet Navy had carried out those sinkings using the PLO as cover.

Difficult as it was to believe that the Russians would perpetrate such an act of aggression, the executive committee nevertheless unanimously recommended to the president that he should discuss the matter with the Soviet government, to ask for their assurances that they were not involved. Hansen had accepted that recommendation, saying that he would talk to Chairman Romanov on the hot line as soon as arrangements could be made. The president ended the executive committee meeting at that point, saying, "Even if I get his assurances they weren't involved, I don't know whether I can believe him any more than I can believe Arafat."

27

27 April   5:00 P.M.

Moscow

Chairman Romanov expected that President Hansen would soon want to talk with him on the hot line. He was, therefore, not surprised when his principal secretary entered his office to advise that the President had put in a bid for a talk in one hour, 6 P.M. Moscow time, nine o'clock in the morning in Washington. The secretary reminded the chairman that he had an appointment at six o'clock to meet a delegation from the Georgian party and Politburo member, nonvoting, Shevardnadze, who was responsible for the supervision of that group. They could wait. His conversation with the American would not last long.

At six o'clock Romanov was at his desk, the hot line television transmitter-receiver in front of him. To his right sat his interpreter. At the end of the desk between it and the wall sat a communications technician. Opposite the chairman sat his three key men, Gromyko, Andropov, and Ustinov, each dedicated to the cause and purposes of Marxist-Leninist communism, the party, and the domination of the world by the Soviet Union. These were experienced men and jealous perhaps in their own way of the younger Romanov, but loyal and trustworthy—at least until some face-losing situation transpired, as with Khrushchev.

At the appointed hour, all sat silent, impassive, waiting for the initiating contact, which came a few seconds after the hour when the face of the new president, Hansen, with whom none of them had any previous contact, appeared on the television screen. Hansen's opening remarks were friendly, as protocol demanded between the leaders of the world's two ascendant superpowers. The preliminaries between the two men, both of an age, were quickly disposed of. Each knew an enormous amount about the other through briefings by their respective intelligence agencies, supplemented by the State Department in America and Gromyko's own foreign affairs ministry in Moscow. It was, therefore, a challenge in evaluation and assessment for Chairman Romanov as he listened to the deep, modulated voice of the towering six-foot five-inch man speaking to him from his Oval Office at the White House. The challenge for John Hansen was equally trying.

But it was not so difficult for them as such discussions had been for their predecessors because, for the first time, the encounter was televised through a special satellite recently launched in a space venture jointly mounted by both countries. Even though the words and images were scrambled for security during transmission, they appeared at both ends in the clear. Thus, for the first time in history, the president of the United States and the chairman of the Soviet Union could see each other during a hot line discussion, an advantage to both in the critical business of long-distance negotiations concerning matters of world-shaking import.

From the very outset, Romanov was favorably impressed by the handsome, white-haired Hansen. As they began their conversation, he could sense that in other circumstances there could be a good rapport between them.

The conversation moved slowly because of the necessary intervention of the translators. Finally, both men knew that it was time to move to the main arena.

"And now, Mr. President, I assume you wish to talk with me about Pakistan and to tell me that the United States is prepared to abandon this indiscreet act of aggression. If so, perhaps there is some form of quid pro quo that might be considered. I can tell you in no uncertain terms what has already been related to you through our diplomatic channels: that I regard the United States intervention in Pakistan in the same light as President Carter regarded any intervention we might have made in Iran or the Persian Gulf countries. He said the United States would use military force to prevent us from so doing. He regarded any such action on our part, therefore, as being a *causus belli*. I want to make it perfectly clear that my colleagues and I look upon Pakistan as a vital area of interest to the Soviet Union and any military intervention there by the United States will be regarded as a *causus belli*."

Hansen nodded. "I understand your position. I do not believe you're justified in taking it. But I understand it. However, Pakistan is not the reason for my call. Perhaps we can talk about it in the next few days . . ."

"There are not too many days left, Mr. President."

"There are enough. I want to talk about the tanker sinkings yesterday. Mr. Chairman, I'm sure you and all of your colleagues have been fully briefed on the PLO action yesterday, the blowing up of the ten loaded tankers in the Indian Ocean and the other fifteen in the South Atlantic, the ones that were in ballast and apparently sank without trace, although some confirming debris has been found at each of their plotted locations."

Hansen paused to let Romanov's interpreter do his work.

Romanov acknowledged. "Yes, Mr. President, we have been fully briefed."

"You will know, therefore, Mr. Chairman, that Arafat has disclaimed any responsibility for the fifteen that went down in the Atlantic."

The chairman's acknowledgment was a nod. But he followed with a question: "But what is your interest in these vessels, Mr. President? They weren't American and they carried the flags of Liberia except one which was Panamanian. And if I recall my facts correctly, they were all in international waters, thousands of miles away from the United States."

Romanov could see the novice president shift uneasily.

"You're quite right. But every one of those ships was owned by American corporations or individuals."

Romanov held up his hand. "It is a capitalist device, an American capitalist device, to register ships in Liberia and Panama in order to avoid your law that requires American registered ships to use only American crews, a law which, if not avoided, would double or even triple the crew cost. Furthermore, Mr. President, most of those ships are owned by multinational corporations who range across the world plundering its economies. They have their head offices of convenience, like their flags of convenience, in the United States, the country that provides the most advantages and luxuries for their management groups. Those multinationals do no more than suck on the economic blood of the oil producers, of your government, and of the people of the Western world."

He went on when the interpreter was finished. "So I find it difficult, Mr. President, to accept the validity of your position that you are interested in the fate of those tankers simply because they are purported to be owned by U.S. interests."

The chairman could feel a touch on this left hand, a finger asking for attention. He turned to listen to Gromyko, then looked back at the screen and with it the television camera. "I have also been reminded that none of the crews of any of the ships were American. So I ask, Mr. President, what is your interest, what is the interest of the United States, in this matter?" He held up his hand to indicate that he had an addition to that question when the interpreter was finished.

"And if you have an interest that I am prepared to recognize, then the next question is, what is it that you want of me?"

Hansen responded, choosing his words carefully. "The

fact of ownership of those vessels, American ownership, not only gives me a legitimate interest but very deep concern. The mass destruction of American property anywhere in the world through an act of war or an act of aggression must be viewed seriously by the Government of the United States and is a matter of substantial concern. That is a fact, regardless of your apparent wish to reject it. But quite apart from the legalities, it is of vital interest to us that the flow of oil from the Persian Gulf to the United States not be cut off or, for that matter, that the supply of oil from any of the OPEC countries, whether in the Persian Gulf, Venezuela, Malaysia, or elsewhere, not be cut off by blockade or threats of naval aggression. We constantly face the possibility of a major supplier nation terminating its flow of oil because of political instability, as in Iran. That risk is inherent in dealing with most OPEC members. We could probably compensate, make up for the flow of lost oil from one country by getting increased supplies from others. Really, what I am concerned about is the preservation of the transportation system, the world tanker fleet, that carries the OPEC and Mexican crude oil to our shores. As you know, we import more than forty percent of our consumption and all of it comes in by tanker."

"I understand your concern about the tankers," Romanov assured him, "but surely you don't think the PLO could threaten the world's tanker fleet?"

"No, I don't. They might try to blockade the Strait of Hormuz by mining it, but we could look after that situation quickly. Or they could sink a group of tankers with your support, just as they did yesterday."

Romanov bristled. "Are you accusing us of being involved in those sinkings?"

"I'm not accusing you of anything, Mr. Chairman. But we do know that the mines the PLO terrorists used were of Soviet manufacture. The same PLO terrorist group used the same type of mine at Haifa early last month."

The chairman waited for Hansen to drop the other shoe about the leader of the PLO group, whom the Israelis had killed in Durban, being a KGB officer. But that did not come. He wondered whether the president knew.

"We also know that the Soviet government has been an active supporter of the PLO for many years. There is a difference between support and direct involvement in an action. I am not making any accusation that there was a Soviet involvement with yesterday's sinkings.

"What I'm concerned about . . . the reason I want to talk with you is this: Arafat has denied any PLO responsibility for the fifteen tankers that went down in the South Atlantic. If the PLO didn't do it, perhaps it was another revolutionary group. But if it wasn't such a group, then the only country in the world with the capability of sinking those ships and at exactly the same time as the PLO blew up the group in the Indian Ocean, is the Soviet Union. Let me hasten to assure you, Chairman Romanov, that I don't believe Arafat. I think he was responsible for the whole thing. On the other hand, it would be helpful to the government of the United States if I could have your assurances, sir, that the Soviet Union . . . your navy has a large number of submarines in the South Atlantic at this time . . . if you could assure us that the Soviet navy did not sink the fifteen tankers in the Atlantic."

Stunned by the bluntness of the question but showing no evidence of it, Romanov made his response immediately. He knew what the answer was. It was part of the Andropov Plan. Furthermore, there was precedent for it, in the assurances Chairman Khrushchev gave to President Kennedy as the Cuban missile crisis was developing in 1962.

"You should know, Mr. President, that I deeply resent the arrogance implicit in your belief that I should account to the United States for any action that the Soviet navy might or might not have taken. But having said that, and in pursuit of the goal of peaceful coexistence, a goal which the Soviet Union has always sought, you have my assurance on the question."

28

1 May

Atlantic Ocean

The surface of the Atlantic fifty miles west of Cape Town on the morning of the first of May, May Day, had a heavy roll but was without waves. The sky was dotted with flat-based cumulus clouds sitting at about 3,000 feet, their white tops brilliant in the morning sun as they moved eastward, carried by the steady five knot wind.

Splendid, still keeping 150 feet, was pronounced by Pilot at 08:36 Zulu to be abeam Cape Town, fifty-two miles west of her light. At that moment the communications officer appeared in the control room to hand the captain a signal. "It's from the flag officer submarines, sir."

From the flag officer! The pink sheet of paper marked Top Secret had Commander Marcus Leach's immediate and full attention. The body of the signal read:

Splendid will make rendezvous with VLCC *Esso Atlantic* to carry out inspection of her hull for limpets. Technical instructions to deactivate and neutralize Soviet-type expected to be found will follow. The *Esso Atlantic*'s real time position is 14° 10' 15" east, 34° 8' 2" south, making 16 knots.

She's very close. Should be on the sonar screen any minute now, thought Leach as he read on:

Approach *Esso Atlantic* with maximum caution. Cause of mass Atlantic sinkings April 26 still not certain. Largest ever deployment of Soviet submarines now in South Atlantic and Indian Ocean. Positions on them cannot be plotted.

You're bloody right they're here! Leach's mind agreed. From the time *Splendid* had entered the tanker lane off Durban on the twenty-seventh, her active sonar had picked up twelve of them, one for each hundred miles of the distance from Durban to Cape Town. Furthermore, they appeared to be running slowly, as if on station, and were spaced roughly one hundred miles apart. Leach didn't like it one bit. But it was up to the brains at Whitehall to figure what was going on. They still hadn't.

Recommend *Splendid* reconnoiter *Esso Atlantic* area carefully before surfacing to carry out inspection. Urgent you report any Soviet submarine activity. Captain *Esso Atlantic* expects contact. Report ETA for rendezvous soonest.

"Keep seventy-five feet." He would go to periscope depth and raise the radar mast so he could transmit.

"Pilot give me an ETA for us from here to . . ." he rhymed off the latitude and longitude set out in the signal. "Subtract one hour's steaming southbound at sixteen knots in your calculation." That would take care of the *Esso Atlantic*'s southbound progress toward them during a one-hour period.

"Aye, aye, sir."

The communications officer stood ready to take the captain's message. Without looking up from his chart table, Pilot quickly came up with the answer. "Fifty-two minutes, sir. ETA 09:32 Zulu."

"Good!" To the communications officer he said, "Make a signal to the flag officer submarines. Message re *Esso Atlantic* received. Wilco. ETA 09:32 Zulu. That's it." The communications officer scuttled out of the control room.

"Keeping seventy-five feet, sir."

"Up search periscope. Pilot, what's the heading to the location I gave you?"

"Three degrees port will do it, sir."

"Right. Three degrees port."

"Three degrees port, sir." The boat swung imperceptibly to the left to take up the new heading.

"Sonar, keep an eye for a contact. Should be dead ahead coming on your screen shortly. Let me know as soon as you've got it." Leach realized that was a useless order. The sonar watchkeepers would give it to him almost the split second it appeared on the screen without his having to tell them to do so.

To the messenger of the watch, Leach said, "Smith, get Chief up here, chop, chop." It would be up to the ship's technical officer to get the divers organized and to sort out the instructions on how to handle the limpet mines when that message came in.

The periscope handles were in his hands. He scanned the horizon, looking intently ahead through the clear morning air. Still nothing. A precautionary sweep of the entire horizon showed the same result.

When Chief arrived in the control room the captain left the periscope to show him the message. "We have two clearance divers on board, have we not?"

"Yes, sir, Parkin and James, but I have half a dozen men who can operate with our scuba diving equipment. The same men who cut the cables."

"How many sets of scuba diving gear, oxygen bottles, that sort of thing, do you have?"

"Six, sir, and at least six men."

"Right. Ask for volunteers. Tell them what they're going to have to do. And tell them it'll be risky as hell."

At that moment Pots appeared with the technical signal from the flag officer submarines outlining the method of neutralizing the limpet mines and the device that would have to be used to do it.

"Simple," Chief pronounced. "It's a quarter-inch square metal rod nine inches long. I can make a dozen of those in ten minutes."

Leach clapped Chief on the shoulder. "Good chap. Now hop to it. We haven't got much time. Get your volunteers. Brief them. Get them into their wetsuits in half an hour. Our ETA for the tanker is 09:32 Zulu but I'm going to spend perhaps an hour doing a wide swing around her and run alongside of her a bit before we surface."

The captain then picked up the broadcast microphone and told the ship's crew what was going on. He believed that as part of his team they should know everything he knew—well, almost everything. His discourse to the crew was cut short by words from the sonar watchkeeper.

"Contact dead ahead, range forty-five miles." The sonar man did not hear the captain's briefing message over the broadcast system because his ears were glued to his headset. Thus he did not know that his target was one of the largest tankers in the world, the *Esso Atlantic*, 1,334 feet long. "And Christ, sir, she's big. The biggest thing I've ever seen on the screen!"

Leach chuckled to himself. He then ordered active sonar. He wanted to see if there was a Soviet submarine lurking in the area, waiting silently so that passive sonar would not pick her up. The pinging active sonar would find her but at the same time it would give away the presence of the British submarine. He timed three minutes. Then, picking up the action broadcast microphone he said, "Report, sonar crew."

The watchkeeper replied immediately. "Listening all around, sir. No contacts."

He was satisfied for the moment. "Secure active sonar."

"Secure active sonar, sir."

Beckoning to the first lieutenant and also the officer of the watch, Leach went to the chart table to stand just to the right of Pilot who was seated, busily working. With the other two gathered so they could see, he outlined his tactics as his finger stabbed at the chart.

"Here's the position of the *Esso Atlantic* and here we are. What I propose to do is to keep periscope depth and do a wide swing out to the west about ten miles beyond her. Then we'll turn north and sweep around behind her, coming up alongside keeping 150 feet. I want to run alongside her about fifty yards out to her port." He didn't say so but he intended to keep *Splendid* running parallel to and in formation with the *Esso Atlantic*'s stern where her mighty engines and propeller generated maximum ship noise.

"We'll stay at periscope depth. I'll have attack scope up but not above the surface. I'll use it to keep station with the tanker. During this part of the maneuver we'll sit next to her for probably an hour, perhaps an hour and a half."

The first lieutenant ventured, "What's the game, sir? Surely if a Russian sub attempts to move in to attack the *Esso Atlantic* it won't attack if we're on the surface or if it sees us. Shouldn't we be on the surface?"

Leach explained. "We've been ordered to try to find out, if the opportunity presents itself, if it's the Soviets who are doing the Atlantic sinkings. The point is, if they see us they won't attack. If they don't see us, then we'll soon know whether they're going to attack or not."

"And if we're in the way, sir?"

"No sweat. We'll just put on the brakes." His officers laughed and Leach with them. But in his own mind he was deadly serious. Besides, it was impossible to think that the Russians would risk starting World War III by sinking tankers. They just wouldn't do it. In any event . . .

"I want to make absolutely sure that before we surface and get both the *Esso Atlantic* and ourselves stopped and into a totally vulnerable spot, totally immobile . . . I want to make sure we haven't put ourselves into the station area of a Russian submarine."

"But, sir," said Pilot, "even if we do, surely they're only going to be there to watch us and monitor what we're doing."

The captain looked down at the naive young face. "Of course that's all they'll do, Pilot. But remember, there's something afoot out here. Five days ago fifteen tankers disappeared without trace in these waters. Like everyone else, I'm quite certain that the PLO is responsible. But right now, the way the world is going . . . Today is May Day, the big day for the Russians. Six days from now the

698

Americans start landing in Pakistan whether the Russians like it or not . . . As a matter of fact, I think it's safe to say that the next six days will be the most critical between the Americans and the Russians since World War II.

"Today, Pilot, I'm taking nothing for granted, least of all any goddamn Russian submarine captain. If there's one in the area he'll make his move either when we're doing our big circle or in the period that we're running in formation with the tanker, up close." A flaw in his tactics occurred to Leach. "On second thought I think that instead of being on the port side—that would blanket our sonar's ability to see out to the starboard side of the tanker—I think we should be in formation with her in line astern as close as we can get. That way we'll be able to see with our sonar in all directions except dead ahead and perhaps thirty degrees to either side of that position."

To the messenger of the watch he called, "Fetch Lieutenant Pritchard."

When Pritchard, the sonar officer, arrived at the control room the captain explained to him where he wanted to position the submarine behind the tanker. Would that interfere with the operation of *Splendid*'s passive sonar? No, it would not. Nor would it interfere with the active sonar.

"From this moment, I do not intend to use the active sonar. It would give away our presence and our position. One final thing, old chap. When we're in position behind the tanker, tucked in right up her bum, if we get a contact with a Soviet submarine, say from the port side, then as soon as we do we'll move up to the port side of the tanker in the station that I originally told you about, next to the engine and propeller and about fifty yards out. Vice versa if the contact's on the starboard side. That'll make doubly sure the Russki can't tell that we're there. Any questions?"

There were none.

"Right, we will go to diving stations immediately. First Lieutenant, have the attack team close up at the double. Bring all tubes to the action state. Let's go, gentlemen!"

In short order H.M.S. *Splendid* was at full fighting

pitch, ready to attack or counter an attack. The captain was at his position in the control room. All communications channels in the ship were open to the sound of his voice, which could demand immediate response from sonar, the tube stations, or whatever compartment he wanted to talk with.

"Now what's our heading, Pilot?" Leach demanded.

"Three-thirty, sir. The tanker's on a reciprocal."

"Sonar, what's the range of the tanker now?"

"Coming up to twenty miles, sir."

"Right. We'll take a fifty degree cut to port to begin our wide circle around her. Steer 290."

"Steer 290, sir." *Splendid* began banking gently to the left to begin the planned sonar sweep westward of the *Esso Atlantic*.

At 09:32 Zulu, her advertised ETA, the submerged *Splendid* was ten miles to port of the *Esso Atlantic* and abeam her. Leach went into the sonar room to take another look. He was still amazed by the size of the white blob the huge tanker made on the screen.

"Bloody marvelous!" he muttered.

Back in the control room keeping an anxious, overseeing eye on everything going on, he said to Tait, "That poor bloody tanker captain will be wondering what's happened to us. By the time we surface . . ."

"About two hours from now?"

"Right. He'll have given us up for lost. Pity."

One hour later *Splendid* had completed her sonar sweep of the waters to the west and north of the *Esso Atlantic*. No contacts were reported. Leach began to move her into close line-astern formation behind the tanker.

For an undistorted view ahead as he prepared to execute this most delicate, precise station-keeping maneuver, Leach had put up his attack periscope with its nonmagnifying lenses. Its eye sat only two feet above the top of the tower. He calculated that at that position he would be able to judge accurately where the uppermost part of his boat and, most important, her nose were in relation to the *Esso Atlantic*.

Leach caught his first glimpse of the roiling turbulence from the tanker's propeller when *Splendid* was some 800 yards astern of the *Esso Atlantic*. By the time he had closed to 400 yards, with an overtaking speed of two knots over the tanker's sixteen, the captain realized that the foaming white turbulence from the big ship's screw was blinding him. He would have to settle for tucking the *Splendid*'s nose up under the keel so that his periscope eye sat perhaps ten feet below and behind the rudder, clear of the vision-destroying turbulence. He was satisfied that, sitting in that position, his own boat's cavitation noise would be lost in the sound of the *Esso Atlantic*'s 45,000-horsepower steam turbine power plant and her enormous propeller. *Splendid* would be safe from the prying sonar eyes of any Soviet submarine.

Taking his boat below the wake of the tanker, he gradually edged her forward. Sonar called one hundred yards range. At that moment Leach had his first glimpse of the *Esso Atlantic*'s stern gear. He was amazed at the scale of what he saw. Her rudder stood as tall as a six-storey building. Immediately behind it was her five-bladed propeller, thirty feet in diameter. At eighty revolutions per minute it rotated so slowly that he could distinctly see each of its gleaming blades.

The crew of *Splendid* had picked up the propeller and engine noise of the massive tanker at maximum range. Now, as the submarine edged her nose under the big vessel's stern with the periscope sitting exactly where Leach wanted it, ten feet down and slightly back from the rudder, the thumping roar from above was deafening. So loud was the noise that Leach, who could not for one second take his eyes away from the periscope, had to scream out his instructions. The first lieutenant stood immediately next to him in order to hear what his captain was saying so he could repeat it. As they approached the stern of the tanker, Tait had realized that the volume of noise coming up would probably destroy all normal voice control over the ship, so he had broken out the ship's bullhorn. Thus, when Leach screamed out an order, the first lieutenant boomed it through his bullhorn over the pervasive din of the *Esso Atlantic*'s machinery and screw.

When *Splendid* was in the exact position, close under the *Esso Atlantic*, that Leach wanted, he screamed out a request for a stool to perch on. While that was being tucked under his butt, he asked, "Is sonar scanning all right?"

The first lieutenant shouted in his ear, "I'll check."

Tait quickly took the few steps to the sonar compartment, had a shouting conversation with Pritchard and returned to his post beside the captain.

"Sonar's scanning okay, sir. Pritchard will bring me any contact as soon as it's made."

"Good-o."

For close to an hour the *Esso Atlantic* and *Splendid* moved in tight formation like an enormous gray whale with her calf tucked under her belly.

"Coming up to one hour in thirty seconds, sir," Tait bellowed into the captain's ear.

Leach started giving the orders that would move *Splendid* down fifty feet and then swing her out to the port to surface running alongside the tanker. "Keep 125 feet." He shouted the order to take her down. But there was no bullhorn repeat from the first lieutenant at his elbow. Instead, over the din he could hear scraps of screamed words. Then Tait's mouth was at his ear.

"Contact, sir. It's another Victor at range forty miles. Bearing green one hundred. Closing at thirty-five knots. Course 110 degrees. She's headed right for us."

No doubt about it, she was on an intercept. Leach calculated the Victor would be in an ideal attack position at say three miles in about forty minutes. Time to move.

He took *Splendid* down to 150 feet, well clear of the tanker's gargantuan keel. Then he swung his boat off to the starboard side of the big craft until the submarine was about fifty yards away, running in line abeam of the propeller and engine room at the stern. Next he eased her up to periscope level, maintaining the positioning of his attack periscope eye just above the tower. He would not put either of his periscopes above the surface. At the right moment he would raise only the radar mast.

Leach had *Splendid*'s propeller and motor exactly where he wanted them, fifty yards away from the thundering engines and propeller of the *Esso Atlantic* and in a direct line between those powerful noise generators and the oncoming Victor. As the Soviet submarine's position changed he would maneuver his boat to maintain that line.

At her new station, the volume of the tanker's noise inside the hull of *Splendid* diminished considerably, sufficiently that Leach could give his orders directly to his control room crew. He turned the periscope over to the first lieutenant and picked up the broadcast microphone.

"All compartments, this is the captain. We have a Victor class submarine moving in from the starboard. She is at 095 degrees to our heading and about thirty-five miles on an intercept course. We're running next to the *Esso Atlantic*, as you can hear. We're about fifty yards to her starboard beside her propeller and engine room and in a line between them and the Russian submarine. The tanker's noise will mask our sound so the Victor won't know we're here. I expect she'll be in an ideal attack position in an hour from now, at 11:40."

He then told the crew what his plan of action was, depending upon what the Soviet submarine did. From that moment it was a matter of watching and waiting. At 11:30 the Victor, approaching the three-mile range, changed from its intercept course to run parallel to the *Esso Atlantic* and moved ahead until it was abeam of the tanker. There it sat, a constant blip on the sonar screen. At 11:34 the radar watchkeeper reported, "Periscope, sir. Green 085. Range 3 miles." The Soviet captain was ready for visual contact with the supertanker.

At 11:55 the Russian submarine altered its heading again to an intercept course.

In the control room of *Splendid*, Marcus Leach received the report he wanted to hear.

"All tubes reported in the action state, sir. Guidance systems in computer control, sir."

Leach acknowledged.

"Up radar mast."

"Up radar mast, sir."

"Communications center."

"Communications center. Go ahead, sir."

"Be prepared to transmit in the clear a running account of everything you hear if the Victor attacks. But don't transmit unless I tell you to."

"Aye, aye, sir."

Throughout the length and breadth of *Splendid*, the next words of the captain caused everyone to tense.

"Stand by to start the attack and watches." *Splendid*'s complex computers, electronic equipment, and instruments had been locked onto the advancing submarine by the attack crew, the sonar information being fed into the system giving it the Victor's depth, speed, range, and course. That information was fed directly into the torpedo control settings. When he made his final decision to attack and gave the order to launch the torpedos, the timing watches would be started to clock their estimated run time to impact with the target.

Finally, on the fire-control computer the five red Torpedo Ready lights flashed on.

The *Splendid* was set. If Leach had to shoot, the torpedos would leave their tubes in the bow of the boat, then turn on their computer set headings to the target. Their own sonar and heat-sensing devices would lead them into it for the impact. In case something went wrong and a torpedo turned back against *Splendid* itself or the *Esso Atlantic*, the torpedo's warheads would not be armed until they had run several hundred yards.

It was coming up to 12:00 Zulu. Leach watched the sweephand go by on the control room clock.

In the control room of the atomic submarine 501, its captain, Boris Chernavin, kept the hairline aiming cross on the exact point on the *Esso Atlantic*'s bridge where he wanted his submerged-launch SS-N-7 surface-to-surface rocket to strike, enter, and destroy. His clear eyes absorbed the scene presented to him through the boat's periscope, as he listened to his executive officer's voice giving him the countdown of seconds to 12:00 noon. On the precise second he gave the order: "Fire!"

Instantly there was a growling, rumbling sound from the forward launch compartment. The surface of the sea immediately in front of the periscope burst in a showering cascade of foam and smoke as the rocket, flung out of its tube by compressed air, ignited its propulsion pod. Its retracted wings sprang out as it began its flat trajectory toward the tanker. Trailing behind it was a guidance wire that was optically and electronically locked to the periscope sighting mechanism controlled by the eye and hands of the captain.

As the clock recorded 12:00 Zulu aboard *Splendid*, the radar watchkeeper shouted, "A rocket, sir. She's launched a rocket!"

Leach couldn't believe it. But he had to.

"Hard to starboard!" If torpedos were to follow the rocket to the *Esso Atlantic*, he had to be out of their path.

"Stop engines! Up attack periscope," Leach had to track the rocket. "Paul, get on the periscope. Tell me what happens with the rocket!"

The combination of the hard bank to starboard and the quick pulling off of power put the *Splendid* astern of the tanker. But would it be enough?

At the instant Chernavin observed the rocket's impact exactly on target he called out, "Fire all torpedos!" He could feel the submarine shudder as she disgorged her lethal package of eight computer preset torpedos toward the helpless supertanker. At that moment, its entire stern superstructure was being ripped apart by the devastating explosion of the powerful rocket. No one could survive that blast. As planned, the communications center of the *Esso Atlantic* was destroyed without warning.

The *Splendid* was only halfway through her turn to face the Victor head on when Leach heard the sonar report,

"Torpedo HE, bearing 040." Pratt's voice was edged with anxiety. "I have eight of them running, sir. Range three miles!"

That was it. The rocket and now the torpedos. It was the Soviets who had sunk the fifteen on April 26!

"Communications center, start broadcasting!"

"Aye, aye, sir."

At that instant the sound of a heavy explosion shook the hull of *Splendid*. At the same time the first lieutenant shouted, "Christ, it hit just below the funnel. It's taken the whole bridge area out and her communications center would be right there." The Russian tactic was clear: hit the communications center first. That explained why there was no word from those that disappeared six days before.

Leach looked at his Torpedo Ready lights. They had gone out as the attack team reset their information. Suddenly they glowed red again.

"On, sir . . ."

"Shoot!"

The impact of having the five torpedos leaving the bow of *Splendid* finished off her remaining forward motion.

"Torpedos running, sir."

"Running time?"

"Two minutes fifty-two seconds to three minutes, sir."

Within ten seconds after the Victor II's torpedos had been launched, all eight tracking with deadly accuracy toward the hull of the tanker, the sonar michman's voice on the loudspeaker system had cut through the hot fetid air of the control room with words that jolted the captain.

There was a contact just behind the tanker. The computer said it was British of the Swiftsure class. It must have been running beside the tanker. The submarine was falling behind the *Esso Atlantic* rapidly. Its bow was swinging toward the 501. The michman's voice did not stop but its pitch became higher as he began to realize what was happening. The port torpedo originally programed to strike the *Esso Atlantic* in the stern, engine room, rudder, propeller area, had locked onto the British submarine and was tracking directly for it.

Then came the chilling shock when the sonar michman's voice with a high shrill of panic screamed that the British sub had just launched five torpedos at the 501.

Captain Second Class Boris Chernavin reacted quickly. He shouted an order to the wheelsman to turn hard to the left. That would put the 501's bow head on toward the running torpedos, minimizing their target profile. That order was followed in the same breath by "Full speed ahead! Dive! Dive!"

That done, the captain said to himself, "It can't happen to you, Chernavin!" He could do nothing now but wait.

On *Splendid*, Pratt's voice again contained a hint of panic. "Sonar, sir. Torpedos halfway to tanker. Seven are tracking to the tanker and one of them is heading for us!"

Leach's reaction was instantaneous. "Dive! Dive! Full ahead!"

In the two minutes left of the Soviet torpedo's running time, diving was the only escape maneuver left to *Splendid*. Agonizingly slowly the ponderous bulk of the huge submarine began to move forward. The planesman had the hydroplane control wheel shoved hard forward as the main ballast tank inlets opened wide to allow emergency flooding in the desperate attempt to avoid the oncoming torpedo.

In two strides Leach was in the sonar room, eyes fixed on the screen, its winking lights instantly conveying the story to him. There was the torpedo, two miles away, speeding toward *Splendid* with the accuracy of an arrow. His own torpedos had completed their turn toward the Victor and were almost a quarter of the way to it. Tracking toward the *Esso Atlantic*, already half a mile south of the stopped British submarine, were seven dots running fast and parallel. They would strike the tanker at spaced intervals from the bow to the stern.

In the communications center, the communications officer was monitoring the voices in the control room. He knew exactly what was happening and he was broadcasting it to the world.

Commander Marcus Leach RN, the captain of H.M.S. *Splendid*, his eyes fixed on the image of the lethal torpedo hurtling through the water toward his boat, thought for an instant about warning the crew. But why panic them? If they were going to buy it they were going to buy it.

Watching the white streak on the sonar screen traverse the last inch toward the bright, shining *Splendid* dot on the sonar screen, Commander Marcus Leach's thoughts raced. "It's going to miss us. Surely it's going to miss us. After all, it's only a Russian torpedo. Primitive construction. Probably a dud. It can't happen to you, Leach. No way."

29

1 May   5:40 P.M.

Moscow

The scene in Chairman Romanov's office was much the same as it had been five days before. The players were the same, the chairman in his dark suit behind his desk looking grim, the translator by his side, the communications technician, and opposite, Marshal Ustinov looking splendid in his uniform, Gromyko bland as ever, and General Andropov looking agitated, nervous.

It was May Day, glorious May Day, the day the Soviet Union celebrated the victory of the revolution, the day that thousands of army, navy and air force troops paraded proudly through Red Square, marching with their tanks, guns, missiles, and all the modern paraphernalia of war, while overhead screeched squadrons of the newest fighters and bombers. It was a showcase into which, through the magic of television, the eyes of the world could look in awe at the increasing might of the Soviet armed forces.

The parade that day had lasted for three hours as it moved past the saluting base where Romanov and his colleagues stood in their formless, dark overcoats and matching wide-brimmed fedoras worn by all except Ustinov, who was in uniform. The spectators that day and the world press were quick to notice that instead of fourteen Politburo members standing behind the white balustrade to take the salute, there were only ten. That was the first clue to Romanov's emerging ruthlessness. On April 28, four members of the Politburo, Pelshe, Kirilenko, Suslov, and the premier, Kosygin, all in their late seventies and old men even by Romanov's standards, had asked for an audience with the chairman and were promptly received. Romanov was horrified when he found that they wanted to abort the Andropov Plan even though they had earlier approved it and stage one had been executed with huge success. The old men were shaken by the devastation wrought by the sinking of the American supertankers on April 26, stage one of the plan. They had convinced themselves that the consequences of stage two would be suicidal for the people of the Mother Country and contrary to the previously established pattern of securing Marxist-Leninist world domination by the socialist peoples in carefully planned and managed incremental steps rather than by the giant step that was implicit in the Andropov scheme.

Unable to dissuade the little group of patriarchs, Romanov decided that he simply could not have in the Politburo a clutch of weak-kneed old men who were totally opposed to any change in the status quo. Such men would chew away at the vitals of the successful execution of the Andropov Plan. He needed men of iron will and determination who were prepared to accept the prospect of a thermonuclear war, knowing that if it occurred, the Soviet Union would be victorious, that its society would survive and that of the enemy would be totally destroyed. He needed men who, at the same time, had total faith in the Andropov Plan and had faith that it would take the Soviet Union to a glorious victory over the capitalistic imperialists of the United States and their NATO and Western world minions. He would replace those old fools with such men. He had so informed them. The flabbergasted four had slunk from his office with no hope of turning back the clock. The next morning, as Romanov had judged, his motion to terminate their membership was carried in a full session of the Politburo. The decision was unanimous, the victims being unable to vote on their own fates. By May Day, however, Romanov had not yet decided which among the nonvoting members of the Politburo, or for that matter, from his loyal friends and supporters outside it, he would nominate to replace the four purged ancient ones.

Thus, only ten members of the Politburo had stood that May Day to receive the salute of the passing military might. During the parade Romanov stood in the center of the line of Politburo members, assured now that all the others knew how ruthless their chairman was. That quality would soon be discovered by the president of the United States.

The completion of stage two of the Andropov Plan was scheduled for three o'clock in the afternoon, Moscow time, noon GMT. Romanov had, therefore, asked for a hotline conference with President Hansen for three hours later, six o'clock in Moscow and 9 A.M. in Washington. In the three-hour interval he would have confirmation that stage two had, in fact, been executed. He and his colleagues would have a chance to rest after the grueling hours-long stand on the inspection platform, and he could polish his notes for the message he was going to deliver to the president. From his perspective of history it would probably be the most important statement delivered by one head of government to another in the history of mankind.

The chairman had been working at his desk alone in his office at 5:35 P.M., carefully going over his statement, when his principal secretary burst in, saying that Hansen urgently wanted to speak with the chairman. It was of the highest priority and could not wait for the appointed hour of six o'clock. Romanov agreed.

"Tell the Americans to give me five minutes." He waved his hands at the television gear at the end of his desk. "Everything is set. Fetch my colleagues."

At 5:42 when contact was established and the face of each leader appeared on his respective television screen, Romanov's trio, Gromyko, Andropov, and Ustinov, were in place opposite him, witnesses to the impending confrontation.

This time Hansen wasted no time on preliminaries.

"Mr. Chairman, I have in my hand," his huge right hand thrust toward the camera a single, long piece of paper, "conclusive and absolute evidence that, just forty minutes ago, one of your Victor class submarines not only sank a British submarine, it also, and without warning to the crew, sank the American-owned *Esso Atlantic* using a rocket and torpedos. My evidence is a broadcast from the sub before it sank. And I also have evidence that as of this moment, another twenty American-owned supertankers have disappeared in the South Atlantic. They were sunk by your submarines just as the fifteen were sunk five days ago." His thundering, accusatory voice rose in pitch and volume. "You lied to me, Romanov, you lied to me—just as Khrushchev lied to Kennedy—when you assured me that the Soviet Union had nothing to do with those sinkings. You have committed an act of war against both the United States of America and Great Britain and don't give me that business about flags of convenience and international waters!"

Romanov was tempted to taunt with "What are you going to do about it?" but he denied himself the pleasure. After all, he held the winning cards. Instead he replied passively, coldly.

"You must understand, Hansen," he would reciprocate the president's rudeness by also using his surname alone, "that if it serves the interests of the nation I lead, I am as prepared as any of my predecessors to say truths which are not true and even to die in the cause of our Mother Country."

Romanov intended to take the initiative away from the emotionally overwrought president. "The United States, you, Hansen, are in the process of committing an act of aggression against the Soviet Union by your entry into Pakistan. You refuse to back off. We have given you every opportunity to do so. The United Nations has censured your action. Yes, 110 countries voted to censure you, whereas

712

only 104 censured us when we entered Afghanistan to protect our own interests on our own borders. We have given you every opportunity to retreat from your active military madness of putting a hundred thousand men on Asian soil in Pakistan at our very throat."

His eyes dropped to his notes as he began to follow them, from time to time looking up into the television screen where President Hansen's haggard image sat clearly before him. Hansen made an effort to intervene in protest but Romanov waved him down, saying, "It would be best if you heard what I have to say. Hear me out and you will have every opportunity to respond."

Hansen remained silent as the Russian went on.

"As a result of your intended act of aggression in Pakistan, and for other reasons which I will outline, the Soviet Union has decided upon a course of action to preserve its own security, to preserve the peace of the world and, at the same time, to gain permanent access to a commodity essential to the economy of the Soviet Union and its East European allies.

"That commodity is crude oil. As far back as October of 1979, economic analysts of your Central Intelligence Agency—and we have the highest regard for the CIA, Mr. President, it is almost as good as the KGB—those analysts told a congressional committee that the Soviet oil industry, then a net exporter of a million barrels a day to Eastern and Western Europe, had peaked in its production and the supply was starting to fall off. Those analysts testified that by 1982, in the face of increased Soviet demand and resources, Moscow would be forced to import 700,000 barrels of crude oil a day and that there was only one place to obtain it—the Middle East. There was much controversy in your country about the validity and accuracy of the CIA estimate, but I can assure you, Mr. President, they were wrong. Our daily shortfall is not 700,000 barrels a day, but 1,200,000, and rapidly rising to crisis figures for our economy and that of our European allies. On the other hand, the CIA analysts were also right. We have had no new major discoveries in the Soviet Union in recent times and the prospects do not look good and, therefore, the only place we can secure the crude oil we need is—as the CIA put it—the Middle East.

"It is apparent, therefore, that assured access to Middle East oil is a matter of paramount concern to the Soviet Union at this moment, just as continued access must be of paramount concern to the United States and to Western Europe, which receives ninety-three percent of its crude oil from the OPEC producers of which sixty percent comes from the Persian Gulf. It is obvious that if that supply of crude oil from all the OPEC countries was cut off, Western Europe would face the total annihilation of its industrial and economic base and indeed the civilization that it now knows. To a lesser degree, but only slightly, the consequences of the cut-off of Persian Gulf oil to Western Europe would be similar. For you in the United States, the result of a cut-off of your oil imports of nine million barrels a day out of a consumption of twenty would be no less catastrophic. Even the termination of your supplies from the Persian Gulf alone would be a major disaster.

"However, at this moment I speak to you not of a termination of the supply to you of Persian Gulf crude but a termination of all crude oil supplied to you and to Western Europe by tanker from whatever source in the world, Venezuela, Mexico, Malaysia, and for that matter, even from Alaska in your own country, where you made the foolish decision to take the production there, 1,200,000 barrels a day—the equivalent of our shortfall at this moment—by tanker down the west coast of Canada rather than in a secure pipeline by land."

Hansen had slumped back in his chair, totally absorbed in what he was hearing. There would be a punch line. Of that he was certain.

Romanov pressed on. "At this moment I have 381 submarines of all classes at sea, my entire serviceable fleet. At this moment 256 of them are locked on to tanker targets in the Cape of Good Hope route from the Persian Gulf up into the South Atlantic."

Romanov was happy with the look of appalled astonishment on Hansen's face when he heard those numbers.

The president sat up instantly, looking off camera to his people as if for confirmation or denial. Apparently, he had no satisfaction. Relentlessly, Romanov pressed on.

"Similarly, I have thirty-five submarines locked on targets moving between Venezuela and the United States, and Mexico and the United States. In the Pacific I have another thirty on targets running in from Malaysia. Of the world tanker fleet of 4,200 vessels, the supertankers of more than 200,000 tons, which carry most of the crude oil on the major runs to your country and to Western Europe, number only 700. In the last five days, quite apart from the PLO sinkings of ten in the Indian Ocean, my submarines have sunk thirty-five of them. All were swiftly dealt with, disappearing below the surface of the ocean within a minute or two minutes of being hit."

Romanov no longer glanced up from time to time. He pushed his gold-rimmed glasses further back on his nose and went on. "The reason for those sinkings? It was to demonstrate to the Government of the United States and to the NATO powers in no uncertain terms that the Red Navy has the capability of destroying in short order the entire supertanker fleet upon which the economy and future of the capitalist world depends. Mr. President, you and your NATO allies are powerless to stop us. Your numbers of surface and submarine antisubmarine vessels are far from sufficient. Furthermore, even if you had adequate numbers they would not be in place because of the NATO restriction at the Tropic of Cancer. The fact is, there is no defense against our capability to destroy the Western world's energy lifeline from the OPEC countries."

Romanov shifted and straightened then bent back again to his paper. "Mr. President, the United States has put us in a position where we have no choice but to act in defense of our Mother Country and to secure our position in the Middle East so that we can have a guarantee of access to its vast reservoirs of crude oil. Accordingly, I am authorized by the Supreme Soviet to inform you as follows:

"At 1200 hours Greenwich mean time tomorrow, the second of May, 0800 hours eastern daylight saving time in the U.S., the Soviet forces in strength will cross the borders into Iran from the Soviet Union and from Afghanistan, and from Afghanistan into Pakistan. Those forces are under orders to take those countries and to drive on through Iraq, Kuwait, Saudi Arabia, Yemen, Oman, the United Arab Emirates, Qatar and Bahrain. In other words, to seize the entire Persian Gulf."

Romanov paused to let that statement have its fullest impact on the reeling mind of the inexperienced president.

"You should know that my authorization from the Politburo is irrevocable. In the interests of the security of the Soviet Union and in the interests of its urgently needed energy supply, we will begin our military action precisely on the time scheduled, noon GMT tomorrow.

"You have some choices, Mr. President. Let me spell them out to you. First, you can go thermonuclear between now and then. You can order the pushing of the button that will rain nuclear warheads down upon our cities and military installations and ports, knowing full well that the instant you do our ICBMs will be launched in immediate total response. Millions upon millions of our people, yours and mine, will die. That is your first choice.

"Your next is to attempt to stop us in the Middle East by conventional warfare. I pause to add here that any use of nuclear tactical weapons will be tantamount to the use of intercontinental nuclear missiles and will be responded to accordingly by us. You can attempt to land your Pakistan Task Force on the seventh of May. You can attempt to throw in your 82nd Airborne Division as soon as you can get it ready.

"The final choice is to not intervene in our Persian Gulf initiative and to recall your Pakistan Task Force."

Romanov's hands moved as he shifted to the next page of his notes. "I suggest that you and your advisers give the utmost consideration to that course of action, Mr. President, because if you do intervene in our Persian Gulf initiative with military forces of any kind—air, sea, or land—then I will forthwith proceed to sink every supertanker on the high seas, all 700 of them, and sufficient of the remaining smaller and medium capacity ships to ensure that all OPEC crude oil supplies to you and Western Europe are cut off for the foreseeable future. Bear in mind, also, Mr. President, that if I destroy those tankers, neither you, Western Europe, nor Japan will have the industrial capacity even to begin to rebuild that fleet for the next ten years.

"So as I see it, you can go nuclear, or you can go conventional, or you can abstain. If you choose to abstain, if you leave us a free hand in the Persian Gulf, stay out of Pakistan, then I will give you this quid pro quo.

"I can assure you that, firstly, my navy will sink no more tankers; secondly, the Soviet Union will guarantee the United States, Canada, Western Europe, and Japan a continued flow of crude oil from the Persian Gulf countries in amounts equivalent to those being shipped today, less an amount equal to the shortfall between the Soviet Union's domestic output and its overall demand including those of its Eastern Bloc allies calculated yearly. The price will be the equivalent of today's average OPEC contract price plus an amount equal to the annual inflation rate averaged between the United States, United Kingdom, and West Germany calculated every six months."

It was done. The future of the civilized world lay squarely in the hands of John Hansen, president of the United States of America. The lives of tens of millions of people, unknown to them, were dependent on his decision.

Romanov slipped off his glasses, looked into the television screen and camera and asked in an arrogantly condescending way, "Do you have any questions, Hansen?"

The big man in Washington was shaken to the core. He sat erect in his chair. "You've lied to me once, Romanov. How can I trust your promise not to sink the tankers and to provide a continued supply of crude oil?"

Romanov shrugged. "The answer to that is for you to decide. No matter what conclusion you come to, the armed forces of the Soviet Union will begin their move toward the Persian Gulf at midday tomorrow."

Romanov ordered the communications technician to

turn off the set as President Hansen belligerently leaned forward shouting, "Romanov, you're a lying, unprincipled, inhumane, absolutely ruthless . . ."

As the screen went blank, the chairman could not but agree with the president's harsh description of him, except that he did not consider himself to be inhumane. On the contrary.

30

1 May   10:28 A.M.

The White House

Washington, D.C.

The eyes of the president and everyone in the Oval Office—Vice-President James, Levy, Kruger and Crane— remained on the television screen for many moments after Romanov's image had disappeared. The five men sat speechless, stunned by what they had heard. It was beyond belief.

Slowly, the president turned to look at the others sitting across the desk. "Gentlemen, some decisions have to be made and quickly. There's no doubt in my mind that Romanov isn't bluffing." His mind was turning over what had to be done. He said to Crane, "I want a meeting in half an hour in the cabinet room. I want the director of the CIA, Cootes. There isn't time to get the approval of Congress, but I want the majority and minority leaders of both the Senate and the House and the Speaker of the House and," to the others present, "all of you."

The secretary of defense asked, "What about General Young?" It was a suggestion.

Crane broke in. "He and the three chiefs are at Colorado Springs, the North American Air Defense headquarters. I checked with his secretary this morning. Something about a conference with their senior generals and admirals."

The president waved a hand. "It doesn't matter. Get hold of him immediately. Tell him what's going on. I want him and his people to stay put next to a telephone and keep the line clear so we can talk to him any time. And get Peterson to arrange time with all the television networks. Say six o'clock. Fifteen minutes. The American people have a right to know what's going on. By the time we're finished, I may have to tell them to evacuate the cities."

"You don't really think it's going to go that far," John Eaton protested.

The president pointed toward the blank screen. "You heard what the man said."

The secretary of state had no further comment.

Hansen flicked his secretary's switch on the intercom box sitting at the end of his desk. "Margaret, get Prime Minister Thrasher and the West German chancellor for me on a conference call immediately. It's urgent. Top priority. We'll talk in the clear."

"What about Canada? If we go, they'll be involved." Eaton knew how sensitive the Canadians were.

"Okay. Include the Canadian prime minister. You'd better get going, Jim." As his chief of staff left the Oval Office, the president said to his colleagues, "There used to be a sign on this desk, 'The buck stops here.' Right now I'd like to have old Harry Truman looking over my shoulder."

Half an hour later, when the president entered the cabinet room to get the emergency meeting underway, he was relieved to see that all the people he had asked for were present. They were standing, waiting for his appearance. There were no amiable greetings. Hansen went directly to his chair at the center of the table and lowered his huge body into it. As he did so, he turned to Crane standing behind him, then pointed to the telephone on the table to the right of his place. "Did you get General Young?"

"Yes, sir, he's standing by with the three chiefs. They can hear what's being said and can talk without the phone being lifted."

Hansen opened the meeting with a thorough update on the situation, going over in detail the ultimatum that Romanov had given him.

"What I have to decide is how we respond. And when I say 'I', I mean just that. We have until 12:00 GMT, 8 A.M. our time, tomorrow. There's no possible way I can get any approval from Congress for whatever action I propose to take. There just isn't time. So I'm most grateful to the congressional leaders, my old colleagues, for being here and I hope they'll support whatever I decide to do."

It was the portly, white-haired old Dan O'Brien, the Speaker of the House of Representatives, who spoke for his colleagues, saying, "We're pleased that you asked us to sit in, Mr. President. It seems to me that what Chairman Romanov said to you, the ultimatum, is, in fact, a declaration of war against the United States. Would you agree with that, Mr. President?"

Hansen shook his head. "Not quite. I see it as a statement of intent to declare war or create war, if certain things are or are not done. The Russian sinking of the fifteen American-owned ships I technically regard as an act of war against Liberia and Panama and not against the United States. And it's a clear act of war against the British. Whatever the legal technicalities are, Dan, the fact is that the Russians are going to move against Iran and the Persian Gulf countries tomorrow morning. They're not going to attack the United States, but they are going to attack the Persian Gulf countries."

Secretary Eaton interjected. "But surely the sinking of the world tanker fleet, the sinking of American ships flying the American flag, would be an act of war against the United States."

"It would indeed. And it would be an act of war against any other nation whose ships were sunk—the United Kingdom, West Germany, France. There's one point I want to get cleared up." He pointed toward the telephone saying to Crane, "Jim, can I talk to Admiral Taylor on that thing?" Admiral Crozier Taylor, the chief of naval operations, was at NORAD headquarters in Colorado Springs with General Young.

"Yes, Mr. President. Just talk at the machine. Ask for him."

"Admiral Taylor, this is the president speaking. Can you hear me?"

"Yes, Mr. President." The admiral's voice came clearly through the loudspeaker attached to the phone.

"Good. Then you've heard my briefing on what's going on. We know the Soviets have some 381 submarines at sea at this moment. Romanov says he can sink the world's tanker fleet. In your opinion, admiral, could he do it?"

There was no hesitation in Taylor's reply. "No question about it, sir. We believe he has close to 300 of his submarines locked onto target ships right now. He could take out almost half the world fleet of 700 on the first shot. I would say that within a week, the Russians could destroy between eighty and ninety percent of all the supertankers and probably thirty percent of the smaller tankers, that's between eight and nine hundred of those. You see, Mr. President, none of the tankers that are at sea, and there are hundreds of them, have any protection whatsoever. With their satellites, the Russians know exactly where they are. Each sub carries between twelve and twenty-one torpedos, say an average of fifteen torpedos per sub. With 300 tasked for tanker sinking, that gives you 4,500 shots. In two weeks there probably wouldn't be a single supertanker afloat and probably three-quarters of the smaller ones would be gone."

"Couldn't we stop them?"

Once more there was no hesitation. "Not a hope, Mr. President. In a week or ten days, we might be able to take out say eighty out of their 381 at sea. We have 148 submarines. Only seventy-six of those have antisubmarine capability. Furthermore, the Soviet submarines are on station right now and ready to shoot. Our antisubmarine subs are thousands of miles away. I think we have thirty at sea at the moment, and all of them are in the North Atlantic."

"You've got nothing in the South Atlantic?" The President shook his head in frustration.

"No, sir, but I have six working with the Fifth Fleet in the Arabian Sea."

"What about the British? They're in this with us. The Soviets' sinking of their submarine today took care of that. At least they nailed the Russian sub at the same time."

"The Brits have a few antisubmarine submarines. They've got lots of surface ship capability but, like ours, they're not deployed. Their surface ships at sea are in the North Atlantic and there's a flotilla working with the Fifth Fleet. The problem is, Mr. President, the Soviets have taken us by surprise. If we'd only known they put their whole submarine fleet to sea . . ."

"They aced us, Admiral, with their goddamn sonar interference and dummy submarines to fool our satellite cameras. They aced us. Thank you, Admiral. We'll be back to you if we have other questions."

The president had earlier been fully briefed by his experts on what would happen if the Red Navy destroyed the world's tanker fleet. He had been appalled by what he had been told. He summarized the main points of the report for the men assembled that morning.

"The U.S. imports nine million barrels a day out of a consumption of twenty million. The loss of imported crude would, within six months, cause the shut-down of at least fifty percent of the industries that rely on petroleum products for their operation and maintenance or on oil derivatives for their raw materials. Gasoline would be even more severely rationed to allow the consumption of only five gallons per week by any automobile and heavy restrictions would have to be placed on the transportation industry and agriculture. Food production would be cut by more than half.

"The automobile industry, the heart of America's economy, would be forced to shut down because of the inability of suppliers to manufacture parts, either metal or plastic, and because the market for new cars would totally disappear. Exports of manufactured goods would drop by between eighty-five and ninety percent because of the total collapse of the economies of Japan and Western Europe except for that of Great Britain, which is now self-sufficient in crude oil. Norway, with its North Sea reserves, is also capable of self-sufficiency. Unemployment throughout the United States would be in the fifty percent range, with inflation rising to an annual rate of between thirty and forty percent.

"Ninety-three percent of Western Europe's consumed crude oil is imported. The result of a cut-off there would be a total collapse of the economy of all the constituent countries except Norway and the U.K. Eighty percent of the work force would be unemployed. Automobiles would not be driven. All petroleum would be needed for the operation of basic utilities and the transportation of people and goods. The export and import of manufactured goods would cease because of lack of domestic manufacturing capability and the lack of money in the hands of consumers caused by the eighty percent unemployment level. For Japan, which relies totally on imported crude oil, the effects of a cut-off would be even more devastating than in Western Europe. All manufacturing would cease, including the building of tankers and ships of all classes.

"The shut-down of ship building, not only in Japan but elsewhere in the Western world, would preclude the rebuilding of the world tanker fleet for several years. The keel of the first replacement might be laid in some country, perhaps the United States, within a year after the destruction of the world fleet, but it would take about twenty years to reestablish world tanker tonnage capacity that would be equivalent to the amount destroyed.

"Domestic air travel in the United States would be cut back by eighty percent with travel permits having to be secured justifying travel for business or compassionate reasons. In Japan, all domestic and international flights would be stopped. A similar situation would prevail in Western Europe except for those airlines that could refuel in the United Kingdom or Norway inside a safe radius of operation."

The president took off his glasses and rubbed the

bridge of his nose between the thumb and forefinger of his right hand.

"As I see it, if the world tanker fleet were destroyed, there would be a total economic collapse in Western Europe and Japan. It would be of such magnitude as to mean the end of today's civilization and lifestyle in those parts of the world. It would mean poverty, starvation, revolution, violence. It would mean, certainly in Western Europe, that communism, which thrives on poverty and unrest, that communism would prevail in a short period of time. Furthermore, the military forces of our NATO allies and indeed our own, standing before massive Soviet forces across the Iron Curtain, would quickly be immobilized. You can't operate an army or an air force without fuel.

"In my judgment, the sinking of the world's tanker fleet and the resulting total cut-off of crude oil to the Western world and Japan would be a calamity, a disaster of the first magnitude, its consequences almost equal to those of an all-out thermonuclear war . . ."

Eaton broke in. "Except that tens of millions of people would not die."

"But life for more millions would be a living hell," Hansen responded.

Vice-President Mark James, who usually said very little at such meetings, decided to speak up.

"I wonder if it would be useful to take a look at the options that are open. First, we know that Romanov is going to act tomorrow morning. Let's take that as a fact. He says that no matter what we do, he's going to put his troops into Iran and Iraq, Saudia Arabia, and all the rest of those countries. If we don't interfere, he will continue to supply us with crude oil, but on a sliding downward scale as his own requirements increase. Frankly, Mr. President, I don't think that option is worth a damn. The man is a congenital liar. He lied to you on the twenty-sixth when he gave you assurances that the Russians weren't involved in the tanker sinkings. Once he has the Persian Gulf under his heel, he could make the Western world dance to any tune he wanted. So as I see it, making any deal with that son of a bitch is out, absolutely out." Uncharacteristically, he pounded the table with his right fist to emphasize his point.

He cleared his throat and went on. "If that's out, then the only way to go is to meet force with force!"

The defense secretary jumped in. "I agree. But if we go conventional, we're in real trouble. We've got ourselves handcuffed and Romanov knows it. By straining everything to the absolute limit in an all-out effort, we've scraped together a task force of 120,000 men. And where is it? It's sitting on ships in the Indian Ocean, 2,500 miles south of Pakistan. That's where it is, steaming toward where the Soviet Indian Ocean fleet has been doing its big OKEAN exercise. The only thing I could throw in would be the 82nd Airborne and two marine battalions. We'd have to put them in God knows where. Maybe even the Iranians would let us in if they knew the Soviets were going to attack, which I'm quite sure they do by now . . ."

The president nodded toward John Eaton. "Secretary Eaton's people notified the embassies of all Middle East countries as soon as I was off the hot line."

Secretary Levy continued. "The 82nd is on standby readiness, but it would still take two days to get there and the Russians' are going to launch tomorrow at noon GMT. Aircraft from the Fifth Fleet haven't got the range to reach the Soviet-Iran border, or to get into Afghanistan, for that matter." Levy had been addressing his remarks to Vice-President James. Now he shifted his gaze to look at the man who would make the decision.

"What I'm saying, Mr. President, is this. If we use force against force, the conventional route is hopeless. There's nothing we can do to stop them. Even if we did get to Pakistan by the sixth, we'd never get ashore because the Soviets would have taken the entire country by then."

The president held up his right hand momentarily to ask for silence. Speaking toward the telephone with its ear and mouth piece unit sitting in the trough that enabled a two-way conversation, he asked, "General Young, have you been able to hear what's being said?"

The general's clipped voice came back immediately. "Yes, sir."

"Do you agree with Secretary Levy?"

"Yes, Mr. President, I do, and so do my colleagues."

The president looked across the table at Levy. "I think you're telling me that the only force option we really have is thermonuclear. Do I read you correctly?"

There was total silence in the cabinet room. Not one man in that room ever believed he would live to hear that question put by the president of the United States of America. Thermonuclear? Absolutely unthinkable—up to that moment. Surely the answer could not be yes.

There was a long silence as Levy, confronted by that horrific question, decided how he would handle the answer. Finally he replied, "Before I say yes or no to that question, Mr. President, I want to put some numbers on the table that will help me to give you a qualified answer. The numbers have to do with cities and people."

It was Levy's turn to put on the reading glasses. From the pile of material he had brought with him, he extracted the notes he wanted and read from them:

"The Soviet Union stands a chance of surviving an all-out nuclear war. The United States does not. The Soviet population is much more thinly spread than ours. Nearly half our people are close together in big cities. If we wiped out the nine Soviet cities with more than a million people, they'd only lose 8.5 percent of their population. They lost twelve, percent in World War Two and survived. And they're more used to losing people than we are, with all the famines, purges, and wars they've been through.

"I find it difficult, Mr. President, to cope with the thought of one hundred million Americans dying in an instant."

The somber president did not smile when he said, "You have no monopoly on that difficulty, Bob."

Levy was ready to state his position. "But my answer to your question, Mr. President, is yes. If we're going to use force, the only alternative now is the ICBM or the submarine-launched ballistic missiles. However. I think we should confine ourselves to the military option. Under the military option, our missiles are targeted only for army bases, airfields, and naval installations. Those military targets that are associated with cities, such as Leningrad or Murmansk, are not included. So we stay away from all the cities. Also included in the military option are the major Russian crude oil production centers and fields in the Pechora and the huge Samotlor field in western Siberia."

Vice-President James could sense a problem. "Surely if you took out their major oil production fields, wouldn't that tempt the Soviets to do the same with the Persian Gulf in retaliation?"

"The very point I wanted to make," Levy acknowledged. "If you go for the military option, Mr. President, I suggest you take out the oil field targets."

The president wondered, "Could we go for targets of opportunity—the Soviet divisions along the Iran border and the Soviet surface fleets in the Atlantic, Indian Ocean, and the Pacific?"

"No problem, Mr. President," Levy assured him. "Although we should stay away from the Indian Ocean. Right now there's far too much traffic in the Arabian Sea. Our Pakistan Task Force is in the area and our Fifth Fleet with the British flotilla."

The president said he had one final question. "If I decide to go thermonuclear, take the limited military option, what should the timing be and should I try to threaten Romanov, get some leverage on him to force him to give up his Persian Gulf invasion? Having put the question, let me give you my view as to time and we'll see if anybody has any comments on it. And I can tell you, gentlemen, that right now I haven't decided what to do except I know that we've got only two choices: We can let the Soviets move into the Persian Gulf without a fight, in return for which they will refrain from sinking the world tanker fleet and allow the Western world continued access to the crude oil supplies in the area, subject to their own escalating requirements. Or we can take the other choice, the limited military option, the thermonuclear route."

The others nodded grimly.

"The crucial time is eight o'clock tomorrow morning," the president went on. "If we go thermonuclear, we should start immediately to get our people out of the cities in case the Soviets retaliate by an all-out attack against us. I've already asked for network time for six this evening."

"With great respect, Mr. President," it was Mark James, "whichever of the two paths you choose to follow, I think the American people should be warned immediately. They should be told the Russians have given us an ultimatum; that the possibility of an all-out thermonuclear war is a real one; that there is truly no need for panic, but that between now and tomorrow morning by six at the latest, they should get out of the cities."

Eaton suggested, "The time limit for completion of the evacuation should be the time you set for launching our ICBMs, which I suggest should be as late in the game as possible. If the ICBMs take roughly twenty minutes from time of launch to time of arrival on target, you want to give Romanov time to consider and to hold his troops back. I think seven o'clock should be your time of launching, Mr. President, and the absolute deadline for all people to be out of the cities. They should know enough to keep away from military installations."

Tom Jackman, the Senate majority leader from Florida, his voice thin and reedy like his body, spoke up. "I agree with the vice-president. It's now quarter to twelve. To wait until tonight to warn the people means that millions of people who could be on the move will have lost six precious hours. I'm sure the networks will clear for you anytime, Mr. President, anytime."

Hansen agreed. "You're right, Tom." He turned to Crane. "Get Peterson to tell the networks I want to go in half an hour, at 12:30." Crane practically ran to the door.

"Now what about bargaining with that bastard Romanov? If I elect to go nuclear, should I threaten him first or just go?"

Old Dan O'Brien, reputedly the best poker player on Capitol Hill, harrumphed from his seat down the table.

"From where I sit, Mr. President, you and Romanov are playing a game with the highest stakes the world has ever seen. He's sure the United States hasn't got enough guts to go nuclear, thermonuclear or whatever you want to call it. He's sitting there positive about that. So he's going to be the most surprised son of a bitch in the world if his radar and surveillance screens tell him at seven tomorrow morning or whenever it is you decide to go, that a hundred or two hundred ICBMs are on their way. You'll catch him with the most important weapon in any battle—surprise. Get him on that hot line two minutes before you launch. Then the moment your big birds are up and on their way, let him have it, then tell him that you're putting in a limited military strike but you're ready to go with a mass attack if he retaliates. And tell him you want three things. Number one, no nuclear retaliation; number two, no submarine attacks on the tankers; number three, no invasion of the Persian Gulf."

"Your scenario sounds good, Dan." Defense Secretary Levy liked what he heard, but it opened up another possibility. "If you're right, the president would have more bargaining leverage in those critical moments if he was able to tell Romanov that even though he could have taken out the Soviet troops massed along the Iranian border in his first ICBM shoot, he had held back. The president could tell Romanov that if he didn't immediately agree to his terms, the ICBMs to obliterate his entire force in that area would be launched."

The president, who had been concentrating totally on what was being said, his body tensed, his mind working at its maximum, decided he had heard enough. "Gentlemen, I'd like about ten minutes to talk this over with the vice-president. If all of you will wait here, please."

With that, President Hansen stood up, as did everyone else around the table. With his vice-president by his side, he made his way out of the room toward the temporary sanctuary of the Oval Office. There he was informed by an agitated Crane that the CIA had reported that the Russians had started to evacuate their cities.

At the stroke of twelve noon, both men returned to the cabinet room. The decision had been made.

When he was settled in his chair, the president spoke toward the telephone to confirm that the chairman of the Joint Chiefs of Staff and the chiefs were on the line and listening.

For the record, the president gave an explanation of his line of reasoning. That done, he stated his decision. "For those reasons, I have decided that at 7 A.M. Washington time tomorrow, I have no choice but to launch an intercontinental ballistic missile assault upon limited military objectives in the USSR. In the first strike, ICBMs programed for the Soviet-Iran border will be withheld, subject to immediate launch in the event negotiations with Chairman Romanov fail. Those negotiations will commence on the hot line as soon as the ICBMs are launched. At that time I will demand Romanov's agreement that there will be no nuclear retaliation; that no Soviet forces will invade Iran or the Persian Gulf; that all troops concentrated against the Soviet-Iran border and Afghanistan will be forthwith withdrawn; that there will be no further submarine attacks against any of the world tanker fleet; and that there be a personal meeting between Chairman Romanov and myself at the earliest possible moment. If he agrees, I will disarm our missiles before impact."

"Let's hope you can," someone muttered.

The president of the United States could scarcely believe the words he himself was uttering. It was like a vivid nightmare.

"General Young?"

"Yes, sir."

"You heard my decision?"

"Yes, sir."

"I'd like you to be in my office here tonight by nine with a list of your recommended military targets and maps showing the locations. Unless countermanded by voice personally by me, you will launch the ICBM attack at precisely seven o'clock tomorrow morning."

The president waited for the general's acknowledgement. When none came, he demanded, "General, did you hear what I said?"

When the general's voice came through the telephone it was filled with contempt. He could not hide his feelings for the bungling, inept politicians he had been listening to.

"Yes, Mr. President, I heard what you said. All four of us here heard what you said. While you were having your ten-minute session with the vice-president to decide what *you* were going to do, we had a little meeting at this end to decide what *we're* going to do. Mr. President, in our opinion, you've been badly advised by people who don't know what the hell they're talking about. If we launched an ICBM attack on limited military targets, the Soviets would blow the United States off the face of the earth. Being able to disarm them at the last minute wouldn't matter a damn. The Soviets would put up a retaliatory launch the instant they saw ours coming. You don't know what you're doing Mr. President!

"What I'm telling you is that the Joint Chiefs of Staffs Committee of the United States of America has decided that there will be *no* launching of any ICBMs or any other ballistic missiles against the Soviet Union tomorrow morning at eight or at any other time until *we're* satisfied it is in the interests of the people of the United States that the launch button should be pushed. In other words, when we're damned well good and ready!"

The president could not believe what he was hearing. "You're telling me you refuse to carry out my order? That's treason, general, absolute naked treason against the Government of the United States."

The general's harsh voice filled the cabinet room. His words stunned his listeners.

"Not if it's a military government, Mr. Hansen. Not if *we*—my colleagues and I—take over."